OF GODS AND MEN

DAISY DUNN is an author, historian and critic. She read Classics at Oxford, before winning a scholarship to the Courtauld and completing a doctorate in Classics and History of Art at University College London. She writes and reviews for many publications, including the *Daily Telegraph*, *Evening Standard*, and *Standpoint*, and is editor of *Argo*, a Greek culture magazine. She is the author of *Catullus' Bedspread* (2016) and an accompanying volume of the poems in translation, *The Poems of Catullus*, and *In the Shadow of Vesuvius: A Life of Pliny* (2019).

OF GODS AND MEN

100 STORIES
FROM ANCIENT GREECE & ROME

Selected and introduced by

Daisy Dunn

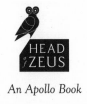

HEAD
of ZEUS

An Apollo Book

ISBN (HB) 9781788546744
ISBN (E) 9781788546737

Typeset by Adrian McLaughlin

Printed and bound in Germany
by CPI Books GmbH, Leck

Head of Zeus Ltd
First Floor East
5–8 Hardwick Street
London EC1R 4RG
WWW.HEADOFZEUS.COM

For Lucy Purcell

CONTENTS

INTRODUCTION

T here are a few things to be done before the stories can begin. A slave must fetch a jug of water and pour it into a silver basin. The visitors shall wash their hands. A table is to be pulled up beside them and laid with bread and meat. Everyone shall eat and drink until they're full. Then, and only then, will the hosts ask the guests about themselves. Who are they? Where have they come from? What is their story?

When I read Homer's *Odyssey* for the first time, more than twenty years ago, what struck me most was how trusting people could be. The most civilized characters in the poem welcome strangers into their homes before they know so much as their names. As a child I found this extremely worrying. What if they were thieves? What if they were murderers? What if they ate all the bread and left their hosts wanting? Students of Homer are taught that such generosity is in keeping with established laws of hospitality: treat strangers as if they are your friends. But over the years I've come to see these acts as also redolent of the fact that the Greeks considered a good story worth waiting for. The bread-and-basin rituals outlined above usually serve as a prelude to storytelling. Odysseus, tossed across the sea after his raft is shattered in a sea-storm, washes up on an island called Scheria, where he is welcomed into a royal palace, fed, and prompted to speak. Relieved that he has finally reached civilization, he settles in to tell his hosts of the terrifying beings he has encountered on his journey home from Troy: one-eyed Cyclopes and singing Sirens, sleepy Lotus-Eaters and cannibalistic Laestrygonians, tricksy temptresses Circe and Calypso, the whims of tempestuous gods.

Homer's *Iliad* and *Odyssey* are at once products and celebrations of a history of storytelling. Two of the oldest works of literature from the Western world, they were passed down orally before being written down in the late eighth or early seventh century BC, and continued to be performed down the centuries. It was in the course of assembling this anthology that I came to appreciate just how richly layered with stories they are. The *Odyssey* gives us stories as told by Odysseus, stories sung to Odysseus, stories told of Odysseus as he wends his way home to Ithaca. Many of the men who fight at Troy in the *Iliad* are skilled tellers of tales, not least of all Achilles, the mightiest fighter for the Greeks.

The richness and variety of Homer's storytelling were my inspiration as I set about compiling this collection of tales from antiquity. Homer marks the beginning but is also the thread that runs through so much of the literature of Greece and Rome, from the 'Epic Cycle' of poems which developed in his wake to provide continuations of his stories, to the tragedies of fifth-century BC Greece, and the poetry of the Roman Empire. Time and again classical authors challenged themselves to explore what became of Homer's heroes after the Trojan War. It is partly as a result of this that ancient stories are seldom self-contained. Sharing common roots, such as Homer or the myths of his near contemporary, a poet from central Greece named Hesiod, they frequently weave into and out of each other like trees in a forest. A great number of the stories included in this anthology collide and overlap, even when separated by hundreds of years.

One of the things that makes ancient tales so mesmerizing is the possibility that they were founded in reality – or at least contain a kernel of truth. When stories are as old as the ones in this collection it feels only natural to imagine the scenarios that might have inspired them. Did anything like the Trojan War take place? Was there ever a man who unwittingly fell in love with his own mother, as Oedipus did in Greek tragedy? So many characters seem thrillingly real. We cannot help but feel Oedipus' pain in Sophocles' play, *Oedipus Rex*, as he begins to comprehend who he really is. When a drunk man suggests to him that his father is not really his father, Oedipus questions his parents: 'They were indignant at the taunt and that comforted me – and yet the man's words rankled'. The line, elegantly rendered by W. B. Yeats, captures an important moment in Oedipus' journey of self-discovery. The Oedipus story is dire and extreme but strangely relatable.

The line between story and history was frequently indeterminate. Ancient history books brim with accounts which are, to our eyes, patently mythical. Herodotus, a writer born in Halicarnassus (modern Bodrum in Turkey) in the fifth century BC, earned the sobriquet 'Father of History' for his celebrated *Histories* of Greece's wars with Persia in spite of his numerous flights of fancy. Herodotus wove into his accounts what was known in Greek as 'logoi' – stories, spoken things, words which might be fictional or might equally be factual. While there is no doubt that the Persian Wars took place, and that much of what Herodotus wrote of them is true, there are also passages in his books which read like pure fiction. Inspired by Herodotus, I have included in this anthology a number of stories from the ancient history books, regardless of whether they are wholly or only partially fictional. It can be so difficult to separate fact from fiction that there is much to be said for enjoying passages in these books on their own terms as vivid stories.

The Romans were particularly partial to this blending of history and story as they sought to establish their own place in the world. In order to trace the origins of their people to the heroes of Homer's epics, they developed the myth that Aeneas, one of the Trojans who fought in the *Iliad*, had led a band of refugees free from burning Troy to found a new home in Italy. The *Aeneid*, a Latin epic by the poet Virgil, provided the Romans with an exciting foundation story. Even Roman historians such as Livy were willing to incorporate it into their accounts of Rome's past. Such was the power of the story.

Myth, the basis for much storytelling, was the common language through which the ancients defined themselves. Even scientists who rejected myths and the gods who populated them found that they were a useful means of communicating their ideas. Lucretius, a Roman philosopher and atomicist of the first century BC, drew on stories surrounding the love goddess Venus to explain his theories of genesis on earth. The ideas in his account are very different from those proffered by Hesiod in the seventh century BC, but the mythology surrounding Venus provided a link between ancient Greece and late-Republican Rome.

We speak of 'The Greeks and Romans' even though the Greek and Roman world extended far beyond Greece and Rome. I hope this anthology will reveal something of its scale. Included are stories by authors from Alexandria and Panopolis (Akhmim) in Egypt, Carthage and Libya in North Africa, Samosata (Samsat), Smyrna (İzmir) and Halicarnassus (Bodrum) in what is now Turkey, Lesbos, Rhodes and Sicily, and an account by the Jewish historian

Josephus, who defected to the Romans in the Jewish War of the first century AD. I've frequently broken the chronological arrangement of the stories in this anthology in order to reflect the development of themes between authors across time and space. The superiority of the countryside over the city, for instance, is a theme that occupies the fables of Aesop, who is thought to have been born in the sixth century BC, a second-century BC comedy by a Carthage-born former slave, and the Latin poetry of Horace.

The two youngest stories in this collection sit on the cusp of a new world. One is taken from the rather saucy mid-sixth-century AD *Secret History* by an historian named Procopius. The other comes from the *Consolation* of Boethius, who was born in Rome at around the same time the last emperor, Romulus Augustulus, was deposed. These texts, though written by Christians, are still pagan enough to warrant a place in a collection of classical literature. For Boethius, in particular, it was almost a case of clinging on to the achievements of classicism lest they fell with Rome itself.

This anthology features many of the celebrated writers of Greece and Rome – but not every single one of them. My guiding principle has been to select from only such works as provide interesting and arresting stories. Classical literature, it must be said, requires us to widen our expectations of what a story is. The short story, for instance, was not a genre the Greeks and Romans recognised. Even the novel was a late development and comparatively rare. Far more common was literature written in dialogue form: tragedies, comedies, philosophical discussions, legal speeches, all of which typically extended to thousands of lines. This means that, while this anthology contains a number of complete, standalone stories, it also features plenty of extracts from longer works, some of which conform more readily than others to what we may imagine a 'story' to be.

Every piece of literature is different and demands its own treatment. I found that an ancient novel, for example, can be précised in a series of episodes. A speech in a play often tells a story in itself; it can hold its own. A section of dialogue can provide a window onto a longer tale. I have also selected a few stories from ancient books of myths told in summary. These are typically very short. Extracting from something longer, such as the *Aeneid* or *Argonautica* – an epic tale of Jason and the Argonauts – has its challenges, but I have tried through my selections to give a flavour of the whole. I decided not to include fragments from ancient anthologies and the Greek lyric poets on the grounds that they seldom of themselves tell satisfyingly complete or accessible stories, but broke my own rules on a couple of occasions, primarily to give a taste of some of the women writers of antiquity. So little of their work survives that a fragmentary poem by Sappho, while not possessed of the liveliest story, is the more tantalizing for its rarity.

The principal joy of working on this anthology has been the opportunity to read the breadth of Greek and Latin literature and moreover to discover the most appealing translations of the hundred stories I liked most. The pages ahead contain a mixture of the familiar and the esoteric. Samuel Butler's translation of Homer's story of Odysseus and the Cyclops, 'a horrid creature, not like a human being at all, but resembling rather some crag that stands out boldly against the sky on the top of a high mountain', has an early starring role. While following the Greek closely, Butler was unafraid of omitting the odd word (for example 'sitophagus' – 'corn-eating' – before 'human being') to maintain the story's pace.

In the twentieth century, E. V. Rieu revealed a similar aptitude for translating the monumentalism of Homer into natural English. 'How strangely the Trojan and Achaean soldiers are behaving', he wrote of the soldiers at Troy, 'strangely' replacing 'wondrous deeds' in the Greek of the *Iliad*. We might expect T. E. Shaw – Lawrence of Arabia – to have relished translating passages of Homeric heroism, but I was intrigued as to how he would have handled the delightfully domestic scene of Odysseus' reunion with his wife Penelope in the *Odyssey*. It turns out rather well. His lively and often colloquial turn of phrase – 'my heart is dazed', 'these shabby clothes' – finds a contemporary counterpart in Emily Wilson's 2018 translation of the poem.

Many more male translators of the classics have been published through history than female. While recent years have witnessed the release of some fantastic translations by women, several of which have found a place in this anthology, it would have been unrepresentative to have sought a 50:50 ratio in a collection that spans the sixteenth to the twenty-first centuries. In making my selections I chose the texts which most appealed to me on their own merit.

I haven't always chosen the translation that is closest to the ancient text. Sometimes a looser translation can capture the spirit of a piece in a way that a strictly accurate one cannot. Ted Hughes's telling of Ovid's story of Pygmalion, a man who fell in love with a statue of his own creation, is masterly even where it deviates from the Latin. In his *Metamorphoses*, Ovid stated that Pygmalion was disgusted by women's vices. Hughes tells us what those vices were. His Pygmalion is deeply psychological, picturing 'every woman's uterus' as a 'spider', her perfume as a 'floating horror'. Ovid's Pygmalion fears bruising her lifelike flesh. Hughes's grips her 'to feel flesh yield under the pressure/That half wanted to bruise her/Into a proof of life, and half did not/Want to hurt or mar or least of all/Find her the solid ivory he had made her'.

I find that the best translators respect the ancient texts while making them their own. One of my favourites is based on a Latin comic novel about a wealthy former slave called Trimalchio who hosts a dinner party. The mysterious translation I have chosen was originally – but deceptively – attributed to Oscar Wilde. Though this attribution has since been retracted, the story still reads like a celebration of Victorian decadence. You can almost hear the voice of Wilde – or even Huysmans – in the description of Trimalchio, the louche protagonist of the story, being 'carried in to the sound of music… bolstered up among a host of tiny cushions'. It is not surprising that the Roman story went on to inspire F. Scott Fitzgerald's *The Great Gatsby* in the twentieth century.

Elsewhere in this collection, early modern England encroaches upon Francis Hickes's seventeenth-century translation of a story about a dream by the ancient satirist Lucian. 'After I had given over going to schoole', wrote Hickes, merging his own voice with that of the Greek satirist, 'and was grown to be a stripling of some good stature, my father advised with his friends, what it were best for him to breed mee to: and the opinion of most was, that to make mee a scholler, the labour would be long, the charge great, and would require a plentifull purse…' When a translator accommodates a story to his own times and tongue he helps to keep it alive.

The hundred stories from classical literature included in this collection owe their survival to the lasting impression they made upon the minds of those who read them. I have tried to strike a balance between what we might call 'classic classics', such as John Dryden's translation of the *Aeneid*, and the less familiar or expected. I have included old translations, new ones, verse and prose, and a handful of my own. There are erudite but highly readable contributions from classical scholars such as Benjamin Jowett, Aubrey de Sélincourt, Martin West and the poet Robert Graves – on Caligula rather than his uncle (I) Claudius – as well as writers better known for their works of English literature. Louis MacNeice offers a fine translation of Aeschylus' *Agamemnon*. Walter Pater's translation of 'Cupid and Psyche' from Apuleius' *Golden Ass* is to my mind unparalleled. Percy Bysshe Shelley clearly had great fun digesting Plato's description of the primordial separation of man from woman, in which the king of the gods 'cut human beings in half, as people cut eggs before they salt them, or as I have seen eggs cut with hairs'.

I close this anthology with a penetrating translation of Boethius' *Consolation of Philosophy* by Queen Elizabeth I. I found the monarch's apparent sympathy with the protagonist of the story incredibly moving. It brought home to me the fact that, for all the centuries that separate us, we might just as easily find ourselves in the characters of an ancient story as those of our own world.

DAISY DUNN, 2019

Author's note

I envisaged this anthology as a kind of grown-up version
of the books of myths and legends I enjoyed as a child. While
some of the stories are suitable for children, a good number
of them contain sexual themes, as found in the original texts,
or are stylistically aimed at the adult reader.

Within the extracts themselves, [*italic type within square
brackets*] denotes a stage direction or other observation in
the original translated text. My own occasional editorial
interpolations in the texts – mainly in the form of linking
passages to connect a sequence of extracts from the same
text or, very occasionally, in footnotes, appear in *unbracketed
italic type*.

THE BIRTH OF LOVE

Theogony

Hesiod

Translated by Barry B. Powell, 2017

In the beginning there was nothing but Chaos. Then came Gaia (Earth), Tartaros (the Underworld), and Eros (Love). Later, from Gaia, came Ouranos (Sky or the Heavens). As early as the seventh century BC, a Greek poet named **Hesiod** composed a poem on the origins of the cosmos entitled the *Theogony* ('Birth of the gods'). He described the often violent geneses of the familiar ancient Greek gods out of these primordial deities. This extract from his superbly sprawling poem culminates with the dramatic birth of Aphrodite, the goddess of love, out of her father Ouranos' severed genitals.

From Chaos came Darkness and black Night, and from Night came
Brightness and Day, whom Night conceived and bore by uniting in love
with Darkness. Earth bore starry Sky first, like to her in size, so that
he covered her all around, everywhere, so that there might always
be a secure seat for the blessed gods. And Earth gave birth to the blessed
Mountains, the pleasant halls of the gods, the nymphs who live in the wooded
hills. She bore the barren waters, raging with its swell, Sea, without making
delightful love.
            But then, uniting with Sky, Earth bore deep-swirling Ocean,
and Koios, and Kreios, and Hyperion, and Iapetos, and Theia, and Rhea,
and Themis, and Mnemosynê, and golden-crowned Phoibê, and beloved
Tethys. After them was born crooked-counseled Kronos, the youngest
and most terrible of these children, who hated his powerful father.
            She bore too the Cyclopês with their overweening spirit – Brontês
and Steropês and mighty Argês, who gave to Zeus the thunderbolt
and manufactured the lightning. These creatures were like the gods
in all other ways, but they had a single eye in the middle of their foreheads:
So they were called "Round-Eyes," because there was a single round
eye in their foreheads. Strength and power and device were in their works.
            Earth and Sky had three other children, great and strong,
scarcely to be named—Kottos and Briareos and Gygês, prodigal children.
One hundred arms sprang from their shoulders, scarcely to be imagined,
and fifty heads grew out of the shoulders of each, mounted on powerful

limbs. Their strength was unapproachable, mighty in their great forms.
Of all the offspring of Earth and Sky, these were the most terrible children.

Their father, Sky, hated them from the beginning. And as soon
as one of his children was born, he would hide them all away in a hiding place
of Earth and would not allow them to come into the light, and Sky took
delight in his evil deed. But huge Earth groaned within from the strain,
and she devised an evil trick. Quickly making a gray unconquerable
substance, she fashioned a huge sickle, and she spoke to her dear children.
She said, encouragingly, but sorrowing in her own heart; "My children,
begotten by a mad father, if you are willing to listen to me,
let us take vengeance for your father's wicked outrage. For he first
devised unseemly deeds." So she spoke, but fear seized them all, nor did
any of them speak. Then, taking courage, the crooked-counseling Kronos
answered his excellent mother. "Mother, I will undertake this deed
and I will bring it to completion, for I do not like our father and his evil
name. It was *he* who first began unseemly deeds."

So he spoke,
and vast Earth rejoiced greatly in her heart. She took Kronos and hid
him in an ambush. She placed the saw-toothed sickle in his hands.
She laid out the whole plot. Great Sky came, dragging night, and he lay
all over Earth, wanting to make love, and he was spread out all over her.
Then the child reached out from his ambush with his left hand,
and with his right hand he held the huge sickle, long and saw-toothed,
and furiously he cut off his father's genitals, and he threw them away,
to fall backwards. They did not flee from his hand for nothing!

Earth received all the bloody drops that shook free, and as the years
rolled around, she bore Erinys and the great and mighty Giants, shining
in their armor and holding long spears in their hands, and she bore
the nymphs that people call the Ash Nymphs upon the boundless earth.
When he first cut off the genitals with his sickle made of an unconquerable
substance, he threw them from the land into the churning sea, where they
were borne for a long time over the waves, and a white foam [*aphros*]
arose around the deathless flesh. And in it a young woman was raised up.

She first came to holy CYTHERA, and then from there she arrived in
CYPRUS, wrapped in waves. She came forth an awful and beautiful goddess,
and around her slender feet grass grew. Men and gods call her Aphrodite,
a goddess born from the foam, and also lovely-crowned Cythereia—
because she was born of the foam, and Cythereia because she came
to Cythera. And Cyprogenea, because she was born on stormy Cyprus,
and Lover of Laughter because she came to light from the genitals.

THE ORIGINS OF THE TROJAN WAR

Cypria

Epic Cycle

Translated by Martin L. West, 2003

Homer's epics describe the events and aftermath of a legendary war fought between the Greeks and Trojans in the Late Bronze Age. The ten-year conflict began after Paris, a prince of Troy, judged Aphrodite to be the most beautiful goddess, and as his reward absconded with Helen, wife of King Menelaus of Sparta. Menelaus and his brother Agamemnon consequently marched a Greek army against Troy. A host of poets working in Homer's wake produced sequels and prequels and adjuncts to these stories. The poems of this so-called 'Epic Cycle' are fragmentary, but this one, the *Cypria*, which is thought to have been composed in the sixth century BC, survives in detailed summary. The poem described Paris meeting Helen for the very first time and the Greeks arriving in Troy. It also included this intriguing backstory, recorded by an ancient scholar on the *Iliad*, as an additional explanation for the cause of the Trojan War.

There was a time when the countless races [of men] roaming [constantly] over the land were weighing down the [deep-]breasted earth's expanse. Zeus took pity when he saw it, and in his complex mind he resolved to relieve the all-nurturing earth of mankind's weight by fanning the great conflict of the Trojan War, to void the burden through death. So the warriors at Troy kept being killed, and Zeus' plan was being fulfilled.

THE TRUCE

Iliad, Book III

Homer

Translated by E. V. Rieu, 1950

The story of the *Iliad* of **Homer** is set in the tenth and final year of the Trojan War. At the beginning of this extract from the poem, the messenger goddess Iris comes to tell Helen that the Greeks ('Achaeans' or 'Argives') and Trojans have agreed to a truce. Her lover Paris is to fight her forsaken husband Menelaus, King of Sparta ('Lacedaemon') man to man for her and her goods. We meet Priam, King of Troy ('Ilium'), and a great many of the characters who predominate on the battlefield, including Menelaus' brother Agamemnon, the leader of the Greek army.

Meanwhile Iris brought the news to white-armed Helen, disguising herself as Helen's sister-in-law, Laodice, the most beautiful of Priam's daughters, who was married to the lord Helicaon, Antenor's son. She found Helen in her palace, at work on a great purple web of double width, into which she was weaving some of the many battles between the horse-taming Trojans and the bronze-clad Achaeans in the war that had been forced upon them for her sake. Iris of the Nimble Feet went up to her and said: 'My dear sister, come and see how strangely the Trojan and Achaean soldiers are behaving. A little while ago they were threatening each other with a terrible battle in the plain and looked as though they meant to fight to the death. But now the battle is off, and they are sitting quietly there, leaning on their shields, with the long javelins stuck on end beside them, while Paris and the redoubtable Menelaus are to fight a duel for you with their great spears, and the winner is to claim you as his wife.'

This news from the goddess filled Helen's heart with tender longing for her former husband and her parents and the city she had left. She wrapped a veil of white linen round her head, and with the tear-drops running down her cheeks set out from her bedroom, not alone, but attended by two waiting-women. Aethre daughter of Pittheus, and the ox-eyed lady Clymene. In a little while they reached the neighbourhood of the Scaean Gate.

At this gate, Priam was sitting in conference with the Elders of the city, Panthous and Thymoetes, Lampus and Clytius, Hicetaon, offshoot of the War-god, and his two wise counsellors, Ucalegon and Antenor. Old age had brought their fighting days to an end, but they were excellent speakers, these Trojan Elders, sitting there on the tower, like cicadas perched on a tree in the woods chirping delightfully.

When they saw Helen coming to the tower, they lowered their voices. 'Who on earth,' they asked one another, 'could blame the Trojan and Achaean men-at-arms for suffering so long for such a woman's sake? Indeed, she is the very image of an immortal goddess. All the same, and lovely as she is, let her sail home and not stay here to vex us and our children after us.'

Meanwhile, Priam had called Helen to his side. 'Dear child,' he said, 'come here and sit in front of me, so that you may see your former husband and your relatives and friends. I bear you no ill will at all: I blame the gods. It is they who brought this terrible Achaean war upon me. And now you can tell me the name of that giant over there. Who is that tall and handsome Achaean? There are others taller by a head, but I have never set eyes on a man with such good looks or with such majesty. He is every inch a king.'

'I pay you homage and reverence, my dear father-in-law,' replied the gracious lady Helen. 'I wish I had chosen to die in misery before I came here with your son, deserting my bridal chamber, my kinsfolk, my darling daughter and the dear friends with whom I had grown up. But things did not fall out like that, to my unending sorrow. However, I must tell you what you wished to know. The man you pointed out is imperial Agamemnon son of Atreus, a good king and a mighty spearman too. He was my brother-in-law once, shameless creature that I am – unless all that was a dream.'

When he heard this the old man gazed at Agamemnon with envious admiration. 'Ah, lucky son of Atreus,' he exclaimed, 'child of fortune, blessed by the gods! So you are the man whom all these thousands of Achaeans serve! I went to Phrygia once, the land of vines and galloping horses, and learnt how numerous the Phrygians are when I saw the armies of Otreus and King Mygdon encamped by the River Sangarius. I was their ally and I bivouacked with them that time the Amazons, who fight like men, came up to the attack. But even they were not as many as these Achaeans with their flashing eyes.'

The old man, noticing Odysseus next, said: 'Tell me now, dear child, who that man is. He is shorter than King Agamemnon by a head, but broader in the shoulders and the chest. He has left his armour lying on the ground, and there he goes, like a bellwether, inspecting the ranks. He reminds me of a fleecy ram bringing a great flock of white sheep to heel.'

'That,' said Helen, child of Zeus, 'is Laertes' son, Odysseus of the nimble wits. Ithaca, where he was brought up, is a poor and rocky land; but he is a master of intrigue and stratagem.'

The wise Antenor added something to Helen's picture of Odysseus. 'Madam,' he said, 'I can endorse what you say, for Odysseus has been here. He came with Menelaus on an embassy in your behalf, and I was their host. I entertained them in my own house, and I know not only what they look like but the way they think. In conference with the Trojans, when all were standing, Menelaus with his broad shoulders overtopped the whole company; but Odysseus was the more imposing of the two when both were seated. When their turn came to express their views in public, Menelaus spoke fluently, not at great length, but very clearly, being a man of few words who kept to the point, though he was the younger of the two. By contrast, when the nimble-witted Odysseus took the floor, he stood there with his head bent firmly down, glancing from under his brows, and he did not swing his staff either to the front or back, but held it stiffly, as though he had never handled one before. You would have taken him for a sulky fellow and no better than a fool. But when that great voice of his came booming from his chest, and the words poured from his lips like flakes of winter snow, there was no man alive who could compete with Odysseus. When we looked at him then, we were no longer misled by appearances.'

Aias was the third man whom the old king noticed and enquired about. 'Who is that other fine and upstanding Achaean,' he asked, 'taller than all the rest by a head and shoulders?'

'That,' said the gracious lady Helen of the long robe, 'is the huge Aias, a tower of strength to the Achaeans. And there on the other side is Idomeneus, standing among the Cretans like a god, with his Cretan captains gathered round him. My lord Menelaus often entertained him in our house, when he paid us a visit from Crete. And now I have picked out all the Achaeans whom I can recognize and name, except two chieftains whom I cannot find, Castor, the tamer of horses and Polydeuces the great boxer, my own brothers, borne by the same mother as myself. Either they did not join the army from lovely Lacedaemon, or if they crossed the seas and came here with the rest, they are unwilling to take part in the fighting on account of the scandal attached to my name and the insults they might hear.'

She did not know, when she said this, that the fruitful Earth had already received them in her lap, over there in Lacedaemon, in the country that they loved.

Heralds, meanwhile, were bringing through the town the wherewithal for the treaty of peace, two sheep and a goatskin bottle full of mellow wine, the fruit of the soil. The herald Idaeus, who carried a gleaming bowl and golden cups, came up to the old king and roused him to action. 'Up, my lord,' he said. 'The commanders of the Trojan and Achaean forces are calling for you to come down onto the plain and make a truce. Paris and the warrior Menelaus are going to fight each other with long spears for Helen. The winner is to have the lady, goods and all, while the rest make a treaty of peace, by which we stay in deep-soiled Troy, and the enemy sail home to Argos where the horses graze and Achaea land of lovely women.'

The old man shuddered when he heard this; but he told his men to harness horses to his chariot, and they promptly obeyed. Priam mounted and drew back the reins, Antenor got into the splendid chariot beside him, and they drove their fast horses through the Scaean Gate towards the open country.

When they reached the assembled armies, they stepped down from their chariot onto the bountiful earth and walked to a spot midway between the Trojans and Achaeans. King Agamemnon and the resourceful Odysseus rose at once; and stately heralds brought the victims for the sacrifice together, mixed wine in the bowl, and poured some water on the kings' hands. Then Agamemnon drew the knife that he always carried beside the great scabbard of his sword, and cut some hair from the lambs' heads. The hair was distributed among the Trojan and Achaean captains by the heralds. And now Agamemnon lifted up his hands and prayed aloud in the hearing of all: 'Father Zeus, you that rule from Mount Ida, most glorious and great; and you, the Sun, whose eye and ear miss nothing in the world; you Rivers and you Earth; you Powers of the world below that make the souls of dead men pay for perjury; I call on you all to witness our oaths and to see that they are kept. If Paris kills Menelaus, let him keep Helen and her wealth, and we shall sail away in our seagoing ships. But if red-haired Menelaus kills Paris, the Trojans must surrender Helen and all her possessions, and compensate the Argives suitably, on a scale that future generations shall remember. And if, in the event of Paris' death, Priam and his sons refuse to pay, I shall stay here and fight for the indemnity until the war is finished.'

Agamemnon now slit the lambs' throats with the relentless bronze and dropped them gasping on the ground, where the life-force ebbed and left them, for the knife had done its work. Then they drew wine from the bowl in cups, and as they poured it on the ground they made their petitions to the gods that have been since time began. The watching Trojans and Achaeans prayed as well – the same prayer served them both. 'Zeus, most glorious and great, and you other immortal gods; may the brains of whichever party breaks this treaty be poured out on the ground as that wine is poured, and not only theirs but their children's too; and may foreigners possess their wives.' Such were their hopes of peace, but Zeus had no intention yet of bringing peace about.

Dardanian Priam now made himself heard. 'Trojans and Achaean men-at-arms,' he said, 'attend to me. I am going back to windy Ilium, since I cannot bear to look on while my own son fights the formidable Menelaus. All I can think is that Zeus and the other immortal gods must know already which of the two is going to his doom.'

With these words, the venerable king put the lambs in the car and himself mounted and drew back the reins. Antenor took his place beside him in the splendid chariot, and the two drove off on their way back to Ilium.

Priam's son Hector and the admirable Odysseus proceeded to measure out the ground, and then to cast lots from a metal helmet to see which of the two should throw his bronze spear first. The watching armies prayed, with their hands raised to the gods – the same prayer served them both. 'Father Zeus, you that rule from Mount Ida, most glorious and great; let the man who brought these troubles on both peoples die and go down to the House of Hades; and let peace be established between us.'

They made their prayers; and now great Hector of the flashing helmet shook the lots, turning his eyes aside. One of the lots leapt out at once. It was that of Paris.

The troops sat down in rows, each man by his high-stepping horses, where his ornate arms were piled; and Prince Paris, husband of Helen of the lovely hair, put on his beautiful armour. He began by tying round his legs a pair of splendid greaves, which were fitted with silver clips for the ankles. Next he put a cuirass on his breast. It was his brother Lycaon's and he had to adjust it. Over his shoulder he slung a bronze sword with a silver-studded hilt, and then a great thick shield. On his sturdy head he set a well-made helmet. It had a horse-hair crest, and the plume nodded grimly from the top. Last, he took up a powerful spear, which was fitted to his grip.

Battle-loving Menelaus also equipped himself in the same way; and when both had got themselves ready, each behind his own front line, they strode out between the two forces, looking so terrible that the spectators were spellbound, horse-taming Trojans and Achaean men-at-arms alike. The two men took their stations not far from one another on the measured piece of ground, and in mutual fury brandished their weapons. Paris was the first to hurl his long-shadowed spear. It landed on the round shield of Menelaus. But the bronze did not break through; the point was bent back by the stout shield. Then Menelaus son of Atreus brought his spear into play, with a prayer to Father Zeus: 'Grant me revenge, King Zeus, on Paris, the man who wronged me in the beginning. Use my hands to bring him down, so that our children's children may still shudder at the thought of injuring a host who has received them kindly.'

With that, he balanced his long-shadowed spear and hurled it. The heavy weapon struck the round shield of Priam's son. It pierced the glittering shield, forced its way through the ornate cuirass, and pressing straight on tore the tunic on Paris' flank. But Paris swerved, and so avoided death. Menelaus then drew his silver-mounted sword, swung it back, and brought it down on the ridge of his enemy's helmet. But the sword broke on the helmet into half a dozen pieces and dropped from his hand. Menelaus gave a groan and looked up at the broad sky. 'Father Zeus,' he cried, 'is there a god more spiteful than yourself? I thought I had paid out Paris for his infamy, and now my sword breaks in my hand, when I have already cast a spear for nothing and never touched the man!'

With that he hurled himself at Paris, seized him by the horsehair crest, and swinging him round, began to drag him into the Achaean lines. Paris was choked by the pressure on his tender throat of the embroidered helmet-strap, which he had fitted tightly round his chin; and Menelaus would have hauled him in and covered himself with glory, but for the quickness of Aphrodite Daughter of Zeus, who saw what was happening and broke the strap for Paris, though it was made of leather from a slaughtered ox. So the helmet came away empty in the great hand of the noble Menelaus. He tossed it, with a swing, into the Achaean lines, where it was picked up by his own retainers, and flung himself at his enemy again, in the hope of despatching him with his bronze-pointed spear. But Aphrodite used her powers once more. Hiding Paris in a dense mist, she whisked him off – it was an easy feat for the goddess – and put him down in his own perfumed fragrant bedroom. Then she went herself to summon Helen.

She found Helen on the high tower, surrounded by Trojan women. Aphrodite put out her hand, plucked at her sweet-scented robe, and spoke to her in the disguise of an old woman she was very fond of, a wool-worker who used to make beautiful wool for her when she lived in Lacedaemon. 'Come!' said the goddess, mimicking this woman. 'Paris wants you to go home to him. There he is in his room, on the inlaid bed, radiant in his beauty and his lovely clothes. You would never believe that he had just come in from a duel. You would think he was going to a dance or had just stopped dancing and sat down to rest.'

Helen was perturbed and looked at the goddess. When she observed the beauty of her neck and her lovely breasts and sparkling eyes, she was struck with awe. But she made no pretence of being deceived. 'Lady of mysteries,' she said, 'what is the object of this mummery? Now that Menelaus has beaten Paris and is willing to take home his erring wife, you are plotting, I suppose, to carry me off to some still more distant city, in Phrygia or in lovely Maeonia, for some other favourite of yours who may be living in those parts? So you begin by coming here, and try to lure me back to Paris. No; go and sit with him yourself. Forget that you are a goddess. Never set foot in Olympus again, but devote yourself to Paris. Pamper him well, and one day you may be his wife – or else his slave. I refuse to go and share his bed again – I should never hear the end of it. There is not a woman in Troy who would not curse me if I did. I have enough to bear already.'

The Lady Aphrodite rounded on her in fury. 'Obstinate wretch!' she cried. 'Do not provoke me, or I might desert you in my anger, and hate you as heartily as I have loved you up till now, rousing the Trojans and Achaeans to such bitter enmity as would bring *you* to a miserable end.'

Helen was cowed, child of Zeus though she was. She wrapped herself up in her white and glossy robe, and went off without a sound. Not one of the Trojan women saw her go: she had a goddess to guide her.

When they reached the beautiful house of Paris, the maids in attendance betook themselves at once to their tasks, while Helen, the great lady, went to her lofty bedroom. There the goddess herself, laughter-loving Aphrodite, picked up a chair, carried it across the room and put it down for her in front of Paris. Helen, daughter of aegis-bearing Zeus, sat down on it, but turned her eyes aside and began by scolding her lover: 'So you are back from the battlefield – and I was hoping you had fallen there to the great soldier who was once my husband! You used to boast that you were a better man than the mighty Menelaus, a finer spearman, stronger in the arm. Then why not go at once and challenge him again? Or should I warn you to think twice before you offer single combat to the red-haired Menelaus? Do nothing rash – or you may end by falling to his spear!'

Paris had his answer ready. 'My dear,' he said, 'do not try to put me on my mettle by abusing me. Menelaus has just beaten me with Athene's help. But I too have gods to help me, and next time I shall win. Come, let us go to bed together and be happy in our love. Never has such desire overwhelmed me, not even in the beginning, when I carried you off from lovely Lacedaemon in my seagoing ships and we spent the night on the isle of Cranae in each other's arms – never till now have I been so much in love with you or felt such sweet desire.'

As he spoke, he made a move towards the bed, leading her to it. His wife followed him; and the two lay down together on the well-made wooden bed.

Meanwhile Menelaus was prowling through the ranks like a wild beast, trying to find Prince Paris. But not a man among the Trojans or their famous allies could point him out to the warrior Menelaus. Not that if anyone had seen him he would have hidden him for love: they loathed him, all of them, like death. In the end King Agamemnon made a pronouncement: 'Trojans, Dardanians and allies, listen to me. The great Menelaus has won: there is no disputing that. Now give up Argive Helen and her wealth, and compensate me suitably on a scale that future generations shall remember.'

Atreides had spoken. The Achaeans all applauded.

The truce, alas, does not last. The gods ensure that it is broken and that the Trojan War continues until many more people have lost their lives.

HECTOR VERSUS ACHILLES

Iliad, Book XXII

Homer

Translated by Martin Hammond, 1987

Hector's parents, Priam, King of Troy, and Hecuba, have tried to dissuade him from meeting Achilles (Achilleus) in combat. Hector (Hektor) feels he has no choice. For Achilles, too, the decision to fight Hector in a duel is fraught. He knows from his mother, a nymph named Thetis, that his own death is sure to follow that of Hector. Achilles' father, Peleus, was only mortal. This passage comes from the twenty-second of the twenty-four books of Homer's *Iliad* but is very much the dramatic finale of the poem. It contains some of the most beautiful similes in the epic. It begins with Hector criticising himself for Troy's ill fortunes and his failure to heed the advice of his friend Poulydamas, who favoured caution over direct attack. Hector shoulders far too much of the blame. If any man is guilty of 'arrant folly' it is his brother Paris ('Alexandros') who ran off with Helen in the first place.

But he spoke in dismay to his own great heart: 'What am I to do? If I go back inside the gates and the wall, Poulydamas will be the first to lay blame on me, because he urged me to lead the Trojans back to the city during this last fatal night, when godlike Achilleus had roused himself. But I did not take his advice – it would have been far better if I had. Now that I have destroyed my people through my own arrant folly, I feel shame before the men of Troy and the women of Troy with their trailing dresses, that some man, a worse man than I, will say: "Hektor trusted in his own strength and destroyed his people." That is what they will say: and then it would be far better for me to face Achilleus and either kill him and return home, or die a glorious death myself in front of my city. But suppose I put down my bossed shield and heavy helmet, and lean my spear against the wall, and go out as I am to meet the excellent Achilleus, and promise to return Helen and all her property with her to the sons of Atreus for their keeping, all that Alexandros brought away in his hollow ships to Troy and was the first cause of our quarrel: and also to share equally with the Achaians all the rest of the property stored in this city – then afterwards I could make the Trojans take an oath in their council that they will hide nothing, but divide everything in two parts, all the possessions that the lovely city contains within it. But what need for this debate in my heart? I fear that if I go up to him he will not show me any pity or regard for my appeal, but will simply kill me unarmed like a woman, when I have taken off my armour. There can be no sweet murmuring with him now, like boy and girl at the trysting-tree or rock, the way a boy and girl murmur sweetly together. Better to close and fight as soon as can be. We can see then to which of us the Olympian is giving the victory.'

Such were his thoughts as he waited. And Achilleus came close on him like Enyalios the god of war, the warrior with the flashing helmet, shaking his terrible spear of Pelian ash over his right shoulder: and the bronze on his body shone, like the light of a blazing fire or the sun when it rises. And trembling took hold of Hektor when he saw him. Now he no longer had the courage to stand his ground where he was, but he left the gates behind him and ran in terror: and the son of Peleus leapt after him, confident in the speed of his legs. As a hawk in the mountains, quickest of all flying things, swoops after a trembling dove with ease: she flies in terror before him, but he keeps close behind her, screaming loud, and lunging for her time after time as his heart urges him to kill. So Achilleus flew straight for Hektor in full fury, and Hektor fled away from him under the walls of Troy, setting his legs running fast. They sped past the look-out place and the wind-tossed fig-tree, keeping all the time to the wagon-track a little way out from the wall, and came to the two well-heads of lovely water: here the twin springs of swirling Skamandros shoot up from the ground. One spring runs with warm water, and steam rises all round it as if a fire were burning there. But the other even in summer flows out cold as hail, or frozen snow, or water turned to ice. There close beside these springs are the fine broad washing-troughs made of stone, where the Trojans' wives and their lovely daughters used to wash their bright clothes, in earlier times, in peace, before the sons of the Achaians came. The two men ran past here, one in flight, the other chasing him. A brave man was running in front, but a far greater one was in pursuit, and they ran at speed, since it was no sacrificial beast or ox-hide shield they were competing for – such as are the usual prizes that men win in the foot-race – but they were running for the life of Hektor the tamer of horses. As when champion strong-footed horses wheel round the turning-posts running at full stretch, when a great prize is there to be won, a tripod or a woman, in the funeral games for a man who has died: so those two raced round the city of Priam, circling it three times with all the speed of their legs, and all the gods looked on. The father of men and gods was the first of them to speak: 'Oh, I love this man who is being pursued around the wall under the gaze of my eyes. My heart is saddened for Hektor, who has burned the thigh-bones of many oxen to me on the peaks of valleyed Ida, and again on the city's height. But now godlike Achilleus on his swift feet is chasing him round the city of Priam. Well then, give thought to it, gods, and consider whether we shall save him from death, or bring him down now, for all his bravery, at the hands of Achilleus son of Peleus.'

Then the bright-eyed goddess Athene said to him: 'Father, master of the bright lightning and the dark clouds, what is this you are saying? Do you intend to take a man who is mortal and long ago doomed by fate, and release him from grim death? Do it then – but we other gods will not all approve you.'

Then Zeus the cloud-gatherer answered her: 'Do not worry, Tritogeneia, dear child. I do not speak with my heart in full earnest, and my intention to you is kind. Do as your purpose directs, and do not hold back any longer.'

With these words he urged on Athene what she herself already desired, and she went darting down from the peaks of Olympos. And swift Achilleus kept driving Hektor on with his relentless pursuit. As when a dog has started the fawn of a deer from its lair in the mountains, and chases it on through the hollows and the glens: even if it takes to cover and crouches hidden under a bush, the dog smells out its track and runs on unerringly until he finds it. So Hektor could not throw off the swift-footed son of Peleus. Whenever he tried to make a dash for the Dardanian gates, to get under the well-built walls and give the men above a chance of defending him with their weapons, every time Achilleus would be there in time to block his way and head him back out towards the plain, while he himself kept always on the city side as he flew onwards. As a man in a dream is unable to pursue someone trying to escape, and the other cannot run away just as he cannot give chase: so Achilleus could not catch him with his running, nor Hektor get away. And how could Hektor have kept clear of the fates of death, if Apollo had not come close to him for the last and final time, and spurred strength in him and speed to his legs? And godlike Achilleus had been shaking his head at his own people to stop them shooting their bitter arrows at Hektor, in case one of them should win the glory with a hit, and he himself reach Hektor too late. But when they came round to the well-heads for the fourth time, then the Father opened out his golden scales. In the pans he put two fates of death's long sorrow, one for Achilleus and one for Hektor the tamer of horses, and he took the scales in the middle and lifted them up: and Hektor's day of doom sank down, away into Hades, and Phoibos Apollo left him. Then the bright-eyed goddess Athene came to the son of Peleus, and stood close by him and spoke winged words to him: 'Now, glorious Achilleus loved of Zeus, now I think that we two will bring great glory for the Achaians back to the ships – we will kill Hektor, for all his lust for battle. There is no possibility now that he can escape us any longer, even if Apollo the far-worker goes through agonies of grovelling before father Zeus who holds the aegis. So you stand still now and get your breath, while I go and persuade him to fight with you face to face.'

So Athene spoke, and Achilleus was happy at heart, and did as she told him: so he stood there leaning on his bronze-barbed ash spear. She then left him and caught up with godlike Hektor, taking the form and tireless voice of Deïphobos. She came close and spoke winged words to him: 'Brother, swift Achilleus is pressing you very hard now, chasing you round the city of Priam with all his speed. Come then, let us face him together and beat him off where we stand.'

Then great Hektor of the glinting helmet said to her: 'Deïphobos, you have always been the brother I loved far the most of all the sons born to Hekabe and Priam. And now my heart is minded to honour you yet more highly, since you have had the courage, when your eyes saw my trouble, to come outside the wall on my account, while all the others stay inside.'

Then the bright-eyed goddess Athene said to him: 'Brother, our father and honoured mother, and my friends around me, did indeed beseech me one after the other, and implored me again and again to stay where I was inside – such is the terror on them all. But my heart within me was chafed with painful sorrow for you. Now let us charge straight in and fight, and not be sparing with our spears, so we can see whether Achilleus will kill us both and carry away our bloody spoils to the hollow ships, or else be beaten down under your spear.'

So speaking Athene led him forward in her treachery. When the two men had advanced to close range, great Hektor of the glinting helmet was first to speak: 'Son of Peleus, I shall not run from you any more, as I did when you chased me three times round the great city of Priam, and I did not dare to stop and take your attack. But now my heart prompts me to stand and face you – I shall kill or be killed. But first let us swear here before our gods – they will be the best witnesses to keep watch on our agreement. I swear that I will inflict no outrage on you, if Zeus grants me the endurance and I take away your life: but after I have stripped you of your famous armour, Achilleus, I will give your body back to the Achaians – and you do the same.'

Then swift-footed Achilleus scowled at him and said: 'Hektor, do not talk to me of agreements, you madman. There are no treaties of trust between lions and men: wolves and lambs share no unity of heart, but are fixed in hatred of each other for all time – so there can be no friendship for you and me, there will be no oaths between us, before one or the other falls and gives his glut of blood to Ares, the fighter with the bull's-hide shield. Call to mind now all your fighting skills: now is the time above all to show yourself a spearman and a brave warrior. But I tell you there is no escape for you any longer, but soon Pallas Athene will beat you down under my spear. And now you will make me lump payment for the pain of my companions' deaths, all those you killed when your spear was raging.'

So he spoke, and steadying his long-shadowed spear he let it fly. But glorious Hektor had looked ahead and avoided it. He watched it come and crouched down, and the bronze spear flew over him and fixed in the earth: and unseen by Hektor, shepherd of the people, Pallas Athene pulled up the spear and gave it back to Achilleus. Hektor then spoke to the excellent son of Peleus: 'You missed! So, godlike Achilleus, it seems you knew nothing from Zeus about my death – and yet you said you did. No, you turn out a mere ranter – all your talk is bluff, to frighten me and make me lose my courage for the fight. Well, I shall not run and let you fix your spear in my back, but you must drive it through my chest as I charge straight for you, if that is what god has granted you. But now you try to avoid this bronze spear of mine – how I hope you take it entire in your flesh! Then the war would go lighter for the Trojans, with you dead, their greatest danger.'

So he spoke, and steadying his long-shadowed spear he let it fly, and did not miss, hitting in the centre of the son of Peleus' shield: but the spear rebounded far from the shield. Hektor was angered that his swift spear had flown wasted from his hand, and stood there in dismay, as he had no second ash spear. He called in a great shout to Deïphobos of the white shield, and asked him for a long spear. But Deïphobos was not there near him. Then Hektor realised in his heart, and cried out: 'Oh, for sure now the gods have called me to my death! I thought the hero Deïphobos was with me: but he is inside the wall, and Athene has tricked me. So now vile death is close on me, not far now any longer, and there is no escape. This must long have been the true pleasure of Zeus and Zeus' son the far-shooter, and yet before now they readily defended me: but now this time my fate has caught me. Even so, let me not die ingloriously, without a fight, without some great deed done that future men will hear of.'

So speaking he drew the sharp sword that hung long and heavy at his side, gathered himself, and swooped like a high-flying eagle which darts down to the plain through the dark clouds to snatch up a baby lamb or a cowering hare. So Hektor swooped to attack, flourishing his sharp sword. And Achilleus charged against him, his heart filled with savage fury. In front of his chest he held the covering of his lovely decorated shield, and the bright four-bossed helmet nodded on his head, with the beautiful golden hairs that Hephaistos had set thick along the crest shimmering round it. Like the Evening Star on its path among the stars in the darkness of the night, the loveliest star set in the sky, such was the light gleaming from the point of the sharp spear Achilleus held quivering in his right hand, as he purposed death for godlike Hektor, looking over his fine body to find the most vulnerable place. All the rest of his body was covered by his bronze armour, the fine armour he had stripped from mighty Patroklos when he killed him. But flesh showed where the collar-bones hold the join of neck and shoulders, at the gullet, where a man's life is most quickly destroyed. Godlike Achilleus drove in there with his spear as Hektor charged him, and the point went right through his soft neck: but the ash spear with its weight of bronze did not cut the windpipe, so that Hektor could still speak and answer Achilleus. He crashed in the dust, and godlike Achilleus triumphed over him: 'Hektor, doubtless as you killed Patroklos you thought you would be safe, and you had no fear of me, as I was far away. You fool – behind him there was I left to avenge him, a far greater man than he, waiting there by the hollow ships, and I have collapsed your strength. Now the dogs and birds will maul you hideously, while the Achaians will give Patroklos full burial.'

Then with the strength low in him Hektor of the glinting helmet answered: 'I beseech you by your life and knees and by your parents, do not let the dogs of the Achaian camp eat me by the ships, but take the ransom of bronze and gold in plenty that my father and honoured mother will offer you, and give my body back to my home, so that the Trojans and the wives of the Trojans can give me in death my due rite of burning.'

Then swift-footed Achilleus scowled at him and said: 'Make me no appeals, you dog, by knees or parents. I wish I could eat you myself, that the fury in my heart would drive me to cut you in pieces and eat your flesh raw, for all that you have done to me. So no man is going to keep the dogs away from your head, not even if they bring here and weigh out ten times or twenty times your ransom, not even if Dardanian Priam offers to pay your own weight in gold. Not even so will your honoured mother lay you on the bier and mourn for you, her own child, but the dogs and birds will share you for their feast and leave nothing.'

Then, dying, Hektor of the glinting helmet said to him: 'Yes, I can tell it – I know you well, and I had no chance of swaying you: your heart is like iron in your breast. But take care now, or I may bring the gods' anger on you, on that day when for all your bravery Paris and Phoibos Apollo will destroy you at the Skaian gates.'

THE DEATH OF ACHILLES

Posthomerica, Book III

Quintus Smyrnaeus

Translated by Alan James, 2004

This story was written around a millennium after the Homeric epics.
Little is known of its author, **Quintus Smyrnaeus** (third century AD),
other than that he came from Smyrna (modern İzmir), in what is now
Turkey. He would probably have been familiar with the ancient Epic
Cycle (see Story 2), which included a poem on Achilles' death called the
Aethiopis. Homer had merely foreshadowed the death of Achilles, son
of Peleus, allowing later poets to imagine how the episode would have
played out. Quintus Smyrnaeus dispensed with Paris and made Apollo
solely responsible for Achilles' death.

Quickly from either side on common ground converged
The tribes of Trojans and of Argives firm in the fray,
Eager for fighting now that the battle was set in motion.
There the son of Peleus destroyed a mighty host
Of his foes. All round the life-giving earth was drenched
With blood, and the waters of Xanthos and Simoeis
Were choked with corpses. Achilles still pursued and slaughtered
All the way to the city, since panic possessed the army.
He would have killed them all and dashed their gates to the ground,
Tearing them from their hinges, or would have smashed the bolts
With a sideward blow and opened a way for the Danaans
Into Priam's city and would have plundered its wealth,
If anger had not filled the merciless heart of Phoibos
At the sight of those countless throngs of warriors slaughtered.
Down from Olympos he came with the speed of a savage beast;
Over his shoulders his quiver was filled with deadly arrows.
Facing Aiakos' grandson he stood, while on his back
Loudly rattled his bow in its case and from his eyes
Came constant flashes of fire; the ground shook under his feet.
The great god gave a terrible shout, to deter Achilles
From the battle for fear of the supernatural voice
Of a god and so to save the Trojans from being killed:
"Back off, son of Peleus, away from the Trojans. No longer

May you inflict the evil Fates upon your foes,
Or one of the deities of Olympos may destroy you."
But Achilles did not quail at the god's immortal voice;
Already the merciless Fates were hovering over him.
So without respect for the god he shouted back at him;
"Phoibos, why do you rouse me, even against my will,
To fight against gods, in order to save the arrogant Trojans?
Once before you tricked and decoyed me from the fighting,
The first time that you rescued Hektor from death,
The man the Trojans exalted so highly in their city.
Back off now, far away, and join the rest of the gods
At home, or I will strike you, immortal though you are."

With that he left the deity far behind, pursuing
The Trojans who were still in flight before the city.
While he was chasing them, the heart of Phoibos Apollo
Was filled with anger and to himself he spoke these words:
"Alas, the man has taken leave of his mind. But now
Not even the son of Kronos himself or anyone else
Can tolerate such insane defiance of the gods."
That said, he made himself invisible with cloud
And from his cloak of mist he shot a baleful shaft,
Which sped and struck Achilles' ankle. Immediately pain
Penetrated his heart and toppled him, like a tower
That from the force of a subterranean vortex
Collapses on top of the deeply shaken earth;
So fell to the ground the handsome frame of Aiakos' grandson.
Looking all about him he uttered this deadly curse:
"Who was it shot a dreadful arrow at me by stealth?
Let him have the courage to face me openly,
To have his blood and all his bowels come gushing out
Around my spear, to send him off to sorrowful Hades.
For well I know there is no warrior in the world
Who at close quarters can overcome me with his spear,
Even with an utterly dauntless heart in his breast,
A totally dauntless heart and a body of bronze.
Stealth is the weakling's way to snare a better man.
Just let him face me, even if he says he's a god
Who's angry with the Danaans; I suspect in my heart
It is Apollo concealed in sinister darkness.
So my beloved mother once revealed to me
That by Apollo's arrows I'd die a miserable death
Close to the Skaian Gate, and they were no idle words."
That said, with unflinching hands he pulled the fatal arrow
Out of a wound that could not heal. Out gushed the blood,
As he was gripped with pain and his heart was yielding to death.

~

In anguish he threw the weapon away, when a sudden gust
Of wind came and snatched it up and gave it back to Apollo
On his way to Zeus's hallowed ground, for it could not be
That a deathless bolt should go missing from a deathless god.
Apollo caught it and quickly gained the height of Olympos,
The general assembly of the immortals, the place where most
They gathered in force to watch the fighting of mortal men.
Some were eager to grant a triumph to the Trojans
And others to the Danaans. Such was their division
As they viewed the killing and dying in the battle.
As soon as Zeus's wise consort caught sight of him
She reproached him with these words of bitterness:
"Phoibos, what monstrous crime have you committed today,
Forgetful of that marriage which we immortals ourselves
Arranged for godlike Peleus? Amid the dining gods
Your sweet song told how Thetis of the silver feet
Left the depths of the sea to be the bride of Peleus.
As you played the lyre all creatures came together:
The savage beasts and birds, the hills with towering crags,
The rivers and all the deeply shaded forest came.
You've forgotten all that and done a heartless thing
In killing a great man, one who you and the other immortals,
Pouring libations of nectar, prayed would be the son
Of Peleus by Thetis. You've forgotten that prayer of yours
Just to oblige the race of the tyrant Laomedon,
For whom you kept the cattle. Mortal though he was,
He troubled you who are a god. You're fool enough
To forget your former labor and oblige the Trojans.
You wretch, is your pitiful mind unable to see
Which man for his wickedness deserves to suffer
And which the gods should hold in honor? For Achilles
Was well disposed to us and belonged to our race.
But I don't think the Trojans' labor will be lighter
For the fall of Aiakos' grandson, because his son
Shall very soon come from Skyros to help the Argives
In this harsh and bitter conflict, in his strength
His father's equal, bringing disaster to many a foe.
You're not really concerned for the Trojans, but are envious
Of Achilles' greatness as the best of men.
You fool, how will you face the daughter of Nereus now,
When she comes to the house of Zeus to join the immortals?
She used to honor you and regard you as her son."
Thus did Hera in her bitterness sharply rebuke
The son of almighty Zeus. He answered her not a word
Because of his respect for his powerful father's spouse.
He couldn't so much as look her in the face,
But sat apart from the gods who live forever,

His eyes upon the ground. Resentment against him was strong
From all the Olympian gods who supported the Danaan cause,
While those who were eager to grant a triumph to the Trojans
Held Apollo in honor, exulting in their hearts,
But out of Hera's sight, since all the heavenly beings
Were awed by her anger.

Meanwhile Achilles remembered still
His fighting spirit. Still in his invincible limbs
The crimson blood was seething with eagerness for the fight.
Not a single Trojan had courage to approach him,
Struck though he was. They stood well back, as from a lion
Rustics in a wood draw back afraid when a hunter
Has struck it; though a shaft has pierced its heart, it remembers
Still its courage; as it rolls its glaring eyes
It utters a terrible roar from its savage jaws.
So anger and his painful wound inflamed the spirit
Of Peleus' son, though dying from Apollo's arrow.
In spite of all he sprang and fell upon his foes,
His huge spear poised. He killed the noble Orythaon,
Hektor's brave comrade, with a blow below the temple.
His helmet failed to stop the long lance as intended.
It shot straight through both metal and bone, to penetrate
The nerves of his brain and so to spill his vital force.
He slew Hipponoos with a spear thrust under the brow
Into the roots of his eye. His eyeball fell from its socket
Onto the ground and his spirit flew away to Hades.
Next he penetrated the jaw of Alkithoos
And severed all of his tongue. He slumped upon the ground
Breathing his last, the spearpoint sticking out of his ear.
All these were slain by the hero as they hurried forth
To face him, while he took the lives of many others
In flight, for still the blood was seething in his heart.

When his limbs grew cold and his spirit ebbed away,
He stopped to lean on his spear. The Trojans continued their flight
In general panic, leaving him to rebuke them thus:
'You cowardly Trojans, Dardanians, even when I'm dead
You won't escape my merciless spear; the lot of you
Will pay the price of death to my avenging spirits."
They shuddered when they heard him speak, as in the mountains
Fawns will tremble at the sound of a roaring lion,
Making their timid escape from the beast. Likewise the army
Of the Trojan horsemen and their foreign allies
Trembled in terror of Achilles' final threat,
Supposing him unwounded still. But with the weight
Of doom upon his gallant spirit and sturdy frame,

He fell among the dead with the fall of a lofty mountain.
The earth resounded with the mighty crash of armor
At the fall of Peleus' peerless son. Yet abject terror
Shook the hearts of those who saw their fallen foe.
Just as when a savage beast is killed by herdsmen;
The sight of it fallen beside the fold so fills the flock
With fear that they haven't even the heart to approach it;
They shudder at the corpse as though it were alive;
Such was the Trojans' fear for Achilles after his death.

Despite that Paris used strong words to stir the people's
Spirits, because his heart was happy in the hope
That the Argives would give up the deadly fighting
After the fall of Peleus' son, who was their strength.
"My friends, if truly and sincerely you support me,
Let us either die today at the hands of the Argives
Or save ourselves and drag away to Ilion
The fallen body of Peleus' son with the horses of Hektor,
Which since the death of my brother bear me into battle,
Feeling still the grief of losing their true master.
If with their help we drag away the dead Achilles,
Great glory we would win for the horses as well as for Hektor
Himself, if really in Hades mortals retain their minds
Or sense of justice, in view of the harm he did to Troy,
Great will be the joy in the hearts of Trojan women
When they gather round him in the city, like fearsome
Lionesses or leopards furious for their cubs
Around a man experienced and skilled in dangerous hunting.
Thus round the body of slain Achilles the women of Troy
Will rush together to show their overwhelming hatred,
Some enraged for loss of fathers, some for husbands,
Some for children, and others for their honored kinsmen.
But happiest of all will be my father and the elders,
Those kept by age against their will inside the walls,
If we can only drag Achilles into the city
And leave him to be devoured by the birds of the air."
At these words round the body of Aiakos' valiant grandson
Quickly gathered those who'd feared him previously,
Glaukos, Aineias, Agenor the brave of heart,
And others who were skilled in the deadly art of war,
Eager to drag him off to Ilion's holy city.

Achilles, though, was not abandoned by godlike Ajax,
Who swiftly bestrode him and with his long lance drove them all
Away from him. And yet they persisted in their attack,
Fighting Ajax on every side and making assaults
One after the other, like so many long-lipped bees,

Which hover round their hive in countless swarms
To drive away a man; he disregards their attacks
While cutting out their honeycombs, and they are distressed
By both the man and the billowing smoke; and still they make
Their frontal assaults, although he heeds them not the least.
So Ajax disregarded all these rapid attacks.
First of all he killed with a blow above the breast
Maion's son Agelaos and next the noble Thestor;
Then Okythoos, Agestratos, Aganippos,
Zoros, Nissos, and the famous Erymas,
Who came from Lykia under valiant Glaukos' command.
His home was steep Melanippion sacred to Athena,
Which faces Massikytos near Cape Chelidon;
Seafaring sailors tremble in awe of that place
Whenever they have to round its jagged rocks.
The killing of that Lykian chilled with horror the heart
Of Hippolochos' famous son, because he was his friend.
Quickly stabbing Ajax's shield of many oxhides,
He was not able to penetrate to his fair flesh.
The hides of his shield protected him and under that
The breastplate that was fitted to his tireless body.
Glaukos, however, did not abandon the mortal combat
In his desire to vanquish Aiakos' grandson Ajax
He was so foolish as to make this boastful challenge:
"Ajax, since men claim that you are far the best
Of all the Argives and they are exceedingly proud of you,
No less than of brave Achilles, now that he is dead
You too will join him in death this very day, I reckon."
The words he uttered he could not fulfill; he did not know
The greater worth of the man at whom he aimed his spear
The steadfast fighter Ajax scowling at him replied:
"Don't you know, wretch, how much better than you in battle
Hektor was? And yet he avoided the force of this spear
Of mine, for with his brawn he had a prudent brain.
Your thoughts are clearly of death and darkness, since you dare
To face in combat one who is so much your better.
You cannot claim to be a family friend of mine,
Nor with your persuasive gifts will you divert me
From fighting as you did the mighty son of Tydeus.
You may have eluded that man's power, but I at least
Will not allow you to escape alive from the battle.
Perhaps you put your trust in others on this field,
Who together with you are flitting like worthless flies
Around the body of peerless Achilles. To them also,
If they attack, I'll give the dismal doom of death."

~

Ajax turned upon the Trojans, like a lion
Among a pack of hounds in a deep and wooded glen.
He quickly dispatched a host who were eager to win some glory,
Trojans and Lykians alike. Those round him trembled with fear,
Just like a shoal of fish in the ocean at the attack
Of a terrible whale or mighty dolphin of the sea.
So shrank the Trojans before the might of Telamon's son
Attacking them time and again in the battle. Even so
They fought on, so that on every side of Achilles' body
Numberless men lay dead in the dust like so many boars
Around a lion, for deadly was the fighting between them.
There too the warlike son of Hippolochos was slain
By stouthearted Ajax. Over Achilles he fell on his back,
Just like a mountain shrub beside a solid oak.
Such was the fall of Glaukos upon the son of Peleus
When struck by the spear. For him Anchises' powerful son
Labored long, and with the help of his warrior friends
Dragged him to the Trojan lines for his grieving comrades
To carry him back to the holy city of Ilion.
Aineias kept fighting over Achilles, till with his spear
The warlike Ajax wounded him above the muscle
Of his right arm. He leapt with rapid motion
Clear of the deadly fray and returned at once to the city.
Men skilled in the art of healing worked upon him,
Cleaning first the blood from his wound and then performing
All else that's needed to cure the suffering of the wounded.
Ajax fought on, as though with bolts of lightning
Killing in all directions, for great was his distress
And long the grief he felt for the death of his cousin.

Nearby the peerless son of the warrior Laertes
Engaged the enemy, who in terror fled before him.
He killed the swift Peisandros and Areios the son
Of Mainalos, whose home was the famous land of Abydos.
Next Odysseus slew Atymnios, who was borne
To strong Emathion by the fair-tressed nymph Pegasis
Beside the river Granikos. Close to that man
He struck dawn Proteus' son Oresbios, who lived
Below the vales of lofty Ida, but whose mother,
The famous Panakeia, never welcomed him home,
Slain as he was by the hands of Odysseus, who also took
The lives of many others with his raging spear,
Killing any he met near the body. But then Alkon,
Son of fleet-foot Megaldes, struck him with his spear
Beside the right knee and round his glittering greave
Dark blood came welling. He, though, disregarding the wound,
At once was the death of the eager fighter who wounded him.

Stabbing him with his spear clean through the shield.
With all the force of his powerful arm he pushed him
Backward onto the ground. The armor on him clashed
As he fell in the dust; the breastplate round his body
Was drenched with gore. Odysseus pulled the fatal spear
Out of both his flesh and his shield, and with the spearpoint
Breath left his limbs and life immortal abandoned him.
Though wounded, Odysseus made a rush at Alkon's comrades
And wouldn't relax the noisy struggle.

Likewise the other
Danaans, all in a compact mass round great Achilles,
fought keenly on and at their hands a host of men
Were rapidly slaughtered with their spears of polished ashwood.
As when leaves are strewn upon the ground by winds
That press with violent blasts on woods and groves,
When autumn wanes toward the closing of the year,
So they were felled by the spears of the resolute Danaan warriors.
The concern of everyone was for the dead Achilles,
But especially that of warlike Ajax. That was why
He slew so many Trojans like an evil Fate.
Then Paris drew his bow at Ajax, who saw at once
And hurled a deadly rock that hit him on the head
And smashed his double-crested helmet, so that darkness
Engulfed him and he collapsed in the dust, his arrows failing
To achieve his purpose, scattered in all directions
In the dust and the quiver lying empty with them,
His bow escaping from his hands. His comrades seized him
And carried him away to Troy on Hektor's chariot,
Hardly drawing breath and groaning in his pain.
Nor were his weapons left without their master; they too
Were gathered from the plain and brought back to the prince.
Ajax shouted after him in his vexation:
"You dog, you have evaded the heavy hand of death
Today, but very soon your final hour shall come,
Either at another Argive's hands or at mine.
Now a different matter weighs on my mind, to rescue
Achilles' body for the Danaans from this slaughter."

THE CYCLOPS

Odyssey, Book IX

Homer

Translated by Samuel Butler, 1900

Odysseus, who fought for the Greeks in the Trojan War, was renowned for his cleverness. It was his idea to build an enormous wooden horse to carry the Greeks into Troy so that they could finally sack the citadel (see Story 48). Unfortunately, he was the last of the men to return home after the war. Odysseus' travels, described in **Homer**'s *Odyssey*, took him over many seas and to many lands, including that of the Cyclopes – one-eyed monsters with a disgusting appetite for human flesh. This famous story is told by Odysseus himself to his hosts on a magical island named Scheria. In Story 3, Priam likened Odysseus to a ram. In this story, a ram saves his life. This lively and highly intelligent translation is by the great novelist Samuel Butler who, in 1897, reached the bold conclusion that the author of the *Odyssey* was a woman. The full title of this edition of his translation is perhaps rather patronising for modern tastes: 'The Odyssey: Rendered into English prose for the use of those who cannot read the original'.

"Now the Cyclopes neither plant nor plough, but trust in providence, and live on such wheat, barley, and grapes as grow wild without any kind of tillage, and their wild grapes yield them wine as the sun and the rain may grow them. They have no laws nor assemblies of the people, but live in caves on the tops of high mountains; each is lord and master in his family, and they take no account of their neighbours.

"Now off their harbour there lies a wooded and fertile island not quite close to the land of the Cyclopes, but still not far. It is over-run with wild goats, that breed there in great numbers and are never disturbed by foot of man; for sportsmen—who as a rule will suffer so much hardship in forest or among mountain precipices—do not go there, nor yet again is it ever ploughed or fed down, but it lies a wilderness untilled and unsown from year to year, and has no living thing upon it but only goats. For the Cyclopes have no ships, nor yet shipwrights who could make ships for them; they cannot therefore go from city to city, or sail over the sea to one another's country as people who have ships can do; if they had had these they would have colonised the island, for it is a very good one, and would yield everything in due season. There are meadows that in some places come right down to the sea shore, well watered and full of luscious grass; grapes would do there excellently; there is level land for ploughing, and it would always yield heavily at harvest time, for the soil is deep. There is a good harbour where no cables are wanted, nor yet anchors, nor need a ship be moored, but all one has to do is to beach one's vessel and stay there till the wind becomes fair for putting out to sea again. At the head of the harbour there is a spring of clear water coming out of a cave, and there are poplars growing all round it.

"Here we entered, but so dark was the night that some god must have brought us in, for there was nothing whatever to be seen. A thick mist hung all round our ships; the moon was hidden behind a mass of clouds so that no one could have seen the island if he had looked for it, nor were there any breakers to tell us we were close in shore before we found ourselves upon the land itself; when, however, we had beached the ships, we took down the sails, went ashore and camped upon the beach till daybreak.

"When the child of morning, rosy-fingered dawn appeared, we admired the island and wandered all over it, while the nymphs Jove's daughters roused the wild goats that we might get some meat for our dinner. On this we fetched our spears and bows and arrows from the ships, and dividing ourselves into three bands began to shoot the goats. Heaven sent us excellent sport; I had twelve ships with me, and each ship got nine goats, while my own ship had ten; thus through the livelong day to the going down of the sun we ate and drank our fill, and we had plenty of wine left, for each one of us had taken many jars full when we sacked the city of the Cicons, and this had not yet run out. While we were feasting we kept turning our eyes towards the land of the Cyclopes, which was hard by, and saw the smoke of their stubble fires. We could almost fancy we heard their voices and the bleating of their sheep and goats, but when the sun went down and it came on dark, we camped down upon the beach, and next morning I called a council.

"'Stay here, my brave fellows,' said I, 'all the rest of you, while I go with my ship and exploit these people myself: I want to see if they are uncivilized savages, or a hospitable and humane race.'

"I went on board, bidding my men to do so also and loose the hawsers; so they took their places and smote the grey sea with their oars. When we got to the land, which was not far, there, on the face of a cliff near the sea, we saw a great cave overhung with laurels. It was a station for a great many sheep and goats, and outside there was a large yard, with a high wall round it made of stones built into the ground and of trees both pine and oak. This was the abode of a huge monster who was then away from home shepherding his flocks. He would have nothing to do with other people, but led the life of an outlaw. He was a horrid creature, not like a human being at all, but resembling rather some crag that stands out boldly against the sky on the top of a high mountain.

"I told my men to draw the ship ashore, and stay where they were, all but the twelve best among them, who were to go along with myself. I also took a goat-skin of sweet black wine which had been given me by Maron son of Euanthes, who was priest of Apollo the patron god of Ismarus, and lived within the wooded precincts of the temple. When we were sacking the city we respected him, and spared his life, as also his wife and child; so he made me some presents of great value—seven talents of fine gold, and a bowl of silver, with twelve jars of sweet wine, unblended, and of the most exquisite flavour. Not a man nor maid in the house knew about it, but only himself, his wife, and one housekeeper: when he drank it he mixed twenty parts of water to one of wine, and yet the fragrance from the mixing bowl was so exquisite that it was impossible to refrain from drinking. I filled a large skin with this wine, and took a wallet full of provisions with me, for my mind misgave me that I might have to deal with some savage who would be of great strength, and would respect neither right nor law.

"We soon reached his cave, but he was out shepherding, so we went inside and took stock of all that we could see. His cheese-racks were loaded with cheeses, and he had more lambs and kids than his pens could hold. They were kept in separate flocks; first there were the hoggets, then the oldest of the younger lambs and lastly the very young ones all kept apart from one another; as for his dairy, all the vessels, bowls, and milk pails into which he milked, were swimming with whey. When they saw all this, my men begged me to let them first steal some cheeses, and make off with them to the ship; they would then return, drive down the lambs and kids, put them on board and sail away with them. It would have been indeed better if we had done so but I would not listen to them, for I wanted to see the owner himself, in the hope that he might give me a present. When, however, we saw him my poor men found him ill to deal with.

"We lit a fire, offered some of the cheeses in sacrifice, ate others of them, and then sat waiting till the Cyclops should come in with his sheep. When he came, he brought in with him a huge load of dry firewood to light the fire for his supper, and this he flung with such a noise on to the floor of his cave that we hid ourselves for fear at the far end of the cavern. Meanwhile he drove all the ewes inside, as well as the she-goats that he was going to milk, leaving the males, both rams and he-goats, outside in the yards. Then he rolled a huge stone to the mouth of the cave—so huge that two and twenty strong four wheeled waggons would not be enough to draw it from its place against the doorway. When he had so done he sat down and milked his ewes and goats, all in due course, and then let each of them have her own young. He curdled half the milk and set it aside in wicker strainers, but the other half he poured into bowls that he might drink it for his supper. When he had got through with all his work, he lit the fire, and then caught sight of us, whereon he said:—

"'Strangers, who are you? Where do you sail from? Are you traders, or do you sail the sea as rovers, with your hands against every man, and every man's hand against you?'

"We were frightened out of our senses by his loud voice and monstrous form, but I managed to say, 'We are Achaeans on our way home from Troy, but by the will of Jove, and stress of weather, we have been driven far out of our course. We are the people of Agamemnon, son of Atreus, who has won infinite renown throughout the whole world, by sacking so great a city and killing so many people. We therefore humbly pray you to show us some hospitality, and otherwise make us such presents as visitors may reasonably expect. May your excellency fear the wrath of heaven, for we are your suppliants, and Jove takes all respectable travellers under his protection, for he is the avenger of all suppliants and foreigners in distress.'

"To this he gave me but a pitiless answer, 'Stranger,' said he, 'you are a fool, or else you know nothing of this country. Talk to me, indeed, about fearing the gods or shunning their anger. We Cyclopes do not care about Jove or any of your blessed gods, for we are ever so much stronger than they. I shall not spare either yourself or your companions out of any regard for Jove, unless I am in the humour for doing so. And now tell me where you made your ship fast when you came on shore. Was it round the point, or is she lying straight off the land?'

"He said this to draw me out, but I was too cunning to be caught in that way, so I answered with a lie; 'Neptune,' said I, 'sent my ship on to the rocks at the far end of your country, and wrecked it. We were driven on to them from the open sea, but I and those who are with me escaped the jaws of death.'

"The cruel wretch vouchsafed me not one word of answer, but with a sudden clutch he gripped up two of my men at once and dashed them down upon the ground as though they had been puppies. Their brains were shed upon the ground, and the earth was wet with their blood. Then he tore them limb from limb and supped upon them. He gobbled them up like a lion in the wilderness, flesh, bones, marrow, and entrails, without leaving anything uneaten. As for us, we wept and lifted up our hands to heaven on seeing such a horrid sight, for we did not know what else to do; but when the Cyclops had filled his huge paunch, and had washed down his meal of human flesh with a drink of neat milk, he stretched himself full length upon the ground among his sheep, and went to sleep. I was at first inclined to seize my sword, draw it, and drive it into his vitals, but I reflected that if I did we should all certainly be lost, for we should never be able to shift the stone which the monster had put in front of the door. So we staid sobbing and sighing where we were till morning came.

"When the child of morning rosy-fingered dawn appeared, he again lit his fire, milked his goats and ewes, all quite rightly, and then let each have her own young one; as soon as he had got through with all his work, he clutched up two more of my men, and began eating them for his morning's meal. Presently, with the utmost ease, he rolled the stone away from the door and drove out his sheep, but he at once put it back again—as easily as though he were merely clapping the lid on to a quiver full of arrows. As soon as he had done so he shouted, and cried 'Shoo, shoo,' after his sheep to drive them on to the mountain; so I was left to scheme some way of taking my revenge and covering myself with glory.

"In the end I deemed it would be the best plan to do as follows:—The Cyclops had a great club which was lying near one of the sheep pens; it was of green olive wood, and he had cut it intending to use it for a staff as soon as it should be dry. It was so huge that we could only compare it to the mast of a twenty oared merchant vessel of large burden, and able to venture out into open sea. I went up to this club and cut off about six feet of it; I then gave this piece to the men and told them to fine it evenly off at one end, which they proceeded to do, and lastly I brought it to a point myself, charring the end in the fire to make it harder. When I had done this I hid it under the dung, which was lying about all over the cave, and told the men to cast lots which of them should venture along with myself to lift it and bore it into the monster's eye while he was asleep. The lot fell upon the very four whom I should have chosen, and I myself made five. In the evening the wretch came back from shepherding, and drove his flocks into the cave—this time driving them all inside, and not leaving any in the yards; I suppose some fancy must have taken him, or a god must have prompted him to do so. As soon as he had put the stone back to its place against the door, he sat down, milked his ewes and his goats all quite rightly, and then let each have her own young one; when he had got through with all this work, he gripped up two more of my men, and made his supper off them. So I went up to him with an ivy-wood bowl of black wine in my hands:—

"'Look here, Cyclops,' said I, 'you have been eating a great deal of man's flesh, so take this and drink some wine, that you may see what kind of liquor we had on board my ship. I was bringing it to you as a drink-offering, in the hope that you would take compassion upon me and further me on my way home, whereas all you do is to go on ramping and raving most intolerably. You ought to be ashamed of yourself; how can you expect people to come and see you any more if you treat them in this way?'

"He then took the cup and drank. He was so delighted with the taste of the wine that he begged me for another bowl full. 'Be so kind,' he said, 'as to give me some more, and tell me your name at once. I want to make you a present that you will be glad to have. We have wine even in this country, for our soil grows grapes and the sun ripens them, but this drinks like Nectar and Ambrosia all in one.'

"I then gave him some more; three times did I fill the bowl for him, and three times did he drain it without thought or heed; then, when I saw that the wine had got into his head, I said to him as plausibly as I could:—'Cyclops, you ask my name and I will tell it you; give me, therefore, the present you promised me; my name is Noman; this is what my father and mother and my friends have always called me.'

"But the cruel wretch said, 'Then I will eat all Noman's comrades before Noman himself, and will keep Noman for the last. This is the present that I will make him.'

"As he spoke he reeled, and fell sprawling face upwards on the ground. His great neck hung heavily backwards and a deep sleep took hold upon him. Presently he turned sick, and threw up both wine and the gobbets of human flesh on which he had been gorging, for he was very drunk. Then I thrust the beam of wood far into the embers to heat it, and encouraged my men lest any of them should turn faint-hearted. When the wood, green though it was, was about to blaze, I drew it out of the fire glowing with heat, and my men gathered round me, for heaven had filled their hearts with courage. We drove the sharp end of the beam into the monster's eye, and bearing upon it with all my weight I kept turning it round and round as though I were boring a hole in a ship's plank with an auger, which two men with a wheel and strap can keep on turning as long as they choose. Even thus did we bore the red hot beam into his eye, till the boiling blood bubbled all over it as we worked it round and round, so that the steam from the burning eyeball scalded his eyelids and eyebrows, and the roots of the eye sputtered in the fire. As a blacksmith plunges an axe or hatchet into cold water to temper it—for it is this that gives strength to the iron—and it makes a great hiss as he does so, even thus did the Cyclops' eye hiss round the beam of olive wood, and his hideous yells made the cave ring again. We ran away in a fright, but he plucked the beam all besmirched with gore from his eye, and hurled it from him in a frenzy of rage and pain, shouting as he did so to the other Cyclopes who lived on the bleak headlands near him; so they gathered from all quarters round his cave when they heard him crying, and asked what was the matter with him.

"'What ails you, Polyphemus,' said they, 'that you make such a noise, breaking the stillness of the night, and preventing us from being able to sleep? Surely no man is carrying off your sheep? Surely no man is trying to kill you either by fraud or by force?'

"But Polyphemus shouted to them from inside the cave, 'Noman is killing me by fraud; no man is killing me by force.'

"'Then,' said they, 'if no man is attacking, you must be ill; when Jove makes people ill, there is no help for it, and you had better pray to your father Neptune.'

"Then they went away, and I laughed inwardly at the success of my clever stratagem, but the Cyclops, groaning and in an agony of pain, felt about with his hands till he found the stone and took it from the door; then he sat in the doorway and stretched his hands in front of it to catch anyone going out with the sheep, for he thought I might be foolish enough to attempt this.

"As for myself I kept on puzzling to think how I could best save my own life and those of my companions; I schemed and schemed, as one who knows that his life depends upon it, for the danger was very great. In the end I deemed that this plan would be the best; the male sheep were well grown, and carried a heavy black fleece, so I bound them noiselessly in threes together, with some of the withes on which the wicked monster used to sleep. There was to be a man under the middle sheep, and the two on either side were to cover him, so that there were three sheep to each man. As for myself there was a ram finer than any of the others, so I caught hold of him by the back, ensconced myself in the thick wool under his belly, and hung on patiently to his fleece, face upwards, keeping a firm hold on it all the time.

"Thus, then, did we wait in great fear of mind till morning came, but when the child of morning rosy-fingered Dawn appeared, the male sheep hurried out to feed, while the ewes remained bleating about the pens waiting to be milked, for their udders were full to bursting; but their master in spite of all his pain felt the backs of all the sheep as they stood upright, without being sharp enough to find out that the men were underneath their bellies. As the ram was going out, last of all, heavy with its fleece and with the weight of my crafty self, Polyphemus laid hold of it and said:—

"'My good ram, what is it that makes you the last to leave my cave this morning? You are not wont to let the ewes go before you, but lead the mob with a run whether to flowery mead or bubbling fountain, and are the first to come home again at night; but now you lag last of all. Is it because you know your master has lost his eye, and are sorry because that wicked Noman and his horrid crew has got him down in his drink and blinded him? But I will have his life yet. If you could understand and talk, you would tell me where the wretch is hiding, and I would dash his brains upon the ground till they flew all over the cave. I should thus have some satisfaction for the harm this no-good Noman has done me.'

"As he spoke he drove the ram outside, but when we were a little way out from the cave and yards, I first got from under the ram's belly, and then freed my comrades; as for the sheep, which were very fat, by constantly heading them in the right direction we managed to drive them down to the ship. The crew rejoiced greatly at seeing those of us who had escaped death, but wept for the others whom the Cyclops had killed. However, I made signs to them by nodding and frowning that they were to hush their crying, and told them to get all the sheep on board at once and put out to sea; so they went aboard, took their places, and smote the grey sea with their oars. Then, when I had got as far out as my voice would reach, I began to jeer at the Cyclops.

"'Cyclops,' said I, 'you should have taken better measure of your man before eating up his comrades in your cave. You wretch, eat up your visitors in your own house? You might have known that your sin would find you out, and now Jove and the other gods have punished you.'

"He got more and more furious as he heard me, so he tore the top from off a high mountain, and flung it just in front of my ship so that it was within a little of hitting the end of the rudder. The sea quaked as the rock fell into it, and the wash of the wave it raised carried us back towards the mainland, and forced us towards the shore. But I snatched up a long pole and kept the ship off, making signs to my men by nodding my head, that they must row for their lives, whereon they laid out with a will. When we had got twice as far as we were before, I was for jeering at the Cyclops again, but the men begged and prayed of me to hold my tongue.

"'Do not,' they exclaimed, 'be mad enough to provoke this savage creature further; he has thrown one rock at us already which drove us back again to the mainland, and we made sure it had been the death of us; if he had then heard any further sound of voices he would have pounded our heads and our ship's timbers into a jelly with the rugged rocks he would have heaved at us, for he can throw them a long way.'

"But I would not listen to them, and shouted out to him in my rage, 'Cyclops, if any one asks you who it was that put your eye out and spoiled your beauty, say it was the valiant warrior Ulysses, son of Laertes, who lives in Ithaca.'

"On this he groaned, and cried out, 'Alas, alas, then the old prophecy about me is coming true. There was a prophet here, at one time, a man both brave and of great stature, Telemus son of Eurymus, who was an excellent seer, and did all the prophesying for the Cyclopes till he grew old; he told me that all this would happen to me some day, and said I should lose my sight by the hand of Ulysses. I have been all along expecting some one of imposing presence and super-human strength, whereas he turns out to be a little insignificant weakling, who has managed to blind my eye by taking advantage of me in my drink; come here, then, Ulysses, that I may make you presents to show my hospitality, and urge Neptune to help you forward on your journey—for Neptune and I are father and son. He, if he so will, shall heal me, which no one else neither god nor man can do.'

"Then I said, 'I wish I could be as sure of killing you outright and sending you down to the house of Hades, as I am that it will take more than Neptune to cure that eye of yours.'

"On this he lifted up his hands to the firmament of heaven and prayed, saying, 'Hear me, great Neptune; if I am indeed your own true begotten son, grant that Ulysses may never reach his home alive; or if he must get back to his friends at last, let him do so late and in sore plight after losing all his men [let him reach his home in another man's ship and find trouble in his house.']

"Thus did he pray, and Neptune heard his prayer. Then he picked up a rock much larger than the first, swung it aloft and hurled it with prodigious force. It fell just short of the ship, but was within a little of hitting the end of the rudder. The sea quaked as the rock fell into it, and the wash of the wave it raised drove us onwards on our way towards the shore of the island.

"When at last we got to the island where we had left the rest of our ships, we found our comrades lamenting us, and anxiously awaiting our return. We ran our vessel upon the sands and got out of her on to the sea shore; we also landed the Cyclops' sheep, and divided them equitably amongst us so that none might have reason to complain. As for the ram, my companions agreed that I should have it as an extra share; so I sacrificed it on the sea shore, and burned its thigh bones to Jove, who is the lord of all. But he heeded not my sacrifice, and only thought how he might destroy both my ships and my comrades.

"Thus through the livelong day to the going down of the sun we feasted our fill on meat and drink, but when the sun went down and it came on dark, we camped upon the beach. When the child of morning rosy-fingered Dawn appeared, I bade my men go on board and loose the hawsers. Then they took their places and smote the grey sea with their oars; so we sailed on with sorrow in our hearts, but glad to have escaped death though we had lost our comrades."

THE SONG OF DEMODOCUS

Odyssey, Book VIII

Homer

Translated by Emily Wilson, 2018

At the palace on Scheria, Odysseus is entertained by a blind bard called Demodocus, who sings this story of Hephaestus, the skilled but physically lame craftsman god, who caught his wife Aphrodite in bed with the war god Ares. This much-admired translation is by a contemporary scholar.

The poet strummed and sang a charming song
about the love of fair-crowned Aphrodite
for Ares, who gave lavish gifts to her
and shamed the bed of Lord Hephaestus, where
they secretly had sex. The Sun God saw them,
and told Hephaestus—bitter news for him.
He marched into his forge to get revenge,
and set the mighty anvil on its block,
and hammered chains so strong that they could never
be broken or undone. He was so angry
at Ares. When his trap was made, he went
inside the room of his beloved bed,
and twined the mass of cables all around
the bedposts, and then hung them from the ceiling,
like slender spiderwebs, so finely made
that nobody could see them, even gods:
the craftsmanship was so ingenious.
when he had set that trap across the bed,
he traveled to the cultured town of Lemnos,
which was his favorite place in all the world.
Ares the golden rider had kept watch.
He saw Hephaestus, famous wonder-worker,
leaving his house, and went inside himself;
he wanted to make love with Aphrodite.
She had returned from visiting her father,

the mighty son of Cronus; there she sat.
Then Ares took her hand and said to her,

"My darling, let us go to bed. Hephaestus
is out of town; he must have gone to Lemnos
to see the Sintians whose speech is strange."

She was excited to lie down with him;
they went to bed together. But the chains
ingenious Hephaestus had created
wrapped tight around them, so they could not move
or get up. Then they knew that they were trapped.
The limping god drew near—before he reached
the land of Lemnos, he had turned back home.
Troubled at heart, he came towards his house.
Standing there in the doorway, he was seized
by savage rage. He gave a mighty shout,
calling to all the gods,

        "O Father Zeus,
and all you blessed gods who live forever,
look! It is funny—and unbearable.
See how my Aphrodite, child of Zeus,
is disrespecting me for being lame.
She loves destructive Ares, who is strong
and handsome. I am weak. I blame my parents.
If only I had not been born! But come,
see where those two are sleeping in my bed,
as lovers. I am horrified to see it.
But I predict they will not want to lie
longer like that, however great their love.
Soon they will want to wake up, but my trap
and chains will hold them fast, until her father
pays back the price I gave him for his daughter.
Her eyes stare at me like a dog. She is
so beautiful, but lacking self-control."

The gods assembled at his house: Poseidon,
Earth-Shaker, helpful Hermes, and Apollo.
The goddesses stayed home, from modesty.
The blessed gods who give good things were standing
inside the doorway, and they burst out laughing,
at what a clever trap Hephaestus set.
And as they looked, they said to one another,

"Crime does not pay! The slow can beat the quick,
as now Hephaestus, who is lame and slow,

has used his skill to catch the fastest sprinter
of all those on Olympus. Ares owes
the price for his adultery." They gossiped.

Apollo, son of Zeus, then said to Hermes,
"Hermes my brother, would you like to sleep
with golden Aphrodite, in her bed,
even weighed down by mighty chains?"

                    And Hermes
the sharp-eyed messenger replied, "Ah, brother,
Apollo lord of archery: if only!
I would be bound three times as tight or more
and let you gods and all your wives look on,
if only I could sleep with Aphrodite."

Then laughter rose among the deathless gods.
Only Poseidon did not laugh. He begged
and pleaded with Hephaestus to release
Ares. He told the wonder-working god,

"Now let him go! I promise he will pay
the penalty in full among the gods,
just as you ask."

          The famous limping god
replied, "Poseidon, do not ask me this.
It is disgusting, bailing scoundrels out.
How could I bind you, while the gods look on,
if Ares should escape his bonds and debts?"

Poseidon, Lord of Earthquakes, answered him,
"Hephaestus, if he tries to dodge this debt,
I promise I will pay."

            The limping god
said, "Then, in courtesy to you, I must
do as you ask." So using all his strength,
Hephaestus loosed the chains. The pair of lovers
were free from their constraints, and both jumped up.
Ares went off to Thrace, while Aphrodite
smiled as she went to Cyprus, to the island
of Paphos, where she had a fragrant altar
and sanctuary. The Graces washed her there,
and rubbed her with the magic oil that glows
upon immortals, and they dressed her up
in gorgeous clothes. She looked astonishing.

AND SO TO BED

Odyssey, Book XXIII

Homer

Translated by T. E. Shaw (Colonel T. E. Lawrence), 1935

After marvelling at Odysseus' tales, the people of Scheria (see previous story) finally conveyed him safely home to Ithaca. To punish them, the sea god Poseidon, father of the blinded Cyclops Polyphemus, turned their ship to stone. Odysseus' troubles were far from over. First he needed to defeat the evil suitors who had been pursuing his loyal wife Penelope. Then he needed to convince her that he was indeed her husband come home to her after an absence of twenty years. In this translation, T. E. Shaw – Lawrence of Arabia – proved that he was as capable of mastering the tender scenes in **Homer** as he was the most thrilling episodes of derring-do. The 'old dame' is Eurycleia, the nurse of the household. Telemachus is Odysseus and Penelope's son.

But it was with a cackle of laughter that the old dame climbed towards the upper room, to warn her mistress of the beloved husband's return. Her knees moved nimbly and her feet tripped along to the lady's bed-head where she stood and spoke her part. "Awake dear child, Penelope: open your eyes upon the sight you have yearned for all these days. Odysseus has appeared, at this end of time. He has reached his home and in it slaughtered the recalcitrant suitors who for so long vexed the house, ate his stored wealth and outfaced his son."

Circumspect Penelope replied to this: "Dear mother, the Gods have driven you frantic. They turn to foolishness the ripest judgements and the flighty into sober ways. From them comes this derangement of your old true understanding:—but why tease with fantasies a heart already brimmed with grief? Why wake me from this sleep whose sweetness held me in thrall and veiled my eyelids; the best sleep I have enjoyed since Odysseus went away to view that ill city never-to-be-named. Off with you below, instantly, to the women's quarters. Had any other of my housemaidens roused me with news of this sort I should have sent her smartly back into her place. Just for this once your great age shall excuse you."

Eurycleia persisted. "Dear child, I am in very earnest with you. Odysseus, I say, is here. He came back to the house as that stranger who met such scurvy treatment at all hands. Telemachus long since learnt his identity but very properly hid the knowledge, to let his father's revenge take shape against those proud rough men."

This time her word transported Penelope who leaped from the couch and clasped the old woman, crying shrilly through the tears that rained from her eyes: "Ah, dear mother, but tell me, tell me truly—if as you say he is really come home, how has he coped single-handed with the shameless suitors, who mobbed our house continually?" And the good nurse told her, "I did not see, I do not know: but I heard the groans of their slaying. We all shrank trembling into a corner of our safe room—its doors wedged fast—until your son Telemachus came and called me forth at his father's bidding. There in the hall I found Odysseus, stalking amidst the bodies of his slain that littered the beaten floor. Your heart would have glowed to see him so lion-like, all battle-stained and steeped in blood. Now the corpses are piled up outside, by the courtyard gates, while he has had a great fire lighted and purges the lovely house. He sent me to summon you; so come, that at the end of all the sorrow you two may enter your hearts' gladness hand in hand. Surely your lingering hope is now fulfilled. He reaches his fireside alive and finds you and your son still there; while upon each and every one of those suitors who served him ill in the house he has wreaked revenge."

"Hush, mother," said Penelope the decorous. "Do not sing too loud or soon. You know how grateful his reappearance in the house would be to everybody, particularly to me and to his son and mine: but what you proclaim does not ring true. This massacre of the overbearing suitors has been the work of some Immortal, inflamed by their heart-breaking wanton insolence which had regard for no soul they met, neither the bad nor the good: so they have been punished according to their sins. But meantime Odysseus in some far land has lost his way to Achaea—yea, lost himself." Nurse Eurycleia replied: "My child, why let fall that dull word of your husband's never coming home, when he is here already and by his fireside? Your heart was always stubborn in unbelief. Why I can quote you a sure proof, that scar from the boar's white tusk long years ago, which I noted as I washed him. I wanted to tell you upon the instant; but he, careful for his own interests put his hand over my jaw and silenced me. Come with me now—and I pledge my life on it. If I mislead you, then slay me by the meanest death you know."

Penelope responded: "Even your storied wisdom, mother dear, hardly equips you to interpret the designs of the eternal Gods. Howbeit let us away to my son, for I would see the suitors lying in death; and their slayer." She was going down as she spoke, her heart in a turmoil of debate whether to keep her distance while she examined her dear lord, or go straight up at once to kiss his head and clasp his hand. So when at length she came in across the stone threshold it was to take a seat in the fire-light facing Odysseus, but over against the further wall. He sat at the base of a tall pillar, waiting with drooping eyelids to hear his stately consort cry out when she caught sight of him. But she sat there in a long silence, with bewildered heart. One moment she would look and see him in his face; and the next moment fail to see him there, by reason of the foul rags he wore—till Telemachus named her in disapproval. "Mother mine," he cried, "un-motherly mother and cruel-hearted, how dare you hold aloof from father, instead of running to sit by his side and ply him with questions? No other woman could in cold blood keep herself apart, when her man got home after twenty years of toil and sorrow. Your heart remains harder than a stone."

But Penelope explained: "Child, my heart is dazed. I have no force to speak, or ask, or even stare upon his face. If this is Odysseus in truth and at last, then shall we soon know each other better than well by certain private signs between us two, hidden from the rest of the world." At which the glorious, long-suffering Odysseus smiled and said hastily to Telemachus, "After that, leave your mother alone for the test in her room with me presently. Soon she will come to fuller understanding. The filth of my body, these shabby clothes—such things make her overlook me and deny it can be myself. Meanwhile you and I must discuss our best policy. In a community the slaying of even a single man with few surviving connections to avenge him entails outlawry from home and family; and we have been killing best part of the young men of Ithaca, its pillars of state. I would have you ponder it"—but Telemachus rejoined, "Let that be your business, father dear. They call you the clearest-headed man alive, supreme in your generation. We others will support you whole-heartedly: and I fancy whatever our strength may be, courage at least will not fail us."

Said Odysseus, "Then hear what I think best. Wash now and dress, and have the house-women deck themselves. Then let the inspired minstrel with his resounding lyre lead off for us in a dance so merry that all hearing it from outside the walls, neighbours or passers-by, will say, 'There is a wedding toward.' Thus rumour of the suitors' deaths will not spread across the city before we have got away to our tree-clad country place, there to weigh what means of advantage the Olympian may offer to our hands." They had all listened intently and moved to do his bidding. They washed and put on tunics: the women were arrayed: the revered musician took his hollow lyre and awoke their appetite for rhythm and the gay dance, till the great house around them rang with the measured foot-falls of men and well-gowned women. Outside the house one and another hearing the harmony did say, "I swear someone has wedded the much-courted queen! Callous she was, and lacked the fortitude and constancy to keep the house of her lawful husband until he came," Such was the gossip, in ignorance of the real event.

Meanwhile, within, old Eurynome washed and anointed Odysseus, draping upon him a fair tunic and cloak, while Athene crowned him with an especial splendour that filled the eye; she made the hair of his head curl downward floridly, like bloom of hyacinth. As a craftsman lavishly endowed with skill by Hephaestus and Pallas washes his silverwork with fine gold until its mastery shines out, so the grace from Athene glorified his head and shoulders and made his figure, when he left the bath-chamber, seem divine. He retook his former throne opposite his wife and declared, "Proud lady, the heart that the lords of Olympus gave you is harder than any true woman's. None but you would pitilessly repulse the husband who had won his way home after twenty years of toil. Old dame, favour me now by arranging my bed somewhere apart, that I may lie solitary: for the heart in her breast has turned to iron."

Said Penelope with reserve, "Proud lord, I neither set myself too high nor esteem you too low: nor am I confused out of mind. It is that I remember only too well how you were when you sailed from Ithaca in your long-oared ship. So Eurycleia, when you make up his great bed for him, move it outside the bridal chamber that he built so firmly. Have forth the heavy bed-frame and pile it high with fleeces and rugs and glossy blankets." This she said to draw her husband out;

and indeed Odysseus was ruffled into protesting to his wife, "Woman, this order pains my heart. Who has changed my bed? It would task the cunningest man—forbye no God happened to shift it in whim—for not the stoutest wight alive could heave it up directly. That bed's design held a marvellous feature of my own contriving. Within our court had sprung a stem of olive, bushy, long in the leaf, vigorous; the bole of it column-thick. Round it I plotted my bed-chamber, walled entire with fine-jointed ashlar and soundly roofed. After adding joinery doors, fitting very close, I then polled the olive's spreading top and trimmed its stump from the root up, dressing it so smooth with my tools and so knowingly that I got it plumb, to serve for bed-post just as it stood. With this for main member (boring it with my auger wherever required) I went on to frame up the bed, complete; inlaying it with gold, silver and ivory and lacing it across with ox-hide thongs, dyed blood-purple. That was the style of it, woman, as I explain: but of course I do not know whether the bed stands as it did; or has someone sawn through the olive stem and altered it?"

As Odysseus had run on, furnishing her with proof too solid for rejection, her knees trembled, and her heart. She burst into tears, she ran to him, she flung her arms about his neck and kissed his head and cried, "My Odysseus, forgive me this time too, you who were of old more comprehending than any man of men. The Gods gave us sorrow for our portion, and in envy denied us the happiness of being together throughout our days, from the heat of youth to the shadow of old age. Be not angry with me, therefore, nor resentful, because at first sight I failed to fondle you thus. The heart within me ever shook for terror of being cheated by some man's lie, so innumerable are those who plot to serve greedy ends. See, it was that way our life's sorrow first began. Argive Helen, the daughter of Zeus, did not in her own imagination invent the ruinous folly that let a strange man lie with her in love and intercourse. A God it was that tempted her astray. Never would she have done it had she known how the warrior sons of the Achaeans would fetch her back once more to her native land. But now with those authentic details of our bed, seen by no human eye but yours, mine and my maid's (Actor's daughter, given me by my father before I came here and ever the sole keeper of our closed bedchamber-door) you have convinced my heart, slow though you may think it to believe."

This word increased by so much his inclination to tears that he wept, even with his arms about his faithful, lovely wife. So at sea when Poseidon has swamped a good ship by making her the target of his winds and mighty waves, the sight of land appears wonderfully kind to the few men of her crew who have escaped by swimming. How they swarm ashore from the grey sea, their bodies all crusted with salt spume, but happy, happy, for the evil overpassed! Just so was she happy to have her husband once more in sight and clasped in her white arms which lingered round his neck, unable to let him go. Rosy dawn might have found them thus, still weeping, only that grey-eyed Athene otherwise ordained. She retarded the night a long while in transit and made Dawn, the golden-throned, tarry by the eastern Ocean's edge; not harnessing Lampus and Phaethon, the sharp-hooved young horses that carry her and bring daylight to the world.

At last provident Odysseus said to his wife: "My dear one, we have not yet reached the issue of our trials. In store for us is immeasurable toil prescribed, and needs must I fulfil it to the end. The day I went down into Hades' realm, the ghost of Teiresias warned me of everything when I asked after my home-coming and my company's. Wherefore let us to bed, dear wife, there at long last to renew ourselves with the sweet meed of sleep." To which Penelope answered, "Bed is yours the instant your heart wills, for have not the Gods restored you to your own great house and native land? But now that Heaven has put it in your mind, tell me of this ordeal remaining. Later I must know; and forewarned is forearmed."

Odysseus in reply assured her, "Brave spirit, I shall tell you, hiding nothing: but why press me insistently for knowledge that will no more please you than me? He gave me word that I must take my shapely oar and wander through many places of men, until I find a people that know not the sea and have no salt to season their food, a people for whom purple-prowed ships are unknown things, as too the shaped oars which wing their flight. An infallible token of them he told me, and I make you wise to it. When another wayfarer passes me and says I have a winnowing fan on my stout shoulder, even there am I to strike my oar into the ground and offer for rich sacrifice to King Poseidon a ram, a bull and a ramping boar. Thence I may turn homeward, to celebrate the Gods of high heaven with hecatombs of victims, and all things else in order due. While death shall come for me from the sea, very mildly, ending me amidst a contented people after failing years have brought me low. He assured me all this would be fulfilled." And Penelope's wise comment was, "If the Gods will make old age your happier time, then there is prospect of your ill-luck passing."

Thus they chatted while Eurynome and the nurse under the flaring torchlight arranged the soft coverlets upon the bed. When they had busily made it comfortable and deep, the old nurse returned to her sleeping-place, while Eurynome the chambermaid conducted them bedward with her torch. She ushered them to their chamber and withdrew; and gladsomely they performed their bed-rites in the old fashion: Telemachus and the herdsmen staying their feet from the dance and staying the women, so that all slept in the darkling halls.

PROMETHEUS AND PANDORA

Theogony & Works and Days

Hesiod

Translated by Richmond Lattimore, 1959

There was no one quite like Prometheus. A Titan, or giant, he stole fire from the gods, and gave it to mankind. The seventh-century BC poet **Hesiod** told his story across two poems, the *Theogony* and *Works and Days*. On the one hand Prometheus' gift of fire was a blessing for humans since it enabled them to live self-sufficiently from the gods. On the other, it spelled the end of their Golden Age, in which they had lived happy lives free from work and suffering. Another consequence of Prometheus' actions was the creation of the first woman, Pandora ('all-gifted'). Epimetheus, Prometheus' less intelligent brother, was quick to fall for her charms.

Theogony

for Prometheus once had matched wits
    against the great son of Kronos.
It was when gods, and mortal men,
    took their separate positions
at Mekone, and Prometheus,
    eager to try his wits, cut up
a great ox, and set it before Zeus,
    to see if he could outguess him.
He took the meaty parts and the inwards
    thick with fat, and set them
before men, hiding them away
    in an ox's stomach,
but the white bones of the ox he arranged,
    with careful deception,
inside a concealing fold of white fat,
    and set it before Zeus.
At last the father of gods
    and men spoke to him, saying:

"Son of Iapetos, conspicuous among all Kings,
old friend, oh how prejudicially
   you divided the portions."
So Zeus, who knows imperishable counsels,
   spoke in displeasure,
but Prometheus the devious-deviser,
   lightly smiling,
answered him again, quite well aware
   of his artful deception:
"Zeus most high, most honored
   among the gods everlasting,
choose whichever of these the heart within
   would have you."
He spoke, with intent to deceive, and Zeus,
   who knows imperishable
counsels, saw it, the trick
   did not escape him, he imagined
evils for mortal men in his mind,
   and meant to fulfil them.
In both his hands he took up the portion
   of the white fat. Anger
rose up about his heart
   and the spite mounted in his spirit
when he saw the white bones of the ox
   in deceptive arrangement.

Ever since that time the races of mortal men
   on earth have burned
the white bones to the immortals
   on the smoky altars.

Then Zeus the cloud-gatherer
   in great vexation said to him:
"Son of Iapetos, versed in planning
   beyond all others,
old friend, so after all you did not forget
   your treachery."
So Zeus, who knows imperishable counsels,
   spoke in his anger,
and ever remembering this deception
   thereafter, he would not
give the force of weariless fire
   to the ash-tree people,
not to people who inhabit the earth
   and are mortal,
no, but the strong son of Iapetos
   outwitted him

and stole the far-seen glory
   of weariless fire, hiding it
in the hollow fennel stalk;
   this bit deep into the feeling
of Zeus who thunders on high,
   and it galled the heart inside him
when he saw the far-seen glory of fire
   among mortal people,
and next, for the price of the fire,
   be made an evil thing for mankind.

Works and Days

He told glorious Hephaistos to make haste, and plaster
earth with water, and to infuse it with a human voice
and vigor, and make the face
   like the immortal goddesses,
the bewitching features of a young girl;
   meanwhile Athene
was to teach her her skills, and how
   to do the intricate weaving,
while Aphrodite was to mist her head
   in golden endearment
and the cruelty of desire and longings
   that wear out the body,
but to Hermes, the guide, the slayer of Argos,
   he gave instructions
to put in her the mind of a hussy,
   and a treacherous nature.
So Zeus spoke. And all obeyed Lord Zeus,
   the son of Kronos.
The renowned strong smith modeled her figure of earth,
   in the likeness
of a decorous young girl, as the son of Kronos
   had wished it.
The goddess gray-eyed Athene dressed and arrayed her;
   the Graces,
who are goddesses, and hallowed Persuasion
   put necklaces
of gold upon her body, while the Seasons,
   with glorious tresses,
put upon her head a coronal of spring flowers,
[and Pallas Athene put all decor upon her body].
But into her heart Hermes, the guide,
   the slayer of Argos,

put lies, and wheedling words
    of falsehood, and a treacherous nature,
made her as Zeus of the deep thunder wished,
    and he, the gods' herald,
put a voice inside her, and gave her
    the name of woman,
Pandora, because all the gods
    who have their homes on Olympos
had given her each a gift, to be a sorrow to men
who eat bread. Now when he had done
    with this sheer, impossible
deception, the Father sent the gods' fleet messenger,
    Hermes,
to Epimetheus, bringing her, a gift,
    nor did Epimetheus
remember to think how Prometheus had told him never
to accept a gift from Olympian Zeus,
    but always to send it
back, for fear it might prove
    to be an evil for mankind.
He took the evil, and only perceived it
    when he possessed her.
    Since before this time the races of men
    had been living on earth
free from all evils, free from laborious work,
    and free from
all wearing sicknesses that bring
    their fates down on men
[for men grow old suddenly
    in the midst of misfortune];
but the woman, with her hands lifting away the lid
    from the great jar,
scattered its contents, and her design
    was sad troubles for mankind.
Hope was the only spirit that stayed there
    in the unbreakable
closure of the jar, under its rim,
    and could not fly forth
abroad, for the lid of the great jar
    closed down first and contained her;
this was by the will of cloud-gathering Zeus
    of the aegis;

Theogony

And in ineluctable, painful bonds
    he fastened Prometheus
of the subtle mind, for he drove a stanchion
    through his middle. Also
he let loose on him the wing-spread eagle,
    and it was feeding
on his imperishable liver, which by night
    would grow back
to size from what the spread-winged bird
    had eaten in the daytime.

WHATEVER ONE LOVES

'Fragment 16'

Sappho

Translated by Diane J. Rayor, 2014

Sappho was born on the island of Lesbos in the seventh century BC. Although she is said to have married a man and had a daughter by him named Cleïs, the poems in which she divulged her feelings for women have ensured that she has remained the 'Lesbian' poet in the popular imagination. In this fragmentary poem, her beloved Anaktoria has left her. Sappho compares her favourably to Helen of Troy. The implication is not simply that Anaktoria is beautiful, but that she has been led away almost against her will – like Helen, whom Paris took as his prize through the machinations of Aphrodite. Sappho hereby ingeniously avoids placing the blame on Anaktoria, and leaves the door open for a reconciliation.

Some say an army of horsemen, others
say foot soldiers, still others say a fleet
is the finest thing on the dark earth.
I say it is whatever one loves.

Everyone can understand this – consider
that Helen, far surpassing the beauty
of mortals, left behind
the best man of all

to sail away to Troy. She remembered
neither daughter nor dear parents,
as [Aphrodite] led her away

… [un]bending … mind
          … lightly … chinks.
… reminding me now
of Anaktoria gone.

I would rather see her lovely step
and the radiant sparkle of her face

than all the war chariots in Lydia
and soldiers battling in arms.

Impossible ... to happen
... human, but to pray for a share
... and for myself

PERSEPHONE AND THE POMEGRANATE SEEDS

Homeric Hymn to Demeter

Anon.

Translated by Peter McDonald, 2016

Demeter, goddess of the harvest, is devastated when her daughter Persephone is snatched away. Who is guilty of the crime? None other than Zeus' brother Hades, god of the Underworld. As Demeter pines for her loss, the earth's crops stop growing. This story, told in the form of a hymn in the seventh or sixth century BC, provides an explanation for the seasons. Peter McDonald's translation is suitably emotionally charged.

Hymn 2: To Demeter

This is about Demeter, the long-haired goddess
Demeter, and about her child, a skinny-legged
little girl who was just taken away
one morning by Hades, Death himself, on the say-so
of his brother Zeus, the deep- and wide-bellowing God.

She was apart from her mother, and from Demeter's
protecting sword, made all of gold, when he came;
she was running about in an uncut spring meadow
with her friends, the daughters of the god Ocean,
and picking flowers here and there – crocuses and wild roses,
with violets and tiny irises, then hyacinths
and one narcissus planted there by Gaia, the Earth,
as Zeus demanded, and as a favour to Death,
to trap the girl, whose own eyes were as small and bright
as the buds of flowers: it blazed and shone out
with astonishing colours, a prodigy as much for
the immortal gods as for people who die.
A hundred flower-heads sprung from the root
with a sweet smell so heavy and overpowering
that the wide sky and the earth, even the salt waves
of the sea lit up, as though they were all smiling.

The girl was dazzled; she reached out with both hands
to gather up the brilliant thing; but then the earth
opened, the earth's surface with its level roads
buckled, there on the plain of Nysa, and up from below
rushed at her, driving his horses, the king of the dead.
He snatched her up, struggling, and he drove her away
in his golden chariot as she wailed and shrieked
and called out loud to her father to help her,
to Zeus, the highest of high powers;
yet nobody – not one god, not one human being,
not even the laden olive-trees – paid heed to her;
but from deep in a cave, the young night-goddess
Hecatē, Perses' daughter, in her white linen veil,
could hear the child's cries; and so could the god Helios
– god of the Sun, like his father Hyperion –
hear the girl screaming for help to Zeus, her own father:
Zeus, who was keeping his distance, apart from the gods,
busy in a temple, taking stock there of the fine
offerings and the prayers of mortal men.

For all her struggling, it was with the connivance of Zeus
that this prince of the teeming dark, the god with many titles,
her own uncle, with his team of unstoppable horses
took away the little girl: she, as long as she kept in sight
the earth and the starry night sky, the sun's day-beams
and the seas pulled by tides and swimming in fish,
still hoped, hoped even now to see her mother again
and get back to her family of the eternal gods.

From the mountain tops to the bottom of the sea, her voice
echoed, a goddess's voice; and, when her mother heard
those cries, pain suddenly jabbed at her heart: she tore
in two the veil that covered her perfumed hair,
threw a dark shawl across her shoulders, and shot
out like a bird across dry land and water,
frantic to search; but nobody – neither god, nor human –
was ready to tell her what had happened, not even
a solitary bird would give Demeter the news.
For nine whole days, with a blazing torch in each hand,
the goddess roamed the earth, not touching, in her grief,
either the gods' food or their drink, ambrosia or nectar,
and not stopping even to splash her skin with water.
On the tenth day, at the first blink of dawn, Hecatē
came to help her, carrying torches of her own,
and gave her first what news she could: 'Royal Demeter,
bringer of seasons, and all the gifts the seasons bring,
what god in heaven, or what man on this earth

can have snatched away Persephone, and broken your heart?
I heard the sound of her crying, but I couldn't see
who it was; I'm telling you everything I know.'
Hecatē said this, and received not one word in reply:
instead, Demeter rushed her away, and the pair of them
soon reached Helios, the watcher of gods and men.

Demeter stopped by his horses, and spoke to him from there.
'If ever I have pleased you, Helios, or if ever
I have done you a favour, do this one for me now:
my daughter's voice was lost on the trackless air,
shrill with distress; I heard, but looked and saw nothing.
You gaze down all day from the broad sky,
and see everything on dry land and the ocean:
so if you have seen who forced away my child
from me, and who went off with her, whether
a man or a god, please, quickly, just tell me.'
She said this, and the son of Hyperion replied:
'Holy Demeter, daughter of Rhea with her long hair,
you are going to hear it all – for I think highly
of you and, yes, I pity you, grieving as you are
for the loss of your skinny-legged little girl. So:
of all the immortal gods, none other is responsible
than the master of the clouds, Zeus himself, who gave her
to Hades his brother to call his own
as a beautiful wife. Hades with his team of horses
snatched her, and dragged her to the thickening dark
as she cried and cried. But come now; you are a goddess:
call an end to this huge sorrow; be reasonable:
there is no need for such uncontrollable rage.
Hades, the lord of millions, is hardly, after all,
the worst son-in-law amongst the immortals,
and he is your own flesh and blood, your own brother.
As for his position – well, he has what was allotted
originally when things were split three ways,
the master of those amongst whom he dwells.'

So saying, Helios took up the reins, and his horses
were away all at once, bearing up the chariot
like birds with slender wings. And now grief fastened
– a harsher, a more dreadful pain – at Demeter's heart.
Furious with the black cloud-god, the son of Cronos,
she abandoned the gods' city, and high Olympus,
to travel through rich fields and the towns of men,
changing her face, wiping all its beauty away,
so that nobody, neither man nor woman, when
they saw her could recognise her for a goddess.

She wandered a long time, until she came to the home
at Eleusis of the good man Celeus, master there.

Heartsore, heart-sorry, Demeter stopped by the roadside
at the well they called the Maiden's Well, where people
from the town would come for water; sat in the shade
cast over her by heavy branches of olive,
and looked for all the world like a very old lady,
one long past childbearing or the gifts of love,
just like a nurse who might care for the children
of royalty, or a housekeeper in their busy house.
The daughters of Celeus caught sight of her as they came
that way to draw water, and carry it back
to their father's place in great big pitchers of bronze:
Callidicē and Clisidicē, beautiful Dēmō
and Callithoē, the eldest girl of all four,
more like goddesses in the first flower of youth.
They had no idea who she was – it's hard for people
to recognise gods – so they came straight up to her
and demanded, 'Madam, where have you come from
and who, of all the old women here, are you?
Why is it that you've walked out past the town
and don't go to its houses? Plenty of ladies
the same age as you, and others who are younger,
are there now, in buildings sheltered from the heat,
to welcome you with a kind word and a kind turn.'

When they had done, the royal goddess replied:
'Good day to you, girls, whoever you may be;
I'll tell you what you want to know, for it's surely
not wrong, when you're asked, to explain the truth.
I am called Grace – my mother gave me that name –
and I have travelled on the broad back of the sea
all the way from Crete – not wanting to, but forced
to make the journey by men who had snatched me,
gangsters, all of them. In that fast ship of theirs
they put in at Thoricos, where the women
disembarked together, and they themselves began
making their supper down by the stern-cables.
But I had no appetite for any meal that they made,
and when their backs were turned I disappeared
into dark country, and escaped from those men
before they could sell me, stolen goods, at a
good price, bullies and fixers that they were.
That's how I arrived like a vagrant, and I
don't know what country it is, or who lives here.
May the gods who have their homes on Olympus

send you good husbands and plenty of children
to please the parents; but now, spare a thought
for me, like the well brought-up girls that you are,
and maybe I can come to one of your houses
to do some honest work for the ladies and gentlemen
living there, the kind of thing a woman of my age
does best: I can nurse a new baby, and hold
him safe in my arms; I can keep the place clean;
I can make up the master's bed in a corner
of the great bedchamber, and give all the right
instructions to serving women in the house.'

It was the goddess who said this; immediately
the girl Callidicē, loveliest of Celeus' daughters,
spoke back to her, calling her Grandma, and saying:
'Whatever the gods give, however grievous the hardship,
people put up with it, as they must, for the gods
are that much stronger: it's just how things are.
But something I can do is tell you the names
of men who have power and prestige in this town,
who keep its walls in good shape, whose decisions
count for much, and whose advice is listened to here:
wise Triptolemus and Diocles, that good man
Eumolpus, then Polyxeinus, and Dolichus,
and our own dear father of course, all have
wives kept busy with the care of their houses;
not one of them would take a dislike to you
and turn you away from the door – they would welcome
you in, for there *is* something special about you.
Stay here, if you will, and we'll all run back
to tell our mother, Metaneira, the whole story,
then see whether she'll suggest that you come
to ours, and not go looking for another home.
She has a new baby in the house now, a son
born later in life, hoped for and prayed for:
if you were to take care of him, and see him through
to manhood, you would be the envy of any
woman, so well would that childcare be paid.'

Demeter simply nodded her head, and the girls
filled their shiny pitchers up with fresh water
and carried them away, their heads held high.
Soon they were at the family home, where they told
their mother all they had seen, all they had heard.
She ordered them to hurry back, and request this woman
to come and work for a good wage. So then
like deer, or like young calves in springtime,

happy and well-fed, running around in the fields,
they pulled up the folds of their long dresses
and dashed down the cart-track; the long hair,
yellow as saffron, streamed back over their shoulders.
They found Demeter where they had left her, by the road,
and they led her then towards their father's house
while she walked a little way behind, troubled at heart,
her head veiled, and with the dark dress fluttering
this way and that over her slender legs.

They got back to Celeus' house, and went in
through the hallway, where their mother was waiting,
seated by a pillar that held up the strong roof,
with her child, the new son and heir, at her breast.
The girls ran straight to her: slowly Demeter placed
a foot over the threshold, her head touched the rafters,
and around her the entire doorway lit up.
Astonishment and draining fear together shook
Metaneira; she gave up her couch to the visitor
and invited her to sit. But Demeter, who brings
the seasons round, and brings gifts with the seasons,
had no wish to relax on that royal couch, and she
maintained her silence, with eyes fixed on the floor,
until Iambe came up, mindful of her duty,
and offered a low stool, which she had covered
with a sheep's white fleece. The goddess
sat down now, and with one hand she drew
the veil across her face; and there she remained,
sunk in her quiet grief, giving to no one
so much as a word or a sign, sitting on there
without a smile, accepting neither food nor drink
for an age, as she pined for her beautiful daughter,
until Iambe, resourceful as ever, took
her mind off things with jokes and funny stories,
making her smile first, then laugh, and feel better,
and Metaneira offered her the cup she had filled
with wine, sweet as honey: but she shook her head
and announced that, for her, it was not proper now
to take wine – instead, she asked Metaneira
to give her some barley-water and pennyroyal
mixed up together: the queen made this, and served it
to the great goddess, to Demeter,
who accepted it solemnly, and drank it down.
Only then did Metaneira begin to speak:
'Madam, you are welcome here; all the more so
for coming from no ordinary stock
but, I'd say, from the best – for your every glance

is full of modesty and grace, you have something
almost royal about you. But what the gods give us,
hard though it is, we mere human beings
endure: all our necks are under that yoke.
You are here now, and whatever is mine shall be yours.
This little boy – my last born, scarcely hoped for,
granted me by the gods only after much prayer –
nurse him for me now, and if you raise him
to be a healthy, strong man, then any woman
at all will be jealous to see you, so great
will be the reward I give you for your work.'
Demeter replied: 'Accept my greetings, good lady,
and may the gods be kind to you. I will indeed
take care of this fine boy of yours, as you ask.
I shall rear him, and neglect nothing: sudden sickness
will never harm him, and never will some witch
of the forest, who taps roots for magic or poison,
touch a single hair of his head; for I know
stronger sources to tap, and I know the remedy
for all such assaults: a sure one, unfailing.'

Then with her two arms, the arms of a goddess,
she drew the baby in close to her own bosom,
and its mother smiled at the sight. In the big house
from then on Demeter looked after the son
of Celeus and Metaneira, while he grew up
at a god's rate, not eating solids, or taking
milk, but fed by her with ambrosia, as if
he were indeed a god, born of a god;
she breathed gently over him and kept him close,
and at night, unknown to anyone, she smuggled him
into the burning fire, like a new log of wood.
He was thriving so well, and looking so much more
than a human child, that both the parents were amazed.

And the goddess Demeter would have delivered him
from age and from death, had not Metaneira
been up one night and, without so much as
giving it a thought, from her own bedroom
looked into the hall: in sheer terror for the child
she screamed, and did her best to raise the alarm,
seeing the worst and believing it, she called out
to her little boy, half-keening: 'Demophoön,
my own baby, this stranger is hiding you
in the big fire, she's the one making my voice shrill
with pain, 'Demophoön, my darling, my child.'

~

She cried all this out, and the goddess heard her.
Furious that instant, mighty Demeter
took the child – their last born, scarcely hoped for –
and with her own immortal hands she brought him
out of the fire, set him gently on the floor,
then, brimming with anger, turned on Metaneira:
'You stupid creatures, you witless and ignorant
humans, blind to the good as well as the bad
things in store for you, and no use to each other:
I swear to you here, as gods do, by the rippling
dark waters of Styx, that I would have made
this child of yours immortal, honoured, a man
untouched by age for eternity; but nothing now
can keep the years back, or keep death from him.
There is one mark of honour that will always be his:
because he once slept in my arms, and lay in my lap,
all the young men at Eleusis, at the set time
each year, as their scared duty, will gather
for the sham fight, and stage that battle forever.
For I am Demeter, proud of my own honours
as the bringer of joy to the gods, and of blessings
to mortal men. Everyone now has to build me
a spacious temple, with its altar underneath,
by the steep walls of your city, where a hill
rises just above the Maidens' Well. The rites
will be as I instruct, when I teach you the ways
to calm my anger, and be good servants to me.'

And with that, instantly the goddess changed form –
her height, her whole appearance – shuffling away
old age, so that sheer beauty blazed and spread
in and around her; from her robes a gorgeous perfume
drifted, and from her immortal flesh there came
pure light, with the reach of moonbeams; her hair
flashed over her shoulders, and the entire house
was flooded with a sudden brilliance of lightning
as she stepped out through the hall. Metaneira's
knees went from beneath her, and for an age
she sat there speechless, not even thinking
to pick that dear child of hers up from the floor.

When his sisters heard the boy starting to cry
they jumped straight out of their beds, and one
caught him up in her arms, and held him close,
while another stoked the fire, and a third
dashed on bare feet to take hold of her mother
and help her away. As the girls huddled round him,

trying to comfort him and dab his skin clean,
the baby wriggled and fretted, knowing full well
these nurses were hardly the kind he was used to.

That whole night long, shaking with fear, the women
did their best to appease the great goddess.
When dawn came at last, they told everything
to Celeus, exactly as Demeter had instructed,
and he, as their ruler, lost no time
in calling the citizens together, and giving them
the order to build the goddess her temple
and to put her altar just where the hill rises.
They listened to him, and they did all that he said,
so that a temple rose up, as the goddess required.
When the job was done, and the people stopped working,
they all went home; but golden Demeter
installed herself in her temple, apart from the other gods,
and stayed there, eaten up with grief for her daughter.

She made that year the worst for people living
on the good earth, the worst and the hardest: not one
little seed could poke its head up from the soil,
for Demeter had smothered them all; the oxen
broke their ploughs and twisted them, scraping
across hardened furrows; and all the white barley
that year was sown in vain. She would have destroyed
every single human being in the world
with this famine, just to spite the gods on Olympus,
had not Zeus decided to intervene: first
he dispatched Iris, on her wings the colour of gold,
to give Demeter his orders, and she did as he asked,
covering the distance in no time, and landing
at Eleusis, where the air was filled with incense.
She found Demeter wearing dark robes in the temple,
and spoke to her urgently: 'Zeus, our father
who knows everything, summons you back now
to join the family of the immortal gods:
come quick, don't let his command be in vain.'
But her pleas had no effect at all on Demeter:
then Zeus sent out all of the gods, one by one,
to deliver his summons, bringing the best of gifts,
with whatever fresh honours she might desire;
but Demeter was so furious then that she
dismissed every speech out of hand, and told them all
that she would neither set foot again
on Olympus, nor let anything grow on the earth,
unless she could see her beautiful daughter once more.

~

When he heard this, Zeus, the deep- and wide-bellowing God,
sent Hermes with his golden staff down into the dark
to talk to Hades there, and ask his permission
to lead Persephone back up from the shadows
and into daylight again, where her mother
could set eyes on her, and so be angry no longer.
Hermes agreed to do this: he hurried away
from his place on Olympus, down into the earth's
crevasses and crannies, down, till he reached
the king of all the dead in his underground palace,
stretched out at his ease, and by his arm a trembling
bride, who pined still for the mother she had lost.
Coming up close to him, the god Hermes began:
'Hades, dark-haired lord and master of the dead,
my father Zeus orders me now to take away
from Erebus the royal Persephone, back
to the world, so that Demeter, when she sees
with her own eyes her daughter returning
may relent, and give up her implacable grudge
against the gods – for what she now intends
is terrible, to wipe from the face of the earth
the whole defenceless species of mortal men
by keeping crops under the ground, and then starving
heaven of its offerings. In her rage, Demeter
will have nothing to do with the gods, and she sits
closed in her own temple, apart, holding sway
there over the rocky citadel of Eleusis.'

Hades listened, with just the hint of a smile
on his face, but did not disobey the express
order of Zeus the king, and he spoke at once:
'Go, Persephone, go back now to your mother,
go in good spirits, and full of happiness,
but don't feel too much anger or resentment.
You know, I won't be the worst of all the gods
to have for a husband, brother to your father Zeus;
and here you could be the mistress of everything
that lives and moves, have the finest of honours
among the gods, while for all those failing to pay
their dues by keeping you happy with sacrifice,
proper respect and generous gifts, there will be
nothing in store but punishment forever.'

Persephone jumped straight up, full of excitement,
when she heard what he said; but Hades, looking
around him, and then back over his shoulder,

gave her the tiny, sweet seed of a pomegranate
for something to eat, so that she would not stay
up there forever with the goddess Demeter.
Then Hades got ready his gold-covered chariot,
hitching up his own horses, and in stepped
Persephone, with the strong god Hermes beside her,
who took the reins and the whip in his hands
as both of the horses shot forward obediently
out and away, making good speed on their journey,
untroubled by the sea, or by flowing rivers,
or grassy glens, or freezing mountain tops:
they sliced thin air beneath them as they flew.

When they came to a stop, it was in front of the temple
where Demeter kept vigil; and, at the sight of them,
she ran forward wildly like someone possessed.
At the sight of her mother, Persephone leapt out
and into her arms, and hugged her, and she wept,
and the two of them, speechless, clung hard
to each other, until suddenly Demeter
sensed something wrong, and broke the embrace,
'My darling,' she said, 'I hope that down there
you didn't eat anything when he took you away?
Tell me, and tell me now: for, if you didn't,
you can stay with me forever, and with the gods,
and Zeus, your father; but, if you did eat
anything at all, then you'll have to go back
underground for the third part of every year,
spending the rest of the time at my side: when
flowers come up in spring, and bloom in the summer,
you will rise too from the deep mists and darkness –
to the amazement of men, as well as the gods.
But how did Hades abduct you? What tricks
did he use to bring you away to the dark?'
'Mother,' Persephone answered, 'I will tell you it all.
When Hermes came for me on the orders of Zeus,
to take me out of Erebus, so you could see me
and abandon your vendetta against the gods,
I jumped for joy; but then Hades, unnoticed,
gave me the seed of a pomegranate to eat,
and made me taste it: it was sweet like honey.
I'll explain, just as you ask me to, how he
snatched me away in the first place, when Zeus
planned everything to bring me down under the earth.
We were playing together in an uncut meadow
– me and all my friends – and gathering for fun
handfuls of the wild flowers that were growing there:

saffron and irises, hyacinths, and young roses,
lilies gorgeous to look at, and a narcissus
that bloomed, just like a crocus, in the soil.
While I was taken up with that, from nowhere
the ground beneath me split apart, and out
came the great king of millions of the dead
who dragged me, as I screamed, into his gold-
covered chariot, and took me down into the earth.
Now you've heard what it hurts me to remember.'

That whole day long, they were completely at one:
each warmed the other's heart, and eased it of sorrow,
the two of them brimming over with happiness
as they hugged one another for joy again and again.
The goddess Hecatē came to them and joined them;
still wearing her veil of white linen, she caught
Demeter's little daughter over and over
in her arms, and became her companion forever.

Only then did Zeus, the deep- and wide-bellowing God,
send down to speak to Demeter her own mother,
Rhea, to reconcile her with her family.
On his behalf, she could offer whatever new honours
were needed, and guarantee that Persephone
would stay down in the darkness for only a season,
the third of a year, and the rest with her mother
and all of the gods. Rhea hurried to the task,
reaching the fields, near Eleusis at Rarion
where harvests once were abundant, but now
no harvest could come up from the cropless plain
where Demeter had hidden away the white barley,
though afterwards, as the spring went on, it would
thicken and move with long corn, and the furrows
would be filled in due course with cut stalks
while all the rest was gathered up into sheaves.

Here the goddess first came down from the trackless air
and she and Demeter greeted one another with joy.
Rhea delivered her message from Zeus, and the promises
he made for Demeter, and for Persephone,
urging her daughter, 'Now, child, you must
do the right thing, and not venture too far
by keeping up this grudge of yours against Zeus:
let food grow again for people on the earth.'
Demeter could say nothing against this: she allowed
crops then and there to come from the fertile ground;
she freighted the wide world with flowers and leaves.

~

She went then to the men in power – Diocles,
Triptolemus, Eumolpus, and Celeus himself,
the people's leader, to give them instruction
in her liturgy and rites: all of the mysteries
neither to be questioned, nor departed from,
and not to be spoken about for fear of the gods,
a fear so great as to stop every mouth.
Whoever has witnessed these is blessed among men:
whoever has not been inducted, whoever
has taken no part in them, can expect no good
fortune when death fetches him to the darkness.

Once she had revealed all of this, Demeter
returned to Olympus and the company of the gods;
there she and Persephone, holy and powerful,
live beside Zeus himself, where he plays with thunder.
Anyone whom they favour is deeply blessed,
for they send the god Wealth to his own hearth
dispensing affluence to mortal men.

You who protect the people of fragrant Eleusis,
rocky Antron, and Paros surrounded by the sea,
Lady Demeter, mistress, bountiful goddess,
both you and your lovely child Persephone,
favour me for this hymn, give me a living,
and I will heed you in my songs, now and always.

THE LIFE OF AESOP

The Life of Aesop

Anon.

Translated from the Spanish by John E. Keller and L. Clark Keating, 1993

A number of classical writers gathered together collections of fables under his name, but very little is known of Aesop himself. Legend has it that he was born a slave in the sixth century BC and earned his freedom before carrying his stories across the Greek world. The following two extracts come from an anonymous *Life of Aesop*, which is something of a fable in itself. Thought to have been assembled some time before the second century AD, the fictional biography was translated widely and proved very popular down the ages. This translation is wonderfully seamless despite being a few stages removed from the earliest texts. It is an English translation of a Spanish version of the story from the fifteenth century.

I

The young Aesop, a disabled slave, proves his cunning.

In the region of Phrygia, where the ancient city of Troy was located, there was a small village called Amonia in which was born a deformed boy, ugly of countenance and with a body more deformed than any other boy of his time. He had a large head and piercing black eyes; he was long of jaw and had a twisted neck; he had fat calves and big feet; he was large of mouth, hump-backed and bepaunched; he stuttered, and his name was Aesop. As he grew, in time he surpassed all others in astuteness. He was soon captured and removed to a foreign country, where he was sold to a rich citizen of Athens named Aristes. And as this gentleman thought him useless and of no profit to serve in his house, he assigned him to work and dig in the fields and on his property.

One day Zenas, to whom was entrusted the administration of the property for his lord, arose from his sleep to go to work, as he usually did on the aforesaid lands. In a short while his lord came with a lad named Agathopus. And as Zenas was showing his master how hard he worked, it happened that he came upon a fig tree in which there were a few figs that had ripened earlier than those on the other fig trees. From this tree Zenas carefully picked the figs and presented them with great courtesy to his lordship, saying: "To you belong the first fruits of your land." And the lord, seeing the beauty of the figs, said: "I thank you, sincerely, Zenas, for the great affection you have for me."

As it was the time at which he was accustomed on such a day to bathe and cleanse himself, he said: "Oh, Agathopus, take and guard these figs carefully, for when I return from the bath I shall begin my meal with them." But as Agathopus took the figs and looked at them, an uncontrollable urge to gluttony arose within him; he looked again and again at the figs in the presence of one of his comrades, and the two of them together looked at them. And he said; "If I were not afraid of our master I would eat these figs one after another." His companion replied: "I will tell you how to do it in such a way that we will suffer no harm on their account." Agathopus said: "How can this be?" Said the other: "This is easy for us, for Aesop comes every day to get the bread you are accustomed to give him. And when the lord asks for his figs, we will say that Aesop, coming in from his toil and finding the figs in the pantry, ate them. And when Aesop is sent for, with that slowness and stammer of his, he will not be able to defend himself or make any excuse, and the lord will beat him, and we will get what we want." Agathopus, having heard this advice, with his desire for the figs began without further thought to eat, and as he ate them with great pleasure and joy Agathopus said laughing: "Grief and sadness will be your lot, Aesop, for upon your shoulders our lord will furiously avenge our guilt." And so, talking and laughing, they ate up all the figs.

When the lord came from his bath, he asked them to bring him the figs for the first course of his dinner. And Agathopus said: "My lord, Aesop came from his work and, as he found the pantry open, he went in and, not listening to reason, ate them all." Hearing this, the lord, moved by anger, said: "Who will send for this Aesop for me?" And when Aesop came before the lord, he said to Aesop: "Tell me, mean rascal, shameless one, is this the way you respect me? So little do you fear me that you have had the boldness to eat the figs that were kept in the pantry for me?" Aesop, not being able to answer his master because of his speech impediment, was afraid. And the lord ordered him stripped. But as he was sharp, clever, and astute and knew that he was being falsely accused by those present, he got down on his knees before his master and, making signs, requested a bit of time before he should be beaten, knowing that he could not counter with words the trick his accusers had laid upon him and that he would have to defend himself by cleverness. Whereupon he went to the fire, picked up a pot of hot water he found there, tossed the contents into a basin, and drank it. Then shortly he stuck his fingers into his throat and threw up only the water that he had drunk, for during that day he had had no other food. Then he begged his lord as a favor to have his accusers drink hot water. By command of their lord they drank it, and to keep from vomiting they held their hands to their mouths, but as their stomachs were swollen with hot water they threw up water mixed with figs. And the lord saw plainly, by the experiment, that they had eaten the figs. Turning to them he said: "Because you lied about this man who is not glib, I order you stripped and publicly beaten, that whosoever shall by deceit raise up an accusation against another will have his hide tanned and burnished for a reward."

II

*Aesop has gained his freedom and embarks upon a series of travels
as a fable-maker.*

But when the Egyptians saw Aesop, they considered him a monster and
without knowledge, a fakir and jokester, for they did not realize that in
ugly and dull vessels there is sometimes contained a balsam that is the
most precious of all liquids, and if sometimes the bottles are not clean, they
contain clean wines. So Aesop went to the palace and threw himself at the feet
of the king, who in all his majesty received him in kindly fashion. And when he
said to him: "Tell me, Aesop, with whom do you compare me and mine?" And
Aesop replied: "I compare you to the sun, and your followers to the rays of the
sun, for certainly you shine in no other manner than the sun and the solar circle
and disk, and your people shine like the rays of the sun that surround it." Then
Nectanabo said to him: "What is the kingdom of Licurus like, as compared with
ours?" And Aesop smiling said: "In no way is it lower, but much higher. Just as
the sun exceeds the moon and astonishes with its splendor, so the kingdom of
Licurus exceeds and overwhelms yours." The king, marveling at such prompt
and skillful reply, and impressed by Aesop's speaking, said: "Bring me the masters who are to build the tower." Aesop replied: "After one other thing: show
me the place where you want it built." Going straightaway out of the city, the
king then showed him the place in the country. And Aesop, in the four corners
of the appointed place, put the eagles with the money bags fastened to their
feet and with the children in them, who held their tongues in one hand and the
food in the other. As the children were borne aloft by the eagles, they called out,
showing their tongues and saying: "Give us mortar and give us bricks and wood
and the things necessary for building." When Nectanabo saw this he said: "Why
are there men among you who have wings?" And Aesop replied: "For many
reasons, yet you, a man, wish to contend with he who is a demigod?"

Then the king of Egypt said: "I confess myself beaten. But I urge you, Aesop,
to answer me this: How is it that the mares I brought from Greece, from hearing
the neighing of the horses in Babylon, became pregnant and conceived?" And
Aesop asked for a day to reply. Going to his house, he ordered his boys to
bring him a cat, and they brought it before Aesop, who caused it to he publicly
whipped with a stick. The Egyptians, hearing this, tried to free and defend the
cat, but not being able to, went to the king and told him of this serious incident.
Then the king ordered Aesop to come before him, and when Aesop came before
the king he asked him: "Why did you act in this fashion, Aesop? Do you not
know that we honor God in the person of a cat?" For the Egyptians honored
such an idol. Aesop replied: "This cat this night offended Licurus, for he killed
a valiant and generous cock who crowed the hours of the night." And the king
said: "I did not think that you would lie this way, for it cannot be that in one
night that cat should go to Babylon and come back here." Smiling, Aesop said:
"The cat went to and returned from Babylon in the same way as the mares who
are here get pregnant on hearing the neighing of the horses that are in Babylon."
For these words the king praised and commended the learning of Aesop.

But the following day King Nectanabo had all the learned men and men of philosophic science summoned to the city of the sun. Informing them of Aesop's wisdom, he invited them to dine, and Aesop with them. When they were at table, one of them said to Aesop: "I greet you in peace. I am sent by God to talk to you. What do you say to that?" Aesop answered: "God by no means wishes men to learn to lie; since your word says that you fear and honor God but little." Another said: "There is a great temple, one column of which holds up twelve cities, and each city is covered with thirty beams which represent two women." Aesop said: "In Babylon the children can solve this question. For the temple is the roundness of the earth, the column is the year, the twelve cities are the twelve months, the thirty columns are the days thereof, and the two women tell day and night. For the two continuously run after each other." King Nectanabo said to his lords: "It is right for me to send tribute to the king of Babylon."

One of the learned men said: "Let us ask Aesop yet another question: What thing is it that we never see or hear?" And the king said: "I ask you, Aesop, to tell us what thing it is that we never hear or see?" Aesop replied: "Allow me to answer tomorrow." And when he went to his house, he pretended to write a contract and obligation in which Nectanabo confessed to having received as a loan from King Licurus one thousand silver marks, which he obliged himself to repay at a time already past. And the next morning Aesop took that contract and showed it to the king. After reading it the king marveled and said to his powerful men; "You hear and see that I received some money a while ago which King Licurus of Babylon lent to me." They said, "We have never heard or seen such a thing." Then, said Aesop: "If what you say is true, the question is resolved." The king, hearing this, said: "Happy art thou, Licurus, to possess such a man." And so he sent the tribute with Aesop. And he, having returned to Babylon, told King Licurus all that he had done in Egypt and then presented the tribute which the king had sent. And for this King Licurus ordered a gold statue of Aesop raised in public.

After a few days, desiring to see Greece, Aesop asked leave of the king, promising to return and spend the rest of his life in Babylon. And thus traveling through the cities of Greece, showing his wisdom through fables, he earned a great reputation and increased in wisdom. Finally Aesop came to a city called Delphi, which was a much honored city and the chief place of the region. As the people heard him and followed him there was no honor they did not do him. And Aesop said to them: "Men of Delphi, you certainly are like a tree that is brought to the sea. The wood, when it is far from the sea, seems a large object, but when it is near it knows itself to be small, just as I was when I was distant from your city: I thought that you were the most excellent of all, but now, being near you, I know you for the least discreet of all." The people of Delphi, hearing these and similar words, said among themselves; "This fellow is feared and followed in many other towns. If we are not careful, certainly by his fables and stories he will take away and diminish the authority of our city. Therefore let us take counsel concerning this affair." So they agreed to kill Aesop by a trick, claiming that he was evil and sacrilegious. But on account of the people they did not dare to kill him publicly without reason, so they detained Aesop's servant, who had to prepare his affairs for his departure. And they placed secretly within his luggage a golden vessel that came from the temple of the sun. Aesop, not knowing the tricks and treason that had been prepared against him, left that place for another, called Focida, and to that place the men of Delphi followed him and there took him prisoner with great clamor. When Aesop asked them why they detained him, they shouted loudly: "O evil one, O villainous, wicked man. Why did you steal from the Temple of Apollo and the Sun?" This Aesop denied freely, maintaining it with a heavy heart. But the men of Delphi, unpacking his luggage, found in it in the golden goblet, and showed it to everyone with great tumult and noise and resolutely dragged him to prison.

Aesop, not yet knowing their deceit and treason, asked them to let him go his way. And they pressed and constrained him more than ever, and kept him in prison more determinedly. Then Aesop, seeing no way to escape and knowing that they had decided to kill him, groaned and complained of his bad fortune. A friend of his, whose name was Demas, coming into the prison and seeing Aesop wailing, said to him: "Why are you moaning in this fashion, Aesop? Be stout-hearted and have hope and console yourself." But the people of Delphi publicly sentenced him to death as a thief and guilty of sacrilege of the temple. And coming together as one man, they took Aesop out of the prison to throw him over a cliff. Realizing this, Aesop said: "In the days when dumb animals were in agreement, the mouse and the frog made peace and concluded a friendship. The former invited the latter to dinner. And as they were entering a room where there were bread, honey, figs, and other good things to eat, the mouse said to the frog: 'Choose of this food and eat what suits you best, and you will have a better appetite.' After they had pleased themselves with those foods, the frog said to the mouse: 'Since I have had pleasure and joy with you, it is but right that you should see my house and company and should partake of my goods as a friend and brother. But so that you may proceed most surely, tie your foot to mine.' The mouse believed him and so, with their feet tied, the frog jumped into the river and took the mouse with him, swimming. And the mouse, seeing that he was drowning, said loudly: 'By your treachery I am killed. Some among the living must avenge me upon you.' And while they were locked in this struggle, a kite, seeing the mouse in the water, seized both him and the frog and ate them both. And now, without guilt and against justice, I am to die at your hands and am punished. But Babylon and Greece will avenge me upon you who do this evil deed to me."

The men of Delphi, hearing this, had no wish to let Aesop go, but rather struggled to carry him to the cliff from which they meant to throw him. But Aesop, struggling, fled from their hands and repaired to the Temple of Apollo and climbed up the altar. But it did him no good, for those of Delphi by force and cruelty took him from there with great wrath, determination, roughness, and beatings and carried him off to throw him over the cliff. Now Aesop, seeing himself thus carried off dishonorably, said to them: "Citizens of Delphi, look upon this your god. Although his dwelling is small, you do not wish to dishonor it, but look with shame and moderation toward Apollo, to whom I had resorted when you dragged me forth." But they, not heeding his words, with great zeal carried him off to death. And Aesop, seeing his end near, said very quickly: "Evil and cruel men, since I cannot make you understand my counsels, at least listen carefully to this story: A woman had a mad virgin for a daughter, and she continually begged the gods to give her daughter some brains. The mother offered this prayer many times and even in public that her mad daughter might recover her mind. And a few days later, being in a village where she had gone with her mother, the daughter went out of the house and saw how a village boy wished to have indecent carnal knowledge of a she-ass. The girl came up to the boy and asked, 'What are you doing, good fellow?' And he replied: 'I am giving some brains to this she-ass.' The mad girl, remembering her mother's words, said: 'Oh, good lad, I wish you would give me some brains also, and if you do so, you will not labor in vain, for my mother will be very grateful to you.' The country boy left the she-ass and violated and corrupted the virgin. And she, thus corrupted and happy, ran to her mother saying: 'Rejoice, mother, for on account of your prayers I have been given brains.' The mother replied: 'And thus the gods have answered my prayers, or what is this?' The daughter answered: 'Just now a boy put a rather long thing with balls hanging below it into my stomach, taking it out and returning it quickly. I received it gladly for certain, and thus he gave me brains, and I feel it so in my heart.' Then said the mother: 'Woe to you, my daughter, rather you have lost the few brains you had.'

"Similarly I urge you to hear another fable in this manner: A farmer, as he was growing old in the country and had never seen a city, and desiring to see one, asked his relatives to take him to the city. They put the old man in a cart pulled by two yoked asses, and they said: 'Now spur them and by themselves they will take you to the city.' But as the old man was going toward the city, a whirlwind came up suddenly so that the sky was dark, and the asses, wandering from the road, took him to a high and dangerous place. The old man, seeing he was in danger of death, called upon Jupiter, saying: 'O Jupiter, how did I offend your temples and majesty that I thus perish miserably? For would that I were dragged and killed or cast down from a cliff by valuable and excellent horses rather than by such vile asses.' "And so," said Aesop, "I am not tormented by distinguished and illustrious men, but by useless and perverse servants am I killed."

Reaching the place where he was to be thrown over, he spoke to them again in this way: "A man, being obsessed by love of his daughter, sent his wife to town, and he had the daughter in the house, whom he violated and ravished. The daughter said to him: 'You are doing forbidden and ugly things. I had rather suffer this crime and evil from a hundred others than from you alone.' "And so," said Aesop, "wicked and perverse men of Delphi, I would prefer to besiege all of Cicilia and suffer all the perils of the sea rather than die thus wrongly at your hands. I beg you and your gods, and your land, and I admonish all of you to hear me who am dying unjustly that you may receive from them other, more just vengeance in the form of torments and penalties." But, unwilling to hear anything, the men of Delphi had him thrown over a steep cliff, and thus ended the life of the harassed Aesop.

After Aesop's death, pestilence and hunger and a great furor and madness of heart fell upon those of Delphi, concerning which they asked advice of Apollo; and the reply came that they should build an oratory for Aesop to placate and appease the gods. Thus, with compunction and repentance in their hearts for having killed Aesop unjustly, they built a temple to him. By this means the princes of Greece and the important persons and presidents of the provinces heard of Aesop's death. Coming to Delphi and having made diligent inquiry and learned the truth, they summoned to justice and suitably punished those who had caused his death. Thus they avenged Aesop's death. Here concludes the life of Aesop.

THE BATTLE OF THE FROGS AND MICE

Battle of Frogs and Mice

Anon.

Translated by Joel P. Christensen and Erik Robinson, 2018

In antiquity, this story was often attributed to Homer. Although the poem is almost certainly not Homeric, its origins remain unclear, with some dating it to the fifth century BC and others to the early Roman Empire. The inspiration for the tale is Aesop's fable of the mouse and the frog (see previous story). A frog, the fable goes, promised to teach a mouse to swim by binding his leg to his. Sadly, the mouse drowned, and in his dying breath threatened to take revenge on the frog from beyond the grave. True to his word, a bird swooped down and snatched the dead mouse before gobbling up the frog still tethered to his corpse. The author of the *Battle of Frogs and Mice* clearly knew Aesop's fable but decided to take it in his own direction.

Once upon a time, a thirsty mouse escaped the weasel's danger
and then lowered his greedy chin down to a pond
to take pleasure in the honey-sweet water. A pond-loving frog,
a big-talker, saw him and uttered something like this:

"Friend, who are you? From where have you come to our shore?
Who sired you?
Tell me everything truly so I don't think you're a liar.
If I consider you a worthy friend, I'll take you home,
where I will give you many fine gifts of friendship.
I am King Bellowmouth and I am honored
throughout the pond as leader of frogs for all days.
My father Mudman raised me up after he had sex
with Watermistress along the banks of the Eridanus.
I see that you are noble and brave beyond the rest,
and also a scepter-bearing king and a warrior in battles.
Come closer and tell me of your lineage."

~

Then Crumbthief answered and spoke:
"Why do you seek out my lineage? It's known
to all men, gods and flying things in the sky.
I am known as Crumbthief. I am the son
of great-hearted Bread nibbler and my mother Mill-licker,
who was daughter of King Hamnibbler.
She birthed me in a hidey-hole and nourished me with food
like figs and nuts and all kinds of choice sweets.
How could you make me your friend when our nature is so different?
Your life is in the water—but it is my custom
to nibble away at the foods of men. And I never miss out
on thrice-kneaded bread in the well-rounded basket.
Nor does a long-robed flat cake dressed out with plenty sesame and cheese
ever escape me. Neither does a ham-slice, a white-robed liver
nor just-curdled cheese from sweet-milk,
nor the holy honey-cake which even the gods desire,
nor the things cooks carve out for mortals' feasts
when they season the dishes with every kind of spice.
I have never fled the dread song of war
but instead I head straight into the danger and join the forefighters.
I don't fear people, even though they have such great size;
no, I run up to their beds and bite the tip of their fingers.
Then I take their ham and no pain overtakes the man,
no one wakes from sleep when I bite him.
But I do really fear two things over the whole earth:
the hawk and the weasel who bring me great grief
and also the grievous mousetrap where a deceptive fate awaits me.
But I fear the weasel more than anything, that beast who is best
at ferreting a hole-dweller out of his hole.

I don't eat radishes, cabbage, and pumpkins;
and I don't munch on pale beets or parsley.
Such things are the delicacies of pond-dwellers like you."

Grinning at this, Bellowmouth responded:
"Friend, you brag too much about your belly. We also
have many marvels to see in the pond and on the shore.
Zeus gave the frogs an amphibious realm
to dance upon the earth or cover our bodies in water
and to inhabit homes divided doubly in parts.
If you wish to learn about these things too, it's simple.
Climb on my back, hold on tight so you don't slip
and then you can come happily to my home."

Thus he spoke and offered up his back. Crumbthief hopped on quickly,
holding his hands around Bellowmouth's delicate neck with a light embrace.
At first he was rejoicing as he looked upon the neighboring harbors

and delighted in Bellowmouth's swimming. But, then, when he was
splashed by the roiling waves, he poured forth a flood of tears
and reproached his useless decision. He tore at his hairs,
squeezed his feet around his stomach and his heart
shook at the novelty and he wished to get back to land.
He wailed dreadfully under the oppression of chilling fear.
First, he set his tail into the water as though guiding a rudder,
and prayed to the gods to make it to the shore.
He was splashed again by the murky water, and kept shouting out for help.
Then he made a speech like this as he proclaimed:

"Didn't the bull carry his cargo of love in this way
when he led Europa over the waves to Krete?
Such is the way this frog set out and led a mouse to his house
after raising his pale body on the white wave."

Suddenly, a water snake appeared, a bitter sight to both,
holding his throat up straight out of the water.
When he saw him, Bellowmouth went under water, considering not
what sort of friend he was about to abandon to death.
He submerged in the depth of the pond, and avoided black death.
But the mouse, as he was let go, fell backward into the water,
clenched his hands, and squeaked as he was dying.
Several times he went down below the water, and several times
he kicked and came back up. But it was not possible to ward off fate.
His wet hair put more weight on him,
and dying in the water, he shouted out these words:

"You won't evade the gods in doing these deceitful things,
tossing me shipwrecked from your body as if off a crag.
You rotten bastard, you were not better than me upon land
at fighting or wrestling or running, so you brought me to the water
and hurled me into it! God has an eye for vengeance.
You will not avoid paying a penalty and
righteous payback to the host of mice who honor me."

As he said this, he gasped in the water. And Platelicker
saw him as he sat upon the luxuriant banks.
Then he wailed terribly, ran, and informed the mice.
A dread wrath fell upon them as they learned his fate,
and they ordered their heralds to summon their kin
to the assembly at the home of Breadmuncher at dawn.
He was father of pitiful Crumbthief who floated on the pond
as a corpse facing upward, no longer struggling
on the banks but raised up in the middle of the sea.
And so they came hurrying at dawn and among them first
Breadmuncher rose enraged over his son to make this speech:

~

"Friends, even if I alone suffered these many evils from the frogs,
it would still be a vile crime against us all.
I am wretched because I have lost three children:
a most hateful weasel snatched up the first and killed him
as she dragged him from his hole.
Harsh men dragged the second to his doom
once they designed a wooded trick with their newfangled arts—
that thing they call the trap, the destroyer of mice.
[A mouse-eating great beast made my first son into dinner
as he chanced upon him spinning on his fat heel.]
The third was beloved to me and his prized mother,
Bellowmouth drowned him once he dragged him to the deep.
Come, let us arm ourselves and go out to face them
once we've arrayed our bodies in our well-worked arms."
In saying this, he persuaded everyone to arm themselves;
and so, Ares who loves war armed them.
First, they fit their greaves to their two legs,
after breaking some pale beans and fitting them well,
beans they nibbled clean by working on them all night.
They had chestpieces made of reed-bound hides
which they made skillfully after flaying a weasel.
Their shield was the middle-section of a lamp. And their spear
was a well-measured needle, a completely bronze work of Ares.
The helmet on their temples was the husk of chick pea.

And this is the way the mice were armed. When the frogs noticed
they rose up from the water: and once they gathered in the same place
they summoned a council for wicked war.
While they were examining the conflict and noise,
a herald approached carrying a staff in his hand:
Bowldiver, the son of great-hearted Cheeseborer,
in announcing the evil report of war said these kind of things:

"My frogs: the mice threaten you and send me
to tell you to arm yourselves for war and battle.
They saw Crumbthief, whom your king
Bellowmouth killed in the water. But fight,
all of you who were born best among the frogs."
He explained it, speaking in this way. The report entered all their ears
and disturbed the minds of the arrogant frogs.
While they were reproaching, Bellowmouth stood and said:

"Friends, I didn't kill the mouse, nor did I witness him dying.
He drowned altogether because he was playing near the shore
trying to mimic the swimming of frogs. These villains

are blaming me when I am not at fault. But let us seek
a plan so that we may kill those treacherous mice.
I will announce the strategy that seems best to me.
Let all of us stand after adorning ourselves in arms
on the top of the banks where the land is steep.
Whenever they come rushing against us—
Once we have snatched them by their helmets as each approaches—
we will throw them straight into the water with their weapons.
When we drown those unaccustomed to the water in this way,
we will happily dedicate a trophy to the murder of mice."

So speaking he persuaded everyone to arm themselves.
First, they covered their shins with the leaves of reeds
and they had breastplates from fine yellow beets
while they fitted the leaves of cabbage into shields well
and a great sharp reed was worked as a spear for each.
The horns of polished snails covered their heads.
They stood on the high banks defending themselves;
and as they brandished their spears, courage filled each of them.

Zeus called the gods to starry heaven
and showed them the mass of war and strong warriors
so many, so great, carrying enormous spears
just as the army of centaurs or giants had once approached them.
Then, laughing sweetly, he asked who among the immortals
were supporters for the frogs or mice. And he addressed Athena:

"Daughter, won't you go forth to help the mice?
For they all continuously dance around your temple
Delighting in the smell and every kind of treat."
So Kronos' son asked and Athena responded:

"Father, I would never come to the aid of the distressed mice
because they have done me many evils
by ruining my garlands and lamps to get at the oil.
One thing they did really wears at my thoughts.
They ate up at the robe which I wore myself out weaving
from tender weft I spun myself on a great warp—
they fill it with holes. The mender waits for me
and makes me his debtor, a thing horrible for the gods.
For I spun it in debt and I can't pay it back.
But there is no way I want to help the frogs.
For these creatures are not of sound mind: yesterday
when I was returning from war and really worn out
and needing sleep, they did not allow me to nap even a little,
as they made a ruckus. And I lay there sleepless,
with a headache until the rooster crowed.

Come on, let us gods avoid helping them,
lest one of us get wounded by a sharp missile,
for they fight up close, even if a god should confront them.
Let's all instead enjoy watching this battle from heaven."

So she spoke and the other gods assented to her
and they all came gathered together in one spot.
Then some mosquitoes bearing great trumpets
sounded the dread song of battle. And from heaven
Kronos' son, Zeus, thundered the portent of wicked war.

First, Croakmaster struck Lickman with a spear
through his stomach, mid-liver, as he stood among the forefighters.
And he fell down headlong and dirtied his delicate hair.
He thundered as he fell, and his weapons clattered about him.
Hole-dweller next hurled at Muddy's son
and fixed a stout spear in his chest. Then black death took him
as he fell and his soul flew from his body.
Bowldiver killed Beeteater when he struck him in the heart
and Breadmuncher struck Sir Croaks-a-lot in the stomach—
and he then fell headlong, and his soul flew from his limbs.
When Pondlubber saw Sir Croaks-a-lot dying
he acted first in crushing Holedweller's tender neck
with a rock like a mill-stone. Then darkness covered his eyes.
Grief overtook Basilson and he drove him through with a sharp reed
as the other didn't raise his spear against him. When Lickman saw this,
he took aim at him with his own shining spear
and hurled it: he didn't miss his liver. Then, when he noticed
that Spice-eater was fleeing, he rushed upon the lush banks.
And he did not let up from battle, no, he ran him through.
He fell and didn't look up again: then the pond was dyed
with purple blood even as he was stretched out on the shore
as he tried to rise with his intestines and trailing loins.
Then he despoiled Cheesenibbler on the same banks.
When Minty saw Hamcarver he went into flight
and he was driven into the pond while rushing, after abandoning his shield.
Blameless Mudbedder killed Poundweight.
Watergrace killed King Hameater
after striking him with a stone on the top of his head. And his brains
dribbled from his nose and the earth was spattered with blood.

Platelicker then killed blameless Mudbedder
as he sprung at him with his spear. Then darkness covered his eyes.
When Greenstalk saw this, he dragged Smokehunter by the foot,
overpowered him, and drowned him in the pond as he reached out his hand.
Crumbthief defended his dead friend
and hurled at Greenstalk through his stomach into his liver—

then he fell forward and his soul descended to Hades.
Cabbagetreader saw this and threw a lump of mud at him;
it smeared his face and he nearly blinded him.
When he was enraged by this, he grabbed a heavy rock
lying on the ground, a burden to the earth, with his stout hand
and he struck Cabbagetreader with it below the knees. His right greave
was completely shattered and he fell face-up into the dust.
Croakerson defended him and went straight at the other guy,
striking him in the middle of the stomach. The whole sharp reed
pierced into him and all of his guts poured out on the ground
because of the spear as it was withdrawn by the strong hand.
When Holedweller saw this from the banks of the river,
he retreated, limping from the battle to rest, since he was terribly
        worn out.
He rushed into the ditches in order to flee the sheer destruction.
Breadmuncher struck Bellowmouth on the top of the foot.
He retreated to the furthest part of the pond, terribly worn out.
And when Greenstalk saw him falling still half-alive,
again he then ran out, desiring to kill,
and he went through the champions and hurled his sharp-reed.

He didn't break the shield and the tip of the spear held fast.
Shining Oregano, as he imitated Ares himself,
and was the only one who prevailed through the engagement among the
        frogs,
did not strike the four-measured, blameless helm
but he rushed at him. But when the frog saw him, he didn't wait for
the strong heroes, but he dived into the depths of the pond.

There was a child among the mice who stood out from all others,
Pieceplunder, the dear son of blameless Grater, the Bread-councilor.
He was on his way home; he had ordered the child to join in the war.
But he was threatening to eliminate the race of the frogs
as he stood nearby desiring to fight with force.
First, he split a nut along its middle into two halves
and set them on both his bare hands as defense,
then everyone feared him and scattered around the pond.
He would have achieved his goal since his strength was so great
if the father of men and gods had not taken note.
Kronos' son pitied the dying frogs;
he spoke this kind of speech as he shook his head.

"O wretches, I really see a wonder with my eyes!
Pieceplunder worries me not a little as he crosses like
a thief among the frogs. But quickly then,
let's send war-rousing Pallas or even Ares
to restrain him from battle, even though he is mighty."

~

So Zeus spoke and Ares responded with a speech:

"Son of Kronos, neither the power of Athena nor Ares
is able to ward steep destruction from the frogs.
Let's all go as allies. Or maybe you should
brandish your arms. Whoever is best will be caught in this way,
as when you killed the stout man Kapaneus,
great Enkelados, and the fierce tribes of the giants."

So he spoke and the son of Kronos threw down shining lightning
and thundered first and shook great Olympos.
Then he hurled and threw the frightening weapon of Zeus
and it flew from the master's hand
and frightened all the frogs and mice as he threw.
But the army of the mice did not let up—they even more
hoped to eradicate the race of spear-bearing frogs—
unless Kronos' son took pity on the frogs from Olympos
and sent helpers straight away to the frogs.

Suddenly, the armor-backed, crooked-clawed
bow-waling, twisted, scissor-mouthed, hard-shelled,
bone-built, broad-backed, with shining shoulders,
crooked-legged, lip-stretching, with eyes set in their chest,
eight-footed, two-headed, handless creatures who are called
crabs, went to war. They easily cut off the mice's tails with their mouths
along with their feet and hands. And their spears were bent back.
The cowardly mice were frightened of them and waited no longer
to turn to flight. The sun was already setting.
And the end of this war was accomplished in a single day.

THE VENGEANCE OF CLYTEMNESTRA

Agamemnon

Aeschylus

Translated by Louis MacNeice, 1936

Agamemnon, King of Mycenae and leader of the Greek army in the Trojan War, sacrificed his own daughter Iphigenia to secure a favourable wind for his journey to Troy. His father before him killed his brother's children and fed him their remains by concealing them in his dinner. In **Aeschylus**' (*c.* 525/524–456/455 BC) tragedy, the first in his *Oresteia* trilogy, the past comes back to haunt Agamemnon. As the Chorus reveals at the beginning of this extract from the play, Agamemnon has survived and triumphed in the Trojan War. He has now returned home with Cassandra, prophetess daughter of King Priam of Troy, as his concubine. Little does Agamemnon know that his wife Clytemnestra has also taken a lover, Aegisthus, in his absence. Cassandra, whose misfortune is to never be believed, has accurately foretold the devastating events of this scene. The poet Louis MacNeice captures the stateliness of Aeschylus' Greek in his translation.

CHORUS.
>Prosperity in all men cries
>For more prosperity. Even the owner
>Of the finger-pointed-at palace never shuts
>His door against her, saying 'Come no more'.
>So to our king the blessed gods had granted
>To take the town of Priam, and heaven-favoured
>He reaches home. But now if for former bloodshed
>>He must pay blood
>And dying for the dead shall cause
>>Other deaths in atonement
>What man could boast he was born
>>Secure, who heard this story?

AGAMEMNON. [*Within*]
>Oh! I am struck a mortal blow—within!

LEADER.
> Silence! Listen. Who calls out, wounded with a mortal stroke?

AGAMEMNON.
> Again—the second blow—I am struck again.

LEADER.
> You heard the king cry out. I think the deed is done.
> Let us see if we can concert some sound proposal.

2ND OLD MAN.
> Well, I will tell you my opinion—
> Raise an alarm, summon the folk to the palace.

3RD OLD MAN.
> I say burst in with all speed possible,
> Convict them of the deed while still the sword is wet.

4TH OLD MAN.
> And I am partner to some such suggestion.
> I am for taking some course. No time to dawdle.

5TH OLD MAN.
> The case is plain. This is but the beginning.
> They are going to set up dictatorship in the state.

6TH OLD MAN.
> We are wasting time. The assassins tread to earth
> The decencies of delay and give their hands no sleep.

7TH OLD MAN.
> I do not know what plan I could hit on to propose.
> The man who acts is in the position to plan.

8TH OLD MAN.
> So I think, too, for I am at a loss
> To raise the dead man up again with words.

9TH OLD MAN.
> Then to stretch out our life shall we yield thus
> To the rule of these profaners of the house?

10TH OLD MAN.
> It is not to be endured. To die is better.
> Death is more comfortable than tyranny.

11TH OLD MAN.

    And are we on the evidence of groans
    Going to give oracle that the prince is dead?

12TH OLD MAN.

    We must know the facts for sure and then be angry.
    Guesswork is not the same as certain knowledge.

LEADER.

    Then all of you back me and approve this plan—
    To ascertain how it is with Agamemnon.

[*The doors of the palace open, revealing the bodies of* AGAMEMNON
and CASSANDRA. CLYTEMNESTRA *stands above them.*]

CLYTEMNESTRA.

    Much having been said before to fit the moment,
    To say the opposite now will not outface me.
    How else could one serving hate upon the hated,
    Thought to be friends, hang high the nets of doom
    To preclude all leaping out?
    For me I have long been training for this match,
    I tried a fall and won—a victory overdue.
    I stand here where I struck, above my victims;
    So I contrived it—this I will not deny—
    That he could neither fly nor ward off death;
    Inextricable like a net for fishes
    I cast about him a vicious wealth of raiment
    And struck him twice and with two groans he loosed
    His limbs beneath him, and upon him fallen
    I deal him the third blow to the God beneath the earth,
    To the safe keeper of the dead a votive gift,
    And with that he spits his life out where he lies
    And smartly spouting blood he sprays me with
    The sombre drizzle of bloody dew and I
    Rejoice no less than in God's gift of rain
    The crops are glad when the ear of corn gives birth.
    These things being so, you, elders of Argos,
    Rejoice if rejoice you will. Mine is the glory.
    And if I could pay this corpse his due libation
    I should be right to pour it and more than right;
    With so many horrors this man mixed and filled
    The bowl—and, coming home, has drained the draught himself.

LEADER.

    Your speech astonishes us. This brazen boast
    Above the man who was your king and husband!

CLYTEMNESTRA.

> You challenge me as a woman without foresight
> But I with unflinching heart to you who know
> Speak. And you, whether you will praise or blame,
> It makes no matter. Here lies Agamemnon,
> My husband, dead, the work of this right hand,
> An honest workman. There you have the facts.

CHORUS.

> Woman, what poisoned
> Herb of the earth have you tasted
> Or potion of the flowing sea
> To undertake this killing and the people's curses?
> You threw down, you cut off—The people will cast you out,
> Black abomination to the town.

CLYTEMNESTRA.

> Now your verdict—in my case—is exile
> And to have the people's hatred, the public curses,
> Though then in no way you opposed this man
> Who carelessly, as if it were a head of sheep
> Out of the abundance of his fleecy flocks,
> Sacrificed his own daughter, to me the dearest
> Fruit of travail, charm for the Thracian winds.
> He was the one to have banished from this land.
> Pay off the pollution. But when you hear what I
> Have done, you judge severely. But I warn you—
> Threaten me on the understanding that I am ready
> For two alternatives—Win by force the right
> To rule me, but, if God brings about the contrary,
> Late in time you will have to learn self-discipline.

CHORUS.

> You are high in the thoughts,
> You speak extravagant things,
> After the soiling murder your crazy heart
> Fancies your forehead with a smear of blood.
> Unhonoured, unfriended, you must
> Pay for a blow with a blow.

CLYTEMNESTRA.

> Listen then to this—the sanction of my oaths:
> By the Justice totting up my child's atonement,
> By the Avenging Doom and Fiend to whom I killed this man,
> For me hope walks not in the rooms of fear
> So long as my fire is lit upon my hearth
> By Aegisthus, loyal to me as he was before.

The man who outraged me lies here.
The darling of each courtesan at Troy,
And here with him is the prisoner clairvoyante,
The fortune-teller that he took to bed,
Who shares his bed as once his bench on shipboard,
A loyal mistress. Both have their deserts.
He lies so; and she who like a swan
Sang her last dying lament
Lies his lover, and the sight contributes
An appetiser to my own bed's pleasure.

CHORUS.

Ah would some quick death come not overpainful,
Not overlong on the sickbed,
Establishing in us the ever-
Lasting unending sleep now that our guardian
Has fallen, the kindest of men,
Who suffering much for a woman
By a woman has lost his life.
　　O Helen, insane, being one
　　One to have destroyed so many
　　And many souls under Troy,
　　Now is your work complete, blossomed not for oblivion,
　　Unfading stain of blood. Here now, if in any home
　　Is Discord, here is a man's deep-rooted ruin.

CLYTEMNESTRA.

Do not pray for the portion of death
Weighed down by these things, do not turn
Your anger on Helen as destroyer of men.
One woman destroyer of many
Lives of Greek men,
　　A hurt that cannot be healed.

CHORUS.

O Evil Spirit, falling on the family.
On the two sons of Atreus and using
Two sisters in heart as your tools.
A power that bites to the heart—
See on the body
Perched like a raven he gloats
Harshly croaking his hymn.

CLYTEMNESTRA.

Ah, now you have amended your lips' opinion.
Calling upon this family's three times gorged
Genius—demon who breeds

Blood-hankering lust in the belly:
Before the old sore heals, new pus collects.

CHORUS.

It is a great spirit—great—
You tell of, harsh in anger,
A ghastly tale, alas,
Of unsatisfied disaster
Brought by Zeus, by Zeus,
Cause and worker of all.
For without Zeus what comes to pass among us?
Which of these things is outside Providence?
O my king, my king,
How shall I pay you in tears,
Speak my affection in words?
You lie in that spider's web,
In a desecrating death breathe out your life,
Lie ignominiously
Defeated by a crooked death
And the two-edged cleaver's stroke.

CLYTEMNESTRA.

You say this is *my* work—mine?
Do not cozen yourself that I am Agamemnon's wife.
Masquerading as the wife
Of the corpse there the old sharp-witted Genius
Of Atreus who gave the cruel banquet
Has paid with a grown man's life
The due for children dead.

CHORUS.

That you are not guilty of
This murder who will attest?
No, but you may have been abetted
By some ancestral Spirit of Revenge.
Wading a millrace of the family's blood
The black Manslayer forces a forward path
To make the requital at last
For the eaten children, the blood-clot cold with time.
O my king, my king.
How shall I pay you in tears,
Speak my affection in words?
You lie in that spider's web,
In a desecrating death breathe out your life,
Lie ignominiously
Defeated by a crooked death
And the two-edged cleaver's stroke.

EDUCATING CYRUS

Cyropaedia

Xenophon

Translated by Wayne Ambler, 2001

The *Cyropaedia* or 'Education of Cyrus' is a glorifying life of Cyrus the Great (*c.* 600–530 BC), the founding king of the Persian Empire, centred on the southwestern part of modern Iran. Often likened to Machiavelli's *The Prince*, it was written by **Xenophon** (*c.* 431–354 BC), a pupil of Socrates, in the first half of the fourth century BC – more than a century and a half after Cyrus lived. In this passage, Cyrus, son of Cambyses and Mandane, is around twelve years old. He accompanies his mother on a visit to see his grandfather Astyages, a king of the Medes, who lived to the north of the Persians. This extract reveals the cultural differences between the Medes and their southern neighbours.

As soon as he arrived and Cyrus knew Astyages to be his mother's father, he immediately—since he was by nature an affectionate boy—hugged him as one would have done if he had been raised with him and had been friendly with him for a long time. And he saw him adorned with eye shadow, rouge, and a wig—as was, of course, customary among the Medes (for all these things were Median: purple coats, cloaks, necklaces, and bracelets on their wrists; but among the Persians who are at home, their clothes are even now much more ordinary and their diet much cheaper). So seeing the adornment of his grandfather, he said while looking at him, "Mother, how handsome my grandfather is!"

And when his mother asked him whom he thought more handsome, Astyages or his father, Cyrus then answered, "Of the Persians, my father is the most handsome by far; of the Medes, however, this grandfather of mine is by far the most handsome of those I have seen both in the streets and at court."

Hugging him in return, the grandfather put a beautiful robe on him and honored and adorned him with necklaces and bracelets, and if ever he went out somewhere, he took him along on a horse with a golden bridle, in just the way he himself was accustomed to travel. Since he was a boy who loved beauty and honor, Cyrus was pleased with the robe and exceedingly delighted at learning how to ride a horse. For among the Persians, it was very rare even to see a horse, because it is difficult to raise horses and difficult to ride them in so mountainous a country.

When at dinner with his daughter and Cyrus, Astyages wished the boy to dine as pleasantly as possible so that he might yearn less for what he had left at home. He thus put before him fancy side dishes and all sorts of sauces and meats; and they say that Cyrus said, "Grandfather, how many troubles you have at dinner, if it is necessary for you to stretch out your hands to all these little dishes and taste all these different sorts of meat!"

"What?" Astyages said. "Does it not seem to you that this dinner is much finer than that among the Persians?"

To this Cyrus answered, "No, grandfather, for the road to satisfaction is much more simple and direct among us than among you, for bread and meat take us to it. You hurry to the same place as we do, yet only after wandering back and forth on many curves do you arrive with difficulty at the point we reached long ago."

"But child," Astyages said, "we are not distressed to wander as we do. Taste them, and you too will realize that they are pleasant."

"And yet I see that even you, grandfather, are disgusted with these meats," he said.

And Astyages asked again, "And on what evidence do you say this, my child?"

"Because," he said, "I see that you too, whenever you touch your bread, do not wipe your hand on anything; but whenever you touch any of these, you wipe your hand on your napkin as if you were most distressed that it became soiled with them."

To this Astyages said, "If you are so resolved, my child, feast at least upon these meats, so that you may go home a vigorous youth." As he was saying this, he had a great deal of meat brought to him, of both wild and tame animals.

When he saw all this meat, Cyrus said, "Are you giving me all this meat, grandfather, to use however I want?"

"Yes, my child, by Zeus I am," he said.

Then Cyrus, taking the meat, distributed it to his grandfather's servants and said to each, "This is for you, because you teach me to ride with enthusiasm; for you, because you gave me a javelin, and now I have it; for you, because you serve my grandfather nobly; for you, because you honor my mother." He proceeded like this until he distributed all the meat that he received.

"But to Sakas, my cupbearer, whom I honor most," Astyages said, "do you give nothing?" Now Sakas happened to be handsome and to have the honor of admitting those who sought Astyages and of excluding such as he did not think it opportune to admit.

And Cyrus answered rashly, as would a boy not yet afraid. "Why, grandfather, do you honor him so?"

And Astyages replied jokingly, "Do you not see how nobly and gracefully he pours out my wine?" The cupbearers of these kings carry the cup with refinement, pour the wine cleanly, hand over the cup while holding it with three fingers, and present the cup in the way it is most easily grasped by the one who is about to drink.

"Order Sakas to give me the cup, grandfather," he said, "that I too, by nobly pouring wine for you to drink, may win you over if I can." And he ordered him to give it. Cyrus, they say, taking the cup, rinsed it so well, as he had seen Sakas do, made such a serious face, and brought and presented it to his grandfather so gracefully that he afforded much laughter to his mother and Astyages. Cyrus himself laughed out loud, leaped up onto his grandfather, kissed him, and said, "Sakas, you are done for; I will cast you out of honor, for I will both pour the wine more nobly than you in other respects and I will not drink of the wine myself." Now the cupbearers of the kings, when they present the cup, draw out some of it with a small cup and, pouring it into their left hand, swallow it down, so that they might not profit if they have added poison.

Upon this Astyages said jokingly, "Cyrus, since you imitated Sakas in other respects, why did you not swallow some of the wine?"

"Because, by Zeus," he said, "I was afraid there might have been some poison mixed in the cup, for when you entertained your friends on your birthday, I learned quite clearly that he had added poison for you all."

"And how, my child," he said, "did you come to know this?"

"Because, by Zeus, I saw you all making mistakes, both in your judgments and with your bodies, for in the first place, you yourselves were doing such things as you do not allow us boys to do, for you all shouted at the same time, and you did not comprehend each other at all. Then you sang very ridiculously, and even though you did not listen to the singer, you all swore that he sang most excellently. Then, after each spoke of his own strength, when you stood up to dance, far from dancing in time with the rhythm, you were not even able to stand up straight. You all forgot yourselves entirely, you that you were king, the others that you were their ruler. Then I learned for the first time that what you were practicing was that liberty of speech; at least you were never silent."

And Astyages said, "My child, has not your father gotten drunk from drinking?"

"No, by Zeus," he said.

"But what does he do?"

"He quenches his thirst and suffers no harm, for a Sakas, grandfather, certainly does not pour his wine."

And his mother said, "But why ever, my child, do you make war on Sakas like this?"

"Because I hate him, by Zeus," said Cyrus, "for often when I desire to run up to my grandfather, this most wretched fellow shuts me out. But I beg you, grandfather, give me three days to rule over him."

And Astyages said, "And how would you rule him?"

And it is said that Cyrus said, "Standing at the entrance, just as he does, whenever he wished to come in for lunch, I would say that it is not possible to have lunch yet, 'for he is busy with certain others.' Then, when he came for supper, I would say, 'He is washing.' If he were very much in earnest to eat, I would say, 'He is with his women.' I would detain him so long, just as he detains me, keeping me from you."

Such amusement did he afford them at meals. At other times of the day, if he perceived either his grandfather or his mother's brother in need of anything, it was difficult for anyone else to take care of it before he did, for Cyrus was extremely delighted to gratify them in any way within his power.

When Mandane was preparing to go back to her husband again, Astyages asked her to leave Cyrus behind. She answered that she wished to gratify her father in all things, but that she believed it to be difficult to leave the boy behind against his will. At this point Astyages said to Cyrus, "My child, if you stay with me, in the first place, Sakas will not govern your access to me, but it will be up to you to come to me whenever you wish. And I will be more grateful to you to the extent that you come to me more often. Next, you will use my horses and as many others as you wish, and when you leave, you may take the ones you your-self want. Next, at meals, you may take whatever path you wish to what seems to you to be a measured [diet]. Next, I give you the wild animals that are now in the park, and I will collect others of all kinds, which, as soon as you learn how to ride a horse, you may pursue and strike down with your bow and spear, just as the grown men do. I will also get you boys for playmates, and, if only you tell me, you will not fail to get whatever else you wish."

After Astyages said this, his mother asked Cyrus whether he wished to stay or go. He did not hesitate but quickly said that he wished to stay. Again being asked by his mother as to why, it is said that he said, "Because at home, mother, among those of my age, I both am and am thought to be the best at throwing spears and shooting the bow, but here I know quite well that I am inferior to those of my age at riding. Be well assured, mother, that this vexes me greatly. But if you leave me here and I learn how to ride a horse, when I am in Persia, I think that I will easily be victorious for you over those who are good on foot; but when I come to Media, I shall try for grandfather to be an ally to him by being the best horseman among these good horsemen."

Cyrus accepted Astyages' invitation to stay behind in Media for some time in the hope of becoming an expert horseman. Later, in his adult years, he united the empires of the Medes and the Persians.

DARIUS AND THE SCYTHIANS

Histories, Book IV

Herodotus

Translated by Aubrey de Sélincourt, 1954

Herodotus, popularly hailed as the 'Father of History', was born in Halicarnassus (modern Bodrum) in what is now Turkey, in the early fifth century BC. He was fascinated by the customs of different peoples, and his account of the Scythians, nomads who ranged the Russian steppe in the period 900–200 BC, is among the most colourful in the whole of his *Histories*. The Scythians were tattooed, pot-smoking horsemen who scalped their enemies and attached the remains to their horses. In this story Herodotus describes how they reacted when Darius I, king of Persia, invaded their territory with his formidable army in the late sixth century BC.

The Scythians, after discussing the situation and concluding that by themselves they were unequal to the task of coping with Darius in a straight fight, sent off messengers to their neighbours, whose chieftains had already met and were forming plans to deal with what was evidently a threat to their safety on a very large scale. The conference was attended by the chieftains of the following tribes: the Tauri, Agathyrsi, Neuri, Androphagi, Melanchlaeni, Geloni, Budini, and Sauromatae. It is the custom of the Tauri to sacrifice to the Maiden Goddess all shipwrecked sailors and such Greeks as they happen to capture upon their coasts; their method of sacrifice is, after the preliminary ceremonies, to hit the victim on the head with a club. Some say that they push the victim's body over the edge of the cliff on which their temple stands, and fix the head on a stake; others, while agreeing about the head, say the body is not pushed over the cliff, but buried. The Tauri themselves claim that the goddess to whom these offerings are made is Agamemnon's daughter, Iphigenia. Any one of them who takes a prisoner in war, cuts off his head and carries it home, where he sets it up high over the house on a long pole, generally above the chimney. The heads are supposed to act as guardians of the whole house over which they hang. War and plunder are the sources of this people's livelihood.

The Agathyrsi live in luxury and wear gold on their persons. They have their women in common, so that they may all be brothers and, as members of a single family, be able to live together without jealousy or hatred. In other respects their way of life resembles that of the Thracians.

The Neuri share the customs and beliefs of Scythia. A generation before the campaign of Darius they were forced to quit their country by snakes, which appeared all over the place in great numbers, while still more invaded them from the uninhabited region to the north, until life became so unendurable that there was nothing for it but to move out, and take up their quarters with the Budini. It is not impossible that these people practise magic; for there is a story current amongst the Scythians and the Greeks in Scythia that once a year every Neurian turns into a wolf for a day or two, and then turns back into a man again. Of course, I do not believe this tale; all the same, they tell it, and even swear to the truth of it. The Androphagi are the most savage of men, and have no notion of either law or justice. They are herdsmen without fixed dwellings; their dress is Scythian, their language peculiar to themselves, and they are the only people in this part of the world to eat human flesh. The Melanchlaeni all wear black cloaks – hence their name. In all else, they resemble the Scythians. The Budini, a numerous and powerful nation, all have markedly blue-grey eyes and red hair; there is a town in their territory called Gelonus, all built of wood, both dwelling-houses and temples, with a high wooden wall round it, thirty furlongs each way. There are temples here in honour of Greek gods, adorned after the Greek manner with statues, altars, and shrines – though all constructed of wood; a triennial festival, with the appropriate revelry, is held in honour of Dionysus. This is to be accounted for by the fact that the Geloni were originally Greeks, who, driven out of the seaports along the coast, settled amongst the Budini. Their language is still half Scythian, half Greek. The language of the Budini is quite different, as, indeed, is their culture generally: they are a pastoral people who have always lived in this part of the country (a peculiarity of theirs is eating lice), whereas the Geloni cultivate the soil, eat grain, and keep gardens, and resemble them neither in appearance nor complexion. In spite of these facts the Greeks lump the Budini and Geloni together under the name of the latter; but they are wrong to do so.

The country here is forest with trees of all sorts. In the most densely wooded part there is a big lake surrounded by reedy marshland; otters and beavers are caught in the lake, and another sort of creature with a square face, whose skin they use for making edgings for their jackets; its testicles are good for affections of the womb.

About the Sauromatae there is the following story. In the war between the Greeks and the Amazons,* the Greeks, after their victory at the river Thermodon, sailed off in three ships with as many Amazons on board as they had succeeded in taking alive. Once at sea, the women murdered their captors, but, as they had no knowledge of boats and were unable to handle either rudder or sail or oar, they soon found themselves, when the men were done for, at the mercy of wind and wave, and were blown to Cremni – the Cliffs – on Lake Maeotis, a place within the territory of the free Scythians. Here they got ashore and made their way inland

---

* The Scythians call the Amazons *Oeorpata*, the equivalent of mankillers, *oeor* being the Scythian word for 'man', and *pata* for 'kill'.

to an inhabited part of the country. The first thing they fell in with was a herd of horses grazing; these they seized, and, mounting on their backs, rode off in search of loot. The Scythians could not understand what was happening and were at a loss to know where the marauders had come from, as their dress, speech, and nationality were strange to them. Thinking, however, that they were young men, they fought in defence of their property, and discovered from the bodies which came into their possession after the battle that they were women. The discovery gave a new direction to their plans; they decided to make no further attempt to kill the invaders, but to send out a detachment of their youngest men, about equal in number to the Amazons, with orders to camp near them and take their cue from whatever it was that the Amazons then did: if they pursued them, they were not to fight, but to give ground; then, when the pursuit was abandoned, they were once again to encamp within easy range. The motive behind this policy was the Scythians' desire to get children by the Amazons. The detachment of young men obeyed their orders, and the Amazons, realizing that they meant no harm, did not attempt to molest them, with the result that every day the two camps drew a little closer together. Neither party had anything but their weapons and their horses, and both lived the same sort of life, hunting and plundering.

Towards midday the Amazons used to scatter and go off to some little distance in ones and twos to ease themselves, and the Scythians, when they noticed this, followed suit; until one of them, coming upon an Amazon girl all by herself, began to make advances to her. She, nothing loth, gave him what he wanted, and then told him by signs (being unable to express her meaning in words, as neither understood the other's language) to return on the following day with a friend, making it clear that there must be two men, and that she herself would bring another girl. The young man then left her and told the others what had happened, and on the next day took a friend to the same spot, where he found his Amazon waiting for him and another one with her. Having learnt of their success, the rest of the young Scythians soon succeeded in getting the Amazons to submit to their wishes. The two camps were then united, and Amazons and Scythians lived together, every man keeping as his wife the woman whose favours he had first enjoyed. The men could not learn the women's language, but the women succeeded in picking up the men's; so when they could understand one another, the Scythians made the following proposal: 'We', they said, 'have parents and property. Let us give up our present way of life and return to live with our people. We will keep you as our wives and not take any others.' The Amazons replied: 'We and the women of your nation could never live together; our ways are too much at variance. We are riders; our business is with the bow and the spear, and we know nothing of women's work; but in your country no woman has anything to do with such things – your women stay at home in their waggons occupied with feminine tasks, and never go out to hunt or for any other purpose. We could not possibly agree. If, however, you wish to keep us for your wives and to behave as honourable men, go and get from your parents the share of property which is due to you, and then let us go off and live by ourselves.' The young men agreed to this, and when they came back, each with his portion of the family possessions, the Amazons said: 'We dread the prospect of settling down here, for we have done much damage to the country by our raids, and we have robbed you of your parents. Look now – if you think fit to keep us for your wives, let us get out of the country altogether and settle somewhere on the other side of the Tanais.' Once again the Scythians agreed, so they crossed the Tanais and travelled east for three days, and then north, for another three, from Lake Maeotis, until they reached the country where they are to-day, and settled down there. Ever since then the women of the Sauromatae have kept to their old ways, riding to the hunt on horseback sometimes with, sometimes without, their menfolk, taking part in war and wearing the same sort of clothes as men. The language of these people is the Scythian, but it has always been a corrupt form of it because the Amazons were never able to learn to speak it properly. They have a marriage law which forbids a girl to marry until she has killed an enemy in battle; some of their women, unable to fulfil this condition, grow old and die in spinsterhood.

These, then, were the nations whose chieftains had met together to discuss the common danger; and to them the envoys from Scythia brought the news that the Persian king, having overrun the whole of the other continent, had bridged the Bosphorus and crossed into Europe, where he had already brought Thrace into subjection and was now engaged in throwing a bridge across the Danube, with the intention of making himself master of all Europe too. 'We beg you,' they said, 'not to remain neutral in this struggle; do not let us be destroyed without raising a hand to help us. Let us rather form a common plan of action, and meet the invader together. If you refuse, we shall be forced to yield to pressure and either abandon our country or make terms with the enemy. Without your help, what else could we do? What will become of us? Moreover, if you stand aside, you will not on that account get out of things any more lightly; for this invasion is aimed at you just as much as at us, and, once we have gone under, the Persians will never be content to leave you unmolested. There is plain proof of the truth of this: for had the Persian attack been directed against us alone in revenge for the old wrong we did them when we enslaved their country, they would have been bound to come straight for Scythia without touching any other nation on the way. By doing that they would have made it plain to everyone that the object of their attack was Scythia, and Scythia alone; but, as things are, they no sooner crossed into Europe than they have begun to bring under their heel in turn every nation through whose territory they pass. Not to mention the other Thracians, even our neighbours the Getae have been enslaved.'

The assembled chieftains deliberated upon what the Scythian envoys had reported, but failed to reach a unanimous conclusion. Those of the Geloni, Budini, and Sauromatae agreed to stand by the Scythians, but the rest – the chieftains, namely, of the Agathyrsi, Neuri, Androphagi, Melanchlaeni, and Tauri – returned the following answer. 'Had you not yourselves been the aggressors in your trouble with Persia, we should have considered your request justified; we should have granted what you ask and been willing enough to fight at your side. But the fact is, you invaded Persia without consulting us, and remained in possession of it as long as heaven allowed you, and now the same power is urging the Persians to pay you back in your own coin. We did the Persians no injury on that former occasion, and we will not be the first to start trouble now. Of course, should they prove to be the aggressors and actually invade us, we shall do our best to keep them out; but until we see that happen, we shall stay where we are and do nothing. In our opinion, the invasion is directed not against us, but against you, who were the aggressors in the first place.'

This reply was reported to the Scythians, who proceeded to lay their plans accordingly. Seeing that these nations refused to support them, they decided to avoid a straight fight, and to retire before the advance of the invader, blocking up all the wells and springs which they passed on the march and stripping the country of all green stuff which might serve as forage. They organized their forces in two divisions, one of which, under the command of Scopasis, was to be joined by the Sauromatae, and had orders to counter any movement the Persians might make against them by withdrawing along the coast of Lake Maeotis toward the river Tanais, and, should the Persians themselves retreat, to attack them in their turn. This was one division, and this was the route it was to take. Of the other, the two sections – the greater under Idanthyrsus and the second under Taxacis – were to unite forces and, after joining up with the Geloni and Budini, were, like the first division, to withdraw before the Persian advance at the distance of a day's march, and carry out as they went the same strategy of destroying the sources of supply. This second division was to begin by retiring in the direction of those nations who had refused to join the alliance, with the object of involving them in the war against their will – the idea being, if they would not fight on their own initiative, to force them into doing so. Subsequently, this second force was to go back to its own part of the country and launch an attack on the Persians, should the situation seem to justify it.

Having determined on this plan of action, the Scythians sent their best horsemen to reconnoitre in advance of the army. They themselves then marched out to meet Darius, and arranged for the waggons which served as houses for the women and children, and all the cattle, except what they needed for food, to move northward at once, in advance of their future line of retreat. The scouts made contact with the Persians about three days' march from the Danube, and at once encamped at a distance of a single day's march in front of them, destroying everything which the land produced. The Persians, on the appearance of the Scythian cavalry, gave chase and continued to follow in their tracks as they withdrew before them. The Persian advance was now directed against the single division of the Scythian army under Scopasis, and was consequently eastward towards the Tanais. The Scythians crossed the river, and the Persians followed in pursuit, until they had passed through the territory of the Sauromatae and reached that of the Budini, where they came across the wooden fortified town of Gelonus, abandoned and empty of defenders, and burnt it. Previously, so long as their route lay through the country of the Scythians and Sauromatae, they had done no damage, because the country was barren and there was nothing to destroy. After burning the town, they continued to press forward on the enemy's heels until they reached the great uninhabited region which lies beyond the territory of the Budini. This tract of land is seven days' journey across, and on the further side of it lies the country of the Thyssagetae, from which four great rivers, Lycus, Oarus, Tanais, and Syrgis, flow through the region occupied by the Maeotae to empty themselves into Lake Maeotis.

When he reached this uninhabited area, Darius called a halt on the banks of the Oarus, and began to build eight large forts, spaced at regular intervals of approximately eight miles. The remains of them were still to be seen in my day. While these forts were under construction, the Scythians whom he had been following changed the direction of their march, and by a broad sweep through the country to the northward returned to Scythia and completely disappeared. Unable to see any sign of them, Darius left his forts half finished and himself turned back towards the west, supposing that the Scythians he had been chasing were the whole nation, and that they were now trying to escape in that direction. He made the best speed he was capable of, and on reaching Scythia fell in with the other two combined divisions of the Scythian army; at once he gave chase, and they, as before, withdrew a day's march in front of him. As Darius continued to press forward in hot pursuit, the Scythians now carried out their plan of leading him into the territory of the people who had refused, in the first instance, to support them in their resistance to Persia. The first were the Melanchlaeni, and the double invasion of their country, first by the Scythians and then by the Persians, caused great alarm and disturbance; the turn of the Androphagi came next, and then the Neuri, and in both cases the result was the same – chaos and dismay. Finally, still withdrawing before the Persian advance, the Scythians approached the frontiers of the Agathyrsi. These people, unlike their neighbours, of whose terrified attempt to escape they had been witness, did not wait for the Scythians to invade them, but sent a representative to forbid them to cross the frontier, adding a warning that, if they attempted to do so, they would be resisted by force of arms. This challenge they followed up by putting their frontiers into a state of defence. The other tribes – the Melanchlaeni, Androphagi, and Neuri – offered no resistance to the successive invasions of Scythians and Persians, but forgot their former threats and in great confusion made the best of their escape to the uninhabited regions of the north. The Scythians, finding the Agathyrsi prepared to keep them out, did not attempt to penetrate into their territory, but turned back and drew the Persians into Scythia.

This ineffective and interminable chase was too much for Darius, who at last dispatched a rider with a message for Idanthyrsus, the Scythian king. 'Why on earth, my good sir,' the message ran, 'do you keep on running away? You have, surely, a choice of two alternatives; if you think yourself strong enough to oppose me, stand up and fight, instead of wandering all over the world in your efforts to escape me; or, if you admit that you are too weak, what is the good, even so, of running away? You should rather send earth and water to your master, as the sign of your submission, and come to a conference.'

'You do not understand me, my lord of Persia,' Idanthyrsus replied. 'I have never yet run from any man in fear; nor do I do so now from you. There is, for me, nothing unusual in what I have been doing; it is precisely the sort of life I always lead, even in times of peace. If you want to know why I will not fight, I will tell you: in our country there are no towns and no cultivated land; fear of losing a town or seeing crops destroyed might indeed provoke us to hasty battle – but we possess neither. If, however, you are determined upon bloodshed with the least possible delay, one thing there is for which we will fight – the tombs of our forefathers. Find those tombs, and try to wreck them, and you will soon know whether or not we are willing to stand up to you. Till then – unless the fancy – we shall continue to avoid a battle. This is my reply to your challenge; and as for your being my master, I acknowledge no masters but Zeus from whom I sprang, and Hestia the Scythian queen. I will send you no gifts of earth and water, but others mote suitable; and your claim to be my master is easily answered – be damned to you!' This was the message which was carried back to Darius.

The mere suggestion of slavery filled the Scythian chieftains with rage, and they dispatched the division under Scopasis, which included the Sauromatae, with orders to seek a conference with the Ionians, who were guarding the bridge over the Danube. Those who remained decided to stop leading the Persians the usual dance, and to attack them whenever they found them at a meal. This policy they carried out, waiting for the proper opportunities to present themselves. On every occasion the Scythian cavalry proved superior to the Persian, which would give ground and fall back on the infantry for support; this checked the attack, for the Scythians knew the Persian infantry would be too much for them, and regularly turned tail after driving in the cavalry. Similar raids were made at night.

I must mention one very surprising thing which helped the Persians and hampered the Scythians in these skirmishes: I mean the unfamiliar appearance of the mules and the braying of the donkeys. As I have already pointed out, neither donkeys nor mules are bred in Scythia – indeed, there is not a single specimen of either in the whole country, because of the cold. This being so, the donkeys' braying caused great confusion amongst the Scythian cavalry; often, in the course of an attack, the sound of it so much upset the horses, which had never heard such a noise before or seen such a creature as that from which it proceeded, that they would turn short round, ears pricked in consternation. This gave the Persians some small advantage in the campaign.

Seeing the Persians disorganized by these continual raids, the Scythians hit upon a stratagem to keep them longer in the country and reduce them in the end to distress from lack of supplies. This was to slip away from time to time to some other district leaving behind a few cattle in the charge of shepherds; the Persians would come and take the animals, and be much encouraged by the momentary success. This happened again and again, until at last Darius did not know where to turn, and the Scythians, seeing his acute embarrassment, sent him the promised presents – a bird, a mouse, a frog and five arrows. The Persians asked the man who brought these things what they signified, but got no reply. The man's orders – so he said – were merely to deliver them, and to return home as quickly as he could: the Persians themselves, if they had any sense, could find out what the presents meant. Thereupon the Persians put their heads together, and Darius expressed the view that, the Scythians were giving him earth and water and intended to surrender: mice, he reasoned, live on the ground and eat the same food as men; frogs live in water; birds are much like horses – and the arrows symbolized the Scythian power, which they were giving into his hands. Gobryas, however (one of the seven conspirators who put down the Magus), by no means agreed with him, but interpreted the gifts in a very different way. 'My friends,' he said, 'unless you turn into birds and fly up in the air, or into mice and burrow under ground, or into frogs and jump into the lakes, you will never get home again, but stay here in this country, only to be shot by the Scythian arrows.'

While the Persians were puzzling their heads over the significance of the gifts, the division of the Scythian force which had previously had orders to keep watch along the shore of Lake Maeotis, and had now been sent to confer with the Ionians on the Danube, made its way to the bridge and opened negotiations. 'Men of Ionia,' began the Scythian spokesman, 'we bring you freedom, if only you will do what we suggest. We understand that your orders from Darius were to guard the bridge for sixty days – no more; and after that if he failed to put in an appearance, to go home. Now, therefore, the obvious thing for you to do is to wait till the sixty days have passed and then clear out – neither Darius nor ourselves will have anything to reproach you for in that.' The Ionians agreed and the Scythians rode back without loss of time.

After the presents had been sent to Darius, the Scythians who had not gone to the Danube drew up their cavalry and infantry with the apparent intention of offering the Persians battle. But as soon as their dispositions were made, a hare started up between the two armies and began running. The Scythians were after it in a moment – company after company of them, directly they caught sight of it – while the array was reduced to a shouting rabble. Darius inquired what all the noise and fuss were about, and upon learning that the enemy was engaged in hunting a hare, he turned to those of his officers he was in the habit of talking with, and said: 'These fellows have a hearty contempt for us, and I am now ready to believe that Gobryas' interpretation of those things they sent me was the right one. Well then – as I have come round to his opinion, it is time to think of the best way of getting out of this country in safety.'

'My lord,' Gobryas answered. 'I already knew pretty well from hearsay how difficult the Scythians were to deal with, and now that I am on the spot and can see how they fool us with their tricks, I know it all the better. As to our next move, my proposal is this: as soon as it is dark, I suggest that we should light the camp-fires as usual, and then, tethering the donkeys and leaving behind on some pretext or other those of our men who are least fit to face the hardship and privation, clear out before the Scythians advance to the Danube and destroy the bridge, and before the Ionians on guard can take any measures which may lead to our destruction.'

Darius adopted this proposal, and as soon as night fell began the homeward march, leaving behind the sick and such other of his troops as he could most easily spare, as well as the donkeys all tethered in their usual places.

The next morning the Scythians realise that the Persians have left and set off to pursue them on horseback. Having overtaken the Persians, the Scythians instruct the Ionians guarding the bridge to destroy it. The Greek leaders, however, elect to remain loyal to Darius, fearing they will lose their power if he is defeated. The surviving Persians are thus able to flee the Scythians in safety.

XERXES' CHOICE

Histories, Book VII

Herodotus

Translated by Aubrey de Sélincourt, 1954

The Persians met many more defeats under their king Darius after the abortive expedition against the Scythians (see Story 16). After invading Greece for the first time in 490 BC they were overcome by the Athenians at the Battle of Marathon. Darius hoped to avenge their losses by launching a further assault against Greece, and another on the Egyptians, who had revolted against Persia, but died in 486 BC before he could accomplish either. This is **Herodotus'** historical account of how Darius' son Xerxes came to decide what to do next.

Xerxes began his reign by building up an army for a campaign in Egypt. The invasion of Greece was at first by no means an object of his thoughts; but Mardonius – the son of Gobryas and Darius' sister and thus cousin to the king – who was present in court and had more influence with Xerxes than anyone else in the country, used constantly to talk to him on the subject. 'Master,' he would say, 'the Athenians have done us great injury, and it is only right that they should be punished for their crimes. By all means finish the task you already have in hand; but when you have tamed the arrogance of Egypt, then lead an army against Athens. Do that, and your name will be held in honour all over the world, and people will think twice in future before they invade your country.' And to the argument for revenge he would add that Europe was a very beautiful place; it produced every kind of garden tree; the land there was everything that land should be – it was, in short, too good for anyone in the world except the Persian king. Mardonius' motive for urging the campaign was love of mischief and adventure and the hope of becoming governor of Greece himself; and after much persistence he persuaded Xerxes to make the attempt. Nevertheless he might not have succeeded in doing so, had it not been for certain other occurrences which came to his aid. In the first place, messengers arrived from the Aleuadae in Thessaly* with an invitation to Xerxes, couched in the most urgent terms, to invade Greece; at the same time the Pisistratidae in Susa spoke to the same purpose and worked upon him even more strongly through

---

* The Aleuadae were the Thessalian reigning family.

the agency of an Athenian named Onomacritus, a collector of oracles, who had arranged and edited the oracles of Musaeus. The Pisistratidae had not been on good terms with this man, but they had made up the quarrel before coming with him to Susa. He had been expelled from Athens by Pisistratus for inserting in the verses of Musaeus a prophecy that the islands off Lemnos would disappear under water – Lasus of Hermione had caught him in the very act of the forgery. Before his banishment he had been a close friend of Hipparchus. Anyway, he went to Susa; and now, whenever he found himself in the king's presence, the Pisistratidae would talk big about his wonderful powers and he would recite selections from his oracles. Any prophecy which implied a setback to the Persian cause he would carefully omit, choosing for quotation only those which promised the brightest triumphs, describing to Xerxes how it was fore-ordained that the Hellespont should be bridged by a Persian, and how the army would march from Asia into Greece. Subjected, therefore, to this double pressure, from Onomacritus' oracles on the one side, and the advice of the Pisistratidae and Aleuadae on the other, Xerxes gave in and allowed himself to be persuaded to undertake the invasion of Greece.

First, however, in the year after Darius' death, he sent an army against the Egyptian rebels and decisively crushed them; then, having reduced the country to a condition of worse servitude than it had ever been in in the previous reign, he turned it over to his brother Achaemenes, who not long afterwards, while he was still Governor, was murdered by Inarus the Libyan, a son of Psammetichus.

After the conquest of Egypt, when he was on the point of taking in hand the expedition against Athens, Xerxes called a conference of the leading men in the country, to find out their attitude towards the war and explain to them his own wishes. When they met, he addressed them as follows: 'Do not suppose, gentlemen, that I am departing from precedent in the course of action I intend to undertake. We Persians have a way of living, which I have inherited from my predecessors and propose to follow. I have learned from my elders that ever since Cyrus deposed Astyages and we took over from the Medes the sovereign power we now possess, we have never yet remained inactive. This is God's guidance, and it is by following it that we have gained our great prosperity. Of our past history you need no reminder; for you know well enough the famous deeds of Cyrus, Cambyses, and my father Darius, and their additions to our empire. Now I myself, ever since my accession, have been thinking how not to fall short of the kings who have sat upon this throne before me, and how to add as much power as they did to the Persian empire. And now at last I have found a way to win for Persia not glory only but a country as large and as rich as our own – indeed richer than our own – and at the same time to get satisfaction and revenge. That, then, is the object of this meeting – that I may disclose to you what it is that I intend to do. I will bridge the Hellespont and march an army through Europe into Greece, and punish the Athenians for the outrage they committed upon my father and upon us. As you saw, Darius himself was making his preparations for war against these men; but death prevented him from carrying out his purpose. I therefore on his behalf, and for the benefit of all my subjects, will not rest until I have taken Athens and burnt it to the ground, in revenge for the injury which the Athenians without provocation once did to me and my father. These men, you remember, came to Sardis with Aristagoras the Milesian – a mere slave of ours – and burnt the temples, and the trees that grew about them; and you know all too well how they served our troops under Datis and Artaphernes, when they landed upon Greek soil. For these reasons I have now prepared to make war upon them, and, when I consider the matter, I find several advantages in the venture: if we crush the Athenians and their neighbours in the Peloponnese, we shall so extend the empire of Persia that its boundaries will be God's own sky. With your help I shall pass through Europe from end to end and make it all one country, so that the sun will not look down upon any land beyond the boundaries of what is ours. For if what I am told is true, there is not a city or nation in the world which will be able to withstand us, once Athens and Sparta are out of the way.

'If, then, you wish to gain my favour, each one of you must present himself willingly and in good heart on the day which I shall name; whoever brings with him the best equipped body of troops I will reward with those marks of distinction held in greatest value by our countrymen. Those are the orders I give you; nevertheless I am no tyrant merely to impose my will – I will throw the whole matter into open debate, and ask any of you who may wish to do so, to express his views.'

The first to speak after the king was Mardonius. 'Of all Persians who have ever lived,' he began, 'and of all who are yet to be born, you, my lord, are the greatest. Every word you have spoken is true and excellent, and you will not allow the wretched Ionians in Europe to make fools of us. It would indeed be an odd thing if we who have defeated and enslaved the Sacae, Indians, Ethiopians, Assyrians, and many other great nations for no fault of their own, but merely to extend the boundaries of our empire, should fail now to punish the Greeks who have been guilty of injuring us without provocation. Have we anything to fear from them? The size of their army? Their wealth? The question is absurd; we know how they fight; we know how slender their resources are. People of their race we have already reduced to subjection – I mean the Greeks of Asia, Ionians, Aeolians, and Dorians. I myself before now have had some experience of these men, when under orders from your father I invaded their country; and I got as far as Macedonia – indeed almost to Athens itself – without a single soldier daring to oppose me. Yet, from what I hear, the Greeks are pugnacious enough, and start fights on the spur of the moment without sense or judgement to justify them. When they declare war on each other, they go off together to the smoothest and levellest bit of ground they can find, and have their battle on it – with the result that even the victors never get off without heavy losses, and as for the losers – well, they're wiped out. Now surely, as they all talk the same language, they ought to be able to find a better way of settling their differences: by negotiation, for instance, or an interchange of views – indeed by anything rather than fighting. Or if it is really impossible to avoid coming to blows, they might at least employ the elements of strategy and look for a strong position to fight from. In any case, the Greeks, with their absurd notions of warfare, never even thought of opposing me when I led my army to Macedonia.

'Well then, my lord, who is likely to resist you when you march against them with the millions of Asia at your back, and the whole Persian fleet? Believe me, it is not in the Greek character to take so desperate a risk. But should I be wrong – should the courage born of ignorance and folly drive them to do battle with us, then they will learn that we are the best soldiers in the world. Nevertheless, let us take this business seriously and spare no pains; success is never automatic in this world – nothing is achieved without trying.'

Xerxes' proposals were made to sound plausible enough by these words of Mardonius, and when he stopped speaking there was a silence. For a while nobody dared to put forward the opposite view, until Artabanus, taking courage from the fact of his relationship to the king – he was a son of Hystaspes and therefore Xerxes' uncle – rose to speak. 'My lord,' he said, 'without a debate in which both sides of a question are expressed, it is not possible to choose the better course. All one can do is to accept whatever it is that has been proposed. But grant a debate, and there is a fair choice to be made. We cannot assess the purity of gold merely by looking at it; we test it by rubbing it on other gold – then we can tell which is the purer. I warned your father – Darius my own brother – not to attack the Scythians, those wanderers who live in a cityless land. But he would not listen to me. Confident in his power to subdue them he invaded their country, and before he came home again many fine soldiers who marched with him were dead. But you, my lord, mean to attack a nation greatly superior to the Scythians: a nation with the highest reputation for valour both on land and at sea. It is my duty to tell you what you have to fear from them: you have said you mean to bridge the Hellespont and march through Europe to Greece. Now suppose – and it is not impossible – that you were to suffer a reverse by sea or land, or even both. These Greeks are said to be great fighters – and indeed one might well guess as much from the fact that the Athenians alone destroyed the great army we sent to attack them under Datis and Artaphernes. Or, if you will, suppose they were to succeed upon one element only – suppose they fell upon our fleet and defeated it, and then sailed to the Hellespont and destroyed the bridge: then, my lord, you would indeed be in peril. It is no special wisdom of my own that makes me argue as I do; but just such a disaster as I have suggested did, in fact, very nearly overtake us when your father bridged the Thracian Bosphorus and the Danube to take his army into Scythia. You will remember how on that occasion the Scythians went to all lengths in their efforts to induce the Ionian guard to break the Danube bridge, and how Histiaeus, the lord of Miletus, merely by following the advice of the other Ionian despots instead of rejecting it, as he did, had it in his power to ruin Persia. Surely it is a dreadful thing even to hear said, that the forunes of the king once wholly depended upon a single man.

'I urge you, therefore, to abandon this plan; take my advice and do not run any such terrible risk when there is no necessity to do so. Break up this conference; turn the matter over quietly by yourself, and then, when you think fit, announce your decision. Nothing is more valuable to a man than to lay his plans carefully and well; even if things go against him, and forces he cannot control bring his enterprise to nothing, he still has the satisfaction of knowing that it was not his fault – the plans were all laid; if, on the other hand, he leaps headlong into danger and succeeds by luck – well, that's a bit of luck indeed, but he still has the shame of knowing that he was ill prepared.

'You know, my lord, that amongst living creatures it is the great ones that God smites with his thunder, out of envy of their pride. The little ones do not vex him. It is always the great buildings and the tall trees which are struck by lightning. It is God's way to bring the lofty low. Often a great army is destroyed by a little one, when God in his envy puts fear into the men's hearts, or sends a thunderstorm, and they are cut to pieces in a way they do not deserve. For God tolerates pride in none but Himself. Haste is the mother of failure – and for failure we always pay a heavy price; it is in delay our profit lies – perhaps it may not immediately be apparent, but we shall find it, sure enough, as times goes on.

'This, my lord, is the advice I offer you. And as for you, Mardonius, I warn you that the Greeks in no way deserve disparagement; so say no more silly things about them. By slandering the Greeks you increase the king's eagerness to make war on them, and, as far as I can see, this is the very thing you yourself most passionately desire. Heaven forbid it should happen! Slander is a wicked thing: in a case of slander two parties do wrong and one suffers by it. The slanderer is guilty in that he speaks ill of a man behind his back; and the man who listens to him is guilty in that he takes his word without troubling to find out the truth. The slandered person suffers doubly – from the disparaging words of the one and from the belief of the other that he deserves the disparagement.

'Nevertheless, if there is no avoiding this campaign in Greece, I have one final proposal to make. Let the king stay here in Persia; and you and I will then stake our children on the issue, and you can start the venture with the men you want and as big an army as you please. Now for the wager: if the king prospers, as you say he will, then I consent that my sons should be killed, and myself with them; if my own prediction is fulfilled, *your* sons forfeit their lives – and you too – if you ever get home.

'Maybe you will refuse this wager, and still persist in leading an army into Greece. In that case I venture a prophecy: the day will come when many a man left at home will hear the news that Mardonius has brought disaster upon Persia, and that his body lies a prey to dogs and birds somewhere in the country of the Athenians or the Spartans – if not upon the road thither. For that is the way you will find out the quality of the people against whom you are urging the king to make war.'

Xerxes was exceedingly angry. 'Artabanus,' he replied, 'you are my father's brother, and that alone saves you from paying the price your empty and ridiculous speech deserves. But your cowardice and lack of spirit shall not escape disgrace: I forbid you to accompany me on my march to Greece – you shall stay at home with the women, and everything I spoke of I shall accomplish without help from you. If I fail to punish the Athenians, let me be no child of Darius, the son of Hystaspes, the son of Arsames, the son of Ariaramnes, the son of Teispes, the son of Cyrus, the son of Cambyses, the son of Teispes, the son of Achaemenes! I know too well that if we make no move, the Athenians will – they will be sure to invade our country. One has but to make the inference from what they did before; for it was they who marched into Asia and burnt Sardis. Retreat is no longer possible for either of us: if we do not inflict the wound, we shall assuredly receive it. All we possess will pass to the Greeks, or all they possess will pass to us. That is the choice before us; for in the enmity between us there is no middle course. It is right, therefore, that we should now revenge ourselves for the injury we once received; and no doubt in doing so I shall learn the nature of this terrible thing which is to happen to me, if I march against men whom Pelops the Phrygian, a mere slave of the Persian kings, once beat so soundly that to this very day both people and country hear the conqueror's name.'

And so began the second Persian invasion of Greece. Although Xerxes would enjoy some successes, most notably in the Battle of Thermopylae, the conflict would ultimately result in victory for the Greek peoples.

THE FALL OF THE BARBARIANS

Persians

Aeschylus

Translated by Janet Lembke and C. John Herington, 1981

Aeschylus' *Persians* is the earliest surviving Greek tragedy. First performed in 472 BC, eight years after the Greeks defeated the Persians in a naval battle at Salamis, the play won first prize at the annual theatre festival in Athens. You can see why. Written from the Greek perspective, the play characterizes the Persians as indulgent over-reachers and 'barbarians'. Darius was not without his faults (see Story 16), but by comparison with his hubristic and headstrong son Xerxes, he is depicted as a man of wisdom and integrity. At Susa, the Persian capital, Darius' widow Atossa awaits news of their son Xerxes' progress. She is joined by a Chorus of elder statesmen.

ATOSSA. [*In unaccompanied iambic verse*] Night after night
       since my son left with the army he mustered
I am joined with many dreams
                  He's gone,
gone to Greece,
    bent on making it Persian and *his*.
But never has a vision showed more clear
than what I saw last night
    in the kind-hearted dark.
I'll tell you:
        It seemed to me
two well-dressed women—
one robed with Persian luxury,
the other in a plain Greek tunic—
came into view, both
taller far than any woman now living,
and flawless in beauty,
and sisters from the one same
parentage.
      And for a fatherland, a home,

one was allotted Greek soil,
the other, the great world beyond.

          Then I saw
the two of them build bitter quarrels,
      one against the other,
and when my son learned this,
he tried to curb and gentle them:
      under his chariot
he yokes the two, and on their necks
he straps broad leather collars.
And the one towered herself
      proud in this harness
and she kept her mouth
      well-governed by the reins.
But the other bucked stubborn
      and with both hands
she wrenches harness from the chariot fittings
and drags it by sheer force,
      bridle flung off, and she
shatters the yoke, mid-span
and he falls,
        my son falls,
and his father is standing beside him—
Darius, pitying him
      and when Xerxes sees that
he shreds around his body
the clothes that a king wears.

        I tell you
I did see these things last night.

Today, when I'd risen
and dipped both hands in a clear-rippling spring
      to cleanse me of bad dreams,
hands busy with offerings,
I stood by Phoibos' altar
wanting to give mixed honey and wine,
      their expected due,
to the undying Powers that turn away evil.
And I see
        an eagle
fleeing toward the altar's godbright flame.
Frightened, mute, my friends, I
      just stood there,
and soon I see a hawk in downstoop
raising wings to break the fall and working

talons in the eagle's head, and the eagle did
nothing,
        only cringed and offered up
its flesh.
                        Terrors! I saw them!
Now you've heard them.
        And you surely know
that if my son succeeds, he'll be marveled at,
but if he fails,
        his people cannot call him to account.
When he is safely home,
        he'll rule the country as he always has.

CHORUS. Mother,
            here's advice
                    meant neither to alarm
nor overgladden you.
        Gods abide:
                turn toward them suppliant,
if anything you saw stirs faintest doubt,
        praying them
                to turn it away and bring
goodness to its peak
        for you and
                children in your line,
for Persia, too,
        and those you love.
                Afterward, pour out
the drink due Earth
        and give the thirsty dead their sip
                and pray, appeasing him,
your husband Darius—
        you say you saw him
                in the kind-hearted night—
asking him to send up
        from his depth into our light
                blessings for you and your son
and hold the reverse back
        earth-coffined
                till it molders in that dark.

For this advice
        I have consulted
                my prophetic heart.
Be appeased,
        for as we
                read the signs,

everything
    shall
        turn out well.

ATOSSA. Yes, you
    the first
        to read my dream,
with goodwill toward my son and house,
    have found
        its true interpretation.
Would that the omens
    turn out well!
        I'll do all you say
for gods and old friends under earth
    when I go home.
        But first
I'd like to know, dear friends,
    where
        Athens is.

CHORUSLEADER. Far west where the Lord Sun fades out.

ATOSSA. My son really wanted to hunt down this city?

CHORUSLEADER. Yes, so all Greece would bend beneath a Shah.

ATOSSA. Does it field a manhorde of an army?

CHORUSLEADER. Such that it has worked evils on the Medes.

ATOSSA. Then bowtugging arrows glint in their hands?

CHORUSLEADER. No. Spears held steady, and heavy shields.

ATOSSA. What else? Wealth in their houses?

CHORUSLEADER. Treasure, a fountain of silver, lies in their soil.

ATOSSA. But who herds the manflock? Who lords the army?

CHORUSLEADER. They're not anyone's slaves or subjects.

ATOSSA. Then how can they resist invaders?

CHORUSLEADER. So well that they crushed Darius' huge and shining army.

ATOSSA. Terrible words! You make the parents of those gone shudder.

CHORUS. [*Severally*]
> But I think you will soon hear the whole story.
> Someone's coming!
>
>   He's ours—
> a Persian clearly by the way he runs.
>
> Something's happened. Good or bad,
> he brings the plain truth.

[The MESSENGER *enters left.]*

MESSENGER.
> Listen! cities that people vast Asia.
> Listen! Persian earth, great harbor of wealth.
> One stroke, one single stroke has smashed
> great prosperity,
>   and Persia's flower is gone, cut down.
> Bitter, being first to tell you bitter news,
> But need presses me to unroll the full disaster.
> Persians,
>   our whole expedition is lost.

CHORUS.
> Cruel cruelest evil
>   newmade, consuming Oh
>   weep, Persians, who hear
> this pain

MESSENGER. Everything over there has ended. And I—
> against all hope, I'm here, seeing this light.

CHORUS. Life stretches long
>   too long for grey old men
>   who hear of all hope
> undone

MESSENGER. I was *there. I* can tell you, no hearsay,
> the evils that sprang up hurtling against us.

CHORUS. No nonono
>   That bright storm
> of arrows showing Asia's massed colors
> advanced
>   all for NOTHING
>   into hostile Greece?

MESSENGER. They met hard deaths. The corpses
    pile on Salamis and every nearby shore.

CHORUS. No nonono
          You're saying
    those we love are floating, foundering
    awash
          DEAD MEN shrouded
              in sea-drowned cloaks?

MESSENGER. Our arrows didn't help. The whole force
    went down, broken, when ship rammed ship.

CHORUS. Rage
         for the Persians killed
    Wail the death howl
         All that began well
             comes to the worst end   CRY!
   CRY OUT
         For the army slaughtered!

MESSENGER. Salamis, I hate that hissing name.
    And Athens, remembering makes me groan.

CHORUS. Athens
         bears Persia's hate
    We will recall
         wives she has widowed
            mothers with no sons   NO!
   and all
      ALL FOR NOTHING!

ATOSSA. Silence has held me till now
    heartsore,
        struck by the blows of loss,
    for this disaster so exceeds all bounds
    that one can neither tell,
    nor ask,
        about the suffering.
    Yet there is terrible need
        for people to bear pain
    when gods send it down.
              You must
    compose yourself: speak out,
    unrolling *all* the suffering,
        though you groan at our losses.
    Who is not dead?

And whom shall we mourn?
Of all the leaders
     whose hands grip authority
which one
     left his post unmanned, deserted
when he died?

MESSENGER. Xerxes—he lives and sees light—

ATOSSA. You speak: light blazes in my house,
     and white day after a black-storming night!

MESSENGER. —but Artembares,
          commander of ten thousand horse,
is hammered along Sileniai's raw coast
and thousand-leader Dadakes,
     spearstuck,
danced back without any effort I could see
     overboard
and Tenagon,
     pureblooded Bactrian and chief,
scrapes against Ajax' sea-pelted island.

Lilaios,
Arsames,
and a third, Argestes,
     wave-tumbled around that dove-broody island,
kept butting resistant stones
and so did Pharnoukhos
     whose home was Egypt, by Nile's fresh flow,
and so did they
     who plunged from one same ship,
Arkteus,
Adeues,
and a third, Pheresseues.
And Matallos from a golden city,
     leader of ten thousand,
dying, stained his full beard's tawny brush
     changing its color with sea-purple dye.
And the Arab, Magos,
with Artabes the Bactrian,
     who led thirty thousand black horse,
took up land as an immigrant
by dying there
     on that harsh ground.

Amistris
and Amphistreus,
     whose spear delighted in trouble,
and bright-souled Ariomardos,
     whose loss brings Sardis down grieving,
and Seisames the Mysian,
Tharybis, too,
     sealord of five times fifty ships,
     Lyrnaian by descent, a hard-bodied man,
lies dead,
     a wretch whose luck went soft,
and Syennesis,
     first in courage, the Cilicians' chief,
     one man who made most trouble for the enemy,
died with glory.

          These are the leaders
of whom I bring my memories.
But we suffered many losses there.
I report a mere few.

         [*The* CHORUS *cry out sharply.*]

ATOSSA. Noooo!
        These words I hear
lift evil to its height.
O the shame cast on Persians,
and the piercing laments!

But tell me,
        turn back again,
was the count of Greek ships so great
they dared launch their rams
      against Persia's fleet?

MESSENGER. If numbers were all, believe me,
    Asia's navy would have won,
for Greek ships counted out
at only ten times thirty
      and ten selected to lead out that line.
But Xerxes, this I know,
commanded a full thousand,
     two hundred and seven
     the fastest ever built.
That is our count. Perhaps you thought
we were outnumbered?
        No.

It was some Power—
     Something not human—
whose weight tipped the scales of luck
and cut our forces down.
Gods keep Athens safe for her goddess.

ATOSSA. You're saying that Athens is not yet sacked?

MESSENGER. Long as her men live, her stronghold can't be shaken.

ATOSSA. But at the beginning, when ship met ship,
    tell me, who started the clash?
                         Greeks?
Or my son
     who exulted in his thousand ships?

MESSENGER. My lady,
     the first sign of the whole disaster came
when Something vengeful—
     or evil and not human—
appeared from somewhere out there.

For a Greek,
     who came in stealth from the Athenian fleet,
whispered this to your son Xerxes:
As soon as black night brought its darkness on,
Greeks would not maintain their stations, no,
but springing on the rowing benches,
     scattering here, there in secret flight,
would try to save their own skins.
And at once,
     for he had listened not understanding
     the man's treachery nor the gods' high jealousy,
he gave all his captains this command:
As soon as Sun's hot eye let go of Earth
and darkness seized the holy vault of Sky, then
they should deploy ships
     in three tight-packed ranks
to bar outsailings and the salt-hammered path,
while others circled Ajax' island.
And if the Greeks should somehow slip the trap
     by setting sail, finding a hidden route,
Xerxes stated flatly
     that every last captain would lose his head.
So he commanded in great good spirits.
He could not know the outcome set by gods.

There was no disorder. Obediently
the crews prepared their suppers,
and each sailor, taking a thong,
      made his oar snug to the tholepin.
And when Sun's glow faded and Night
was coming on,
              each oarlord,
each expert man-at-arms
      boarded his ship.
Squadron on squadron, cheers for the warships
roared from the decks,
              and they sailed,
each captain maintaining his position.
And all night long the lords of the fleet
kept fully manned vessels plying the channel.
And night was wearing on.
              The Greek forces never
tried sailing out secretly.
Not once.

But when Day rode her white colt
dazzling the whole world,
           the first thing we heard
was a roar, a windhowl, Greeks
singing together, shouting for joy,
and Echo at once hurled back
that warcry
      loud and clear from island rocks.
Fear churned in every Persian.
We'd been led off the mark:
              the Greeks
weren't running, no,
but sang that eerie triumph-chant
as men
      racing toward a fight
          and sure of winning.

Then the trumpet-shriek blazed
      through everything over there.
A signal:
         instantly
their oars struck salt.
         We heard
that rhythmic rattle-slap.
It seemed no time till they
all stood in sight.
        We saw them sharp.

First the right wing,
        close-drawn, strictly ordered,
led out, and next we saw
the whole fleet bearing down, we heard
a huge voice

> *Sons of Greece, go!*
> *Free fatherland,*
> *free children, wives,*
> *shrines of our fathers' gods,*
> *tombs where our forefathers lie.*
> *Fight for all we have!*
> *Now!*

Then on our side shouts in Persian
rose to a crest.
                We didn't hold back.
That instant, ship rammed
bronzeclad beak on ship.
                        It was
a Greek ship started the attack
shearing off a whole Phoenician
stern. Each captain steered his craft
        straight on one other.
At first the wave of Persia's fleet
rolled firm, but next, as our ships
        jammed into the narrows and
                no one could help any other and
                        our own bronze teeth bit into
our own strakes,
                        whole oarbanks shattered.
Then the Greek ships, seizing their chance,
swept in circling and struck and overturned
our hulls,
        and saltwater vanished before our eyes—
shipwrecks filled it, and drifting corpses.
Shores and reefs filled up with our dead
and every able ship under Persia's command
broke order,
        scrambling to escape.
We might have been tuna or netted fish,
for they kept on, spearing and gutting us
        with splintered oars and bits of wreckage,
while moaning and screams drowned out
the sea noise till
        Night's black face closed it all in.

Losses by thousands!
        Even if I told

the catalogue for ten full days I
could not complete it for you.
But this is sure:
         never before in one day
have so many thousands died.

*In the second half of the play, Darius' spirit is summoned from his tomb. His
wife tells him that Persia is ruined. Darius considers Xerxes a fool for bridging
the Hellespont and bringing ruin on the Persian army. He recommends that the
Persians never march against the Greeks again.*

THE FAIREST OF THEM ALL

Various Histories, XII

Aelian

Translated by Thomas Stanley, 1665

Aelian was an historian of the second century AD who lived in Rome but wrote in Greek. Here he describes a beautiful woman named Aspasia, from Phocis in Greece, who entered the court of Cyrus the Younger of Persia in the fifth century BC and captivated all those who saw her with her beauty. She is not to be confused with the more famous Aspasia who became the common-law wife of Pericles. In this seventeenth-century translation, by the poet and classical scholar Thomas Stanley, the first part of her story reads like a fairy tale.

Chap I: Of Aspasia

Aspasia a Phocian, Daughter of Hermotimus, was brought up an Orphan, her Mother dying in the pains of Child-birth. She was bred up in poverty, but modestly and vertuously. She had many times a Dream which foretold her that she should be married to an excellent person. Whilest she was yet young, she chanced to have a swelling under her chin, loathsome to sight, whereat both the Father and the Maid were much afflicted. Her Father brought her to a Physician: he offered to undertake the Cure for three Staters; the other said he had not the Money. The Physician replied, he had then no Physick for him. Hereupon Aspasia departed weeping; and holding a Looking-glass on her knee, beheld her face in it, which much increased her grief. Going to rest without Supping, by the reason of the trouble she was in, she had an opportune Dream; a Dove seemed to appear to her as she slept, which being changed to a Woman, said, "Be of good courage, and bid a long farewel to Physicians and their Medicines: Take of the dried Rose of Venus Garlands, which being pounded apply to the swelling." After the Maid had understood and made trial of this, the tumor was wholly asswaged; and Aspasia recovering her beauty by means of the most beautiful Goddess, did once again appear the fairest amongst her Virgin-companions, enriched with Graces far above any of the rest. Of hair yellow, locks a little curling, she had great eyes, somewhat hawk-nosed, ears short, skin delicate, complexion like Roses; whence the Phocians, whilest she was yet a child, called her Milto. Her lips

were red, teeth whiter then snow, small insteps, such as of those Women whom
Homer calls καλλισφύρυς. Her voice sweet and smooth, that whosoever heard her
might justly say he heard the voice of a Siren. She was averse from Womanish
curiosity in dressing: Such things are to be supplied by wealth. She being poor, and
bred up under a poor Father, used nothing superfluous or extravagant to advantage her Beauty. On a time Aspasia came to Cyrus, Son of Darius and Parysatis,
Brother of Artaxerxes, not willingly nor with the consent of her Father, but by
compulsion, as it often happens upon the taking of Cities, or the violence of
Tyrants and their Officers. One of the Officers of Cyrus brought her with other
Virgins to Cyrus, who immediately preferred her before all his Concubines, for
simplicity of behaviour, and modesty; whereto also contributed her beauty with-
out artifice, and her extraordinary discretion, which was such, that Cyrus many
times asked her advice in affairs, which he never repented to have followed.
When Aspasia came first to Cyrus, it happened that he was newly risen from
Supper, and was going to drink after the Persian manner: for after they have done
eating, they betake themselves to Wine, and fall to their cups freely, encountring
Drink as an Adversary. Whilest they were in the midst of their drinking, four
Grecian Virgins were brought to Cyrus, amongst whom was Aspasia the Phocian.
They were finely attired; three of them had their heads neatly drest by their own
Women which came along with them, and had painted their faces. They had been
also instructed by their Governesses how to behave themselves towards Cyrus, to
gain his favour; not to turn away when he came to them, not to be coy when he
touched them, to permit him to kiss them, and many other amatory instructions
practised by Women who exposed their beauty to sale. Each contended to outvie
the other in handsomeness. Onely Aspasia would not endure to be clothed with a
rich Robe, nor to put on a various-coloured Vest, nor to be washed; but calling
upon the Grecian and Eleutherian Gods, she cried out upon her Father's name,
execrating herself to her Father. She thought the Robe which she should put on
was a manifest sign of bondage. At last being compelled with blows she put it on,
and was necessitated to behave herself with greater liberty then beseemed a Virgin.
When they came to Cyrus, the rest smiled, and expressed chearfulness in their
looks. But Aspasia looking on the ground, her eyes full of tears, did every way
express an extraordinary bashfulness. When he commanded them to sit down by
him, the rest instantly obeyed; but the Phocian refused, until the Officer caused
her to sit down by force. When Cyrus looked upon or touched their eyes, cheeks
and fingers, the rest freely permitted him; but she would not suffer it: For if Cyrus
did but offer to touch her, she cried out, saying, he should not goe unpunished for
such actions. Cyrus was herewith extremely pleased; and when upon his offering
to touch her breast, she rose up, and would have run away, Cyrus much taken
with her native ingenuity, which was not like the Persians, turning to him that
bought them, "This Maid onely, saith he, of those which you have brought me is
free and pure; the rest are adulterate in face, but much more in behaviour." Hereupon Cyrus loved her above all the Women he ever had. Afterwards there grew a
mutual love between them, and their friendship proceeded to such a height that it
almost arrived at parity, not differing from the concord and modesty of Grecian
Marriage. Hereupon the fame of his affection to Aspasia was spread to Ionia and
throughout Greece; Peloponnesus also was filled with discourses of the love

betwixt Cyrus and her. The report went even to the great King [of Persia,] for it was conceived that Cyrus, after his acquaintance with her, kept company with no other Woman. From these things Aspasia recollected the remembrance of her old Apparition, and of the Dove, and her words, and what the Goddess foretold her. Hence she conceived that she was from the very beginning particularly regarded by her. She therefore offered Sacrifice of thanks to Venus. And first caused a great Image of Gold to be erected to her, which she called the Image of Venus, and by it placed the picture of a Dove beset with Jewels, and every day implored the favour of the Goddess with Sacrifice and Prayer. She sent to Hermotimus her Father many rich Presents, and made him wealthy. She lived continently all her life, as both the Grecian and Persian Women affirm. On a time a Neck-lace was sent as a Present to Cyrus from Scopas the younger, which had been sent to Scopas out of Sicily. The Neck-lace was of extraordinary workmanship, and variety. All therefore to whom Cyrus shewed it admiring it, he was much taken with the Jewel, and went immediately to Aspasia, it being about noon. Finding her asleep, he lay down gently by her, watching quietly whilest she slept. As soon as she awaked, and saw Cyrus, she imbraced him after her usual manner. He taking the Neck-lace out of a Boxe, said, "This is worthy either the Daughter or the Mother of a King." To which she assenting; "I will give it you, said he, for your own use, let me see your neck adorned with it." But she received not the Gift, prudently and discreetly answering, "How will Parysatis your Mother take it, this being a Gift fit for her that bare you? Send it to her, Cyrus, I will shew you a Neck handsome enough without it." Aspasia from the greatness of her minde acted contrary to other Royal Queens, who are excessively desirous of rich Ornaments. Cyrus being pleased with this answer, kissed Aspasia. All these actions and speeches Cyrus writ in a Letter which he sent together with the Chain to his Mother; and Parysatis receiving the Present was no less delighted with the News than with the Gold, for which she requited Aspasia with great and Royal Gifts; for this pleased her above all things, that though Aspasia were chiefly affected by her Son, yet in the love of Cyrus she desired to be placed beneath his Mother. Aspasia praised the Gifts, but said she had no need of them; (for there was much money sent with the Presents) but sent them to Cyrus, saying, "To you who maintain many men this may be useful: For me it is enough that you love me and are my ornament." With these things, as it seemeth, she much astonished Cyrus. And indeed the Woman was without dispute admirable for her personal beauty, but much more for the noble-ness of her mind. When Cyrus was slain in the fight against his Brother, and his Army taken Prisoners, with the rest of the prey she was taken; not falling acci-dentally into the Enemies hands, but fought for with much diligence by King Artaxerxes, for he had heard her fame and vertue. When they brought her bound, he was angry, and cast those that did it into Prison. He commanded that a rich Robe should be given her: which she hearing, intreated with tears and lamentation that she might not put on the Garment the King appointed, for she mourned exceedingly for Cyrus. But when she had put it on, she appeared the fairest of all Women, and Artaxerxes was immediately surprised and inflamed with love of her. He valued her beyond all the rest of his Women, respecting her infinitely. He endeavoured to ingratiate himself into her favour, hoping to make her forget Cyrus, and to love him no less then she had done his Brother; but it was long before he could compass it. For the affection of Aspasia to Cyrus had taken so deep impression, that it could not easily be rooted out. Long after this, Teridates the Eunuch died, who was the most beautiful youth in Asia. He had full surpassed his childhood, and was reckoned among the youths. The King was said to have loved him exceedingly: he was infinitely grieved and troubled at his death, and there was an universal mourning throughout Asia, every one endeavouring to gratify the King herein; and none durst venture to come to him and comfort him, for they thought his passion would not admit any consolation. Three daies being past, Aspasia taking a mourning Robe as the King was going to the Bath, stood weeping, her eyes cast on the ground. He seeing her, wondred, and demanded the reason of her coming. She said, "I come, O King, to comfort your grief and affliction, if you so please; otherwise I shall goe back." The Persian pleased with this care, commanded that she should retire to her Chamber, and wait his coming. As soon as he returned, he put the Vest of the Eunuch upon Aspasia, which did in a manner fit her: And by this means her beauty appeared with greater splendour to the King's eye, who much affected the youth. And being once pleased herewith, he desired her to come alwaies to him in that dress, until the height of his grief were allayed: which to please him she did. Thus more then all his other Women, or his own Son and Kindred, she comforted Artaxerxes, and relieved his sorrow; the King being pleased with her care, and prudently admitting her consolation.

A BEAST OF INDIA

Indica

Ctesias

Translated by Andrew Nichols, 2011

Ctesias of Cnidus was a doctor who worked at the royal court in Persia in the late fifth century BC. He was also the author of *Indica*, a fascinating book about India which, while clearly intended to be documentary, featured fantastical elements, including accounts of feathered and four-footed 'griffins' that guard huge hoards of gold and armies that charge into battle accompanied by 120,000 war elephants. The work sadly no longer survives but a number of ancient authors describe its contents. This is Ctesias' story, as paraphrased by the writers Aelian (author of Story 19) and the geographer Pausanias, of a curious creature known as the manticore.

From Aelian

There seems to be an Indian beast of irresistible strength which is the size of the largest lion, red in colour like cinnabar, and as hairy as a dog. In Indian it is called the martichora. It has a face that more closely resembles a man than a beast. It has three rows of teeth on its upper and lower jaws which are very sharp at their cutting edge and larger than a dog's. Its ears also appear human in shape, but they are larger and hairy. It has blue eyes which also look human. I think its feet and claws resemble a lion's. The stinger of a scorpion is attached to the tip of the tail which is a cubit long and has stingers on either side. The tip of the tail pricks its victim when close at hand and instantly kills him. If someone pursues it, then it discharges its stingers horizontally like arrows and can shoot them very far. When it unleashes its stingers toward the front its tail bends back, and when it aims them toward the rear it stretches its tail out flat like the Saka. Whatever it hits it kills, with the exception of elephants. The stingers used for shooting measure one foot in length and are as thick as a rope. Ctesias claims and maintains that the Indians corroborate this, that in place of the discharged stingers a new one grows as if it were the offspring of this dreadful item. As Ctesias himself says, it is especially fond of human flesh and it kills many. It does not lay in wait for one person, but chases after two or three and vanquishes all of them by itself. It prevails upon the rest of the animal kingdom, but could never overpower a lion. This animal takes great pleasure in having its fill of human flesh living up to its name, for the Indian name in Greek means 'man-eater' and is so-called from this habit. It is as swift as a deer and the Indians hunt their young before they develop a stinger and smash their tails with stones so they are never able to grow them. It emits a sound most closely resembling that of a salpinx. Ctesias claims to have seen one such creature which was brought to the Persian king as a gift, if he is a credible witness about these matters. However, when one hears of the peculiar characteristics of this animal, his attention is drawn to the Cnidian's history.

From Pausanias

In the account given by Ctesias there is a beast in India called the martichora by the Indians and the 'man-eater' by the Greeks which I take to refer to the tiger. It has three rows of teeth on each jaw and a stinger on the tip of its tail. It defends itself with these stingers in close combat and discharges them when fighting at a distance like a bowman's arrow. I think excessive fear for the beast has led the Indians to receive a false account from each other. They were also deceived as to the colour of its skin. When the tiger appeared before them in the rays of the sun, they thought it was red and either because of its speed or, if it were not running, its continuous twisting and turning, they could not see it up close.

THE ECSTASY

Bacchae

Euripides

Translated by William Arrowsmith, 1959

The Athenian tragedian **Euripides** (*c.* 480–*c.* 406 BC) was born, by tradition, on the island of Salamis. In his *Bacchae*, first performed posthumously in around 405, at the Theatre of Dionysus Eleuthereus, Dionysus, god of wine and revelry, has come to Thebes in Greece in mortal guise. His mother Semele was born here and conceived him when she was visited by Zeus (see Story 98). Dionysus has driven her sisters and other women of Thebes to the mountains because they denied he was Zeus' child. Here they rave in orgiastic frenzy. Against better advice, Pentheus, the young new ruler of Thebes, tries to stamp out Dionysus' influence on his city. But while Pentheus detests the god's wild and effeminate ways, he is also rather intrigued by them. A Messenger describes what happens when Dionysus, 'that stranger', agrees to take Pentheus to watch the orgiastic scenes on Mount Cithaeron. Pentheus' own mother, Agave, is among the 'Maenads' or female followers of Dionysus. Euripides captures in his play the struggle between our inner wildness and outer propriety.

MESSENGER.
    There were three of us in all: Pentheus and I,
    attending my master, and that stranger who volunteered
    his services as guide. Leaving behind us
    the last outlying farms of Thebes, we forded
    the Asopus and struck into the barren scrubland
    of Cithaeron.
                There in a grassy glen we halted,
    unmoving, silent, without a word,
    so we might see but not be seen. From that vantage,
    in a hollow cut from the sheer rock of the cliffs,
    a place where water ran and the pines grew dense
    with shade, we saw the Maenads sitting, their hands
    busily moving at their happy tasks. Some
    wound the stalks of their tattered wands with tendrils
    of fresh ivy; others, frisking like fillies
    newly freed from the painted bridles, chanted

in Bacchic songs, responsively.
                              But Pentheus—
unhappy man—could not quite see the companies
of women. "Stranger," he said, "from where I stand,
I cannot see these counterfeited Maenads.
But if I climbed that towering fir that overhangs
the banks, then I could see their shameless orgies
better."
          And now the stranger worked a miracle.
Reaching for the highest branch of a great fir,
he bent it down, down, down to the dark earth,
till it was curved the way a taut bow bends
or like a rim of wood when forced about the circle
of a wheel. Like that he forced that mountain fir
down to the ground. No mortal could have done it.
Then he seated Pentheus at the highest tip
and with his hands let the trunk rise straightly up,
slowly and gently, lest it throw its rider.
And the tree rose, towering to heaven, with my master
huddled at the top. And now the Maenads saw him
more clearly than he saw them. But barely had they seen,
when the stranger vanished and there came a great voice
out of heaven—Dionysus', it must have been—
crying: "Women, I bring you the man who has mocked
at you and me and at our holy mysteries.
Take vengeance upon him." And as he spoke
a flash of awful fire bound earth and heaven.
The high air hushed, and along the forest glen
the leaves hung still; you could hear no cry of beasts.
The Bacchae heard that voice but missed its words,
and leaping up, they stared, peering everywhere.
Again that voice. And now they knew his cry,
the clear command of god. And breaking loose
like startled doves, through grove and torrent,
over jagged rocks, they flew, their feet gladdened
by the breath of god. And when they saw my master
perching in his tree, they climbed a great stone
that towered opposite his perch and showered him
with stones and javelins of fir, while the others
hurled their wands. And yet they missed their target,
poor Pentheus in his perch, barely out of reach
of their eager hands, treed, unable to escape.
Finally they splintered branches from the oaks
and with those bars of wood tried to lever up the tree
by prying at the roots. But every effort failed.
Then Agave cried out: "Maenads, make a circle
about the trunk and grip it with your hands.

Unless we take this climbing beast, he will reveal
the secrets of the god." With that, thousands of hands
tore the fir tree from the earth, and down, down
from his high perch fell Pentheus, tumbling
to the ground, sobbing and screaming as he fell,
for he knew his end was near. His own mother,
like a priestess with her victim, fell upon him
first. But snatching off his wig and snood
so she would recognize his face, he touched her cheeks,
screaming, *"No, no, Mother! I am Pentheus,
your own son, the child you bore to Echion!
Pity me, spare me, Mother! I have done a wrong,
but do not kill your own son for my offense."*
But she was foaming at the mouth, and her crazed eyes
rolling with frenzy. She was mad, stark mad,
possessed by Bacchus. Ignoring his cries of pity,
she seized his left arm at the wrist; then, planting
her foot upon his chest, she pulled, wrenching away
the arm at the shoulder—not by her own strength,
for the god had put inhuman power in her hands.
Ino, meanwhile, on the other side, was scratching off
his flesh. Then Autonoë and the whole horde
of Bacchae swarmed upon him. Shouts everywhere,
he screaming with what little breath was left,
they shrieking in triumph. One tore off an arm,
another a foot still warm in its shoe. His ribs
were clawed clean of flesh and every hand
was smeared with blood as they played ball with scraps
of Pentheus' body.

          The pitiful remains lie scattered,
one piece among the sharp rocks, others
lying lost among the leaves in the depths
of the forest. His mother, picking up his head,
impaled it on her wand. She seems to think it is
some mountain lion's head which she carries in triumph
through the thick of Cithaeron. Leaving her sisters
at the Maenad dances, she is coming here, gloating
over her grisly prize. She calls upon Bacchus:
he is her "fellow-huntsman," "comrade of the chase,
crowned with victory." But all the victory
she carries home is her own grief.

                   Now,
before Agave returns, let me leave
this scene of sorrow. Humility,
a sense of reverence before the sons of heaven
of all the prizes that a mortal man might win,
these, I say, are wisest; these are best.   [*Exit* MESSENGER.]

HIPPOLYTUS AND HIS HORSES

Hippolytus

Euripides

Translated by Anne Carson, 2006

Euripides' *Hippolytus* – first performed in 428 BC, more than two decades before his *Bacchae* – also explores the conflict between different aspects of the human spirit. The love goddess Aphrodite is furious because a young man named Hippolytos repudiates her while worshipping Artemis, the goddess of the hunt. In this story from Euripides' tragedy, which is set in the town of Troezen in the Peloponnese, Aphrodite determines to punish him for his unfailing chastity. Hippolytos' father is Theseus, the founding king of Athens, who is now married to Phaidra. A daughter of King Minos and Pasiphaë, who conceived the Minotaur when she fell in love with a bull (see Story 44), poor Phaidra succumbs to the family curse. Aphrodite ('Cypris') is nothing if not vengeful. Seneça's *Phaedra* (first century AD) and Jean Racine's neoclassical tragedy *Phèdre* (1677) would draw on the same myth. Anne Carson is a celebrated Canadian poet and classicist and her translation is wonderfully rich.

HIPPOLYTOS.
　For you
　　this crown
　　　from a field uncut
　O queen I wove and bring—
　from a virgin field where no shepherd dares to graze his animal,
　no knife comes near it—
　　　　field uncut,
　just a bee dozing by in spring.
　And Shame
　　waters it with river dews.
　No one can cut a flower there
　except those who have
　　purity absolute in their nature,
　　　　untaught, all the time.
　The bad are kept out.

But O
    beloved queen
        for your golden hair
accept this crown from a reverent hand.
For I alone of mortals have the privilege:
with you I stay, with you I talk,
I hear your voice,
although I do not see you.
So may my finish-line match my start.

                [*Enter (male)* SERVANT *from palace.*]

SERVANT.
    You are my prince but gods are our masters, all.
    So will you accept some advice from me?

HIPPOLYTOS.
    Yes. Or seem unwise.

SERVANT.
    Do you know there is a law among men?

HIPPOLYTOS.
    What law?

SERVANT.
    To hate high pride and bad manners.

HIPPOLYTOS.
    Of course, what proud man is not annoying?

SERVANT.
    And is there some charm in being courteous?

HIPPOLYTOS.
    Very much. And profit too.

SERVANT.
    And would you expect the same among gods?

HIPPOLYTOS.
    If mortals use gods' laws.

SERVANT.
    How is it then you refuse courtesy to a proud goddess?

HIPPOLYTOS.
    Which goddess? Be careful.

SERVANT.

   The goddess who stands at your gates. Aphrodite.

HIPPOLYTOS.

   From afar I greet that one, since I am pure.

SERVANT.

   Yet she is proud and important to men.

HIPPOLYTOS.

   No god adored at night is pleasing to me.

SERVANT.

   To honor gods, child, is an *obligation*.

HIPPOLYTOS.

   Different men like different gods.

SERVANT.

   I wish you good luck and good sense. You'll need them.

HIPPOLYTOS.

   Go, servants, into the house and to your supper.
   Sweet after hunting is a full table.
   My horses need a rubdown,
   then after I've had my fill of food
   I'll yoke them and give them a run.
   You, Aphrodite,
   keep out of my way!

           [*Exit* HIPPOLYTOS *with attendants into palace.*]

SERVANT.

   We must not imitate the young in thoughts like these.
   As becomes a slave, I shall bow
   to your statue, Aphrodite be compassionate!
   If someone who is stretched tight inside himself
   talks reckless talk, best not to listen.
   Gods should have more wisdom than men.

           [*Exit* SERVANT *into palace.*]

      [*Enter* CHORUS *from both side entrances into orchestra.*]

CHORUS. (*Entrance song*)
   Water from the river Okeanos drips
       down a certain rock
   (so it is said) and

at its edge a stream
     where pitchers are dipped.
There
someone I know
was soaking her redpurple robes
in river dew,
     spreading them on flat rocks in the sun.
From her to me
first came the story of my lady

wasting herself on a bed of pain:
     she hides her body
in the house,
covers her yellow hair.
Three days
(so I hear)
she is without food,
keeps her body
     pure of bread, longs to
run herself aground
in a sad secret death.

Is it a god inside you, girl?
Deranged by Pan, by Hekate?
Or the holy mountain mother?
Or does Artemis, mistress of wild things,
devastate you?
For she ranges the lake
   and the sand
     near the sea and the wet salt places.

Or is it your husband, the king of Athens,
the highborn one—
is someone in your house coaxing him
to secret sex?
Or has some sailor out from Krete
brought to the queen
   harsh news
     that binds her soul to its bed with grief?

Woman has a wrongturned harmony:
   some evil sad helplessness
     comes to dwell in her
   when she has pain or despair.
That breeze shot through my womb once.
   But to Artemis of childbirth,
     the heavenly one

who rules arrows,
I cried out
and praise god!
she came to me.

But here is the old Nurse at the door,
bringing Phaidra out of the house.
What is it—my soul longs to know—
what has so changed the body of my queen?

[*Enter* NURSE *from palace with* PHAIDRA *on a bed
carried by (female) Servants.*]

NURSE.
Ah, humans and their ailments! Gas and gloom!
What should I do for you? Or not do?
Here is your daylight, here is your bright open air,
here is your sickbed brought out of the house—
"Outside!" you said. "Take me outside!"—
but any minute you'll rush back in.
Every joy disappoints.
What's here doesn't please you,
what's far off you crave.
Better to be sick than tend the sick.
The one is simple, the other
work, work, work, work and worry.
Now every mortal life has pain
and sweat is constant,
but if there is anything dearer than being alive
it's dark to me.
We humans seem disastrously in love with this thing
(whatever it is) that glitters on the earth—
we call it life. We know no other.
The underworld's a blank
and all the rest just fantasy.

PHAIDRA.
Lift my body, raise my head.
I've gone loose in the joints of my limbs.
Take my hands, servants.
This headbinder is heavy,
take it away, let down my hair on my shoulders.

NURSE.
There, child, don't throw yourself around so.
The disease will feel lighter
if you stay calm.
We all must suffer.

PHAIDRA.

AIAI! [*cry of pain*] How I long for a dewcold spring
and pure running water!
To lie back
beneath black poplars,
to sink deep in the long grass of a field!

NURSE.

Child, what are you shouting?
Don't say such things where people can hear.
Your words ride toward madness.

PHAIDRA.

Send me to the mountains! I will go to the woods,
to the pine woods
where
hunting dogs race to the kill,
closing in on dappled deer.
How I long
to cry the hounds onward
and let fly a spear fly
from alongside my yellow hair,
floating
the weapon in my hand!

NURSE.

Why harm yourself like this?
What do you care about hunting?
What do you want with cold running springs?
Right next to the wall is a stream where you can drink.

PHAIDRA.

Queen of the salt lake,
Artemis,
lady of racetracks
where horses' hooves pound,
how I long to be on your ground
riding,
breaking
wild northern colts!

NURSE.

Crazy talk!
One minute you're gone to the mountains to hunt,
the next you want colts and flat beaches!
It would take a mighty prophet to say
what god is pulling back the reins on you

and riding your mind off its track.
Oh child.

PHAIDRA.

    I am a sad one! What have I done?
    Where have I gone from my own good mind?
    I went mad, a god hurt me, I fell.
    PHEU PHEU TLEMON! [*cry*]
    Woman, hide my head again.
    I am ashamed of my own words.
    Hide me.
    Tears fall
    and my eye turns back for shame.
    To think straight is agony.
    But this madness is evil.
    Best to die unaware.

NURSE.

    Yes I am covering you. But when
    will death cover me?
    Long life teaches many things.
    Mortals must measure their love for one another,
    not let it cut right through to the marrow of the soul.
    Keep affections of the mind flexible, I say—
    easy to let them go or pull them tight.
    But when one soul feels the pain of two,
    as mine for hers,
    what a burden.
    You know strict rules of life do more harm
    than giving in to pleasure—
    unhealthy, they say.
    Excess is your culprit.
    "Nothing too much," that's my advice.
    And wise men agree with me.

CHORUS.

    Old woman, trusted Nurse of the queen,
    we see Phaidra in a bad state
    but no sign of the disease.
    Please tell us, what is it?

NURSE.

    I don't know. She wont say.

CHORUS.

    What started it?

NURSE.
Same answer. She is silent.

CHORUS.
How weak and worn her body is.

NURSE.
Well yes, three days without food.

CHORUS.
Is she in a delusion or trying to die?

NURSE.
Who knows? She doesn't eat, she dies.

CHORUS.
Astonishing her husband approves.

NURSE.
She hides her pain, won't say she is ill.

CHORUS.
Does he not see the proof on her face?

NURSE.
In fact he's away from home right now.

CHORUS.
Then won't you use force, try to find out
what is making her sick, drifting her mind?

NURSE.
I've tried everything! Got nowhere!
But I'm not giving up.
You can bear witness
what kind of woman I was for my mistress in trouble.
Come, dear child, let's both forget
what we said before: you be sweeter,
clear your brow, open your mind,
and I'll start again trying to reason with you.
Even if your illness is something unspeakable
there are women here who could help.
Or if it's decent for men to hear,
speak up! tell a doctor!
Silent now? What use is silence?
Correct me if I'm wrong
or agree if I'm right.

Say something! Look at me! Ah,
women, our effort is futile.
We are miles off.
She was not touched, she is not persuaded.
Well, know this—stubborn as the sea!—
if you die you betray your own children.
They will get no share of their father's house.
I swear by the horseriding Amazon queen
whose son is master of your sons—
that bastard who thinks he's the true son,
you know him well,
Hippolytos—

PHAIDRA.
OIMOI! [*cry*]

NURSE.
[*Silence, waits*]

PHAIDRA.
You destroy me, woman. By the gods
I beg you do not say his name again.

NURSE.
You see? you are quite sane, yet unwilling
to help your children or save yourself.

PHAIDRA.
I love my children. But I'm caught in the storm of a different fate.

NURSE.
Your hands are clean of blood, child?

PHAIDRA.
Hands are clean. The mind is filth.

NURSE.
Is it bad magic, a spell cast by some enemy?

PHAIDRA.
A loved one destroys me, although he doesn't mean to.

NURSE.
Theseus has done you wrong?

PHAIDRA.
Oh no—and may I never seem evil to him!

NURSE.

Well what is this dread thing that pulls you toward death?

PHAIDRA.

Leave me to my sins, they are not against you.

NURSE.

No I will not give up on you.

PHAIDRA.

What then—force me? cling to my hand?

NURSE.

Your knees too, I will not let go.

PHAIDRA.

Evil, you unlucky woman, evil is what you will find.

NURSE.

What greater evil than watching you die?

PHAIDRA.

To hear it will kill you. My honor is in this.

NURSE.

And you hide it though I plead with you!

PHAIDRA.

Out of what is shameful I am contriving something good.

NURSE.

Won't you get more honor if you tell it?

PHAIDRA.

Get back, by the gods, let go my right hand!

NURSE.

No I will not. You must tell it.

PHAIDRA.

Yes. I must. I will. I respect your suppliant hand.

NURSE.

I am silent. It's your story now.

PHAIDRA.

O my poor mother, what a love you fell into!

NURSE.
You mean her lust for the bull?

PHAIDRA.
O my sad sister, wife of Dionysos!

NURSE.
Child, what's wrong? Why talk old family scandal?

PHAIDRA.
And third—me. Oh I am a sad one. I am lost.

NURSE.
You frighten me. Where is this going?

PHAIDRA.
To where our sorrows began long ago.

NURSE.
Maybe I don't want to hear.

PHAIDRA.
PHEU! [*cry*]
If only you could say it for me!

NURSE.
I am no prophet of the invisible.

PHAIDRA.
What is this thing they call falling in love?

NURSE.
Something absolutely sweet and absolutely bitter at the same time.

PHAIDRA.
I feel only the second.

NURSE.
You're in love? Child! Who is it?

PHAIDRA.
That one, whoever he is, the Amazon's—

NURSE.
Hippolytos?

PHAIDRA.
  You say it, not I.

Phaidra asks the Nurse to promise not to tell Hippolytos of her feelings. The Nurse cannot hold back. Hippolytos hears the truth.

PHAIDRA.
  O you agent of ruin! Corrupter of trust!
  What have you done to me!
  May Zeus
  my forefather
  grind you to nothing,
  blast you in fire from the face of the earth!
  Didn't I see this coming—did I not command you
  to keep silent? And now my humiliation!
  You would not hold back.
  Because of you I'll die in shame.
  Oh I need all new plans!
  That man bitten to the brains with anger as he is
  will speak against me to his father—tell your crimes—
  and fill the land with my disgrace.
  Curse you!
  Curse anyone eager
  to help a friend to ruin!

NURSE.
  Go ahead and blame my failures, lady,
  for the sting is stronger than your judgment now.
  But I have answers too, if you allow.
  I reared you, I am on your side.
  I sought a cure
  for your disease and found one not so nice.
  Yet if I had succeeded you'd call me smart.
  Smartness is relative to winning, isn't it.

PHAIDRA.
  So this is justice? This is supposed to be enough for me?
  You cut me to the nerves and then say "Sorry!"

NURSE.
  We're wasting words. I went too far.
  But, child, there is a way to save the situation even now.

PHAIDRA.
  No more advice.
  It was bad before.
  Go—look to your own affairs, I'll manage mine.

[*Exit* NURSE *into palace.*]

And you, noble women of Trozen,
grant me this favor I beg.
Keep in silence what you heard here.

CHORUS.
I swear by reverend Artemis daughter of Zeus,
I'll show none of this to the light of day.

PHAIDRA.
Ladies, thank you.
One last thing.
I've got an idea
how I can leave my children a respectable name
and allow myself a way out.
For I will not shame my Kretan home
nor come to Theseus charged with corruption,
just to save one life.

CHORUS.
What do you intend?

PHAIDRA.
To die. How I'm not sure.

CHORUS.
Hush.

PHAIDRA.
Hush nothing.
I will pleasure Aphrodite, the one who destroys me,
by releasing myself from life this very day.
Bitter the love by which I'm beaten.
But I shall become
disaster for another
as I die—may he learn
not to swell himself on my misfortune.
If he gets a share of this disease he'll learn self-control.
[*Exit* PHAIDRA *into palace.*]

Theseus finds a tablet in his dead wife's hand. It falsely accuses Hippolytos of raping her. Hippolytos denies the accusation and stresses his chastity. His father Theseus refuses to believe him and resolves to send him into exile.

THESEUS.
PHEU [*cry*] the human mind! To what lengths will it not go?
Where will its reckless impudence end?

For if it swells from life to life
and each one exceeds the one before in evildoing,
the gods will have to add another world to this one
to make room for the unjust and the bad.
Look at this man: my own son yet
he shames my bed! And stands denounced
by this dead woman
as plain and utter evil.
Show your face to your father, polluted as you are!
Are you the one who walks with gods as if you were
    something special?
You, the model of purity, uncut by sin?
No—to credit your boasts
is to call the gods stupid.
Go ahead, exalt yourself, sell your story—
the vegetarian diet, the Orphic jargon,
all that Bacchic business and spooky writings!
You stand exposed. I tell the world:
avoid such men.
She is dead. You think that will save you?
No, you are caught, you thing of evil.
What kind of oaths, what words
could exonerate you?
Will you say she hated you, that a bastard
is always the enemy of legitimate sons?
She made a bad bargain, the way you tell it,
destroying her own dear life just to discomfit you.
Or do you claim that lust isn't natural to men,
just women? I don't see
young men are any more controlled than females
when Aphrodite mixes up their blood.
The fact of being male is good in itself but—
oh why do I bother to argue with you?
Isn't her corpse right here the clearest witness in the world?
Get yourself out of this land as fast as you can.
You are exiled!
Don't come near godbuilt Athens,
don't cross any frontier I rule!
If after suffering this I am bested by you,
I'll lose my reputation as a scourge of bad men,
they'll say
no scoundrel ever felt my punishing hand.

CHORUS.
Who can call any mortal happy?
Look how beginnings are turned upside down.

HIPPOLYTOS.
  Father, the passion and set of your mind are terrifying.
  But the case you make, although elegant,
  is wrong.
  Now I boast no skill at public speaking
  (I prefer to address a few of my peers,
  and I guess this makes sense—
  if you think what kind of people impress a crowd!)
  still, there is a necessity. I must
  loose my tongue. I'll begin
  from the first accusation you made,
  which you presumed I could not answer.
  You see this daylight, this earth?
  Nowhere in it is there a man—
  go ahead deny it!—more purehearted than I.
  I know how to worship gods,
  and I choose my friends from honorable people,
  people ashamed to connive at evil
  or do dirty favors.
  I am not a man to mock my companions, father,
  I am the same to friends absent or present.
  And there is one sin that has never touched me—that sin
  in which you think me caught—
  my body is pure of sex to this day.
  I do not know the deed except from hearsay, pictures.
  Nor do I want to.
  I have a virgin soul.
  No doubt my chastity fails to persuade you—well,
  explain then how I was seduced.
  Was this woman's body more lovely than any other in the world?
  Or did I
  take the heiress to bed to get your house?
  Then I was a fool—mad, really!
  But men who crave royal power are scarcely sane, are they?
  No, never, never in the world! those who find
  power sweet have had their wits turned by it.
  Sure I'd like to win at the Olympic Games
  but in politics second place is fine.
  I am happy with men of virtue as my friends—
  the kind of influence that brings no risk—
  much more pleasant than tyranny.
  Nothing left to say but this:
  if I had a character witness here,
  or if I were pleading my case with her alive,
  the facts would show you who is evil.
  But now I swear an oath to you
  by Zeus who guards oaths,

by the plain of earth.
I never touched your marriage bed.
I never wanted to.
I never took the thought in mind.
May I perish unknown and nameless,
may neither sea nor land receive my flesh when dead,
if I was an evil man.
What despair drove this woman to end her life
I don't know.
I can say no more.
She was not pure but she did one pure thing.
Whereas I—my purity has ruined me.

CHORUS.
Good. The oath was a nice touch.

THESEUS.
Swindler! Sorcerer!—thinks
to rule my soul with his mild manners,
though he has put his own father to shame!

HIPPOLYTOS.
I wonder at your manners too, father.
If you were my child and I your father
and I thought you'd touched my wife,
I'd murder you, not sentence you to exile.

THESEUS.
How like you to say that! But no,
you won't die so.
Quick death is too kind.
I want you outcast from your father's country
bleeding a bitter life away in alien places.

HIPPOLYTOS.
OIMOI! [cry]
Is that your intention? You won't
wait for time to condemn me, just
throw me out?

THESEUS.
Beyond the Black Sea and the boundary of Atlas if I could,
I hate you so.

HIPPOLYTOS.
Without any test of oath or pledge or oracle,
without trial, you'll cast me out?

THESEUS.

    This letter denounces you plainly. No need
    for divination! Let the birds of omen
    fly over my head—be gone!

HIPPOLYTOS.

    O gods! why not speak out—
    I am being destroyed for honoring you!
    No. He would never believe me.
    I'd break my oath in vain.

THESEUS.

    OIMOI! [*cry*]
    Your piety will kill me!
    Out of my land! Go!

HIPPOLYTOS.

    Where shall I turn? Whose house
    can I enter, exiled on a charge like this?

THESEUS.

    Go to someone who wants his women defiled,
    one cozy with evil.

HIPPOLYTOS.

    ALAI! [*cry*]
    That goes to the heart. This is near tears,
    if I seem evil and you think me so.

THESEUS.

    The time for tears was before
    you raped your father's wife.

HIPPOLYTOS.

    O house! If only you could speak for me,
    bear witness!

THESEUS.

    Wise of you to turn to voiceless witnesses.
    But your deed speaks aloud.

HIPPOLYTOS.

    PHEU! [*cry*]
    I wish that I could stand apart, observe myself
    and weep for my own suffering.

THESEUS.
    You are much more adept at self-worship
    than at piety toward parents.

HIPPOLYTOS.
    O most miserable mother! O bitter birth!
    Pity anyone who is a bastard!

THESEUS.
    Drag him out, servants!
    Do you not hear me pronounce him exiled?

HIPPOLYTOS.
    No.
    You do it. You do it.

THESEUS.
    I will if you don't obey.
    Your exile stirs no pity in me.

HIPPOLYTOS.
    So, it is fixed.
    Sad, what I know I cannot tell.

Hippolytos is wounded when his horses rear, frightened by a divinely-inspired sea monster. The goddess Artemis tells Theseus the truth. Hippolytos forgives his father. Hippolytos slips away.

EURIPIDES THE WOMAN-HATER

Thesmophoriazusae

Aristophanes

Translated by William James Hickie, 1883

A comedy by **Aristophanes** (*c.* 446–*c.* 386 BC), *Thesmophoriazusae* was first performed in Athens in or around 411 BC. Its tongue-twister of a title translates as 'The Women Celebrating the Thesmophoria'. Held in honour of Demeter and her daughter Persephone (see Story 11) each year, the Greek festival of the Thesmophoria was celebrated exclusively by women. In this extract, the playwright Euripides attempts to infiltrate the festival to save his own skin. The women of the city have taken umbrage at his harsh characterisation of their sex in his tragedies. Medea (Story 43) and Phaidra in *Hippolytus* (Story 22) are just two of the many flawed women from his oeuvre. The very idea that women of the fifth century BC might have taken issue with the apparent misogyny of a leading playwright is striking. As Euripides seeks a stooge to do his dirty work for him, the misogyny of which he is accused becomes only too apparent.

EURIPIDES. A great evil is ready kneaded for me.

MNESILOCHUS. Of what kind?

EURIPIDES. On this day will be decided whether Euripides still lives or is undone.

MNESILOCHUS. Why, how? For now neither the courts are about to judge causes, nor is there a sitting of the Senate; for it is the third day, the middle of the Thesmophoria.

EURIPIDES. In truth, I expect this very thing even will destroy me. For the women have plotted against me, and are going to hold an assembly to-day about me in the temple of Demeter and Persephone for my destruction.

MNESILOCHUS. Wherefore? why, pray?

EURIPIDES. Because I represent them in tragedy and speak ill of them.

MNESILOCHUS. And justly too would you suffer, by Neptune! But, as this is the case, what contrivance have you?

EURIPIDES. To persuade Agathon the tragic poet to go to the temple of Demeter and Persephone.

MNESILOCHUS. What to do? Tell me!

EURIPIDES. To sit in assembly among the women, and to speak whatever is necessary in my defence.

MNESILOCHUS. Openly, or secretly?

EURIPIDES. Secretly, clothed in a woman's stole.

MNESILOCHUS. The device is a clever one, and exceedingly in conformity with your disposition; for ours is the prize for trickery. [*The creaking of machinery is heard.*]

Agathon refuses to help Euripides so the task falls to his elderly father-in-law Mnesilochus. Dressed up as a woman, Mnesilochus joins the festival where the women are holding a meeting

HERALD. Hear, every one! [*Unfolds a paper and begins to read the preliminary decree*] "These things have been determined on by the Senate of the women: Timoclea was Epistates, Lysilla was secretary, Sostrata moved the decree; to convene an assembly in the morning in the middle of the Thesmophoria, when we are most at leisure; and to debate first about Euripides, what he ought to suffer, for he has been adjudged guilty by us all." Who wishes to speak?

FIRST WOMAN. I.

HERALD. Then first put on this crown before you speak. [*To the meeting.*] Be silent! Be quiet! Give attention! for she is now expectorating, as the orators do. She seems to be going to make a long speech.

FIRST WOMAN. Through no ostentatiousness, by the two goddesses, have I stood up to speak, O women; but indeed I have been vexed, unhappy woman, now for a long time, seeing you treated with contumely by Euripides the son of the herb-woman, and abused with much abuse of every kind. For what abuse does he not smear upon us? And where has he not calumniated us, where, in short, are spectators, and tragic actors, and choruses? calling us adulteresses in disposition, lovers of the men, wine-bibbers, traitresses, gossips, masses of wickedness, great pests to men. So that, as soon as they come in from the wooden-benches, they look askance at us, and straightway search, lest any paramour be concealed in the house. And we are no longer able to do any of those things which we formerly did: such badness has he taught our husbands. So that, if even any woman weave a crown, she is thought to be in love; and if she let fall any vessel while roaming about the house, her husband asks her, "In whose honour is the pot broken? It must be for the Corinthian stranger." Is any girl sick; straightway her brother says, "This colour in the girl does not please me." Well; does any woman, lacking children, wish to substitute a child; it is not possible even for this to go undiscovered; for now the husbands sit down beside them. And he has calumniated us to the old men, who heretofore used to marry girls; so that no old man is willing to marry a woman, on account of this verse, "For a woman is ruler over an old bridegroom." In the next place, through him they now put seals and bolts upon the women's apartments, guarding us; and moreover they keep Molossian dogs, a terror to paramours. And this, indeed, is pardonable; but as for what was permitted us heretofore, to be ourselves the housekeepers, and to draw forth and take barley-meal, oil, and wine; not even this is any longer permitted us. For the husbands now themselves carry secret little keys, most ill-natured, certain Spartan ones with three teeth. Previously, indeed, it was possible at least to secretly open the door, if we got a three-obol seal-ring made. But now this home-born slave Euripides has taught them to have rings of worm-eaten wood, having them suspended about them. Now therefore I move that we mix up some destruction in some way or other for him, either by poison, or by some one artifice, so that he shall perish. These I speak openly; but the rest I will draw up in the form of a motion in conjunction with the secretary.

[...]

MNESILOCHUS. It is not wonderful, O women, that you who are so abused should be exceedingly exasperated at Euripides, nor yet that your bile should boil over; for I myself hate that man, if I be not mad,—so may I be blessed in my children! But nevertheless we must grant the privilege of speaking amongst each other; for we are by ourselves, and there is no blabbing of our conversation. Why thus do we accuse him, and are vexed, if, being cognizant of two or three misdeeds of ours, he has said them of us who perpetrate innumerable? For I myself, in the first place,—not to speak of any one else,—am conscious with myself of many shameful acts: at all events of that most shameful one, when I was a bride of three days, and my husband was sleeping beside me. Now I had a friend, who had debauched me when I was seven years of age. He, through love of me, came and began scratching at the door; and then I immediately understood it; and then I was for going down secretly, but my husband asked me, "Whither are you going down?" "Whither?—A colic and pain, husband, possesses me in my stomach;

therefore I am going to the necessary." "Go then!" said he. And then he began pounding juniper berries, anise, and sage. But after I had poured some water on the hinge, I went out to my paramour; and then I conversed with him beside the statue of Apollo, holding by the bay-tree. These, you see, Euripides never yet at any time spoke of. Nor does he mention how we give ourselves up to our slaves and to muleteers, if we have not any other. Nor how, when we junket ever so much during the night, we chew up garlic in the morning, in order that the husband having smelt it when he comes in from the wall, may not suspect us of doing any thing bad. These things, you see, he has never at any time spoken of. And if he does abuse a Phaedra, what is this to us? Neither has he ever mentioned that, how that well-known woman, while showing her husband at day-break how beautiful her upper garment is, sent out her paramour hidden in it—*that* he has never yet mentioned. And I know another woman, who for ten days said she was in labour, till she purchased a little child; while her husband went about purchasing drugs to procure a quick delivery. But the child an old woman brought in a pot with its mouth stopped with honeycomb, that it might not squall. Then, when she that carried it nodded, *the wife* immediately cried out, "Go away, husband, go away, for methinks I shall be immediately delivered." For *the child* kicked against the bottom of the pot. And he ran off delighted, while she drew out *the stoppage* from the mouth of the child, and it cried out. And then the abominable old woman who brought the child, runs smiling to the husband, and says, "A lion has been born to you, a lion! your very image, both in all other respects whatever, and its nose is like yours, being crooked like an acorn-cup." Do we not practise these wicked acts? Yea, by Diana, do we! And then are we angry at Euripides, "who have suffered nothing greater than we have committed?"

CHORUS. This certainly is wonderful, where the creature was found, and what land reared this so audacious *woman*. For I did not think the villanous *woman* would even ever have dared thus shamelessly to say this publicly amongst us. But now every thing may take place. I commend the old proverb, "For we must look about under every stone, lest an orator bite us." But indeed there existeth not any thing more wicked for all purposes than women shameless by nature,—unless perhaps it be women.

The women continue to be shocked by Mnesilochus' utterings. News arrives that Euripides has sent an in-law of his in women's guise to eavesdrop on them. The women decide to hunt him out. Their suspicions are raised when Mnesilochus gives an inaccurate account of the previous year's festival.

FIFTH WOMAN. Strip him; for he says nothing that is right.

MNESILOCHUS. And will you then strip the mother of nine children?

CLISTHENES. Unloose your girdle quickly, you shameless creature!

FIFTH WOMAN. How very stout and strong she appears! and, by Jove, too, she has no breasts, as we have.

MNESILOCHUS. For I am barren, and have never been pregnant.

FIFTH WOMAN. Now; but you were the mother of nine children a while ago.

CLISTHENES. Stand upright! Whither are you thrusting down your hand?

FIFTH WOMAN. See there, it peeped out! and very fresh-coloured it is, you rogue.

CLISTHENES. Why, where is it?

FIFTH WOMAN. It's gone again to the front. [CLISTHENES *goes in front of* MNESILOCHUS.]

CLISTHENES. It is not here.

FIFTH WOMAN. Nay, but it has come hither again.

CLISTHENES. You've a kind of an isthmus, fellow; you're worse than the Corinthians.

FIFTH WOMAN. Oh the abominable fellow! On this account then he reviled us in defence of Euripides.

Mnesilochus is punished by being fastened to a board so that an archer can shoot arrows at him.

[*Enter* EURIPIDES *as an old procuress, accompanied by a dancing-girl and a boy with a flute.*]

EURIPIDES. Women, if you are willing to make peace with me for the future, it is now in your power; I make you these proposals of peace on the understanding that you are to be in no wise abused by me at all henceforth.

CHORUS. On account of what matter do you bring forward this proposal?

EURIPIDES. This man in the plank is my father-in-law. If therefore I recover him, you shall never be abused at all. But if you do not comply, I will accuse you to your husbands when they come home from the army of those things which you do secretly.

With a little help Euripides eventually sets Mnesilochus free.

OEDIPUS LEARNS THE TRUTH

Oedipus Rex

Sophocles

Translated by W. B. Yeats, 1928

Sophocles (497/6–406/5 BC) was the third in the triumvirate of great Athenian tragedians, Aeschylus and Euripides being the other two. *Oedipus Rex* was the second of his surviving 'Theban Plays' to be written (after *Antigone*, see Story 25), but chronologically the first in the sequence of events portrayed. A terrible plague has swept across Thebes. A prophecy suggests that respite will come only when the Thebans have avenged the murder of their previous king, Laius. Oedipus (literally 'swollen foot'), who married Laius' widow Jocasta and had four children by her, seeks to discover who was responsible and punish him. Oedipus is incredulous when the blind prophet Teiresias reveals to him that *he*, Oedipus, is the blind one, since the murderer he is seeking is none other than himself. This extract from Sophocles' play, which features a Chorus of elders, describes Oedipus' terrible moment of realisation. It opens with Jocasta speaking.

[…] An oracle came to Laius once,
I will not say from Phoebus, but from his ministers,
that he was doomed to die by the hand of his own
child sprung from him and me. When his child was
but three days old, Laius bound its feet together and
had it thrown by sure hands upon a trackless mountain; and when Laius was murdered at the place
where three highways meet, it was, or so at least the
rumour says, by foreign robbers. So Apollo did not
bring it about that the child should kill its father,
nor did Laius die in the dreadful way he feared by
his child's hand. Yet that was how the message of
the seers mapped out the future. Pay no attention
to such things. What the God would show he will
need no help to show it, but bring it to light himself.

OEDIPUS. What restlessness of soul, lady, has come upon me since I heard you speak, what a tumult of the mind!

JOCASTA. What is this new anxiety? What has startled you?

OEDIPUS. You said that Laius was killed where three highways meet.

JOCASTA. Yes: that was the story.

OEDIPUS. And where is the place?

JOCASTA. In Phocis where the road divides branching off to Delphi and to Daulia.

OEDIPUS. And when did it happen? How many years ago?

JOCASTA. News was published in this town just before you came into power.

OEDIPUS. O Zeus! What have you planned to do unto me?

JOCASTA. He was tall; the silver had just come into his hair; and in shape not greatly unlike to you.

OEDIPUS. Unhappy that I am! It seems that I have laid a dreadful curse upon myself, and did not know it.

JOCASTA. What do you say? I tremble when I look on you, my King.

OEDIPUS. And I have a misgiving that the seer can see indeed. But I will know it all more clearly, if you tell me one thing more.

JOCASTA. Indeed, though I tremble I will answer whatever you ask.

OEDIPUS. Had he but a small troop with him; or did he travel like a great man with many followers?

JOCASTA. There were but five in all—one of them a herald; and there was one carriage with Laius in it.

OEDIPUS. Alas! It is now clear indeed. Who was it brought the news, lady?

JOCASTA. A servant—the one survivor.

OEDIPUS. Is he by chance in the house now?

JOCASTA. No; for when he found you reigning instead of Laius he besought me, his hand clasped in mine, to send him to the fields among the cattle that he might be far from the sight of this town; and I sent him. He was a worthy man for a slave and might have asked a bigger thing.

OEDIPUS. I would have him return to us without delay.

JOCASTA. Oedipus, it is easy. But why do you ask this?

OEDIPUS. I fear that I have said too much, and therefore I would question him.

JOCASTA. He shall come, but I too have a right to know what lies so heavy upon your heart, my King.

OEDIPUS. Yes: and it shall not be kept from you now that my fear has grown so heavy. Nobody is more to me than you, nobody has the same right to learn my good or evil luck. My father was Polybus of Corinth, my mother the Dorian Merope, and I was held the foremost man in all that town until a thing happened—a thing to startle a man, though not to make him angry as it made me. We were sitting at the table, and a man who had drunk too much cried out that I was not my father's son—and I, though angry, restrained my anger for that day; but the next day went to my father and my mother and questioned them. They were indignant at the taunt and that comforted me—and yet the man's words rankled, for they had spread a rumour through the town. Without consulting my father or my mother I went to Delphi, but Phoebus told me nothing of the thing for which I came, but much of other things —things of sorrow and of terror: that I should live in incest with my mother, and beget a brood that men would shudder to took upon; that I should be my father's murderer. Hearing those words I fled out of Corinth, and from that day have but known where it lies when I have found its direction by the stars. I sought where I might escape those infamous things—the doom that was laid upon me. I came in my flight to that very spot where you tell me this king perished. Now, lady, I will tell you the truth. When I had come close up to those three roads, I came upon a herald, and a man like him you have described seated in a carriage. The man who held the reins and the old man himself would not give me room, but thought to force me from the path, and I struck the driver in my anger. The old man, seeing what I had done, waited till I was passing him and then struck me upon the head. I paid him back in full, for I knocked him out of the carriage with a blow of my stick. He rolled on his back, and after that I killed them all. If this stranger were indeed Laius, is there a more miserable man in the world than the man before you? Is there a man more hated of Heaven? No stranger, no citizen, may receive him into his house, not a soul may speak to him, and no mouth but my own mouth has laid this curse upon me. Am I not wretched? May I be swept from this world before I have endured this doom!

A Messenger comes to tell Oedipus that Polybus, his father – or at least, the man he thought was his father – has died. His conversation with Oedipus is revelatory.

OEDIPUS. I am afraid lest Phoebus has spoken true.

MESSENGER. You are afraid of being made guilty through Merope?

OEDIPUS. That is my constant fear.

MESSENGER. A vain fear.

OEDIPUS. How so, if I was born of that father and mother?

MESSENGER. Because they were nothing to you in blood.

OEDIPUS. What do you say. Was Polybus not my father?

MESSENGER. No more or less than myself.

OEDIPUS. How can my father be no more to me than you who are nothing to me?

MESSENGER. He did not beget you any more than I.

OEDIPUS. No? Then why did he call me his son?

MESSENGER. He took you as a gift from these hands of mine.

OEDIPUS. How could he love so dearly what came from another's hands?

MESSENGER. He had been childless.

OEDIPUS. If I am not your son, where did you get me?

MESSENGER. In a wooded valley of Cithaeron.

OEDIPUS. What brought you wandering there?

MESSENGER. I was in charge of mountain sheep.

OEDIPUS. A shepherd—a wandering, hired man.

MESSENGER. A hired man who came just in time.

OEDIPUS. Just in time—had it come to that?

MESSENGER. Have not the cords left their marks upon your ankles?

OEDIPUS. Yes, that is an old trouble.

MESSENGER. I took your feet out of the spancel.

OEDIPUS. I have had those marks from the cradle.

MESSENGER. They have given you the name you bear.

OEDIPUS. Tell me, for God's sake, was that deed my mother's or my father's?

MESSENGER. I do not know—he who gave you to me knows more of that than I.

OEDIPUS. What? You had me from another? You did not chance on me yourself?

MESSENGER. No. Another shepherd gave you to me.

OEDIPUS. Who was he? Can you tell me who he was?

MESSENGER. I think that he was said to be of Laius' household.

OEDIPUS. The king who ruled this country long ago?

MESSENGER. The same—the man was herdsman in his service.

OEDIPUS. Is he alive, that I might speak with him?

MESSENGER. You people of this country should know that.

OEDIPUS. Is there any one here present who knows the herd he speaks of? Any one who has seen him in the town pastures? The hour has come when all must be made clear.

CHORUS. I think he is the very herd you sent for but now; Jocasta can tell you better than I.

JOCASTA. Why ask about that man? Why think about him? Why waste a thought on what this man has said? What he has said is of no account.

OEDIPUS. What, with a clue like that in my hands and fail to find out my birth?

JOCASTA. For God's sake, if you set any value upon your life, give up this search—my misery is enough.

OEDIPUS. Though I be proved the son of a slave, yes, even of three generations of slaves, you cannot be made base-born.

JOCASTA. Yet, hear me, I implore you. Give up this search.

OEDIPUS. I will not hear of anything but searching the whole thing out.

JOCASTA. I am only thinking of your good—I have advised you for the best.

OEDIPUS. Your advice makes me impatient.

JOCASTA. May you never come to know who you are, unhappy man!

OEDIPUS. Go, some one, bring the herdsman here—and let that woman glory in her noble blood.

JOCASTA. Alas, alas, miserable man! Miserable! That is all that I can call you now or for ever.

[She goes out.]

CHORUS. Why has the lady gone. Oedipus, in such a transport of despair? Out of this silence will burst a storm of sorrows.

OEDIPUS. Let come what will. However lowly my origin I will discover it. That woman, with all a woman's pride, grows red with shame at my base birth. I think myself the child of Good Luck, and that the years are my foster-brothers. Sometimes they have set me up, and sometimes thrown me down, but he that has Good Luck for mother can suffer no dishonour. That is my origin, nothing can change it, so why should I renounce this search into my birth?

CHORUS. Oedipus' nurse, mountain of many a hidden glen,
Be honoured among men;
A famous man, deep-thoughted, and his body strong;
Be honoured in dance and song.

Who met in the hidden glen? Who let his fancy run
Upon nymph of Helicon?
Lord Pan or Lord Apollo or the mountain Lord
By the Bacchantes adored?

OEDIPUS. If I, who have never met the man, may venture to say so, I think that the herdsman we await approaches; his venerable age matches with this stranger's, and I recognise as servants of mine those who bring him. But you, if you have seen the man before, will know the man better than I.

CHORUS. Yes, I know the man who is coming; he was

indeed in Laius' service, and is still the most trusted of the herdsmen.

OEDIPUS. I ask you first, Corinthian stranger, is this the man you mean?

MESSENGER. He is the very man.

OEDIPUS. Look at me, old man! Answer my questions. Were you once in Laius' service?

HERDSMAN. I was; not a bought slave, but reared up in the house.

OEDIPUS. What was your work—your manner of life?

HERDSMAN. For the best part of my life I have tended flocks.

OEDIPUS. Where, mainly?

HERDSMAN. Cithaeron or its neighborhood.

OEDIPUS. Do you remember meeting with this man there?

HERDSMAN. What man do you mean?

OEDIPUS. This man. Did you ever meet him?

HERDSMAN. I cannot recall him to mind.

MESSENGER. No wonder in that, master; but I will bring back his memory. He and I lived side by side upon Cithaeron. I had but one flock and he had two. Three full half-years we lived there, from spring to autumn, and every winter I drove my flock to my own fold, while he drove his to the fold of Laius. Is that right? Was it not so?

HERDSMAN. True enough; though it was long ago.

MESSENGER. Come, tell me now—do you remember giving me a boy to rear as my own foster-son?

HERDSMAN. What are you saying? Why do you ask me that?

MESSENGER. Look at that man, my friend, he is the child you gave me.

HERDSMAN. A plague upon you! Cannot you hold your tongue?

OEDIPUS. Do not blame him, old man; your own words are more blameable.

HERDSMAN. And how have I offended, master?

OEDIPUS. In not telling of that boy he asks of.

HERDSMAN. He speaks from ignorance, and does not know what he is saying.

OEDIPUS. If you will not speak with a good grace you shall be made to speak.

HERDSMAN. Do not hurt me for the love of God, I am an old man.

OEDIPUS. Some one there, tie his hands behind his back.

HERDSMAN. Alas! Wherefore! What more would you learn?

OEDIPUS. Did you give this man the child he speaks of?

HERDSMAN. I did: would I had died that day!

OEDIPUS. Well, you may come to that unless you speak the truth.

HERDSMAN. Much more am I lost if I speak it.

OEDIPUS. What! Would the fellow make more delay?

HERDSMAN. No, no. I said before that I gave it to him.

OEDIPUS. Where did you come by it? Your own child, or another?

HERDSMAN. It was not my own child—I had it from another.

OEDIPUS. From any of those here? From what house?

HERDSMAN. Do not ask any more, master, for the love of God do not ask.

OEDIPUS. You are lost if I have to question you again.

HERDSMAN. It was a child from the house of Laius.

OEDIPUS. A slave? Or one of his own race?

HERDSMAN. Alas! I am on the edge of dreadful words.

OEDIPUS. And I of hearing: yet hear I must.

HERDSMAN. It was said to have been his own child. But your lady within can tell you of these things best.

OEDIPUS. How? It was she who gave it to you?

HERDSMAN. Yes, King.

OEDIPUS. To what end?

HERDSMAN. That I should make away with it.

OEDIPUS. Her own child?

HERDSMAN. Yes: from fear of evil prophecies.

OEDIPUS. What prophecies?

HERDSMAN. That he should kill his father.

OEDIPUS. Why, then, did you give him up to this old man?

HERDSMAN. Through pity, master, believing that he would carry him to whatever land he had himself come from—but he saved him for dreadful misery; for if you are what this man says, you are the most miserable of all men.

OEDIPUS. O! O! All brought to pass! All truth! Now, O light, may I look my last upon you, having been found accursed in bloodshed, accursed in marriage, and in my coming into the world accursed!

ONE GIRL VERSUS THE LAW

Antigone

Sophocles

Translated by H. D. F. Kitto, 1962

Oedipus' troubles did not end there. In the final scenes of *Oedipus Rex*, his wife Jocasta kills herself and he blinds himself with her brooch pins before leaving Thebes. Jocasta's brother Creon is now guardian of the city. **Sophocles'** play, *Antigone*, sees Creon at odds with Oedipus' daughter Antigone. Her brothers, Eteocles and Polyneices, have killed one another. Creon has forbidden the burial of Polyneices on the grounds that he was a traitor. Antigone urges her sister Ismene to help her lay Polyneices to rest. Ismene is afraid to break Creon's law. The only law Antigone recognises is divine law. She therefore proceeds to bury her brother alone. In this scene her act of defiance is reported to Creon.

Strophe 1

CHORUS. [*Sings*] Wonders are many, yet of all
    Things is Man the most wonderful.
    He can sail on the stormy sea
    Though the tempest rage, and the loud
    Waves roar around, as he makes his
    Path amid the towering surge.

    Earth inexhaustible, ageless, he wearies, as
    Backwards and forwards, from season to season, his
      Ox-team drives along the ploughshare.

Antistrophe 1

    He can entrap the cheerful birds,
    Setting a snare, and all the wild
    Beasts of the earth he has learned to catch, and
    Fish that teem in the deep sea, with
    Nets knotted of stout cords; of

Such inventiveness is man.
Through his inventions he becomes lord
Even of the beasts of the mountain: the long-haired
Horse he subdues to the yoke on his neck, and the
Hill-bred bull, of strength untiring.

Strophe 2

And speech he has learned, and thought
So swift, and the temper of mind
To dwell within cities, and not to lie bare
Amid the keen, biting frosts
Or cower beneath pelting rain;
Full of resource against all that comes to him
Is Man. Against Death alone
He is left with no defence.
But painful sickness he can cure
   By his own skill.

Antistrophe 2

Surpassing belief, the device and
Cunning that Man has attained,
And it bringeth him now to evil, now to good.
If he observe Law, and tread
The righteous path God ordained,
Honoured is he; dishonoured, the man whose reckless heart
Shall make him join hands with sin:
May I not think like him,
Nor may such an impious man
   Dwell in my house.

[*Enter* GUARD, *with* ANTIGONE.]

CHORUS. What evil spirit is abroad? I know
   Her well: Antigone. But how can I
   Believe it? Why, O you unlucky daughter
   Of an unlucky father, what is this?
   Can it be you, so mad and so defiant,
   So disobedient to a King's decree?

GUARD. Here is the one who did the deed, this girl;
   We caught her burying him.—But where is Creon?

CHORUS. He comes, just as you need him, from the palace.

[*Enter* CREON, *attended.*]

CREON. How? What occasion makes my coming timely?

GUARD. Sir, against nothing should a man take oath,
    For second thoughts belie him. Under your threats
    That lashed me like a hailstorm, I'd have said
    I would not quickly have come here again;
    But joy that comes beyond our dearest hope
    Surpasses all in magnitude. So I
    Return, though I had sworn I never would,
    Bringing this girl detected in the act
    Of honouring the body. This time no lot
    Was cast; the windfall is my very own.
    And so, my lord, do as you please: take her
    Yourself, examine her, cross-question her.
    I claim the right of free and final quittance.

CREON. Why do you bring this girl? Where was she taken?

GUARD. In burying the body. That is all.

CREON. You know what you are saying? Do you mean it?

GUARD. I saw her giving burial to the corpse
    You had forbidden. Is that plain and clear?

CREON. How did you see and take her so red-handed?

GUARD. It was like this. When we had reached the place,
    Those dreadful threats of yours upon our heads,
    We swept aside each grain of dust that hid
    The clammy body, leaving it quite bare,
    And sat down on a hill, to the windward side
    That so we might avoid the smell of it.
    We kept sharp look-out; each man roundly cursed
    His neighbour, if he should neglect his duty.
    So the time passed, until the blazing sun
    Reached his mid-course and burned us with his heat.
    Then, suddenly, a whirlwind came from heaven
    And raised a storm of dust, which blotted out
    The earth and sky; the air was filled with sand
    And leaves ripped from the trees. We closed our eyes
    And bore this visitation as we could.
    At last it ended; then we saw the girl.
    She raised a bitter cry, as will a bird
    Returning to its nest and finding it
    Despoiled, a cradle empty of its young.
    So, when she saw the body bare, she raised

A cry of anguish mixed with imprecations
Laid upon those who did it; then at once
Brought handfuls of dry dust, and raised aloft
A shapely vase of bronze, and three times poured
The funeral libation for the dead.
We rushed upon her swiftly, seized our prey.
And charged her both with this offence and that.
She faced us calmly; she did not disown
The double crime. How glad I was!—and yet
How sorry too; it is a painful thing
To bring a friend to ruin. Still, for me,
My own escape comes before everything.

CREON. You there, who keep your eyes fixed on the ground,
   Do you admit this, or do you deny it?

ANTIGONE. No, I do not deny it. I admit it.

CREON. [*To* GUARD] Then you may go; go where you like. You have
   Been fully cleared of that grave accusation.

                                        [*Exit* GUARD.]

   You: tell me briefly—I want no long speech:
   Did you not know that this had been forbidden?

ANTIGONE. Of course I knew. There was a proclamation.

CREON. And so you dared to disobey the law?

ANTIGONE. It was not Zeus who published this decree,
   Nor have the Powers who rule among the dead
   Imposed such laws as this upon mankind;
   Nor could I think that a decree of yours—
   A man—could override the laws of Heaven
   Unwritten and unchanging. Not of today
   Or yesterday is their authority;
   They are eternal; no man saw their birth.
   Was I to stand before the gods' tribunal
   For disobeying them, because I feared
   A man? I knew that I should have to die,
   Even without your edict; if I die
   Before my time, why then, I count it gain;
   To one who lives as I do, ringed about
   With countless miseries, why, death is welcome.
   For me to meet this doom is little grief;
   But when my mother's son lay dead, had I
   Neglected him and left him there unburied,

That would have caused me grief; this causes none.
And if you think it folly, then perhaps
I am accused of folly by the fool.

CHORUS. The daughter shows her father's temper—fierce,
Defiant; she will not yield to any storm.

CREON. But it is those that are most obstinate
Suffer the greatest fall; the hardest iron,
Most fiercely tempered in the fire, that is
Most often snapped and splintered. I have seen
The wildest horses tamed, and only by
The tiny bit. There is no room for pride
In one who is a slave! This girl already
Had fully learned the art of insolence
When she transgressed the laws that I established;
And now to that she adds a second outrage—
To boast of what she did, and laugh at us.
Now she would be the man, not I, if she
Defeated me and did not pay for it.
But though she be my niece, or closer still
Than all our family, she shall not escape
The direst penalty; no, nor shall her sister:
I judge her guilty too; she played her part
In burying the body. Summon her.
Just now I saw her raving and distracted
Within the palace. So it often is:
Those who plan crime in secret are betrayed
Despite themselves; they show it in their faces.
But this is worst of all: to be convicted
And then to glorify the crime as virtue.

[*Exeunt some* GUARDS.]

ANTIGONE. Would you do more than simply take and kill me?

CREON. I will have nothing more, and nothing less.

ANTIGONE. Then why delay? To me no word of yours
Is pleasing—God forbid it should be so!—
And everything in me displeases you.
Yet what could I have done to win renown
More glorious than giving burial
To my own brother? These men too would say it,
Except that terror cows them into silence.
A king has many a privilege: the greatest,
That he can say and do all that he will.

CREON. You are the only one in Thebes to think it!

ANTIGONE. These think as I do—but they dare not speak.

CREON. Have you no shame, not to conform with others?

ANTIGONE. To reverence a brother is no shame.

CREON. Was he no brother, he who died for Thebes?

ANTIGONE. One mother and one father gave them birth.

CREON. Honouring the traitor, you dishonour him.

ANTIGONE. He will not bear this testimony, in death.

CREON. Yes! if the traitor fare the same as he.

ANTIGONE. It was a brother, not a slave who died!

CREON. He died attacking Thebes; the other saved us.

ANTIGONE. Even so, the god of Death demands these rites.

CREON. The good demand more honour than the wicked.

ANTIGONE. Who knows? In death they may be reconciled.

CREON. Death does not make an enemy a friend!

ANTIGONE. Even so, I give both love, not share their hatred.

CREON. Down then to Hell! Love there, if love you must.
    While I am living, no woman shall have rule.

                [*Enter* GUARDS, *with* ISMENE.]

CHORUS. [*Chants*] See where Ismene leaves the palace-gate,
    In tears shed for her sister. On her brow
    A cloud of grief has blotted out her sun,
    And breaks in rain upon her comeliness.

CREON. You, lurking like a serpent in my house,
    Drinking my life-blood unawares; nor did
    I know that I was cherishing two fiends,
    Subverters of my throne; come, tell me this:
    Do you confess you shared this burial.
    Or will you swear you had no knowledge of it?

ISMENE. I did it too, if she allows my claim;
    I share the burden of this heavy charge.

ANTIGONE. No! Justice will not suffer that; for you
    Refused, and I gave you no part in it.

ISMENE. But in your stormy voyage I am glad
    To share the danger, travelling at your side.

ANTIGONE. Whose was the deed the god of Death knows well;
    I love not those who love in words alone.

ISMENE. My sister, do not scorn me, nor refuse
    That I may die with you, honouring the dead.

ANTIGONE. You shall not die with me, nor claim as yours
    What you rejected. My death will be enough.

ISMENE. What life is left to me if I lose you?

ANTIGONE. Ask Creon! It was Creon that you cared for.

ISMENE. O why taunt me, when it does not help you?

ANTIGONE. If I do taunt you, it is to my pain.

ISMENE. Can I not help you, even at this late hour?

ANTIGONE. Save your own life. I grudge not your escape.

ISMENE. Alas! Can I not join you in your fate?

ANTIGONE. You cannot: you chose life, and I chose death.

ISMENE. But not without the warning that I gave you!

ANTIGONE. Some thought *you* wise; the dead commended me.

ISMENE. But my offence has been as great as yours.

ANTIGONE. Be comforted; you live, but I have given
    My life already, in service of the dead.

CREON. Of these two girls, one has been driven frantic,
    The other has been frantic since her birth.

ISMENE. Not so, my lord; but when disaster comes
  The reason that one has can not stand firm.

CREON. Yours did not, when you chose to partner crime!

ISMENE. But what is life to me, without my sister?

CREON. Say not 'my sister': sister you have none.

Antigone hangs herself. Creon's son Haemon, who was engaged to her, kills himself. Haemon's devastated mother kills herself. For his hubris, Creon has witnessed the devastating collapse of his household.

A version of this story by Jean Anouilh was performed in Paris in 1944. Its juxtaposition of rejection of authority (by Antigone) and acceptance of it (by Creon) offered parallels with life under the German Occupation of France.

THE PLAGUE AT ATHENS

The History of the Peloponnesian War, Book II

Thucydides

Translated by Paul Woodruff, 1993

The Greek historian **Thucydides** (*c.* 460–400 BC) wrote a riveting account of the Peloponnesian War, which was fought between Athens and Sparta and their respective allies from 431 to 404 BC. He was also an eyewitness to the devastating plague that hit Athens in the second year of the conflict. The timing could hardly have been worse, for the inhabitants of the surrounding countryside of Attica had poured into the city to seek protection from the Spartans ('Lacedaemonians') behind the walls, meaning that the plague could spread at terrifying speed. It has been estimated that a third of the population perished from the disease, which modern historians have interpreted variously as typhus, bubonic plague, smallpox or ebola. Some readers view Thucydides' description of the wild behaviour that spread with the plague as needless moralising, but difficult times have often prompted the desperate to seize the day. The unfortunate Athenians went on to lose the Peloponnesian War.

In the very beginning of summer the Peloponnesians and their allies, with two-thirds of their forces as before, invaded Attica under the command of Archidamus, King of Lacedaemon. After they had settled in, they started wasting the country around them.

They had not been in Attica for many days when the plague first began among the Athenians. Although it was said to have broken out in many other places, particularly in Lemnos, no one could remember a disease that was so great or so destructive of human life breaking out anywhere before. Doctors, not knowing what to do, were unable to cope with it at first, and no other human knowledge was any use either. The doctors themselves died fastest, as they came to the sick most often. Prayers in temples, questions to oracles—all practices of that kind turned out to be useless also, and in the end people gave them up, defeated by the evil of the disease.

They say it first began in the part of Ethiopia that is above Egypt, and from there moved down to Egypt and Libya and into most of the Persian Empire. It hit

Athens suddenly, first infecting people in Piraeus [the port of Athens], with the result that they said the Peloponnesians must have poisoned the water tanks (they had no wells there at the time). Afterwards the plague moved inland to the city, where people died of it a good deal faster. Now anyone, doctor or layman, may say as much as he knows about where this probably came from, or what causes he thinks are powerful enough to bring about so great a change. For my part, I will only say what it was like: I will show what to look for, so that if the plague breaks out again, people may know in advance and not be ignorant. I will do this because I had the plague myself, and I myself saw others who suffered from it.

This year of all years was the most free of other diseases, as everyone agrees. If anyone was sick before, his disease turned into this one. If not, they were taken suddenly, without any apparent cause, and while they were in perfect health. First they had a high fever in the head, along with redness and inflammation of the eyes; inside, the throat and tongue were bleeding from the start, and the breath was weird and unsavory. After this came sneezing and hoarseness, and soon after came a pain in the chest, along with violent coughing. And once it was settled in the stomach, it caused vomiting, and brought up, with great torment, all the kinds of bile that the doctors have named. Most of the sick then had dry heaves, which brought on violent spasms which were over quickly for some people, but not till long after for others. Outwardly their bodies were not very hot to the touch, and they were not pale but reddish, livid, and flowered with little pimples and ulcers; inwardly they were burning so much with fever that they could not bear to have the lightest clothes or linen garments on them—nothing but mere nakedness, and they would have loved to throw themselves into cold water. Many of them who were not looked after did throw themselves into water tanks, driven mad by a thirst that was insatiable, although it was all the same whether they drank much or little. Sleeplessness and total inability to rest persisted through everything.

As long as the disease was at its height, the body did not waste away, but resisted the torment beyond all expectation, so that they either died after six or eight days from the burning inside them, or else, if they escaped that, then the disease dropped down into the belly, bringing severe ulceration and uncontrollable diarrhea; and many died later from the weakness this caused, since the disease passed through the whole body, starting with the head and moving down. And if anyone survived the worst of it, then the disease seized his extremities instead and left its mark there: it attacked the private parts, fingers, and toes. Many people escaped with the loss of these, while some lost their eyes as well. Some were struck by total amnesia as soon as they recovered, and did not know themselves or their friends.

This was a kind of disease that defied explanation, and the cruelty with which it attacked everyone was too severe for human nature. What showed more clearly than anything else that it was different from the diseases that are bred among us was this: all the birds and beasts that feed on human flesh either avoided the many bodies that lay unburied, or tasted them and perished. Evidence for this was the obvious absence of such birds: they were not to be seen anywhere, and certainly not doing that. But this effect was more clearly observed in the case of dogs, because they are more familiar with human beings.

Now this disease was generally as I have described it, if I may set aside the many variations that occurred as particular people had different experiences.

During that time no one was troubled by any of the usual sicknesses, but whatever sickness came ended in this. People died, some unattended, and some who had every sort of care. There was no medical treatment that could be prescribed as beneficial, for what helped one patient did harm to another. Physical strength turned out to be of no avail, for the plague carried the strong away with the weak, no matter what regimen they had followed.

But the greatest misery of all was the defection of mind in those who found themselves beginning to be sick, for as soon as they made up their minds it was hopeless, they gave up and made much less resistance to the disease. Another misery was their dying like sheep, as they became infected by caring for one another; and this brought about the greatest mortality. For if people held back from visiting each other through fear, then they died in neglect, and many houses were emptied because there was no one to provide care. If they did visit each other, they died, and these were mainly the ones who made some pretense to virtue. For these people would have been ashamed to spare themselves, and so they went into their friends' houses, especially in the end, when even family members, worn out by the lamentations of the dying, were overwhelmed by the greatness of the calamity. But those who had recovered had still more compassion, both on those who were dying and on those who were sick, because they knew the disease first-hand and were now out of danger, for this disease never attacked anyone a second time with fatal effect. And these people were thought to be blessedly happy, and through an excess of present joy they conceived a kind of light hope never to die of any other disease afterwards.

The present affliction was aggravated by the crowding of country folk into the city, which was especially unpleasant for those who came in. They had no houses, and because they were living in shelters that were stifling in the summer, their mortality was out of control. Dead and dying lay tumbling on top of one another in the streets, and at every water fountain lay men half-dead with thirst. The temples also, where they pitched their tents, were all full of the bodies of those who died in them, for people grew careless of holy and profane things alike, since they were oppressed by the violence of the calamity, and did not know what to do. And the laws they had followed before concerning funerals were all disrupted now, everyone burying their dead wherever they could. Many were forced, by a shortage of necessary materials after so many deaths, to take disgraceful measure for the funerals of their relatives: when one person had made a funeral pyre, another would get before him, throw on his dead, and give it fire; others would come to a pyre that was already burning, throw on the bodies they carried, and go their way again.

The great lawlessness that grew everywhere in the city began with this disease, for, as the rich suddenly died and men previously worth nothing took over their estates, people saw before their eyes such quick reversals that they dared to do freely things they would have hidden before—things they never would have admitted they did for pleasure. And so, because they thought their lives and their property were equally ephemeral, they justified seeking quick satisfaction in easy pleasures. As for doing what had been considered noble, no one was eager to take any further pains for this, because they thought it uncertain whether they should die or not before they achieved it. But the pleasure of the moment, and whatever contributed to that, were set up as standards of nobility and usefulness. No one was held back in awe, either by fear of the gods or by the laws of men: not by the gods, because men concluded it was all the same whether they worshipped or not, seeing that they all perished alike; and not by the laws, because no one expected to live till he was tried and punished for his crimes. But they thought that a far greater sentence hung over their heads now, and that before this fell they had a reason to get some pleasure in life.

Such was the misery that weighed on the Athenians. It was very oppressive, with men dying inside the city and the land outside being wasted. At such a terrible time it was natural for them to recall this verse, which the older people said had been sung long ago:

> A Dorian war will come.
> and with it a plague.

People had disagreed about the wording of the verse: some said it was not *plague (loimos)* but *famine (limos)* that was foretold by the ancients; but on this occasion, naturally, the victory went to those who said 'plague,' for people made their memory suit their current experience. Surely, I think if there is another Dorian war after this one, and if a famine comes with it, it will be natural for them to recite the verse in that version.

Those who knew of it also recalled an oracle that was given to the Lacedaemonians when they asked the god [Apollo] whether they should start this war or not. The oracle had said: *they would win if they fought with all their might, and that he himself would take their part.* Then they thought that their present misery was a fulfillment of the prophecy; the plague did begin immediately when the Peloponnesians invaded, and it had no appreciable effect in the Peloponnesus, but preyed mostly on Athens and after that in densely populated areas. So much for the plague.

THE MURDER OF ERATOSTHENES

On the Murder of Eratosthenes

Lysias

Translated by S. C. Todd, 2011

This is a gripping tale of murder embedded in a speech by **Lysias** (*c.* 445 BC–*c.* 380 BC), one of the great orators of ancient Athens. Euphiletus stands accused of killing Eratosthenes for having an affair with his wife. The defendant, the narrator of this piece, maintains that his act was justified by Athenian law, which he cites as permitting a man to kill with impunity an adulterer caught in the act with his wife. Did Euphiletus get away with the murder? Frustratingly we do not know. But it is worth noting that the murdered Eratosthenes was one of the Thirty Tyrants who subjected Athens to harsh rule after its defeat in the Peloponnesian War in 404 BC.

After I decided to get married, men of Athens, and brought my bride home, for a while my attitude was not to trouble her too much but not to let her do whatever she wanted either. I watched her as best I could and gave her the proper amount of attention. But from the moment my son was born, I began to have full confidence in her and placed everything in her hands, reckoning that this was the best relationship. In those early days, men of Athens, she was the best of women: a good housekeeper, thrifty, with a sharp eye on every detail. But my mother's death was the cause of all my troubles. For it was while attending her funeral that my wife was seen by this fellow and eventually corrupted by him: he kept an eye out for the slave girl who did the shopping, put forward proposals, and seduced her.

Now before continuing, gentlemen, I need to explain something. My house has two stories, and in the part with the women's rooms and the men's rooms, the upper floor is the same size as the floor below. When our baby was born, his mother nursed him. To avoid her risking an accident coming down the stairs whenever he needed washing, I took over the upstairs rooms, and the women moved downstairs. Eventually we became so used to this arrangement that my wife would often leave me to go down and sleep with the baby, so that she could nurse it and stop it crying. Things went on in this way for a long time, and I never had the slightest suspicion; indeed, I was so naive that I thought my wife was the most respectable woman in Athens.

Some time later, gentlemen, I returned unexpectedly from the country. After dinner, the baby began to cry and was restless. (He was being deliberately teased by the slave girl, to make him do this, because the man was inside the house: I later found out everything.) So I told my wife to go down and feed the baby, to stop it crying. At first she refused, as if glad to see me home after so long. When I became angry and ordered her to go, she said, "You just want to stay here and have a go at the slave girl. You had a grab at her once before when you were drunk." I laughed at this, and she got up and left. She closed the door behind her, pretending to make a joke out of it, and bolted it. I had no suspicions and thought no more of it, but gladly went to bed, since I had just returned from the country. Towards morning, she came and unlocked the door. I asked her why the doors had creaked during the night, and she claimed that the baby's lamp had gone out, so she had to get it relit at our neighbors'. I believed this account and said no more. But I noticed, gentlemen, that she had put on makeup, even though her brother had died less than a month earlier. Even so, I did not say anything about it but left the house without replying.

After this, gentlemen, there was an interval of some time, during which I remained completely unaware of my misfortunes. But then an old woman came up to me. She had been secretly sent, or so I later discovered, by a lady whom this fellow had seduced. This woman was angry and felt cheated, because he no longer visited her as before, so she watched until she found out why. The old woman kept an eye out and approached me near my house. "Euphiletus," she said, "please do not think that I am being a busybody by making contact with you. The man who is humiliating you and your wife is an enemy of ours as well. Get hold of your slave girl, the one who does the shopping and waits on you, and torture her: you will discover everything. It is," she continued, "Eratosthenes of the deme Oe who is doing this. He has seduced not only your wife but many others as well. He makes a hobby of it." She said this, gentlemen, and left. At once I became alarmed. Everything came back into my mind, and I was filled with suspicion. I remembered how I had been locked in my room, and how that night both the door of the house and the courtyard door had creaked (which had never happened before), and how I had noticed that my wife had used makeup. All these things flashed into my mind, and I was full of suspicion. I returned home, and told the slave girl to come shopping with me, but I took her to the house of one of my friends and told her that I had found out everything that was going on in my house. "So it is up to you," I said, "to choose the fate you prefer: either to be flogged and put out to work in the mill, and never have any rest from such sufferings; or else to admit the whole truth and suffer no punishment, but instead to be forgiven for your crimes. No lies now: I want the full truth." At first she denied it and told me to do whatever I pleased, because she knew nothing. But when I mentioned the name Eratosthenes to her and declared that this was the man who was visiting my wife, she was astonished, realizing that I knew everything. She immediately fell at my knees and made me promise she would suffer no harm. She admitted, first, how he had approached her after the funeral, and then how she had eventually acted as his messenger, and how my wife had in the end been won over, and the various ways he had entered the house, and how during the Thesmophoria,* when I was in the country, my wife had attended the shrine with his mother. She gave me a full and accurate account of everything else that had happened. When she had finished, I said, "Make sure that nobody at all hears about this; otherwise nothing in our agreement will be binding. I want you to show me them in the act. I don't want words; I want their actions to be clearly proved, if it is really true." She agreed to do this.

After this there was an interval of four or five days, as I shall bring clear evidence to show. But first, I want to tell you what happened on that last day. There is a man called Sostratus, who was a close friend of mine. I happened to meet him, at sunset, on his way back from the country. I knew that if he arrived at that time, he would find none of his friends at home, so I invited him to dine with me. We returned to my house, went upstairs, and had supper. After he had had a good meal, he left, and I went to bed. Eratosthenes entered the house, gentlemen, and the slave girl woke me at once to say he was inside. I told her to take care of the doors, and going downstairs, I went out silently. I called at the houses of various friends: some I discovered were out, and others were not even in town. I gathered as many as I could find at home and came back. We collected torches from the nearest shop and made our way in; the door was open, because it had been kept ready by the slave girl. We burst open the door of the bedroom, and those of us who were first to enter saw him still lying next to my wife. The others, who came later, saw him standing on the bed naked. I struck him, gentlemen, and knocked him down. I twisted his arms behind him and tied them, and asked why he had committed this outrage against my house by entering it. He admitted his guilt, and begged and entreated me not to kill him but to accept compensation. I replied, "It is not I who will kill you, but the law of the city. You have broken that law and have had less regard for it than for your own pleasure. You have preferred to commit this crime against my wife and my children rather than behaving responsibly and obeying the laws."

So it was, gentlemen, that this man met the fate which the laws prescribe for those who behave like that. He was not snatched from the street, nor had he taken refuge at the hearth, as my opponents claim. How could he have done so? It was inside the bedroom that he was struck, and he immediately fell down, and I tied his hands. There were so many men in the house that he could not have escaped, and he did not have a knife or a club or any other weapon with which to repel those coming at him. I am sure you realize, gentlemen, that men who commit crimes never admit that their enemies are telling the truth, but instead they themselves tell lies and use tricks to provoke their hearers to anger against the innocent.

So, first of all, please read out the law.

[LAW]

He did not dispute it, gentlemen. He admitted his guilt, he begged and pleaded not to be killed, and he was ready to pay money in compensation. But I did

* *On the Thesmophoria, a women's festival, see Story 23.*

not accept his proposal. I reckoned that the law of the city should have greater authority; and I exacted from him the penalty that you yourselves, believing it to be just, have established for people who behave like that.

Will my witnesses to these facts please come forward.

[WITNESSES]

Read me this law also, the one from the inscribed stone on the Areopagus.*

[LAW]

You hear, gentlemen, how the court of the Areopagus (to which the ancestral right of judging homicide cases belongs, as has been reaffirmed in our own days) has expressly decreed that a man is not to be convicted of homicide if he captures an adulterer in bed with his wife and exacts this penalty from him. Indeed, the lawgiver was so convinced that this is appropriate in the case of married women that he has established the same penalty in the case of concubines, who are less valuable. Clearly if he had had a more severe penalty available in the case of married women, he would have imposed it; but in fact he was unable to find a more powerful sanction than death to use in their case, so he decided the penalty should be the same as in the case of concubines.

Read me this law as well.

[LAW]

You hear, gentlemen: if anybody indecently assaults a free man or boy, he shall pay twice the damages; if he assaults a woman (in those categories where the death sentence is applicable), he shall be liable to the same penalty. Clearly therefore, gentlemen, the lawgiver believed that those who commit rape deserve a lighter penalty than those who seduce: he condemned seducers to death, but for rapists he laid down double damages. He believed that those who act by violence are hated by the people they have assaulted, whereas those who seduce corrupt the minds of their victims in such a way that they make other people's wives into members of their own families rather than of their husbands'. The victim's whole household becomes the adulterer's, and as for the children, it is unclear whose they are, the husband's or the seducer's. Because of this the lawgiver laid down the death penalty for them.

In my case, gentlemen, the laws have not only acquitted me of crime but have actually commanded me to exact this penalty. It is for you to decide whether the law is to be powerful or worthless. In my opinion, every city enacts its laws in order that when we are uncertain in a situation, we can go to them to see what to do, and in such cases the law commands the victims to exact this penalty. So I ask you now to reach the same verdict as the law does. If not, you will be giving adulterers such immunity that you will encourage burglars to call themselves adulterers too. They will realize that if they describe adultery as their object and

* The Areopagus (consisting of former Archons) was the most famous Athenian homicide court.

claim that they have entered somebody else's house for this purpose, nobody will dare touch them. Everyone will know that we must say good-bye to the laws on adultery and take notice only of your verdict—which is the sovereign authority over all the city's affairs.

THE POWER OF LOVE

Symposium

Plato

Translated by Percy Bysshe Shelley, 1818

In this philosophical dialogue by Socrates' most celebrated pupil, **Plato** (420s–340s BC), Socrates, Alcibiades, Aristophanes and a number of others are invited to a symposium or party at the house of Agathon. The guests eat, pour libations to the gods, and sing hymns. The conversation then turns to love. In this extract, the comedian Aristophanes (author of Story 23) playfully expounds his understanding of human sexuality. While Plato wrote a great many dialogues in the fourth century BC, this speech from his *Symposium* has to be one of the most entertaining. The Romantic poet Percy Bysshe Shelley, who turned his hand to a number of classical texts in his lifetime, brought out the liveliness of the original in this translation from 1818.

"You ought first to know the nature of man, and the adventures he has gone through; for his nature was anciently far different from that which it is at present. First, then, human beings were formerly not divided into two sexes, male and female; there was also a third, common to both the others, the name of which remains though the sex itself has disappeared. The androgynous sex, both in appearance and in name, was common both to male and female; its name alone remains, which labours under a reproach.

"At the period to which I refer, the form of every human being was round, the back and the sides being circularly joined, and each had four arms and as many legs; two faces fixed upon a round neck, exactly like each other; one head between the two faces; four ears, and everything else as from such proportions it is easy to conjecture. Man walked upright as now, in whatever direction he pleased; but when he wished to go fast he made use of all his eight limbs, and proceeded in a rapid motion by rolling circularly round,—like tumblers, who, with their legs in the air, tumble round and round. We account for the production of three sexes by supposing that, at the beginning, the male was produced from the sun, the female from the earth; and that sex which participated in both sexes, from the moon, by reason of the androgynous nature of the moon. They were round, and their mode of proceeding was round, from the similarity which must needs subsist between them and their parent.

"They were strong also, and had aspiring thoughts. They it was who levied war against the Gods; and what Homer writes concerning Ephialtus and Otus, that they sought to ascend heaven and dethrone the Gods, in reality relates to this primitive people. Jupiter and the other Gods debated what was to be done in this emergency. For neither could they prevail on themselves to destroy them, as they had the giants, with thunder, so that the race should be abolished; for in that case they would be deprived of the honours of the sacrifices which they were in the custom of receiving from them; nor could they permit a continuance of their insolence and impiety. Jupiter, with some difficulty having desired silence, at length spoke, 'I think,' said he, 'I have contrived a method by which we may, by rendering the human race more feeble, quell the insolence which they exercise, without proceeding to their utter destruction. I will cut each of them in half; and so they will at once be weaker and more useful on account of their numbers. They shall walk upright on two legs. If they show any more insolence, and will not keep quiet, I will cut them up in half again, so they shall go about hopping on one leg.'

"So saying, he cut human beings in half, as people cut eggs before they salt them, or as I have seen eggs cut with hairs. He ordered Apollo to take each one as he cut him, and turn his face and half his neck towards the operation, so that by contemplating it he might become more cautious and humble; and then, to cure him, Apollo turned the face found, and drawing the skin upon what we now call the belly, like a contracted pouch, and leaving one opening, that which is called the navel, tied it in the middle. He then smoothed many other wrinkles, and moulded the breast with much such an instrument as the leather-cutters use to smooth the skins upon the block. He left only a few wrinkles in the belly, near the navel, to serve as a record of its former adventure. Immediately after this division, as each desired to possess the other half of himself, these divided people threw their arms around and embraced each other, seeking to grow together; and from this resolution to do nothing without the other half, they died of hunger and weakness: when one half died and the other was left alive, that which was thus left sought the other and folded it to its bosom; whether that half were an entire woman (for we now call it a woman) or a man; and thus they perished. But Jupiter, pitying them, thought of another contrivance. In this manner is genera-tion now produced, by the union of male and female; so that from the embrace of a man and woman the race is propagated.

"From this period, mutual love has naturally existed between human beings; that reconciler and bond of union of their original nature, which seeks to make two one, and to heal the divided nature of man. Every one of us is thus the half of what may be properly termed a man, and like a [flatfish] cut in two, is the imperfect portion of an entire whole, perpetually necessitated to seek the half belonging to him.

"Such as I have described is ever an affectionate lover and a faithful friend, delighting in that which is in conformity with his own nature. Whatever, there-fore, any such as I have described are impetuously struck, through the sentiment of their former union, with love and desire and the want of community, they are unwilling to be divided even for a moment. These are they who devote their whole lives to each other, with a vain and inexpressible longing to obtain from each other something they know not what; for it is not merely the sensual delights of their intercourse for the sake of which they dedicate themselves to each other with such serious affection; but the soul of each manifestly thirsts for, from the other, something which there are no words to describe, and divines that which it seeks, and traces obscurely the footsteps of its obscure desire. If Vulcan should say to persons thus affected, 'My good people, what is it that you want with one another?' And if, while they were hesitating what to answer, he should proceed to ask, 'Do you not desire the closest union and singleness to exist between you, so that you may never be divided night or day? If so, I will melt you together, and make you grow into one, so that both in life and death ye may be undivided. Consider, is this what you desire? Will it content you if you become that which I propose?' We all know that no one would refuse such an offer, but would at once feel that this was what he had ever sought; and intimately to mix and melt and to be melted together with his beloved, so that one should be made out of two.

"The cause of this desire is, that according to our original nature, we were once entire. The desire and the pursuit of integrity and union is that which we all love. First, as I said, we were entire, but now we have been dwindled through our own weakness, as the Arcadians by the Lacedaemonians. There is reason to fear, if we are guilty of any additional impiety towards the Gods, that we may be cut in two again, and may go about like those figures painted on the columns, divided through the middle of our nostrils, as thin as lispae. On which account every man ought to be exhorted to pay due reverence to the Gods, that we may escape so severe a punishment, and obtain those things which Love, our general and commander, incites us to desire; against whom let none rebel by exciting the hatred of the Gods. For if we continue on good terms with them, we may discover and possess those lost and concealed objects of our love; a good-fortune which now befalls to few.

"I assert, then, that the happiness of all, both men and women, consists singly in the fulfilment of their love, and in that possession of its objects by which we are in some degree restored to our ancient nature. If this be the completion of felicity, that must necessarily approach nearest to it, in which we obtain the possession and society of those whose natures most intimately accord with our own. And if we would celebrate any God as the author of this benefit, we should justly celebrate Love with hymns of joy; who, in our present condition, brings good assistance in our necessity, and affords great hopes, if we persevere in piety towards the Gods, that he will restore us to our original state, and confer on us the complete happiness alone suited to our nature."

THE AGEING PROCESS

Republic

Plato

Translated by Benjamin Jowett, 1888

Socrates is the main protagonist in the majority of **Plato**'s thirty-odd dialogues. In the *Republic*, he encounters a group of men at the Piraeus, the port of Athens. They later reconvene at the house of Polemarchus, whose elderly father, Cephalus, Socrates engages in conversation. Let the sea of Greek names wash over you as you witness Socrates drawing out intelligent thought from his interlocutor as only he can. The pair talk about the pleasures and pains of growing old. Their words are an entrée to the discussion of justice and the ideal state for which this dialogue is famous. As well as translating Plato's dialogues, Benjamin Jowett – intellectual titan of Victorian Oxford where he was Regius Professor of Greek for thirty-eight years – also translated works by Aristotle and Thucydides.

Persons of the Dialogue

SOCRATES, who is the narrator.
GLAUCON.
ADEIMANTUS.
POLEMARCHUS.
CEPHALUS.
THRASYMACHUS.
CLEITOPHON.
And others who are mute auditors.

The scene is laid in the house of Cephalus at the Piraeus; and the whole dialogue is narrated by Socrates the day after it actually took place to Timaeus, Hermocrates, Critias, and a nameless person, who are introduced in the Timaeus.

I went down yesterday to the Piraeus with Glaucon the son of Ariston, that I might offer up my prayers to the goddess*; and also because I wanted to see in what manner they would celebrate the festival, which was a new thing. I was delighted with the procession of the inhabitants; but that of the Thracians

---

*   Bendis, the Thracian Artemis

was equally, if not more, beautiful. When we had finished our prayers and viewed the spectacle, we turned in the direction of the city; and at that instant Polemarchus the son of Cephalus chanced to catch sight of us from a distance as we were starting on our way home, and told his servant to run and bid us wait for him. The servant took hold of me by the cloak behind, and said: Polemarchus desires you to wait.

I turned round, and asked him where his master was.

There he is, said the youth, coming after you, if you will only wait.

Certainly we will, said Glaucon; and in a few minutes Polemarchus appeared, and with him Adeimantus, Glaucon's brother, Niceratus the son of Nicias, and several others who had been at the procession.

Polemarchus said to me: I perceive, Socrates, that you and your companion are already on your way to the city.

You are not far wrong, I said.

But do you see, he rejoined, how many we are?

Of course.

And are you stronger than all these? for if not, you will have to remain where you are.

May there not be the alternative, I said, that we may persuade you to let us go?

But can you persuade us, if we refuse to listen to you? he said.

Certainly not, replied Glaucon.

Then we are not going to listen; of that you may be assured.

Adeimantus added: Has no one told you of the torch-race on horseback in honour of the goddess which will take place in the evening?

With horses! I replied: That is a novelty. Will horse-men carry torches and pass them one to another during the race?

Yes, said Polemarchus, and not only so, but a festival will be celebrated at night, which you certainly ought to see. Let us rise soon after supper and see this festival; there will be a gathering of young men, and we will have a good talk. Stay then, and do not be perverse.

Glaucon said: I suppose, since you insist, that we must.

Very good, I replied.

Accordingly we went with Polemarchus to his house; and there we found his brothers Lysias and Euthydemus, and with them Thrasymachus the Chalcedonian, Charmantides the Paeanian, and Cleitophon the son of Aristonymus. There too was Cephalus the father of Polemarchus, whom I had not seen for a long time, and I thought him very much aged. He was seated on a cushioned chair, and had a garland on his head, for he had been sacrificing in the court; and there were some other chairs in the room arranged in a semicircle, upon which we sat down by him. He saluted me eagerly, and then he said:—

You don't come to see me, Socrates, as often as you ought: If I were still able to go and see you I would not ask you to come to me. But at my age I can hardly get to the city, and therefore you should come oftener to the Piraeus. For let me tell you, that the more the pleasures of the body fade away, the greater to me is the pleasure and charm of conversation. Do not then deny my request, but make our house your resort and keep company with these young men; we are old friends, and you will be quite at home with us.

I replied: There is nothing which for my part I like better, Cephalus, than conversing with aged men; for I regard them as travellers who have gone a journey which I too may have to go, and of whom I ought to enquire, whether the way is smooth and easy, or rugged and difficult. And this is a question which I should like to ask of you who have arrived at that time which the poets call the 'threshold of old age'—Is life harder towards the end, or what report do you give of it?

I will tell you, Socrates, he said, what my own feeling is. Men of my age flock together; we are birds of a feather, as the old proverb says; and at our meetings the tale of my acquaintance commonly is—I cannot eat, I cannot drink; the pleasures of youth and love are fled away: there was a good time once, but now that is gone, and life is no longer life.

Some complain of the slights which are put upon them by relations, and they will tell you sadly of how many evils their old age is the cause. But to me, Socrates, these complainers seem to blame that which is not really in fault. For if old age were the cause, I too being old, and every other old man, would have felt as they do. But this is not my own experience, nor that of others whom I have known. How well I remember the aged poet Sophocles, when in answer to the question, How does love suit with age, Sophocles,—are you still the man you were? Peace, he replied; most gladly have I escaped the thing of which you speak; I feel as if I had escaped from a mad and furious master. His words have often occurred to my mind since, and they seem as good to me now as at the time when he uttered them. For certainly old age has a great sense of calm and freedom; when the passions relax their hold, then, as Sophocles says, we are freed from the grasp not of one mad master only, but of many. The truth is, Socrates, that these regrets, and also the complaints about relations, are to be attributed to the same cause, which is not old age, but men's characters and tempers; for he who is of a calm and happy nature will hardly feel the pressure of age, but to him who is of an opposite disposition youth and age are equally a burden.

I listened in admiration, and wanting to draw him out, that he might go on— Yes, Cephalus, I said; but I rather suspect that people in general are not convinced by you when you speak thus; they think that old age sits lightly upon you, not because of your happy disposition, but because you are rich, and wealth is well known to be a great comforter.

You are right, he replied; they are not convinced: and there is something in what they say; not, however, so much as they imagine. I might answer them as Themistocles answered the Seriphian who was abusing him and saying that he was famous, not for his own merits but because he was an Athenian: 'If you had been a native of my country or I of yours, neither of us would have been famous.' And to those who are not rich and are impatient of old age, the same reply may be made; for to the good poor man old age cannot be a light burden, nor can a bad rich man ever have peace with himself.

May I ask, Cephalus, whether your fortune was for the most part inherited or acquired by you?

Acquired! Socrates; do you want to know how much I acquired? In the art of making money I have been midway between my father and grandfather: for my grandfather, whose name I bear, doubled and trebled the value of his patrimony, that which he inherited being much what I possess now; but my father Lysanias reduced the property below what it is at present: and I shall be satisfied if I leave to these my sons not less but a little more than I received.

That was why I asked you the question, I replied, because I see that you are indifferent about money, which is a characteristic rather of those who have inherited their fortunes than of those who have acquired them; the makers of fortunes have a second love of money as a creation of their own, resembling the affection of authors for their own poems, or of parents for their children, besides that natural love of it for the sake of use and profit which is common to them and all men. And hence they are very bad company, for they can talk about nothing but the praises of wealth.

That is true, he said.

Yes, that is very true, but may I ask another question?—What do you consider to be the greatest blessing which you have reaped from your wealth?

One, he said, of which I could not expect easily to convince others. For let me tell you, Socrates, that when a man thinks himself to be near death, fears and cares enter into his mind which he never had before: the tales of a world below and the punishment which is exacted there of deeds done here were once a laughing matter to him, but now he is tormented with the thought that they may be true: either from the weakness of age, or because he is now drawing nearer to that other place, he has a clearer view of these things; suspicions and alarms crowd thickly upon him, and he begins to reflect and consider what wrongs he has done to others. And when he finds that the sum of his transgressions is great he will many a time like a child start up in his sleep for fear, and he is filled with dark forebodings. But to him who is conscious of no sin, sweet hope, as Pindar charmingly says, is the kind nurse of his age:

‘Hope,’ he says, ‘cherishes the soul of him who lives in justice and holiness, and is the nurse of his age and the companion of his journey;—hope which is mightiest to sway the restless soul of man.’

How admirable are his words! And the great blessing of riches, I do not say to every man, but to a good man, is, that he has had no occasion to deceive or to defraud others, either intentionally or unintentionally; and when he departs to the world below he is not in any apprehension about offerings due to the gods or debts which he owes to men. Now to this peace of mind the possession of wealth greatly contributes; and therefore I say, that, setting one thing against another, of the many advantages which wealth has to give, to a man of sense this is in my opinion the greatest.

THREE TYPES

Characters

Theophrastus

Translated by James Diggle, 2004

Theophrastus (371 BC–*c*. 287 BC) was born on Lesbos and succeeded Aristotle as head of the Lyceum – the Peripatetic school of philosophy. His book of *Characters* consists of a series of pen portraits of human character types. Whilst capturing the realities of ancient Athens, Theophrastus' caricatures are truly timeless. Who hasn't encountered a Shabby Profiteer or Tactless Man? Here are three of his most dynamic and familiar personalities.

XXI: The Man of Petty Ambition

[Petty Ambition would seem to be a mean desire for prestige.]

The Man of Petty Ambition is the kind who, when he gets an invitation to dinner, is eager to sit next to the host. He takes his son to Delphi to have his hair cut. He goes to the trouble of acquiring an Aethiopian attendant. When he pays back a *mina* of silver he pays it back in new coin. He is apt to buy a little ladder for his domestic jackdaw and make a little bronze shield for it to carry when it hops onto the ladder. When he has sacrificed an ox he nails up the skull opposite the entrance to his house and fastens long ribbons around it, so that his visitors can see that he has sacrificed an ox. After parading with the cavalry he gives his slave the rest of his equipment to take home, then throws back his cloak and strolls through the marketplace in his spurs. On the death of his Maltese dog he builds a funeral monument and sets up a little slab with the inscription '** from Malta'. He dedicates a bronze finger in the sanctuary of Asclepius and does not let a day pass without polishing, garlanding and oiling it. And you can be sure that he will arrange with the executive committee of the Council that he should be the one to make the public report on the conduct of religious business, and will step forward wearing a smart white cloak, with a crown on his head, and say 'Men of Athens, my colleagues and I celebrated the Milk-Feast with sacrifices to the Mother of the Gods. The sacrifices were propitious. We beg you to accept your blessings.' After making this report he goes home and tells his wife that he had an extremely successful day.

XXX: The Shabby Profiteer

[Shabby profiteering is desire for shabby profit.]

The Shabby Profiteer is the kind who does not provide enough bread when he entertains. He borrows money from a visitor who is staying with him. When he is serving out helpings he says that it is right and proper that the server should be given a double helping and so he proceeds to give himself one. When he has wine for sale he sells it to a friend watered down. He takes his sons to the theatre only when there is free admission. When he goes abroad on public service he leaves his official travel allowance at home and borrows from the other delegates, loads his attendant with more baggage than he can carry and provides him with shorter rations than anyone else, and asks for his share of the presents and then sells them. When he is oiling himself in the baths he says to his slave 'The oil you bought is rancid' and he uses someone else's. If his slaves find a few coppers in the street he is liable to demand a portion of them, saying 'Fair shares for all'. He takes his cloak to the cleaner's and borrows one from an acquaintance and puts off returning it for several days until it is demanded back. [And the like.] He measures out the rations for the household in person, using a measuring jar set to the old Pheidonian standard, that has had its bottom dinted inwards, and rigorously levels off the top. ******************. And you can be sure that when he repays a debt of thirty minae he pays it back four drachmas short. When his sons do not attend school for the full month because of illness he deducts a proportion of the fees, and he does not send them for lessons during Anthesterion, to avoid the expense, because there are so many shows. When he collects his share of a slave's earnings he charges him for the cost of exchanging the copper coin; and when he gets an account from <   >. When he entertains members of his phratry he asks for food for his slaves from the communal meal, but he has an inventory made of the radish-halves left over from the table, so that the slaves waiting at the table won't get them. When he is abroad with acquaintances he uses their slaves and lets his own slave out for hire and doesn't put the proceeds towards the joint account. And, needless to say, when the dining club meets at his house he charges for the firewood, beans, vinegar, salt and lamp-oil that he is providing. When a friend is getting married or marrying off a daughter he leaves town some time before, so that he won't have to send a present. And he borrows from acquaintances the kinds of thing which nobody would demand back or be in a hurry to take back if offered.

XII: The Tactless Man

[Tactlessness is choosing a time which annoys the people one meets.]

The Tactless Man is the kind who comes for a discussion when you are busy. He serenades his girlfriend when she is feverish. He approaches a man who has just forfeited a security deposit and asks him to stand bail. He arrives to give evidence after a case is closed. As a guest at a wedding he delivers a tirade against the female sex. When you have just returned home after a long journey he invites you to go for a walk. He is liable to bring along a higher bidder when you have already completed a sale. When the audience has taken the point he gets up to explain it all over again. He will enthusiastically try to secure what you don't want but haven't the heart to refuse. When people are engaged in a sacrifice and inclining heavy expense he arrives with a request for payment of interest. He stands watching while a slave is being whipped and announces that a boy of his own once hanged himself after such a beating. When he assists at an arbitration he puts the parties at loggerheads, though they are both eager for a reconciliation. When he wants to dance he takes hold of a partner who is still sober.

THE MISANTHROPE

Dyskolos

Menander

Translated by Norma Miller, 1987

> **Menander** (*c.* 342/41 – *c.* 290 BC) was a Greek writer of comic plays. Most
> of his work has vanished but his *Dyskolos* or 'Misanthrope' is largely
> extant. Knemon, the misanthrope of this comedy, despises all company.
> When a wealthy man named Sostratos attempts to marry his daughter,
> he is none too pleased.

Characters

PAN, the god of country life
SOSTRATOS, a young man about town
CHAIREAS, his friend
PYRRHIAS, his servant
KNEMON, a cantankerous old farmer
A GIRL, his daughter
GORGIAS, his step-son
DAOS, Gorgias's servant
SIMICHE, Knemon's servant
KALLIPIDES, Sostratos's father
GETAS, his servant
SIKON, a cook

Sostratos's MOTHER and MYRRHINE, Knemon's estranged wife
also appear

ACT ONE

[SCENE: *a village in Attica, about fourteen miles from Athens. In the centre of
the stage is the shrine of Pan and the Nymphs, with statues at its entrance.
On the audience's left of this is Knemon's house, on the right that of
Gorgias. A statue of Apollo of the Ways stands by Knemon's door.*]

[*Enter* PAN *from shrine*]

PAN. [*Addresses audience*] Imagine, please, that the scene is set in Attica, in
fact at Phyle, and that the shrine I'm coming from is the one belonging

to that village (Phylaeans are able to farm this stony ground). It's a holy place, and a very famous one. This farm here on my right is where Knemon lives: he's a real hermit of a man, who snarls at everyone and hates company – 'company' isn't the word: he's getting on now, and he's never addressed a civil word to anyone in his life! He's never volunteered a polite greeting to anyone except myself (I'm the god Pan): and that's only because he lives beside me, and can't help passing my door. And I'm quite sure that, as soon as he does, he promptly regrets it.

Still, in spite of being such a hermit, he did get married, to a widow whose former husband had just died, leaving her with a small son. Well, he quarrelled with his wife, every day and most of the night too – a miserable life. A baby daughter was born, and that just made things worse. Finally, when things got so bad that there was no hope of change, and life was hard and bitter, his wife left him and went back to her son, the one from her former marriage. He owns this smallholding here, next door, and there he's now struggling to support his mother, himself and one loyal family servant. The boy's growing up now, and shows sense beyond his years: experience matures a man.

The old man lives alone with his daughter, and an old servant woman. He's always working, fetching his own wood and doing his own digging – and hating absolutely everyone, from his neighbours here and his wife, right down to the suburbs of Athens. The girl has turned out as you'd expect from her upbringing, innocent and good. She's careful in her service to the Nymphs who share my shrine, and so we think it proper to take some care of her, too. There's a young man. His father's well-off, farms a valuable property here. The son's fashionable and lives in town, but he came out hunting with a sporting friend, and happened to come here. I've cast a spell on him, and he's fallen madly in love.

There, that's the outline. Details you'll see in due course, if you like – and please do like. Ah! I think I see our lover coming with his friend; they're busily discussing this very topic.

[*Exit* PAN *into shrine. Enter* CHAIREAS *and* SOSTRATOS *right.*]

CHAIREAS. *What?* You saw a girl here, a girl from a respectable home, putting garlands on the Nymphs next door, and you fell in love at first sight, Sostratos?

SOSTRATOS. At first sight.

CHAIREAS. That was quick! Or was that your idea when you came out, to fall for a girl?

SOSTRATOS. You think it's funny. But I'm suffering, Chaireas.

CHAIREAS. I believe you.

SOSTRATOS. That's why I've brought you in on it. For I reckon you're a good friend, and a practical man, too.

CHAIREAS. In such matters, Sostratos, my line is this. A friend asks me for help – he's in love with a call-girl. I go straight into action, grab her, carry her off, get drunk, burn the door down, am deaf to all reason. Before even asking her name, the thing to do is to get her. Delay increases passion dangerously, but quick action produces quick relief.

But if a friend is talking about marriage and a 'nice' girl, then I take a different line. I check on family, finance and character. For now I'm leaving my friend a permanent record of my professional efficiency.

SOSTRATOS. Great. [*Aside*] But not at all what I want.

CHAIREAS. And now we must hear all about the problem.

SOSTRATOS. As soon as it was light, I sent Pyrrhias my huntsman out.

CHAIREAS. What for?

SOSTRATOS. To speak to the girl's father, or whoever is head of the family.

CHAIREAS. Heavens, you can't mean it!

SOSTRATOS. Yes, it was a mistake. It's not really done to leave a job like that to a servant. But when you're in love, it's not too easy to remember propriety. He's been away for ages, too, I can't think what's keeping him. My instructions were to report straight back home to me, when he'd found how things stood out there.

[*Enter* PYRRHIAS, *running as if pursued.*]

PYRRHIAS. Out of the way, look out, everyone scatter! There's a maniac after me, a real maniac.

SOSTRATOS. What on earth, boy—?

PYRRHIAS. Run!

SOSTRATOS. What *is* it?

PYRRHIAS. He's pelting me with lumps of earth, and stones. Oh, it's terrible.

SOSTRATOS. Pelting you? Where the devil are you going?

PYRRHIAS. [*Stopping and looking round*] He's not after me any more, perhaps?

SOSTRATOS. He certainly isn't.

PYRRHIAS. Oh, I thought he was.

SOSTRATOS. What on earth are you talking about?

PYRRHIAS. Let's get out of here, please.

SOSTRATOS. Where to?

PYRRHIAS. Away from this door here, as far as possible. He's a real son of pain, a man possessed, a lunatic, living here in this house, the man you sent me to see – oh, it's terrible! I've banged my toes and pretty well broken the lot.

SOSTRATOS. And your errand?

PYRRHIAS. What? He beat me up! This way [*moving towards exit, right*].

SOSTRATOS. This chap's off his head.

PYRRHIAS. It's true, sir, I swear it, on my life. For goodness' sake, keep your eyes open. I can hardly talk, I'm so out of breath.
　　Well, I knocked at the house door, and asked to see the owner. A miserable old crone answered the door, and from the very spot where I stand speaking to you now, she pointed him out. He was trailing around on that hill there, collecting wild pears – or a real load of trouble for his back.

CHAIREAS. He's in a proper tizz. [*To* PYRRHIAS] So, my friend...?

PYRRHIAS. Well, I stepped on to his land and made my way towards him. I was still quite a way off, but I wanted to show some courtesy and tact, so I called to him and said, 'I've come to see you, sir, on a business matter. I want to talk to you about something that's to your advantage.' But 'You horrible heathen,' he promptly replied, 'trespassing on *my* land! What's the idea?' And he picks up a lump of earth and lets fly with it, right in my face.

CHAIREAS. The hell he did.

PYRRHIAS. And while I had my eyes shut, muttering 'Well, God damn you', he picks up a stick and sets about me, saying 'Business is it – what business is there between you and me? Don't you know where the public highway is?' And he was shouting at the top of his voice.

CHAIREAS. From what you say, the farmer's a raving lunatic.

PYRRHIAS. To finish my story: I took to my heels, and he ran after me for the better part of two miles, round the hill first, then down here to this wood. And he was slinging clods and stones at me, even his pears when he'd nothing else left. He's a proper violent piece of work, a real old heathen. For goodness' sake, move off!

SOSTRATOS. Chicken!

PYRRHIAS. You don't realize the danger. He'll eat us alive.

CHAIREAS. [*Edging away*] He seems to be a bit upset at the moment. Put off your visit to him, Sostratos, that's my advice. I assure you that in any sort of business, finding the psychological moment is the secret of success.

PYRRHIAS. Yes, do show some sense.

CHAIREAS. A poor farmer's always a bit touchy – not just this one, but nearly all of them. Tomorrow morning early. I'll go and see him on my own, now that I know where he lives. For the moment, you go home and stay there. It'll be all right. [*Exit* CHAIREAS, *hurriedly, right.*]

PYRRHIAS. Yes, let's do that.

SOSTRATOS. He was delighted to find an excuse. It was quite clear from the start that he didn't want to come with me, and that he didn't approve at all of my notion of marriage. [*To* PYRRHIAS] But as for you, you devil, God rot you entirely, you sinner.

PYRRHIAS. Why, what have *I* done, sir?

SOSTRATOS. Some damage to property, obviously.

PYRRHIAS. I swear I never touched a thing.

SOSTRATOS. And a man beat you although you were doing no wrong?

PYRRHIAS. Yes, and [*looking to the left*] here he comes. [*Calling to* KNEMON] I'm just off, sir. [*To* SOSTRATOS] You talk to him. [*Exit* PYRRHIAS, *right.*]

SOSTRATOS. Oh, I couldn't. I never convince anyone when I talk. [*Looks to left*] How can one describe a man like this? He doesn't look at all amiable to me, by God he doesn't. And he means business. I'll just move a bit away from the door: that's better. He's actually yelling at the top of his voice, though he's all on his own. I don't think he's right in the head. To tell the truth, I'm afraid of him, I really am.

[*Enter* KNEMON, *left.*]

KNEMON. Well, wasn't Perseus the lucky one, twice over, too. First, he could fly, so he never had to meet any of those who walk the earth: and then he had this marvellous device with which he used to turn anyone who annoyed him into stone. I wish I had it now [*looking at audience*]. There'd be no shortage of stone statues all round here.

Life is becoming intolerable, by God it is. People are actually walking on to my land now, and *talking* to me. [*Ironically*] Of course, I'm used to hanging about on the public highway – sure I am! When I don't even work this part of my land any longer, I've abandoned it because of the traffic. But now they're following me up to the tops, hordes of them. Heavens, here's another one, standing right beside the door.

SOSTRATOS. [*Aside*] I wonder if he'll hit me?

KNEMON. Privacy – you can't find it anywhere, not even if you want to hang yourself.

SOSTRATOS. [*Addressing him*] Am I offending you, sir? I'm waiting here for someone, I arranged to meet him.

KNEMON. What did I tell you? Do you and your friends think this is a public walk-way? or Piccadilly Circus? Sure, make a date to meet at my door, if you want to see someone. Feel free, put up a bench if you want, build yourselves a club-house. What I suffer! Sheer impertinence, that's the whole trouble, in my opinion. [*Exit* KNEMON *into his house.*]

Sostratos befriends Gorgias, the misanthrope's stepson, who suggests that he prove his diligence by coming to work the fields. The misanthrope then falls down a well.

[*Enter* SOSTRATOS, *from* KNEMON'*s house.*]

SOSTRATOS. [*Addressing audience*] My friends, by all the gods of heaven I swear, I have never in my whole life seen a man so conveniently half-drowned. That episode was a delight! As soon as we got there, Gorgias jumped straight down into the well, and the girl and I did nothing in particular up top. Well, what could we do? Except that she was tearing her hair, crying and pounding away at her breast, and I was standing there like a nanny – I really was, and a fine fool I looked – pleading with her to stop it, worshipping at her shrine and feasting my eyes on a perfect picture. For the victim down below I cared less than nothing, except for trying all the time to haul him up – that did inconvenience me a bit! And I tell you, I very nearly did for him. For as I gazed into the girl's eyes, I let the rope go, two or three times. But

Gorgias was a veritable Atlas: he kept a grip on him and eventually, with considerable difficulty, got him up.

When he was safely out, I came out, and here I am. I couldn't control myself any longer – I very nearly went up to the girl and kissed her. That's how madly in love I am. I'm preparing the ground – but the door's opening. God in heaven, look at that!

[KNEMON *is wheeled out on a couch,* GORGIAS *and the girl with him.*]

GORGIAS. Can I do anything for you, sir? You only have to ask.

KNEMON. Oh, I'm in a very bad way.

GORGIAS. Cheer up!

KNEMON. Don't worry, Knemon will never trouble any of you again, ever.

GORGIAS. Look, this is the kind of thing that happens when you live like a hermit. You came very close to death just now. A man of your age should end his days with someone to look after him.

KNEMON. I know I'm in a bad way, Gorgias. Ask your mother to come, tell her it's urgent. We only learn from bitter experience, it seems. Little daughter, please help me to sit up.

SOSTRATOS. [*Viewing process*] Lucky fellow!

KNEMON. [*To* SOSTRATOS] Why are you hanging about there, you miserable man?

[*Several lines are missing here, but it is clear that Gorgias has fetched Myrrhine, and that Knemon has begun his great speech.*]

KNEMON. ... and not one of you could change my views on that, make up your minds to it. One mistake I did perhaps make, in thinking that I could be completely self-sufficient, and would never need anyone's assistance. Now that I've seen how sudden and unexpected death can be, I realize I was stupid to take that line. You always need to have – and to have handy – someone to help you. When I saw how people lived, calculating everything for profit, I swear I grew cynical, and I never even imagined that any man would ever do a disinterested kindness to another.

I was wrong. By his noble efforts Gorgias, all by himself, has managed to demonstrate that. I never let him come near my door, never did him the slightest service, never said 'good morning' or gave him a kind word. And yet he's saved my life. Another man might (with some justification) have said 'You don't let me come near you; I'm keeping well away. You've never done anything for my family: I'm doing nothing for you now.' [*To* GORGIAS, *who is looking embarrassed*] What's the matter, boy? Whether I die now (which seems only too likely, I'm not at all well), or whether I live, I'm adopting you as my son, and anything I have, consider it all your own. My daughter here I entrust to your care. Find her a husband. Even if I make a complete recovery, I won't be able to do that, for I'll never find anyone I approve of. If I live, leave me to live my own life, but take over and manage everything else.

You've got some sense, thank God, and you're your sister's natural protector. Divide my property, give half for her dowry, and use the other half to provide for her mother and myself. [*To his daughter*] Lay me down again, my dear. I don't think a man should ever say more than is strictly necessary, so I'll add only this, my child: I want to tell you a little about myself and my ways. If everyone was like me, there'd be no law-suits or dragging one another off to gaol, and no wars: everyone would be satisfied with a moderate competence. But you may like things better as they are. Then live that way. The cantankerous and bad-tempered old man won't stop you.

GORGIAS. I accept all that. But, with your assistance, we must find a husband for the girl without delay, if you agree.

KNEMON. Look, I've told you my intentions. Leave me alone, for goodness' sake.

GORGIAS. Someone wants a word with you –

KNEMON. For God's sake, NO!

GORGIAS. ... to ask for your daughter's hand in marriage.

KNEMON. I've no further concern with that.

GORGIAS. But it's the man who helped to rescue you.

KNEMON. Who?

GORGIAS. He's here. Come on, Sostratos.

KNEMON. He's certainly been in the sun. A farmer, is he?

GORGIAS. Yes, and a good one, Father. He's not soft, not the kind that strolls idly round all day.

[*In two badly damaged lines, Knemon probably gives his consent to the marriage.*]

KNEMON. Wheel me in. You see to him. And look after your sister.

[He is wheeled into his house.]

GORGIAS. You'd better consult your family about this, Sostratos.

SOSTRATOS. My father will make no difficulties.

GORGIAS. [*Formally*] Then I betroth her to you, Sostratos, giving her to you in the sight of heaven, as is right and proper. You've been frank and straightforward in approaching the business, without any deceit in your courtship. And you were ready to do anything to win the girl. You've lived soft, but you took a mattock and dug the land, you were willing to *work*. A man really proves his true worth when, although he's well-off, he's ready to treat a poor man as his equal. A man like that will bear any change of fortune with a good grace. You've given adequate proof of your character. Just stay that way!

THE CONTEST OF TWO MOUNTAINS

Fragmentary Poems

Corinna

Translated by I. M. Plant, 2004

This rare fragment comes from a poem by **Corinna**, a female poet from central Greece, and describes two mountains, Helicon and Cithaeron, engaging in a song contest. The mountains have just sung their songs, one of which described Rhea hiding her son Zeus away in a cave so that his father Kronos would not swallow him as he did his other children. It is now time for the gods to decide which mountain is the winner. Historically, Corinna was believed to have been a near contemporary of a sixth–fifth-century BC male poet named Pindar, and this poem a sort of allegory of the rivalry between them, but many scholars now believe that she lived hundreds of years later, in the third century BC.

The Contest of Helicon and Cithaeron

At once the Muses told the blessed gods
to cast their secret votes
in the golden-glowing urns
and together they all rose up.

Cithaeron took the majority
and at once Hermes shouted out and proclaimed
that he had taken the victory he so desired,
and the blessed gods crowned him
with a victor's garland of fir,
and his mind was full of joy.

But Helicon was seized
by bitter pains and
ripped out a shinning rock
and the mountain shook. In pain
he cried and from above he smashed it down
into ten thousand pieces of stone.

HERCULES AND THE TWELVE LABOURS

Library of History, Book IV

Diodorus Siculus

Translated by G. Booth, 1814

> Hercules, the son of Zeus and a mortal named Alcmene, married Megara, the daughter of King Creon of Thebes. When a neighbouring king named Eurystheus grew envious of Hercules' authority, he challenged him to complete Twelve Labours, much to the pleasure of Zeus' wife Hera (Juno). Although Hercules was reluctant, an oracle confirmed that the gods desired him to do as Eurystheus bade. They would reward him with immortality if he succeeded in the quest. **Diodorus Siculus**, a Greek historian of the first century BC from Sicily, describes the fiendish Labours in full.

Perseus (they say) was the son of Jupiter by Danaë, the daughter of Acrisius, and that Perseus begat Electryon of Andromeda, the daughter of Cepheus, and that Electryon begat Alcmena of Eurydice the daughter of Pelops, and that Jupiter (deceiving Alcmena) lay with her, and begat Hercules: so that by this genealogy Hercules descended from the chiefest of the gods, both immediately by his mother, and more remotely by his great grandfather Perseus. His virtue and valour were not only evident from his acts, but might be concluded and foreseen by what happened before he was born: for when Jupiter lay with Alcmena, he lengthened the night threefold, so that, spending so much time in procreating this child was a sign how extraordinary strong he was likely to be. They say that Jupiter lay not with her out of any amorous pang of love, as with other women, but merely for procreation sake: and therefore, willing that his embraces at this time should be lawful, he forbore all violence; and knowing that the woman's chastity was such, that no arguments would prevail with her, he deceived her by taking upon him the shape of Amphitryon.

And now the time of her delivery drew nigh, when Jupiter, full of thoughts concerning the birth of Hercules, in the presence of all the gods declared, that he would make him king of the Persians, who was to be born that day. Whereupon Juno, enraged with jealousy, with the assistance of Ilithyia* her daughter, gave

---

* Ilithyia, a goddess, assistant to those in travail.

a check to the delivery of Alcmena, and brought forth Eurystheus before his full time. But though Jupiter was thus outwitted by Juno, yet, that he might perform his promise, he took care to preserve the honour and reputation of Hercules; and therefore it is reported, that he prevailed with Juno to consent, that Eurystheus being made king according to his promise, Hercules, (who should be subject to him), performing twelve labours, (such as Eurystheus should impose upon him), should be taken into the society of the immortal gods.

Alcmena being delivered (out of fear of Juno's jealousy) exposed the child in a place which is now, from him, called Hercules's Field. About which time Minerva, together with Juno, walking abroad, found the infant, and, much admiring his beauty, Minerva persuaded Juno to give it suck: the child drawing the breast with more violence than at his age was usual, Juno, not able to endure the pain, cast away the infant, whom Minerva took up, and brought home to his mother, to be nursed by her. The accident here seems very strange and remarkable: for the mother, who owed a natural affection to her own child, exposed him to destruction; but she who hated him, as a step-mother, (unknowingly) preserved her natural enemy.

Afterwards Juno sent two serpents to devour the child: but he took them with both his hands by their throats, and strangled them. Upon which account the Argives (coming to understand what was done) called him Hercules*, because Juno was the occasion of his glory and fame, for he was before called Alcides. Others are named by their parents, but he gained his name by his valour.

In after times it happened that Amphitryon, being banished from Tyrinthe, settled himself in Thebes; here Hercules was educated, here he was instructed and greatly improved in all laudable exercises, insomuch that he excelled all others in strength of body, and also in the excellent endowments of his mind.

Being now grown up to man's estate, he first freed Thebes from tyrannical slavery, and thereby made a grateful return to the country where he was bred. The Thebans at that time were under the tyranny of Erginus, king of the Minyans†, who every year exacted tribute from them, not without scorn and contempt. Hercules, therefore, not at all discouraged with the greatness of the bondage they laboured under, attempted a glorious piece of service. For when those who were sent from the Minyae to collect the tribute carried it insolently towards the people, he cut off their ears, and cast them out of the city; whereupon Erginus demanded the delivery up of the malefactor, and Creon, the prince of Thebes, (dreading the potency of Erginus) resolved to deliver him up; but Hercules stirred up the young men of the city to arm themselves, in order to recover the liberty of their country, and to that end took away all the arms that were in the temples, formerly dedicated to the gods by their ancestors, of the spoils of their enemies: for none of the citizens had any arms of their own, by reason the Minyans had disarmed the city; so that the Thebans had not the least thought of a revolt.

Intelligence being brought that Erginus with an army approached the city, Hercules set upon him in a strait passage (where a multitude was of little use)

---

* Hercules signifies, the glory of Juno, who is called in Greek, Hera.
† Or Orchemonians; a people of Thessaly.

and killed Erginus, and cut off almost his whole army. He fell likewise suddenly upon the city of the Orchomenians, entering unexpectedly, and burnt the palace of the Minyae, and razed the city to the ground.

The fame of this notable exploit was presently noised over all Greece, while such a sudden and unexpected achievement was the subject of every man's admiration, and Creon the king (wonderfully taken with the valour of the young man) gave him his daughter Megaera to wife, and committed to him the care and charge of the city, as if he had been his own son.

But Eurystheus, king of Argos (jealous of Hercules's growing greatness, sent for him to perform the labours he was to impose upon him, which he refusing, Jupiter commanded him to obey king Eurystheus; whereupon Hercules went to Delphos, and inquired of the oracle concerning this matter, who answered him—That it was the pleasure of the gods, that he should perform twelve labours at the command of Eurystheus, and that when he had finished them, he should receive the reward of immortality. Hereupon Hercules became exceeding sad and melancholy; for he judged it very much below him to be at the beck of his inferior, and to disobey his father Jupiter a second time he concluded was both unprofitable and impossible. While he was in this perplexity, Juno struck him with madness; being therefore, through the discomfiture of his mind, become distracted, and by the growth of his distemper altogether a madman, he designed to murder Iolaus, who saving himself by flight, he fell upon his own children by Megaera, who were next in his way, and struck them through with his darts, as if they had been his enemies.

As soon as he came again to himself, and understood his error, he almost sunk under the weight of his misery, (being pitied by every body), and shut himself up in his own house a long time from the converse and society of men.

At length, time moderating his grief, resolving to undergo all the difficulties that were enjoined him, he went to Eurystheus, who in the first place commanded him to kill the lion in the forest of Nemaea*, which was of a monstrous bigness, not to be pierced or wounded by sword, spear, or stones, and therefore not to be dealt with but by mere force and strength of hand. His walks were commonly between Mycenae and Nemaea, near the mountain (from what happened to it) called Tretos†. For at the foot of this hill there was a den, in which this monster used to lurk. Hercules here meeting with him, laid hold of him, whereupon the beast beginning to fly to his den, he resolutely pursued him, (having before stopped up one of the mouths of the den), and so both closed, where he got the lion by the throat, and strangled him with his arms. Then he clothed himself with his skin, (which was big enough to cover his whole body, and ever after wore it as a defence in all conflicts.

His second task was to kill the hydra of Lerna. This monster had a hundred necks rising out of one body, and upon every neck a serpentine head, and when one of these was cut off, two others grew up in its stead; and therefore this monster was accounted invincible, and not without good reason, for, from the part that was lost, arose a double assistance in its room. Against this difficulty he

---

* This forest was in Achaia.
† Tretos, bored through.

invented this stratagem; he commanded Iolaus to sear the part that was cut off with a firebrand, that thereby the blood might be stopped, by which means the beast was killed, and he dipped the points of his darts in the monster's gall, that wherever they struck, the wound might be incurable.

The third command was, that he should bring the Erymanthean boar (which roved about in the plains of Arcadia) to him alive. This seemed to be a most difficult task: for he that fought with this beast ought to be so subtle as diligently to watch the exact time and fittest opportunity in the management of the conflict; for if he should let him go while he was in his full strength, the champion was in danger to be rent in pieces with his tushes; and if he wounded him too sore, and so killed him, his labour was lost, and his victory imperfect. However, he so prudently managed the combat, that he brought the boar alive to Eurystheus, who was so terrified to see him come hurrying with the boar upon his shoulders, that he hid himself in a brazen hogshead.

In the mean time Hercules subdued the centaurs, upon this occasion: there was one Pholus among the centaurs, from whom the neighbouring mountain was called Pholoe; this same having entertained Hercules as his guest, took up an hogshead of wine that had for a long time been buried in the earth: for it is reported, that this wine was antiently deposited in the hands of a certain centaur by Bacchus, who commanded that it should be broached at that very time when Hercules came thither; who now happening to be there, the fourth age after, Pholus, remembering Bacchus's command, opened the hogshead; whereupon, the wine being old, and exceeding strong, the flavour of it reached to the neighbouring centaurs, and struck them all with a fit of fury and madness; whereupon they all came in troops, and in a terrible tumult assaulted Pholus's house, to carry away the prey, insomuch that Pholus, in a great fright, hid himself.

But Hercules unexpectedly set upon the aggressors; for he was to fight with those who from the mother partook of the nature of the gods, were as swift as horses, as strong as double-bodied beasts, and were endued with the understanding and prudence of men.

Some of these centaurs assailed him with fir-trees plucked up by the roots, others with huge and massy stones, some with lighted firebrands, and others with axes, with whom he undauntedly entered the list, and fought with that bravery as was agreeable to the glory of his former actions.

Their mother Nephele* assisted them by a violent storm of rain, which was no prejudice to them that were four-footed, but he, that had but two, had by this means a troublesome and slippery standing: however Hercules, with wonderful valour, overcame them that had so many and great advantages above him, killing most of them, and putting the rest to flight. Of those that were slain, the most remarkable were Daphnis, Argeus, Amphion, Hippotion, Oreus, Isoples, Melanchetes, Thereus, Dupo, and Phrixus: and every one of those that fled came afterwards to condign punishment; for Homadus (because he ravished, in Arcadia, Atalcyona, the sister of Eurystheus) was slain by Hercules, for which his generosity was greatly admired: for, though he hated his enemy upon his own private account, yet he judged it a commendable piece of humanity to have

* A cloud.

compassion on a woman in her afflicted condition, upon the account of her dishonour and disgrace.

Somewhat remarkable likewise happened to Pholus, Hercules's friend: for, burying the centaurs that were killed, (upon the account of his kindred and relation to them) plucking a dart out of one of them, he chanced with the point mortally to wound himself, of which he died, whom Hercules with great pomp and state buried at the foot of the mount, which fell out to be far more glorious than the most stately monument; for the mountain being called Pholoe, preserves the memory of him buried there, not by characters and inscriptions, but by similitude of name. In the same manner he killed Chiron* (eminent for his art in physic) by chance, with the throwing of a dart. But this that has been said of the centaurs shall suffice.

Afterwards Hercules received a further command, that he should take the swift hart that had golden horns, and bring him to the king. This he performed more by art and subtlety, than strength of body: for some say he took her in a net, others by tracing her to the place where she rested, and there laying hold of her when she was asleep; but others say that he ran her down, and so gained her by swiftness of foot. However it were, it is certain he performed this labour not by force or any hazard, but by art and skill.

Being next commanded to drive away the birds that were about the Stymphalian lake, by art and contrivance he easily performed this: for there were an innumerable number of birds in those places, which destroyed and ate up all the fruits in the neighbourhood, and they were so numerous, that no force could prevail to get rid of them. Being, therefore, there was need of art and contrivance in this matter, he invented a brazen pan, and, by the mighty sound it made, by striking upon it, frighted the birds, and by the continual noise drove them at length quite away, so that the lake was never infested with them afterwards.

This labour being now at an end, Eurystheus, in contempt of him, commanded him, without any assistant, to cleanse Augias's stable, in which were vast heaps of muck and dirt, which had been gathering together for many years. Hercules, therefore, to avoid the ignominy of this contempt cast upon him, scorned to carry out the muck and dung upon his shoulders, but in one day's time, without any disgrace to himself, cleansed the stable, by turning the course of the river Peneus through it; in which thing the ingenuity of Hercules is admirable, who so executed the proud command of his domineering master as to avoid every thing that was base and unbecoming the glory of his immortal honour.

Next was imposed upon him the bringing the bull out of Crete, with which (they say) Pasiphae fell in love. To this end, therefore, he sailed into the island, and, by the assistance of king Minos, transported the beast (for which he had made so long a voyage) into Peloponnesus.

Having performed this task, he instituted the Olympic games, and for that purpose chose out a place he judged most convenient for the reception of such a pompous assembly, which were the fields all along the banks of the river Alpheus. Here he ordered the solemnity of these games to the honour of his father Jupiter, and appointed to the victors a crown for a reward, minding the general good

* Another centaur.

and benefit of mankind, without taking any advantage to himself. In every exercise he was victor, without any opposition; for, by reason of his remarkable strength and valour, none durst contend with him, although the contests were of a contrary and different nature one from another: for it is a hard matter even for a mighty champion in combat always to win the prize in a course, and as difficult for those that are usually victors in small contentions to prevail against them that are eminent in greater contests. Hercules, therefore, prevailed in all these games, carrying away the prize from the chiefest among them.

And here we are not to omit giving an account of the rewards given to him by the gods for his virtue; for, when he retired himself from wars, and betook himself to his ease and quietness, and to follow sports, panegyrics, and festivals, every one of the gods presented him with their several gifts.

Minerva gave him an embroidered hood, Vulcan a club and a breast-plate; and between these two was a contest who should excel in their several arts, whilst the one wrought and bestowed what was for pleasure and ornament in time of peace, and the other what was for defence in time of war. Neptune presented him with horses. Mercury with a sword, Apollo a bow, and taught him the art of archery. And Ceres, to expiate the slaughter of the centaurs, instituted in honour of Hercules some small mysteries. But concerning the birth of this god, this is remarkable; for the first woman upon earth that Jupiter lay with was Niobe, the daughter of Pharoneus, and the last was Alcmena, who was in the sixteenth age after Niobe, as the mythologists say. From the time of her ancestors, he began to beget men, and at length ended in this Alcmena, and would never after have any thing to do with any mortal, or beget any issue, never expecting to beget a more excellent offspring.

Afterwards, when the giants fought with the immortal gods at Pallene, Hercules aided the gods, and, after a great slaughter made by him of those sons of the earth, he became greatly renowned. For Jupiter called those only gods of Olympus who assisted him in the war, by this title of honour to distinguish the courageous from the coward; which surname he gave to Bacchus and Hercules, though their mothers were mortals, not only because they were the offspring of Jove, but likewise for that they were like him in virtuous qualifications, doing good generally to all mankind.

But Prometheus, because he stole fire from heaven, and handed it to men, was clapped in chains by Jupiter, who caused an eagle to seize and feed continually upon his liver; but Hercules, seeing that he suffered so much for his kindness to mankind, shot the bird with an arrow, and then, having pacified Jove, freed this common benefactor from all further trouble.

Afterwards he was enjoined to bring away Diomedes king of Thrace's mares, which were kept in stalls of brass, and (by reason of their strength and fierceness) tied up in iron chains. Their provender was not from the product of the earth, but they were fed with the flesh of miserable strangers that came thither, cut in small pieces for that purpose. Hercules, to gain possession of them, laid their own master Diomedes before them, who, satiating their hunger by his flesh who had wickedly taught them to feed upon flesh, thereby became tame and manageable. Eurystheus, when they were brought to him, dedicated them to

Juno, and their breed continued to the time of Alexander the Great. When he had performed this labour, he sailed with Jason to Colchis, to bring away the golden fleece by force of arms. But of this we shall speak when we come to the expedition of the Argonauts.

Then he was commanded to strip Hippolyta the Amazon of her belt. Hereupon, resolving upon a war against the Amazons, he sailed into Pontus, from him called Euxinus*, and, arriving at the mouth of the river Thermodon, he encamped near the city Themiscyra, the seat-royal of the Amazons; and first he demanded the belt to be delivered to him, which being refused, he joined battle with them.

The choice and most noble of the Amazons were drawn up against Hercules, the rest of the army opposed the other ordinary troops, so that there was a very sharp engagement. The first that fought hand to hand with him was Aella, so called from her swiftness; but she found her enemy swifter than herself: the second was Philippis, who upon the first onset received a mortal wound, and fell down dead. Then Prothoe entered the list, who, they say, seven times baffled her enemy in single combat; but she being at length slain, he killed the fourth, called Eribea. She was so confident in her strength and feats of arms, that she used to boast she needed none to second her; but, meeting with one stronger than herself, she presently experienced the vanity of her boasting.

After these Celaenus, Eurysea, and Phoebe, companions with Diana in hunting, (who never used to miss their mark, yet now could none of them hit one), in defending one another, were all killed together upon the spot. Then he overcame Deianita, Asteria, Marpes, Tecmessa, and Alcippe. The last mentioned had vowed perpetual virginity, and kept their oaths, but could not preserve their lives. Melanippe also, the queen of the Amazons, (who was famous and highly admired every where for her valour), then lost her kingdom. The chief of the Amazons being thus cut off, he forced the rest to fly, and killing most of them in the pursuit, wholly destroyed and rooted up that nation. Of the prisoners he gave Antiope to Theseus, but Melanippe he discharged, having first taken from her her belt.

After this, a tenth labour was imposed upon him by Eurystheus, and that was to drive away the oxen of Gerion that pastured in Iberia near to the ocean. Hercules, perceiving he could not perform this task without much trouble and great preparation, set forth a brave fleet, and manned it with such a number of seamen and soldiers as such an expedition justly required: for it was noised abroad through the whole world, that Chrysaor (so called from his riches) king of Iberia†, had three sons‡, strong bodied men, and famous for martial affairs, and that each of them had great armies of valiant men constantly at hand attending upon them, which was the reason Eurystheus imposed this task upon him, conceiving this expedition was greater than he was ever able to perform: but Hercules undertook this with as much confidence as he had done those before, and commanded forces to be raised in Crete, whence he resolved to

* The Euxine sea.
† Spain.
‡ Of whom this Gerion was one, whom the poets feign to have three bodies.

set forth, this island being the most convenient port from whence to make any expedition into any part of the world. Before he set sail, mighty honours were conferred upon him by the inhabitants; in grateful return for which favours he freed the island from wild beasts, so that no hurtful creatures, such as bears, wolves, serpents, and such like, remained there ever after. He did these things in reverence to the island, because it was reported that Jupiter was bred and born there. Loosing thence, he arrived at Libya. Here, in the first place, he challenged and slew Antaeus (famous for his great strength and skill in wrestling), who was used to kill the strangers he wrestled with, after he had mastered them. Then he destroyed the wild beasts in the deserts, and made Africa so quiet and improveable, (which was before full of hurtful creatures), that every part was fit for tillage, and planting of fruit-trees; the whole country productive of wine and oil. In short, he so improved Libya, (which, by reason of the multitude of wild beasts, was before uninhabitable), that no country in the world afterwards exceeded it for fertility and richness of soil. In like manner he so purged the nation from wicked men and insolent tyrants, that he put all the cities into a flourishing state and condition. It is therefore reported that he was prosecuted with the hatred and opposition of all sorts of dreadful wild beasts, and of wicked men; for, when he was an infant in his cradle, he was assaulted by serpents, and, when he was a man, he was vexed and perplexed with the commands of a proud and unjust tyrant.

After the killing of Antaeus, he went into Egypt, where he slew the tyrant Busiris, who murdered all strangers that landed there. After he had passed over the sandy deserts of Libya, he found a fertile and well watered country, in which he built an extraordinary great city, from the number of its gates called Hecatompylon*, which continued in a flourishing condition till of latter times that the Carthaginians, with a great army, (commanded by eminent captains), took it.

Hercules having passed through a great part of Africa, arrived in the ocean near Gades†, where he erected two pillars, one on each side the strait upon the continent.

Thence (with his fleet sailing along with him) he passed over into Iberia, where he found the sons of Chrysaor with three mighty armies. These at a distance he challenged to a single combat, and having at length slain the three generals, he gained Iberia, and drove away those remarkable herds of cattle.

In the mean time, as he travelled through Spain, he was magnificently entertained by a petty prince in the country, (who was a pious and just man), in return for which, he bestowed upon him some of the cattle; and he again consecrated them all to Hercules, and every year sacrificed to him one of the fairest bulls that were bred of them, some of which sacred breed remain in Iberia to this day.

And now, because we have before made mention of Hercules's pillars, we conceive it fit in this place to say something further concerning them.

Hercules, when he arrived at the utmost coasts of both continents adjoining to the ocean, resolved to set up these pillars as lasting monuments of his expedition. That his work, therefore, might be famous to all posterity, it is said, that

---

* Hecatompylon, a hundred gates.
† Or in the straits near Cadiz.

he much enlarged both the mountains on each side, by making great mounds for a long way into the sea; so that, whereas before they lay in the sea at a great distance one from another, he made the passage so narrow, that the great whales from that time could not pass out of the ocean through those straits into the Mediterranean; and, by the greatness of the work, the glory of the workman is preserved in everlasting remembrance.

But there are some of a contrary opinion, and affirm that the continents once joined together, and that he cut a trench through them, whereby he opened a passage, and so brought the ocean into our sea. But every man may judge of this matter as he thinks fit. The like he did before in Greece: for, when the large champaign country about Tempe was all over a standing lake, he cut sluices through the lower grounds, and through those trenches drained all the water out of the lake, by which means were gained all those pleasant fields of Thessaly as far as to the river Peneus. But in Boeotia he did quite contrary; for he caused the river which ran through the country of the Minyae to overflow the whole region, and turn all into a standing pool. What he did in Thessaly was to gain the favour of the Grecians, but that in Boeotia he did to punish the Minyae, because they oppressed the Thebans.

Hercules having committed the government of the kingdom of Iberia to the chiefest of the inhabitants, marched away with his army into Celtica*, and over-ran the whole country, and put an end to their usual impieties and murdering of strangers.

And whereas a vast multitude from all nations came and listed themselves of their own accord in his army, having such a number, he built a famous large city, which he called, from his wandering expedition, Alesia†. But because many of the barbarians from the neighbouring places were mixed among the citizens, it happened that the rest of the inhabitants (being much inferior in number) learnt the barbarian manners of the other. The Celtae at this day have a great esteem and honour for this city, as being the chief and metropolis of all Gaul; and ever since the time of Hercules it has remained free, never taken by any, to our very days; till at length Caius Caesar, who (by reason of the greatness of his actions) was called Divus, took it by storm, and so it came into the hands of the Romans. With the rest of the Gauls Hercules, marching out of Gaul into Italy, as he passed over the Alps, levelled and opened those rough and difficult ways (that were scarce passable) to make way for his army and carriages. The barbarians who inhabited those mountainous parts were used to kill and rob armies, in the strait and craggy places, as they happened to pass this way; but he subdued them, and put to death the perpetrators of those wicked practices, and so made the passage safe this way to all posterity. Having passed the Alps, he continued his march through Gaul, as it is now called, and came into Liguria. The Ligurians inhabit a rough and barren soil, but being forced by continual labour and toil, it produces some little corn and other fruits: the people here are short and low, but by reason of their constant labours well set and strong; for they are far from being idle and luxurious livers, and therefore are very active and valiant in

---

* France.
† Or Alexia, Arras.

time of war. To conclude, because all these neighbouring regions are plied with continual labours and pains, (for that the land requires it), it is the custom for the women to work and labour in that kind as well as the men; and whereas the women as well as the men work for hire, there fell out a remarkable accident concerning one of these women, strange and unusual to any of our female sex. Being great with child, and falling in labour in the midst of her work amongst the men, without any noise or complaint she withdrew herself into a certain grove there near at hand, and there being delivered, she covered the infant with leaves, and hid it among the shrubs, and then returned to her work again, without the least sign of having borne a child, and continued with her fellow-labourers in her work as she did before. But the infant, crying and bawling, discovered the whole matter; yet the overseer of the workmen would by no means be persuaded to suffer her to leave her miserable employment, till he that hired her, pitying her condition, paid her her wages, and discharged her.

Hercules, after he had gone through Liguria and Tuscany, encamped at Tiber, where Rome now stands, built many ages after by Romulus, the son of Mars. The natural inhabitants at that time inhabited a little town upon a hill, now called Mount Palatine. Here Potitius* and Pinarius, the most eminent persons of quality among them, entertained Hercules with all the demonstrations of kindness imaginable, and presented him with many noble presents. There are now at Rome antient monuments of these men; for the most noble family, called the Pinarii, remains still among the Romans, and is accounted the most antient at this day. And there are Potitius's stone stairs to go down from Mount Palatine, (called after his name), adjoining to that which was antiently his house.

Hercules being much pleased with the civil entertainment of the Palatines, foretold them, that whosoever should dedicate the tenth of their goods to him, after he was translated to the gods, should be ever after more prosperous; and this dedication has been ever since constantly used to this day: for many of the Romans, not only such as are of mean estates, but the great and rich men, (having experienced how riches have flowed in upon them after the decimation of their goods to Hercules), have dedicated the tenth part of their substances, which have been of the value of four thousand talents: for Lucullus (the richest almost of all the Romans in his time) valued his estate, and consecrated the tenths to this god, and feasted continually with prodigious charge and expence. The Romans afterwards built a magnificent temple near the river Tiber, in honour of this god, and instituted sacrifices to him out of the tenths.

Hercules marching from Mount Palatine, passed through the maritime coasts of Italy, as they are now called, and came into the champaign country of Cumae, where (it is said) there were men infamous for their outrages and cruelties, called giants. This place is also called the Phlegraean plain, from a hill which antiently vomited out fire, like unto Aetna in Sicily, now called Vesuvius, which retains many signs and marks of its antient irruptions.

These giants, hearing of Hercules's approach, met him in battle array, and, fighting with the force and cruelty of giants, Hercules (with the assistance of the gods) overcame them, and cutting off most of them, quieted that country. These

* Cacius in the Greek.

giants were called sons of the earth, by reason of the vast bulk of their bodies. These are the things that some report (whom Tiuneus follows) concerning the destruction of the giants of Phlegraea.

Leaving the plains of Phlegraea, he came to the sea, where he performed some remarkable works about the lake Avernus, (as it is called), which is consecrated to Proserpine. It is situated between Micenus and Diciarchcos, near the hot baths, five furlongs in circuit, and of an incredible depth. The water of this lake is exceeding clear, and the mighty depth of it casts a blue colour upon the surface.

It is reported that there was antiently here an oracle, where they conjured the infernal spirits, which the latter ages abolished. Whereas this lake extended as far as to the sea, it is said Hercules, by casting up of earth, so stopped up its current, that he made the way near the sea, now called the Herculean way. And these are the things he did there.

Marching thence, he came to a certain rock in the country of the Posidonians, where, they report, a kind of a miracle happened. A certain huntsman (famous all over the country for his brave exploits) was used formerly to fix the heads and feet of all the game he took to trees, as an offering to Diana: but having then taken a great wild boar, (in contempt of the goddess), he boasted, and declared he would only consecrate the head to her; and forthwith, according to what he said, hung it upon a tree. It being then summer-time, about noon, he laid him down to sleep, during which time, the band that fastened the head broke, and so it fell down upon him as he slept, and killed him. And there is no reason to wonder at this, when many of the like kind are reported to have happened, by which the goddess has revenged herself on the impious. But the contrary happened to Hercules, for the sake of his piety; for, when he came to the borders of Rhegium and Locris, being wearied with his march, and laid down to rest, they say he was disturbed with the noise and creaking of the grasshoppers, whereupon he entreated the gods to free him from that disturbance, who heard his prayers: for the grasshoppers flew away, not only for that time, but none were ever seen there at any time after.

When he came to the narrowest passage over the sea, he caused the cattle to swim over before him into Sicily, and he himself catched hold of one of the horns of the oxen, and in that manner swam along for the space of thirteen furlongs, as Timreus reports the matter. Afterwards, desiring to go round the island, he went on his journey from Peloriados to Eryx, and, passing along the shore, the nymphs opened the hot baths for him, where he refreshed himself after his tedious journey. These baths were two in number, the Hemerian and Egestean, so called from the places. After Hercules came into the country of Eryx, Eryx the son of Venus and Bula, the king of the country, challenged Hercules to wrestle with him. Both sides proposed the wager to be won and lost; Eryx laid to stake his kingdom, but Hercules his oxen; Eryx at first disdained such an unequal wager, not fit to be compared with his country; but when Hercules, on the other side, answered, that if he lost them, he should lose together with them immortality, Eryx was contented with the condition, and engaged in the contest: but he was overcome, and so was stripped out of the possession of his country, which Hercules gave to the inhabitants, allowing them to take the fruits to their own use, till some one of his posterity came to demand it, which afterwards happened: for, many ages after, Dorieus the Lacedaemonian (sailing into Sicily) recovered his ancestor's dominion, and there built Heraclea, which, growing great on a sudden, became the object of the Carthaginians' envy and fear, lest, growing stronger than Carthage itself, it should deprive them of their sovereignty; and for that reason they besieged it with a mighty army, and took it by force, and razed it to the ground; of which we shall speak particularly in its proper place.

Hercules having viewed Sicily round, came to the city now called Syracuse, where, when he came to be informed of the rape of Proserpine, he offered magnificent sacrifices to the goddesses, and at Cyane sacrificed the goodliest of his bulls, and ordered the inhabitants to sacrifice yearly to Proserpine, and observe an anniversary festival at Cyane. Then travelling through the heart of the country with his oxen, he was set upon by the Sicani, with a strong body of men; whom, after a cruel battle, he routed, and cut off most of them, amongst whom (it is reported) there were captains of extraordinary valour, who are honoured as demi-gods to this day; to wit, Leucaspis, Pedicrates, Buphonas, Caugates, Cygaus, and Crytidas. Thence he passed through the country of the Leontines, and much admired the pleasantness of the territory; and, by reason of the singular respect he found from the inhabitants, he left there eternal monuments of his presence.

Among the Agyrineans something remarkable happened concerning him; for they kept magnificent festivals, and offered sacrifices to him, as to the gods themselves, which was the first time he approved of such worship, never before allowing any sacrifice to himself: but now the deity itself ratified his divinity; for, not far from the city, in a rocky way, the oxen made impressions with their feet, as if it had been in wax; and the same thing likewise happening to Hercules himself, caused him to conclude, that (his tenth labour being now perfected) his immortality was in part sealed to him, and therefore he refused not the yearly solemnity of sacrifices instituted in honour of him by the inhabitants. That he might, therefore, manifest his gratitude to them for the honours conferred upon him, he caused a pond to be sunk near the city, four furlongs in compass, which he called after his own name. The impressions, likewise, made by the hoofs of his oxen, he named after himself, and consecrated a grove* to Gerion, as to a demi-god, whom the inhabitants religiously worship at this day. He built likewise there a famous temple in honour of Iolaus, his associate in his expedition, and appointed he should be honoured with yearly sacrifices, which are observed at this day: for all the inhabitants of this city let their hair grow, without cutting, from their very births, in honour of Iolaus, till they make an offering of them to him, and gain the favour of the god by costly and magnificent sacrifices. Such is the holiness and majesty of this temple, that whosoever do not observe these holy rites, they are stricken dumb, and are like dead men: but as soon as any recollects himself, and vows to offer his sacrifices, and gives a pledge to the god for that purpose, they are presently restored to their former health. The inhabitants, therefore, very fitly call the gate where these sacred solemnities are performed Heraclea. They every year, likewise, with great earnestness, celebrate the Gymnic

* Or built a temple.

sports*, and horse-races; whither all the people, both bond and free, flocking, they privately taught their servants how to worship this god, how to celebrate the solemn sacrifices, and to perform when they met together the sacred rites and festivals.

After this, Hercules passed over his oxen again into Italy, and in his marching along by the sea-coasts, he killed one Lacinius that was stealing some of his oxen. There he buried Croton, and erected a stately monument over him, whom he had unfortunately slain, and foretold that in time to come there should be built a famous city; called after the name of him that was there buried. Having at length marched round about Adria, and all the coasts of that gulf, on foot, he passed through Epirus into Peloponnesus.

Having finished his tenth labour, Eurystheus imposed another task upon him, and that was, that he should bring Cerberus out of hell. Preparing himself, therefore, to perform this, to be better enabled thereunto, he went to Athens to be initiated into the mysterious rites of Elusina, where Musaeus the son of Orpheus was then high priest.

And because we have now occasion to mention Orpheus, we conceive it will not be amiss here to give a short account of him. He was the son of Oeagrus, and by birth a Thracian, for in the art of music and poetry far excelling all that ever were recorded. For he composed a poem, for sweetness and smoothness, the subject of all men's admiration: and he grew so eminent in this art, that, by the melody of his music, he was said to draw even wild beasts and trees after him; and being naturally very studious, he attained to an extraordinary degree of knowledge in the antient theology. He improved himself, likewise, very much by travelling into Egypt, so that he was accounted to excel the most accomplished person among all the Grecians for his knowledge both in divinity and sacred mysteries, in music, and in poetry. He was one, likewise, in the expedition of the Argonauts, and for the exceeding love he had to his wife, (with an admirable courage) descended into hell, and there so enchanted Proserpine with the sweetness of his music, that she gratified him so far as to suffer him to carry back his wife along with him, that died a little before.

In like manner, they say, Bacchus hereupon raised his mother Semele from the shades below, and, enduing her with immortality, surnamed her Thyone.

Having now done with this digression relating to Orpheus, we return to Hercules: when he entered the infernal regions, (the mythologists say), Proserpine kindly received him as her brother, and gave him liberty to loose Theseus and Pirithous from their chains; and at length, contrary to the expectations of all men, brought up the dog† tied in his chain, and presented him to open view.

The last labour enjoined him was to fetch away the golden apples of the Hesperides, to which purpose he passed over a second time into Africa. The mythologists vary in their writings concerning this; for some affirm that there were really golden apples in some of the gardens of the Hesperides, guarded continually by a terrible dragon. Others say, that there are sheep of exquisite beauty in the Hesperides, and that from thence they are poetically called golden

---

* Wrestlings, quoitings, &c.
† Cerberus.

apples, as Venus, from her beauty, is called golden Venus. Others will have it, that the fleeces upon the sheep's backs are of that admirable colour, that they glitter like gold, and thence have been so called. And by the dragon they understand the shepherd of the flocks, who, being a man of a strong body and stout heart, preserved the flocks, and killed the thieves that attempted to steal them.

But let every one judge of this matter as he thinks best himself: for Hercules killed the keeper, and brought away the apples or sheep (which soever they were) to Eurystheus, trusting now, that since all his tasks were performed, (according to the oracle of Apollo), he should be rewarded with immortality.

ALEXANDER THE GREAT MEETS THE RAM GOD

The Anabasis of Alexander, Book III

Arrian

Translated by E. J. Chinnock, 1884

> Alexander the Great (356–323 BC), ruler of Macedon, is said to have visited the oracle of Ammon, a ram-headed god, during his expedition to Siwa, near the Egyptian–Libyan border. He was associated thereafter with the ram's horn, and is depicted wearing one on coins minted by his successors. The Old Testament Book of Daniel mentions a 'king of Grecia' with a 'great horn between his eyes'. If only we knew what message Alexander received from the oracle. This story comes from a biography written hundreds of years after his death by the Greek historian **Arrian** of Nicomedia (c. AD 86/89 – after 146/160).

III. Alexander Visits the Temple of Ammon

After these transactions, Alexander was seized by an ardent desire to visit Ammon in Libya, partly in order to consult the god, because the oracle of Ammon was said to be exact in its information, and Perseus and Heracles were said to have consulted it, the former when he was despatched by Polydectes against the Gorgons, and the latter, when he visited Antaeus in Libya and Busiris in Egypt. Alexander was also partly urged by a desire of emulating Perseus and Heracles, from both of whom he traced his descent. He also deduced his pedigree from Ammon, just as the legends traced that of Heracles and Perseus to Zeus. Accordingly he made the expedition to Ammon with the design of learning his own origin more certainly, or at least that he might be able to say that he had learned it. According to Aristobulus, he advanced along the seashore to Paraetonium through a country which was a desert, but not destitute of water, a distance of about 1,600 stades. Thence he turned into the interior, where the oracle of Ammon was located. The route is desert, and most of it is sand and destitute of water. But there was a copious supply of rain for Alexander, a thing which was attributed to the influence of the deity; as was also the following occurrence. Whenever a south wind blows in that district, it heaps up the sand upon the route far and wide, rendering the tracks of the road invisible, so that it is impossible to discover where one ought to direct one's course in the sand, just as if one were at sea; for there are no landmarks along the road, neither mountain anywhere, nor tree, nor permanent hill standing erect, by which travellers might be able to form a conjecture of the right course, as sailors do by the stars. Consequently, Alexander's army lost the way, and even the guides were in doubt about the course to take. Ptolemy, son of Lagus, says that two serpents went in front of the army, uttering a voice, and Alexander ordered the guides to follow them, trusting in the divine portent. He says too that they showed the way to the oracle and back again. But Aristobulus, whose account is generally admitted as correct, says that two ravens flew in front of the army, and that these acted as Alexander's guides. I am able to assert with confidence that some divine assistance was afforded him, for probability also coincides with the supposition; but the discrepancies in the details of the various narratives have deprived the story of certainty.

IV. The Oasis of Ammon

The place where the temple of Ammon is located is entirely surrounded by a desert of far-stretching sand, which is destitute of water. The fertile spot in the midst of this desert is not extensive; for where it stretches into its greater expanse, it is only about forty stades broad. It is full of cultivated trees, olives and palms; and it is the only place in those parts which is refreshed with dew. A spring also rises from it, quite unlike all the other springs which issue from the earth. For at midday the water is cold to the taste, and still more so to the touch, as cold as cold can be. But when the sun has sunk into the west, it gets warmer, and from the evening it keeps on growing warmer until midnight, when it reaches the warmest point. After midnight it goes on getting gradually colder; at daybreak it is already cold; but at midday it reaches the coldest point. Every day it undergoes these alternate changes in regular succession. In this place also natural salt is procured by digging, and certain of the priests of Ammon convey quantities of it into Egypt. For whenever they set out for Egypt they put it into little boxes plaited out of palm, and carry it as a present to the king, or some other great man. The grains of this salt are large, some of them being even longer than three fingers' breadth; and it is clear like crystal. The Egyptians and others who are respectful to the deity use this salt in their sacrifices, as it is clearer than that which is procured from the sea. Alexander then was struck with wonder at the place, and consulted the oracle of the god. Having heard what was agreeable to his wishes, as he himself said, he set out on the journey back to Egypt by the same route, according to the statement of Aristobulus; but according to that of Ptolemy, son of Lagus, he took another road, leading straight to Memphis.

THE DEATH OF ALEXANDER

The Alexander Romance

Pseudo-Callisthenes

Translated by Albert Mugrdich Wolohojian, 1969

The following story derives from one in a series of fictional biographies
of Alexander the Great composed in antiquity. Fancifully attributed to
Alexander's court historian, **Callisthenes**, *The Alexander Romance* was
passed down in several versions over many centuries, but the Armenian,
on which this translation is based, is believed to be particularly close to
the lost Greek original. Alexander is described in the story not as the son
of Philip II of Macedon and his wife Olympias, but as the son of Olympias
and the ram god Ammon (see previous story). Alexander is presented as
strong and heroic but prone to violent outbursts. He has campaigned
against the 'barbarians', subdued Persia, travelled to India and arrived
in Babylon, where this portion of the story is set. The Chaldeans – local
astrologers – are summoned to interpret a peculiar omen. Alexander's
mother writes to him complaining of her ill-treatment by Antipater, the
regent of Macedonia, prompting Alexander to send his general Krateros
to investigate. Antipater's response is to forge a plot against Alexander.

When one of the local women gave birth to a child, the upper part of
its body, as far as the navel, was completely human and according to
nature, but the lower extremities were those of a wild beast. And its
general appearance was like that of Scylla except that it differed in the kinds of
animals and in the great number of them. For there were the shapes of leopards
and lions, wolves and wild boars and dogs. And these forms moved, and each
was clearly recognizable to all. And the child was dead and his body blue. And
immediately upon giving birth to the above-mentioned baby, the woman put it in
the fold of her robe and hid it. And she came to the palace of Alexander, and told
the chamberlain to announce her to the king, "for I have something of importance
to show and tell him." And he happened to be resting in his room at midday. And
when he awoke and heard from the chamberlain about the woman who had
come, he ordered that she be brought in. And when she entered, the king ordered
those who were there to leave. And when they had gone out, she uncovered and
showed him the marvel that had been begotten, saying that she herself had given

birth to it. When Alexander saw it, he was filled with wonder and great amazement. And he called together the magi and the Chaldean sign-readers and ordered them to make a reading concerning it, promising them either death or harm if they did not tell the truth. And they were famous and widely reputed and the most learned of the Chaldeans. But the one who was more able in his art than all the rest happened not to be there. Those who were present said that Alexander was the greatest of men and the terror of his enemies and that he held sway over land and sea. And they said that the mighty and terrible monsters placed beneath the human body meant this: that he is to rule the mightiest men and that no one shall be mightier than he. And after they had explained how it was, they left him and went away. And after them, the other Chaldean returned from his trip and came to the king. And upon seeing the state of the omen, he gave a great outcry and rent his clothing and was greatly troubled and saddened at the transformation that was to befall the great king. And when the king saw that the man was so smitten by the happenings, he was greatly frightened; and he ordered him to explain frankly what the omen looked like. And he said this to him: "King, hereafter, you are no longer among the living; rather your body has left its mortal state. For such is the meaning of the marvelous omen." And Alexander asked him about these words. And the omen solver answered and said: "O bravest of all men, you are the human body, and the wild animal forms are the soldiers who are with you. If the human part of the body were alive and moving, as are the animals beneath it, you would have been destined to rule all men. But it is this very part that is dead; and the beasts are alive. So just as it has left its living state, so have you too departed to those who are no more. For example, the animals that are bound to the human body have no kind consideration toward man. In the same way, do those who surround you love you. And there will be many upheavals in the world when you depart; and those about you will fall out with one another and will bloodily slaughter one another." The philosopher spoke thus and left. And the Chaldean thought it best to burn the child.

When Alexander heard this, he was touched to the very heart and saddened. He said: "Aramazd, you have brought the fraudulent game to an end for me. So if such is your desire, take me, this mortal man, to you also." And this is what he meant: that Dionysos, when the evil deeds done him by those under his rule were revealed, was judged to be one of the gods. So, too, Heracles, since he had distinguished himself to the whole world, was considered in the same way, for his deeds, to be a companion of all the gods. And his mother, Olympias, wrote many times to him about Antipater, saying that he had deeply humiliated and spurned and dishonored her because she was Alexander's mother; and that Antipater was still doing as he pleased and was writing slanderous accusations about her. Because Olympias was once again complaining, Alexander wanted to cross to Epirus, for he knew how to put an end to Antipater's hostility to his mother. And he sent forth and summoned Antipater to him from Macedon by sending Krateros. And since Antipater was aware of Alexander's cleverness, he plotted the death of the world conqueror to be administered by the soldiers, for he was afraid that some evil might befall himself. For he had heard and he bore in mind the fact that Alexander had grown very proud as a result of the successes that had befallen him. And he sent out and brought the gentian drug whose power he knew was very deadly. And he put it in the hoof of a mule and he boiled it in order to be able to keep the strength of the drug alive. For no other dish, be it of copper or of clay, could support the strength of the drug, but was broken by it. And he put it in an iron box, and gave it to Kasandros with instructions to discuss with Iollas, his brother, the administration of the drug.

And when Kasandros arrived in Babylon, he found Alexander making sacrifices and receiving foreigners. He spoke with Iollas who was Alexander's chief cupbearer. And it so happened that a few days earlier Alexander had hit him on the head with a club for some misdemeanor. Thus, since the boy was prone to anger, he gladly listened to the suggestion of committing the crime. And he took as his helper Mandios, a Thessalonian, who was a friend of Alexander and his own lover. And this fellow considered it a criminal injustice that his Iollas had received a caning. So, of his own will and desire, he agreed that they would give him the poison to drink.

Meanwhile, Alexander was enjoying himself with his close friends and the Dionysian artists. For many had come to Babylon to crown Alexander ceremoniously and to take part personally in the ceremony because of the notable glories of the very happy king.

And then when he got up and wanted to go to rest, Medios came to him and beseeched him to come to his friends, telling him, "Your important friends are all gathered together and are awaiting you." He said this, and Alexander was persuaded by Medios' cunning. He went to the party.

And twenty men were gathered there: Perdikkas, Meleadros, Pichon, Leonatos, Kasandros, Pokestes, Ptlomeos, Lysimachos, Philip, Olkias, Eumenes, Philip the doctor, Nearchos the Crete, Heraclides, Europpeos, Ariston, Pharsalios, Philip who had mechanical skills, Philotas, Menandres, Dardana. Of these men, Perdikkas and Ptlomeos, Olkias and Lysimachos, Eumenes and Asandros did not know what had been planned. But all the others were associated in the act and in agreement with Iollas and Kasandros and had given their oath. For they longed for material possessions, and they were wary of Alexander; and in their hearts, they were greatly dismayed by his overweening pride.

When the king had stretched out, Iollas offered him the drink. And then, those who were there behaved in this fashion. They busily added remarks to the conversation to draw out as long as possible the taking of the drugs. Suddenly, Alexander cried out as though he had been hit in the liver by an arrow. For a short while, he controlled himself and, supporting the pain, went off by himself, bidding those who were there to drink. And they were very frightened, and then and there broke up the party and observed the turn of events. Alexander wanted very badly to bring up the wine and asked for a feather, for this is the way he used to do it. And Iollas contaminated it with the drug and offered it to him. Because of this, the drug overcame him all the more effectively, passing undiluted through the body. And Alexander was very ill and trying in vain to vomit, he passed the entire night in awful pain, in dolorous groaning, and in patient suffering.

And on the next day, he realized his bad state, for he was uttering indistinct and unclear sounds because his tongue was already growing stiff. He sent everyone out, so that he might be quiet and alone to talk about what he wanted to. And Kasandros conferred with his brothers, and at night, rushed off to the hills, boldly taking his cup from Iollas. For he had made a pact with Iollas that if the king died, he would be freed from all responsibility. And he sent it to his parent in Macedonia, having written to him in code that the deed was done.

And at nightfall, Alexander ordered everyone to leave the house. Among those he dismissed were Kombaphe and Roxiane, his wife. And from the house there was an exit toward the river called the Euphrates, which runs through Babylon. He ordered it opened and that no one be at the places they customarily stood guard. And when it was the middle of the night, he got up from his bed, put out the light, and crawled on all fours toward the river. And he saw his wife, Roxiane, advancing toward him. He had been planning to act in a manner worthy of his great courage. She followed his final journey in the dark. And Alexander, scarcely making a sound, would groan, and Roxiane was directed to the cry. And he stopped and was still. And his wife embraced him and said, "Are you abandoning and leaving me, Alexander, by committing suicide?" And he said: "Roxiane, it is a small deprivation for you that my glory be taken away from you. But still let no one hear about this." And he turned away from Roxiane and went back home in concealment.

And when it was day, he ordered Perdikkas and Ptlomeos and Lysimachos to come in. He told them that no one else should approach him until he wrote a will about his affairs. And they went out. And then he seated near him the will makers, Kombaphe and Hermogenes, who were young men. And Perdikkas thought that Alexander would leave all his goods to Ptlomeos because he had often spoken to him of Ptlomeos' lucky birth. And Olympias, too, had made it clear that Ptlomeos had been fathered by Philip. So he had made him promise privately that he would in turn be a recipient of Alexander's possessions at the time of the division of his goods. And when night fell, the secretaries began to write. And the king ordered that Perdikkas and Loukias and Ptlomeos and Lysimachos be summoned to him. And they came into the palace.

And suddenly a great shout arose from all the Macedonians. And they all rushed upon the palace saying that they would kill the guards unless they showed them their king. And Alexander heard the noise of the uproar and Perdikkas came and informed him of what the Macedonians were saying. He ordered that his couch be lifted and put in a place where the army might pass and see him and that the soldiers be brought in, clad in a single garment, and taken out the other door, so that they make no trouble amongst themselves and start fighting. The Macedonians entered and passed close by him and gave him encouragement. And there was no one who was not grieved over what had happened to such a great and world-conquering king.

Alexander, still ailing, reads out his will, appointing as king any son born of him and his wife posthumously or, should none be born, his brother, a son of the late Philip of Macedon, until the Macedonians elect a new ruler. Alexander then dies. Historically, Alexander the Great died in Babylon in 323 BC after a night of heavy drinking. His intoxication might have masked the true cause of his death, which some believe was malaria, others alcohol-induced pancreatitis, and others still, poison.

THE CONSTELLATION OF THE MAIDEN

Phaenomena

Aratus

Translated by Douglas Kidd, 1997

> The night sky inspired many stories in antiquity. **Aratus** (*c.* 315 BC/
> 310 BC–240 BC), a poet from Asia Minor, wrote an entire book of
> *Phaenomena* or 'Things That Appear'. Underpinned by Stoic philosophy
> and Greek myth, it describes the positions, and the rising and setting,
> of the constellations. In the seventh century BC, the poet Hesiod (see
> Stories 1 and 9) had described Justice (also known as 'the Maiden' or
> 'Virgo' in Latin) as abandoning mortals as they grew ever more violent
> and degenerate. His tale of the decline of man over five ages – Golden,
> Silver, Bronze, Heroic, and Iron – provides the backbone of Aratus' story.

Beneath the two feet of Bootes you can observe the Maiden, who carries in
her hand the radiant Spica.* Whether she is the daughter of Astraeus, who,
they say, was the original father of the stars, or of some other, may her
way be peaceful! There is, however, another tale current among men, that once
she actually lived on earth, and came face to face with men, and did not ever
spurn the tribes of ancient men and women, but sat in their midst although she
was immortal. And they called her Justice: gathering together the elders, either in
the market-place or on the broad highway, she urged them in prophetic tones to
judgements for the good of the people. At that time they still had no knowledge
of painful strife or quarrelsome conflict or noise of battle, but lived just as they
were; the dangerous sea was far from their thoughts, and as yet no ships brought
them livelihood from afar, but oxen and ploughs and Justice herself, queen of the
people and giver of civilised life, provided all their countless needs. That was as
long as the earth still nurtured the Golden Age. But with the Silver she associated
little, and now not at all willingly, as she longed for the ways of the earlier folk.
But nevertheless she was still with this Silver Age too. She would emerge from
the sounding mountain towards evening all alone, and not engage anyone in
friendly conversation. But filling the broad hillsides with people, she would then
speak menacingly, rebuking them for their wickedness, and say she would never

---

*   The 'Spica' is an ear of grain.

more come face to face with them, even if they called her: 'What an inferior generation your golden fathers have left! And you are likely to beget a still more evil progeny. There will surely be wars, yes, and unnatural bloodshed among men, and suffering from their troubles will come upon them.' So saying she made for the mountains, and left the people all staring after her. But when these men also had died and there were born the Bronze Age men, more destructive than their predecessors, who were the first to forge the criminal sword for murder on the highways, and the first to taste the flesh of ploughing oxen, then Justice, conceiving a hatred for the generation of these men, flew up to the sky and took up her abode in that place, where she is still visible to men by night as the Maiden near conspicuous Bootes.

THE MERCHANT

The Merchant

Plautus

Translated by Henry Thomas Riley, 1852

The Merchant, by the Roman playwright **Plautus** (*c.* 254–184 BC), is a classic comedy of errors after a Greek original, dating from around 200 BC. A young man named Charinus has returned to Athens from Rhodes with a secret lover. No sooner has his father Demipho spied her on the ship than he falls hopelessly in lust with her. The woman pretends that Charinus has brought her as attendant to his mother. Unaware that she is in fact his son's beloved, Demipho decides to pursue her. To keep this from his wife, he persuades his friend Lysimachus to purchase the woman and take her back to his house. But then Lysimachus' wife returns unexpectedly from the country.

[*Enter* DEMIPHO.]

DEMIPHO. [*To himself*]

In wondrous ways do the Gods make sport of men, and in wondrous fashions do they send dreams in sleep. As, for instance, I, this very last night that has passed, have sufficiently experienced in my sleep, and, mortal that I am, was much occupied therewith. I seemed to have purchased for myself a beautiful she-goat. That she might not offend that other she-goat which I had at home before, and that they mightn't disagree if they were both in the same spot, after that I had purchased her, I seemed to entrust her to the charge of an ape. This ape, not very long afterwards, came to me, uttered imprecations against me, and assailed me with reproaches; he said that by her means and through the arrival of the she-goat he had suffered injury and loss in no slight degree; he said that the she-goat, which I had entrusted to him to keep, had gnawed away the marriage-portion of his wife. This seemed extremely wonderful to me, how that this single she-goat could possibly have gnawed away the marriage-portion of the wife of the ape. The ape, however, insisted that it was so, and, in short, gave me this answer, that if I didn't make haste and remove her away from his own house, he would bring her home into my house to my wife. And, by my troth, I seemed very greatly to take an interest in her, but not to have any one to whom to entrust this she-goat; wherefore the more, in my distress, was I tormented with anxiety what to do. Meanwhile, a kid appeared to address me, and began to tell me that he had carried off the she-goat from the ape, and began to laugh at me. But I began to lament and complain that she was carried off. To what reality I am to suppose that this vision points, I can't discover; except that I suspect that I have just now discovered this she-goat, what she is, or what it all means. This morning, at daybreak, I went away hence down to the harbour. After I had transacted there what I wanted, suddenly I espied the ship from Rhodes, in which my son arrived here yesterday. I had an inclination, I know not why, to visit it; I went on board a boat, and put off to the ship; and there I beheld a woman of surpassing beauty, whom my son has brought as a maid-servant for his mother. After I had thus beheld her, I fell in love with her, not as men in their senses, but after the fashion in which madmen are wont. I' faith, in former times, in my youthful days, I fell in love, 'tis true; but after this fashion, according as I'm now distracted, never. Now beyond a doubt, surely thus this matter stands; this is that she-goat. But what that ape and that kid mean, I'm afraid. One thing, i' faith, I really do know for certain, that I'm undone for love; [*to the* AUDIENCE] consider yourselves the other point, what a poor creature I am. But I'll hold my tongue; lo! I see my neighbour; he's coming out of doors. [*Stands aside*]

[...]

LYSIMACHUS.
Well met! and greetings to you, Demipho. How are you? How goes it?

DEMIPHO.
As with one that's most wretched.

LYSIMACHUS.
May the Gods grant better things.

DEMIPHO.
As for the Gods, it's they that do this.

LYSIMACHUS.
What's the matter?

DEMIPHO.
I'd tell you, if I saw that you had time or leisure.

LYSIMACHUS.
Although I have business in hand, if you wish for anything, Demipho, I'm never too busy to give attention to a friend.

DEMIPHO.

You speak of your kindness to myself who have experienced it. How do I seem to you as to age?

LYSIMACHUS.

A subject for Acheron – an antiquated, decrepit old fellow.

DEMIPHO.

You see in a wrong light. I am a child, Lysimachus, of seven years old.

LYSIMACHUS.

Are you in your senses, to say that you are a child?

DEMIPHO.

I'm telling what's true.

LYSIMACHUS.

I' faith, it has this moment come into my mind what you mean to say; directly a person is old, no longer has he sense or taste; people say that he has become a child again.

DEMIPHO.

Why, no; for I'm twice as hearty as ever I was before.

LYSIMACHUS.

I' faith, it's well that so it is, and I'm glad of it.

DEMIPHO.

Aye, and if you did but know; with my eyes, too, I see even better now than I did formerly.

LYSIMACHUS.

That's good.

DEMIPHO.

Of a thing that's bad, I'm speaking.

LYSIMACHUS.

Then that same is not good.

DEMIPHO.

But, if I wished at all, could I venture to disclose something to you?

LYSIMACHUS.

Boldly.

DEMIPHO.
Give heed, then.

LYSIMACHUS.
It shall be carefully done.

DEMIPHO.
This day, Lysimachus, I've begun to go to school to learn my letters. I know three letters already.

LYSIMACHUS.
How? Three letters?

DEMIPHO. [*Spelling*]
A M O [I am in love].

LYSIMACHUS.
What! you, in love, with your hoary head, you most shocking old fellow?

DEMIPHO.
Whether that is hoary, or whether red, or whether black, I'm in love.

LYSIMACHUS.
You're now playing upon me in this, I fancy, Demipho.

DEMIPHO.
Cut my throat, if it's false, what I'm saying. That you may be sure I'm in love, take a knife, and do you cut off either my finger, or my ear, or my nose, or my lip: if I move me, or feel that I'm being cut, then, Lysimachus, I give you leave to torture me to death here with being in love.

Charinus is beside himself when he is given to believe that his father intends to sell his mistress. Cue a number of terrible misunderstandings.

LYSIMACHUS. [*To himself*]
I've lent my assistance to my friend in a friendly manner; this piece of goods, which my neighbour requested me, I've purchased. [*Turning to* PASICOMPSA] You are my own; then follow me. Don't weep. You are acting very foolishly; spoiling such eyes. Why, really you have more reason to laugh than to be crying.

PASICOMPSA.
In the name of heaven, prithee, my good old gentleman, do tell me—

LYSIMACHUS.
Ask me what you please.

PASICOMPSA.
Why have you bought me?

LYSIMACHUS.
What, I, bought you? For you to do what you are bidden; in like manner what you bid me, I'll do.

PASICOMPSA.
I am determined, to the best of my ability and skill, to do what I shall think you desire.

LYSIMACHUS.
I shall bid you do nothing of laborious work.

PASICOMPSA.
Why, really, for my part, my good old gentleman, I haven't learnt, i' faith, to carry burdens, or to feed cattle at the farm, or to nurse children.

LYSIMACHUS.
If you choose to be a good girl, it shall be well for you.

PASICOMPSA.
Then, i' faith, to my sorrow, I'm undone.

LYSIMACHUS.
Why so?

PASICOMPSA.
Because in the place from which I have been conveyed hither, it used to be well with the worthless.

LYSIMACHUS. [Aside]
By my troth, her talk alone is worth more than the sum that she was purchased at. [To PASICOMPSA] As though you would say that no woman is good.

PASICOMPSA.
Indeed I don't say so; nor is it my way, to say a thing which I believe all people are acquainted with.

LYSIMACHUS.
I want to ask this one thing of you.

PASICOMPSA.

I'll answer you when you ask.

LYSIMACHUS.

What say you now? What am I to say your name is?

PASICOMPSA.

Pasicompsa.

LYSIMACHUS.

The name was given you from your good looks. But what say you, Pasicompsa? Can you, if occasion should arise, spin a fine woof?

PASICOMPSA.

I can.

LYSIMACHUS.

If you know how to do a fine one, I'm sure you can spin a coarser one.

PASICOMPSA.

For spinning, I fear no woman that's of the same age.

LYSIMACHUS.

Upon my faith, I take it that you are good and industrious, since, young woman, now that you are grown up, you know how to do your duty.

PASICOMPSA.

I' faith, I learned it from a skilful mistress. I won't let my work be called in question.

LYSIMACHUS.

Well, thus the matter stands, i' faith. Look now, I'll give you a sheep for your own, one sixty years old.

PASICOMPSA.

My good old gentleman, one so old as that?

LYSIMACHUS.

It's of the Grecian breed. If you take care of it, it is a very good one; it is shorn very easily.

PASICOMPSA.

For the sake of the compliment, whatever it is that shall be given me, I shall receive it with thanks.

LYSIMACHUS.

Now, damsel, that you mayn't be mistaken, you are not mine; so don't think it.

PASICOMPSA.

Prithee, tell me, then, whose I am?

LYSIMACHUS.

You've been bought back for your own master. I've bought you back for him; he requested me to do so.

PASICOMPSA.

My spirits have returned, if good faith is kept with me.

LYSIMACHUS.

Be of good courage; this person will give you your liberty. I' troth, he did so dote upon you this day as soon as ever he had seen you.

PASICOMPSA.

I' faith, it's now two years since he commenced his connexion with me. Now, as I'm sure that you are a friend of his, I'll disclose it.

LYSIMACHUS.

How say you? Is it now two years since he formed the connexion with you?

PASICOMPSA.

Certainly, it is; and we agreed, on oath, between ourselves, I with him, and he with me, that I would never have intercourse with any man except himself, nor he with any woman except myself.

LYSIMACHUS.

Immortal Gods! Isn't he even to sleep with his wife?

PASICOMPSA.

Prithee, is he a married man? He neither is nor will he be.

LYSIMACHUS.

Indeed, I wish he wasn't. I' faith, the fellow has been committing perjury.

PASICOMPSA.

No young man do I more ardently love.

LYSIMACHUS.

Why, really he's a child, you simpleton; for, in fact, it's not so very long a time since his teeth fell out.

PASICOMPSA.

What? His teeth?

LYSIMACHUS.

It's no matter? Follow me this way, please; he requested that I would find you room for one day in my house, since my wife is away in the country. [*He goes into his house, followed by* PASICOMPSA]

[...]

DEMIPHO.

[*to himself*] At last I've managed to ruin myself; a mistress has been purchased for me without the knowledge of my wife and son. I'm resolved on it; I'll have recourse again to former habits and enjoy myself. In my allotment of existence, almost now run through, the little that there remains of life, I'll cheer up with pleasure, wine, and love. For it's quite proper for this time of life to enjoy itself. When you are young, then, when the blood is fresh, it's right to devote your exertions to acquiring your fortune; and then when at last, you are an old man, you may set yourself at your ease; drink, and be amorous; this, the fact that you are living, is now so much profit. This, as I say, I'll carry out in deed.

Meanwhile a friend of Charinus tells him that the girl has been sold. And Lysimachus, who is holding the girl in his house for Charinus' father, Demipho, comes in for a nasty surprise when his wife Dorippa arrives home.

[*Enter* DORIPPA.]

DORIPPA. [*To herself*]

Since a messenger came to me in the country from my husband, that he couldn't come into the country, I made up my mind, and came back to follow after him who fled from me. But [*looking round*] I don't see our old woman Syra following. Aye, look, there she comes at last [*with a bundle of green sprigs*].

DORIPPA.

Why don't you go quicker?

SYRA.

By my troth, I cannot; so great is this burden that I'm carrying.

DORIPPA.

What burden?

SYRA.

Fourscore years and four, and to that are added servitude, sweat, and thirst; these things as well which I am carrying weigh me down.

DORIPPA.

Give me something, Syra, with which to decorate this altar of our neighbour.

SYRA. [*Holding out a sprig*]

Present this sprig of laurel, then.

DORIPPA.

Now do you go into the house.

SYRA.

I'm going. [*Goes into the house of* LYSIMACHUS]

DORIPPA. [*Laying the sprig on the altar*]

Apollo, I pray thee that thou wilt propitiously grant peace, safety, and health, unto our household, and that in thy propitiousness thou wilt show favour to my son. [*Rushes out of the house, clapping her hands*]

SYRA.

I'm utterly undone! Wretch that I am, I'm ruined! Ah! wretched me!

DORIPPA.

Prithee, are you quite in your senses? What are you howling for?

SYRA.

Dorippa, my dear Dorippa!

DORIPPA.

Prithee, why are you crying out?

SYRA.

Some woman, I know not who, is here in-doors in the house.

DORIPPA.

What? A woman?

SYRA.

A harlot woman.

DORIPPA.

Is it so, really?

SYRA.

In serious truth. You know how to act very prudently, in not remaining in the country. A fool even could have found it out that she was the mistress of your very pretty husband.

DORIPPA.

By heavens, I believe it.

SYRA. [*Taking her arm*]

Step this way with me, that you, my Juno, may see as well your rival Alcmena.

DORIPPA.

I' troth, I certainly shall go there, as fast as I can. [*They go into the house of* LYSIMACHUS]

[*Enter* LYSIMACHUS.]

LYSIMACHUS. [*To himself*]

Is this too little of a misfortune that Demipho's in love, that he must be extravagant as well? If he had been inviting ten men of highest rank to dinner, he has provided too much. But the cooks he directed in such a way just as at sea the time-keeper is wont to direct the rowers. I hired a Cook myself, but I'm surprised that he hasn't come as I directed him. But who's this, I wonder, that's coming out of my house? The door's opening. [*He stands aside*]

[...]

DORIPPA. [*Continuing*]

I cannot remain at home; my eyes cannot abide that pretty young harlot; I would have shut her out of doors, but my son Eutychus prevented me. Still, I shan't altogether believe the news he brings.

[...]

PERISTRATA.

I'm not a nuisance, but a well-wisher; and it's your friend Peristrata addresses you. Prithee, do stay.

DORIPPA.

Why, Peristrata – i' faith, I didn't know you: dreadful vexation is tormenting and agitating me.

PERISTRATA.

This I enquire about – prithee don't deny me. I heard you just now; tell me what annoyance is troubling you.

DORIPPA.

Peristrata, so may the Gods prosper your only son, do kindly lend me your attention; none could be given me more agreeably: our ages are alike; together we grew up; we have husbands alike in age; with no one do I converse with greater pleasure. I'm really annoyed with good reason. What now would your feelings be, if at this time of life your husband Demipho were to bring a mistress before your eyes?

PERISTRATA.
Has he brought one?

DORIPPA.
So it is.

PERISTRATA.
She's at your house?

DORIPPA.
At my house [...]

Lysimachus' son Eutychus confronts his friend Charinus' father Demipho.

EUTYCHUS. [*To* DEMIPHO]
I bring you word that you have got no mistress.

DEMIPHO.
The Gods confound you. Why, prithee, what affair is this?

EUTYCHUS.
I'll tell you. Give your attention then, both of you.

LYSIMACHUS.
Well then, we are giving you our attention, both of us.

EUTYCHUS.
Those who are born of a good family, if they are of bad tendencies, by their own faultiness withdraw nobleness from their rank, and disgrace their disposition.

DEMIPHO.
He says what's true.

LYSIMACHUS.
Then it's to yourself he says it.

EUTYCHUS.
For this reason is this the more true; for at this time of life, it wasn't just for you to take away from your son, a young man, his mistress, purchased with his own money.

DEMIPHO.

How say you? Is she the mistress of Charinus?

EUTYCHUS. [*Aside*]

How the rogue does dissemble.

DEMIPHO.

Why, he said that he had bought her as a maidservant for his mother.

EUTYCHUS.

Was it for that reason, then, you bought her, you young lover, you old boy?

LYSIMACHUS.

Very well said, i' troth! Proceed, proceed. I'll stand by him here on the other side. Let's both load him well with such speeches as he's worthy of.

DEMIPHO. [*Aside*]

I'm done for.

EUTYCHUS.

Who has done an injustice so great to his blameless son; whom, in fact, upon my faith, I brought back home just when he was setting out in self-banishment; for he was going into exile.

DEMIPHO.

Has he gone then?

LYSIMACHUS.

What, do you speak, you hobgoblin? At this time of life you ought to abstain from those pursuits.

DEMIPHO.

I confess it; undoubtedly I've acted wrong.

EUTYCHUS.

What, do you speak, you hobgoblin? You ought at this time of life to have done with these guilty practices. Just as the seasons of the year, so different lines of conduct befit different ages; but if this is proper, that old fellows should be wenching in their old age, where in the world is our common welfare?

DEMIPHO.

Alas! wretch that I am! I'm undone.

EUTYCHUS.

The young men are more in the habit of giving their attention to following those pursuits.

DEMIPHO.

Troth, now, prithee, do take her to yourselves, with pigs and with basket.

EUTYCHUS.

Restore her to your son; let him have her, now, as he wishes.

DEMIPHO.

So far as I'm concerned, he may have her.

EUTYCHUS.

High time, i' faith, since you haven't the power of doing otherwise.

DEMIPHO.

For this injury let him take what satisfaction he likes; only do you make peace, I beg of you, that he mayn't be angry with me. I' faith, if I had known it, or if, indeed, he had told me in the slightest way of joke that he was in love with her, I should never have proceeded to take her away from him so in love. Eutychus, you are his companion, preserve and rescue me, I beg of you. Make this old fellow your client. You shall say that I'm mindful of a kindness.

And all's well that ends well.

EUROPA AND THE BULL

'Idyll II'

Moschus

Translated by Andrew Lang, 1892

In this pastoral *Idyll* by **Moschus**, a bucolic poet born in Syracuse, in Sicily, in the mid-second century BC, a young virgin named Europa is sent a curious dream by Aphrodite ('Cypris'). Her fate is sealed. There are echoes here of the tale of young Persephone (see Story 11), among others. The story of Europa and the bull was particularly popular among artists of the Renaissance.

To Europa, once on a time, a sweet dream was sent by Cypris, when the third watch of the night sets in, and near is the dawning; when sleep more sweet than honey rests on the eyelids, limb-loosening sleep, that binds the eyes with his soft bond, when the flock of truthful dreams fares wandering.

At that hour she was sleeping, beneath the roof-tree of her home, Europa, the daughter of Phoenix, being still a maid unwed. Then she beheld two Continents at strife for her sake, Asia, and the farther shore, both in the shape of women. Of these one had the guise of a stranger, the other of a lady of that land, and closer still she clung about her maiden, and kept saying how 'she was her mother, and herself had nursed Europa.' But that other with mighty hands, and forcefully, kept haling the maiden, nothing loth; declaring that, by the will of Aegis-bearing Zeus, Europa was destined to be her prize.

But Europa leaped forth from her strown bed in terror, with beating heart, in such clear vision had she beheld the dream. Then she sat upon her bed, and long was silent, still beholding the two women, albeit with waking eyes; and at last the maiden raised her timorous voice:—

'Who of the gods of heaven has sent forth to me these phantoms? What manner of dreams have scared me when right sweetly slumbering on my strown bed, within my bower? Ah, and who was the alien woman that I beheld in my sleep? How strange a longing for her seized my heart, yea, and how graciously she herself did welcome me, and regard me as it had been her own child.

'Ye blessed gods, I pray you, prosper the fulfilment of the dream.'

Therewith she arose, and began to seek the dear maidens of her company, girls of like age with herself, born in the same year, beloved of her heart, the daughters of noble sires, with whom she was always wont to sport, when she was arrayed for the dance, or when she would bathe her bright body at the mouths of the rivers, or would gather fragrant lilies on the leas.

And soon she found them, each bearing in her hand a basket to fill with flowers, and to the meadows near the salt sea they set forth, where always they were wont to gather in their company, delighting in the roses, and the sound of the waves. But Europa herself bore a basket of gold, a marvel well worth gazing on, a choice work of Hephaestus. He gave it to Libya, for a bridal-gift, when she approached the bed of the Shaker of the Earth, and Libya gave it to beautiful Telephassa, who was of her own blood; and to Europa, still an unwedded maid, her mother, Telephassa, gave the splendid gift.

Many bright and cunning things were wrought in the basket: therein was Io, daughter of Inachus, fashioned in gold; still in the shape of a heifer she was, and had not her woman's shape, and wildly wandering she fared upon the salt sea-ways, like one in act to swim; and the sea was wrought in blue steel. And aloft upon the double brow of the shore, two men were standing together and watching the heifer's sea-faring. There too was Zeus, son of Cronos, lightly touching with his divine hand the cow of the line of Inachus, and her, by Nile of the seven streams, he was changing again, from a horned heifer to a woman. Silver was the stream of Nile, and the heifer of bronze and Zeus himself was fashioned in gold. And all about, beneath the rim of the rounded basket, was the story of Hermes graven, and near him lay stretched out Argus, notable for his sleepless eyes. And from the red blood of Argus was springing a bird that rejoiced in the flower-bright colour of his feathers, and spreading abroad his tail, even as some swift ship on the sea doth spread all canvas, was covering with his plumes the lips of the golden vessel. Even thus was wrought the basket of the lovely Europa.

Now the girls, so soon as they were come to the flowering meadows, took great delight in various sorts of flowers, whereof one would pluck sweet-breathed narcissus, another the hyacinth, another the violet, a fourth the creeping thyme, and on the ground there fell many petals of the meadows rich with spring. Others again were emulously gathering the fragrant tresses of the yellow crocus; but in the midst of them all the princess culled with her hand the splendour of the crimson rose, and shone pre-eminent among them all like the foam-born goddess among the Graces. Verily she was not for long to set her heart's delight upon the flowers, nay, nor long to keep untouched her maiden girdle. For of a truth, the son of Cronos, so soon as he beheld her, was troubled, and his heart was subdued by the sudden shafts of Cypris, who alone can conquer even Zeus. Therefore, both to avoid the wrath of jealous Hera, and being eager to beguile the maiden's tender heart, he concealed his god head, and changed his shape, and became a bull. Not such a one as feeds in the stall nor such as cleaves the furrow, and drags the curved plough, nor such as grazes on the grass, nor such a bull as is subdued beneath the yoke, and draws the burdened wain. Nay, but while all the rest of his body was bright chestnut, a silver circle shone between his brows, and his eyes gleamed softly, and ever sent forth lightning of desire. From his brow branched horns of even length, like the crescent of the horned moon, when her disk is cloven in twain. He came into the meadow, and his coming terrified not the maidens, nay, within them all wakened desire to draw nigh the lovely bull, and to touch him, and his heavenly fragrance was scattered afar, exceeding even the sweet perfume of the meadows. And he stood before the feet of fair Europa, and kept licking her neck, and cast his spell over the maiden. And she still caressed him, and gently with her hands she wiped away the deep foam from his lips, and kissed the bull. Then he lowed so gently, ye would think ye heard the Mygdonian flute uttering a dulcet sound.

He bowed himself before her feet, and, bending back his neck, he gazed on Europa, and showed her his broad back. Then she spake among her deep-tressed maidens, saying—

'Come, dear playmates, maidens of like age with me, let us mount the bull here and take our pastime, for truly, he will bear us on his back, and carry all of us; and how mild he is, and dear, and gentle to behold, and no whit like other bulls. A mind as honest as a man's possesses him, and he lacks nothing but speech.'

So she spake, and smiling, she sat down on the back of the bull, and the others were about to follow her. But the bull leaped up immediately, now he had gotten her that he desired, and swiftly he sped to the deep. The maiden turned, and called again and again to her dear playmates, stretching out her hands, but they could not reach her. The strand he gained, and forward he sped like a dolphin, faring with unwetted hooves over the wide waves. And the sea, as he came, grew smooth, and the sea-monsters gambolled around, before the feet of Zeus, and the dolphin rejoiced, and rising from the deeps, he tumbled on the swell of the sea. The Nereids arose out of the salt water, and all of them came on in orderly array, riding on the backs of sea-beasts. And himself, the thund'rous Shaker of the World, appeared above the sea, and made smooth the wave, and guided his brother on the salt sea path; and round him were gathered the Tritons, these hoarse trumpeters of the deep, blowing from their long conches a bridal melody.

Meanwhile Europa, riding on the back of the divine bull, with one hand clasped the beast's great horn, and with the other caught up the purple fold of her garment, lest it might trail and be wet in the hoar sea's infinite spray. And her deep robe was swelled out by the winds, like the sail of a ship, and lightly still did waft the maiden onward. But when she was now far off from her own country, and neither sea-beat headland nor steep hill could now be seen, but above, the air, and beneath, the limitless deep, timidly she looked around, and uttered her voice, saying—

'Whither bearest thou me, bull-god? What art thou? how dost thou fare on thy feet through the path of the sea-beasts, nor fearest the sea? The sea is a path meet for swift ships that traverse the brine, but bulls dread the salt sea-ways. What drink is sweet to thee, what food shalt thou find from the deep? Nay, art thou then some god, for godlike are these deeds of thine? Lo, neither do dolphins of the brine fare on land, nor bulls on the deep, but dreadless dost thou rush o'er land and sea alike, thy hooves serving thee for oars.

'Nay, perchance thou wilt rise above the grey air, and flee on high, like the swift birds. Alas for me, and alas again, for mine exceeding evil fortune, alas for me that have left my father's house, and following this bull, on a strange sea-faring I go, and wander lonely. But I pray thee that rulest the grey salt sea, thou Shaker of the Earth, propitious meet me, and methinks I see thee smoothing this path of mine before me. For surely it is not without a god to aid, that I pass through these paths of the waters!

So spake she, and the horned bull made answer to her again—

'Take courage, maiden, and dread not the swell of the deep. Behold I am Zeus, even I, though, closely beheld, I wear the form of a bull, for I can put on the semblance of what thing I will. But 'tis love of thee that has compelled me to measure out so great a space of the salt sea, in a bull's shape. Lo, Crete shall presently receive thee, Crete that was mine own foster-mother, where thy bridal chamber shall be. Yea, and from me shalt thou bear glorious sons, to be sceptre-swaying kings over earthly men.'

So spake he, and all he spake was fulfilled. And verily Crete appeared, and Zeus took his own shape again, and he loosed her girdle, and the Hours arrayed their bridal bed. She that before was a maiden straightway became the bride of Zeus, and she bore children to Zeus, yea, anon she was a mother.

TROUBLE COMES TO TOWN

The Brothers

Terence

Translated by Betty Radice, 1965

The Brothers is a Roman comedy by **Terence** (*c.* 195/185–*c.* 159 BC), who was born in Carthage to Libyan parents in the second century BC and came as a slave to Rome, where he was later freed. A man named Demea has two sons, the younger of whom, Ctesipho, he has raised in the countryside. Demea's brother Micio, meanwhile, has raised the elder, his nephew Aeschinus, in the city of Athens. While Demea has been a severe father, Micio has taken a rather hands-off approach to parenting, and his ward Aeschinus is consequently something of a reprobate. This play, which was based on a Greek comedy by Menander (author of Story 31), has a characteristically elaborate plot. Aeschinus has impregnated a girl called Pamphila and promised to marry her. But then his brother Ctesipho comes to town, lets loose, and has him procure a Music Girl for him. Aeschinus agrees to cover for his brother and conceal the Music Girl but is then suspected of taking her for himself. His future mother-in-law, Sostrata, hears about the Music Girl as Pamphila is giving birth to his child. In this extract from the play, Aeschinus considers his options and is confronted by his father, who playfully feigns ignorance of recent events.

AESCHINUS. This is sheer torture! I never thought to receive such a cruel blow. I just can't think what I'm to do with myself or what to do at all. I'm numb with terror, dazed with fear, robbed of reasoning power! How can I find a way out of this confusion? This awful suspicion – it all seemed so natural! Sostrata is convinced I bought this girl for myself – so I discovered from the old woman when I caught sight of her on her way to fetch the midwife; I ran up and asked her how Pamphila was, whether labour had started and the midwife had been sent for. 'Get out!' was all she said. ' Clear off, Aeschinus, we've had enough of your lying words and your broken promises!' 'What on earth do you mean by that?' I said. 'Good-bye, you can keep the girl you've chosen.' I guessed at once what they suspected, but held my tongue – one word about my brother to that old gossip and all would be out.

Now what can I do? Say the girl is my brother's? But this mustn't get abroad at all costs. I can't let it out if it's still possible to keep the secret.... Besides, I doubt if they would believe me: it all hangs together and sounds likely enough. It was I who carried off the girl and I who paid the money, and our house she was brought to. This at least was all my doing, I admit. If only I'd told it all to my father however I'd managed it! I could have persuaded him to let me marry Pamphila.... [*After a pause*] Here I am, still putting things off! Now's the time, Aeschinus, to pull yourself together! And first of all I'll go to the women and clear myself. [*He moves towards* SOSTRATA'*s house.*] Here's the door.... No, I can't face it.... I'm a poor thing, I can never raise a hand to this door without a shudder.... [*He makes a tremendous effort and knocks loudly*] Anyone there? It's Aeschinus. Open the door, somebody, at once! Someone's coming out; I'll stay over here.

[MICIO *comes out of* SOSTRATA'*s house speaking back to her.*]

MICIO. Do as I say, Sostrata, both of you, while I find Aeschinus and tell him our arrangements. [*Coming forward*] Someone knocked – who was it?

AESCHINUS. [*Aside*] Heavens, it's my father; I'm done for!

MICIO. Aeschinus!

AESCHINUS. [*Aside*] What can he want?

MICIO. Was it you who knocked? [*Aside*] No reply; I think I must tease him a bit – he deserves it for never wanting to trust me over this. [*Aloud*] Can't you answer me?

AESCHINUS. [*In confusion*] I didn't knock – at least I don't think I did.

MICIO. No? I was just wondering what you were doing here. [*Aside*] He's blushing: all's well.

AESCHINUS. Excuse me, father, but what took you there? [*pointing to* SOSTRATA'*s house*].

MICIO. No business of mine. A friend brought me here just now – to act as a witness.

AESCHINUS. Witness for what?

MICIO. [*Watching him closely*] I'll tell you. There are some women living here, in a poor way. I don't think you know them, in fact I am sure you can't, for they have not been here long.

AESCHINUS. Well, what then?

MICIO. There is a girl with her mother –

AESCHINUS. Go on –

MICIO. The girl has lost her father, and this friend of mine is her next-of-kin; so he must marry her. That's the law.

AESCHINUS. [*Aside*] No – I can't bear it.

MICIO. What was that?

AESCHINUS. Nothing: it's all right: go on.

MICIO. He has come to take her away to Miletus – where he lives.

AESCHINUS. What, to take the girl away with him ?

MICIO. That's right.

AESCHINUS. All the way to Miletus did you say?

MICIO. I did.

AESCHINUS. [*Aside*] Oh my head reels! [*Aloud*] But the women – what do they say?

MICIO. What do you expect? Nothing, in fact. The mother has a trumped-up story about the girl having a baby by another man, whom she won't name. He came first, she says, so the girl ought not to be married to my friend.

AESCHINUS. Then don't you think that's right?

MICIO. No, I don't.

AESCHINUS. You don't? And will he really take her away, father?

MICIO. Why on earth shouldn't he?

AESCHINUS. [*In a passionate outburst*] It was cruel of you both, it was heartless, and if I must speak plainly, father, it was – it was – downright dishonourable!

MICIO. But why?

AESCHINUS. You ask me why? What about the unhappy man who first loved her and for all I know, poor wretch, still loves her desperately? What do you suppose he will feel when he sees her torn from his arms and carried off before his very eyes? I tell you, father, it's a sin and a scandal!

MICIO. How do you make that out? Who promised this girl in marriage and who gave her away? Who was the bridegroom and when was the wedding? Who witnessed it? She was meant for another – why did this man take her?

AESCHINUS. Then was this girl to sit at home, at her age, waiting for a relative to turn up from heaven knows where? You could have said that, father, and stuck to it.

MICIO. Nonsense! I had come to help a friend; was I to turn against him? In any case, Aeschinus, the girl is no concern of ours. Why should we bother about them? Let us go... But what's the matter? Why are you crying?

AESCHINUS. Father, please listen...

MICIO. [*Gently*] My son, I have heard the whole story; I understand, for I love you, so all you do touches my heart.

AESCHINUS. Then I'll try to deserve your love in future all your life, father – I feel so guilty and ashamed of what I've done that I can't look you in the face.

MICIO. I believe you; I know you are honourable at heart. But I worry about you and your heedless ways. What sort of a country do you think you live in? You seduced a girl you should never have touched. That was your first fault, and quite bad enough, though no more than human: honest men have done the same before you. But afterwards, tell me, did you give it a thought? Or did you look ahead at all and think what you should do and how to do it? If you were ashamed to confess to me yourself, how was I to find out? You delayed and did nothing while nine months went by. This was the greatest wrong you could do, to yourself, to that poor girl, and the child. Well: did you think you could leave everything to the gods and go on dreaming? And that she would be brought to you as a bride without your lifting a finger? I trust you are not so thoughtless in all your personal affairs. [*Changing his tone, after a pause*] Cheer up, you shall marry her.

AESCHINUS. What?

MICIO. I said, Cheer up.

AESCHINUS. Father, for pity's sake, are you making fun of me now?

MICIO. No, I'm not. Why should I?

AESCHINUS. I don't know, except that I'm so desperately anxious for this to be true that I'm afraid it isn't.

MICIO. Go indoors, and pray the gods to help you bring home your wife. Off with you.

AESCHINUS. What? My wife? Will it be soon?

MICIO. Yes.

AESCHINUS. How soon?

MICIO. As soon as possible.

AESCHINUS. [*Hugging him*] Damn me, father, if I don't love you more than my own eyes!

MICIO. [*Gently disengaging himself*] What, more than – her?

AESCHINUS. Well, just as much.

MICIO. [*Ironically*] Very kind of you.

AESCHINUS. [*Suddenly remembering*] But where's that man from Miletus?

MICIO. [*Airily*] Lost, gone, on board his ship… Now what's stopping you?

AESCHINUS. Father, you go, you pray to the gods. They'll be more likely to listen to you, I know; you're so much better than I.

MICIO. I am going in: there are preparations to be made. You be sensible and do what I say. [*He goes into* MICIO's *house.*]

AESCHINUS. [*Coming forward*] What do you think of that? Is this what it means to be a father or a son? A brother or a friend couldn't do more for me. Oh, he's a man to love and cherish in one's heart! Wonderful! If he can be so kind I'll be sure never to be foolish again or do anything he doesn't like.

PHILOCTETES

Fabulae

Hyginus

Translated by R. Scott Smith and Stephen M. Trzaskoma, 2007

In his *Fabulae*, the Latin writer **Hyginus** (64 BC–AD 17) reduced hundreds
of ancient myths to a paragraph or two each. The *Fabulae* may lack the
colour of the Greek epics and tragedies, but they provide useful over-
views of their plots. The playwright Sophocles had written at length of the
wretched plight of the Greek warrior Philoctetes in a tragedy in the fifth
century BC. The story is set during the Trojan War and brings home just
how unsympathetically the ancients looked upon physical disabilities.

When Philoctetes, the son of Poeas and Demonassa, was on the island
of Lemnos, a snake bit him on his foot. This snake had been sent by
Juno, who was angry at him because he was the only one who had
the nerve to build a pyre for Hercules when he discarded his human body and
was made immortal. In return for his service, Hercules bequeathed to him his
divine arrows. But when the Achaeans could no longer put up with the foul
odor that was coming from the wound, on King Agamemnon's orders he was
abandoned on Lemnos along with his divine arrows. A shepherd of King Actor
named Iphimachus, the son of Dolopion, found him abandoned and took care
of him. Later it was revealed to the Greeks that Troy could not be taken without
Hercules' arrows. Agamemnon then sent Ulysses and Diomedes to find him.
They convinced him to let bygones be bygones and help them sack Troy, and
they took him back to Troy with them.

SLAUGHTER OF THE HUSBANDS

Thebaid, Book V

Statius

Translated by William Lillington Lewis, 1767

The Aegean island of Lemnos, where Philoctetes was abandoned in the previous story, also features in the *Thebaid* of **Statius** (*c.* AD 45–*c.* 96). A Latin epic composed in the 80s or early 90s AD, the *Thebaid* retells the legend of the struggle of the sons of Oedipus for the throne of Thebes – dramatized some five centuries earlier by the Greek tragedian Aeschylus in his *Seven Against Thebes*. In Book V, Hypsipyle, daughter of the Lemnian king, tells her story to Adrastus, King of Argos. She describes how Venus took vengeance on the Lemnians for their failure to worship her by inspiring the women to murder the men. Hypsipyle alone saved her father. William Lillington Lewis's verse translation of 1767, dedicated to Henry, Duke of Beaufort, brings out the sheer horror of the ensuing bloodbath.

> Encircled by the Deep fair Lemnos lies;
> Here weary Vulcan wastes his leisure Hours,
> And recollects in Sleep his scatter'd Pow'rs.
> The Cloud-capt Athos from his length'ning Steep
> O'erlooks our Isle; his Groves o'ershade the Deep.
> Each fronting Tract of Land the Thracian plows,
> The Thracian, fatal to each Lemnian Spouse.
> Once great in Arms and useful Arts it shone,
> Fertile in Chiefs of Valour and Renown:
> Not Delos, or the Samian Isle could claim
> A greater Share of Riches and of Fame;
> Till Heav'n to punish our Offence decreed.
> Nor were we wanting to promote the Deed:
> No Temples to the Queen of Love were rais'd,
> Nor Incense on the sacred Altars blaz'd.
> Thus sometimes Anger stings a heav'nly Mind,
> And Vengeance sure, tho' tardy, creeps behind.
> From Paphos, where a hundred Altars smoke,

And love-sick Votaries her Aid invoke,
Careless of Dress and Ornament she moves,
And leaves behind her Cestus and her Doves.
The Moon had measur'd half the starry Frame,
When the fierce Goddess with the Furies came:
Far other Flames, than those of Love she bears,
And high in Air the Torch of Discord rears.
Soon as the Fiend-engendred Serpents roam,
Diffusing Terrors o'er each wrangling Dome,
The Loves, or willing, or compell'd by Force,
From guilty Lemnos bend their airy Course;
Lemnos, which dearer to her Consort stands
Than all the Cities rear'd by mortal Hands.
                                        Thus
Urg'd by no Cause, the sullen Bridegroom fled
From blooming Beauty, and the genial Bed;
No more he pays the pleasing Debt of Love,
When conscious Cynthia rules the Realms above:
Nor Sleep surprizes with unnotic'd Pace
The clasping Pair, and strengthens their Embrace:
But Rage and Hate in every Breast arise,
And with his Torch inverted Hymen flies.
The Men (a Plea for Absence) oft complain
Of Thracian Insults, and demand the Plain:
And tho' from Camp their Eyes with Ease command
Their native City, and the Lemnian Strand,
Tho' Nature, oft recoiling, chides their Stay,
And their sad Children beckon them away;
Stretch'd on the Banks, they rather wish to bear
The wintry Storm, th' Inclemencies of Air,
And listen to the hoarse-resounding Roar
Of nightly Surges, breaking on the Shore.
Our Sex in social Converse seek Relief,
And point to Thrace, the Object of their Grief:
From Morn to Night the Stream of Sorrow flows,
And Sol but sets to rise upon their Woes.
How blest was I, a Stranger then to Love,
And all the Pangs, which widow'd Matrons prove.
Now thro' the Zenith flaming Sol had driv'n
His panting Steeds, and gain'd the middle Heav'n,
When, tho' no gath'ring Clouds the Day controul
Thro' Skies serene portentous Thunders roll;
                                        And
The Caverns of the smoky God display
Thick-steaming Flames, and choak the Face of Day:
Tho' mute each Blast, the rough Aegean roars,
And heavy Surges lash the plaintive Shores:

Then grave Polyxo thro' the City roves,
And mourns her widow'd Bed and slighted Loves.
Mad as the Thracian Bacchanal appears,
When from afar the vocal Pipe she hears,
Evoe she cries, and shakes the solid Ground,
While ecchoing Mountains answer to the Sound.
Flush'd are her Cheeks, and haggard roll her Eyes,
She rends the desart Town with frantic Cries,
And, while the Gates resound beneath her Strokes,
To join in Aid th' assembling Dames invokes,
Four death-devoted Babes, (sad Scene of Grief;)
Hung at her Side, and sought to give Relief.
Swift as our Leader, to Minerva's Fane
We bend our Course, a wild disorder'd Train.
Silence enjoin'd, with Confidence arose
The daring Authoress of all our Woes;
Her better Hand a naked Dagger press'd,
And thus her Speech the wrathful Fair address'd.
Ye Lemnian Dames, dissolv'd in barren Ease,
If Venus yet retains the Pow'r to please,
If empty Marriage-Forms ye disapprove,
And hate the Name without the Joys of Love;
Hear and attend: when Fortune points the Way,
And Heav'n inspires, 'tis impious to delay:
To Vengeance rise; nor let your Sex be known
By Want of Courage, but by Form alone.
Yet Hymen's Privilege we may regain,
And Love and genial Joys revive again,
Would each the Toil with just Division share,
And join her private with the public Care.
Three Years have past, since each deserted Bride
Has lost the sullen Partner of her Side:
No more each Debt of Love and Duty's paid,
Nor more Lucina yields her timely Aid.
Prompted by Nature, and by Love inclin'd,
The Fishes, Birds, and Beasts increase their Kind.
Stern Danaus his Progeny could rouse
To Vengeance for the Breach of Marriage-Vows,
And, unrestrain'd with Fears, dismiss the Foe,
In Dreams of Terror, to the Shades below:
But we, a worthless, servile, heartless Train,
Had rather brook tyrannic Hymen's Chain.
Yet should these old Examples fail to move
Your just Revenge of alienated Love;
Copy the Thracian Dame, who durst explore;
Her Spouse's Heart, and drink the rushing Gore.
Each Doubt, and each Objection to remove,

Myself will first the guilty Labour prove.
Four Babes, the Boast and Solace of their Sire,
Shall first beneath the ruthless Sword expire:
Nor shall their Blandishments a Respite gain,
But interposing Nature plead in vain:
While yet they breath, the Author of their Birth
Shall crown the Heap, and stain the loaded Earth.
What Heroine dares thus far in Guilt engage,
And second my Design with equal Rage?
Mean while the Lemnian Fleet, in all the Pride
Of swelling Canvass, cleaves the yielding Tide.
This with pleas'd Eyes the fierce Polyxo view'd.
And thus in Height of Joy her Theme pursu'd.
When Fortune calls, what farther can detain,
And shall the Gods afford their Aid in vain.
Our Foes advance, impell'd by adverse Fate,
To stain the Sword, and glut in Death our Hate.
Late slighted Venus in a Dream appear'd,
And o'er my Head a naked Falchion rear'd.
Why waste thus the Bloom of Youth? (she said)
Arise, arise, and purge the Marriage Bed;
On me alone for other Flames rely;
Each vacant Bed will I myself supply.
The Goddess spoke, and on the Pillow laid
This same (believe me) this same vengeful Blade,
But linger on, when fair Occasion calls.
And their Ships ride in Prospect of our Walls:
At ev'ry Stroke they raise the briny Foam,
And bring, perhaps, their Thracian Consorts Home.
Her Words their Hearts with manly Rage inspire,
And spread from Breast to Breast the vengeful Fire.
Not greater Shouts the Plains of Scythia rend,
When the fierce Amazons to Fight descend,
When their stern Patron summons from afar
His Virgin-Troops, and frees th' imprison'd War.
Nor Discord, rising from a various Choice,
Disturbs their Councils with tumultuous Voice;
But equal was their Will, the fame their Haste
To desolate, and lay each Mansion waste,
To strike the Youth, and Sire with Age opprest
To tear the wailing Infant from the Breast,
And subject to their unexcepting Rage
Each Stage of Life, and each Degree of Age.
There grew a Forest near Minerva's Fane,
Whose gloomy Boughs obscure the subject Plain,
A steepy Mount o'erhangs the nether Glade,
And Sol is loft between the double Shade.

Here they repair, and at the Rites obscene
Attest Bellona, and the Stygian Queen.
From Acheron their Course the Furies bend,
And, uninvok'd, the Sacrifice attend.
The Paphian Goddess turns on ev'ry Side
Her Steps unknown, and fires each youthful Bride.
Spontaneous then fell Caropeia brought
Her Son (his Sex, alas, his only Fault)
A Throng of armed Priestesses surrounds,
The Victim falls beneath unnumber'd Wounds:
The Life-Blood issuing from a thousand Strokes,
With horrid Imprecations each invokes:
The recent Shade from its dark Prison springs,
And haunts the Mother with encircling Wings.
Struck at the Sight, my Limbs with Horror shook,
The Blood at once my ghastly Cheeks forsook.
Thus fares the Hind, by rav'ning Wolves pursu'd,
As first she seeks the Covert of the Wood;
Much she distrusts a safe Retreat in Flight,
But more her Strength and Fortune in the Fight.
Now, now she seems to feel her seizing Foes,
And hears with Dread their Jaws eluded close.
Mean while, their Anchors dropt, the Ships restore
The Lemnian Warriors to their native Shore:
With Emulation on the Deck they stand,
Contending, who should first attain the Strand.
Far happier! had they press'd the Thracian Plain,
Or sunk beneath the Fury of the Main,
The lofty Fanes are hid in ambient Smoke,
And votive Victims grace the fatal Stroke:
But the black Flame and unsound Entrails prove
Th' unfav'ring Purpose of the Gods above.
Late and unwilling to his watry Bed
The Sun retir'd, and veil'd his radiant Head,
Detain'd by Jove; nor ever did the Day
So long before survive his letting Ray.
The Stars awhile withheld their gleamy Light,
And sicken'd to behold the fatal Night.
While other Isles enjoy their usual Share
Of Light, and glitter with the distant Glare,
O'er guilty Lemnos gath'ring Clouds arise,
And low-hung Vapours choak the lab'ring Skies.
Lemnos, in circling Darkness lost, alone
Was to the sorrowing Mariner unknown.
Now from the finish'd Rites they bend their Way,
To drown in Wine the Labours of the Day;
And, while the sprightly Essence of the Bowl

Glows in each Vein, and opens ev'ry Soul,
With Rapture they recount their recent Toils,
Their Victories, and long-contested Spoils.
Their Wives alike indulge the genial Hour,
Studious to please, and call forth Beauty's Pow'r;
Then Love's soft Queen (to crown the short Repast,
And bless the Night of all their Nights the last)
Breath'd in each Husband's Breast a fierce Desire
Of am'rous Joys that quickly must expire.
T'was dead of Night; the Matrons cease to sing,
Dumb was each Voice, and mute the tuneful String;
When Sleep, Half-Brother of approaching Death,
Steep'd in soft Dews exhal'd from Styx beneath,
Safe under Covert of the silent Hours,
With lavish Hand his opiate Juices pours,
But not on all: their Ardour to destroy,
And watchful Cares the female Part employ.
At length, no longer patient of Delay,
They rush impetuous on their helpless Prey:
And each (a Fury lodg'd within her Breast,)
Invades her Man, with downy Sleep opprest.
Thus Scythian Tigresses the Herd surround,
And leap amidst them with a furious Bound,
When, press'd with Hunger, they desert the Wood,
Or their fierce Whelps demand the promis'd Food.
What Act of Guilt, or whose untimely Fate
Amidst a Thousand shall I first relate?
O'er Helimus, with leafy Honours crown'd,
Rash Gorge stands, and meditates a Wound.
Cloy'd with the Banquet, he retir'd to Rest,
And puff'd the fumy God from out his Breast;
But Sleep forsook him, e'er depriv'd of Breath,
And starting at the cold Approach of Death,
He wakes, confounded at the sudden View,
And round her Neck his Arms in Transport threw,
But mourns the social Greeting ill repaid,
As in his Chest he feels the driving Blade.
Nor yet resenting of his Wound, he prest
Th' unworthy Object closer to his Breast,
And, struggling in the griping Arms of Death,
On Gorge dwells, and wastes his parting Breath.
Dire as they were, I cannot now relate
The Vulgar's countless Deaths and various Fate:
Suffice it private Evils to disclose,
And measure by my own another's Woes.
Craeneus fell, a Warrior fair and bold,
And youthful Cydon, grac'd with Locks of Gold.

With these, the Product of an Alien's Bed,
I pass'd my early Days, together bred.
Next Gyas bled, design'd with me to prove,
Had Heav'n prolong'd his Date, the Joys of Love.
Then fair Aepopeus met his Mother's Blade,
As at the Feast the wanton Stripling play'd.
Lycaste of her Rage disarm'd, appears
And sheds o'er Cydimus a Flood of Tears;
As she beheld a Face of her own Mold,
And Hair which she herself had trick'd with Gold,
Her Consort slain, her Mother near her Stands,
Impells with Threats, and arms her trembling Hands.
As when the Lion, or the spotted Pard,
Long from the Woods and Forests are debarr'd,
With equal Pain and Labour is renew'd
Their savage Nature, as at first subdu'd.
The fair Lycaste thus resists in vain;
She rushes on him, as he press'd the Plain.
Catches the welling Blood, and to renew
His Wounds, by the loose Hair his Body drew.
But as Alcimede I first survey'd,
Her Sire's pale Visage fix'd upon the Blade,
Fear shrunk my Sinews, and congeal'd my Blood,
And on my Head my Hair erected stood.
My Father's Image fill'd my pious Mind,
Lest equal Years might equal Fortune find.
From thence in Haste I seek the regal Seat;
Fear aids my Course, and wings my tardy Feet:
My Sire I found perplex'd with Doubts and Fears,
(For now the Shouts and Groans awak'd his Ears,
And broke his Slumbers, tho' the Palace stood
Sequester'd, and encompass'd with a Wood)
The Motives of my Flight I soon disclose,
And all the Series of preceding Woes:
'Arise, arise, or you for ever fall;
'Our female Foes approach the regal Hall:
'Nor on our utmost Speed I much rely;
'The Shaft may yet arrest us as we fly.'
Struck at the News, the hoary King arose,
And left the silent Mansion of Repose.
Thro' the least peopled Parts we speed our Way,
And, in a sable Cloud obscur'd, survey
The Passages, and Streets around dispread
With Streams of Blood and Mountains of the dead.

Salvation for the now partnerless women of Lemnos came with the arrival of the Argonauts, the subject of the next story.

THE GOLDEN FLEECE

Argonautica

Apollonius Rhodius

Translated by E. V. Rieu, 1959

The Greek writer **Apollonius** was once head of the Great Library of Alexandria, in Egypt. He later settled at Rhodes. His *Argonautica*, which dates to the third century BC, is perhaps the most thrilling Greek epic to have been composed since Homer's *Iliad* and *Odyssey*. The poem is spread over only four books, reflecting the so-called 'Hellenistic' poets' preference for concision over length. The extracts below reflect some key moments of the unfolding story.

It was King Pelias who sent them out. He had heard an oracle which warned him of a dreadful fate – death through the machinations of the man whom he should see coming from the town with one foot bare. The prophecy was soon confirmed. Jason, fording the Anaurus in a winter spate, lost one of his sandals, which stuck in the bed of the flooded river, but saved the other from the mud and shortly after appeared before the king. He had come for a banquet that Pelias was giving in honour of his father Poseidon and all the other gods, except Pelasgian Here to whom he paid no homage. And no sooner did the king see him than he thought of the oracle and decided to send him on a perilous adventure overseas. He hoped that things might so fall out, either at sea or in outlandish parts, that Jason would never see his home again.

The ship was built by Argus, under Athene's eye. But as poets before me have told that tale, I will content myself by recounting the names and lineage of her noble crew, their long sea voyages, and all they achieved in their wanderings. Muses, inspire my lay.

Jason and his sailor Argonauts, among them Heracles, Peleus and Orpheus, accept a mission to steal the golden fleece of a ram from Colchis on the coast of what is now Georgia, in the Caucasus. Before they set out across the Black Sea they receive a prophecy that they will succeed but suffer along the way.

Jason wept as he turned his eyes away from the land of his birth. But the rest struck the rough sea with their oars in time with Orpheus' lyre, like young men bringing down their quick feet on the earth in unison with one another and the lyre, as they dance for Apollo round his altar at Pytho, or in Ortygia, or by the waters of Ismenus. Their blades were swallowed by the waves, and on either side the dark salt water broke into foam, seething angrily in answer to the strong men's strokes. The armour on the moving ship glittered in the sunshine like fire; and all the time she was followed by a long white wake which stood out like a path across a green plain.

All the gods looked down from heaven that day, observing *Argo* and the spirit shown by her heroic crew, the noblest seamen of their time; and from the mountain heights the Nymphs of Pelion admired Athene's work and the gallant Argonauts themselves, tugging at the oars. Cheiron son of Philyra came down from the high ground to the sea and wading out into the grey surf waved his great hand again and again and wished the travellers a happy home-coming. His wife came too. She was carrying Peleus' little boy Achilles on her arm, and she held him up for his dear father to see.

Till they had left the harbour and its curving shores behind them, the ship was in the expert hands of Tiphys, wise son of Hagnias, who used the polished steering-oar to keep her on her course. But now they stept the tall mast in its box and fixed it with forestays drawn taut on either bow; then hauled the sail up to the masthead and unfurled it. The shrill wind filled it out; and after making the halyards fast on deck, each round its wooden pin, they sailed on at their ease past the long Tisaean headland, while Orpheus played his lyre and sang them a sweet song of highborn Artemis, Saver of ships and Guardian of those peaks that here confront the sea, and of the land of Iolcus. Fish large and small came darting out over the salt sea depths and gambolled in their watery wake, led by the music like a great flock of sheep that have had their fill of grass and follow their shepherd home to the gay sound of some rustic melody from his high-piping reed. And the wind, freshening as the day wore on, carried *Argo* on her way.

The Argonauts encounter many peoples on their journey to Colchis, including Hypsipyle and the Lemnian women, who hope they will stay (see Story 41). They at last reach their destination and the magnificent palace of King Aeëtes, son of the Sun god Helios. The king's daughter, Medea, is struck by Eros' arrow and falls in love with Jason. With her help he might complete his quest. Aeëtes addresses Jason:

'Sir, there is no need for me to hear you out. If you are really children of the gods or have other grounds for approaching me as equals in the course of your piratical adventure, I will let you have the golden fleece – that is, if you still want it when I have put you to the proof. For I am not like your overlord in Hellas, as you describe him; I am not inclined to be ungenerous to men of rank.

'I propose to test your courage and abilities by setting you a task which, though formidable, is not beyond the strength of my two hands. Grazing on the plain of Ares, I have a pair of bronze-footed and fire-breathing bulls. These I yoke and drive over the hard fallow of the plain, quickly ploughing a four-acre field up to the ridge at either end. Then I sow the furrows, not with corn, but with the teeth of a monstrous serpent, which presently come up in the form of armed men, whom I cut down and kill with my spear as they rise up against me on all sides. It is morning when I yoke my team and by evening I have done my harvesting. That is what I do. If you, sir, can do as well, you may carry off the fleece to your king's palace on the very same day. If not, you shall not have it – do not deceive yourself. It would be wrong for a brave man to truckle to a coward.'

Jason listened to this with his eyes fixed on the floor; and when the king had finished, he sat there just as he was, without a word, resourceless in the face of his dilemma. For a long time he turned the matter over in his mind, unable boldly to accept a task so clearly fraught with peril. But at last he gave the king an answer which he thought would serve:

'Your Majesty, right is on your side and you leave me no escape whatever. Therefore I will take up your challenge, in spite of its preposterous terms, and though I may be courting death. Men serve no harsher mistress than Necessity, who drives me now and forced me to come here at another king's behest.'

Jason entreats the love-struck Medea. She issues him some advice about what to do when he receives the teeth of the serpent slayed by Cadmus, founder-king of Thebes.

At one moment both of them were staring at the ground in deep embarrassment; at the next they were smiling and glancing at each other with the love-light in their eyes. But at last Medea forced herself to speak to him. 'Hear me now,' she said. 'These are my plans for you. When you have met my father and he has given you the deadly teeth from the serpent's jaws, wait for the moment of midnight and after bathing in an ever-running river, go out alone in sombre clothes and dig a round pit in the earth. There, kill a ewe and after heaping up a pyre over the pit, sacrifice it whole, with a libation of honey from the hive and prayers to Hecate, Perses' only Daughter. Then, when you have invoked the goddess duly, withdraw from the pyre. And do not be tempted to look behind you as you go, either by footfalls or the baying of hounds, or you may ruin everything and never reach your friends alive.

'In the morning, melt this charm, strip, and using it like oil, anoint your body. It will endow you with tremendous strength and boundless confidence. You will feel yourself a match, not for mere men, but for the gods themselves. Sprinkle your spear and shield and sword with it as well; and neither the spear-points of the earthborn men nor the consuming flames that the savage bulls spew out will find you vulnerable. But you will not be immune for long – only for the day. Nevertheless, do not at any moment flinch from the encounter.

'And here is something else that will stand you in good stead. You have yoked the mighty bulls; you have ploughed the stubborn fallow (with those great hands and all that strength it will not take you long); you have sown the serpent's teeth in the dark earth; and now the giants are springing up along the furrows. Watch till you see a number of them rise from the soil, then, before they see you, throw a great boulder in among them; and they will fall on it like famished dogs and kill one another. That is your moment; plunge into the fray yourself.

'And so the task is done and you can carry off the fleece to Hellas – a long,

long way from Aea, I believe. Go none the less, go where you will; go where the fancy takes you when you part from us.'

After this, Medea was silent for a while. She kept her eyes fixed on the ground, and the warm tears ran down her lovely cheeks as she saw him sailing off over the high seas far away from her. Then she looked up at him and sorrowfully spoke again, taking his right hand in hers and no longer attempting to conceal her love. She said:

'But do remember, if you ever reach your home. Remember the name of Medea, and I for my part will remember you when you are far away. But now, pray tell me where you live. Where are you bound for when you sail across the sea from here? Will your journey take you near the wealthy city of Orchomenus or the Isle of Aea? Tell me too about that girl you mentioned, who won such fame for herself, the daughter of Pasiphae my father's sister.'

As he listened to this and noted her tears, unconscionable Love stole into the heart of Jason too. He replied: 'Of one thing I am sure. If I escape and live to reach Achaea; if Acetes does not set us a still more formidable task; never by night or day shall I forget you.'

Jason anoints himself and defeats the bulls and earthborn men grown from the teeth. He then sets his sights on the golden fleece which is protected by an enormous serpent. He and Medea carefully make their approach.

A path led them to the sacred wood, where they were making for the huge oak on which the fleece was hung, bright as a cloud incarnadined by the fiery beams of the rising sun. But the serpent with his sharp unsleeping eyes had seen them coming and now confronted them, stretching out his long neck and hissing terribly. The high banks of the river and the deep recesses of the wood threw back the sound, and far away from Titanian Aea it reached the ears of Colchians living by the outfall of Lycus, the river that parts from the loud waters of Araxes to unite his sacred stream with that of Phasis and flow in company with him till both debouch into the Caucasian Sea. Babies sleeping in their mothers' arms were startled by the hiss, and their anxious mothers waking in alarm hugged them closer to their breasts.

The monster in his sheath of horny scales rolled forward his interminable coils, like the eddies of black smoke that spring from smouldering logs and chase each other from below in endless convolutions. But as he writhed he saw the maiden take her stand, and heard her in her sweet voice invoking Sleep, the conqueror of the gods, to charm him. She also called on the night-wandering Queen of the world below to countenance her efforts. Jason from behind looked on in terror. But the giant snake, enchanted by her song, was soon relaxing the whole length of his serrated spine and smoothing out his multitudinous undulations, like a dark and silent swell rolling across a sluggish sea. Yet his grim head still hovered over them and the cruel jaws threatened to snap them up. But Medea, chanting a spell, dipped a fresh sprig of juniper in her brew and sprinkled his eyes with her most potent drug; and as the all-pervading magic scent spread round his head, sleep fell on him. Stirring no more, he let his jaw sink to the ground, and his innumerable coils lay stretched out far behind, spanning the deep wood. Medea called to Jason and he snatched the golden fleece from the oak. But she herself stayed where she was, smearing the wild one's head with a magic salve, till Jason urged her to come back to the ship and she left the sombre grove of Ares.

Lord Jason held up the great fleece in his arms. The shimmering wool threw a fiery glow on his fair cheeks and forehead; and he rejoiced in it, glad as a girl who catches on her silken gown the lovely light of the full moon as it climbs the sky and looks into her attic room. The ram's skin with its golden covering was as large as the hide of a yearling heifer or a brocket, as a young stag is called by hunting folk. The long flocks weighed it down and the very ground before him as he walked was bright with gold.

MEDEA'S REVENGE

Medea

Euripides

Translated by Gilbert Murray, 1910

Medea was furious when, having helped Jason to steal the golden fleece from her homeland (see previous story), he abandoned her for Glauce, a princess of Corinth. Medea had turned her back on her family to help Jason, even killing her own brother so as to help Jason escape. In this extract from **Euripides'** tragedy, first produced in 431 BC, she exacts revenge not only on young Glauce, to whom she has sent a poisoned robe, but on Jason himself, in the most shocking way imaginable. This translation by Gilbert Murray, Regius Professor of Greek at Oxford, was very popular in its time.

MEDEA. I will endure.—Go thou within, and lay
    All ready that my sons may need to-day.
                      [*The* ATTENDANT *goes into the house.*]

    O children, children mine: and you have found
    A land and home, where, leaving me discrowned
    And desolate, for ever you will stay,
    Motherless children! And I go my way
    To other lands, an exile, ere you bring
    Your fruits home, ere I see you prospering
    Or know your brides, or deck the bridal bed,
    All flowers, and lift your torches overhead.
      Oh, cursèd be mine own hard heart! 'Twas all
    In vain, then, that I reared you up, so tall
    And fair; in vain I bore you, and was torn
    With those long pitiless pains, when you were born.
    Ah, wondrous hopes my poor heart had in you,
    How you would tend me in mine age, and do
    The shroud about me with your own dear hands,
    When I lay cold, blessèd in all the lands
    That knew us. And that gentle thought is dead!
    You go, and I live on, to eat the bread
    Of long years, to myself most full of pain.

And never your dear eyes, never again,
Shall see your mother, far away being thrown
To other shapes of life... My babes, my own,
Why gaze ye so?—What is it that ye see?—
And laugh with that last laughter?... Woe is me,
What shall I do?

                Women, my strength is gone,
Gone like a dream, since once I looked upon
Those shining faces... I can do it not.
Good-bye to all the thoughts that burned so hot
Aforetime! I will take and hide them far,
Far, from men's eyes. Why should I seek a war
So blind: by these babes' wounds to sting again
Their father's heart, and win myself a pain
Twice deeper? Never, never! I forget
Henceforward all I laboured for.

                         And yet,
What is it with me? Would I be a thing
Mocked at, and leave mine enemies to sting
Unsmitten? It must be. O coward heart,
Ever to harbour such soft words!—Depart
Out of my sight, ye twain.   [*The* CHILDREN *go in.*]
                And they whose eyes
Shall hold it sin to share my sacrifice,
On their heads be it! My hand shall swerve not now.

  Ah, Ah, thou Wrath within me! Do not thou,
Do not... Down, down, thou tortured thing, and spare
My children! They will dwell with us, aye, there
Far off, and give thee peace.

                  Too late, too late!
By all Hell's living agonies of hate,
They shall not take my little ones alive
To make their mock with! Howsoe'er I strive
The thing is doomed; it shall not escape now
From being. Aye, the crown is on the brow,
And the robe girt, and in the robe that high
Queen dying.

             I know all. Yet... seeing that I
Must go so long a journey, and these twain
A longer yet and darker, I would fain
Speak with them, ere I go.

            [*A handmaid brings the* CHILDREN *out again.*]

               Come, children; stand
A little from me. There. Reach out your hand,
your right hand—so—to mother: and good-bye!

[*She has kept them hitherto at arm's-length: but at the
touch of their hands, her resolution breaks down,
and she gathers them passionately into her arms.*]

Oh, darling hand! Oh, darling mouth, and eye,
And royal mien, and bright brave faces clear,
May you be blessèd, but not here! What here
Was yours, your father stole... Ah God, the glow
Of cheek on cheek, the tender touch; and Oh,
Sweet scent of childhood... Go! Go! ... Am I blind?...
Mine eyes can see not, when I look to find
Their places. I am broken by the wings
Of evil... Yea, I know to what bad things
I go, but louder than all thought doth cry
Anger, which maketh man's worst misery.

[*She follows the* CHILDREN *into the house.*]

CHORUS. My thoughts have roamed a cloudy land,
    And heard a fierier music fall
    Than woman's heart should stir withal:
    And yet some Muse majestical,
    Unknown, hath hold of woman's hand,
    Seeking for Wisdom—not in all;
    A feeble seed, a scattered band,
    Thou yet shalt find in lonely places,
    Not dead amongst us, nor our faces
    Turned away from the Muses' call.

And thus my thought would speak: that she
    Who ne'er hath borne a child nor known
    Is nearer to felicity:
    Unlit she goeth and alone,
    With little understanding what
    A child's touch means of joy or woe,
    And many toils she beareth not.

But they within whose garden fair
    That gentle plant hath blown, they go
    Deep-written all their days with care—
    To rear the children, to make fast
    Their hold, to win them wealth; and then
    Much darkness, if the seed at last
    Bear fruit in good or evil men!
    And one thing at the end of all
    Abideth, that which all men dread:
    The wealth is won, the limbs are bred
    To manhood, and the heart withal

Honest: and, lo, where Fortune smiled,
Some change, and what hath fallen? Hark!
'Tis death slow winging to the dark,
And in his arms what was thy child.

What therefore doth it bring of gain
To man, whose cup stood full before,
That God should send this one thing more
Of hunger and of dread, a door
Set wide to every wind of pain?

        [MEDEA *comes out alone from the house.*]

MEDEA. Friends, this long hour I wait on Fortune's eyes,
    And strain my senses in a hot surmise
    What passeth on that hill.—Ha! even now
    There comes... 'tis one of Jason's men, I trow.
    His wild-perturbèd breath doth warrant me
    The tidings of some strange calamity.

        [*Enter* MESSENGER.]

MESSENGER. O dire and ghastly deed! Get thee away,
    Medea! Fly! Nor let behind thee stay
    One chariot's wing, one keel that sweeps the seas...

MEDEA. And what hath chanced, to cause such flights as these?

MESSENGER. The maiden princess lieth—and her sire,
    The king—both murdered by thy poison-fire.

MEDEA. Most happy tiding! Which thy name prefers
    Henceforth among my friends and well-wishers.

MESSENGER. What say'st thou? Woman, is thy mind within
    Clear, and not raving? Thou art found in sin
    Most bloody wrought against the king's high head,
    And laughest at the tale, and hast no dread?

MEDEA. I have words also that could answer well
    Thy word. But take thine ease, good friend, and tell,
    How died they? Hath it been a very foul
    Death, prithee? That were comfort to my soul.

MESSENGER. When thy two children, hand in hand entwined,
    Came with their father, and passed on to find
    The new-made bridal rooms, Oh, we were glad,
    We thralls, who ever loved thee well, and had
    Grief in thy grief. And straight there passed a word

From ear to ear, that thou and thy false lord
Had poured peace offering upon wrath foregone.
A right glad welcome gave we them, and one
Kissed the small hand, and one the shining hair:
Myself, for very joy, I followed where
The women's rooms are. There our mistress... she
Whom now we name so... thinking not to see
Thy little pair, with glad and eager brow
Sate waiting Jason. Then she saw, and slow
Shrouded her eyes, and backward turned again,
Sick that thy children should come near her. Then
Thy husband quick went forward, to entreat
The young maid's fitful wrath. "Thou wilt not meet
Love's coming with unkindness? Nay, refrain
Thy suddenness, and turn thy face again,
Holding as friends all that to me are dear,
Thine husband. And accept these robes they bear
As gifts: and beg thy father to unmake
His doom of exile on them—for my sake."
When once she saw the raiment, she could still
Her joy no more, but gave him all his will.
And almost ere the father and the two
Children were gone from out the room, she drew
The flowered garments forth, and sate her down
To her arraying: bound the golden crown
Through her long curls, and in a mirror fair
Arranged their separate clusters, smiling there
At the dead self that faced her. Then aside
She pushed her seat, and paced those chambers wide
Alone, her white foot poising delicately—
So passing joyful in those gifts was she!—
And many a time would pause, straight-limbed, and wheel
Her head to watch the long fold to her heel
Sweeping. And then came something strange. Her cheek
Seemed pale, and back with crooked steps and weak
Groping of arms she walked, and scarcely found
Her old seat, that she fell not to the ground.
    Among the handmaids was a woman old
And grey, who deemed, I think, that Pan had hold
Upon her, or some spirit, and raised a keen
Awakening shout; till through her lips was seen
A white foam crawling, and her eyeballs back
Twisted, and all her face dead pale for lack
Of life: and while that old dame called, the cry
Turned strangely to its opposite, to the
Sobbing. Oh, swiftly then one woman flew
To seek her father's rooms, one for the new

Bridegroom, to tell the tale. And all the place
Was loud with hurrying feet.

                So long a space
As a swift walker on a measured way
Would pace a furlong's course in, there she lay
Speechless, with veilèd lids. Then wide her eyes
She oped, and wildly, as she strove to rise,
Shrieked: for two diverse waves upon her rolled
Of stabbing death. The carcanet of gold
That gripped her brow was molten in a dire
And wondrous river of devouring fire.
And those fine robes, the gift thy children gave—
God's mercy!—everywhere did lap and lave
The delicate flesh; till up she sprang, and fled,
A fiery pillar, shaking locks and head
This way and that, seeking to cast the crown
Somewhere away. But like a thing nailed down
The burning gold held fast the anadem,
And through her locks, the more she scattered them,
Came fire the fiercer, till to earth she fell
A thing—save to her sire—scarce nameable,
And strove no more. That cheek of royal mien,
Where was it—or the place where eyes had been?
Only from crown and temples came faint blood
Shot through with fire. The very flesh, it stood
Out from the bones, as from a wounded pine
The gum starts, where those gnawing poisons fine
Bit in the dark—a ghastly sight! And touch
The dead we durst not. We had seen too much.
    But that poor father, knowing not, had sped,
Swift to his daughter's room, and there the dead
Lay at his feet. He knelt, and groaning low,
Folded her in his arms, and kissed her: "Oh,
Unhappy child, what thing unnatural hath
So hideously undone thee? Or what wrath
Of gods, to make this old grey sepulchre
Childless of thee? Would God but lay me there
To die with thee, my daughter!" So he cried.
But after, when he stayed from tears, and tried
To uplift his old bent frame, lo, in the folds
Of those fine robes it held, as ivy holds
Strangling among young laurel boughs. Oh, then
A ghastly struggle came! Again, again,
Up on his knee he writhed; but that dead breast
Clung still to his: till, wild, like one possessed,
He dragged himself half free; and, lo, the live
Flesh parted; and he laid him down to strive

No more with death, but perish; for the deep
Had risen above his soul. And there they sleep,
At last, the old proud father and the bride,
Even as his tears had craved it, side by side.

　　For thee—Oh, no word more! Thyself will know
How best to baffle vengeance... Long ago
I looked upon man's days, and found a grey
Shadow. And this thing more I surely say,
That those of all men who are counted wise,
Strong wits, devisers of great policies,
Do pay the bitterest toll. Since life began,
Hath there in God's eye stood one happy man?
Fair days roll on, and bear more gifts or less
Of fortune, but to no man happiness.

　　　　　　　　　　　　　　　　[*Exit* MESSENGER.]

CHORUS. [*Some Women*] Wrath upon wrath, meseems, this day shall fall
　　From God on Jason! He hath earned it all.
　　[*Other Women*] O miserable maiden, all my heart
　　Is torn for thee, so sudden to depart
　　From thy king's chambers and the light above
　　To darkness, all for sake of Jason's love!

MEDEA. Women, my mind is clear. I go to slay
　　My children with all speed, and then, away
　　From hence; not wait yet longer till they stand
　　Beneath another and an angrier hand
　　To die. Yea, howsoe'er I shield them, die
　　They must. And, seeing that they must, 'tis I
　　Shall slay them, I their mother, touched of none
　　Beside. Oh, up, and get thine armour on,
　　My heart! Why longer tarry we to win
　　Our crown of dire inevitable sin?
　　Take up thy sword, O poor right hand of mine,
　　Thy sword: then onward to the thin-drawn line
　　Where life turns agony. Let there be naught
　　Of softness now: and keep thee from that thought,
　　'Born of thy flesh,' 'thine own belovèd.' Now,
　　For one brief day, forget thy children: thou
　　Shalt weep hereafter. Though thou slay them, yet
　　Sweet were they... I am sore unfortunate.

　　　　　　　　　　　　　　　[*She goes into the house.*]

CHORUS. [*Some Women*] O Earth, our mother; and thou
　　　　All-seër, arrowy crown
　　　　Of Sunlight, manward now
　　　　Look down, Oh, look down!

Look upon one accurst,
    Ere yet in blood she twine
    Red hands—blood that is thine!
O Sun, save her first!
She is thy daughter still,
    Of thine own golden line;
Save her! Or shall man spill
    The life divine?
Give peace, O Fire that diest not! Send thy spell
    To stay her yet, to lift her afar, afar—
A torture-changèd spirit, a voice of Hell
    Wrought of old wrongs and war!

OTHERS. Alas for the mother's pain
        Wasted! Alas the dear
    Life that was born in vain!
        Woman, what mak'st thou here,
    Thou from beyond the Gate
        Where dim Symplêgades
        Clash in the dark blue seas,
    The shores where death doth wait?
    Why hast thou taken on thee,
        To make us desolate,
    This anger of misery
            And guilt of hate?
For fierce are the smitings back of blood once shed
    Where love hath been: God's wrath upon them that kill,
And an anguished earth, and the wonder of the dead
        Haunting as music still...

                              [*A cry is heard within.*]

A WOMAN. Hark! Did ye hear? Heard ye the children's cry?

ANOTHER. O miserable woman! O abhorred!

A CHILD WITHIN. What shall I do? What is it? Keep me fast
    From mother!

THE OTHER CHILD. I know nothing. Brother! Oh,
    I think she means to kill us.

A WOMAN. Let me go!
    I will—Help! Help!—and save them at the last.

A CHILD. Yes, in God's name! Help quickly ere we die!

THE OTHER CHILD. She has almost caught me now. She has a sword.

[*Many of the Women are now beating at the barred*
door to get in. Others are standing apart.]

WOMEN AT THE DOOR. Thou stone, thou thing of iron! Wilt verily
    Spill with thine hand that life, the vintage stored
        Of thine own agony?

THE OTHER WOMEN. A Mother slew her babes in days of yore,
    One, only one, from dawn to eventide,
      Ino, god-maddened, whom the Queen of Heaven
       Set frenzied, flying to the dark: and she
       Cast her for sorrow to the wide salt sea,
    Forth from those rooms of murder unforgiven,
Wild-footed from a white crag of the shore,
    And clasping still her children twain, she died.

    O Love of Woman, charged with sorrow sore,
    What hast thou wrought upon us? What beside
        Resteth to tremble for?
               [*Enter hurriedly* JASON *and Attendants.*]

JASON. Ye women by this doorway clustering
    Speak, is the doer of the ghastly thing
    Yet here, or fled? What hopeth she of flight?
    Shall the deep yawn to shield her? Shall the height
    Send wings, and hide her in the vaulted sky
    To work red murder on her lords, and fly
    Unrecompensed? But let her go! My care
    Is but to save my children, not for her.
    Let them she wronged requite her as they may.
    I care not. 'Tis my sons I must some way
    Save, ere the kinsmen of the dead can win
    From them the payment of their mother's sin.

LEADER. Unhappy man, indeed thou knowest not
    What dark place thou art come to! Else, God wot,
    Jason, no word like these could fall from thee.

JASON. What is it?—Ha! The woman would kill me?

LEADER. Thy sons are dead, slain by their mother's hand.

JASON. How? Not the children… I scarce understand…
    O God, thou hast broken me!

LEADER. Think of those twain
    As things once fair, that ne'er shall bloom again.

JASON. Where did she murder them? In that old room?

LEADER. Open, and thou shalt see thy children's doom.

JASON. Ho, thralls! Unloose me yonder bars! Make more
    Of speed! Wrench out the jointing of the door.
    And show my two-edged curse, the children dead,
    The woman... Oh, this sword upon her head...
                    [*While the Attendants are still battering at the door*
                    MEDEA *appears on the roof, standing on a chariot of*
                    winged Dragons, in which are the children's bodies.]

MEDEA. What make ye at my gates? Why batter ye
    With brazen bars, seeking the dead and me
    Who slew them? Peace!... And thou, if aught of mine
    Thou needest, speak, though never touch of thine
    Shall scathe me more. Out of his firmament
    My fathers' father, the high Sun, hath sent
    This, that shall save me from mine enemies' rage.

JASON. Thou living hate! Thou wife in every age
    Abhorrèd, blood-red mother, who didst kill
    My sons, and make me as the dead: and still
    Canst take the sunshine to thine eyes, and smell
    The green earth, reeking from thy deed of hell;
    I curse thee! Now, Oh, now mine eyes can see,
    That then were blinded, when from savagery
    Of eastern chambers, from a cruel land,
    To Greece and home I gathered in mine hand
    Thee, thou incarnate curse: one that betrayed
    Her home, her father, her... Oh, God hath laid
    Thy sins on me!—I knew, I knew, there lay
    A brother murdered on thy hearth that day
    When thy first footstep fell on Argo's hull...
    Argo, my own, my swift and beautiful!
      That was her first beginning. Then a wife
    I made her in my house. She bore to life
    Children: and now for love, for chambering
    And men's arms, she hath murdered them! A thing
    Not one of all the maids of Greece, not one,
    Had dreamed of; whom I spurned, and for mine own
    Chose thee, a bride of hate to me and death,
    Tigress, not woman, beast of wilder breath
    Than Skylla shrieking o'er the Tuscan sea.
    Enough! No scorn of mine can reach to thee,
    Such iron is o'er thine eyes. Out from my road,
    Thou crime-begetter, blind with children's blood!

And let me weep alone the bitter tide
That sweepeth Jason's days, no gentle bride
To speak with more, no child to look upon
Whom once I reared... all, all for ever gone!

MEDEA. An easy answer had I to this swell
Of speech, but Zeus our father knoweth well,
All I for thee have wrought, and thou for me.
So let it rest. This thing was not to be,
That thou shouldst live a merry life, my bed
Forgotten and my heart uncomforted,
Thou nor thy princess: nor the king that planned
Thy marriage drive Medea from his land,
And suffer not. Call me what thing thou please,
Tigress or Skylla from the Tuscan seas:
My claws have gripped thine heart, and all things shine.

JASON. Thou too hast grief. Thy pain is fierce as mine.

MEDEA. I love the pain, so thou shalt laugh no more.

JASON. Oh, what a womb of sin my children bore!

MEDEA. Sons, did ye perish for your father's shame?

JASON. How? It was not my hand that murdered them.

MEDEA. 'Twas thy false wooings, 'twas thy trampling pride.

JASON. Thou hast said it! For thy lust of love they died.

MEDEA. And love to women a slight thing should be?

JASON. To women pure!—All thy vile life to thee!

MEDEA. Think of thy torment. They are dead, they are dead!

JASON. No: quick, great God; quick curses round thy head!

MEDEA. The Gods know who began this work of woe.

JASON. Thy heart and all its loathliness they know.

MEDEA. Loathe on... But, Oh, thy voice. It hurts me sore.

JASON. Aye, and thine me. Wouldst hear me then no more?

MEDEA. How? Show me but the way. 'Tis this I crave.

JASON. Give me the dead to weep, and make their grave.

MEDEA. Never! Myself will lay them in a still
    Green sepulchre, where Hera by the Hill
    Hath precinct holy, that no angry men
    May break their graves and cast them forth again
    To evil. So I lay on all this shore
    Of Corinth a high feast for evermore
    And rite, to purge them yearly of the stain
    Of this poor blood. And I, to Pallas' plain
    I go, to dwell beside Pandion's son,
    Aegeus.—For thee, behold, death draweth on,
    Evil and lonely, like thine heart: the hands
    Of thine old Argo, rotting where she stands,
    Shall smite thine head in twain, and bitter be
    To the last end thy memories of me.

        [*She rises on the chariot and is slowly borne away.*]

ARIADNE AND THESEUS

'Poem 64'

Catullus

Translated by Daisy Dunn, 2016

Ariadne, the daughter of King Minos of Crete, has woken alone on the shore of Naxos. She helped an Athenian stranger, Theseus, to navigate a labyrinth to kill her monstrous half-brother, the Minotaur, only to find herself abandoned by him after becoming his lover. The Latin love poet **Catullus** (*c.* 82 BC–*c.* 53 BC), who was born into a wealthy family from Verona and worked in Rome in the mid-first century BC, presented this story as the decoration on a bedspread. We are to imagine each scene as though it were embroidered. Hence the wine god Bacchus is said to fly in 'from another part of the cloth'. Catullus was left broken-hearted when his own lover, Lesbia, abandoned him. He clearly empathised with miserable Ariadne. In the sixteenth century the artist Titian used this story as the inspiration for his exquisite painting *Bacchus and Ariadne*.

On the quietly shifting shore of Naxos
Ariadne watches Theseus
Fading with fast fleet and bears at heart
Fears she cannot temper.
Not yet does she believe she is seeing
What she is seeing,
Barely woken from sleep that deceived
To discover she is abandoned
And pitiful and alone on lonely sands.
But the young man is forgetful and fleeing
And pushes the waves away with oars,
Leaving his promises unfulfilled to the tempest that is stirring.

From afar atop the seaweed, with sad little eyes,
The daughter of Minos watches, ah she watches
Him, like a stone sculpture of a bacchant.
She ebbs on currents swollen with pain,
Losing hold
On the fine band on her fair head

And the cloth that envelops her body in a gentle clinch
And the rounded bra that bounds her milky breasts.
All the coverings which have fallen from her body everywhere
The salt waves make sport of at her feet.
But neither headband nor fluttering veils vexed her
When in the fullness of her heart
She was missing you, Theseus,
With her every thought, in the fullness of her heart
Clinging to you, completely lost.

Poor girl, how Venus felled her with never-ending grief,
Sowing thorny worries in her heart
From the moment Theseus determined
A departure from the port of Piraeus on Athens' arced shore
And reached the palace of the unjust king of Crete.
For they say that Athens, plagued by damnation
To pay the penalty for the murder of Androgeos,
Would at one time provide its pick of youths
And glory of maidens as a feast for the Minotaur.
The fledgling city was suffering the consequences
When Theseus chose to yield his own body
For precious Athens so the living dead of Cecrops
Should not be carried to such deaths in Crete.

And so he put his trust in a light ship and gentle breeze
And came before haughty Minos
And his magnificent enclosure.
The moment the virgin princess clapped her
Widening eyes upon him –
Her pure little bed was still protecting her in a soft
And motherly embrace, breathing sweetly
Over her the flagrant breath
Of myrtle such as the River Eurotas puts forth
Or the breeze spring plucks from flowers of many colours –
And averted her hot eyes from him only when
Her whole body had caught the flame of love
And she burned deep inside to the depths of her marrow.

Wretchedly rousing passions in his cruel heart,
Divine Cupid, weaver of joys with worries among men,
And Venus, ruler of the Golgians and leafy Idalium.
On what waves you inflamed the girl, threw her
From her wits, as she sighed for her fair guest
With breath upon breath.
How huge the fears she carried in her wearied heart.
How many times she paled beyond gleaming gold,
When putting his mind to conquering the savage monster

Theseus sought either death or the fruits of glory.
Promising little gifts to the gods that were not unwelcome
But futile nonetheless, she mouthed vows silently.

Like an oak tree or cone-bearing pine with seeping bark
Shaking its branches on the heights of Mount Taurus
Whose twisting trunk a storm uproots in a flash –
And the tree, torn from the roots,
Falls prostrate and far
Breaking whatever lies in its broad path –
So Theseus laid the beast low, conquering its force
While it tossed its horns ineffectually to the empty breeze.
From there and high on glory the stranger retraced his path,
Steering his wandering course with the delicate thread
So the deception of the enclosure should not defeat him
As he departed from meandering turns of the labyrinth.

But come, I digress from my primary song,
Recollecting further how the girl departed
From the face of her father, the embrace of her sister,
And finally her mother, who tried wretchedly
To feel happy for her lost daughter, who put above
Them all her sweet love for Theseus;
Or how she came to the foaming shore of Naxos
By boat; or how her partner abandoned her as she
Was buried in sleep, sailing away,
Forgetful through and through.

They say that, raging in the passion in her heart,
She would release deeply felt and audible words,
Then climbed the steep mountains in sadness
To extend from there her view over the vast swell
Of sea, then sallied forth into the salt waves
Dancing before her and raising her soft clothes
To bear her calves, uttered in sorrow these final complaints,
Preparing cold little sobs on wet lips:

'Was it for this I was taken from my father's hearth, traitor,
For you to leave me on an empty shore, traitor, Theseus?
So you leave me, heedless of the gods' authority,
Forgetful, ah. Do you carry home your perjured vows?
Could nothing alter the intention in your cruel mind?
Could there be no mercy to tempt you to take
Pity on me for all your hardness of heart?
These were not the promises you once made
Me in a warming tone, these are not what you bade
My wretchedness to hope for, but a happy marriage,

Longed-for wedding songs, everything
The wandering breezes have scattered vain.

May no woman now believe a man when he makes a promise,
May no woman hope the words of her man are true.
While their minds are desirous, desperate to obtain something,
They are afraid of swearing nothing,
There is nothing they won't promise.
But as soon as the lust in their desirous minds is sated,
They remember none of their words,
Have no fear of perjury.

There's no doubt I seized you as you tossed
Mid death throes, and more than that I elected to lose
My half-brother rather than fail you,
Deceitful man, in your final hour.
For that I am to be torn apart by beasts and given to birds
As prey – and no mound of earth will be piled upon my corpse.
What kind of lioness bore you beneath a lonely rock,
What sea conceived you and spat you out from its foaming waves,
What Syrtis, what fierce Scylla, what monstrous Charybdis,
You, who offer such returns for your sweet life?

If a marriage to me was not in your heart
Because you feared the savage reprimands of your aged father
You might still have led me to your home
To be a slave to you in a joyous labour,
Washing your white feet with pure water,
Spreading your bed with a purple bedspread.

But I have been felled by trouble so why pile
Fruitless complaints on the dumb winds which lack
The feelings to hear
My words and respond in kind?
He is almost mid ocean now,
No human shape is visible on dull seaweed.
So far does cruel fate mock me in my desperate
Times and begrudge even ears to my complaints.

All-powerful Jupiter, I wish the ships of Cecrops
Had not touched the shores of Cnossos in the first place,
That the traitor, bringing a gruesome tribute to
The ungovernable bull, had not tethered his ship in Crete,
That the evil man did not hide his cruel plans
Behind a handsome exterior
And stay here as a guest in our home.
For where can I take myself now?

What kind of hope can I cling to? I am lost.
Shall I make for the mountains of Ida?
But the savage sea divides, separates me
From them, swirling far and wide.
Or should I expect my father to help me?
Did I not leave him as I pursued a young man
Spattered with my brother's blood?
Or should I console myself
With the loyalty and love of a husband,
A man who flees, bending heavy oars in the swirling sea?
Worse, I am on a lonely island, a shore with no shelter,
And no way out reveals itself on the circling waves of water.
There is no means of escape, no hope. Everything is silent.
Everything deserted; everything points to death.

But my eyes will not fall shut on me in death,
My senses will not leave my wearied body
Until I demand from the gods rich justice for my betrayal
And in my final hour pray for the loyalty of the gods.

So Eumenides, punishers and avengers of the crimes
Of men, your forehead, fringed with snaky hair,
Exposing the anger exhaled from your chest,
Here, come here, hear my complaints,
Which I am forced in my wretched helplessness
To pour from the depths of my marrow, blazing,
Blinded by mindless madness.
As these truths are born from the bottom of my heart
Please do not allow my grief to turn to dust,
But with the kind of heart Theseus had when he left me,
Goddesses, may he destroy himself and his family.'

After she poured these words from her sad breast,
Troubled, demanding punishment for wicked deeds,
The ruler of the gods
Whose authority goes unchallenged
Nodded his agreement,
At the movement of which the
Earth and choppy seas trembled
And the firmament shook its gleaming stars.

But as for Theseus, his mind gripped by murky darkness,
He released from his forgetful heart all the instructions
Which hitherto he was guarding permanently in his mind,
Nor raising the sweet signs to his sad father
Did he show that he had seen the port of Athens safely.
For they say that once, when Aegeus entrusted his son

To the winds as he left the goddess' walls in his ship,
He embraced the young man and gave him these instructions:

'My only son, dearer to me than life's length,
Son, whom I am forced to send into an uncertain situation,
Returned to me only recently at the height of my old age,
Since my fate and your determined virtue snatch you
Away from me against my will, though my tired eyes are
Not yet drunk with the dear shape of my son,
I shall not send you rejoicing with a happy heart
Or allow you to carry the signs of good fortune,
But first I shall free my heart of countless laments,
And pour soil over my white hair and defile it with ash,
Then hang dyed sails from my bending mast
So that sails dipped in Iberian rust may proclaim
This grief of mine, this blaze in my head.

But if Minerva of sacred Itonus, who agreed to defend our race
And the seat of Erechtheus, allows you to sprinkle your
Right hand with the blood of the bull,
Then see that these commands endure,
Kept safe in your remembering heart –
May no time erase them.
As soon as your eyes light upon our hills
Drop each black cloth from the yards
And let your twisted ropes hoist white sails
So as soon as possible I may see them and know
True happiness in my heart, as the blessed
Hour brings you back to me.'

These instructions, which until now Theseus was holding
Constantly in his thoughts, seeped away
Like clouds struck by a blast of wind
From the high summit of a snowy mountain.
But his father, as he sought a view from the top of the citadel,
Spilt a flood of tears from his anxious eyes
As soon as he caught sight of the billowing sails,
And threw himself headlong from the top
Of the cliffs
Assuming Theseus lost to cruel fate.
So savage Theseus entered a household
Decked in mourning for his father's death
And caught the same sort of grief
He had imposed on the daughter of Minos
Through the neglectfulness of his heart.

Then she, watching in her sorrow his ship

Disappearing, drifted from one worry
To another in her wounded heart.

But from another part of the cloth
Flew in vigorous Bacchus
With his throng of Satyrs and Silenes from Nysa,
Seeking you, Ariadne, burning in love for you.
His followers were raging all over, out of their wits,
'Euhoe!' bacchantes tossing their heads with cries 'Euhoe!'
One section were shaking sticks with covered tips,
Another were hurling the limbs of a dismembered bullock,
Others were dressing themselves in plaits of snakes,
Others were gathering in worship of sacraments
Concealed in hollow baskets,
Rites which the profane long to hear, but in vain.
Others were patting drums with outstretched palms,
Or causing round cymbal tin to ring and ring,
Many had horns which blew booming booms
And the Phrygian flute shrieked in shrill song.

ALCIBIADES

Alcibiades

Cornelius Nepos

Translated by William Casey, 1828

Cornelius Nepos (*c.* 110 BC–*c.* 25 BC) was – like Catullus – born in the region of Verona, and worked in Rome. He was the dedicatee of Catullus' poetry book and wrote a history of the world in three volumes, which no longer survives, as well as a series of biographies, *Of Celebrated Men*. His biography of Alcibiades is not as famous as that of Plutarch, who paralleled his life with that of Coriolanus, a Roman general of the fifth century BC, but it is succinct and captures the dangerous allure of its subject. Alcibiades was one of the most fascinating statesmen of ancient Athens. Born in around 450 BC, he was a ward of Pericles and became a close friend (some suggested more than a friend) of Socrates, whose life he was said to have saved in the Peloponnesian War. Cornelius Nepos reveals a typically Roman disapproval of Alcibiades' indulgent relationships with men.

Alcibiades, the son of Clinias, seems to have been endowed by nature with all the gifts which it could lavish on his person. All writers agree that no one ever excelled him either in virtues or vices. Descended from one of the most illustrious families, born at a stately city, and one of the most comely youths of his age, he possessed an uncommon judgment, and displayed the greatest aptitude for any post. He was a skilful commander both by sea and land, and exhibited such a flow of easy eloquence, aided by the charms of his person, that his speech had an irresistible effect on all who heard him. He was patient and laborious as occasion required; liberal and splendid at home and abroad; affable and condescending in his actions, showing a wonderful address in his conformity to time and circumstance. In his moments of relaxation, and when disengaged from the pursuits of the mind, he was found prodigal and irregular, indulging all sort of luxury and debauchery to such a degree as astonished all on observing in the same person so great an unlikeness in his manners, and so great a difference in his nature.

Alcibiades was brought up in the house of Pericles, to whom he was said to be step-son, and was instructed under the tuition of Socrates. He married the daughter of Hipponicus, the greatest orator then in Greece; so that, had he given free scope to his imagination, he could not have wished for, nor obtained greater favours than those fortune and nature had bestowed on him. According to the customs of the Greeks, he was beloved in his tender age by numbers, and especially by Socrates, as Plato observes in his banquet (symposio), where this philosopher represents Alcibiades *as having spent the whole night with Socrates, and as having left him like a child who quits his father's side.* At a ripe age he conceived a fondness himself for several others, on whom he played many odious tricks, though with as much delicacy and humour as the possibility of the thing allowed of, and which I should not omit mentioning, were I not engrossed by the recital of others of a more important and dignified nature.

In the Peloponnesian war, the Athenians were led by the counsels and authority of Alcibiades to commence hostilities against the Syracusians. He was appointed general, and to conduct the war he was joined by two of his colleagues Nicias and Lamachus. While the preparations for this expedition were going on, before the fleet had sailed, all the effigies of Mercury throughout Athens happened to be pulled down except that which stood before the gate of Andocides, from whence it was styled the Mercury of Andocides. As this event was obviously the prelude of some grand plot, since it closely concerned the republic at large, and not the aims of any particular rank of persons, it excited the astonishment, and awoke the fears of the citizens, lest by some violent and sudden accident they should be deprived of their liberty. As Alcibiades, by his power and exaltation, was now above private persons, all suspicions turned naturally on him. His liberalities had gained him a number of friends, but his eloquence in pleading for them at the bar, many more; so that, whenever he appeared in public, he drew all eyes on himself; nor could he be found a match in the whole city. His presence thus became at once an object of deep fears and sanguine hopes; it being in his power to be productive of great good or evil. His character was, moreover, stigmatized on the report spread of *having celebrated the misteries of Ceres in his own house,* which was a crime among the Athenians, who regarded such meetings as acts of conspiracy rather than of religion.

Alcibiades was charged with this offense by the public assemblies, at the same time that the war urged his departure; but as he was aware of the conduct of his fellow-citizens, he availed himself of that very circumstance, and desired *that if they thought any thing was intended against him, they should inquire into the matter while he was present, to obviate the accusation of the envy to which he might be exposed during his absence.* His enemies finding they could not now injure him, thought proper to remain quiet for the moment, and wait for his departure, in order to asperse him when absent. This was the case; for as soon as they judged he had reached Sicily, they called him to trial as a person guilty of *sacrilegious acts.* Wherefore, he was now arraigned by a decree before the magistrates, to appear again at the city and defend himself from the charges brought against him. Alcibiades, though he had entertained the strongest hopes of succeeding in the expedition, would not disobey, but mounted the galley sent to convey him back. When he arrived at Thurium, a port in Italy, after having duly considered the immoderate licentiousness of his fellow-citizens and their severe proceedings with the nobles, he thought the properest thing to be done, in order to free himself from the impending storm, was to elope; for which purpose, by eluding the vigilance of his guards, he fled to Elis, and after to Thebes.

On learning, therefore, *he had been condemned to death; that his property had been sequestered and that the Eumolpides, constrained by the people, had curst him, as customary then, and, in fine, by way of perpetuating the memory of their malediction, a copy thereof had been engraved on a stone-pillar raised to public view*; he sought refuge in Lacedemonia. There, as he himself used to say, *he made war not on his country, but on his own and his country's enemies, who had driven him out from a knowledge of the important services he was likely to render it; whilst they had only sought the gratification of private animosities, and not the object of public good.* The Lacedemonians, by the advice of Alcibiades, entered into a league with the king of Persia; fortified Decelea, a town in Attica, and, by placing a garrison there on a permanent footing, kept Athens at bay. It was by his endeavours, too, that the alliance subsisting between the Ionians and Athenians, was broken off which circumstance proved highly advantageous to the Lacedemonians in their wars.

These signal services, however, far from inspiring the Lacedemonians with a greater fondness towards Alcibiades, only tended to augment their fears, and preclude their good will. As they were all sensible of the uncommon ability and prudence displayed by this great man in all matters, they now conceived apprehensions, lest the love of his country should induce him some day to abandon them, in case a reconciliation should be brought about between him and his fellow-citizens. Impressed with these ideas, the Lacedemonians now resolved to dispatch him when an opportunity should present itself. Alcibiades, whose penetration could baffle any attempt of surprise, when on his guard, soon saw through their designs, and fled for protection to Tissaphernes, one of Darius' governors.

When he had acquired a thorough intimacy with this chief, and now saw the Athenian power reduced to a low ebb from their reverses in Sicily (whilst that of Sparta was on the rise), he opened an intercourse through the medium of commissioners with Pisander who then commanded an army near Samos, and to whom he expressed a wish of returning to Athens. Pisander was animated with the same sentiments as Alcibiades, an enemy to the overpower of the people, and an advocate for the nobles. Though he failed of success in that quarter, yet, through the influence of Thrasybulus, the son of Lycus, he was received in the army, and appointed to command at Samos, after which, and in consequence of the endeavours of Theramenes, he was recalled by an edict of the people, and invested, though yet absent, with as much authority as Thrasybulus and Theramenes themselves in the command of the army.

Under the directions of these generals affairs assumed so different an aspect, that the Lacedemonians who had hitherto proved victorious and powerful, were now intimidated to such a degree, that they sued for peace. They had now suffered five defeats by land, and three by sea, having lost in the latter two hundred thrireme gallies which fell into their enemy's hands. Besides all this, Alcibiades, acting in conjunction with the other colleagues, had regained Ionia, the Hellespont and several other Grecian cities lying on the coast of Asia; in the recovery whereof, especially of Byzantium, he had recourse to arms; whilst the rest voluntarily surrendered on seeing the political lenity which had been used towards the vanquished. After these great exploits the three commanders returned to Athens, both they and the army being loaded with the rich spoils of conquest.

The whole city flocked down to the Piraeus to receive them; and such was the ardent desire of the people to behold Alcibiades, that his galley attracted the notice of all, as if he alone had only arrived; for he was deemed in public persuasion both as the cause of past mishaps and present success. The loss of Sicily and the victories gained by the enemy, were now imputed to their having banished a man of so much merit; nor did this appear an unjust reproach on their side, for the moment the command of the army was given to Alcibiades, the Lacedemonians were no longer able to cope with the Athenians either by sea or land.

Although Theramenes and Thrasybulus were equals in commanding the warlike operations; and had entered the Piraeus at the same time, yet when Alcibiades went on shore, he was followed by the crowd, and presented on all sides with gold and brazen crowns, an honour which had never been conferred before, except on victors at the Olympic games. Alcibiades, on receiving such testimonies of affection from the people, wept with joy when he called to mind the undeserved severity he had formerly experienced from his fellow-citizens.

IN THE BEGINNING

De Rerum Natura, Book V

Lucretius

Translated by Rev. John Selby Watson, 1880

The Greek philosopher Epicurus was adamant that humans should not fear
death. The keenest proponent of his philosophy in first-century BC Rome,
a poet named **Lucretius** (*c.* 99–*c.* 55 BC), sought to stamp out unhealthy
'superstition' by providing a more scientific explanation for things. In
his *De Rerum Natura* ('On The Nature Of Things') we find references
to atoms as well as to Venus. Lucretius did not reject the myths so much
as use them for his own ends. His story of early mankind, extracted here,
contains an explanation of evolution, but also of the softening of mortal
bodies over time. There is a strong parallel with the ancient Greek myths
that recount man's decline from a pre-agricultural Golden Age to the Iron
Age of the present day. Lucretius dedicated the poem to his patron, a
politician named Gaius Memmius.

In the beginning, *then*, the earth spread over the hills the growth of herbs, and
the beauty of verdure, and the flowery fields, throughout all regions, shone
with a green hue; and then was given, to the various kinds of trees, full power
of shooting upwards through the air. *For* as feathers, and hairs, and bristles, are
first produced over the limbs of quadrupeds and the bodies of the winged tribes,
so the new earth then first put forth herbs and trees; *and* afterwards generated the
numerous races of animals, which arose in various forms and by various modes.
For animals, that were to live on the earth, could assuredly neither have fallen from
the sky, nor have come forth from the salt depths *of the sea*. It remains, *therefore, to
believe* that the earth must justly have obtained the name of MOTHER, since from
the earth all *living creatures* were born. And even now many animals spring forth
from the earth, *which are* generated by means of moisture and the quickening
heat of the sun. It is accordingly less wonderful, if, at that time, *creatures* more
numerous and of larger size arose, *and* came to maturity while the earth and the
air were yet fresh *and vigorous*.

First of all, the race of winged animals, and variegated birds, left their eggs,
being excluded in the season of spring; as grasshoppers, in these days, spontaneously leave their thin coats in the summer, proceeding to seek sustenance and life.

Next, be assured, the earth produced, for the first time, the tribes of men and
beasts; for much heat and moisture abounded through the plains, and hence,

where any suitable region offered itself, *a kind of* wombs sprung up, adhering to the earth by fibres. These, when the age of the infants *within them*, at the season of maturity, had opened, (escaping from their moist-enclosure, and seeking for air,) nature, in those places, prepared the pores of the earth, and forced it to pour from its open veins a liquid like milk; just as every woman at present, when she has brought forth, is stored with sweet milk, because all the strength of the food is directed to the breasts. *Thus* the earth afforded nourishment to the infants; the warmth *rendered* a garment *unnecessary*; and the grass *supplied* a couch abounding with luxuriant and tender down.

But the early age of the world gave forth neither severe cold nor extraordinary heat, nor winds of impetuous violence. For all these alike increase and acquire strength *by time*.

For which cause, *I say* again and again, the earth has justly acquired, *and justly* retains, the name of MOTHER, since she herself brought forth the race of men, and produced, at *this* certain time, almost every kind of animal which exults over the vast mountains, and the birds of the air, at the same period, with *all their* varied forms. But because she must necessarily have some termination to bearing, she ceased, like a woman, exhausted by length of time. For lapse of time changes the nature of the whole world, and one condition after another must succeed to all things, nor does any being continue *always* like itself. All is unsettled; nature alters and impels every thing to change. For one thing decays, and, *grown* weak through age, languishes; another, again, grows up, and bursts forth from contempt. Thus age changes the nature of the whole world, and one condition after another falls upon the earth; *so that* what she could *once bear* she can *bear* no *longer*; *while* she can *bear* what she did not bear of old.

The earth, also, in that age, made efforts to produce various monsters, that sprung up with wonderful faces and limbs; the hermaphrodite, between both *sexes*, and not either, but removed from both; others wanting feet, and others destitute of hands; *some* also were found dumb for want of a mouth, and some blind without *even* a face; *and others again* were shackled by the cohesion of their limbs over their whole bodies, *so* that they could neither do any thing, nor go in any direction; *could* neither avoid harm, nor take what was necessary *to preserve life*.

Other prodigies and portents of this kind she generated; *but* to no purpose; for nature abhorred *and prevented* their increase; nor could they reach the desired maturity of age, or find nutriment, or be united in the pleasures of love. For we see that many *circumstances* must concur with other circumstances, in order that *living creatures* may be able to produce their kinds by propagation. First *it is necessary* that there be food; then that there be genial semen throughout the organs, which may flow when the limbs are relaxed *in union*; and likewise, for the female to be united with the male, *they must both* have correspondent *members*, by which each may combine *in* mutual delight with the other.

Many kinds of animal life, too, must then have perished, not having been able to continue their species by propagation. For whatever *creatures* you see breathing the vital air, *assuredly* either craft, or courage, or at least activity, has preserved and defended their race from the commencement of its existence. And there are many which, from their usefulness *to mankind*, remain, *as it were*, intrusted to us, *and* committed to our guardianship.

In the first place, courage has protected the fierce brood of lions, and the savage races *of other wild animals*; *and* craft *has secured* the fox, as swiftness *has saved* the stag. But the light-slumbering breed of dogs, with their faithful affections, and all the various species of horses, and the woolly flocks, too, and horned cattle, all these, *my dear* Memmius, are committed to the protection of man. For they have anxiously avoided wild beasts, and have sought peace; and plenty of *subsistence* has been provided for them without labour of theirs, which subsistence we secure to them as a reward in return for their service. But of those to whom nature has given no such qualities, that they should either be able to live of themselves, or to afford us any service, why should we suffer the races to be maintained and protected by our support? Indeed all these, rendered helpless by their own fatal bonds, were exposed as a prey and a prize to other *animals*, until nature brought their *whole species* to destruction.

But Centaurs, and such creatures, there neither were, nor ever can be; *for there can never exist* an *animal* formed of a double nature and of two bodies; *an animal* made up of *such* heterogeneous members that the power in the opposite portions *of the frame* cannot possibly be equal. This you may learn, with however dull an understanding, from the following observations.

First, the horse, when three years *of his age* have passed, is flourishing in *full* vigour; the boy, at this time of life, is by no means *so*, but will even often seek in his sleep the milky teats of *his mother's* breast. Afterwards, when, in old age, his lusty vigour and stout limbs are failing the horse, (*growing* torpid as life is departing,) *behold*, at that very period, the young man's age being in its flower, youth prevails in him, and clothes his cheeks with soft down; so that you cannot possibly imagine that Centaurs can be composed or consist of a man and the servile seed of a horse; or *that there can be* Scyllae, of half-marine bodies, cinctured with fierce dogs; or other *monsters* of this sort, whose parts we observe to be incompatible with each other; *parts* which neither grow up together in their bodies, nor acquire vigour *together*, nor lose their strength *together* in old age; and which are neither excited by the same objects of affection, nor agree with the same tempers, nor *find that* the same *kinds of food* are nutritious to their bodies. For you may observe that bearded goats often grow fat on hemlock, which to men is rank poison.

Since, too, the flame of fire is accustomed to scorch and burn up the tawny bodies of lions, as well as every kind *of creature* on earth that consists of flesh and blood, how was it possible that a Chimaera, one *animal compounded* of three bodies, the fore part a lion, the hinder a dragon, the middle a goat, could blow abroad at its mouth a fierce flame out of its body?

For which reason, he who supposes that such animals might have been produced, even when the earth was new and the air fresh, (leaning *for argument* only on this empty term of newness,) may babble, with equal reason, many *other hypotheses of a like nature*. He may say that rivers of gold then flowed everywhere over the earth, and that the groves were accustomed to blossom with jewels; or that men were formed with such power *and bulk* of limbs, that they could extend their steps over the deep seas, and turn the whole heaven around them with their hands. For though, at the time when the earth first produced animal life, there were innumerable seeds of things in the ground, this is yet no proof that creatures could have been generated of mixed natures, and *that heterogeneous* members of animals *could have been* blended together. Since the various kinds of herbs, and fruits, and rich groves, which even now spring up exuberantly from the earth, can nevertheless not be produced with a union of *different* kinds. But *they can readily be produced*, if each proceeds in its own order, and all preserve their distinctions according to the fixed law of nature.

And that *early* race of men upon the earth was much more hardy; as it was natural *that they should be*, for the hard earth *herself* bore them. They were internally sustained with bones both larger and more solid, and furnished with strong nerves throughout their bodies; nor *were they a race* that could easily be injured by heat or cold, or by change of food, or by any corporeal malady.

And during many lustres of the sun, revolving through the heaven, they prolonged their lives after the roving manner of wild beasts. No one was either a driver of the crooked plough, or knew how to turn up the fields with the spade, or to plant young seedlings in the earth, or to cut, with pruning-hooks, the old boughs from the lofty trees. That supply which the sun and rain had afforded, *or* which the earth had yielded of its own accord, sufficiently gratified their desires. They refreshed themselves, for the most part, among the acorn-laden oaks. The earth, too, then furnished abundance of whortle-berries, even larger *than at present*, which you now see ripen in winter, *and become* of a purple colour. And many rude kinds of nourishment besides, ample for hapless mortals, the florid freshness of the world in those days produced.

The rivers and fountains then invited them to quench their thirst, as the echoing fall of waters from the high hills now calls, far and wide, the thirsty tribes of wild beasts. Afterwards they occupied the sylvan temples of the nymphs, well known to the wanderers; from which *the goddesses* sent forth flowing rills of water, to lave with a copious flood the humid rocks, trickling over the green moss, and to swell and burst forth, with a portion *of their streams*, over the level plain.

Nor as yet did they understand how to improve their condition by the aid of fire, or to use skins, and to clothe their bodies with the spoils of wild beasts. But they dwelt in groves, and hollow mountains, and woods; and, when compelled to flee from the violence of the wind and rain, sheltered their rude limbs amid the thickets.

Nor could they have regard to *any* common interest, or understand how to observe any customs or laws among themselves. Whatever prize fortune had thrown in the way of any one, *on that* he seized; each knowing *only* to profit by his own instinct, and to live for himself.

And Venus united the persons of lovers in the woods; for either mutual desire reconciled each female *to the intercourse*, or the impetuous force and vehement lust of the man *overcame her*; or acorns and whortle-berries, or choice crabs, were the purchase *of her favours*.

And, relying on the extraordinary vigour of their hands and feet, they pursued the sylvan tribes of wild beasts with missile stones and ponderous clubs; and many they overcame, *while* a few escaped them in their dens; and, when surprised by night, they threw their savage limbs, like bristly boars, unprotected on the earth, covering themselves over with leaves and branches.

Nor did they, trembling and wandering in the shades of night, seek *to recall* the day and the sun with loud cries throughout the fields, but, silent and buried in sleep, they waited till Phoebus, with his roseate beams, should *again* spread light over the heavens. For since they had always been accustomed, from their infancy, to see darkness and light produced at alternate seasons, it was impossible that they should ever wonder *at the change*, or feel apprehension lest, the beams of the sun being withdrawn for ever, eternal night should keep possession of the earth. But what rather gave *them* trouble, *was*, that the tribes of wild beasts often disturbed the rest of hapless *sleepers*; while, driven from their cell at the approach of a foaming boar or stout lion, they lied from their rocky shelter, and yielded up with trembling, at the dead of night, their couches of leaves to the savage intruders.

Nor *yet* did the race of men, in those days, leave with lamentations the sweet light of life in much greater numbers than at present. For *though* more *frequently* at that period, one individual of their number, being caught by wild beasts, and consumed by their teeth, afforded them living food, and filled, *meanwhile*, the groves, and mountains, and forests, with his shrieks, as he felt his bowels buried in a living tomb; while those whom flight had saved, with their bodies torn, and pressing their trembling hands over their grievous wounds, called on death with horrid cries, until, destitute of relief, and ignorant what their hurts required, cruel tortures deprived them of life. Yet, *in those times*, one day did not consign to destruction many thousands of men under *military* banners; nor did the boisterous floods of the sea dash ships and men upon rocks. But the ocean, *though* often rising *and swelling*, raged in vain and to no purpose, and laid aside its empty threats without effect; nor could the deceitful allurement of its calm water entice, with its smiling waves, any one into danger; *for* the daring art of navigation was then unknown. Want of food then consigned languishing bodies to death; now, on the contrary, abundance of luxuries causes destruction. The men *of those times* often poured out poison for themselves unawares; now *persons* of their own accord give *it* craftily to others.

Afterwards, when they procured huts, and skins, and fire, and the woman, united to the man, came to dwell in the same place *with him*; and when the pure *and* pleasing connexions of undivided love were known, and they saw a progeny sprung from themselves; then first the human race began to be softened *and civilized*. For fire now rendered their shivering bodies less able to endure the cold under the canopy of heaven; and love diminished their strength; and children with their blandishments easily subdued the ferocious tempers of their parents. Then, also, neighbours, feeling a mutual friendship, began to form agreements not to hurt or injure *one another*; and they commended, with sounds and gestures, their children, and the female sex to each other's protection; while they signified, with imperfect speech, that it is right for every one to have compassion on the weak. Such concord, however, could not be established universally; but the better and greater part kept their faith inviolate, or the human race would then have been wholly destroyed, and the species could not have continued its generations to the present period.

SULPICIA'S BIRTHDAY

Elegies

Sulpicia

Translated by John Heath-Stubbs, 2000

Poetry in ancient Rome was not only a man's craft. We know of several female poets, but in most cases we have been deprived of the chance to read their work because it was not preserved. Fortunately, a handful of poems by **Sulpicia**, a poetess of the late first century BC, survived by accident, bundled together with those of a male poet called Tibullus. Although Sulpicia was well-born and well-connected, her poems reach beyond the confines of her status – and indeed her time – to speak clearly to us today. In this poem she writes of her misery at being parted from her beloved Cerinthus for her birthday.

Sulpicia's Birthday

My dreaded birthday is looming, and I've got to spend it
There in the odious country without Cerinthus.
What is more agreeable than the city? Is a country estate
A fit place for a girl or the fields
By the cold river Arno? Stop fussing about me
Messala, my kinsman, you're much too ready
To take me on an unnecessary journey.
Carried hence—I leave my soul and my senses behind
As I cannot exercise my own free will.

She Can Be At Rome, After All

Don't you know that the burden of an unnecessary journey
Is lifted from your poor girl's heart?
I can be at Rome, it now seems, for my birthday—
This comes to you by an unexpected stroke of luck.

THE TROJAN HORSE

Aeneid, Book II

Virgil

Translated by John Dryden, 1697

The Aeneid, a Latin epic by the Augustan poet **Virgil** (70 BC–19 BC), tells
of the fall of Troy and escape of Aeneas, son of Venus, and a group of
survivors, and of their coming to Italy to found a new home. Modelled on
the epics of Homer, the poem provided Romans with the opportunity to
view themselves as descendants of the families of Troy. The final moments
of the Trojan War had been recounted only briefly in flashback in the
Odyssey, allowing Virgil to develop the story in full. In this excerpt from
his poem, translated in the seventeenth century by the great John Dryden,
England's first official Poet Laureate, the Trojans receive the gift of a
wooden horse from the Greeks.

> By destiny compell'd, and in despair,
> The Greeks grew weary of the tedious war,
> And, by Minerva's aid, a fabric rear'd,
> Which like a steed of monstrous height appear'd:
> The sides were plank'd with pine: they feign'd it made
> For their return, and this the vow they paid.
> Thus they pretend, but in the hollow side,
> Selected numbers of their soldiers hide:
> With inward arms the dire machine they load;
> And iron bowels stuff the dark abode.
> In sight of Troy lies Tenedos, an isle
> (While Fortune did on Priam's empire smile)
> Renown'd for wealth; but, since, a faithless bay,
> Where ships expos'd to wind and weather lay,
> There was their fleet conceal'd. We thought, for Greece
> Their sails were hoisted, and our fears release.
> The Trojans, coop'd within their walls so long,
> Unbar their gates, and issue in a throng,
> Like swarming bees, and with delight survey
> The camp deserted, where the Grecians lay:
> The quarters of the several chiefs they show'd—
> Here Phoenix, here Achilles made abode;

Here join'd the battles; there the navy rode.
Part on the pile their wandering eyes employ—
The pile by Pallas rais'd to ruin Troy.
Thymoetes first ('tis doubtful whether hir'd,
Or so the Trojan destiny requir'd)
Mov'd that the ramparts might be broken down,
To lodge the monster fabric in the town.
But Capys, and the rest of sounder mind,
The fatal present to the flames design'd,
Or to the watery deep; at least to bore
The hollow sides, and hidden frauds explore.
The giddy vulgar, as their fancies guide,
With noise say nothing, and in parts divide.
Laocoön, follow'd by a numerous crowd,
Ran from the fort, and cried, from far, aloud:
'O wretched countrymen! what fury reigns?
What more than madness has possess'd your brains?
Think you the Grecians from your coasts are gone?
And are Ulysses' arts no better known?
This hollow fabric either must inclose,
Within its blind recess, our secret foes;
Or 'tis an engine rais'd above the town,
To' o'erlook the walls, and then to batter down.
Somewhat is sure design'd by fraud or force—
Trust not their presents, nor admit the horse.'
Thus having said, against the steed he threw
His forceful spear, which, hissing as it flew,
Pierc'd through the yielding planks of jointed wood,
And trembling in the hollow belly stood.
The sides, transpierc'd, return a rattling sound;
And groans of Greeks inclos'd come issuing through the wound.
And, had not heaven the fall of Troy design'd,
Or had not men been fated to be blind, mind:
Enough was said and done, to' inspire a better
Then had our lances pierc'd the treacherous wood,
And Ilian tow'rs and Priam's empire stood.
Meantime, with shouts, the Trojan shepherds bring
A captive Greek in bands, before the king—
Taken, to take—who made himself their prey,
To' impose on their belief, and Troy betray;
Fix'd on his aim, and obstinately bent
To die undaunted, or to circumvent.
About the captive, tides of Trojans flow;
All press to see, and some insult the foe.
Now hear how well the Greeks their wiles disguis'd:
Behold a nation in a man compris'd.
Trembling the miscreant stood: unarm'd and bound,

He star'd, and roll'd his haggard eyes around;
Then said, 'Alas! what earth remains, what sea
Is open to receive unhappy me?
What fate a wretched fugitive attends,
Scorn'd by my foes, abandon'd by my friends!'
He said, and sigh'd, and cast a rueful eye:
Our pity kindles, and our passions die.
We cheer the youth to make his own defence,
And freely tell us what he was, and whence:
What news he could impart we long to know,
And what to credit from a captive foe.

    His fear at length dismiss'd, he said, 'Whate'er
My fate ordains, my words shall be sincere:
I neither can nor dare my birth disclaim:
Greece is my country, Sinon is my name.
Though plung'd by Fortune's power in misery,
'Tis not in Fortune's power to make me lie.
If any chance has hither brought the name.
Of Palamedes, not unknown to fame,
Who suffer'd from the malice of the times,
Accus'd and sentenc'd for pretended crimes,
Because the fatal wars lie would prevent;
Whose death the wretched Greeks too late lament—
Me, then a boy, my father, poor and bare
Of other means, committed to his care,
His kinsman and companion in the war.
While Fortune favour'd, while his arms support
The cause, and rul'd the counsels of the court,
I made some figure there; nor was my name
Obscure, nor I without my share of fame.
But when Ulysses, with fallacious arts,
Had made impression in the people's hearts,
And forg'd a treason in my patron's name
(I speak of things too far divulg'd by fame),
My kinsman fell. Then I, without support,
In private mourn'd his loss, and left the court.
Mad as I was, I could not bear his fate
With silent grief, but loudly blam'd the state,
And curs'd the direful author of my woes.—
'Twas told again; and hence my ruin rose.
I threaten'd, if indulgent heaven once more
Would land me safely on my native shore,
His death with double vengeance to restore.
This mov'd the murderer's hate; and soon ensued
The' effects of malice from a man so proud.
Ambiguous rumours through the camp he spread,
And sought, by treason, my devoted head;

New crimes invented; left unturn'd no stone,
To make my guilt appear, and hide his own;
Till Calchas was by force and threatening wrought—
But why—why dwell I on that anxious thought?
If on my nation just revenge you seek,
And 'tis to' appear a foe, to' appear a Greek;
Already you my name and country know:
Assuage your thirst of blood, and strike the blow:
My death will both the kingly brothers please,
And set insatiate Ithacus at ease.'
This fair unfinish'd tale, these broken starts,
Rais'd expectations in our longing hearts;
Unknowing as we were in Grecian arts.
His former trembling once again renew'd.
With acted fear, the villain thus pursued:
'Long had the Grecians (tir'd with fruitless care,
And wearied with an unsuccessful war)
Resolv'd to raise the siege, and leave the town:
And, had the gods permitted, they had gone.
But oft the wintry seas, and southern winds,
Withstood their passage home, and chang'd their minds.
Portents and prodigies their souls amaz'd;
But most, when this stupendous pile was rais'd:
Then flaming meteors, hung in air, were seen.
And thunders rattled through a sky serene.
Dismay'd, and fearful of some dire event,
Eurypylus, to' inquire their fate, was sent.
He from the gods this dreadful answer brought:
'O Grecians, when the Trojan shores you sought,
Your passage with a virgin's blood was bought:
So must your safe return be bought again;
And Grecian blood once more atone the main.'
The spreading rumour round the people ran;
All fear'd, and each believ'd himself the man.
Ulysses took the' advantage of their fright;
Call'd Calchas, and produc'd in open sight,
Then bade him name the wretch, ordain'd by fate
The public victim, to redeem the state.
Already some presag'd the dire event,
And saw what sacrifice Ulysses meant.
For twice five days the good old seer withstood
The' intended treason, and was dumb to blood,
Till, tir'd with endless clamours and pursuit
Of Ithacus, he stood no longer mute,
But, as it was agreed, pronounc'd that I
Was destin'd by the wrathful gods to die.
All prais'd the sentence, pleas'd the storm should fall

On one alone, whose fury threaten'd all.
The dismal day was come: the priests prepare
Their leaven'd cakes, and fillets for my hair.
I follow'd nature's laws, and must avow,
I broke my bonds, and fled the fatal blow.
Hid in a weedy lake all night I lay,
Secure of safety when they sail'd away.
But now what further hopes for me remain,
To see my friends or native soil again:
My tender infants, or my careful sire,
Whom they returning will to death require;
Will perpetrate on them their first design,
And take the forfeit of their heads for mine?
Which, O! if pity mortal minds can move,
If there be faith below, or gods above,
If innocence and truth can claim desert,
Ye Trojans, from an injur'd wretch avert.'
    False tears true pity move: the king commands
To loose his fetters, and unbind his hands,
Then adds these friendly words: 'Dismiss thy fears:
Forget the Greeks: be mine as thou wert theirs;
But truly tell, was it for force or guile,
Or some religious end, you rais'd the pile?'
Thus said the king.—He, full of fraudful arts,
This well-invented tale for truth imparts:
'Ye lamps of heaven! (he said, and lifted high
His hands now free)—thou venerable sky!
Inviolable powers, ador'd with dread!
Ye fatal fillets, that once bound this head!
Ye sacred altars, from whose flames I fled!
Be all of you adjur'd; and grant I may,
Without a crime, the' ungrateful Greeks betray,
Reveal the secrets of the guilty state,
And justly punish whom I justly hate!
But you, O king, preserve the faith you gave,
If I, to save myself, your empire save.
The Grecian hopes, and all the' attempts they made,
Were only founded on Minerva's aid.
But from the time when impious Diomede,
And false Ulysses, that inventive head,
Her fatal image from the temple drew,
The sleeping guardians of the castle slew,
Her virgin statue with their bloody hands
Polluted, and profan'd her holy bands;
From thence the tide of fortune left their shore,
And ebb'd much faster than it flow'd before:
Their courage languish'd, as their hopes decay'd:

And Pallas, now averse, refus'd her aid.
Nor did the goddess doubtfully declare
Her alter'd mind, and alienated care.
When first her fatal image touch'd the ground,
She sternly cast her glaring eyes around,
That sparkled as they roll'd, and seem'd to threat:
Her heavenly limbs distill'd a briny sweat.
Thrice from the ground she leap'd, was seen to wield
Her brandish'd lance, and shake her horrid shield.
Then Calchas bade our host for flight prepare,
And hope no conquest from the tedious war,
Till first they sail'd for Greece; with prayers besought
Her injur'd power, and better omens brought.
And, now their navy ploughs the watery main,
Yet, soon expect it on your shores again,
With Pallas pleas'd; as Calchas did ordain.
But first, to reconcile the blue-eyed maid
For her stol'n statue and her tower betrayed,
Warn'd by the seer, to her offended name
We rais'd and dedicate this wondrous frame,
So lofty, lest through your forbidden gates
It pass, and intercept our better fates:
For, once admitted there, our hopes are lost;
And Troy may then a new Palladium boast:
For so religion and the gods ordain,
That, if you violate with hands profane
Minerva's gift, your town in flames shall burn;
(Which omen, O ye gods, on Graecia turn!)
But if it climb, with your assisting hands,
The Trojan walls, and in the city stands;
Then Troy shall Argos and Mycenae burn,
And the reverse of fate on us return.'

    With such deceits he gain'd their easy hearts,
Too prone to credit his perfidious arts.
What Diomede, nor Thetis' greater son,
A thousand ships, nor ten years' siege, had done—
False tears and fawning words the city won.

    A greater omen, and of worse portent,
Did our unwary minds with fear torment,
Concurring to produce the dire event.
Laocoön, Neptune's priest by lot that year,
With solemn pomp then sacrific'd a steer:
When (dreadful to behold!) from sea we spied
Two serpents, rank'd abreast, the seas divide,
And smoothly sweep along the swelling tide.
Their flaming crests above the waves they show;
Their bellies seem to burn the seas below;

Their speckled tails advance to steer their course,
And on the sounding shore the flying billows force.
And now the strand, and now the plain, they held;
Their ardent eyes with bloody streaks were fill'd;
Their nimble tongues they brandish'd as they came,
And lick'd their hissing jaws, that sputter'd flame.
We fled amaz'd; their destin'd way they take,
And to Laocoön and his children make;
And first around the tender boys they wind,
Then with their sharpen'd fangs their limbs and bodies grind.
The wretched father, running to their aid
With pious haste, but vain, they next invade;
Twice round his waist their winding volumes roll'd;
And twice about his gasping throat they fold.
The priest thus doubly chok'd—their crests divide,
And tow'ring o'er his head in triumph ride.
With both his hands he labours at the knots;
His holy fillets the blue venom blots:
His roaring fills the flitting air around.
Thus, when an ox receives a glancing wound,
He breaks his bands, the fatal altar flies,
And with loud bellowings breaks the yielding skies.
Their tasks perform'd, the serpents quit their prey,
And to the tower of Pallas make their way:
Couch'd at her feet, they lie protected there,
By her large buckler and protended spear.
Amazement seizes all: the general cry
Proclaims Laocoön justly doom'd to die,
Whose hand the will of Pallas had withstood,
And dar'd to violate the sacred wood.
All vote to' admit the steed, that vows be paid,
And incense offer'd, to the' offended maid.
A spacious breach is made: the town lies bare:
Some hoising-levers, some the wheels, prepare,
And fasten to the horse's feet: the rest
With cables haul along the' unwieldy beast.
Each on his fellow for assistance calls:
At length the fatal fabric mounts the walls,
Big with destruction. Boys with chaplets crown'd,
And choirs of virgins, sing and dance around.
Thus rais'd aloft, and then descending down,
It enters o'er our heads, and threats the town.
O sacred city, built by hands divine!
O valiant heroes of the Trojan line!
Four times he struck: as oft the clashing sound
Of arms was heard, and inward groans rebound.
Yet, mad with zeal, and blinded with our fate,

We haul along the horse in solemn state;
Then place the dire portent within the tower.
Cassandra cried, and curs'd the' unhappy hour;
Foretold our fate; but, by the gods' decree,
All heard, and none believ'd the prophecy.
With branches we the fanes adorn, and waste,
In jollity, the day ordain'd to be the last.
Meantime the rapid heavens roll'd down the light,
And on the shaded ocean rush'd the night:
Our men, secure, nor guards nor centries held;
But easy sleep their weary limbs compell'd.
The Grecians had embark'd their naval powers
From Tenedos, and sought our well-known shores,
Safe under covert of the silent night,
And guided by the' imperial galley's light;
When Sinon, favour'd by the partial gods,
Unlock'd the horse, and op'd his dark abodes;
Restor'd to vital air our hidden foes,
Who joyful from their long confinement rose.

DIDO AND AENEAS

Aeneid, Book IV

Virgil

Translated by Sarah Ruden, 2008

The Trojan refugees, led by Aeneas, travelled to Carthage in North Africa, and met its queen, Dido. She had arrived here from Phoenician Tyre after her brother Pygmalion killed her husband Sychaeus because he coveted his gold. Naturally she fell in love with Aeneas and hoped he might stay on with her. He would not. Like many a hero, Aeneas loved her and left her to continue in his quest. The gods were calling him onwards. It was his destiny to found a new home for his people. One cannot help but pity poor Dido, whose melancholy story inspired opera composers from Henry Purcell in the seventeenth century (*Dido and Aeneas*) to Hector Berlioz in the nineteenth (*Les Troyens*).

He burned to run—however sweet this land was.
The gods' august command had terrified him.
But how? What would he dare say to the queen
In her passion? What beginning could he make?
His mind kept darting and his thoughts dividing
Through the whole matter and each baffling question.
After much wavering, this seemed the best plan:
He called Mnestheus and brave Serestus
And Sergestus: they must get the men together
Quietly, rig the fleet, and hide the reason
For the stirring. Meanwhile the good lady Dido
Would not expect such strong love could be broken.
He would approach her, seeking out the best words
At the kindest time. With great alacrity,
These men obeyed in everything he ordered.
But who can fool a lover? Soon the queen—
Even in safety anxious—sensed the trick,
Though no ship moved yet. Evil Rumor told her
The fleet was being fitted for a journey.
She raved all through the town in helpless passion,
Like a Bacchant the biennial mysteries rouse
With shrieks of ritual and brandished emblems

And shouts that summon her to dark Cithaeron.
She faced off with Aeneas and accused him:
"You traitor, did you think that you could hide
Such a great crime, that you could sneak away?
The pledge you made, our passion for each other,
Even your Dido's brutal death won't keep you?
Monster, you toil beneath these winter skies
And rush to cross the deep through northern blasts,
For a strange home on someone else's land?
If ancient Troy still stood today to sail to,
Would you make off across that surging plain?
You run from me? By your pledged hand, my tears
(Since I am stripped of everything but these),
Our union, and the wedding we embarked on—
If I have ever earned it through my kindness,
Have pity on my tottering house and me.
If pleading has a chance still, change your mind.
The Libyan clans and Nomad rulers hate me;
So do the Tyrians, because of you.
You ruined me and my good name—my one path
To heaven. My guest leaves me here to die.
Now I must call you guest instead of husband.
Pygmalion my brother will raze my walls,
Gaetulian Iarbas lead me off, a captive.
If only, though deserting me, you gave me
A child—if I could see a small Aeneas
Play in my palace, with a face like yours—
I wouldn't feel so cheated and abandoned."
She spoke; he kept his eyes down, at Jove's orders,
Struggling to force his feelings from his heart.
Finally, briefly: "Name your favors, list them.
There isn't one I ever could deny.
Never will I regret Elissa's memory
While I *have* memory, while I breathe and move.
A little on the facts, though: don't imagine
I meant to sneak away, and as for 'husband,'
I never made a pact of marriage with you.
If fate would let me live the life I chose;
If I had power over my decisions,
I would have stayed at Troy, where I could tend
Belovèd graves; Priam's high citadel
Would stand; I would restore Troy for the conquered.
But Grynean Apollo and the edicts
Of Lycia drive me into Italy.
My love, my home are there. You are Phoenician,
But love to see your towers in Libya.
How can you then resent us Trojans settling

In Italy—*our* lawful foreign kingdom?
When the night covers earth with drizzling shadows,
When fiery stars rise, then the troubled ghost
Of my father, dear Anchises, hounds my dreams.
I know I cheat my darling son Ascanius
Of fields fate gave him in his western realm.
From Jove himself a heavenly emissary
(On both our heads, I swear it) brought me orders
Down through the air. In the clear day I saw him
Come through the gate, and these ears heard his voice.
Don't goad me—and yourself—with these complaints.
Italy is against my will."
Although her back was turned, she still surveyed
The speaker blankly and distractedly
Over her shoulder. Then her fury broke out.
"Traitor—there is no goddess in your family,
No Dardanus. The sharp-rocked Caucasus
Gave birth to you, Hyrcanian tigers nursed you.
Why pretend now? Is something worse in store?
Was there a sigh for tears of mine? A glance?
Did he give in to tears himself, or pity?
Injustice overwhelms me, which concerns
Great Juno and our father, Saturn's son.
What bond can hold? I helped a castaway,
I shared my kingdom with him, like a fool.
The ships you lost—I saved your friends from death—
Hot madness drives me. Now the fortune-teller
Apollo, Lycian lotteries, Jove dispatching
Dire orders earthward through the gods' own mouthpiece—
As if such cares disturbed the gods' calm heaven!
I will not cling to you or contradict you.
Ride windy waves to chase Italian kingdoms.
I hope that heaven's conscience has the power
To trap you in the rocks and force your penance
Down your throat, as you call my name. I'll send
My black flames there. When cold death draws my soul out,
My ghost will hound you. Even among dead souls
In hell, I'll know when you are finally paying."
In torment, she broke off and turned away,
And ran out of his sight into the palace.
And there he froze—with much he would have said.
She fainted and was lifted by her maids,
And the bed inside the marble walls received her.
Now the right-thinking hero, though he wished
To give some comfort for so great a grief,
Obeyed the gods, returning to his ships,
While he continued groaning, deeply lovesick.

The Trojans fell to work and pulled the vessels
Down from the beach in one long line. Tarred hulls
Floated. The busy crews brought leafy oars
And logs with bark still on.
That rush from everywhere in town resembled
Ants plundering a giant heap of spelt
To store at home in readiness for winter.
Over the grass the thin black phalanx goes,
Loaded with booty. Some are heaving huge grains
Forward, and some are marshaling and prodding,
So the entire pathway hums with work.
What did you feel then, Dido, when you saw?
How did you sob when all that shoreline seethed?
You looked out from your tower, and the sea
Was an industrious uproar and commotion.
Reprobate Love, wrencher of mortal hearts!
He drives her now to tears, and now to beg
And cravenly submit her pride to love—
Whatever leaves her with a hope of life.
"Anna, you see the whole shore in a tumult.
They come from everywhere. Sails draw the breeze.
Sailors in joy hang garlands on the sterns.
As surely as I saw this great grief coming,
So surely I'll endure. But do one favor
In pity, since the traitor was your friend—
Yours only: you were trusted with his secrets;
You know how to approach him when he's weak.
Go, sister, kneel to my proud enemy.
I was no Greek at Aulis when they swore
To smash his race. I sent no fleet to Troy,
Nor made his father's ghost and ashes homeless.
How can he block his ears against my words?
Where is he running? As a last sad love gift,
He ought to wait for winds that make it easy.
I do not plead the marriage he betrayed.
Let the man go be king in charming Latium.
I just want time, a pause to heal my mind
And teach myself to mourn in my defeat.
I ask this final wretched favor, sister—
A loan—and I will give my death as interest."
Weeping, she made this plea. Her grieving sister
Delivered it repeatedly. No tears
Could move him; no words found his sympathy.
His fate and Jove were barriers to his ears,
As in the Alps, the North Wind's blasts assault
A solid, tough, and venerable oak,
Competing to uproot it; with a creak

At the blows, it strews its high leaves on the ground
But clasps the cliff with roots that go as far
Toward hell as its top reaches into heaven:
Just as relentless were the words that battered
The hero. In his noble heart he suffered,
But tears did nothing. His resolve endured.
Appalled now by her fate, poor Dido prayed
For death; she wished to see the sky no longer.
Other things also drove her from the daylight:
Her gifts on incense-burning altars rotted,
Horrible to describe: wine turned to black
And filthy gore the second that she poured it.
No one was told. Her sister did not know it.
There stood inside her home a marble shrine
To her late husband: there she worshiped him,
Spreading white fleece and hanging holy wreaths.
She thought she heard his voice there, echoing, calling.
When the night's darkness covered all the earth,
She listened to a lone owl on the rooftree
Whose song of death kept trailing into sobs.
Many grim warnings of the long-dead seers
Panicked her too. In dreams a fierce Aeneas
Chased her. She raved in fear or was abandoned,
Friendless, forever walking a long road,
Seeking her Tyrians in a lifeless land.
It was like Pentheus seeing bands of Furies,
And a pair of Thebes, and a sun split in two;
As in a play the son of Agamemnon
Runs from his mother's torches and black snakes
While vengeful demons lurk outside the door.
Madness and grief filled her defeated heart,
And she chose death. She had a time and method,
But hid her plan behind a face of peace
And hope, in speaking to her wretched sister.
"Anna, I've found a way—congratulate me!—
To bring him back or set me free from love.
Next to the setting sun and Ocean's boundary,
In Ethiopia, where giant Atlas
Turns the star-blazing heavens on his shoulder,
Lived a Massylian priestess I've now found,
Who guarded the Hesperides' temple there,
Nourished the snake, preserved the sacred branches,
And strewed sleep-bringing poppy and moist honey.
She says her spells soothe any minds she wishes
Or else bring grueling troubles into others,
Stop rivers and turn stars back in their courses,
And call out ghosts at night. The earth will roar

Beneath your feet, ash trees will rush down mountains.
Sister, I swear it by your darling life
And by the gods—I would not choose such weapons.
Build me a pyre in secret in the courtyard.
The arms that evil man hung in our bedroom—
The clothes I stripped from him, our bed of union,
My death—put it all there. I want the leavings
Of the criminal destroyed. She's shown me how."
Now she was silent, and her face went pale.
But Anna did not guess her sister's funeral
Hid in these strange rites, or suspect such frenzy—
What could be worse than when Sychaeus died?
She did as she was told.
Deep in the house, beneath the sky, a pyre
Now towered high with logs of pine and oak.
The queen festooned the walls with funeral garlands.
Conscious of what must be, she put his picture
On the bed, above his sword and cast-off clothes.
Altars encircled her. The loose-haired priestess
Shouted three hundred gods' names—Erebus, Chaos,
Three-faced Diana, who is triple Hecate.
She sprinkled drops she said were from Avernus.
Herbs appeared, cut with bronze knives at the full moon,
Swollen and oozing coal-black milk of poison;
A love charm too, torn from a new foal's forehead
Before the mare could get it.
Dido, with sacred meal in clean hands, robes loose,
One sandal off, now stood at the high altar,
Called gods, called fate-wise stars as witnesses.
She prayed to anything in heaven that sees
And punishes a broken bond of love.

Now it was night, and all earth's weary creatures
Slept peacefully. The woods and savage waters
Were still. The stars were halfway through their journeys
Above the tranquil fields. Cattle and bright birds
Of the broad lakes and brambly wilderness
All lay asleep beneath the noiseless sky,
Their troubles soothed, their sufferings forgotten—
But not the desolate Phoenician queen.
Her heart and eyes shunned darkness and the ease
Of sleep. Her torments thronged, her love ran wild—
They came and went on seething tides of madness.
Her heart was churning with unceasing questions:
"What should I do? Go back where I'll be laughed at,
And beg to marry a Numidian prince
After I turned those suitors all away?

Follow the Trojan ships and do whatever
The Trojans order? Surely they'll recall
The help I gave and, for the past's sake, help me.
But then again, would they allow the outcast
On their proud ships? Poor fool, you're not familiar
With the treachery of Laomedon's descendants?
Would I trail those cheering sailors all alone,
A deserter? Would I take my Tyrian ranks
As escorts? Would those barely torn from Sidon
Endure another sea voyage on my orders?
No, die—you've earned it. Give the sword your sorrow.
But you, my sister, weakened by my tears,
Turned folly to disaster and defeat.
I could not live a blameless life, unmarried,
Like a wild thing, and be spared this agony:
I broke my promise to the dead Sychaeus."
Out of her heart these words of sorrow broke.
Aeneas was asleep on the high stern,
In confidence that everything was ready—
When in a dream he saw the god again:
The form had Mercury's face and his complexion,
His yellow hair and handsome young man's body.
And it renewed the warning from before:
"You sleep, child of the goddess, while disaster
Teeters above, and perils lurk around?
Fool, can't you hear your guide, the West Wind, breathing?
The woman, who now knows that she will die,
Is tossed in scheming, heaving tides of rage.
While you still can, you need to run for it,
Or you'll see storms of wreckage and the glare
Of brutal torches. Flames will fill the beach
If the dawn finds you loitering in this land.
Be quick and go! A woman is a changing
And fitful thing." The form ebbed into black night.
The sudden vision of this chilling shade
Ripped him from sleep. He shook his comrades too.
"Wake—now!—and take your places on the benches.
Hurry! Unfurl the sails. Once more from heaven
A god's come, driving our escape: start cutting
The twisted ropes! We follow you, whichever
God you might be—again we cheer your orders.
Be with us, guide us graciously, and bring us
Favoring stars." He drew his flashing sword
And struck the mooring line. A single passion
Seized all of them. They ran and snatched their gear up
And quit the beach. The blue plain now was hidden
By skimming ships. The oars raised twists of foam.

Dawn, risen from her husband's saffron bed,
Was scattering her light across the world.
The sky grew white above the queen's high tower.
Below, the sails went forward in a row.
The port, the shore were bare, the sailors gone.
Repeatedly she struck her lovely breast
And tore her gold hair. "Jupiter! He's leaving?
A stranger comes—and goes—and mocks my power?
Why doesn't the whole city arm and follow
On ships torn madly from their moorings? Hurry!
Bring torches, pass out arms, ram the oars forward!
What? Where is this new madness taking me?
Poor thing. Your crimes—you feel them only now?
Not when you made him king? This is his pledged word!
They say he brought his household gods with him,
And hauled his frail old father on his shoulders.
I could have scattered the torn pieces of him
Across the waves. I could have killed his friends—
His son—and made a banquet for the father—
A struggle I might not have won—no matter:
I still would die. My torches should have swarmed
His camp and gangways till they made a pyre
For father and son, the whole race, and myself.
Come, Sun, the blazing lamp of all creation—
Juno, the witness and the go-between—
And Hecate, a name shrieked at the crossroads—
Avenging Furies—and my own death demons:
Turn heaven's justice where it should be turned.
This is my prayer now: if that living curse
Must skim his way to harbor in that country,
If Jove and fate require this to happen,
Then let a bold and warlike people drive him
Out of his realm and tear his Iulus from him.
Make him a suppliant, let him see the death
Of blameless friends. Humiliating peace terms
Will bring no happy old age in his kingdom.
He'll fall and lie unburied in the sand.
And now my last plea, gushing with my blood:
Tyrians, hound with hatred for all time
The race he founds. My ashes call from you
This service. Let there be no pacts of friendship.
Out of my grave let an avenger rise,
With fire and iron for Dardanian settlers—
Now—someday—when the power is there to strike.
Our shores will clash, weapons and seas collide.
My curse is war for Trojans and their children."
She finished. Now her thoughts went everywhere,

Seeking the fastest way to leave the light.
She told the old nurse of Sychaeus, Barce
(Her own had died back in the fatherland),
"Darling, please bring my sister Anna—hurry!
Have her splash river water on her body
And bring the beasts and other offerings.
Cover your own brow with a pious fillet.
I'll now round off the ritual I began
For Jove below the earth, to end my pain,
Putting to flame this pyre—the Trojan's life."
Quickly the fond old woman hobbled off.
Now Dido's own grim plans had made her frantic.
Her red eyes darted, and her cheeks were blotched
And shook—but she grew pale in facing death.
She burst into the center of the house,
Frenzied, and climbed the pyre and drew the sword
From Troy—she hadn't asked for it for this.
Here she surveyed the bed she knew so well,
And the Trojan clothes. In tearful contemplation
She lay a little while, and spoke these last words:
"Sweet spoils—while fate and god still kept you sweet—
Receive my breath and free me from this pain.
I lived, I ran the race that fate allotted.
I'll send the underworld a noble ghost.
I saw the walls of my great city standing,
Avenged my husband, made my brother pay.
A happy—no, a more than happy life,
If Trojan ships had never touched these shores."
She kissed the bed. "I die without revenge—
But let me die. I like this path to darkness.
Let the cruel Trojan's eyes take in these flames.
The omen of my death will go with him."
Her maids now saw her falling on her sword,
Still speaking, saw her blood foam down the blade
And fleck her hands. A shout rose to the rooftop,
And through the shaken city Rumor raged.
Long-drawn-out shrieks of grief and women's keening
Brimmed from the buildings. Anguish filled the sky.
As if invading troops brought Carthage down—
Or ancient Tyre were sacked—and flames were scaling
The rooftops of the houses and the temples.
Her sister heard and ran to her in panic.
Clawing her cheeks, bruising her breast with blows.
As she plunged through the crowd, she called that doomed name.
"This was your purpose, sister—to deceive me?
The pyre, the flames, the altars bring me this?
How could you leave me like a cast-off thing

And go alone? You should have called me with you:
One sword, one hour, one agony for both!
I piled this wood, I called our fathers' gods
To let you lie alone here, heartless monster?
You killed yourself and me, your city's people,
And the Phoenician lords. Come, give me water
To wash these wounds—and if a last breath hovers,
My mouth will take it." She had climbed the pyre,
And held her sister now, that fading life,
And moaned and mopped the black blood with her clothes.
Dido now strained to lift her heavy eyes
But failed. Around the sword, her breast's wound hissed.
Three times she rose a little, on her elbow,
Collapsed each time, and with her wandering vision
Searched for the bright, high sky and sighed to find it.
Queen Juno cut this torture short, in pity,
Dispatching Iris earthward from Olympus
To free the struggling spirit from its bonds.
There was no fate or justice in her death.
Her madness brought a wretched, early end.
Proserpina had cut no lock of blond hair
To dedicate this life to Stygian Orcus.
So dewy Iris soared on saffron wings,
Trailing a thousand sun-reflecting colors,
And floated near her head. "I am to take
This gift to Dis and free you from your body."
Her right hand made the stroke. All living heat
Vanished, and life dissolved into the wind.

ROMULUS AND REMUS

Ab urbe condita, Book I

Livy

Translated by Rev. Canon Roberts, 1912

At the beginning of his history of Rome, **Livy** (64 or 59 BC–AD 17) described how Aeneas and the Trojan refugees eventually reached the west coast of Italy. Here Aeneas met King Latinus, married his daughter Lavinia, and built a new town named Lavinium. Lavinia, however, had previously been engaged to another king, who declared war. Although his people prevailed, Aeneas later died, leaving behind his son Ascanius. When he grew up, Ascanius built a new city called 'Alba Longa', and had a son of his own. Many generations down the line, the daughter of his descendant Numitor, Rhea Silvia, was violated, allegedly by the war god Mars, and gave birth to twin boys. In this story Livy explains what happened after her uncle Amulius, who had usurped her father to become king, ordered her infant sons, Romulus and Remus, to be thrown into the river. Livy was an historian, but the early centuries of Rome's history were so steeped in legend that he had little choice but to embrace foundation myths like this one.

By a heaven-sent chance it happened that the Tiber was then overflowing its banks, and stretches of standing water prevented any approach to the main channel. Those who were carrying the children expected that this stagnant water would be sufficient to drown them, so under the impression that they were carrying out the king's orders they exposed the boys at the nearest point of the overflow, where the Ficus Ruminalis (said to have been formerly called Romularis) now stands. The locality was then a wild solitude. The tradition goes on to say that after the floating cradle in which the boys had been exposed had been left by the retreating water on dry land, a thirsty she-wolf from the surrounding hills, attracted by the crying of the children, came to them, gave them her teats to suck and was so gentle towards them that the king's flock-master found her licking the boys with her tongue. According to the story his name was Faustulus. He took the children to his hut and gave them to his wife Larentia to bring up. Some writers think that Larentia, from her unchaste life, had got the nickname of 'She-wolf' amongst the shepherds, and that this was the origin of the marvellous story.

As soon as the boys, thus born and thus brought up, grew to be young men they did not neglect their pastoral duties but their special delight was roaming through the woods on hunting expeditions. As their strength and courage were thus developed, they used not only to lie in wait for fierce beasts of prey, but they even attacked brigands when loaded with plunder. They distributed what they took amongst the shepherds, with whom, surrounded by a continually increasing body of young men, they associated themselves in their serious undertakings and in their sports and pastimes.

It is said that the festival of the Lupercalia, which is still observed, was even in those days celebrated on the Palatine hill. This hill was originally called Pallantium from a city of the same name in Arcadia; the name was afterwards changed to Palatium. Evander, an Arcadian, had held that territory many ages before, and had introduced an annual festival from Arcadia in which young men ran about naked for sport and wantonness, in honour of the Lycaean Pan, whom the Romans afterwards called Inuus. The existence of this festival was widely recognised, and it was while the two brothers were engaged in it that the brigands, enraged at losing their plunder, ambushed them. Romulus successfully defended himself, but Remus was taken prisoner and brought before Amulius, his captors impudently accusing him of their own crimes. The principal charge brought against them was that of invading Numitor's lands with a body of young men whom they had got together, and carrying off plunder as though in regular warfare. Remus accordingly was handed over to Numitor for punishment.

Faustulus had from the beginning suspected that it was royal offspring that he was bringing up, for he was aware that the boys had been exposed at the king's command and the time at which he had taken them away exactly corresponded with that of their exposure. He had, however, refused to divulge the matter prematurely, until either a fitting opportunity occurred or necessity demanded its disclosure. The necessity came first. Alarmed for the safety of Remus he revealed the state of the case to Romulus. It so happened that Numitor also, who had Remus in his custody, on hearing that he and his brother were twins, and comparing their ages, and the character and bearing so unlike that of one in a servile condition, began to recall the memory of his grandchildren, and further inquiries brought him to the same conclusion as Faustulus; nothing was wanting to the recognition of Remus. So the king Amulius was being enmeshed on all sides by hostile purposes. Romulus shrunk from a direct attack with his body of shepherds, for he was no match for the king in open fight. They were instructed to approach the palace by different routes and meet there at a given time, whilst from Numitor's house Remus lent his assistance with a second band he had collected. The attack succeeded and the king was killed.

At the beginning of the fray, Numitor gave out that an enemy had entered the City and was attacking the palace, in order to draw off the Alban soldiery to the citadel, to defend it. When he saw the young men coming to congratulate him after the assassination, he at once called a council of his people and explained his brother's infamous conduct towards him, the story of his grandsons, their parentage and bringing up, and how he recognised them. Then he proceeded to inform them of the tyrant's death and his responsibility for it. The young men marched in order through the midst of the assembly and saluted their grandfather as king; their action was approved by the whole population, who with one voice ratified the title and sovereignty of the king.

After the government of Alba was thus transferred to Numitor, Romulus and Remus were seized with the desire of building a city in the locality where they had been exposed. There was the superfluous population of the Alban and Latin towns, to these were added the shepherds: it was natural to hope that with all these Alba would be small and Lavinium small in comparison with the city which was to be founded. These pleasant anticipations were disturbed by the ancestral curse—ambition—which led to a deplorable quarrel over what was at first a trivial matter. As they were twins and no claim to precedence could be based on seniority, they decided to consult the tutelary deities of the place by means of augury as to who was to give his name to the new city, and who was to rule it after it had been founded. Romulus accordingly selected the Palatine as his station for observation, Remus the Aventine.

Remus is said to have been the first to receive an omen: six vultures appeared to him. The augury had just been announced to Romulus when double the number appeared to him. Each was saluted as king by his own party. The one side based their claim on the priority of the appearance, the other on the number of the birds. Then followed an angry altercation; heated passions led to blood-shed; in the tumult Remus was killed. The more common report is that Remus contemptuously jumped over the newly raised walls and was forthwith killed by the enraged Romulus, who exclaimed, 'So shall it be henceforth with every one who leaps over my walls.' Romulus thus became sole ruler, and the city was called after him, its founder.

THE GEESE ON THE CAPITOL

Ab urbe condita, Book V

Livy

Translated by J. H. Freese, 1893

> This famous story from **Livy**'s history of Rome reveals how the Roman Capitol was once saved from ruin by the cackling of geese. In the fourth century BC, the Romans and Gauls were in conflict with one another. While the Romans laid siege to the nearby city of Veii, the Gauls overran much of Rome before attempting to conquer its Capitoline Hill. A number of geese, sacred to the goddess Juno, were kept here. When the Gauls began to scale the hill in the middle of the night, the birds began to squawk, alerting the Romans to the approaching danger. Could one of the Romans' bravest men, Marcus Furius Camillus, 'the dictator', having returned from exile, now vanquish the Gauls? The Roman people later founded a temple to Juno on the Capitol to honour her and her geese.

It now seemed high time that their country should be recovered and rescued from the hands of the enemy. But a head was wanting to this strong body. The very place put them in mind of Camillus, and a considerable part of the soldiers were men who had fought successfully under his guidance and auspices. Caedicius declared that he would not give occasion for any one, whether god or man, to terminate his command; but, mindful of his own rank, he would rather himself call for the appointment of a general. With universal consent it was resolved that Camillus should be sent for from Ardea, but that first the senate at Rome should be consulted: so far did a sense of propriety regulate every proceeding, and so carefully did they observe proper distinctions in their almost desperate circumstances. Someone had to pass at great risk through the enemy's guards. For this purpose a spirited youth, Pontius Cominius, offered his services, and supporting himself on cork was carried down the Tiber to the city. Then, where the distance from the bank was shortest, he made his way into the Capitol over a portion of the rock that rose abruptly and therefore was neglected by the enemy's guard; and being conducted to the magistrates he delivers the instructions received from the army. Then having received a decree of the senate, that Camillus, recalled from exile by the comitia curiata, should be forthwith appointed dictator by order of the people, and that the soldiers should have the general whom they wished, the messenger passed out the same way and proceeded to Veii. Then deputies were sent to Camillus at Ardea, and conducted him to Veii: or else the law was passed by the curias, and he was nominated dictator in his absence; for I am more inclined to believe that he did not set out from Ardea until he found that the law was passed; because he could neither change the country of his residence without an order from the people, nor hold the auspices in the army until he was nominated dictator.

Meanwhile, whilst these things were going on at Veii, the citadel and Capitol of Rome were in great danger. For the Gauls had either perceived the track of a human foot where the messenger from Veii had passed, or had of themselves remarked the rock with its easy ascent at the temple of Carmentis. So on a starlight night, after they had first sent forward an unarmed man to make trial of the way, they attempted the ascent. Handing over their arms whenever any difficult passage occurred, alternately supported by and supporting each other and drawing each other up according as the ground required, they reached the summit in such silence that they not only escaped the notice of the sentinels, but of the dogs also, an animal extremely vigilant with respect to noises by night. They did not escape the notice of the geese. These, as being sacred to Juno, were spared, though there was the greatest scarcity of food. This circumstance was the cause of their preservation. For Marcus Manlius, who three years before had been consul, a man of great military distinction, being aroused from sleep by their cackling and the clapping of their wings, snatched up his arms, and at the same time calling the others to do the same, proceeds to the spot. Whilst the others were thrown into confusion, he struck with the boss of his shield a Gaul who had already got footing on the summit, and tumbled him down; and since the fall of this man as he tumbled threw down those who were next, Manlius slew others, who in their consternation had thrown away their arms, and were grasping tight the rocks to which they clung. And now the others also having assembled beat down the enemy with javelins and stones, and the whole line of men fell and were hurled down headlong with a crash. The alarm then subsiding, the remainder of the night was given up to repose, as far as could be done considering the disturbed state of their minds, since the danger, even though past, still kept them in a state of anxiety.

Day having appeared, the soldiers were summoned by sound of trumpet to attend the tribunes in assembly, as recompense was due both to merit and to demerit. Manlius was first of all commended for his bravery and presented with gifts, not only by the military tribunes, but by the soldiers with general consent; for they all carried to his house, which was in the citadel, a contribution of half a pound of meal and a gill of wine. This is a matter trifling to relate, but the prevailing scarcity had rendered it a strong proof of esteem, when each man, depriving himself of his own food, contributed in honour of one man a portion subtracted from his own personal requirements. Then the sentinels of the place where the enemy had climbed up unobserved were summoned; and Quintus Sulpicius declared openly that he would punish all according to the usage of military discipline; but being deterred by the unanimous voice of the soldiers, who threw the blame on one sentinel, he spared the rest. The man who was manifestly guilty of the crime he threw down from the rock with general approbation. From this time forth the guards on both sides became more vigilant; on the part of the Gauls because a rumour had spread that messengers passed between Veii and Rome, and on that of the Romans from the recollection of the peril of that night.

But beyond all evils of siege and war, famine distressed both armies; pestilence moreover oppressed the Gauls, since they were encamped in a place lying between the hills that was heated by the burning of the houses and full of exhalations, and that sent up clouds not only of dust but also of ashes whenever the wind rose to any degree; and as that race, accustomed to moisture and cold, is most intolerant of these annoyances, and suffered severely from the heat and suffocation, disease spread as if among cattle, and they died. And now becoming weary of burying separately, they heaped up the bodies promiscuously and burned them. A truce was now made with the Romans, and conferences were held with the permission of the commanders. At these the Gauls frequently alluded to the famine, and made the urgency of that a reason for summoning them to surrender. It is said that for the purpose of removing that opinion bread was thrown in many places from the Capitol to the advanced posts of the enemy. But the famine could neither be dissembled nor endured any longer. Accordingly whilst the dictator was engaged in person in holding a levy at Ardea, in ordering his master of the horse, Lucius Valerius, to bring the troops from Veii, and in raising forces and equipping them, so that he might attack the enemy on equal terms, in the mean time the army of the Capitol was wearied out with keeping guard and with watches. They had surmounted all calamities that man could cause, but famine alone nature would not suffer to be overcome. So after looking forward from day to day to see whether there were any signs of succour coming from the dictator, when at length not only food but hope also failed them, and their arms weighed down their debilitated bodies (since there was constant sentinel duty), they insisted that there should be either a surrender, or that they should be ransomed on whatever terms were possible, as the Gauls were intimating in rather plain terms that they could be induced for no very great compensation to relinquish the siege. Then a meeting of the senate was held and instructions were given to the military tribunes to capitulate. Upon this the matter was settled between Quintus Sulpicius, a military tribune, and Brennus, the chieftain of the Gauls, and one thousand pounds' weight of gold was agreed on as the ransom of a people who were soon after to be the rulers of the world. To a transaction very humiliating in itself insult was added. False weights were brought by the Gauls. On the tribune's objecting, the insolent Gaul threw his sword in in addition to the weight; and these words were heard—so repulsive to the Romans—"Woe to the vanquished!"

But both gods and men interfered to prevent the Romans from owing their lives to a ransom. For by some chance, before the execrable bargain was completed, all the gold being not yet weighed in consequence of the altercation, the dictator comes up, and orders the gold to be removed from their midst, and the Gauls to clear away. The latter, demurring to this, affirmed that they had concluded a treaty; but he denied that the agreement was a valid one which had been entered into with a magistrate of inferior authority without his orders, after he had been nominated dictator; and he gave notice to the Gauls to get ready for battle. He ordered his men to throw their baggage in a heap, and to get ready their arms, and to recover their country with steel, not with gold, having before their eyes the temples of the gods, and their wives and children, and the site of their native city disfigured by the calamities of war, and all that they were solemnly bound to defend, to recover, and to revenge. He then drew up his army, as the nature of the place admitted, on the site of the half-demolished city, which was naturally uneven; and he secured all those advantages for his own men, which could be selected or acquired by military skill. The Gauls, thrown into confusion by this unexpected event, took up arms, and governed by fury rather than prudence rushed upon the Romans. But now fortune had changed; now the aid of the gods and human skill assisted the Roman cause. At the first encounter therefore the Gauls were routed with no greater difficulty than they had found in gaining the victory at the Allia. They were afterwards beaten when the Romans were again under the conduct and auspices of Camillus, in a more regular engagement at the eighth stone on the Gabine road, whither they had betaken themselves after their defeat. There the slaughter was universal: their camp was taken, and not even one person was left to carry news of the defeat. The dictator, after having recovered his country from the enemy, returned into the city in triumph; and in the soldiers' rough jests such as they are wont to make, he was styled, with praises by no means undeserved, "Romulus," and "Parent of the country," and "Second founder of the city."

THE RISE OF HANNIBAL

Punica, Book I

Silius Italicus

Translated by J. D. Duff, 1934

The Second Punic War was fought between Rome and the North African state of Carthage from 218 to 201 BC. Almost three hundred years later, a poet named **Silius Italicus** (*c.* AD 28–*c.* 103) celebrated Rome's ultimate victory in his tremendously long Latin poem, the *Punica*. In this passage he charts the rise of Hannibal, the most fearsome fighter on the Carthaginian side, against the background of Dido's foundation of Carthage in mythical times. Having fled her native Tyre after her brother, Pygmalion, murdered her husband, Sychaeus, Dido ('Elissa') was permitted to establish a territory as large as could be surrounded by a bull's hide. Cleverly, she cut the hide into tiny strips and joined them together to encompass a significant plot. Aeneas, the 'exile of Troy', later arrived in Carthage and became Dido's lover (see Story 49). Silius Italicus describes what inspired Hannibal of Carthage to war against the 'kingdom of Latinus', that is, the Italy Aeneas came to know, and become one of the most memorable enemies the Romans ever encountered.

When Dido long ago fled across the sea from the land of Pygmalion, leaving behind her the realm polluted by her brother's guilt, she landed on the destined shore of Libya. There she bought land for a price and founded a new city, where she was permitted to lay strips of a bull's hide round the strand. Here—so remote antiquity believed—Juno elected to found for the exiles a nation to last for ever, preferring it to Argos, and to Mycenae, the city of Agamemnon and her chosen dwelling-place. But when she saw Rome lifting her head high among aspiring cities, and even sending fleets across the sea to carry her victorious standards over all the earth, then the goddess felt the danger close and stirred up in the minds of the Phoenicians a frenzy for war. But the effort of their first campaign was crushed, and the enterprise of the Carthaginians was wrecked on the Sicilian sea; and then Juno took up the sword again for a fresh conflict. When she upset all things on earth and was preparing to stir up the sea, she found a sufficient instrument in a single leader.

Now warlike Hannibal clothed himself with all the wrath of the goddess; his single arm she dared to match against destiny. Then, rejoicing in that man of blood, and aware of the fierce storm of disasters in store for the realm of Latinus, she spoke thus: "In defiance of me, the exile from Troy brought Dardania to Latium, together with his household gods—deities that were twice taken prisoners; and he gained a victory and founded a kingdom for the Teucrians at Lavinium. That may pass—provided that the banks of the Ticinus cannot contain the Roman dead, and that the Trebia, obedient to me, shall flow backwards through the fields of Gaul, blocked by the blood of Romans and their weapons and the corpses of men; provided that Lake Trasimene shall be terrified by its own pools darkened with streams of gore, and that I shall see from heaven Cannae, the grave of Italy, and the Iapygian plain inundated with Roman blood, while the Aufidus, doubtful of its course as its banks close in, can hardly force a passage to the Adriatic shore through shields and helmets and severed limbs of men." With these words she fired the youthful warrior for deeds of battle.

By nature he was eager for action and faithless to his plighted word, a past master in cunning but a strayer from justice. Once armed, he had no respect for Heaven; he was brave for evil and despised the glory of peace; and a thirst for human blood burned in his inmost heart. Besides all this, his youthful vigour longed to blot out the Aegates, the shame of the last generation, and to drown the treaty of peace in the Sicilian sea. Juno inspired him and tormented his spirit with ambition. Already, in visions of the night, he either stormed the Capitol or marched at speed over the summits of the Alps. Often too the servants who slept at his door were roused and terrified by a fierce cry that broke the desolate silence, and found their master dripping with sweat, while he fought battles still to come and waged imaginary warfare.

When he was a mere child, his father's passion had kindled in Hannibal this frenzy against Italy and the realm of Saturn, and started him on his glorious career. Hamilcar, sprung from the Tyrian house of ancient Barcas, reckoned his long descent from Belus. For, when Dido lost her husband and fled from a Tyre reduced to slavery, the young scion of Belus had escaped the unrighteous sword of the dread tyrant, and had joined his fortunes with hers for weal or woe. Thus nobly born and a proved warrior, Hamilcar, as soon as Hannibal could speak and utter his first distinct words, sowed war with Rome in the boy's heart; and well he knew how to feed angry passions.

In the centre of Carthage stood a temple, sacred to the spirit of Elissa, the foundress, and regarded with hereditary awe by the people. Round it stood yew-trees and pines with their melancholy shade, which hid it and kept away the light of heaven. Here, as it was reported, the queen had cast off long ago the ills that flesh is heir to. Statues of mournful marble stood there—Belus, the founder of the race, and all the line descended from Belus; Agenor also, the nation's boast, and Phoenix who gave a lasting name to his country. There Dido herself was seated, at last united for ever to Sychaeus; and at her feet lay the Trojan sword. A hundred altars stood here in order, sacred to the gods of heaven and the lord of Erebus. Here the priestess with streaming hair and Stygian garb calls up Acheron and the divinity of Henna's goddess. The earth rumbles in the gloom and breaks forth into awesome hissings; and fire blazes unkindled upon the altars. The dead also are called up by magic spells and flit through empty space; and the marble face of Elissa sweats. To this shrine Hannibal was brought by his father's command; and, when he had entered, Hamilcar examined the boy's face and bearing. No terrors for him had the Massylian priestess, raving in her frenzy, or the horrid rites of the temple, the blood-bespattered doors, and the flames that mounted at the sound of incantation. His father stroked the boy's head and kissed him; then he raised his courage by exhortation and thus inspired him:

"The restored race of Phrygians is oppressing with unjust treaties the people of Cadmean stock. If fate does not permit my right hand to avert this dishonour from our land, you, my son, must choose this as your field of fame. Be quick to swear a war that shall bring destruction to the Laurentines; let the Tuscan people already dread your birth; and when you, my son, arise, let Latian mothers refuse to rear their offspring."

With these incentives he spurred on the boy and then dictated a vow not easy to utter: "When I come to age, I shall pursue the Romans with fire and sword and enact again the doom of Troy. The gods shall not stop my career, nor the treaty that bars the sword, neither the lofty Alps nor the Tarpeian rock. I swear to this purpose by the divinity of our native god of war, and by the shade of Elissa." Then a black victim was sacrificed to the goddess of triple shape; and the priestess, seeking an oracle, quickly opened the still breathing body and questioned the spirit, as it fled from the inward parts that she had laid bare in haste.

The Carthaginians lost the First and Second Punic Wars. Years later they were defeated in a third and final war with Rome.

ATTIS AND THE MOTHER GODDESS

'Poem 63'

Catullus

Translated by Daisy Dunn, 2016

The Romans were ailing in the Second Punic War (218–201 BC) against Carthage when they received an oracle advising them to carry their 'mother' to Rome. As was their habit, the oracle was enigmatic, but the Romans worked out that, if they were to defeat Hannibal and his forces, then they needed to establish worship of the Great Mother goddess Cybele in their city. Cybele had been worshipped as an earth goddess across Asia Minor since ancient times. Her priests traditionally castrated themselves in her honour, a custom thoroughly at odds with the Roman way of life. Nonetheless, in 204 BC, the Romans welcomed the goddess, and proceeded to win the war. A century and a half later, **Catullus** wrote this story about Attis, a man who castrated himself to become a priestess of Cybele ('he' becomes 'she') only to regret it. The strange metre ('galliambics') of Catullus' poem brought out the foreignness and frenzy the Romans continued to associate with the goddess' cult.

Driven over high seas in a fast ship Attis
Touched down in the Phrygian grove on quick keen foot
And in woodland approached the goddess' haunts
Veiled by shadow, summoned there in heightened frenzy,
Drifting from his senses,
He freed with sharp flint the weight from his groin.
And when he felt his remaining limbs were male-free,
Still soaking ground below with fresh blood,
She took quickly in her pale hands a light drum –
Your drum – Cybele, for your rites, mother,
And tapping hollow bull hide with slender fingers
Commenced with trembling voice her song to her companions:

   'To the heights, Gallae, come together to Cybele's groves,
Together come, Mistress of Dindymus' vagrant flock,
Who like exiles sought places unknown

As friends of mine and followers of my way
And endured savage salt and wild sea
And unmanned your bodies in deep hatred of Venus.
Hearten the mind of your mistress by meandering quickly,
Let the thought of dallying delay fade from your mind, together come
Let us lead the way to the Phrygian home of Cybele,
The goddess' Phrygian groves,
Where cymbals cry and drums call back,
Where Phrygian flautist plays profoundly on curved reed,
Where ivy-bearing Maenads shake their heads wilfully
And add encouragement to sacred rites with shrill ululations,
Where that nomad troop of the goddess likes to flutter
And where we should hasten with furious dancing.'

   As soon as the counterfeit female Attis sang so to her friends
Her throng suddenly cried with tongues that danced,
The light drum groaned back, the hollow cymbals called back,
The quick chorus approached green Ida on feet that could not wait.
Raging and gasping and drawing breath all at once Attis led the way
To the accompaniment of drums in wandering the shadowy groves
Like an untamed heifer avoiding the weight of the yoke,
The quick Gallae followed their fleet-footed leader.
And so when, quite exhausted, they reached Cybele's home
After much exertion they fell asleep without dinner,
Slow sleep, slipping languidly, covered their eyes.
Fervent fury abandons the mind in soft sleep.

   But when the golden-faced Sun with eyes of rays
Surveyed the white sky, hard ground, wild sea,
And drove off night's shadows with lively loud feet
Sleep woke Attis there and fled quickly.
The goddess Pasithea welcomed Sleep in her trembling bosom.
In the wake of quiet sleep and free from frenzied madness,
The moment Attis replayed in her mind what she had done
And clocked, clear-headed
               Where she was
What she lacked
She made her way back to the shore again.
Her heart was rippling.
Watching, there, a desert of sea with tears in her eyes
She spoke to her country in a voice that was sad, miserable, like this:
'Oh my country, my maker, my mother, my country oh
How rueful when I left you, as runaway slaves escape their masters
So my feet took me to Mount Ida's groves,
To be mid-snow and ice-riven beast lairs
And to approach, quite witless, their dens in the shadows.

~

Where do I believe you lie, my country? Or on which plots?
My very pupils burn to turn their gaze to you
While for sharp season my mind is free of rabidity.
Am I to be uprooted from my home to these backwoods?
Am I to retire from my country, possessions, friends, parents?
Am I to retire from the forum, palaestra, racecourse, gym?
Helpless, helpless, heart, more, more, must you weep.

For what shape or form have I not been at one with?
A woman, now, pubescent, young man, boy
I blossomed at the gym; I was the fat in the olive oil;
My doorways were busy, my porch was warm,
My house was decked with plaits of flowers
When it was time to leave my bed at dawn.
Must I wait today on the gods and suffer in Cybele's service?
A priestess, me, a part of myself, a seedless man, shall I be?
Am I to garden the frozen snow-cuddled soils of green Ida?
Live my life beneath the tall pillars of Phrygia
Where deer farm forest, where boar gad grove?
Now, now, I regret what I did. Now, now, and I grieve.'

        When this sound rushed from her rosy lips
Relaying unprecedented news to the twin ears of the gods
Cybele at once released the yoke from her lions
And goading the enemy of the flock to her left, says this:
'Onwards,' she said, 'Go Fierce One, see that fury drives him on,
Let him be struck by the blow of madness and return to the groves,
Since he so obviously desires to elude my authority,
Come whip your back with your tail, suffer your own lashes,
See everywhere resound with bellow and roar,
Toss the ruddy mane on your taut neck.'
So spoke fearsome Cybele and loosed the yoke with her hand.
Roused, the beast incites himself to speed,
Roams, roars, tramples the vegetation with ranging paw.
And when he approaches the damp ground on the whitening shore
And sees delicate Attis near the marble sea
He makes his attack. She, out of her wits, flees into the wild grove;
There she spent all the rest of her life as a servant to the goddess.

Goddess, great goddess, Cybele, goddess mistress of Dindymus,
May all your madness be far from my home, Mistress,
Urge, incite others, drive others to madness.

A COUNTRY VILLA

De Re Rustica, III

Varro

Translated by W. D. Hooper, 1934

Varro (116–27 BC), a veteran of the Roman civil wars, wrote prolifically on themes as diverse as historical chronology, architecture and agriculture. In *De Re Rustica*, his only complete work to survive, a group of Romans gather to discuss the particulars of country life and villa husbandry while waiting for the results of an election of 'aediles' – junior politicians. Voting in Rome traditionally took place on the Campus Martius. Their conversation centres on luxuries and ways to make profit. Although Varro's dialogue is rather meandering – a sequence of extracts is provided here for ease of reading – it reveals some of the more surprising preoccupations of Romans in the first century BC.

During the election of aediles, Quintus Axius, the senator, a member of my tribe, and I, after casting our ballots, wished, though the sun was hot, to be on hand to escort the candidate whom we were supporting when he returned home. Axius remarked to me: "While the votes are being sorted, shall we enjoy the shade of the Villa Publica, instead of building us one out of the half-plank of our own candidate?"

"Well," I replied, "I think that the proverb is correct, 'bad advice is worst for the adviser,' and also that good advice should be considered good both for the adviser and the advised." So we go our way and come to the Villa. There we find Appius Claudius, the augur, sitting on a bench so that he might be on hand for consultation, if need should arise. There were sitting at his left Cornelius Merula ("Blackbird"), member of a consular family, and Fircellius Pavo ("Peacock"), of Reate; and on his right Minucius Pica ("Magpie") and Marcus Petronius Passer ("Sparrow"). When we came up to him, Axius said to Appius, with a smile:

"Will you let us come into your aviary, where you are sitting among the birds?"

"With pleasure," he replied, "and especially you; I still 'bring up' those hospitable birds which you set before me a few days ago in your villa at Reate, when I was on my way to lake Velinus in the matter of the dispute between the people of Interamna and those of Reate. But," he added, "isn't this villa, which our ancestors built, simpler and better than that elaborate villa of yours at Reate? Do you see anywhere here citrus wood or gold, or vermilion or azure, or any coloured or mosaic work? At your place everything is just the opposite. Also, while this villa is the common property of the whole population, that one belongs to you alone; this one is for citizens and other people to come to from the Campus, and that one is for mares and asses; and furthermore, this one is serviceable for the transaction of public business—for the cohorts to assemble when summoned by the consul for a levy, for the inspection of arms, for the censors to convoke the people for the census."

"Do you really mean," replied Axius, "that this villa of yours on the edge of the Campus Martius is merely serviceable, and isn't more lavish in luxuries than all the villas owned by everybody in the whole of Reate? Why, your villa is plastered with paintings, not to speak of statues; while mine, though there is no trace of Lysippus or Antiphilus, has many a trace of the hoer and the shepherd. Further, while that villa is not without its large farm, and one which has been kept clean by tillage, this one of yours has never a field or ox or mare. In short, what has your villa that is like that villa which your grandfather and great-grandfather had? For it has never, as that one did, seen a cured hay harvest in the loft, or a vintage in the cellar, or a grain-harvest in the bins. For the fact that a building is outside the city no more makes it a villa than the same fact makes villas of the houses of those who live outside the Porta Flumentana or in the Aemiliana."

To which Appius replied, with a smile: "As I don't know what a villa is, I should like you to enlighten me, so that I shall not go wrong from lack of foresight; since I want to buy a villa from Marcus Seius near Ostia. For if buildings are not villas unless they contain the ass which you showed me at your place, for which you paid 40,000 sesterces, I'm afraid I shall be buying a 'Seian' house instead of a seaside villa. My friend here, Lucius Merula, made me eager to own this house when he told me, after spending several days with Seius, that he had never been entertained in a villa which he liked more; and this in spite of the fact that he saw there no picture or statue of bronze or marble, nor, on the other hand, apparatus for pressing wine, jars for olive oil, or mills."

Axius turned to Merula and asked: "How can that be a villa, if it has neither the furnishings of the city nor the appurtenances of the country?"

"Why," he replied, "you don't think that place of yours on the bend of the Velinus, which never a painter or fresco-worker has seen, is less a villa than the one in the Rosea which is adorned with all the art of the stucco-worker, and of which you and your ass are joint owners?" When Axius had indicated by a nod that a building which was for farm use only was as much a villa as one that served both purposes, that of farm-house and city residence, and asked what inference he drew from that admission;

"Why," he replied, "if your place in the Rosea is to be commended for its pasturage, and is rightly called a villa because cattle are fed and stabled there, for a like reason that also should have the name in which a large revenue is derived from pasturing. For if you get a revenue from flocks, what does it matter whether they are flocks of sheep or of birds? Why, is the revenue sweeter on your place from oxen which give birth to bees than it is from the bees which are busy at their task in the hives of Seius's villa? And do you get more from the butcher for the boars born on your place there than Seius does from the market-man for the wild boars from his place?"

"Well," replied Axius, "what is there to prevent me from keeping these at my villa at Reate? You don't think that honey is Sicilian if it is produced on Seius's place, and Corsican if it is produced at Reate? And that if mast which has to be bought feeds a boar on his place it makes him fat, while that which is had for nothing on my place makes him thin?"

Whereupon Appius remarked: "Merula did not say that you could not have husbandry like Seius's on your place; but I have, with my own eyes, seen that you have not. For there are two kinds of pasturing: one in the fields, which includes cattle-raising, and the other around the farmstead, which includes chickens, pigeons, bees, and the like, which usually feed in the steading; the Carthaginian Mago, Cassius Dionysius, and other writers have left in their books remarks on them, but scattered and unsystematic. These Seius seems to have read, and as a result he gets more revenue from such pasturing out of one villa than others receive from a whole farm."

"You are quite right," said Merula; "for I have seen there large flocks of geese, chickens, pigeons, cranes, and peafowl, not to speak of numbers of dormice, fish, boars, and other game. His book-keeper, a freedman who waited on Varro and used to entertain me when his patron was away from home, told me that he received, because of such husbandry, more than 50,000 sesterces from the villa every year."

When Axius expressed his surprise, I remarked to him: "Doubtless you know my maternal aunt's place in the Sabine country, at the twenty-fourth milestone from Rome on the Via Salaria?"

"Of course," he replied; "it is my custom to break the journey there at noon in summer, when I am on my way to Reate from the city, and to camp there at night in winter when I am on my way from there to town."

"Well, from the aviary alone which is in that villa, I happen to know that there were sold 5,000 fieldfares, for three denarii apiece, so that that department of the villa in that year brought in sixty thousand sesterces—twice as much as your farm of 200 iugera at Reate brings in."

"What? Sixty?" exclaimed Axius, "Sixty? Sixty? You are joking!" "Sixty," I repeated. "But to reach such a haul as that you will need a public banquet or somebody's triumph, such as that of Metellus Scipio at that time, or the club dinners which are now so countless that they make the price of provisions go soaring. If you can't look for this sum in all other years, your aviary, I hope, will not go bankrupt on you; and if fashions continue as they now are, it will happen only rarely that you miss your reckoning. For how rarely is there a year in which you do not see a banquet or a triumph, or when the clubs do not feast?"

"Why," said he, "in this time of luxury it may fairly be said that there is a banquet every day within the gates of Rome. Was it not Lucius Abuccius, who is, as you know, an unusually learned man (his writings are quite in the manner of Lucilius), who used to remark likewise that his estate near Alba was always beaten in feeding by his steading? For his land brought in less than 10,000, and his steading more than 20,000 sesterces. He also claimed that if he had got a villa near the sea, where he wanted one, he would take in more than 100,000 from the villa. Come, did not Marcus Cato, when he took over the guardianship of Lucullus recently, sell the fish from his ponds for 40,000 sesterces?" "My dear Merula," said Axius, "take me, I beg, as your pupil in this villa-feeding."

There continues a detailed discussion of aviaries, hare-warrens and fish ponds.

While we were thus conversing, a shouting arose in the Campus. We old hands at politics were not surprised at this occurrence, as we knew how excited an election crowd could become, but still we wanted to know what it meant; thereupon Pantuleius Parra comes to us, and tells us that a man had been caught, while they were sorting the ballots in the office, in the act of casting ballots into the ballot-box; and that he had been dragged off to the consul by the supporters of the other candidates. Pavo arose, as it was the watcher for his candidate who was reported to have been arrested.

"You may speak freely about peafowl," said Axius, "since Fircellius has gone; if you should say anything out of the way about them, he would perhaps have a bone to pick with you for the credit of the family."

To whom Merula said: "As to peafowl, it is within our memory that flocks of them began to be kept and sold at a high price. From them Marcus Aufidius Lurco is said to receive an income of more than 60,000 sesterces a year. There should be somewhat fewer males than females if you have an eye to the financial returns; but the opposite if you look at the pleasure, for the male is handsomer. They should be pastured in flocks in the fields. Across the water they are said to be reared in the islands—on Samos, in the grove of Juno, and likewise in Marcus Piso's island of Planasia. For the forming of a flock they are to be secured when they are young and of good appearance; for nature has awarded the palm of beauty to this fowl over all winged things. The hens are not suited for breeding under two years, and are no longer suited when they get rather old. They eat any kind of grain placed before them, and especially barley; so Seius issues a modius of barley a month per head, with the exception that he feeds more freely during the breeding season, before they begin to tread. He requires of his breeder three chicks for each hen, and these, when they are grown, he sells for fifty denarii each, so that no other fowl brings in so high a revenue. He buys eggs, too, and places them under hens, and the chicks which are hatched from these he places in that domed building in which he keeps his peafowl. This building should be made of a size proportioned to the number of peafowl, and should have separate sleeping quarters, coated with smooth plaster, so that no serpent or animal can get in; it should also have an open place in front of it, to which they may go out to feed on sunny days. These birds require that both places be clean; and so their keeper should go around with a shovel and pick up the droppings and keep them, as they are useful for fertilizer and as litter for chicks. It is said that Quintus Hortensius was the first to serve these fowl; it was on the occasion of his inauguration as aedile, and the innovation was praised at that time rather by the luxurious than by those who were strict and virtuous. As his example was quickly followed by many, the price has risen to such a point that the eggs sell for five denarii each, the birds themselves sell readily for 50 each, and a flock of 100 easily brings 40,000 sesterces—in fact, Abuccius used to say that if one required three chicks to every hen, the total might amount to 60,000.

Meanwhile Appius's bailiff comes with a message from the consul that the augurs are summoned, and he leaves the villa. But pigeons fly into the villa, and Merula, pointing to them, remarks to Axius: "If you had ever built a dove-cote you might think these were your doves, wild though they are. For in a dove-cote there are usually two species of these: one the wild, or as some call them, the rock-pigeon, which lives in turrets and gable-ends (columina) of the farmhouse— whence the name columbae—and these, because of their natural shyness, hunt for the highest peak of the roof; hence the wild pigeons chiefly hunt for the turrets, flying into them from the fields and back again, as the fancy takes them. The other species of pigeon is gentler, and being content with the food from the house usually feeds around the doorstep. This species is generally white, while the other, the wild, has no white, but is variously coloured."

[...]

Meantime Pavo returns to us and says: "If you wish to weigh anchor, the ballots have been cast and the casting of lots for the tribes is going on; and the herald has begun to announce who has been elected aedile by each tribe." Appius arose hurriedly, so as to congratulate his candidate at once and then go on to his home. And Merula remarked: "I'll give you the third act of the husbandry of the steading later, Axius."

[...]

Then a noise on the right, and our candidate, as aedile-elect, came into the villa wearing the broad stripe. We approach and congratulate him and escort him to the Capitoline.

SPARTACUS

Civil Wars

Appian

Translated by John Davies, 1679

Appian (*c.* AD 95–*c.* 165) was born in Alexandria in Egypt and became a lawyer as well as an historian in Rome. His bracing history of Rome is sadly now incomplete. Nonetheless, his seventeenth-century translator John Davies commended his readers to admire 'the excellent method and contrivance of Appian, his composure being such, that though so many of his Books are lost, yet the want of them renders not those left imperfect (as Livy, or other Historians are by so much as is left of them) but by taking the whole Affairs of every Country from the first dealings the Romans had with them, till such time as they were reduced to a Roman Province, he makes every Book independant, [*sic*] and become a perfect History…' Davies's rendering of Appian's account of the slave revolt led by Spartacus in 73 BC is especially masterly.

About the same time *Spartacus* a Thracian by Nation, who had formerly born Arms in the Roman Militia, and was now a Captive in Capua to serve as a Gladiator, persuaded about seventy of his Comrades to fight rather for their own liberty, than to please the spectators, and breaking Prison he gave them such Arms as he took from Passengers, and went and posted himself on Mount *Vesuvius*. Store of fugitive Slaves, and likewise some free people of the Country flocking to him upon the news of his Revolt, he received them, and began to make Incursions and Robberies in the Neighbouring Places, he made *Oenomaus* and *Crixus* two Gladiators his Lieutenants, and because he equally divided the Prey among his Companions, in a short time he gathered together so great Forces, that first *Varinius Glaber* and then *P. Valerius* being sent against him not with formed Bodies, but such men as they could get together as they passed along, were beaten: for the Roman People esteemed these only a concourse of Thieves, and not worth the name of a War. *Spartacus* in the Fight took *Varinius*'s Horse, and there mist little but that the Gladiator had taken the Pretor. After these Victories such multitudes came in to him, that he soon beheld seventy thousand Men under his Command. He then set himself to provide Arms, and to make great Preparations; so that the Consuls were sent against him with two Legions, one of which engaging with *Crixus* near Mount *Gorganus*, the Gladiator was killed with thirty thousand of his Men, scarce a third part of his Army escaping: *Spartacus* having taken his March by the *Aventine* to gain the *Alpes,* and thence pass into *Gaul,* one of the Consuls got before him to stop his passage, and the other Consul followed him at the Heels. He fell upon them one after the other, and made them give ground, and indeed put them to flight, in which the Vanquisher having taken three hundred Roman Prisoners, he cut their Throats, and offered them in Sacrifice to *Crixus*'s Ghost, his forces being afterwards swelled to sixscore thousand Men, he marched directly towards the City, and to make the quicker way, caused all the Baggages to be burnt, his Prisoners murdered, and his Beasts of Loading slain. Upon the way several Runaways offered themselves to him, but he would accept of none. And when the Consuls to stop his March, engaged him once more in the Country of *Picene,* he defeated them with a great loss of their Men. However, he changed his design of going to the City, because he found himself too weak, his Army not being sufficiently furnished with all things necessary for War: for he was not aided by any Commonalty; and all his forces were composed of fugitive Slaves and Runnagate People. He went therefore and seised upon the Mountains, and likewise of the City of *Turine*, and caused Proclamation to be made, that he forbid all sorts of Merchants to bring any Gold or Silver into the Camp, and all Soldiers to keep any: so with what they had they bought Iron and Copper, without doing any wrong to those which brought it; and by this means they got together abundance of Materials, with which they fixed themselves up Arms of all sorts. Mean while they went dayly out a skirmishing, and having once more encountred the Romans, gained the Victory, together with a good store of Spoil and Booty. It was now three years that this formidable War had lasted, which only for having contemned it at first, because of the meanness of the Authors of it, was so prodigiously augmented, and withal the ancient Roman Valour was so bastardised, that when the Assembly was held for naming of Praetors, there was none found that demanded that Dignity, till *Licinius Crassus* a man of Quality, and mighty rich, resolved to accept of the Pretorship offered; and with six other Legions marched against *Spartacus,* there were joyned to him the other two Legions which the Consuls had, but he first decimated them as a punishment of those shameful losses they had suffered: though some say, that going to assault the Enemies with all the Legions together, and being beaten by their fault, he then decimated them without considering the great number of Men, amounting to no less than four thousand by which he weakened his Army. However it were, after having managed so his Affairs, that his own men were more afraid of him, than of the Enemy: ten thousand of *Spartacus*'s Army being encamped severally, he fell suddenly upon them, and made so great a slaughter, that scarce a third part escaped into the Gross, commanded by their Captain. Soon after he undertook *Spartacus* himself, defeated him, and drove him to the Sea side, where, as he laid a design to get over into Sicily, to hinder him, he shut him up with a Circumvallation he drew round his Camp, with a Ditch and Palisade. *Spartacus* seeing himself invested, endeavoured to break his way out, to get into the Country of the Samnites, but *Crassus* made him turn in again, after having killed him six thousand Men in a Morning, and as many in the Evening, with the loss of only three of his own, and seven wounded, so much did the recent memory of their chastisement contribute to the

Victory. After which *Spartacus*, who expected some Horse which were to come to him from elsewhere, durst no more engage with all his Forces, but contented himself to incommode the Besiegers with frequent sallies, which he made sometimes on one side, and sometimes on another, and with throwing flaming Faggots into the Ditch, to burn the Palisade, and hinder the Work. Mean while he caused one of the Roman Prisoners to be hanged up in the middle of the Place between his Camp and *Crassus*'s Trenches, to let his men know what they were to trust to, if they did not gain the Victory. The news of this cruelty coming to the City, moved their spirits to indignation, that a War should last so long against Gladiators. So that judging the Remains of it were not despiseable, they gave order to *Pompey*, newly returned from *Spain*, to go thither. But *Crassus* fearing lest *Pompey* should carry away all the Glory of the end of this War, did all that he could possible to draw *Spartacus* quickly to a Fight. On the other side, *Spartacus*, who thought it not convenient to stay *Pompey*'s coming, lent to demand peace from *Crassus*, which being refused him as a thing unworthy the Grandeur of *Rome*, and some Horse being come to him, he resolved to try the fortune of a Battel, and having with all his Army forced the Circumvallation, he took his way towards *Brundusium*, pursued by *Crassus*: but when he understood that *Lucullus* returning to *Rome* after his Victory against *Mithridates*, was landed, he lost all hopes of Retreat, and drew his Forces (which were yet numerous) into Battalia. The Fight was very fierce, Crassus having to deal with so many thousand desperate people, till such time as *Spartacus* wounded in the Thigh with a Javelin; fell upon his Knees, where still he defended himself for a while, covered with his Buckler, but at last was killed with all that were fighting about him, all the rest were presently routed, and there was so great a Butchery, that the dead could hardly be counted, nor could they find the body of *Spartacus*. The Romans lost scarce a thousand men. Those that remained of *Spartacus*'s Men fled to the Mountains, whither *Crassus* having followed them, to give the last stroke to the Victory, they formed of what were left forty Battalions, and in that posture yet defended themselves valiantly, till they were all killed, save six thousand, who were afterwards hanged along the way between *Capua* and *Rome*. *Crassus* having done all this in six months, thought now he yielded nothing to *Pompey* in Glory, and kept his Army as well as he. They both demanded the Consulate, *Crassus* having passed the charge of Pretor according to *Sylla*'s Law, whereas *Pompey* had neither been Pretor nor so much as Questor, and not above four and thirty years old, but he promised the Tribunes to re-establish their ancient power. Thus these two Generals designed Consuls, did not dismiss their Armies, but kept them near the City, and shewed their reasons for it, *Pompey* that he waited for *Metellus*, who ought to triumph at his return from *Spain*; and *Crassus* that *Pompey* ought first to dismiss his Forces. Now the people seeing this difference tended to new Dissentions, and that the City was besieged by two Armies, besought the Consuls who were eminently seated in the view of all in the great place, to be reconciled, at first both the one and the other rejected their Prayers; but when the Divines told them that the City was threatened with great miseries if the Consuls did not agree, the people weeping, and casting themselves upon their Knees, renewed the same entreaties, for they had not yet lost the memory of those miseries caused by the Dissentions of *Sylla* and *Marius*. Hereupon *Crassus* beginning first to be moved, rises from his Seat, and goes to present his hand to his Colleague, as a sign of reconciliation: the other rising likewise went to meet him, and having joyned hands, all the people made acclamations of joy, wishing them all happiness; so that before the Assembly broke up, both Consuls dismissed their Armies. Thus was the Common-wealth happily delivered from the fear of a Civil War. And this happened sixty years after the death of *Tiberius Gracchus* the first mover of Seditions.

A WOMAN SCORNED?

Pro Caelio

Cicero

Translated by William Guthrie, 1741

A theatrical episode from a real defence speech delivered by the great orator, lawyer and statesman **Cicero** (106–43 BC) in Rome in April 56 BC. A young man named Caelius Rufus has been implicated in the assassination of an Alexandrian. First, it is alleged, Caelius borrowed gold from a woman named Clodia and used it to pay slaves to carry out the murder. Then he supposedly attempted, unsuccessfully, to silence Clodia with poison. Cicero happened to be a mentor to the defendant and an enemy of Clodia's brother. His defence speech provided him with an opportunity to denigrate Clodia and her family. A member of the aristocracy, whose ancestors had ruled Rome for centuries, Clodia was married to a senator named Metellus Celer until he died unexpectedly in 59 BC. Cicero capitalises on the rumours surrounding her private life. Not only did she commit incest with her brother, he suggests, but she murdered her husband, just as Clytemnestra murdered Agamemnon (see Story 14). Cicero's trick is to present Clodia as little more than a common prostitute (a 'quadrans' was the price of entry to the cheap baths). Like Medea, who took vengeance upon her lover Jason when he spurned her (see Story 43), Cicero suggests, Clodia has been spurned by Caelius and is seeking revenge in court. Cicero even goes so far as to adopt the persona of Clodia's illustrious ancestor Appius Claudius Caecus.

There are two charges (one relating to gold, the other to poison) urged against the same person. It is said that gold was borrowed of Clodia, and a poison prepared to despatch her. Every thing else urged is not criminal, but scandalous, and more properly the subject of a scolding, than a public trial. To call adulterer, whoremaster, pimp, is to rail, not to accuse. For such charges there is not so much as a foundation where you can fix them; they are opprobrious terms, rashly poured out, without any grounds, by a passionate accuser.

I have the source, I have the author, I have the precise principle and rise of all these calumnies in my eye. There was a necessity for gold; he borrowed it of Clodia; he borrowed it without any evidence, and he had it as long as he pleased. Here I can perceive a strong presumption of a certain prodigious intimacy.

He had a mind to kill the same lady; he looked out for poison; he applied to all he could; he prepared it; he fixed on the place; he brought it. Here again I can discern the most inveterate hatred, with a most cruel quarrel broken out. In this whole affair, my lords, we have to do with Clodia, a woman not only noble, but notorious; of whom I shall say nothing, but so far as I am obliged for the vindication of my client.

But, Cneius Domitius, your distinguished penetration informs you, that our business lies with her only: if she denies that she lent gold to Caelius, if she does not affirm that he prepared poison for her, we are guilty of slander, by our mentioning the mother of a family, in a manner that is inconsistent with the decency which the sanctity of matrons requires. But since, were that lady out of the question, there neither would be a crime of which my client could be convicted, nor any money to carry on the prosecution, what ought we, are his advocates, to do, but to repel those who attack us? This, indeed, I would do with great keenness, did there not subsist animosities betwixt me and that lady's husband—I mean her brother—I still fall into that mistake. Now I will act coolly, nor advance a step farther than my duty, and the interest of my client, oblige me; for I have always thought it unbecoming me to harbour any resentment against a woman; especially a lady who has the character of extending her good nature to all the world, rather than of showing her spite to any particular male.

But let me ask herself, whether she chooses that I should treat her in a serious, solemn, old-fashioned, or in a gentle, complaisant, gallant manner? If she chooses the sour manner and fashion, then must I raise some of the bearded gentlemen from the shades, and not such a smock-faced gentleman as she is fond of; one of those bristle-beards which we see in old images and statues; one who will bang my lady, and speak for me, if she should scold me into silence. Let some such in her own family start up; there is the blind old gentleman, the most proper that can be; for his not being capable to see her, will save him a great deal of grief. Supposing now he was to start up, such would be his behaviour, and such his language: "Woman! what hast thou to do with Caelius? What with a stripling? What with a stranger? Why was you so intimate with him as to lend him money? Or why such a foe as to dread his poison? Hast thou not seen thy father? Hast thou not heard that thy uncle, thy grandfather, thy great grandfather, and his father, were consuls? Art thou insensible that thou wast married to Quintus Metellus, a brave nobleman, and a worthy patriot? Who no sooner left the threshold of his own house, than he rose superior to almost all his countrymen in merit, in glory, and dignity. When thou thyself, of noble descent, wast by him married into an illustrious family, why was Caelius so much thy intimate? Was he thy cousin, thy relation, or the bosom-friend of thy husband? He was none of these. What could be the reason, but lust, hood-winked lust? If thou art unmoved at seeing the manly images of our family, ought not my descendant, ought not the example of that Quinta Clodia, to have invited thee into a competition for the female glory of domestic virtue? Ought not Clodia, too, that vestal virgin, who, embracing her triumphant father, prevented his being torn from his car by a spiteful tribune of the people? Why art thou more affected with the vices of a brother, than with the virtues of a father and a grandfather, which have developed from me upon the females, as well as the males, of my family? Did I divert my country from the thoughts of a peace with Pyrrhus, and shalt thou daily enter into intrigues of obscene amours? Did I bring in the water that supplies this city, that thou mightest use it to thy incestuous purposes? Did I lay a road, that it might serve as a parade for thee and thy train of gallants?"

What am I doing, my lords! I have introduced so grave a character, that I am afraid the same Appius may suddenly turn to the other side, and, with his censorial severity, begin to school Caelius. But I shall speak of that presently, and in such a manner, my lords, that I hope to vindicate the morals of Marcus Caelius to the severest inquisitors. But you, madam, for now I speak to you not in a borrowed, but my own character, if you dream of proving your actions, your words, your forgeries, your machinations, your arguments, there is a necessity of your accounting for, and laying forth, all this excessive intimacy, this excessive friendship, this excessive familiarity. While our accusers talk so freely of intrigues, amours, adulteries, the Baiae, the banquets, collations, songs, concerts, and pleasure-boats, they at the same time own, that they have their instructions from you. But since you were so blindly, so wilfully, so unaccountably obstinate, as to be brought into the forum, and before this court, you must either disown and disprove all they have advanced, or confess there is no credit to be given either to your accusation, or to your evidence.

But if you would have me accost you in a more polite manner, I will treat you thus; I will remove that grim, that almost savage old fellow; I will pitch upon one of these gentlemen present; your younger brother rather than any, who is quite a master in this kind of politeness; who has a mighty liking for you, and, from a strange natural fearfulness, and haunted, I suppose, by some phantoms in the dark, lay every night with you, like a little master, as he is, with his elder sister. Suppose then that he thus accosts you; "Why, my sister, in this flurry? Why in this distraction of mind? Why shriek out, and make so much ado about a trifle? You have gazed upon your handsome young neighbour; his delicate complexion, his graceful shape, his face and eyes have smitten you. You wish to see him often; sometimes a woman of quality appears in the same gardens; all your riches cannot fix in your arms the young gentleman, though not yet emancipated from an old griping father. He spurns, he rejects, he undervalues your presents. Go somewhere else. You have gardens near the Tiber; and have taken care to fit up an apartment near to where all our young gentlemen bathe; from thence you may read their proposals. Why do you teaze one who loathes you?"

Let me now, Caelius, address you in your turn, and here will I personate the authority and gravity of a father. But in what character of a father am I to act? In that of the passionate unrelenting sire in Caecilius:

> ——Now all my soul is in a blaze,
> And my heart labours with its swelling passion.

Or, shall I assume that other character?

> O wretch! O reprobate!

But these fathers have souls of flint.

What can I say, or what can I propose,
When thy foul deeds defeat my best intentions?

The reproaches of such a father would be almost intolerable.

Why did'st thou court the neighbourhood of whores?
From the gross baits why didst thou not retire?
Why clasp a lewd adulteress to thy bosom?
Here squander, dissipate; you may for me.
If griping want shall seize thee, thou must mourn.
I have a competency that will serve
To prop the stooping remnant of my years.

To this disspirited, decrepit old man, Caelius might answer, that he had been enticed from the right path by no lust of the eye. But how can you prove that?—No extravagance of expense; no diminution of fortune; no running into debt. But the thing was talked of.—But who can help being talked of in a city so full of scandal? Is it surprising that a neighbour of this lady should be scandalized, when her own brother could not escape the slanders of the malicious? But to a gentle, indulgent parent, who should talk at this rate: has he broke open doors? They shall be repaired. Has he torn a garment? It shall be mended. The boy has a ready apology; for in such circumstances, how easy is it for one to be vindicated? I speak nothing of this lady; but if there is one of a character different from hers, who has been a common prostitute; who has always lived in avowed lewdness with some one or other; who orders her gardens, houses, and bagnios, to be thrown open to a promiscuous traffic in every impurity; who even maintains young men, whose purse makes amends for the sparing allowances of close-fisted fathers; if she is wanton in widowhood, insolent in airs, profuse in wealth, and if her lusts should lead her into a keeping-expense, can I think a man an adulterer who shall make some free addresses to such a lady?

I may be told, "Is it thus you train up young gentlemen? Did his father recommend him, when a boy, and deliver him to you, that you might initiate his youth in lewdness and pleasures? Wilt thou be an advocate for such a course of life and studies?" My lords, if there is a man endued with such fortitude of soul, with such dispositions to virtue and chastity, as to reject all pleasures, as to finish his career of life with the toils of the body, and the pursuits of the mind; a man who has no taste for repose, none for relaxation, none for the pleasures of his equals, none for diversions, none for banquets; who is persuaded that in life there ought to be no end proposed, that does not unite the great with the graceful; I shall freely own, that he is furnished, that he is embellished with certain supernatural qualifications: such, I take it, were the Camilli, the Fabricii, the Curii, and all those heroes, who, from a narrow foundation, reared this empire to such glory and greatness.

But virtues such as theirs, are not now to be found in the lives, nay, scarce in the writings, of mankind. Even the very scrolls which contain this severity of former ages, are antiquated, not only with us, who have professed such an institution, and such a method of living, more by our actions than our words, but even with the Greeks, those very learned philosophers, who, when they could no longer practise what was honest and great in life, were still at liberty to recommend it in their speeches and writings. Another system of morality has prevailed since new customs were introduced into Greece.

For this reason some of their sages maintained, that pleasure is the ultimate end of the actions of the wise; nor have even men of learning been averse to that shameful tenet. Others have thought, that dignity ought to be united with pleasure, that they might have an opportunity to talk things, which, in their own natures, had a direct repugnancy to one another, into union. They who maintained, that the only way to glory was through toil, are now left almost solitary within their schools; for many are the blandishments that nature herself has implanted within us, and which the lethargy of virtue indulges; many slippery paths does she point out to youth, in which they can scarce either stand or tread, without a misfortune or a fall; and great is the pleasing variety she affords, with which mankind, not only in their bloom, but even in their maturity, are apt to be enchanted. Therefore, if, by chance, you find a man whose eye despises the beauty of order, who indulges no sensation of smell, touch, or taste, and whose ears shut out all harmony, I, and a few others, perhaps, may think that the gods have blessed such a person; but many more will think that they have cursed him.

Let us, therefore, abandon this path, which is now desert, uncouth, and choked with weeds and briars: let some allowances be made to youth; let it enjoy more liberty; let not pleasure be debarred in every instance; let not reason, uninfluenced and unbiassed by passion, always take place. To passion and pleasure, let reason sometimes give way, provided, when that is the case, they are regulated by decency and moderation. Let the young man be tender of his own chastity; let him not injure that of another; let him not dissipate his fortune; let him not be eaten up by mortgages; let him not invade another man's house, nor his reputation: let him not aim slander at the chaste, defilement at the uncorrupted, nor infamy at the worthy; let him terrify none by violence, nor over-reach them by treachery; let him be free from premeditated guilt. Lastly, when he shall obey the calls of pleasure, when he shall allot some part of his time to the diversions of his age, and these trifling pursuits of youth, let him sometimes recall his thoughts to the concerns of his family, the concerns of the forum, the concerns of his country, that he may seem to have discarded through satiety, and despised from experience, those objects which he had not before viewed with the cool eye of reason.

And, indeed, my lords, there have been many great men, and illustrious citizens, in our days, in the days of our fathers and forefathers, in whom, when the ebullitions of youthful desire have subsided, the most excellent virtues have in more advanced life sprung up. I need not descend to particulars; you yourselves may recollect them; for I am unwilling, while I speak of any brave and honourable man, to join the mention of his smallest failing to the praise of his greatest perfection. Did I think myself at liberty to do this, I might produce instances of many great and accomplished persons, and yet touch on the youthful licentiousness of some, on the extravagant luxury, the enormous debt, and expensive pleasures, of others: vices, which afterwards being effaced by many virtues, might be excused by the craving appetite of youth.

CICERO: FOR HIS DAUGHTER

Letters to Atticus

Cicero

Translated by Evelyn S. Shuckburgh, 1900

Cicero was enormously fond of his daughter, Tullia, who apparently took after him. Her premature death in 45 BC, just a month after giving birth to her second son, left him utterly bereft. He wrote to many friends of his grief. His letters to Atticus, of which a number are extracted here, reveal his difficulty in securing a suburban plot upon which to establish a memorial to Tullia as he came to terms with his bereavement.

You wish me some relaxation of my mourning: you are kind, as usual, but you can bear me witness that I have not been wanting to myself. For not a word has been written by anyone on the subject of abating grief which I did not read at your house. But my sorrow is too much for any consolation. Nay, I have done what certainly no one ever did before me—tried to console myself by writing a book, which I will send to you as soon as my amanuenses have made copies of it. I assure you that there is no more efficacious consolation. I write all day long, not that I do any good, but for a while I experience a kind of check, or, if not quite that—for the violence of my grief is overpowering—yet I get some relaxation, and I try with all my might to recover composure, not of heart, yet, if possible, of countenance. When doing that I sometimes feel myself to be doing wrong, sometimes that I shall be doing wrong if I don't. Solitude does me some good, but it would have done me more good, if you after all had been here: and that is my only reason for quitting this place, for it does very well in such miserable circumstances. And even this suggests another cause of sorrow. For you will not be able to be to me now what you once were: everything you used to like about me is gone.

In this lonely place I have no one with whom to converse, and plunging into a dense and wild wood early in the day I don't leave it till evening. Next to you, I have no greater friend than solitude. In it my one and only conversation is with books. Even that is interrupted by tears, which I fight against as long as I can.

To fly from recollections, which make my soul smart as though it were stung, I take refuge in recalling my plans to your memory. Pray pardon me, whatever you think of this one. The fact is that I find that some of the authors, whom I am now continually reading, suggest as a proper thing to do just what I have often discussed with you, and for which I desire your approval. I mean about the shrine—pray think of it as earnestly as your affection for me should suggest.* About the design I do not feel any doubt, for I like that of Cluatius, nor about the building of it at all—for to that I have made up my mind: but about the site I do sometimes hesitate. Pray therefore think over it. To the fullest capacity of such an enlightened age, I am quite resolved to consecrate her memory by every kind of memorial borrowed from the genius of every kind of artist, Greek or Latin. This may perhaps serve to irritate my wound: but I look upon myself as now bound by a kind of vow and promise. And the infinite time during which I shall be non-existent has more influence on me than this brief life, which yet to me seems only too long. For though I have tried every expedient, I find nothing to give me peace of mind. For even when I was composing that essay, of which I wrote to you before, I was in a way nursing my sorrow. Now I reject every consolation, and find nothing more endurable than solitude, which Philippus did not, as I feared, disturb. For after calling on me yesterday, he started at once for Rome.

[Astura] This is certainly a lovely spot, right in the sea, and within sight of Antium and Cerceii: but in view of the whole succession of owners—who in the endless generations to come may be beyond counting, supposing the present empire to remain—I must think of some means to secure it being made permanent by conse-cration.† For my part, I don't want large revenues at all, and can put up with a little. I think sometimes of purchasing some pleasure-grounds across the Tiber, and principally for the reason that I don't think that there is any other position so much frequented. But what particular pleasure-grounds I shall purchase we will consider when we are together; but it must be on condition that the temple is finished this summer.

As to the suburban pleasure-grounds, as you approve of them, come to some settlement. You know my means. [...]

You urge me to reappear in the forum: that is a place which I ever avoided even in my happier days. Why, what have I to do with a forum when there are no law courts, no senate-house, and when men are always obtruding on my sight whom I cannot see with any patience? You say people call for my presence at Rome, and are unwilling to allow me to be absent, or at any rate beyond a certain time: I assure you that it is long since I have valued your single self higher than all those people. Nor do I undervalue myself even, and I much prefer abiding by my own judgment than by that of all the rest. Yet, after all, I go no farther than the greatest philosophers think allowable, all whose writings of whatever kind

---

* Cicero wished to build a shrine in honour of Tullia's memory. His first idea was to do this at Astura: but he soon changed to the plan of purchasing suburban *horti*.
† If consecrated, the building would not change hands with a change of owners of the property.

bearing on that point I have not only read—which is itself being a brave invalid and taking one's physic—but have transcribed in my own essay. That at least did not look like a mind crushed and prostrate. From the use of these remedies do not call me back to the crowds of Rome, lest I have a relapse.

As to the suburban pleasure-grounds, I am particularly urgent with you. I must employ all my own means, and those of men whom I know will not fail to help me: though I shall be able to do it with my own. I have also some property which I could easily sell. But even if I don't sell, but pay the vendor interest on the purchase money— though not for more than a year—I can get what I want if you will assist me. The most readily available are those of Drusus, for he wants to sell. The next I think are those of Lamia; but he is away. Nevertheless, pray scent out anything you can. Silius does not make any use of his either, and he will be very easily satisfied by being paid interest on the purchase money. Manage the business your own way; and do not consider what my purse demands— about which I care nothing—but what I want.

If we don't come to terms about pleasure-grounds beyond the Tiber, Cotta has some at Ostia in a very frequented situation, though confined as to space. Enough, however, and more than enough for this purpose. Please think the matter over. And don't be afraid of the cost of the pleasure-grounds. I don't want plate, nor rich furniture coverings, nor particular picturesque spots: I want this. I perceive too by whom I can be aided. But speak to Silius about it. There's no better fellow. I have also given Sicca a commission. He has written back to say that he has made an appointment with him. He will therefore write and tell me what he has arranged, and then you must see to it.

Sicca has written to me fully about Silius, and says that he has reported the matter to you—as you too mention in your letter. I am satisfied both with the property and the terms, only I should prefer paying ready money to assigning property at a valuation. For Silius will not care to have mere show-places: while, though I can get on with my present rents, I can scarcely do so with less. How am I to pay ready money? You can get 600 sestertia [about £4,800] from Hermogenes, especially if it is absolutely necessary, and I find I have 600 in hand. For the rest of the purchase money I will even pay interest to Silius, pending the raising of the money from Faberius or from some debtor of Faberius. I shall besides get some from other quarters. But manage the whole business yourself. I, in fact, much prefer these suburban pleasure-grounds to those of Drusus: and the latter have never been regarded as on a level with them. Believe me, I am actuated by a single motive, as to which I know that I am infatuated. But pray continue as before to indulge my aberration. You talk about a "solace for my old age": that is all over and done with; my objects now are quite different.

★

As to the bargain with Silius, though I am acquainted with the terms, still I expect to hear all about it to-day from Sicca. Cotta's property, with which you say that you are not acquainted, is beyond Silius's villa, which I think you do know: it is a shabby and very small house, with no farm land, and with sufficient ground for no purpose except for what I want it. What I am looking out for is a frequented position. But if the bargain for Silius's pleasure-grounds is completed, that is, if you complete it—for it rests entirely with you—there is of course no occasion for us to be thinking about Cotta's.

I have learnt nothing more about Silius from Sicca in conversation than I knew from his letter: for he had written in full detail. If, therefore, you have an interview with him, write and tell me your views. As to the subject on which you say a message was sent to me, whether it was sent or not I don't know; at any rate not a word has reached me. Pray therefore go on as you have begun, and if you come to any settlement on such terms as to satisfy her—though I, for my part, think it impossible—take my son with you on your visit, if you think it right. It is of some importance to him to seem to have wished to do something to please. I have no interest in it beyond what you know, which I regard as important.

You call upon me to resume my old way of life: well, it had long been my practice to bewail the republic, and that I was still doing, though somewhat less violently, for I had something capable of giving me ease. Now I positively cannot pursue the old way of life and old employments; nor do I think that in that matter I ought to care for the opinion of others. My own feeling is more in my eyes than the talk of them all. As to finding consolation for myself in literature, I am content with my amount of success. I have lessened the outward signs of mourning: my sorrow I neither could, nor would have wished to lessen if I could.

About the suburban pleasure-grounds do, I beseech you, come to some conclusion. The main point is what you know it to be. Another thing is that I want something of the sort for myself: for I cannot exist in a crowd, nor yet remain away from you. For this plan of mine I find nothing more suitable than the spot you mention, and on that matter pray tell me what you advise.

Sicca expresses surprise at Silius having changed his mind. He makes his son the excuse, and I don't think it a bad one, for he is a son after his own heart. Accordingly, I am more surprised at your saying that you think he will sell, if we would include something else which he is anxious to get rid of, as he had of his own accord determined not to do so. You ask me to fix my maximum price and to say how much I prefer those pleasure grounds of Drusus. I have never set foot in them. I know Coponius's villa to be old and not very spacious, the wood a fine one, but I don't know what either brings in, and that after all I think we ought to know. But for me either one or the other is to be valued by my occasion for it rather than by the market price. Pray consider whether I could acquire them or not. If I were to sell my claim on Faberius, I don't doubt my being able to settle for the grounds of Silius even by a ready money payment, if he could only be induced to sell. If he had none for sale, I would have recourse to Drusus, even at the large price at which Egnatius told you that he was willing to sell. For Hermogenes can give me great assistance in finding the money. But I beg you to allow me the disposition of an eager purchaser; yet, though I am under the influence of this eagerness and of my sorrow, I am willing to be ruled by you.

To-morrow therefore I shall be in Sicca's suburban villa; thence, as you advise, I think I shall stay in your house at Ficulea.* We will talk about the subject you mention when we meet, as I am coming in person. I am extraordinarily touched by your kindness, thoroughness, and wisdom, both in carrying out my business and in forming and suggesting plans to me in your letters. However, if you come to any understanding with Silius, even on the very day on which I am to arrive at Sicca's house, please let me know, and above all, what part of the site he wishes to withdraw from the sale. You say "the farthest"—take care that it isn't the very spot, for the sake of which I thought about the matter at all.†

The search for a suitable plot rumbled on for some time after Silius' land became unavailable. Cicero even sought to purchase some gardens on the Tiber owned by Clodia, whom he had painted in unflattering terms in a court case some ten years previously (see earlier story). But in the end it seems that his project never bore fruit.

---

* Some villa of Atticus's at Ficulnea, about ten miles from Rome on the Via Nomentana.

† That is, the part of the property on which he would build the memorial fane to Tullia.

CAESAR VERSUS POMPEY

Pharsalia, Book I

Lucan

Translated by A. S. Kline, 2014

In 60 BC, Julius Caesar forged an alliance for power in Rome with Pompey the Great and a wealthy man named Marcus Licinius Crassus. The deal was sealed with the betrothal of Caesar's daughter Julia to Pompey. The three leaders were able to dominate Roman politics for a time. But the relationship between Pompey and Caesar deteriorated rapidly after Julia died in childbirth in 54 BC and Crassus perished in a disastrous war against the Parthians in the east a year later. The short life of the poet **Lucan** (AD 39–65), a nephew of Seneca the Younger, ended when he was forced to commit suicide for allegedly conspiring against the emperor Nero. Happily for us, he had already written his epic *Pharsalia*, one of the great Roman history poems. Here he describes the moment in 49 BC when Caesar crossed the Rubicon with his forces, initiating civil war. The decisive battle was fought at Pharsalus, in central Greece, and led to Pompey being beheaded.

For a short while a discordant harmony was maintained, there was
peace despite the leaders' wills, since Crassus stood between them,
a check to imminent war. So the slender Isthmus divides the waves,
and separates two seas, forbidding their waters to merge; and yet
if the land were withdrawn, the Ionian would break on the Aegean.
Thus when Crassus, who kept those fierce competitors apart, died
pitifully, drenching Syrian Carrhae with Roman blood, that defeat
by Parthia let loose the furies on Rome. In that battle the Parthians
wrought better than they knew, visiting civil war on the defeated.
Power was divided by the sword; the wealth of an imperial people
who ruled the sea, the land, possessed the globe, was not enough
for two. For now, when Julia, Caesar's daughter, Pompey's wife,
was cut down by fate, she bore with her to the Shades the bonds
of affinity, and a marriage turned, by that dread omen, to mourning.
She, if fate had granted her longer life, might alone have restrained
her husband's anger on the one side, and her father's on the other.
She might have struck aside their swords, made them clasp hands,

as the Sabine women stood between their husbands and their fathers
and brought about reconciliation. But at her death bonds of loyalty
were broken, and the generals freed to pursue armed conflict.
A powerful rivalry drove them on: for Pompey feared fresh exploits
might obscure his former triumphs, his ridding the seas of pirates
yielding second place to Caesar's victories in Gaul; while Caesar,
used to battle, inured to endless effort, was driven by an ambition
that yearned for supremacy; Caesar could accept none above him,
Pompey no equal. It is wrong to ask who had the greatest right
to seek war; each had great authority to support him: if the victor
had the gods on his side, the defeated had Cato. The contest was
unequal, Pompey being somewhat past his prime, long used
to the toga and forgetting in peace how to play a general's part;
courting adulation, lavish with his gifts to the people of Rome,
swayed by popularity, overjoyed by the clamour that greeted him
in the theatre he had built, trusting in former claims to greatness,
he did nothing to establish wider power, and stood as the mere
shadow of a mighty name. So some oak-tree towers in a rich grove,
hung with a nation's ancient trophies, sacred gifts of the victors,
and though its clinging roots have lost their strength, their weight
alone holds it, spreading naked branches to the sky, casting shade
not with leaves but its trunk alone, and though it quivers, doomed
to fall at the next gale, among the host of sounder trees that rise
around it, still it alone is celebrated. But Caesar possessed more
than mere name and military fame: his energies were un-resting,
his only shame in battle not to win; alert and unrestrained, every
summons of anger or ambition his strength answered, he never
shrank from an opportunistic use of the sword; intent on pursuing
each success, grasping the gods' favour, pushing aside every
obstacle to his supremacy, happy to clear a path through ruin.
So a storm drives a lightning-bolt through the clouds, its flare
shattering the daylight sky, with the sound of thunderous air,
with a crash of the heavens, filling the human mind with terror,
dazzling the eye with its slanting flame. Rushing to a given
quarter of the skies, nothing material prevents its course;
mighty in its descent and its retreat it spreads destruction
far and wide, before gathering its scattered energies again.
Such were the leaders' motives; but there were those hidden causes
of the war, amongst the people, that will ever destroy powerful
nations. For, the world conquered, and fortune showering excessive
wealth on Rome, virtue yielded to riches, and those enemy spoils drew
men to luxury. They set no bounds to wealth or buildings; greed
disdained its former fare; men wore clothes scarcely decent on women;
austerity, the mother of virtue, fled; and whatever ruined other nations
was brought to Rome. Then estates were increased, until those fields
once tilled by Camillus' iron ploughshare, or Curius' spade, became
vast tracts tended by alien farmers. Such a people took no pleasure

in peace and tranquility, no delight in liberty free from the sword.
Thus they were quick to anger, and crime, prompted by need, was
treated lightly; it was a virtue to take up arms and hold more power
than the State, and might became the measure of right. Thence laws
and statutes of the people passed by force, thence the consuls
and tribunes alike confounding all justice; office snared by bribery,
popular support bought at auction, while corruption, year after year
perpetuating venal elections to the magistracy, destroyed the State;
thence voracious usury, interest greedily seeking payment,
trust readily broken, and multitudes profiting greatly from war.
Now, Caesar, swiftly surmounting the frozen Alps,
had set his mind on vast rebellion and future conflict.
On reaching the banks of the Rubicon's narrow flow
that general saw a vision of his motherland in distress,
her sorrowful face showing clear in nocturnal darkness,
with the white hair streaming from her turreted head,
as with torn tresses and naked arms she stood before him
her speech broken by sobbing: 'Where are you marching,
whither do you bear those standards, my warriors?
If you come as law-abiding citizens, here you must halt.'
Then the general's limbs quaked, his hair stood on end,
faintness overcame him and he halted, his feet rooted
to the river-bank. But soon he spoke: 'O, Jupiter, God
of Thunder, who gazes from the Tarpeian Rock over
the walls of the mighty city; O Trojan household gods
of the tribe of Iulus, and you, sacred relics of Quirinus;
O Jove of Latium, on Alba's heights, and you, fires
of Vesta, and you, O Rome, equal in sanctity, favour
my enterprise; I bring no assault on you in wild warfare;
see me here, victorious by land and sea, always your
champion – now as ever, if that be possible. His
shall be the guilt, who forces me to act as your enemy.'
Then Caesar let loose the bonds of war, and led his
standards swiftly over the swollen stream; so a lion
in the untilled wastes of burning Libya, seeing his foes
nearby, crouches at first, uncertain, rousing himself to rage,
but soon maddened, lashing his tail, his mane erect,
sends out a roaring from his cavernous mouth, such
that if a nimble Moor pierces his flesh with the lance
he brandishes, or a spear lances at his vast chest, he
leaps over the weapons careless of such wounds.
The reddish waters of the Rubicon glide through
the valleys and serve as the boundary between
the land of Gaul and the farms of Italy. Born from
a modest spring it is parched by the heat of summer,
but then its volume was increased by winter, its waters
swollen by the third rising of a rain-bearing moon

with its moisture-laden horns, and by Alpine snows
melted by damp gales. The cavalry first met the flow,
taking position slantwise across the current, lessening
its power so the rest of the army could ford it with ease.
Once Caesar had crossed and reached the Italian shore
on the further side, he halted on territory proscribed to them:
'Here I relinquish peace,' he cried, 'and the law already
scorned, to follow you, my Fortune. Let me hear no more
talk of pacts, I have placed my trust in those for far
too long, now I must seek the judgement of war.'

DIVINE CAESAR

Metamorphoses, Book XV

Ovid

Translated by 'Mr. Dryden and Others', 1700

In 44 BC, four months after Julius Caesar was assassinated, a comet
appeared in the skies above Rome and shone for seven days. It was taken
to represent the soul of Caesar received into the heavens. Two years later
Caesar was officially deified. The description of Caesar's apotheosis by
the poet **Ovid** (43 BC–AD 17/18), a contemporary of Virgil and Horace,
is wonderfully overblown. Although Caesar twice invaded Britain, he
could hardly have been said to have conquered it. The Roman victory
over Mithridates of Pontus, a kingdom in what is now Turkey, was
secured rather by Pompey the Great and a general named Lucullus. In his
lifetime Caesar, who served as Pontifex Maximus (chief priest), claimed
descent from Venus via Aeneas. Ovid emphasises the fact that Caesar's
death does not mark the end of his line. He pays tribute to Caesar's great-
nephew and successor, Octavian, the future emperor Augustus. Hailed
as *divi filius* – son of a god – Octavian secured the help of Mark Antony
in defeating Caesar's assassins, Brutus and Cassius, at Philippi, six years
after Caesar had defeated Pompey at Pharsalus. In 1717 the English
poet Sir Samuel Garth edited a collection of translations of the books of
Ovid's *Metamorphoses* by some of the leading writers of the seventeenth
and eighteenth centuries, including Joseph Addison and John Dryden,
who is the principal translator of this portion of the text.

In his own city, Caesar we adore:
Him arms and arts alike renown'd beheld,
In peace conspicuous, dreadful in the field;
His rapid conquests, and swift-finish'd wars,
The hero justly fix'd among the stars;
Yet is his progeny his greatest fame:
The son immortal makes the father's name.
The sea-girt Britons, by his courage tam'd,
For their high rocky cliffs, and fierceness fam'd;
His dreadful navies, which victorious rode
O'er Nile's affrighted waves and seven-sourc'd flood;

Numidia, and the spacious realms regain'd;
Where Cinyphis or flows, or Juba reign'd;
The pow'rs of titled Mithridatès broke,
And Pontus added to the Roman yoke;
Triumphal shows decreed, for conquests won,
For conquests, which the triumphs still outshone;
These are great deeds; yet less than to have giv'n
The world a lord, in whom, propitious heav'n,
When you decreed the sov'reign rule to place,
You blessed with lavish bounty human race.

   Now, lest so great a prince might seem to rise
Of mortal stem, his sire must reach the skies;
The beauteous goddess that Aeneas bore;
Foresaw it, and, foreseeing, did deplore;
For well she knew her hero's fate was nigh,
Devoted by conspiring arms to die.
Trembling, and pale, to ev'ry god she cry'd,
Behold, what deep and subtle arts are tried,
To end the last, the only branch that springs
From my Iülus, and the Dardan kings!
How bent they are! how desp'rate to destroy
All that is left me of unhappy Troy!
Am I alone by Fate ordain'd to know
Uninterrupted care, and endless woe?
Now from Tydidès' spear I feel the wound:
Now Ilium's tow'rs the hostile flames surround:
Troy laid in dust, my exil'd son I mourn,
Through angry seas, and raging billows borne;
O'er the wide deep his wand'ring course he bends;
Now to the sullen shades of Styx descends.
With Turnus driv'n at last fierce wars to wage,
Or rather with unpitying Juno's rage.
But why record I now my ancient woes?
Sense of past ills in present fears I lose;
On me their points the impious daggers throw;
Forbid it, gods, repel the direful blow:
If by curst weapons Numa's priest expires,
No longer shall ye burn, ye vestal fires.
   While such complainings Cypria's grief disclose;
In each celestial breast compassion rose:
Nor gods can alter fate's resistless will;
Yet they foretold, by signs, th' approaching ill.
Dreadful were heard, among the clouds, alarms
Of echoing trumpets, and of clashing arms;
The sun's pale image gave so faint a light.
That the sad earth was almost veil'd in night;

The Aether's face with fiery meteors glow'd;
With storms of hail were mingled drops of blood!
A dusky hue the morning star o'erspread,
And the moon's orb was stain'd with spots of red;
In ev'ry place portentous shrieks were heard,
The fatal warnings of th' infernal bird:
In ev'ry place the marble melts to tears;
While in the groves, rever'd through length of years,
Boding, and awful sounds, the ear invade;
And solemn music warbles through the shade;
No victim can atone the impious age,
No sacrifice the wrathful gods assuage;
Dire wars and civil fury threat the state:
And ev'ry omen points out Caesar's fate:
Around each hallow'd shrine and sacred dome,
Night-howling dogs disturb the peaceful gloom;
Their silent seats the wand'ring shades forsake,
And fearful tremblings the rock'd city shake.
    Yet could not, by these prodigies, be broke
The plotted charm, or staid the fatal stroke;
Their swords th' assassins in the temple draw;
Their murd'ring hands nor gods nor temples awe;
This sacred place their bloody weapons stain,
And virtue falls before the altar slain.
'Twas now fair Cypria, with her woes opprest,
In raging anguish smote her heav'nly breast;
While with distracting tears the goddess try'd
Her hero in th' ethereal cloud to hide,
The cloud which youthful Paris did conceal,
When Meneläus urg'd the threat'ning steel!
The cloud, which once deceiv'd Tydidès sight,
And sav'd Aeneas in th' unequal fight.
    When Jove:—'In vain, fair daughter, you essay
To o'er-rule destiny's unconquer'd sway:
Your doubts to banish, enter Fate's abode:
A privilege to heav'nly pow'rs allow'd;
There shall you see the records grav'd in length,
On ir'n and solid brass, with mighty strength;
Which heav'n's and earth's concussions shall endure,
Maugre all shocks, eternal, and secure:
There, on perennial adamant design'd,
The various fortunes of your race you'll find:
Well I have mark'd 'em, and will now relate
To thee the settled laws of future fate.

    'He, goddess, for whose death the fates you blame,
Has finish'd his determin'd course with fame:

To thee 'tis giv'n, at length that he shall shine
Among the gods, and grace the worshipp'd shrine:
His son to all his greatness shall be heir,
And worthily succeed to empire's care:
Our self will lead his wars, resolv'd to aid
The brave avenger of his father's shade:
To him its freedom Mutina shall owe,
And Decius his auspicious conduct know:
His dreadful pow'rs shall shake Pharsalia's plain,
And drench in gore Philippi's fields again:
A mighty leader in Sicilia's flood,
Great Pompey's warlike son shall be subdu'd.
Aegypt's soft queen, adorn'd with fatal charms,
Shall mourn her soldier's unsuccessful arms:
Too late shall find, her swelling hopes were vain,
And know, that Rome o'er Memphis still must reign:
Why name I Afric or Nile's hidden head?
Far as both oceans roll, his pow'r shall spread:
All the known earth to him shall homage pay,
And the seas own his universal sway:
When cruel war no more disturbs mankind;
To civil studies shall he bend his mind,
With equal justice guardian laws ordain,
And, by his great example, vice restrain:
Where will his bounty or his goodness end?
To times unborn his gen'rous views extend;
The virtues of his heir our praise engage,
And promise blessings to the coming age:
Late shall he in his kindred orbs be plac'd,
With Pylian years, and crouded honours grac'd.
Meantime, your hero's fleeting spirit bear,
Fresh from his wounds, and change it to a star:
So shall great Julius rites divine assume,
And from the skies eternal smile on Rome.'
    This spoke; the goddess to the senate flew:
Where, her fair form conceal'd from mortal view,
Her Caesar's heav'nly part she made her care,
Nor left the recent soul to waste to air,
But bore it upwards to its native skies:
Glowing with new-born fires she saw it rise;
Forth springing from her bosom up it flew,
And, kindling, as it soar'd, a comet grew;
Above the lunar sphere it took its flight,
And shot behind it a long trail of light.

    Thus rais'd, his glorious offspring Julius view'd.
Beneficently great, and scatt'ring good,

Deeds, that his own surpass'd, with joy beheld,
And his large heart dilates to be excell'd.
What, though this prince refuses to receive
The preference, which his juster subjects give;
Fame uncontroll'd, that no restraint obeys,
The homage, shunn'd by modest virtue, pays,
And proves disloyal only in his praise.
Though great his sire, him greater we proclaim:
So Atreus yields to Agamemnon's fame;
Achilles so superior honours won,
And Peleus must submit to Peleus' son;
Examples yet more noble to disclose,
So Saturn was eclips'd, when Jove to empire rose:
Jove rules the heav'ns; the earth Augustus sways;
Each claims a monarch's and a father's praise.

   Celestials, who for Rome your cares employ;
Ye gods, who guarded the remains of Troy;
Ye native gods, here born and fix'd by fate;
Quirinus, founder of the Roman state;
O parent Mars, from whom Quirinus sprung;
Chaste Vesta, Caesar's household gods among
Most sacred held; domestic Phoebus, thou,
To whom with Vesta chaste alike we bow;
Great guardian of the high Tarpeïan rock;
And all ye pow'rs whom poets may invoke;
O, grant that day may claim our sorrows late,
When lov'd Augustus shall submit to fate;
Visit those seats where gods and heroes dwell;
And leave, in tears, the world he rul'd so well.

ANTONY AND CLEOPATRA

Life of Antony

Plutarch

Translated by Aubrey Stewart and George Long, 1892

In 31 BC, Antony ('Antonius') lost to Octavian ('Caesar'), great-nephew
of Julius Caesar, in a naval battle at Actium in western Greece. Here,
one of Antony's most trusted men, Canidius, informs him that he is now
isolated. Antony's response is to take comfort in his lover Cleopatra,
ruler of Egypt, and the luxuries of her court. Their time is limited. The
Greek writer **Plutarch** (AD 46–120), Antony's biographer – and author of
Parallel Lives (a collection of paired biographies of famous Greeks and
Romans) – describes the lovers as the end draws near.

Canidius himself brought intelligence to Antonius of the loss of his forces
at Actium, and he heard that Herodes, the Jew, who had certain legions
and cohorts, had gone over to Caesar, and that the rest of the princes in
like manner were revolting, and that none of his troops out of Egypt still kept
together. However, none of these things disturbed him; but, as if he gladly laid
aside hope as he did care, he left that dwelling on the sea, which he called Timo-
neium, and being taken by Cleopatra into the palace, he turned the city to feasting
and drinking and distribution of money, registering the son of Cleopatra and
Caesar among the young men, and putting on Antyllus, his son by Fulvia, the
vest without the purple hem, which marked the attainment of full age, on which
occasion banquets and revellings and feasts engaged Alexandria for many days.
They themselves put an end to that famed company of the Inimitable Livers,
and they formed another, not at all inferior to that in refinement and luxury and
expense, which they called the company of those who would die together. For
the friends of Antonius registered themselves as intending to die together, and
they continued enjoying themselves in a succession of banquets. Cleopatra got
together all kinds of deadly poisons, and she tried the painless character of each
by giving them to those who were in prison under sentence of death. When she
discovered that the quick poisons brought on a speedy death with pain, and the
less painful were not quick, she made trial of animals, which in her presence were
set upon one another. And she did this daily; and among nearly all she found
that the bite of the asp alone brought on without spasms and groans a sleepy

numbness and drowsiness, with a gentle perspiration on the face, and dulling of the perceptive faculties, which were softly deprived of their power, and made resistance to all attempts to awake and arouse them, as is the case with those who are in a deep sleep.

At the same time they sent also ambassadors to Caesar into Asia, Cleopatra requesting the dominion of Egypt for her children, and Antonius asking to be allowed to live as a private person at Athens, if he could not be permitted to stay in Egypt. Through the want of friends and their distrust owing to the desertions, Euphronius, the instructor of the children, was sent on the embassy. For Alexas, of Laodiceia, who at Rome had become known to Antonius through Timagenes, and possessed most influence of all the Greeks, who also had been the most active of the instruments of Cleopatra against Antonius, and had overthrown all the reflections which rose in his mind about Octavia, had been sent to King Herodes to keep him from changing; and having stayed there and betrayed Antonius, he had the impudence to go into the presence of Caesar, relying on Herodes. But Herodes helped him not, but being forthwith confined and carried in chains to his own country, he was put to death there by order of Caesar. Such was the penalty for his infidelity that Alexas paid to Antonius in his lifetime.

Caesar would not listen to what was said on behalf of Antonius; but as to Cleopatra, he replied that she should not fail to obtain anything that was reasonable if she would kill Antonius or drive him away. He also sent with the ambassadors of Antonius and Cleopatra one Thyrsus, a freedman of his, a man not devoid of judgment, nor, as coming from a young general, one who would fail in persuasive address to a haughty woman who was wonderfully proud of her beauty. This man, having longer interviews with Cleopatra than the rest, and being specially honoured, caused Antonius to have suspicions, and he seized and whipped him; and he then sent him back to Caesar with a letter to the effect that Thyrsus, by giving himself airs and by his insolent behaviour, had irritated him, who was easily irritated by reason of his misfortunes. "But you," he said, "if you do not like the thing, have my freedman Hipparchus. Hang him up and whip him, that we may be on equal terms." Upon this Cleopatra, with the view of doing away with his cause of complaint and suspicions, paid more than usual court to Antonius: she kept her own birthday in a mean manner and a way suitable to her condition, but she celebrated the birthday of Antonius with an excess of splendour and cost, so that many of those who were invited to the feast came poor and went away rich. Agrippa in the meantime called Caesar back, frequently writing to him from Rome, and urging that affairs there required his presence.

Accordingly for the time the war was suspended; but when the winter was over, Caesar advanced through Syria and his generals through Libya. Pelusium was taken, and it was said that Seleukus gave it up, not without the consent of Cleopatra. But Cleopatra surrendered to Antonius the wife and children of Seleukus to be put to death; and as she had a tomb and a monument constructed of unusual beauty and height, which she had built close to the temple of Isis, she collected there the most precious of the royal treasures, gold, silver, emeralds, pearls, ebony, ivory, and cinnamon, and also a great quantity of fire-wood and tow; so that Caesar, being afraid about the money, lest Cleopatra becoming desperate should destroy and burn the wealth, kept continually forwarding to her hopes of friendly treatment while he was advancing with his army against the city. When Caesar had taken his position near the hippodrome, Antonius sallied forth and fought gallantly, and he put Caesar's cavalry to flight and pursued them to the camp. Elated with his victory, he entered the palace and embraced Cleopatra in his armour, and presented to her one of the soldiers who had fought most bravely. Cleopatra gave the soldier as a reward of his courage a golden breastplate and a helmet. The man took them, and in the night deserted to Caesar.

Again, Antonius sent to Caesar and challenged him to single combat. Caesar replied that Antonius had many ways of dying, on which Antonius, reflecting that there was no better mode of death for him than in battle, determined to try a land battle and a naval battle at the same time. And at supper, it is said, he bade the slaves to pour out and feast him cheerfully, for it was uncertain whether they would do that on the morrow or would be serving other masters, while he should lie a corpse and should be a nothing. Seeing that his friends shed tears at his words, he said that he would not lead them out to a battle from which he would seek for himself a glorious death rather than safety and victory. During this night, it is said, about the middle thereof, while the city was quiet and depressed through fear and expectation of the future, all at once certain harmonious sounds from all kinds of instruments were heard, and shouts of a crowd with Evoes and satyric leapings, as if some company of revellers not without noise were going out of the city; and the course of the procession seemed to be through the middle of the city to the gate leading outwards in the direction of the enemy, and at this point the tumult made its way out, being loudest there. And those who reflected on the sign were of opinion that the god to whom Antonius all along most likened himself and most claimed kinship with was deserting him.

At daybreak Antonius posted his troops on the hills in front of the city, and watched his ships, which were put in motion and advancing against those of the enemy; and as he expected to see something great done by them, he remained quiet. But when the men of Antonius came near, they saluted with their oars Caesar's men, and as they returned the salute, the men of Antonius changed sides, and the fleet becoming one by the junction of all the ships, sailed with the vessels' heads turned against the city. As soon as Antonius saw this, he was deserted by the cavalry, who changed sides, and being defeated with his infantry he retired into the city, crying out that he was betrayed by Cleopatra to those with whom he was warring on her account. Cleopatra, fearing his anger and despair, fled to the tomb and let down the folding doors which were strengthened with bars and bolts; and she sent persons to Antonius to inform him that she was dead. Antonius, believing the intelligence, said to himself, "Why dost thou still delay, Antonius? fortune has taken away the sole remaining excuse for clinging to life." He then entered his chamber, and loosing his body armour and taking it in pieces, he said: "Cleopatra, I am not grieved at being deprived of thee, for I shall soon come to the same place with thee; but I am grieved that I, such an Imperator, am shown to be inferior to a woman in courage." Now Antonius had a faithful slave named Eros, whom he had long before exhorted, if the necessity should arise, to kill him; and he now claimed the performance of the promise. Eros drew his sword and held it out as if he were going to strike his master, but he turned away his face and killed himself. As Eros fell at his master's feet Antonius said, "Well done, Eros, though you are not able to do this for me, you teach me what I ought to do;" and piercing himself through the belly he threw himself on the bed. But the wound was not immediately mortal; and accordingly, as the flow of blood ceased when he lay down, he came to himself and requested the bystanders to finish him. But they fled from the chamber while he was calling out and writhing in pain, till Diomedes the secretary came from Cleopatra with orders to convey him to her to the tomb.

When he learned that she was alive, he eagerly commanded his slaves to take him up, and he was carried in their arms to the doors of the chamber. Cleopatra did not open the doors, but she appeared at a window, from which she let down cords and ropes; and when the slaves below had fastened Antonius to them, she drew him up with the aid of the two women whom alone she had admitted into the tomb with her. Those who were present say that there never was a more piteous sight; for stained with blood and struggling with death he was hauled up, stretching out his hands to her, while he was suspended in the air. For the labour was not light for women, and Cleopatra with difficulty, holding with her hands and straining the muscles of her face, pulled up the rope, while those who were below encouraged her and shared in her agony. When she had thus got him in and laid him down, she rent her garments over him, and beating her breasts and scratching them with her hands, and wiping the blood off him with her face, she called him master and husband and Imperator; and she almost forgot her own misfortunes through pity for his. Antonius, stopping her lamentations, asked for wine to drink, whether it was that he was thirsty or that he expected to be released more speedily. When he had drunk it, he advised her, if it could be done with decency, to look after the preservation of her own interests, and to trust to Procleius most of the companions of Caesar; and not to lament him for his last reverses, but to think him happy for the good things that he had obtained, having become the most illustrious of men and had the greatest power, and now not ignobly a Roman by a Roman vanquished.

Just as Antonius died, Procleius came from Caesar; for after Antonius had wounded himself and was carried to Cleopatra, Derketaeus, one of his guards, taking his dagger and concealing it, secretly made his way from the palace, and running to Caesar, was the first to report the death of Antonius, and he showed the blood-stained dagger. When Caesar heard the news, he retired within his tent and wept for a man who had been related to him by marriage, and his colleague in command, and his companion in many struggles and affairs. He then took the letters that had passed between him and Antonius, and calling his friends, read them, in order to show in what a reasonable and fair tone he had written himself, and how arrogant and insolent Antonius had always been in his answers. Upon this he sent Procleius with orders, if possible, above all things to secure Cleopatra alive; for he was afraid about the money, and he thought it a great thing for the glory of his triumph to lead her in the procession. However Cleopatra would not put herself in the hands of Procleius; but they talked together while he was standing on the outside close to the building near a door on a level with the ground, which was firmly secured, but allowed a passage for the voice. In their conversation Cleopatra entreated that her children might have the kingdom, and Procleius bade her be of good cheer and trust to Caesar in all things.

After Procleius had inspected the place and reported to Caesar, Gallus was sent to have another interview with her; and having come to the door he purposely prolonged the conversation. In the meantime Procleius applied a ladder and got through the window by which the women took in Antonius; and he immediately went down with two slaves to the door at which Cleopatra stood with her attention directed to Gallus. One of the women who were shut up with Cleopatra called out, "Wretched Cleopatra, you are taken alive," on which she turned round, and seeing Procleius, attempted to stab herself, for she happened to have by her side a dagger such as robbers wear: but Procleius, quickly running up to her and holding her with both his hands, said, "You wrong yourself, Cleopatra, and Caesar too by attempting to deprive him of the opportunity of a noble display of magnanimity and to fix on the mildest of commanders the stigma of faithlessness and implacability." At the same time he took away her dagger and shook her dress to see if she concealed any poison. There was also sent from Caesar one of his freedmen, Epaphroditus, whose orders were to watch over her life with great care, but as to the rest to give way in all things that would make her most easy and be most agreeable to her.

Caesar entered the city talking with Areius the philosopher, and he had given Areius his right hand, that he might forthwith be conspicuous among the citizens and be admired on account of the special respect that he received from Caesar. Entering the gymnasium and ascending a tribunal that was made for him, the people the while being terror-struck and falling down before him, he bade them get up, and he said that he acquitted the people of all blame, first on account of the founder Alexander, second because he admired the beauty and magnitude of the city, and third, to please his friend Areius. Such honour Areius obtained from Caesar, and he got the pardon of many others; and among them was Philostratus, a man of all sophists the most competent to speak on the sudden, but one who claimed to be of the Academy without just grounds. Wherefore Caesar, who abominated his habits, would not listen to his entreaties. But Philostratus, letting his white beard grow and putting on a dark vest, followed behind Areius, continually uttering this verse:

Wise save the wise, if wise indeed they be.

Caesar hearing of this, pardoned Philostratus, wishing rather to release Areius from odium than Philostratus from fear.

Of the children of Antonius, Antyllus, the son of Fulvia, was given up by his paedagogus Theodorus and put to death; and when the soldiers had cut off his head, the paedagogus took the most precious stone which he wore about his neck and sewed it in his belt; and though he denied the fact, he was convicted of it and crucified. The children of Cleopatra were guarded together with those who had charge of them, and they had a liberal treatment; but as to Caesarion, who was said to be Cleopatra's son by Caesar, her mother sent him to India with much treasure by way of Ethiopia; but another paedagogus like Theodorus, named Rhodon, persuaded him to return, saying that Caesar invited him to take the kingdom. While Caesar was deliberating about Caesarion, it is said that Areius observed: "Tis no good thing, a multitude of Caesars."

Now Caesar put Caesarion to death after the death of Cleopatra. Though many asked for the body of Antonius to bury it, both kings and commanders,

Caesar did not take it from Cleopatra, but it was interred by her own hands sumptuously and royally, and she received for that purpose all that she wished. In consequence of so much grief and pain, for her breasts were inflamed by the blows that she had inflicted and were sore, and a fever coming on, she gladly availed herself of this pretext for abstaining from food and with the design of releasing herself from life without hindrance. There was a physician with whom she was familiar, Olympus, to whom she told the truth, and she had him for her adviser and assistant in accomplishing her death, as Olympus said in a history of these transactions which he published. Caesar suspecting her design, plied her with threats and alarms about her children, by which Cleopatra was thrown down as by engines of war, and she gave up her body to be treated and nourished as it was wished.

Caesar himself came a few days after to see her and pacify her. Cleopatra happened to be lying on a mattress meanly dressed, and as he entered she sprang up in a single vest and fell at his feet with her head and face in the greatest disorder, her voice trembling and her eyes weakened by weeping. There were also visible many marks of the blows inflicted on her breast; and in fine her body seemed in no respect to be in better plight than her mind. Yet that charm and that saucy confidence in her beauty were not completely extinguished, but, though she was in such a condition, shone forth from within and showed themselves in the expression of her countenance. When Caesar had bid her lie down and had seated himself near her, she began to touch upon a kind of justification, and endeavoured to turn all that had happened upon necessity and fear of Antonius; but as Caesar on each point met her with an answer, being confuted, she all at once changed her manner to move him by pity and by prayers, as a person would do who clung most closely to life. Finally she handed to him a list of all the treasures that she had; and when Seleukus, one of her stewards, declared that she was hiding and secreting some things, she sprang up and laying hold of his hair, belaboured him with many blows on the face. As Caesar smiled and stopped her, she said, "But is it not scandalous, Caesar, that you have condescended to come to me and speak to me in my wretched condition, and my slaves make it a matter of charge against me if I have reserved some female ornaments, not for myself forsooth, wretch that I am, but that I may give a few things to Octavia and your wife Livia, and so through their means make you more favourable to me and more mild." Caesar was pleased with these words, being fully assured that she wished to live. Accordingly, after saying that he left these matters to her care and that in everything else he would behave to her better than she expected, he went away, thinking that he had deceived her; but he had deceived himself.

Now there was Cornelius Dolabella, a youth of rank, and one of the companions of Caesar. He was not without a certain liking towards Cleopatra; and now, in order to gratify her request, he secretly sent and informed her that Caesar himself was going to march with his troops through Syria, and that he had determined to send off her with her children on the third day. On hearing this, Cleopatra first entreated Caesar to permit her to pour libations on the tomb of Antonius; and when Caesar permitted it, she went to the tomb, and embracing the coffin in company with the women who were usually about her, said, "Dear Antonius, I buried thee recently with hands still free, but now I pour out libations as a captive and so watched that I cannot either with blows or sorrow disfigure this body of mine now made a slave and preserved to form a part in the triumph over thee. But expect not other honours or libations, for these are the last which Cleopatra brings. Living, nothing kept us asunder, but there is a risk of our changing places in death; thou a Roman, lying buried here, and I, wretched woman, in Italy, getting only as much of thy country as will make me a grave. But if indeed there is any help and power in the gods there (for the gods of this country have deserted us), do not deliver thy wife up alive, and let not thyself be triumphed over in me, but hide me here with thee and bury thee with me; for though I have ten thousand ills, not one of them is so great and grievous as this short time which I have lived apart from thee!"

After making this lamentation and crowning and embracing the coffin, she ordered a bath to be prepared for her. After bathing, she lay down and enjoyed a splendid banquet. And there came one from the country bringing a basket; and on the guards asking what he brought, the man opened it, and taking off the leaves showed the vessel full of figs. The soldiers admiring their beauty and size, the man smiled and told them to take some, whereon, without having any suspicion, they bade him carry them in. After feasting, Cleopatra took a tablet, which was already written, and sent it sealed to Caesar, and, causing all the rest of her attendants to withdraw except those two women, she closed the door. As soon as Caesar opened the tablet and found in it the prayers and lamentations of Cleopatra, who begged him to bury her with Antonius, he saw what had taken place. At first he was for setting out himself to give help, but the next thing that he did was to send persons with all speed to inquire. But the tragedy had been speedy; for, though they ran thither and found the guards quite ignorant of everything, as soon as they opened the door they saw Cleopatra lying dead on a golden couch in royal attire. Of her two women, Eiras was dying at her feet, and Charmion, already staggering and drooping her head, was arranging the diadem on the forehead of Cleopatra. One of them saying in passion, "A good deed this, Charmion;" "Yes, most goodly," she replied, "and befitting the descendant of so many kings." She spake not another word, but fell there by the side of the couch.

Now it is said that the asp was brought with those figs and leaves, and was covered with them; for that Cleopatra had so ordered, that the reptile might fasten on her body without her being aware of it. But when she had taken up some of the figs and saw it, she said, "Here then it is," and baring her arm, she offered it to the serpent to bite. Others say that the asp was kept in a water-pitcher, and that Cleopatra drew it out with a golden distaff and irritated it till the reptile sprang upon her arm and clung to it. But the real truth nobody knows; for it was also said that she carried poison about her in a hollow comb, which she concealed in her hair; however, no spots broke out on her body, nor any other sign of poison. Nor yet was the reptile seen within the palace; but some said that they observed certain marks of its trail near the sea, in that part towards which the chamber looked and the windows were. Some also say that the arm of Cleopatra was observed to have two small indistinct punctures; and it seems that Caesar believed this, for in the triumph a figure of Cleopatra was carried with the asp clinging to her. Such is the way in which these events are told. Though Caesar was vexed at the death of Cleopatra, he admired her nobleness of mind, and he ordered the body to be interred with that of Antonius in splendid and royal style. The women of Cleopatra also received honourable interment by his orders. Cleopatra at the time of her death was forty years of age save one, and she had reigned as queen two-and-twenty years, and governed together with Antonius more than fourteen.

Octavian went on to cement his position as Augustus, the first emperor of Rome.

TO HEAL AN ASP BITE

On Theriac to Piso

Attr. Galen

Translated by Robert Leigh, 2016

Galen of Pergamon (AD 129–*c*. 200) was a Greek doctor of the Roman Empire, whose ideas about human physiology – most notably the theory of the humours – were still current in the seventeenth century. The following comes from a treatise attributed to him on a particular antidote or 'theriac'. The antidote was originally invented by Mithridates VI Eupator of Pontus, a kingdom south of the Black Sea, which the Romans conquered in the mid-first century BC. Mithridates was famous for taking daily antidotes to protect himself against potential poisoning. The Romans stole his recipes when they conquered his territory and developed some of them further. Nero's private doctor Andromachus improved his so-called 'theriac' by adding the flesh of vipers to the recipe, as he details in the text below. Galen presents his treatise as a response to a request from one Piso, whose son was treated with theriac following a riding accident.

O f the asps, the one called spitter stretches out its neck and measures out the length of the gap and, as if it had at that moment become capable of reason, accurately spits its poison at the body.

They say that it was with one of these sorts of beast (for there are three sorts of asp, this one and the one called the land snake and the one called the swallow snake) that Queen Cleopatra, wanting to escape the notice of her guards, died quickly and in a way which avoided suspicion. For when Augustus had beaten Antony and wanted to take her alive and to guard her carefully, as you would expect, so as to display such a famous woman to the Romans in a triumph. But, they say, she realised this and chose to leave the world of the living while still a queen rather than appear at Rome as a nobody, and so contrived her own death by the agency of one of these creatures. And they say she called her two most trusted women whose job was to tend to the attire of her body so as to display her beauty, called Naeira and Charmione. Naeira did her hair in a fitting manner and Charmione cut her fingernails and she then ordered the snake to be brought in, hidden in some grapes and figs so that, as I have said, it would escape the notice of the guards. She then tried out the snake on these women to see if it could kill swiftly, and after it did she killed herself with the rest and they say that Augustus was completely amazed at this, both that they loved her to the extent of dying with her and that she was unwilling to live like a slave and chose rather to die nobly. And they say she was found with her right hand on her head grasping the diadem, as is likely, so that even up to that point it should be obvious to onlookers that she was the queen. Similarly the tragedian tells us about Polyxena that she also "when she died gave much forethought to falling in a noble manner". And those who want to demonstrate by this story both the cleverness of the woman in evading attention, and the speed of the asp in killing, say that she bit her own arm wide and deep, and after doing this got the asp poison brought to her in some vessel and poured it into the wound, and so after it had been given to her without the guards noticing, she peacefully died.

[...]

We do not put the whole body of the viper into theriac, but cut off the heads and tails and use the rest of the body in the mixture. We do not do this capriciously, nor without reason, but because the head contains the worst of the bodily fluids, the poison itself, and so we try to cut them off so that the drug should have less of their power, since the nature of these heads has a certain power of turning things to poison just as sperm is created by changes occurring in the testicles, and milk in the breast. The female viper has a head more suited for destruction than any other creature. For they say it opens its mouth to receive the male's semen, and then when it has got it to cut off his head; and this is the method of their foul intercourse. Then the creatures born from the sperm by a sort of natural revenge eat through the mother's stomach and emerge into the open and so kill the mother to avenge the father. So the great Nicander writes elegantly in his poetry, and these are his words:

"Do not be at the crossroads when the dusky viper escaping her bite is enraged by the blow of the sooty-coloured she-viper when, as the male mounts her, leaping and fastening her furious bite in him, she cuts off her husband's head. But the little snakes which are born follow up the outrage against their father when they orphan themselves by breaking out of their mother's slender body."

We remove the tails and the whole extremities of the body because they are part of the tail and, in my view, because they drag the more foul part of the body and get more of a dragging because they provide the motion of the snake, just as the parts of a fish towards the tail are said to be more nourishing because of the amount of moving they do. Do not be amazed if after cutting off these parts, the rest of the body of the creatures makes the drug stronger when its inherent power to save is mixed in with their very flesh. In the case of other animals we know that many of their body parts heroically treat many conditions. For example many are helped by the heads of mice, for when burnt and anointed with honey they can cure alopecia. And they say that the head of a kite likewise is a treatment for gout if one dries it without its feathers and sprinkles it in three fingers of water. And sometimes even single subdivisions of parts can cure some diseases. For example a camel's brain dried and drunk with vinegar cures epileptics; likewise that of a weasel. That of a swallow with milk works against cataracts. That of a sheep prepared the same way is a great help against the teething pains of children. The shavings of the horn of a bull, drunk with water, stop haemorrhage, and the burnt thighbones also hold back the blood. The same thing also often stops an upset stomach. The filings of the horn of a deer, when burnt, and ground up with wine, then applied as a plaster, fix loosened teeth; they say the vertebra of an ox can do this too. And drunk with honey it expels roundworm, with vinegar and honey it softens the spleen, and when smeared on to leprosies it softens them, and it is equally aphrodisiac; and the beaver's testicles drunk in the same way cure spasms. And many animals can help men by their bile, their fat, their marrow, their milk, their skin, their very blood, and in the case of snakes their shed skin. We have even known men helped by their excrement. For example cow dung dried and burnt with three snails helps dropsy; mouse dung mixed with vinegar cures alopecia; and taken in a drink it breaks down bladder stones; goose fat with rose water heals the lungs; and deer marrow is a very soothing drug. Drinking cow's milk helps those with bad stomachs. Hyena bile with honey helps to induce sharp-sightedness, and when rubbed on cataracts removes them. Hippopotamus skin, burnt and made into a smooth paste with water, dissipates tumours, just as a smooth paste of snakeskin applied to bald patches wonderfully encourages hair growth. An asp's shed skin rubbed into honey and applied as an ointment gives very sharp sight. There is so much material of this kind that I think now not a good time to write it all down for fear this treatise becomes too long for us, and just as much as I have already written is enough to give you proof of what I say. And you should know this, that the whole bodies of animals are often good for people. For example river crab beaten smooth and applied as a plaster drives out thorns and splinters; similarly shrimp beaten small with bryony root and drunk expels worms. Scorpion roasted and eaten with bread breaks up bladder stones. Again, earth worms drunk in wine do the same thing. And if someone with jaundice beats them up in honey and wine and drinks them he will immediately be purged and relieved of it.

They have often healed the lungs of the gouty when applied with rose salve, and falcon cooked up with lily perfume cures weakness of sight. Dung beetle cures ear ache when boiled up with oil and dripped into the ear. Eating roast lark has often wonderfully helped those suffering from colic. And so that you may wonder more at the power in the bodies of living creatures I will explain something even more remarkable. Many creatures exhibit their power just by being looked at. The gecko fixes scorpions to the spot when they see it and so kills them. The amphisbaena is a two-headed animal like double-ended ships, since nature has done her the unusual favour of giving her two heads, and they say that if a pregnant woman encounters this creature she miscarries, and no wonder if the bodies of these snakes, cut up, still have power to help. For I have diligently shown I think that both the whole bodies sometimes help men, and sometimes just parts of them, and sometimes small parts of the parts themselves.

THE GNAT

Culex

Anon.

Translated by Lucius M. Sargent, 1807

Believed by some to be an early work of Virgil (see Stories 48, 49 and 63),
the *Culex* or 'Gnat' is a lively tale about a shepherd and the adventures
which take him away from his fields. Although Virgil had a keen interest
in rural living, setting both his *Eclogues* and *Georgics* in the countryside,
this sprawling story, written in Latin hexameters, was probably written
by someone else to replace a poem of his that was lost.

But to my song: now fled the shades of night,
And rosy morning open'd on the sight;
From out their folds his flock, as morning gay,
A shepherd drove; and bent his wonted way
Along the vale with various flow'rets spread,
To where the mountain lifts it's grassy head.
Pleas'd at release, in various tracks they rove,
Some wander o'er the vale, some seek the grove;
Some snuff the wanton breeze, some strive amain
To mount the dang'rous steep, and gaze along the plain:
Those crop the lowly grass, while eager these
Roam thro' the wood for shrubs and flow'ring trees;
While this the bud or grateful blossom nips,
Or from the branch the pendent dewdrop sips,
That seeks afar some height, whence fountains flow,
And views its semblance in the stream below.—
Blest is the shepherd's life! ah, happy swain,
Who seeks no joys beyond his native plain;
Nor pants for wealth, nor heaves a wishful sigh
For all the charms of pageant luxury.
For him no joy can Syrian dies impart,
Nor costly bowls, the boast of Alcon's art;
Nor splendid halls, nor stones of fairest hue,
Nor pearls that toil from India's ocean drew.
But oft, when spring and all her charms appear,
And Flora's pencil paints the blooming year,

Full light of heart, from some green bank he views
The various fields, and notes their sev'ral hues;
Or, all at ease, beguiles his hours away,
Whilst with his reed he tunes some past'ral lay.
Vines, curling o'er him, shade the verdant ground,
And rip'ning clusters hang luxurious round.
For him fair flocks their copious udders yield,
And fruitful Pales lives in ev'ry field;
He too has groves; and in the vales below
From cooling grots each day new fountains flow.
Who knows more joy than he, retir'd who lives,
And blest with all approving conscience gives;
Far, far away from war's ensanguin'd plain,
And direful contests midst the raging main?
'Gainst no rude warrior, fierce in arms, he toils,
For splendid trophies, or for sacred spoils.
For him their sweets Panchaean odors yield,
With ev'ry flow'r that decks the fragrant field;
Pan he reveres, invokes for ev'ry good,
Pan guards the cot, and dwells in ev'ry wood.
Delicious ease is thine, ah, happy swain,
With fair content and all her careless train;
Thrice blest indeed, thou know'st no greater wealth
Than gentle slumber, competence and health.
Hail flocks! and groves where gentle breezes swell!
And shady vales where Hamadryads dwell!
Amidst your joys contented shepherds lie,
And lose their hours in rival poesy.
Beside his crook the musing shepherd lay,
And with his reed chas'd summer's cares away:
Bright Phoebus now his middle course had run,
And on each ocean pour'd the burning sun.
Now rose the swain, his flocks before him go,
By mossy banks where murm'ring streamlets flow;
Their thirst appeas'd, they seek the flow'ry glade,
Where Dian's beeches form a cooling shade.
Here once Agave, Cadmus' daughter, fled
Her children's anger, for their father dead.
And here full oft the bristly Fauns are seen
With troops of Satyrs sporting on the green;
Here with the rest appear the Naiad train,
And dancing Dryads skim along the plain.
Such feats were these, that streamlets ceased to glide,
Ev'n wond'ring Peneus curb'd his rolling tide.
A sight more strange than when, at Orpheus' lyre,
Swift Hebrus stops and dancing groves admire.
But, weary with the toil, full oft they rove,

Where various foliage forms a cooling grove;
Here, first of all, where most the vale descends,
The lofty plane its length of shade extends.
Here too the Lotus holds her impious reign,
Whose potent charms beguil'd Ulisses' train.
Here poplars sigh, in whose sad semblance grow
The sister Heliads, on the banks of Po;
Still, still their sorrows float in ev'ry gale,
And amber tears a brother's fate bewail.
With these the tree, in whose green branches drest,
The constant Phyllis mourns her faithless guest.
Here sacred oaks the will of fate reveal'd
Ere golden Ceres turn'd the fruitful field;
These mighty monarchs tow'r'd above the plain,
Till Celeus' son usurp'd their wide domain.
Here rugged pines, the pride of Argos, rise,
Climb the tall hills and emulate the skies.
Here the dark holm and fatal cypress show
Their shady heads: here lofty beeches grow;
Whose spreading arms (lest trembling aspins find
Their neighbours fatal) curling ivies bind;
Still tow'rds the top their little tendrils twine,
Thro' pale green leaves where golden clusters shine.
Here, with the rest, fair Venus' myrtles bloom,
Nor yet unconscious of their former doom.
On spreading branches swell the feather'd choir,
Whose various notes in melody conspire;
Now from afar these various notes resound;
And creaking locusts wake the fields around.
In crystal drops a fount beneath distils,
Whose rippling water forms a thousand rills.
Scatter'd abroad, the weary flocks repose,
On thorny cliffs where gentle zephyr blows.

Here, where a stream divides the flow'ry glade,
The swain at ease enjoy'd the cooling shade;
All unsuspecting, on the grass he lay,
And gentle slumber stole his thoughts away.
But fate o'er man a veil of darkness throws,
Hence ev'ry joy and ev'ry sorrow flows.
Now from his slimy bed, where, all the day,
To shun its ardor, deep conceal'd he lay,
A monstrous Hydra rose; of various hue,
And round the shore his wonted course he drew.
Eager for air, he warns the trembling throng,
Where'er he leads his scaly length along;
Still more sublime his fulgent front he bears,

And ev'ry breeze his loud approach declares.
His lofty head a purple crest displays,
And his fierce eyeballs roll a threat'ning blaze.
At length the monster drew his sinuous way,
Where on a bank the sleeping shepherd lay;
He comes, he sees, he burns with furious ire,
His flaming eyes diffuse a fiercer fire,
Half springing on his prey, he still forbears,
And 'gainst th' intruder all his arms prepares;
With burning rage more bright each colour shines,
And his vast length in bloody folds he twines.
While for th' attack the raging serpent swell'd,
A little gnat his threat'ning form beheld;
Full swift he flew, and bent his anxious way,
Where, lost in sleep, the careless shepherd lay;
Full quick with piercing sting his front assail'd,
And bade him fly, e'er threat'ning fate prevail'd.
Swiftly he rose, and, raging with the wound,
Dash'd the poor gnat all trembling to the ground.
Now the sad gnat expends his latest breath,
And all his stiff'ning limbs grow cold in death.—
But now the swain beholds the serpent's glare,
And sees him furious for the fight prepare;
Trembling and pale, with fearful haste he flew,
And from the wood a tree's vast body drew;
With whose huge bulk (this aid 'tis hard to find
If chance produc'd, or fate itself design'd,)
Enrag'd, he clave the monster's sounding mail
Now blows on blows his nodding crest assail;
Till from his temples pours the purple tide,
And thro' the wound his floating spirits glide.
But when the shepherd saw the foe was slain,
Careless he turn'd, and sought his seat again;
For still his mind the dregs of slumber seal'd.
Nor half his danger to his thoughts reveal'd.

Now tardy Vesper comes o'er Oeta's height;
And hard behind appear the steeds of night.
His flock collected, home the shepherd bears
His weary limbs, and now for rest prepares;
Reclin'd at ease, his languid members lay,
And gentle slumber held her grateful sway;
When, lo! his sight the gnat's pale form assails,
And mournful thus his cruel death bewails:
Hard is my lot! ungrateful swain, declare,
By what desert, these cruel bonds I wear!
You I preserv'd, from you my sorrows flow.

And thus rewarded to the shades I go.
At ease you lie, nor dream of dangers o'er;
Me the sad Manes drag to Lethe's shore,
Vile Charon's prey. In realms of sad despair,
Mark how yon torches shed their frightful glare!
Now the fierce keeper, with his hideous yell,
Salutes my entrance at the gates of hell;
His form new horror from it's snakes acquires,
And from his eyes flash vivid light'ning's fires.
See too! the fury lifts her serpent hair,
Hurls round her flames, and shakes her scourge in air!
'Twas mine your life from instant fate to save,
Ah! how proportion'd the reward you gave!
For deeds like this shall no fair meed remain?
Has justice fled? shall faith forsake the plain?
Careless of self, for you my life I paid;
Shall no sad rites appease an injured shade?
If grateful blood still flows in shepherd's veins,
Let some small tribute grace my poor remains.
In unknown paths, with wilder'd steps I rove,
Along the mazes of the Stygian grove:
Here countless hosts of gloomy souls appear,
And ev'ry shade receives it's sentence here.
Here, bound with serpents, tow'ring Othos stands,
Gazing in grief on Ephialtes' bands;
Compeers in strength, of old these giants hurl'd
Their flaming brands, to burn the mighty world.
Here too, Titania, Tityus owns thy pow'r,
Whom, chain'd for ages, hungry birds devour.
Confounded at the sight, my steps I stay,
And now in terror seek my former way,
Back to the Stygian waves: here, doom'd in Hell,
To feel a thirst he sees the means to quell,
Sad Tantalus remains; condemn'd by Jove,
For stealing nectar from the starry grove.
Why name the wretch, who scorn'd the gods' control,
And now condemn'd a stone's vast weight to roll,
Ceaseless complains? Here too those daughters stand;
Whom fierce Erinnis gave her vengeful brand,
Whose wond'rous pow'r impell'd these impious brides
To quench young Hymen's torch in purple tides.
Full black the crime! yet fair as day, compar'd
With those fell deeds, that shameless Colchis dar'd
Whose bursting rage in twain her bosom rent,
And 'gainst her offspring all its fury bent.
And now I hear Pandion's daughters sing
Their mournful notes. With these, Bistonia's king,

A bird in semblance, wings his airy flight.
And here fell discord hurls the flames of fight
Mid Cadmus' train; with ire the brothers burn,
And, each on each, their kindred weapons turn;
Eternal labor!—Now compell'd to fly,
Th' infernal powers in distant prospect lie;
Now born afar, along th' Elysian tide,
Where Ceres' daughter, Pluto's gloomy bride,
Still urges on her train. Absolv'd from care,
The fair Alcestis roves rewarded there;
Proof of unbounded love! her life she gave,
To save her spouse, Admetus, from the grave.
And here is seen, the grace of womankind,
Ulisses' wife: and, ling'ring far behind,
Transfix'd with spears, the daring suitor train.
Mourn, Orpheus, mourn! here, rack'd with grief and pain,
Curs'd by that fatal lovesick look from thee,
Thy bride remains! All-daring sure was he,
Who hop'd for mercy from the gods of Hell,
Who strove to stop the keeper's horrid yell;
Who dar'd with mortal strength to pierce the gloom,
Where none may go, but those whom Minos doom:
Who trod mid realms of ruin, fire, and blood,
And view'd with living eyes the burning flood.
All this did Orpheus! Mid the fury-throng,
Secure he pass'd; so great the pow'r of song!
Lo, in his train ev'n list'ning beasts appear,
And rapid rivers stay their floods to hear;
Vast oaks, in rapture, hear his heav'nly strains,
Spring from their roots, and leave their native plains:
The lofty forests wave their heads around,
While their tough rinds receive the potent sound.
The monthly maid, along the starry sphere,
Pleas'd with the notes, inclin'd her steeds to hear;
Hell's mighty mother own'd the matchless strain,
And willing gave what force could ne'er obtain;
Ev'n back to life sad Orpheus' bride she gave,
Long try'd with griefs beyond the Stygian wave.
Yet by these ties constrain'd; if, in their flight,
Their eyes reverted to the realms of night;
If mortal voice profan'd the shades below,
Back to her bonds the forfeit bride should go.
Ah, mournful Orpheus! cruel love prevail'd,
And thro' that love thy glorious labor fail'd.
If but one crime Hell's iron lips could move
To speak in pardon, sure that crime were Love.
Yet, constant pair, th' Elysian fields are thine;

Where from afar immortal heroes shine.
Blest in their father, Jove's official son,
Here Peleus stands and virtuous Telamon;
This, by a slave of modest worth caress'd,
That, with her charms immortal Thetis bless'd.
In equal place the youth unshaken stands,
Whose mighty arm repell'd the flaming brands,
With tenfold fury mid the Phrygian bands.
What tongue unborn shall not the tale employ,
The ten years labor and the fall of Troy?
When all her fields and rivers ran with blood,
And fair Sigeum drank the vital flood;
When raging Hector, with his valiant train,
Mid Argos' fleet bade fire and slaughter reign.
Ev'n mother Ida pour'd her pitchy store
'Gainst the tall barks, along the Trojan shore.
Here, dauntless Ajax fought thro' fields of blood;
There, Troy's first honor swell'd the purple flood,
Both fierce in war; their pond'rous armour rung,
While vivid lightning on their falchions hung.
With flaming brands here Hector strove to burn
Their lofty fleet, and stop the Greeks' return;
There, fiercer Ajax rais'd his sword on high,
Hurl'd back their brands, and bade the Trojans fly.
Next, fam'd Pelides flying Hector slew,
And round Troy's walls in cruel triumph drew.
Sad will of Fate! Pelides press'd the ground,
By Paris' hand: his doom great Ajax found,
In that sly chief, by whom, at midnight slain,
Here Dolon lay, there Rhesus press'd the plain.
He too from Troy their great Palladium bore,
And drove the Cicons from their native shore:
'Twas his to pass along the roaring waves,
Where, bound with dogs, the fatal Scylla raves;
Where the rough seas of loud Charybdis swell;
The land of Cyclops, and the shades of Hell.—
Here Atreus' son is seen, the next in place,
The pride of Greece, and honor of his race,
He taught the flames o'er Ilium's walls to rise,
Climb the high tow'rs and seek the distant skies,
But he alas! a mournful tribute gave
To falling Troy, in Asia's fatal wave.
Trust not too far the smile that fortune lends,
Nor blindly follow wheresoe'er she tends:
He, who, elate, some giddy height would gain;
Thrown from that height shall oft lament in vain.
So, flush'd with spoils, from Troy the Grecian bands

Launch'd their tall barks, and sought their native lands:
Now gentle breezes bear them on their way,
And guardian sea nymphs round their vessels play.
When (Fate so will'd, or so some baleful star,)
Waves war with winds, and spurn old ocean's bar:
Now floods on floods in sounding contest rise,
Toss their tall heads, and threat the lofty skies.
Earth echoes back the sound; the Grecians tost,
So late victorious, now forever lost,
Sink in the whelming flood, along the shores,
Where 'gainst Caphareus sounding ocean pours.
Wide o'er the waves the floating relicks fly,
Here, shatter'd ships, there, Trojan treasures lie.—
Here, mid th' Elysian fields, a martial band,
The pride of Rome, in equal honor stand.
Here brave Horatius, and the Fabian name;
And great Camillus, crown'd with deathless fame.
With these the Decii, and that youth, who gave
His life, devoted to the gaping grave,
His country's freedom and her name to save.
Here too is he, who bore the raging flame,
And bade Porsenna dread the Roman name.
With these Flaminius, heir of endless praise,
Who boldly rush'd amid the fatal blaze.
Here faithful Curius: here those heroes dwell,
By whom the walls of Libyan Carthage fell.
Wide o'er the plain the valiant bands extend,
And round their brows perpetual laurels bend.

Ah wretched fate! compell'd to seek my way,
Mid regions banish'd from the smiles of day:
Where Hell's grim lakes the mazy paths enclose,
And burning floods my fearful steps oppose.
Here mighty Minos high enthron'd appears,
And ev'ry shade from him it's sentence hears.
Around the judge th' infernal furies stand,
My life's whole tenor and my death demand.
But you, the cause of all my sorrows here,
Nor grace my shade; nor pay the fun'ral tear;
While endless griefs within my bosom burn,
Fate calls me hence, and Fate forbids return.
Shepherd, farewell! enjoy your peaceful seats,
Your cooling fountains, and your green retreats.
Still live content, mid flow'ry fields reclin'd,
While these sad words are lost in empty wind.
Thus to the swain the gnat lamenting said,
Then from his sight in silent sorrow fled.—

Now, long by slumber's galling chains oppress'd,
The shepherd rose, grief heavy at his breast.
Fresh in his mind the gnat's pale form he view'd,
And his long tale of endless wo renew'd.
Now with what strength his aged limbs retain'd,
(Which o'er the Hydra's force victorious reign'd,)
To clear a spot the mindful swain began,
Where mid the grove a secret river ran.
To raise the turf an iron haft he found,
And drew an orb's fair figure on the ground.
Still on his task intent, the ground he rear'd,
Till the fair mound in symmetry appear'd.
Next round the spot a marble line he drew,
And sow'd the place with flowr's of various hue.
Here the red rose and rough acanthus bloom,
And fragrant vi'lets flourish round the tomb.
With these the myrtle noble Sparta yields;
And golden crocus of Cilician fields.
Here hyacinths and sacred laurels grow;
And here Nonacria's sweetest odors blow.
Here the chrysanthus and buphthalmus spring,
And Bocchus, mindful still of Libya's king.
Here ivies twine; here grows that flow'r of fire,
Whose beauteous form inflam'd with self-desire.
Here amaranths and flow'ring pines appear,
And each fair season spreads it's odor here.
Last o'er the tomb a stone the shepherd rear'd,
Where rudely grav'd these silent lines appear'd.
Poor little gnat, these funeral rites receive,
What thou deserv'st, and all the swain can give.

ORPHEUS AND EURYDICE

Georgics, Book IV

Virgil

Translated by James Rhoades, 1881

This is the story of Orpheus, a proud musician who lost his wife Eurydice
to a snakebite and tried to rescue her from the Underworld. Within
Virgil's poem the tale is told by Proteus, a shape-shifting seer from the
sea, to Aristaeus, a son of the god Apollo, who sought from him the
reasons for his recent lack of good fortune. It transpires that Aristaeus
had been lustily pursuing Eurydice through a forest when she stumbled
upon the snake and died. Orpheus is allowed to enter the Underworld
but can lead Eurydice free of it only if he resists the urge to look behind
him to check she is still following him. In his poignant telling of the
myth, Virgil focuses on the depth of Orpheus' sorrow.

When Proteus seeking his accustomed cave
Strode from the billows: round him frolicking
The watery folk that people the waste sea
Sprinkled the bitter brine-dew far and wide.
Along the shore in scattered groups to feed
The sea-calves stretch them: while the seer himself,
Like herdsman on the hills when evening bids
The steers from pasture to their stall repair,
And the lambs' bleating whets the listening wolves,
Sits midmost on the rock and tells his tale.
But Aristaeus, the foe within his clutch,
Scarce suffering him compose his aged limbs,
With a great cry leapt on him, and ere he rose
Forestalled him with the fetters; he natheless,
All unforgetful of his ancient craft,
Transforms himself to every wondrous thing,
Fire and a fearful beast, and flowing stream.
But when no trickery found a path for flight,
Baffled at length, to his own shape returned,
With human lips he spake, "Who bade thee, then,

So reckless in youth's hardihood, affront
Our portals? or what wouldst thou hence?"—But he,
"Proteus, thou knowest, of thine own heart thou knowest;
For thee there is no cheating, but cease thou
To practise upon me: at heaven's behest
I for my fainting fortunes hither come
An oracle to ask thee." There he ceased.
Whereat the seer, by stubborn force constrained,
Shot forth the gray light of his gleaming eyes
Upon him, and with fiercely gnashing teeth
Unlocks his lips to spell the fates of heaven:
  "Doubt not 'tis wrath divine that plagues thee thus,
Nor light the debt thou payest; 'tis Orpheus' self,
Orpheus unhappy by no fault of his,
So fates prevent not, fans thy penal fires,
Yet madly raging for his ravished bride.
She in her haste to shun thy hot pursuit
Along the stream, saw not the coming death,
Where at her feet kept ward upon the bank
In the tall grass a monstrous water-snake.
But with their cries the Dryad-band her peers
Filled up the mountains to their proudest peaks:
Wailed for her fate the heights of Rhodope,
And tall Pangaea, and, beloved of Mars,
The land that bowed to Rhesus, Thrace no less
With Hebrus' stream; and Orithyia wept,
Daughter of Acte old. But Orpheus' self,
Soothing his love-pain with the hollow shell,
Thee his sweet wife on the lone shore alone,
Thee when day dawned and when it died he sang.
Nay to the jaws of Taenarus too he came,
Of Dis the infernal palace, and the grove
Grim with a horror of great darkness—came,
Entered, and faced the Manes and the King
Of terrors, the stone heart no prayer can tame.
Then from the deepest deeps of Erebus,
Wrung by his minstrelsy, the hollow shades
Came trooping, ghostly semblances of forms
Lost to the light, as birds by myriads hie
To greenwood boughs for cover, when twilight-hour
Or storms of winter chase them from the hills;
Matrons and men, and great heroic frames
Done with life's service, boys, unwedded girls,
Youths placed on pyre before their fathers' eyes.
Round them, with black slime choked and hideous weed,
Cocytus winds; there lies the unlovely swamp
Of dull dead water, and, to pen them fast,

Styx with her ninefold barrier poured between.
Nay, even the deep Tartarean Halls of death
Stood lost in wonderment, the Eumenides,
Their brows with livid locks of serpents twined;
E'en Cerberus held his triple jaws agape,
And, the wind hushed, Ixion's wheel stood still.
And now with homeward footstep he had passed
All perils scathless, and, at length restored,
Eurydice to realms of upper air
Had well-nigh won, behind him following—
So Proserpine had ruled it—when his heart
A sudden mad desire surprised and seized—
Meet fault to be forgiven, might Hell forgive.
For at the very threshold of the day,
Heedless, alas! and vanquished of resolve,
He stopped, turned, looked upon Eurydice
His own once more. But even with the look,
Poured out was all his labour, broken the bond
Of that fell tyrant, and a crash was heard
Three times like thunder in the meres of hell.
"Orpheus! what ruin hath thy frenzy wrought
On me, alas! and thee? Lo! once again
The unpitying fates recall me, and dark sleep
Closes my swimming eyes. And now farewell:
Girt with enormous night I am borne away,
Outstretching toward thee, thine, alas! no more,
These helpless hands." She spake, and suddenly,
Like smoke dissolving into empty air,
Passed and was sundered from his sight; nor him
Clutching vain shadows, yearning sore to speak.
Thenceforth beheld she, nor no second time
Hell's boatman lists he pass the watery bar.
What should he do? fly whither, twice bereaved?
Move with what tears the Manes, with what voice
The Powers of darkness? She indeed e'en now
Death-cold was floating on the Stygian barge!
For seven whole months unceasingly, men say,
Beneath a skyey crag, by thy lone wave,
Strymon, he wept, and in the caverns chill
Unrolled his story, melting tigers' hearts,
And leading with his lay the oaks along.
As in the poplar-shade a nightingale
Mourns her lost young, which some relentless swain,
Spying, from the nest has torn unfledged, but she
Wails the long night, and perched upon a spray
With sad insistence pipes her dolorous strain,
Till all the region with her wrongs o'erflows.

No love, no new desire, constrained his soul:
By snow-bound Tanais and the icy north,
Far steppes to frost Rhipaean for ever wed,
Alone he wandered, lost Eurydice
Lamenting, and the gifts of Dis ungiven.
Scorned by which tribute the Ciconian dames,
Amid their awful Bacchanalian rites
And midnight revellings, tore him limb from limb,
And strewed his fragments over the wide fields.
Then too, e'en then, what time the Hebrus stream,
Oeagrian Hebrus, down mid-current rolled,
Rent from the marble neck, his drifting head,
The death-chilled tongue found yet a voice to cry
"Eurydice! ah! poor Eurydice!"
With parting breath he called her, and the banks
From the broad stream caught up "Eurydice!"

NARCISSUS

Metamorphoses, Book III

Ovid

Translated by David Raeburn, 2004

A nymph named Liriope gives birth to a son by a river-god named
Cephisus. At the beginning of this story from **Ovid**'s *Metamorphoses*, she
consults the prophet Teiresias as to what the future holds for the young
boy, Narcissus. 'Know thyself' was a famous Greek adage inscribed at
the precinct of Apollo at Delphi. But as Teiresias reveals, Narcissus' very
happiness depends upon him *not* knowing himself.

Liriope gave birth to a child, already adorable,
called Narcissus. In course of time she consulted the seer;
'Tell me,' she asked, 'will my baby live to a ripe old age?'
'Yes,' he replied, 'so long as he never knows himself' –
empty words, as they long appeared, but the prophet was proved right.
In the event, Narcissus died of a curious passion.
  Sixteen years went by and already the son of Cephisus
was changing each day from beautiful youth to comely manhood.
Legions of lusty men and bevies of girls desired him;
but the heart was so hard and proud in that soft and slender body,
that none of the lusty men or languishing girls could approach him.
One day he was sighted, blithely chasing the scampering roebuck
into the huntsman's nets, by a nymph whose babbling voice
would always answer a call but never speak first. It was Echo.
Echo still was a body, not a mere voice, but her chattering
tongue could only do what it does today, that is
to parrot the last few words of the many spoken by others.
Juno had done this to her. The goddess would be all ready
to catch her husband Jupiter making love to some nymph
in a mountain dell, when crafty Echo would keep her engaged
in a long conversation, until the nymph could scurry to safety.
When Saturn's daughter perceived what Echo was doing, she said to her,
'I've been cheated enough by your prattling tongue. From now on
your words will be short and sweet!' Her curse took effect at once.
Echo could only repeat the words she heard at the end
of a sentence and never reply for herself. So when

she saw Narcissus wandering over the country fields,
she burned with desire and stealthily followed along his tracks.
The closer she followed, the flames of her passion grew nearer and nearer,
as sulphur smeared on the tip of a pine-torch quickly catches
fire when another flame is brought into close proximity.
Oh, how often she longed, poor creature, to say sweet nothings
and beg him softly to stay! But her nature imposed a block
and would not allow her to make a start. She was merely permitted
and ready to wait for the sounds which her voice could return to the speaker.
    Narcissus once took a different path from his trusty companions.
'Is anyone there?' he said '... one there?' came Echo's answer.
Startled, he searched with his eyes all round the glade and loudly
shouted, 'Come here!' 'Come here!' the voice threw back to the caller.
He looks behind him and, once again, when no one emerges,
'Why are you running away?' he cries. His words come ringing
back. His body freezes. Deceived by his voice's reflection,
the youth calls out yet again, 'This way! We must come together.'
Echo with rapturous joy responds, 'We must come together!'
To prove her words, she burst in excitement out of the forest,
arms outstretched to fling them around the shoulders she yearned for.
Shrinking in horror, he yelled, 'Hands off! May I die before
you enjoy my body.' Her only reply was '... enjoy my body,'
Scorned and rejected, with burning cheeks, she fled to the forest
to hide her shame and live thenceforward in lonely caves.
But her love persisted and steadily grew with the pain of rejection.
Wretched and sleepless with anguish, she started to waste away.
Her skin grew dry and shrivelled, the lovely bloom of her flesh
lost all its moisture; nothing remained but voice and bones;
then only voice, for her bones (so they say) were transformed to stone.
Buried away in the forest, seen no more on the mountains,
heard all over the world, she survives in the sound of the echo.

Not only Echo, the other nymphs of the waves and mountains
incurred Narcissus' mockery; so did his male companions.
Finally one of his scorned admirers lifted his hands
to the heavens: 'I pray Narcissus may fall in love and never
obtain his desire!' His prayer was just and Némesis heard it.
  Picture a clear, unmuddied pool of silvery, shimmering
water. The shepherds have not been near it; the mountain-goats
and cattle have not come down to drink there; its surface has never
been ruffled by bird or beast or branch from a rotting cypress.
Imagine a ring of grass, well-watered and lush, and a circle
of trees for cooling shade in the burning summer sunshine.
Here Narcissus arrived, all hot and exhausted from hunting,
and sank to the ground. The place looked pleasant, and here was a spring!
Thirsty for water, he started to drink, but soon grew thirsty
for something else. His being was suddenly overwhelmed

by a vision of beauty. He fell in love with an empty hope,
a shadow mistaken for substance. He gazed at himself in amazement,
limbs and expression as still as a statue of Párian marble.
Stretched on the grass, he saw twin stars, his own two eyes,
rippling curls like the locks of a god, Apollo or Bacchus,
cheeks as smooth as silk, an ivory neck and a glorious
face with a mixture of blushing red and a creamy whiteness.
All that his lovers adored he worshipped in self-adoration.
Blindly rapt with desire for himself, he was votary and idol,
suitor and sweetheart, taper and fire – at one and the same time.
Those beautiful lips would implore a kiss, but as he bent forward
the pool would always betray him. He plunges his arms in the water
to clasp that ivory neck and finds himself clutching at no one.
He knows not what he is seeing; the sight still fires him with passion.
His eyes are deceived, but the strange illusion excites his senses.
Trusting fool, how futile to woo a fleeting phantom!
You'll never grasp it. Turn away and your love will have vanished.
The shape now haunting your sight is only a wraith, a reflection
consisting of nothing; there with you when you arrived, here now,
and there with you when you decide to go – if ever you can go!
   Nothing could drag him away from the place, not hunger for food
nor need for sleep. As he lay stretched out in the grassy shade,
he never could gaze his fill on that fraudulent image of beauty;
and gazing proved his demise. He raised his body a little,
then stretching his arms in grief to the witnessing trees all round him,
'Wise old trees,' he exclaimed, 'has anyone loved more cruelly?
Lovers have often kissed in secret under your branches.
Here you have stood for hundreds of years. In all that time
has anyone suffered for love like me? Whom can you remember?
I've looked and have longed. But looking and longing is far from enough.
I still have to find!' (His lover's delusion was overpowering.)
'My pain is the more since we're not divided by stretches of ocean,
unending roads, by mountains or walls with impassable gates.
All that keeps us apart is a thin, thin line of water.
He wants to be held in my arms. Whenever I move to kiss
the clear bright surface, his upturned face strains closer to mine.
We all but touch! The paltriest barrier thwarts our pleasure.
Come out to me here, whoever you are! Why keep eluding me,
peerless boy? When I seek you, where do you steal away?
It can't be my looks or my age which makes you want to avoid me;
even the nymphs have longed to possess me!... Your looks of affection
offer a grain of hope. When my arms reach out to embrace you,
you reach out too. I smile at you, and you smile at me back.
I weep and your tears flow fast. You nod when I show my approval.
When I read those exquisite lips, I can watch them gently repeating
my words – but I never can *hear* you repeat them!.....
I know you now and I know myself. Yes, I am the cause

of the fire inside me, the fuel that burns and the flame that lights it.
What can I do? Must I woo or be wooed? What else can I plead for?
All I desire I have. My wealth has left me a pauper.
Oh, how I wish that I and my body could now be parted,
I wish my love were not here! — a curious prayer for a lover.
Now my sorrow is sapping my strength. My life is almost
over. Its candle is guttering out in the prime of my manhood.
Death will be easy to bear, since dying will cure my heartache.
Better indeed if the one I love could have lived for longer,
but now, two soulmates in one, we shall face our ending together.'

    With that he turned distractedly back to his own reflection;
his tears were troubling the limpid waters and blurring the picture
that showed in the ruffled pool. When he saw it fast disappearing,
'Don't hurry away, please stay! You cannot desert me so cruelly.
I love you!' he shouted. 'Please, if I'm not able to touch you,
I must be allowed to see you, to feed my unhappy passion!'
In wild distress he ripped the top of his tunic aside
and bared his breast to the blows he rained with his milk-white hand.
His fist brought up a crimson weal on his naked torso,
like apples tinted both white and red, or a multi-coloured
cluster of grapes just ripening into a blushing purple.
Once the water had cleared again and he saw what his hand
had done, the boy could bear it no longer. As yellow wax
melts in a gentle flame, or the frost on a winter morning
thaws in the rays of the sunshine, so Narcissus faded
away and melted, slowly consumed by the fire inside him.
His face had lost that wonderful blend of red and whiteness,
gone was the physical vigour and all he had looked at and longed for,
broken the godlike frame which once poor Echo had worshipped.

    Echo had watched his decline, still filled with angry resentment
but moved to pity. Whenever the poor unhappy youth
uttered a pitiful sigh, her own voice uttered a pitiful
sigh in return. When he beat with his hand on his shoulders, she also
mimicked the sound of the blows. His final words, as he gazed
once more in the pool, rang back from the rocks: 'Oh marvellous boy,
I loved you in vain!' Then he said, 'Farewell.' 'Farewell,' said Echo.
He rested his weary head in the fresh green grass, till Death's hand
gently closed his eyes still rapt with their master's beauty.
Even then, as he crossed the Styx to ghostly Hades,
he gazed at himself in the river. At once his sister naiads
beat their breasts and cut their tresses in mourning tribute;
the dryads wailed their lament; and Echo re-echoed their wailing.
A pyre was raised, the bier made ready, the funeral torches
brandished on high. The body, however, was not to be found –
only a flower with a trumpet of gold and pale white petals.

DIANA & ACTAEON

Metamorphoses, Book III

Ovid

Translated by David Raeburn, 2004

Actaeon, a grandson of King Cadmus of Thebes, has enjoyed a day's hunting when he stumbles upon an unexpected sight. What happens to him next, **Ovid** assures us, is not his fault: '...you'll find that chance/ was the culprit./ No crime was committed. Why punish a man for a pure/ mistake?' The artist Titian transformed Ovid's story into a pair of exquisite narrative paintings for King Philip II of Spain in the mid-sixteenth century.

Picture a mountain stained with the carnage of hounded beasts.
It was now midday, the hour when the shadows draw to their shortest;
the sun god's chariot was halfway over from east to west.
A band of huntsmen was strolling along through the pathless glades,
when their leader, the young Actaeon, calmly made an announcement:
'Comrades, our nets are soaked, our spears are drenched in our quarry's
blood. Our luck is enough for today. When the goddess Aurora
appears tomorrow and shows the gleam of her rosy wheels,
let us all return to the chase. Now Phoebus is halfway over
from east to west and cutting the fields with his burning rays.
Leave off what you're doing and stow your knotted nets for the moment.'
The men did just as he told them and took a break from their hunting.
Now picture a valley, dense with pine and tapering cypress,
called Gargáphië, sacred haunt of the huntress Diana;
there, in a secret corner, a cave surrounded by woodland,
owing nothing to human artifice. Nature had used
her talent to imitate art: she had moulded the living rock
of porous tufa to form the shape of a rugged arch.
To the right, a babbling spring with a thin translucent rivulet
widening into a pool ringed round by a grassy clearing.
Here the goddess who guards the woods, when weary with hunting,
would come to bathe her virginal limbs in the clear, clean water.
On this occasion she made her entrance and handed her javelin,
quiver and slackened bow to the chosen nymph who carried
her weapons. Another put out her arms to receive her dress
as she stripped it off. Two more were removing her boots, while Crócale,

more of an expert, gathered the locks that were billowing over
her mistress' neck in a knot, though her own stayed floating and free.
Néphele, Hýale, Rhamis, Psecas and Phíale charged
their capacious urns with water and stood all ready to pour it.
And while the virgin goddess was taking her bath in her usual
pool, as fate would have it, Actaeon, Cadmus' grandson,
wandered into the glade. His hunting could wait, he thought,
as he sauntered aimlessly through the unfamiliar woodland.
Imagine the scene as he entered: the grotto, the splashing fountains,
the group of nymphs in the nude. At once, at the sight of a man,
they struck their bosoms in horror, their sudden screams re-echoing
through the encircling woods. They clustered around Diana
to form a screen with their bodies, but sadly the goddess was taller;
her neck and shoulders were visible over the heads of her maidens.
Think of the crimson glow on the clouds when struck by the rays
of the setting sun; or think of the rosy-fingered dawn;
such was the blush on the face of Diana observed quite naked.
Although her companion nymphs had formed a barrier round her,
she stood with her front turned sideways and looked at the rash intruder
over her shoulder. She wished that her arrows were ready to hand,
but used what she could, caught up some water and threw it into
the face of the man. As she splashed his hair with revengeful drops,
she spoke the spine-chilling words which warned of impending disaster:
'Now you may tell the story of seeing Diana naked –
If story-telling is in your power!' No more was needed.
The head she had sprinkled sprouted the horns of a lusty stag;
the neck expanded, the ears were narrowed to pointed tips;
she changed his hands into hooves and his arms into long and slender
forelegs; she covered his frame in a pelt of dappled buckskin;
last, she injected panic. The son of Autónoë bolted,
surprising himself with his speed as he bounded away from the clearing.
But when he came to a pool and set eyes on his head and antlers,
'Oh, dear god!' he was going to say; but no words followed.
All the sound he produced was a moan, as the tears streamed over
his strange new face. It was only his feelings that stayed unchanged.
What could he do? Make tracks for his home in the royal palace?
Or hide in the woodlands? Each was precluded by shame or fear.

  He wavered in fearful doubt. And then his dogs caught sight of him.
First to sound on the trail were Blackfoot and sharp-nosed Tracker –
Tracker of Cretan breed and Blackfoot a Spartan pointer.
Others came bounding behind them, fast as the gusts of the storm wind:
Ravenous, Mountain-Ranger, Gazelle, his Arcadian deerhounds;
powerful Fawnkiller, Hunter the fierce, and violent Hurricane;
Wingdog, fleetest of foot, and Chaser, the keenest-scented;
savage Sylvan, lately gashed by the tusks of a wild boar;
Glen who was dropped from a wolf at birth, and the bitch who gathers
the flocks in, Shepherdess; Harpy, flanked by her two young puppies;

River, the dog from Sícyon, sides all taut and contracted;
Racer and Gnasher; Spot, with Tigress and muscular Valour;
Sheen with a snow-white coat and murky Soot with a pitch-black;
Spartan, wiry and tough; then Whirlwind, powerful pursuer;
Swift, and Wolfcub racing along with her Cypriot brother;
Grabber, who sported an ivory patch midway on his ebony
forehead; Sable, and Shag with a coat like a tangled thicket;
two mongrel hounds from a Cretan sire and Lacónian dam,
Rumpus and Whitefang; Yelper, whose howls could damage the eardrums –
and others too many to mention. Spoiling all for their quarry,
over crag, over cliff, over rocks which appeared to allow no approach,
where access was hard and where there was none, the whole pack followed.
      Actaeon fled where so many times he had been the pursuer.
He fled from the dogs who had served him so faithfully, longing to shout
          to them,
'Stop! It is I, Actaeon, your master. Do you not know me?'
But the words would not come. The air was filled with relentless baying.
Blacklock first inserted his teeth to tear at his back;
Beast-killer next; then Mountain-Boy latched on to his shoulder.
These had started out later but stolen a march by taking
a short cut over the ridge. As they pinned their master down,
the rest of the pack rushed round and buried their fangs in his body,
until it was covered with crimson wounds. Actaeon groaned
in a sound that was scarcely human but one no stag could ever
have made, as he filled the familiar hills with his cries of anguish.
Then bending his legs like a cringing beggar, he gazed all round
with his silently pleading eyes, as if they were outstretched arms.
      What of his friends? In ignorant zeal they encouraged the wild pack
on with the usual halloos. They scanned the woods for their leader,
shouting, 'Actaeon! Actaeon!', as if he were far away,
though he moved his head in response to his name.
        'Why aren't you here,
you indolent man, to enjoy the sight of this heaven-sent prize?'
If only he'd not been there! But he was. He would dearly have loved
to watch, instead of enduring, his own dogs' vicious performance.
Crowding around him, they buried their noses inside his flesh
and mangled to pieces the counterfeit stag who embodied their master.
Only after his life was destroyed in a welter of wounds
is Diana, the goddess of hunting, said to have cooled her anger.

PYGMALION

Metamorphoses, Book X

Ovid

Translated by Ted Hughes, 1997

The sculptor Pygmalion, sickened by the immorality of some of the
women he has seen, resolves to carve his own out of ivory. He soon falls in
love with her. This story from **Ovid**'s *Metamorphoses* is sung by Orpheus
(see Story 63). There are obvious parallels with the ancient myth of
Pandora (see Story 9). The Pygmalion myth has also had a busy afterlife,
inspiring a significant handful of operas, and informing works as diverse
as Mary Shelley's novel *Frankenstein* (1818) and George Bernard Shaw's
eponymous play (1912), which was later re-adapted as the musical *My
Fair Lady* (1956). Ted Hughes's translation is splendidly visual and very
much in Ovid's spirit.

If you could ask the region of Amathis
Where the mines are so rich
Whether it had wanted those women
The Propoetides,
You would be laughed at, as if you had asked
Whether it had wanted those men
Whose horned heads earned them the name Cerastae.

An altar to Zeus,
God of hospitality, stood at the doors
Of the Cerastae, soaked –
A stranger would assume – with the blood
Of the humbly sacrificed
Suckling calves and new lambs of Amathis.
Wrong. They butchered their guests.

Venus was so revolted to see offered
Such desecrated fare
She vowed to desert Ophiusa
And her favoured cities.
But she paused: 'The cities,' she reasoned,

'And the places I love –
What crime have these innocents committed?

'Why should I punish all
For a few? Let me pick out the guilty
And banish or kill them –
Or sentence them to some fate not quite either
But a dire part of both.
The fate for such, I think, is to become
Some vile thing not themselves.'

The horns of the Cerastae suggested
One quick solution for all –
Those men became bullocks. As for the others,
The Propoetides –
Fools who denied Venus divinity –
She stripped off their good names
And their undergarments, and made them whores.

As those women hardened,
Dulled by shame, delighting to make oaths
Before the gods in heaven
Of their every lie, their features hardened
Like their hearts. Soon they shrank
To the split-off, heartless, treacherous hardness
Of sharp shards of flint.

The spectacle of these cursed women sent
Pygmalion the sculptor slightly mad.
He adored woman, but he saw
The wickedness of these particular women
Transform, as by some occult connection,
Every woman's uterus to a spider.
Her face, voice, gestures, hair became its web.
Her perfume was a floating horror. Her glance
Left a spider-bite. He couldn't control it.

So he lived
In the solitary confinement
Of a phobia,
Shunning living women, wifeless.
Yet he still dreamed of woman.
He dreamed
Unbrokenly awake as asleep
The perfect body of a perfect woman –
Though this dream

Was not so much the dream of a perfect woman
As a spectre, sick of unbeing,
That had taken possession of his body
To find herself a life.

She moved into his hands,
She took possession of his fingers
And began to sculpt a perfect woman.
So he watched his hands shaping a woman
As if he were still asleep. Until
Life-size, ivory, as if alive
Her perfect figure lay in his studio.

So he had made a woman
Lovelier than any living woman.
And when he gazed at her
As if coming awake he fell in love.

His own art amazed him, she was so real.
She might have moved, he thought,
Only her modesty
Her sole garment – invisible,
Woven from the fabric of his dream –
Held her as if slightly ashamed
Of stepping into life.

Then his love
For this woman so palpably a woman
Became his life.

Incessantly now
He caressed her,
Searching for the warmth of living flesh,
His finger-tip whorls filtering out
Every feel of mere ivory.

He kissed her, closing his eyes
To divine an answering kiss of life
In her perfect lips.
And he would not believe
They were after all only ivory.

He spoke to her, he stroked her
Lightly to feel her living aura
Soft as down over her whiteness.
His fingers gripped her hard

To feel flesh yield under the pressure
That half wanted to bruise her
Into a proof of life, and half did not
Want to hurt or mar or least of all
Find her the solid ivory he had made her.

He flattered her.
He brought her love-gifts, knick-knacks,
Speckled shells, gem pebbles,
Little rainbow birds in pretty cages,
Flowers, pendants, drops of amber.
He dressed her
In the fashion of the moment,
Set costly rings on her gold fingers,
Hung pearls in her ears, coiled ropes of pearl
To drape her ivory breasts.

Did any of all this add to her beauty?
Gazing at her adorned, his head ached.
But then he stripped everything off her
And his brain swam, his eyes
Dazzled to contemplate
The greater beauty of her naked beauty.

He laid her on his couch,
Bedded her in pillows
And soft sumptuous weaves of Tyrian purple
As if she might delight in the luxury.
Then, lying beside her, he embraced her
And whispered in her ear every endearment.

The day came
For the festival of Venus – an uproar
Of processions through all Cyprus.
Snowy heifers, horns gilded, kneeled
Under the axe, at the altars.

Pygmalion had completed his offerings.
And now he prayed, watching the smoke
Of the incense hump shapelessly upwards.
He hardly dared to think
What he truly wanted
As he formed the words: 'O Venus,
You gods have power
To give whatever you please. O Venus
Send me a wife. And let her resemble –'

He was afraid
To ask for his ivory woman's very self –
'Let her resemble
The woman I have carved in ivory.'

Venus was listening
To a million murmurs over the whole island.
She swirled in the uplift of incense
Like a great fish suddenly bulging
into a tide-freshened pool.
She heard every word
Pygmalion had not dared to pronounce.

She came near. She poised above him –
And the altar fires drank her assent
Like a richer fuel.
They flared up, three times,
Tossing horns of flame.

Pygmalion hurried away home
To his ivory obsession. He burst in,
Fevered with deprivation,
Fell on her, embraced her, and kissed her
Like one collapsing in a desert
To drink at a dribble from a rock.

But his hand sprang off her breast
As if stung.
He lowered it again, incredulous
At the softness, the warmth
Under his fingers. Warm
And soft as warm soft wax –
But alive
With the elastic of life.

He knew
Giddy as he was with longing and prayers
This must be hallucination.
He jerked himself back to his senses
And prodded the ivory. He squeezed it.
But it was no longer ivory.
Her pulse throbbed under his thumb.
Then Pygmalion's legs gave beneath him.
On his knees
He sobbed his thanks to Venus. And there
Pressed his lips

On lips that were alive.
She woke to his kisses and blushed
To find herself kissing
One who kissed her,
And opened her eyes for the first time
To the light and her lover together.

Venus blessed the wedding
That she had so artfully arranged.
And after nine moons Pygmalion's bride
Bore the child, Paphos,
Who gave his name to the whole island.

OVID'S DEFENCE

Tristia, Book I

Ovid

Translated by A. D. Melville, 1992

In AD 8, Emperor Augustus exiled **Ovid** to Tomis (modern Constanţa, in Romania) on the shores of the Black Sea for reasons which are now unclear. The poet blamed his miserable fate on *carmen et error* – 'a poem and a mistake'. The poem was his *Ars Amatoria*, a scandalous guide to love and love-making. Augustus had embarked upon a moral crusade against adultery in Rome, and Ovid's text did not sit well with the legislation passed to revive old-fashioned values. Ovid here embarks upon his journey and pens a heart-breaking self-defence, which forms part of a longer work of *Tristia* ('sad poems'). Whatever 'mistake' Ovid made, it was not forgiven, for he died in exile in AD 17 or 18.

I do not plough the main in greed for endless
    Riches and trade, my wares from shore to shore,
Nor, as in student days, do I seek Athens
    And Asian towns and places seen before.

Nor do I sail to Alexander's city
    To see the merry Nile's delightful strand.
Why I want easy winds—who would believe it?—
    Is that my sails shall reach Sarmatia's land.

To reach the Black, unlucky, Sea I've made my
    Vows—and complain my flight from home's so slow!
I pray my journey's short—to see Tomitans!
    Where in the world that place is, I don't know.

If you gods love me, quell these ghastly billows,
    Bless my poor ship, and keep the waters flat.
Or if you hate me, steer me where I'm ordered,
    Part of my punishment's the place I'm at.

Drive my ship, you swift winds—*here* I've no business—
    Why do my sails hanker for Italy?

Caesar forbids. Whom he expels, don't hamper;
    My face the Black Sea now must surely see.

Those orders—I deserve them. Crimes that Caesar
    Condemned I don't deem proper to deny.
But if gods aren't deceived by human actions,
    You know my fault is free from villainy.

And, if you know, if a mistake has wrecked me,
    If I was foolish, never criminal,
If I accepted Caesar's public edicts
    And backed his house as is allowed to all,

If, in his rule, I sang good times and offered
    Incense to Caesar and his family,
If that was my true mind; ye Gods, have mercy!
    If not, may I be sunk in the deep sea!

Am I deceived or is the cloudbank thinning,
    The ocean changing and its anger laid?
This is no chance. You, called to hear my pledges,
    Who can't be duped, are coming to my aid.

[...]

When in my thoughts that tragic night is pictured
    Which in the City formed my final hour,
That night on which I left so much I treasured,
    Now once again from my sad eyes tears shower.

The dawn was near on which by Caesar's order
    From Italy's last bounds I must depart.
No more delay! My mind was numb: for proper
    Arrangements I had neither time nor heart.

No thought of choosing slaves or a companion,
    No kit or clothes an exile ought to wear.
I was as stunned as someone struck by lightning,
    Who lives, yet of his life is unaware.

But when my pain itself cleared my mind's stormcloud,
    And senses in the end some strength regained,
I spoke to my sad friends last words of parting:
    So many once—now one or two remained.

I was in tears. My wife, in tears more bitter,
    Held me, her blameless sheets wet endlessly.

My daughter, far away on shores of Libya,
    Could not be told the fate befallen me.

Look where you might, it seemed a noisy funeral;
    You heard the sounds of grief and sorrow swell
Inside the house, with tears in every corner,
    As men and women grieved, and slaves as well
If great events may be compared with little,
    Troy had the same appearance when she fell.

The voices now of men and dogs were quiet,
    And through the night the moon was riding high.
Gazing at her and by her light discerning
    The Capitol (my home in vain hard by),

'Ye Powers', I said, 'whose dwellings are my neighbours,
    Ye shrines that now my eyes must never see,
And gods, whom I must leave, of Rome's tall city,
    Take for all time this last farewell from me;

'And though I take my shield too late and wounded,
    Yet free from hatred this my banishment,
And tell that man divine what error duped me,
    That, my fault deemed no crime, he may relent,
And what *you* know my punisher may know too;
    If his godhead's appeased, I'll be content.'

I made that prayer to gods above; my wife made
    Adore, but her sobs cut short the words she said.
She even lay before the hearth, hair flowing;
    Her trembling lips touched embers cold and dead.
She poured her words to Household Gods unhearing;
    No help to him for whom her tears were shed.

The hasting night allowed no time to linger;
    Around the Northern pole the Wain had rolled.
What could I do? I loved my country dearly,
    But that night was my last—go, I was told.

How often I said when someone tried to hurry me,
    Why rush? Think whence and where you're hastening.
How often I said, quite falsely, I had fixed on
    The time convenient for travelling.

Thrice I was on the doorstep, thrice was called back;
    In kindness to my thoughts my *feet* were slow.

Often 'Goodbye', and then again much talking
   And kisses given as if I meant to go.

Often I gave the same instructions, fooling
   Myself, and on my dear ones turned my gaze.
'Why haste?', I said, 'it's Scythia I'm sent to,
   Rome I must leave—both reasons for delays.

'I live, my wife lives, barred from me for ever,
   My home and household too, so loyal to me,
And my companions whom I loved as brothers,
   Hearts bound to me with Theseus' loyalty.
I'll hug while I still may; perhaps I may not
   Ever more. Each hour I'm granted gain will be.'

No lingering! I left my words unfinished
   And in my arms held everything most dear.
While our tears fell, bright in the sky had risen
   The Morning Star, that star to me so drear.

Sundered I was, as if my body'd lost its
   Limbs and I left behind a part of me.
Such was the pain of Mettus when the horses
   Were driven apart to avenge his treachery.

Ah, then arose my dear ones' lamentations
   And on bare breasts fell many a sad blow.
Ah, then, as I was leaving, my wife hugged me
   And mingled with my tears her words of woe:

'We can't be parted. We shall go together:
   An exiled wife, I'll share an exile's fate.
Mine too's the way: there's room for me at the world's end;
   To your ship in its flight I'll add small freight.

'You Caesar's wrath compels to leave our country,
   Me, love. For me that love shall Caesar be.'
She tried, as she had tried before, and hardly
   Surrendered, yielding to expediency.

I left, more like a corpse without a funeral,
   Bedraggled, cheeks unshaven, hanging hair.
She, mad with grief I'm told, and almost lifeless
   Slumped where she was, her mind in darkness there.

And when she rose, the shameful dust befouling
   Her tresses, from the cold ground where she lay,

She mourned herself, mourned Household Gods deserted,
    Called often on her husband snatched away,
Groaning as if she'd seen me and my daughter's
    Corpses upon a pyre prepared that day.

She longed for death to end the pain of evil,
    But, in her care for me, death could not be.
Long may she live, and since Fate thus has borne me
    Afar, may her life ever succour me.

THE TOWN AND THE COUNTRY MOUSE

Satires, II.6

Horace

Translated by Philip Francis, 1746

The poet **Horace** (65–8 BC) divided his time between Rome, where life was always busy, and his idyllic country home beyond the city. His poem begins as a thanksgiving for his modest 'Sabine' farm and the generosity of his patron Maecenas. It then becomes a vivid retelling of the famous Aesopic fable of the town and the country mouse. The eighteenth-century writer, critic and lexicographer Samuel Johnson was full of admiration for his contemporary Philip Francis as a translator of Horace. 'The lyrical part of Horace', he wrote, 'can never be perfectly translated; so much of the excellence is in the numbers and the expression. Francis has done it the best; I'll take his, five out of six, against them all'.

> I often wish'd I had a farm,
> A decent dwelling snug and warm,
> A garden, and a spring as pure
> As crystal running by my door,
> Besides a little ancient grove,
> Where at my leisure I might rove.
>   The gracious gods, to crown my bliss,
> Have granted this, and more than this;
> I have enough in my possessing;
> 'Tis well: I ask no greater blessing,
> O Hermes! than remote from strife
> To have and hold them for my life.
>   If I was never known to raise
> My fortune by dishonest ways,
> Nor, like the spendthrifts of the times,
> Shall ever sink it by my crimes:
> If thus I neither pray nor ponder—
> Oh! might I have that angle yonder,
> Which disproportions now my field,
> What satisfaction it would yield!

O that some lucky chance but threw
A pot of silver in my view,
As lately to the man, who bought
The very land in which he wrought!
If I am pleas'd with my condition,
O hear, and grant this last petition:
Indulgent, let my cattle batten,
Let all things, but my fancy, fatten,
And thou continue still to guard,
As thou art wont, thy suppliant bard.

    Whenever therefore I retreat
From Rome into my Sabine seat,
By mountains fenc'd on either side,
And in my castle fortified,
What can I write with greater pleasure,
Than satires in familiar measure?
Nor mad ambition there destroys,
Nor sickly wind my health annoys;
Nor noxious autumn gives me pain,
The ruthless undertaker's gain.

    Whatever title please thine ear,
Father of morning, Janus, hear,
Since mortal men, by heaven's decree,
Commence their toils, imploring thee,
Director of the busy throng,
Be thou the prelude of my song.

    At Rome, you press me: "Without fail
A friend expects you for his bail;
Be nimble to perform your part,
Lest any rival get the start.
Though rapid Boreas sweep the ground,
Or winter in a narrower round
Contract the day, through storm and snow,
At all adventures you must go."

    When bound beyond equivocation,
Or any mental reservation,
By all the ties of legal traps,
And to my ruin, too, perhaps,
I still must bustle through the crowd,
And press the tardy; when aloud
A foul-mouth'd fellow reimburses
This usage with a peal of curses.
"What madness hath possess'd thy pate
To justle folk at such a rate,
When puffing through the streets you scour
To meet Maecenas at an hour?"

    This pleases me, to tell the truth,

And is as honey to my tooth.
Yet when I reach th' Esquilian Hill
(That deathful scene, and gloomy still),
A thousand busy cares surround me,
Distract my senses, and confound me.
"Roscius entreated you to meet
At court to-morrow before eight—
The secretaries have implor'd
Your presence at their council-board—
Pray, take this patent, and prevail
Upon your friend to fix the seal—"
Sir, I shall try—replies the man,
More urgent, "If you please you can—"

'Tis more than seven years complete,
It hardly wants a month of eight,
Since great Maecenas' favour grac'd me,
Since first among his friends he plac'd me,
Sometimes to carry in his chair,
A mile or two, to take the air,
And might intrust with idle chat,
Discoursing upon this or that,
As in a free familiar way,
"How, tell me, Horace, goes the day?
Think you the Thracian can engage
The Syrian Hector of the stage?
This morning air is very bad
For folks who are but thinly clad."

Our conversation chiefly dwells
On these, and such like bagatelles,
As might the veriest prattler hear,
Or be repos'd in leaky ear.
Yet every day, and every hour,
I'm more enslav'd to envy's power.
"Our son of fortune (with a pox)
Sate with Maecenas in the box,
Just by the stage: you might remark,
They play'd together in the park."

Should any rumour, without head
Or tail, about the streets be spread,
Whoever meets me gravely nods,
And says, "As you approach the gods,
It is no mystery to you,
What do the Dacians mean to do?"
Indeed I know not—"How you joke,
And love to sneer at simple folk!"
Then vengeance seize this head of mine,
If I have heard or can divine—

"Yet, prithee, where are Caesar's bands
Allotted their debenture-lands?"
Although I swear I know no more
Of that than what they ask'd before,
They stand amaz'd, and think me grown
The closest mortal ever known.
    Thus, in this giddy, busy maze
I lose the sun-shine of my days,
And oft with fervent wish repeat—
"When shall I see my sweet retreat?
Oh! when with books of sages deep,
Sequester'd ease, and gentle sleep,
In sweet oblivion, blissful balm!
The busy cares of life becalm?
Oh! when shall I enrich my veins,
Spite of Pythagoras, with beans?
Or live luxurious in my cottage,
On bacon ham and savoury pottage?
O joyous nights! delicious feasts!
At which the gods might be my guests."
My friends and I regal'd, my slaves
Enjoy what their rich master leaves.
There every guest may drink and fill,
As much, or little, as he will,
Exempted from the bedlam-rules
Or roaring prodigals and fools:
Whether, in merry mood or whim,
He fills his bumper to the brim,
Or, better pleas'd to let it pass.
Grows mellow with a moderate glass.
    Nor this man's house, nor that's estate,
Becomes the subject of debate;
Nor whether Lepos, the buffoon,
Can dance, or not, a rigadoon;
But what concerns us more, I trow,
And were a scandal not to know;
Whether our bliss consist in store
Of riches, or in virtue's lore:
Whether esteem, or private ends,
Should guide us in the choice of friends:
Or what, if rightly understood,
Man's real bliss, and sovereign good.
    While thus we spend the social night,
Still mixing profit with delight,
My neighbour Cervius never fails
To club his part in pithy tales:
Suppose, Arellius, one should praise

Your anxious opulence: he says—
   A country mouse, as authors tell,
Of old invited to his cell
A city mouse, and with his best
Would entertain the courtly guest.
Thrifty he was, and full of cares
To make the most of his affairs,
Yet in the midst of his frugality
Would give a loose to hospitality.
In short, he goes, and freely fetches
Whole ears of hoarded oats, and vetches;
Dry grapes and raisins cross his chaps,
And dainty bacon, but in scraps,
If delicacies could invite
My squeamish courtier's appetite,
Who turn'd his nose at every dish,
And saucy piddled, with a—Pish!
   The master of the house, reclin'd
On downy chaff, more temperate din'd
On wheat, and darnel from a manger,
And left the dainties for the stranger.
   The cit, displeas'd at his repast,
Address'd our simple host at last:
"My friend, what pleasure can you find,
To live this mountain's back behind?
Would you prefer the town and men,
To this wild wood, and dreary den,
No longer, moping, loiter here,
But go with me to better cheer.
   "Since animals but draw their breath,
And have no being after death;
Since nor the little, nor the great.
Can shun the rigour of their fate;
At least be merry while you may,
The life of mice is but a day:
Come then, my friend, to pleasure give
The little life you have to live."
Encourag'd thus, the country mouse,
Transported, sallies from his house:
They both set out, in hopes to crawl
At night beneath the city wall;
And now the night, elaps'd eleven,
Possess'd the middle space of heaven,
When in a rich and splendid dome
They stopp'd, and found themselves at home,
Where ivory couches, overspread
With Tyrian carpets, glowing, fed

The dazzled eye. To lure the taste,
The fragments of a costly feast,
Remaining, drest but yesterday,
In baskets, pil'd on baskets, lay.

 The courtier on a purple seat
Had plac'd his rustic friend in state,
Then bustled, like a busy host,
Supplying dishes boil'd and roast,
Nor yet omits the courtier's duty
Of tasting, ere he brings the booty.

 The country-mouse, with rapture strange,
Rejoices in his fair exchange,
And lolling, like an easy guest,
Enjoys the cheer, and cracks his jest—
When, on a sudden, opening gates,
Loud-jarring, shook them from their seats.

 They ran, affrighted, through the room,
And, apprehensive of their doom,
Now trembled more and more; when, hark!
The mastiff-dogs began to bark;
The dome, to raise the tumult more,
Resounded to the surly roar.

 The bumpkin then concludes, Adieu!
This life, perhaps, agrees with you:
My grove, and cave, secure from snares,
Shall comfort me with chaff and tares.

THE EMPEROR'S SLAVE

Aesop's Fables

Phaedrus

Translated by Laura Gibbs, 2002

Phaedrus is said to have been a former slave and tutor in the imperial household at Rome. In the first century AD he set about translating Aesop's fables into Latin verse and gathering them into collections. This is one of his own tales. Set in Misenum, in the Bay of Naples, it describes the condition of slavery in the time of Tiberius, who was Roman emperor from AD 14 to 37. Roman slaves aspired to 'manumission' or freedom, the literal meaning of manumission being 'sending forth from the hand', from the Latin words *manus*, 'hand' and *mittere*, 'to send', which they were granted to the accompaniment of a customary slap from their master.

There is a whole imputation of busybodies at Rome running all over the place excitedly, occupied without any true occupation huffing and puffing at frivolous pursuits, and making much out of nothing. They are an annoyance to each other and utterly despised by everyone else. Yet I would like to try to correct this crowd, if possible, by means of a true story: it is one worth listening to.

Tiberius Caesar was on his way to Naples, and had arrived at his estate in Misenum which had been built by Lucullus* on a high hill overlooking the Sicilian sea on one side and the Tuscan sea on the other. When Caesar was walking about in the cheerful greenery, one of his household stewards turned up, dressed in a fancy-fringed tunic of Egyptian cotton hanging down from his shoulders. The man began to sprinkle the sizzling hot ground with water from a wooden basin, making a great show of his diligence as Caesar's attendant, but everyone just laughed at him. The man then ran ahead to the next walkway, using some shortcuts known only to himself, and he started settling the dust in that spot as well. When Caesar recognized the man and realized what he was doing, he said, 'Hey you!' The man scampered up to Caesar, excited at the joyful prospect of what seemed a sure reward. Then Caesar's majestic person made the

---

* *Lucullus was a general in the first century BC who was notorious for his luxurious lifestyle and fishponds.*

following joke: 'You have not accomplished much and your efforts have come to naught; if you want me to give you the slap that makes you a freedman, it will cost you much more than that!'

THE RICHES OF CALIGULA

Life of Caligula

Suetonius

Translated by Robert Graves, 1957

Robert Graves may be best known for *I, Claudius*, his tremendous novel of 1934, but he was also a keen-eyed translator of classical texts. The following extract comes from his translation of **Suetonius'** (*c*. AD 69–*c*. 122) biography of Claudius' nephew and predecessor, Caligula. Emperor from AD 37 until his assassination in AD 41, Caligula was renowned for his excesses, which frequently defy belief. Suetonius' celebrated *Lives of the Caesars*, which date to the early second century AD, often seem to blur the line between reality and fiction. It is for each of us to decide how much of what Suetonius wrote is true.

No parallel can be found for Caligula's far-fetched extravagances. He invented new kinds of baths, and the most unnatural dishes and drinks—bathing in hot and cold perfumes, drinking valuable pearls dissolved in vinegar, and providing his guests with golden bread and golden meat; and would remark that Caesar alone could not afford to be frugal. For several days in succession he scattered largesse from the roof of the Julian Basilica; and built Liburnian galleys, with ten banks of oars, jewelled poops, multi-coloured sails, and with huge baths, colonnades and banqueting halls aboard—not to mention growing vines and apple-trees of different varieties. In these vessels he used to take early-morning cruises along the Campanian coast, reclining on his couch and listening to songs and choruses. Villas and country-houses were run up for him regardless of expense—in fact, Caligula seemed interested only in doing the apparently impossible—which led him to construct moles in deep, rough water far out to sea, drive tunnels through exceptionally hard rocks, raise flat ground to the height of mountains, and reduce mountains to the level of plains; and all at immense speed, because he punished delay with death. But why give details? Suffice it to record that, in less than a year he squandered Tiberius's entire fortune of 27 million gold pieces, and an enormous amount of other treasure besides.

When bankrupt and in need of funds, Caligula concentrated on wickedly ingenious methods of raising funds by false accusations, auctions, and taxes.

He ruled that no man could inherit the Roman citizenship acquired by any ancestor more remote than his father; and when confronted with certificates of citizenship issued by Julius Caesar or Augustus, rejected them as obsolete. He also disallowed all property returns to which, for whatever reason, later additions had been appended. If a leading centurion had bequeathed nothing either to Tiberius or himself since the beginning of the former's reign, he would rescind the will on the ground of ingratitude; and voided those of all other persons who were said to have intended making him their heir when they died, but had not yet done so. This caused widespread alarm, and even people who did not know him personally would tell their friends or children that they had left him everything; but if they continued to live after the declaration he considered himself tricked, and sent several of them presents of poisoned sweetmeats. Caligula conducted these cases in person, first announcing the sum he meant to raise, and not stopping until he had raised it. The slightest delay nettled him, and he once passed a single sentence on a batch of more than forty men charged with various offences, and then boasted to Caesonia,* when she woke from her nap, that he had done very good business since she dozed off.

He would auction whatever properties were left over from a theatrical show; driving up the bidding to such heights that many of those present, forced to buy at fantastic prices, found themselves ruined and committed suicide by opening their veins. A famous occasion was when Aponius Saturninus fell asleep on a bench, and Caligula warned the auctioneer to keep an eye on the senator of praetorian rank who kept nodding his head. Before the bidding ended Aponius had unwittingly bought thirteen gladiators for a total of 90,000 gold pieces.

While in Gaul Caligula did so well by selling the furniture, jewellery, slaves, and even the freedmen of his condemned sisters at a ridiculous overvaluation that he decided to do the same with the furnishings of the Old Palace. So he sent to Rome, where his agents commandeered public Conveyances, and even draught animals from the bakeries, to fetch the stuff north; which led to a bread shortage in the City, and to the loss of many law-suits, because litigants who lived at a distance were unable to appear in court and meet their bail. He then used all kinds of tricks for disposing of the furniture; scolding the bidders for their avarice, or for their shamelessness in being richer than he was, and pretending grief at this surrender of family property to commoners. Discovering that one wealthy provincial had paid the Imperial secretariat 2,000 gold pieces to be smuggled into a banquet, Caligula was delighted that the privilege of dining with him should be valued so highly and, when next day the same man turned up at the auction, made him pay 2,000 gold pieces for some trifling object—but also sent him a personal invitation to dinner.

The publicans were ordered to raise new and unprecedented taxes, and found this so profitable that he detailed his Guards colonels and centurions to collect the money instead. No goods or services now avoided duty of some kind. He imposed a fixed tax on all foodstuffs sold in any quarter of the City, and a charge of 2½ per cent on the money involved in every lawsuit and legal transaction whatsoever; and devised special penalties for anyone who compounded or

* *Caesonia was Caligula's fourth and final wife.*

abandoned a case. Porters had to hand over an eighth part of their day's earnings and prostitutes their standard fee for a single act of intimacy—even if they had quitted their profession and were respectably married; pimps and ex-pimps also became liable to this public tax.

These new regulations having been announced by word of mouth only, many people failed to observe them, through ignorance. At last he acceded to the urgent popular demand, by posting the regulations up, but in an awkwardly cramped spot and written so small that no one could take a copy. He never missed a chance of making profits; setting aside a suite of Palace rooms, he decorated them worthily, opened a brothel, stocked it with married women and boys, and then sent his pages around the squares and public places, inviting all men, of whatever age, to come and enjoy themselves. Those who appeared were lent money at interest, and clerks wrote down their names under the heading 'Contributors to the Imperial Revenue'.

When Caligula played at dice he would always cheat and lie. Once he interrupted a game by giving up his seat to the man behind him and going out into the courtyard. A couple of rich knights passed; Caligula immediately had them arrested and confiscated their property; then resumed the game in high spirits, boasting that his luck had never been better.

His daughter's birth gave him an excuse for further complaints of poverty. 'In addition to the burden of sovereignty,' he said, 'I must now shoulder that of fatherhood'—and promptly took up a collection for her education and dowry. He also announced that New Year gifts would be welcomed on 1 January; and then sat in the Palace porch, grabbing the handfuls and capfuls of coin which a mixed crowd of all classes pressed on him. At last he developed a passion for the feel of money and, spilling heaps of gold pieces on an open space, would walk over them barefoot, or else lie down and wallow.

THE PUMPKINIFICATION OF EMPEROR CLAUDIUS

Apocolocyntosis

Attr. Seneca the Younger

Translated by Martha C. Nussbaum, 2010

In AD 54, Emperor Claudius died, allegedly after consuming some poisoned mushrooms. The question was, would he be deified after he died? The curious title of this satire, which was in all probability written by **Seneca the Younger** (4 BC–AD 65), is a play on the words for 'apotheosis' and 'gourd' or 'pumpkin'. The story is a parody of the Roman practice of deifying 'good' emperors. Claudius was physically disabled but an able ruler who granted Roman citizenship to many peoples overseas.

Claudius began to gasp for breath, but couldn't find the exit. Then Mercury, who had always been delighted by Claudius's wit, took one of the three Fates aside and said, "You horribly cruel woman! Why do you allow the poor man to be tortured? Won't you ever give him a rest from his long agony? It's been sixty-four years now that he's been wrestling with his life. Why do you hold a grudge against him and against the Republic? Let the astrologers be right for a change. They've been predicting his death every year—no, every month—ever since he became emperor. But still, it's no wonder if they make mistakes and nobody seems clear about his final hour. For nobody ever realized he was alive. Do what has to be done:

Give him to death: let the better king
Reign in the empty hall.

But Clotho replied, "By Hercules! I wanted to give him just a teensy bit more time, so that he could confer citizenship on the last remaining stragglers"—for he had decided to see all Greeks, Gauls, Spaniards, and Britons wearing the toga. "But since you like the idea of keeping some foreigners for breeding stock, and that's what you are insisting on, so be it." Then she opened a small box and brought out three spindles. One belonged to Augurinus, the second to Baba, the third to Claudius. "These three men," she said, "I shall decree to die in the same year, just a few minutes apart. I won't send him away without companions. For it is not right that a man who has been accustomed to seeing so many thousands follow him, precede him, and swarm around him should suddenly be left all alone. He will be satisfied with these pals in the meantime."

> So she spoke; and, spinning the thread of fate
> On a dirty spindle, snapped it, putting an end
> To his royal stupid life. But Lachesis,
> Sweeping her long hair up in a fancy knot,
> And crowning her brow with the Muses' own laurel,
> Pulls from the snow-white skein a shiny thread
> Of white wool, guiding it with happy hand.
> As she spins it out, it magically changes color.
> Her sisters stand amazed: common wool
> Has suddenly been changed to precious metal.
> On that lovely thread a Golden Age spins down.
> There is no end. Spinning the happy fleece
> They joyfully fill their hands. Work is sweet.
> The task goes rapidly, without effort.
> Easily the delicate thread winds round
> The whirling spindle. His years exceed those
> Of Nestor and Tithonus. Phoebus too
> Is there: he helps them on with singing,
> Happy about the times to come. With joy
> He now plucks the lyre, now helps the spinning.
> With his voice he enchants them, making their work easy.
> While they heap praise on their brother's lyre and singing
> They spin out more than was their custom. Praise
> Makes their work exceed the normal human life span.
> "Don't make it shorter, Fates," Apollo says.
> "Let him live beyond the span of mortal years,
> That man so similar to me in grace
> And beauty, and no less skilled at singing.
> He will give happy years to his weary people.
> He will break the long silence of the laws.
> As Lucifer scatters the stars in headlong flight,
> As Hesperus rises when they return at night,
> Or as, when blushing Dawn dissolves the shadows,
> Ushering in the day, Sun in his splendor
> Looks at the world, and speeds his chariot on
> From the starting gate: such a Caesar now
> Approaches. Such a Nero, now, all Rome
> Will gaze upon. His radiant face blazes
> With gentle brilliance; his lovely neck
> Displays the beauty of his flowing hair."

So said Apollo. But Lachesis, since she too had a weakness for such a good-looking man, indulged it lavishly and gave Nero many years from her store. As for Claudius, they told everyone

> With celebration and auspicious words
> To send him out the door.

And in fact he gushed out his life, and from that moment on he ceased to have even the appearance of being alive. (By the way, he died while he was listening to the comic actors, so you can see that it's not without reason that I'm afraid of them.) His last words heard among mortals—after he had let out a louder sound from that part with which he found it easier to communicate—were as follows: "Good heavens. I think I've shat myself." Well, I don't know about that, but he certainly shat up everything else.

It would be superfluous to report the subsequent events on earth. You know them very well, and there's no danger of losing sight of what public joy has impressed on people's memories. Nobody forgets what makes him happy. Listen now to the business transacted in heaven. My informant will be held responsible for the accuracy of this report.

A messenger came to Jupiter saying that a man had arrived, fairly tall with very white hair. He seemed to be making some kind of threat, for he kept shaking his head back and forth. His right foot dragged behind. The messenger said that he had asked him what country he came from. The man stammered something unintelligible; his voice shook and his speech was garbled. The messenger couldn't tell what language he was speaking. He wasn't Greek or Roman or from any other familiar place.

Then Jupiter ordered Hercules, who had wandered all over the world and seemed to be familiar with all its countries, to go and figure out this man's national origin. Hercules was pretty upset at the first sight of him, even though he had always been undismayed by monsters. When he saw that weird face, that strange gait, and heard that voice—which sounded like nothing belonging to a land animal, but the sort of hoarse barking sound that a walrus usually makes—he thought that his thirteenth labor was at hand. When he examined the creature more carefully, it looked rather like a human being. He therefore approached and, as was very easy for a guy from Greece, said:

> Who are you? Where from? Describe your city and your kin.

Claudius was delighted to discover that there were classical scholars there; he hoped that they would appreciate his historical writings. So he too spoke with a line from Homer, signifying that he was Caesar, and said:

> From Troy the wind blew me to the coast of Thrace.

(But the next line would have been truer, and equally Homeric:

> And there I sacked the city and destroyed the people.)

A discussion ensues among the deified as to whether or not Claudius should be made a god, and if so, what kind of a god he should be. Augustus, the deified late first emperor of Rome, is staunchly opposed to Claudius' deification. He sees him as a murderer, who killed members of his family and many others, including his wife Messalina. Claudius witnesses part of his own funeral and is then led down to the Underworld.

The freedman Narcissus had taken a shortcut and gotten there before him. Shining clean, fresh from a bath, he came to meet Claudius and said, "Why do the gods condescend to visit mortals?" "Get going," said Mercury, "And tell them that we are here."

Before he had finished speaking, Narcissus flew off. Everything slanted down, making it an easy trip. So, even though Narcissus had gout, it took him only a moment to get to the door of Dis, where Cerberus was lying—"the hundred-headed beast," as Horace says. Narcissus had a favorite little dog, an off-white bitch, so he was rather upset when he saw that shaggy black hound, not the sort of thing you'd like to meet in the dark. In a loud voice he said, "Claudius will soon be here." Amid cheering they came out singing, "We have found him; let us rejoice." Here were Gaius Silius the consul designate, Juncus the praetor, Sextus Traulus, Marcus Helvius, Trogus, Cotta, Vettius Valens, Fabius, and some Roman knights whom Narcissus had put to death. In the middle of this crowd of singers was Mnester the actor, whom Claudius, observing the proprieties, had made shorter than Messalina by taking off his head.

Soon the rumor spread that Claudius had arrived. The first to rush out were the freedmen Polybius, Myron, Arpocras, Ampheus, and Pheronaotus, all of whom Claudius had sent on ahead of him, so that he would never lack for attendants. Then the two Praetorian prefects Justus Catonius and Rufrius Pollio. Then his advisors Saturninus Lusius, Pedo Pompeius, Lupus, and Celer Asinius, all ex-consuls. Last of all came his brother's daughter, his sister's daughter, his sons-in-law, his fathers-in-law, his mothers-in-law—all relations, clearly. And forming a receiving line they came to greet Claudius. When Claudius saw them, he exclaimed, "'The whole world is full of friends.' How did you all get here?" Then Pedo Pompeius replied, "What are you saying, you paragon of cruelty? You ask how? Who else sent us here but you, you murderer of all your friends. Let's go to court. This time *I* will show *you* the defendant's table and the judge's bench."

Pedo led him to the courtroom of Aeacus, who presided over cases brought under the capital homicide law. Pedo asked for permission to bring a charge against Claudius and read the indictment: thirty-five senators killed, three hundred twenty-one Roman knights, and others "as many as the grains of sand and the motes of dust." Claudius couldn't find a lawyer to represent him. Finally Publius Petronius turned up: an old crony of his, and a man fluent in the Claudian tongue. He asked for a continuance; he was refused. Pedo Pompeius read the accusation to loud cheers. The defense attorney began to try to argue his side of the case. Aeacus, a most fair-minded man, told him he couldn't. Having heard only one side of the case, he condemned Claudius, saying:

> Were you to suffer what you inflicted on others,
> Straight justice would be done.'

There was a long silence. Everyone was struck dumb, stunned by the novelty of the idea. They said that such a thing had never happened. To Claudius, though, the idea seemed more unfair than novel.

There was a long discussion about the sentence, what he ought to suffer. There were those who said that Sisyphus had pushed his load for a long time; that Tantalus would die of thirst unless someone helped him; that at some point poor Ixion ought to have the brake put on his wheel. But it was decided not to give a respite to any of the old-timers, lest Claudius at some point expect the same consideration. A new type of punishment would have to be dreamed up for him: some futile task involving the hope of a goal without any result. Aeacus then ordered him to play dice using a dice-box with a hole drilled in the bottom.

And already Claudius was starting to chase after the dice that always kept falling out, and he was getting nowhere:

> Whenever he tried to throw from the echoing dice-box,
> Both dice escaped from the hole cut in the bottom.
> And when he boldly picked them up and tried
> To throw again, like a man who is always
> On the verge of playing, always trying to play,
> The dice would cheat his hope. Always the stealthy
> Double-dealing die slipped through his fingers.
> Just so, touching the highest mountain peak,
> Sisyphus drops the load from his shoulders,
> But in vain.

Suddenly Gaius Caesar turned up and asked to have Claudius as his slave. He called witnesses who had seen him beating Claudius with whips, canes, and his fists. The decision of the court was read out: Aeacus gave him to Gaius Caesar. He, in turn, gave him to his freedman Menander, to be his law clerk in charge of petitions.

Historically Claudius was in fact deified after his death.

THE STORY OF BRITAIN

Agricola

Tacitus

Translated by Alfred John Church and William Jackson Brodribb, 1876

Agricola, father-in-law of the historian **Tacitus** (*c.* AD 56–*c.* 120), was a highly successful governor of Britain. He conquered the island of Mona (modern Anglesey) and prevailed over the Caledonian tribesmen at the Battle of Mons Graupius in what is now Scotland. After this victory, the Emperor Domitian recalled him to Rome in AD 85, allegedly out of jealousy at his success. Tacitus prefaced his account of Agricola's achievements with a potted history of Rome's involvement in Britain prior to his arrival. Considerable progress had been made since Julius Caesar first invaded in 55 and 54 BC, and Claudius led a more successful expedition in AD 43. Tacitus had a particular interest in the characteristics of foreign peoples. Below we encounter the Silures, a tribe of south-eastern Wales, the Brigantes, of northern England, and Boudicca, who led the tribe of the Iceni in the area surrounding modern Norfolk.

Who were the original inhabitants of Britain, whether they were indigenous or foreign, is, as usual among barbarians, little known. Their physical characteristics are various, and from these conclusions may be drawn. The red hair and large limbs of the inhabitants of Caledonia point clearly to a German origin. The dark complexion of the Silures, their usually curly hair, and the fact that Spain is the opposite shore to them, are an evidence that Iberians of a former date crossed over and occupied these parts. Those who are nearest to the Gauls are also like them, either from the permanent influence of original descent, or, because in countries which run out so far to meet each other, climate has produced similar physical qualities. But a general survey inclines me to believe that the Gauls established themselves in an island so near to them. Their religious belief may be traced in the strongly-marked British superstition. The language differs but little; there is the same boldness in challenging danger, and, when it is near, the same timidity in shrinking from it. The Britons, however, exhibit more spirit, as being a people whom a long peace has not yet enervated. Indeed we have understood that even the Gauls were once renowned in war; but, after a while, sloth following on ease crept over them, and they lost their courage along with their freedom. This too has happened to the long-conquered tribes of Britain; the rest are still what the Gauls once were.

Their strength is in infantry. Some tribes fight also with the chariot. The higher in rank is the charioteer; the dependants fight. They were once ruled by kings, but are now divided under chieftains into factions and parties. Our greatest advantage in coping with tribes so powerful is that they do not act in concert. Seldom is it that two or three states meet together to ward off a common danger. Thus, while they fight singly, all are conquered.

Their sky is obscured by continual rain and cloud. Severity of cold is unknown. The days exceed in length those of our part of the world; the nights are bright, and in the extreme north so short that between sunlight and dawn you can perceive but a slight distinction. It is said that, if there are no clouds in the way, the splendour of the sun can be seen throughout the night, and that he does not rise and set, but only crosses the heavens. The truth is, that the low shadow thrown from the flat extremities of the earth's surface does not raise the darkness to any height, and the night thus fails to reach the sky and stars.

With the exception of the olive and vine, and plants which usually grow in warmer climates, the soil will yield, and even abundantly, all ordinary produce. It ripens indeed slowly, but is of rapid growth, the cause in each case being the same, namely, the excessive moisture of the soil and of the atmosphere. Britain contains gold and silver and other metals, as the prize of conquest. The ocean, too, produces pearls, but of a dusky and bluish hue. Some think that those who collect them have not the requisite skill, as in the Red Sea the living and breathing pearl is torn from the rocks, while in Britain they are gathered just as they are thrown up. I could myself more readily believe that the natural properties of the pearls are in fault than our keenness for gain.

The Britons themselves bear cheerfully the conscription, the taxes, and the other burdens imposed on them by the Empire, if there be no oppression. Of this they are impatient; they are reduced to subjection, not as yet to slavery. The deified Julius, the very first Roman who entered Britain with an army, though by a successful engagement he struck terror into the inhabitants and gained possession of the coast, must be regarded as having indicated rather than transmitted the acquisition to future generations. Then came the civil wars, and the arms of our leaders were turned against their country, and even when there was peace, there was a long neglect of Britain. This Augustus spoke of as policy, Tiberius as an inherited maxim. That Caius Caesar meditated an invasion of Britain is perfectly clear, but his purposes, rapidly formed, were easily changed, and his vast attempts on Germany had failed. Claudius was the first to renew the attempt, and conveyed over into the island some legions and auxiliaries, choosing Vespasian to share with him the campaign, whose approaching elevation had this beginning. Several tribes were subdued and kings made prisoners, and destiny learnt to know its favourite.

~

Aulus Plautius was the first governor of consular rank, and Ostorius Scapula the next. Both were famous soldiers, and by degrees the nearest portions of Britain were brought into the condition of a province, and a colony of veterans was also introduced. Some of the states were given to king Cogidumnus, who lived down to our day a most faithful ally. So was maintained the ancient and long-recognised practice of the Roman people, which seeks to secure among the instruments of dominion even kings themselves. Soon after, Didius Gallus consolidated the conquests of his predecessors, and advanced a very few positions into parts more remote, to gain the credit of having enlarged the sphere of government. Didius was succeeded by Veranius, who died within the year. Then Suetonius Paullinus enjoyed success for two years; he subdued several tribes and strengthened our military posts. Thus encouraged, he made an attempt on the island of Mona, as a place from which the rebels drew reinforcements; but in doing this he left his rear open to attack.

Relieved from apprehension by the legate's absence, the Britons dwelt much among themselves on the miseries of subjection, compared their wrongs, and exaggerated them in the discussion. "All we get by patience," they said, "is that heavier demands are exacted from us, as from men who will readily submit. A single king once ruled us; now two are set over us; a legate to tyrannise over our lives, a procurator to tyrannise over our property. Their quarrels and their harmony are alike ruinous to their subjects. The centurions of the one, the slaves of the other, combine violence with insult. Nothing is now safe from their avarice, nothing from their lust. In war it is the strong who plunders; now, it is for the most part by cowards and poltroons that our homes are rifled, our children torn from us, the conscription enforced, as though it were for our country alone that we could not die. For, after all, what a mere handful of soldiers has crossed over, if we Britons look at our own numbers. Germany did thus actually shake off the yoke, and yet its defence was a river, not the ocean. With us, fatherland, wives, parents, are the motives to war; with them, only greed and profligacy. They will surely fly, as did the now deified Julius, if once we emulate the valour of our sires. Let us not be panic-stricken at the result of one or two engagements. The miserable have more fury and greater resolution. Now even the gods are beginning to pity us, for they are keeping away the Roman general, and detaining his army far from us in another island. We have already taken the hardest step; we are deliberating. And indeed, in all such designs, to dare is less perilous than to be detected."

Rousing each other by this and like language, under the leadership of Boudicea, a woman of kingly descent (for they admit no distinction of sex in their royal successions), they all rose in arms. They fell upon our troops, which were scattered on garrison duty, stormed the forts, and burst into the colony itself, the headquarters, as they thought, of tyranny. In their rage and their triumph, they spared no variety of a barbarian's cruelty. Had not Paullinus on hearing of the outbreak in the province rendered prompt succour, Britain would have been lost. By one successful engagement, he brought it back to its former obedience, though many, troubled by the conscious guilt of rebellion and by particular dread of the legate, still clung to their arms. Excellent as he was in other respects, his policy to the conquered was arrogant, and exhibited the cruelty of one who was avenging private wrongs. Accordingly Petronius Turpilianus was sent out to initiate a milder rule. A stranger to the enemy's misdeeds and so more accessible to their penitence, he put an end to old troubles, and, attempting nothing more, handed the province over to Trebellius Maximus. Trebellius, who was somewhat indolent, and never ventured on a campaign, controlled the province by a certain courtesy in his administration. Even the barbarians now learnt to excuse many attractive vices, and the occurrence of the civil war gave a good pretext for inaction. But we were sorely troubled with mutiny, as troops habituated to service grew demoralised by idleness. Trebellius, who had escaped the soldiers' fury by flying and hiding himself, governed henceforth on sufferance, a disgraced and humbled man. It was a kind of bargain; the soldiers had their licence, the general had his life; and so the mutiny cost no bloodshed. Nor did Vettius Bolanus, during the continuance of the civil wars, trouble Britain with discipline. There was the same inaction with respect to the enemy, and similar unruliness in the camp, only Bolanus, an upright man, whom no misdeeds made odious, had secured affection in default of the power of control.

When however Vespasian had restored to unity Britain as well as the rest of the world, in the presence of great generals and renowned armies the enemy's hopes were crushed. They were at once panic-stricken by the attack of Petilius Cerialis on the state of the Brigantes, said to be the most prosperous in the entire province. There were many battles, some by no means bloodless, and his conquests, or at least his wars, embraced a large part of the territory of the Brigantes. Indeed he would have altogether thrown into the shade the activity and renown of any other successor; but Julius Frontinus was equal to the burden, a great man as far as greatness was then possible, who subdued by his arms the powerful and warlike tribe of the Silures, surmounting the difficulties of the country as well as the valour of the enemy.

THE GREAT FIRE OF ROME

Annals

Tacitus

Translated by J. C. Yardley, 2008

Every schoolchild knows that Nero fiddled while Rome burned. But did he? The historian **Tacitus** records that the emperor was away from the city when the fire actually broke out in AD 64. He also notes the ease with which rumours of Nero's behaviour spread after the conflagration had taken hold. Tacitus' younger contemporary Suetonius (see Story 70) suggested that Nero so despised Rome's old buildings and narrow streets that he decided to burn them down. To deflect blame for the disaster from himself, said Tacitus, Nero pointed his finger at the Christians, whom he proceeded to persecute. Despite writing over half a century after the events, Tacitus captured perfectly in his description the sense of panic and displacement that the fire must have inspired in the people of Rome.

It started in the part of the Circus adjacent to the Palatine and Caelian hills. There, amidst shops containing merchandise of a combustible nature, the fire immediately gained strength as soon as it broke out and, whipped up by the wind, engulfed the entire length of the Circus. For there were no dwellings with solid enclosures, no temples ringed with walls, and no other obstacle of any kind in its way. The blaze spread wildly, overrunning the flat areas first, and then climbing to the heights before once again ravaging the lower sections. It outstripped all defensive measures because of the speed of its deadly advance and the vulnerability of the city, with its narrow streets twisting this way and that, and with its irregular blocks of buildings, which was the nature of old Rome.

In addition, there was the wailing of panic-stricken women; there were people, very old and very young; there were those trying to save themselves and those trying to save others, dragging invalids along or waiting for them; and these people, some hanging back, some rushing along, hindered all relief efforts. And often, as they looked back, they found themselves under attack from the flames at their sides or in front; or if they got away to a neighbouring district, that also caught fire, and even those areas they had believed far distant they found to be in the same plight. Eventually, unsure what to avoid and what to head for, they crowded the roads or scattered over the fields. Even though escape lay open to them, some chose death because they had lost all their property, even their daily livelihood; others did so from love of family members whom they had been unable to rescue. And nobody dared fight the fire: there were repeated threats from numerous people opposing efforts to extinguish it, and others openly hurled in firebrands and yelled that they 'had their instructions'. This was to give them more freedom to loot, or else they were in fact under orders.

Nero was at Antium at the time, and he did not return to the city until the fire was approaching that building of his by which he had connected the Palatium with the gardens of Maecenas. But stopping the fire from consuming the Palatium, Nero's house, and everything in the vicinity proved impossible. However, to relieve the homeless and fugitive population Nero opened up the Campus Martius, the monuments of Agrippa, and even his own gardens, and he erected makeshift buildings to house the destitute crowds. Vital supplies were shipped up from Ostia and neighbouring municipalities, and the price of grain was dropped to three sesterces. These were measures with popular appeal, but they proved a dismal failure. For the rumour had spread that, at the very time that the city was ablaze, Nero had appeared on his private stage and sung about the destruction of Troy, drawing a comparison between the sorrows of the present and the disasters of old.

Finally, after five days, the blaze was brought to a halt at the foot of the Esquiline. Buildings had been demolished over a vast area so that the fire's unremitting violence would be faced only with open ground and bare sky. But before the panic had abated, or the plebs' hopes had revived, the fire resumed its furious onslaught, though in more open areas of the city. As a result, there were fewer human casualties, but the destruction of temples and porticoes designed as public amenities was more widespread. And that particular conflagration caused a greater scandal because it had broken out on Tigellinus' Aemilian estates; and it looked as if Nero was seeking the glory of founding a new city, one that was to be named after him. In fact, of the fourteen districts into which Rome is divided, four were still intact, three had been levelled to the ground, and in the other seven a few ruined and charred vestiges of buildings were all that remained.

To put a figure on the houses, tenement buildings, and temples that were lost would be no easy matter. But religious buildings of the most time-honoured sanctity were burned down: the temple that Servius Tullius had consecrated to Luna; the Ara Maxima and sanctuary that the Arcadian Evander had consecrated to Hercules Praesens; the temple of Jupiter Stator promised in a vow by Romulus; the palace of Numa; and the shrine of Vesta holding the Penates of the Roman people. Other casualties were rich spoils taken through our many victories; fine specimens of Greek art; and antique and authentic works of literary genius. As a result, though surrounded by the great beauty of the city as it grew again, older people still remember many things that could not be replaced. There were those who observed that this fire started on 19 July, which was the date on which the Senones captured and burned the city. Others have taken their interest so far as to compute equal numbers of years, months, and days between the two fires.

In fact, Nero took advantage of the homeland's destruction to build a palace. It was intended to inspire awe, not so much with precious stones and gold (long familiar and commonplace in the life of luxury) as with its fields, lakes, and woods that replicated the open countryside on one side, and open spaces and views on the other. The architects and engineers were Severus and Celer, who had the ingenuity and audacity to attempt to create by artifice what nature had denied, and to amuse themselves with the emperor's resources. For they had undertaken to dig a navigable channel from Lake Avernus all the way to the mouths of the Tiber, taking it along the desolate shoreline or through the barrier of the hills. In fact, one comes across no aquifer here to provide a water supply. There are only the Pomptine marshes, all else being cliffs or arid ground—and even if forcing a way through this were possible, it would have involved an extreme and unjustifiable effort. But Nero was ever one to seek after the incredible. He attempted to dig out the heights next to Avernus, and traces of his futile hopes remain to this day.

As for space that remained in the city after Nero's house-building, it was not built up in a random and haphazard manner, as after the burning by the Gauls. Instead, there were rows of streets properly surveyed, spacious thoroughfares, buildings with height limits and open areas. Porticoes were added, too, to protect the façade of the tenement buildings. These porticoes Nero undertook to erect from his own pocket, and he also undertook to return to their owners the building lots, cleared of debris. He added grants, pro-rated according to a person's rank and domestic property, and established time limits within which houses or tenement buildings were to be completed for claimants to acquire the money.

He earmarked the Ostian marshes as the dumping ground for the debris, and ordered ships that had ferried grain up the Tiber to return downstream loaded with debris. The actual edifices were, for a specific portion of their structure, to be free of wooden beams and reinforced with rock from Gabii or Alba, since such stone is fireproof. In addition, because individuals had had the effrontery to siphon off water, watchmen would be employed to ensure a fuller public supply, and at more points. Everyone was also to have appliances accessible for fighting fires, and houses were not to have party walls but each be enclosed by its own. These measures were welcomed for their practicality, and they also enhanced the aesthetics of the new city. There were, however, those who believed that the old configuration was more conducive to health, inasmuch as the narrowness of the streets and the height of the buildings meant they were less easily penetrated by the torrid sunlight. Now, they claimed, the broad open spaces, with no shade to protect them, were baking in a more oppressive heat.

Such were the precautions taken as a result of human reasoning. The next step was to find ways of appeasing the gods, and the Sibylline Books were consulted. Under their guidance, supplicatory prayers were offered to Vulcan, Ceres, and Proserpina, and there were propitiatory ceremonies performed for Juno by married women, first on the Capitol, and then on the closest part of the shoreline. (From there, water was drawn, and the temple and statue of the goddess were sprinkled with it.) Women who had husbands also held ritual feasts and all-night festivals.

But neither human resourcefulness nor the emperor's largesse nor appeasement of the gods could stop belief in the nasty rumour that an order had been given for the fire. To dispel the gossip Nero therefore found culprits on whom he inflicted the most exotic punishments. These were people hated for their shameful offences whom the common people called Christians. The man who gave them their name, Christus, had been executed during the rule of Tiberius by the procurator Pontius Pilatus. The pernicious superstition had been temporarily suppressed, but it was starting to break out again, not just in Judaea, the starting point of that curse, but in Rome, as well, where all that is abominable and shameful in the world flows together and gains popularity.

And so, at first, those who confessed were apprehended, and subsequently, on the disclosures they made, a huge number were found guilty—more because of their hatred of mankind than because they were arsonists. As they died they were further subjected to insult. Covered with hides of wild beasts, they perished by being torn to pieces by dogs; or they would be fastened to crosses and, when daylight had gone, burned to provide lighting at night. Nero had offered his gardens as a venue for the show, and he would also put on circus entertainments, mixing with the plebs in his charioteer's outfit or standing up in his chariot. As a result, guilty though these people were and deserving exemplary punishment, pity for them began to well up because it was felt that they were being exterminated not for the public good, but to gratify one man's cruelty.

DINNER AT TRIMALCHIO'S

Satyricon

Petronius Arbiter

Translation ascribed to Oscar Wilde, 1902

Petronius (AD 27–66) was 'arbiter of elegance' to the Emperor Nero. In AD 66, however, he was implicated in a plot against the emperor and committed suicide. His brilliant novel, the *Satyricon*, belongs to the last years of his life. Its most famous episode, the *Cena Trimalchionis* or 'Dinner of Trimalchio', sees the young narrator Encolpius and his friends go to dine at the house of the achingly nouveau Trimalchio, a former slave or 'freedman', who earned his fortune by winning his master's favour and exporting goods from Rome. In the twentieth century, the boorish Trimalchio was an inspiration for F. Scott Fitzgerald's character Jay Gatsby.

When this translation was first published in Paris in 1902 it was prefaced by a slip of paper identifying its translator as Sebastian Melmoth – the name Oscar Wilde adopted in exile. Although Wilde was an excellent classicist, he was apparently not the real translator* of this story; the attribution was retracted some years after his death.

Well! at last we take our places, Alexandrian slave-boys pouring snow water over our hands, and others succeeding them to wash our feet and cleanse our toe nails with extreme dexterity. Not even while engaged in this unpleasant office were they silent, but sang away over their work. I had a mind to try whether all the house servants were singers, and accordingly asked for a drink of wine. Instantly an attendant was at my side, pouring out the liquor to the accompaniment of the same sort of shrill recitative. Demand what you would, it was the same; you might have supposed yourself among a troupe of pantomime actors, rather than at a respectable citizen's table.

Then the preliminary course was served in very elegant style. For all were now

---

* *The identity of the translator remains a mystery, but suspicion has fallen on one Alfred Richard Allinson – see Rod Boroughs, 'Oscar Wilde's Translation of Petronius: The Story of a Literary Hoax', English Literature in Transition, 1880–1920, Vol 38, No. 1, 1995, pp. 9–49. The sense of mystery and fun that surrounds the origins of this translation feels very much in Petronius' spirit.*

at table except Trimalchio, for whom the first place was reserved,—by a reversal of ordinary usage. Among the other hors d'oeuvres stood a little ass of Corinthian bronze with a packsaddle holding olives, white olives on one side, black on the other. The animal was flanked right and left by silver dishes, on the rim of which Trimalchio's name was engraved and the weight. On arches built up in the form of miniature bridges were dormice seasoned with honey and poppy-seed. There were sausages too smoking hot on a silver grill, and underneath (to imitate coals) Syrian plums and pomegranate seeds.

We were in the middle of these elegant trifles when Trimalchio himself was carried in to the sound of music, and was bolstered up among a host of tiny cushions,—a sight that set one or two indiscreet guests laughing. And no wonder; his bald head poked up out of a scarlet mantle, his neck was closely muffled, and over all was laid a napkin with a broad purple stripe or laticlave, and long fringes hanging down either side. Moreover he wore on the little finger of his left hand a massive ring of silver gilt, and on the last joint of the next finger a smaller ring, apparently of solid gold, but starred superficially with little ornaments of steel. Nay! to show this was not the whole of his magnificence, his left arm was bare, and displayed a gold bracelet and an ivory circlet with a sparkling clasp to put it on.

After picking his teeth with a silver toothpick, "My friends," he began, "I was far from desirous of coming to table just yet, but that I might not keep you waiting by my absence, I have sadly interfered with my own amusement. But will you permit me to finish my game?" A slave followed him in, carrying a draught-board of terebinth wood and crystal dice. One special bit of refinement I noticed; instead of the ordinary black and white men he had medals of gold and silver respectively.

Meantime, whilst he is exhausting the vocabulary of a tinker over the game, and we are still at the hors d'oeuvres, a dish was brought in with a basket on it, in which lay a wooden hen, her wings outspread round her as if she were sitting. Instantly a couple of slaves came up, and to the sound of lively music began to search the straw, and pulling out a lot of pea-fowl's eggs one after the other, handed them round to the company. Trimalchio turns his head at this, saying, "My friends, it was by my orders the hen was set on the peafowl's eggs yonder; but by God! I am very much afraid they are half-hatched. Still we can but try whether they are still eatable." For our part, we take our spoons, which weighed at least half a pound each, and break the eggs, which were made of paste. I was on the point of throwing mine away, for I thought I discerned a chick inside. But when I overheard a veteran guest saying, "There should be something good here!" I further investigated the shell, and found a very fine fat beccafico swimming in yolk of egg flavoured with pepper.

Trimalchio had by this time stopped his game and been helped to all the dishes before us. He had just announced in a loud voice that any of us who wanted a second supply of honeyed wine had only to ask for it, when suddenly at a signal from the band, the hors d'oeuvres are whisked away by a troupe of slaves, all singing too. But in the confusion a silver dish happened to fall and a slave picked it up again from the floor; this Trimalchio noticed, and boxing the fellow's ears, rated him soundly and ordered him to throw it down again. Then a groom came in and began to sweep up the silver along with the other refuse with his besom.

He was succeeded by two long-haired Ethiopians, carrying small leather skins, like the fellows that water the sand in the amphitheatre, who poured wine over our hands; for no one thought of offering water.

After being duly complimented on this refinement, our host cried out, "Fair play's a jewel!" and accordingly ordered a separate table to be assigned to each guest. "In this way," he said, "by preventing any crowding, the stinking servants won't make us so hot."

Simultaneously there were brought in a number of wine-jars of glass carefully stoppered with plaster, and having labels attached to their necks reading:

FALERNIAN; OPIMIAN VINTAGE
ONE HUNDRED YEARS OLD.

Whilst we were reading the labels, Trimalchio ejaculated, striking his palms together, "Alackaday! to think wine is longer lived than poor humanity! Well! bumpers then! There's life in wine. 'Tis the right Opimian, I give you my word. I didn't bring out any so good yesterday, and much better men than you were dining with me."

So we drank our wine and admired all this luxury in good set terms. Then the slave brought in a silver skeleton, so artfully fitted with its articulations and vertebrae were all movable and would turn and twist in any direction. After he had tossed this once or twice on the table, causing the loosely jointed limbs to take various postures, Trimalchio moralized thus:

Alas! how less than naught are we;
    Fragile life's thread, and brief our day!
What this is now, we all shall be;
    Drink and make merry while you may.

Our applause was interrupted by the second course, which did not by any means come up to our expectations. Still the oddity of the thing drew the eyes of all. An immense circular tray bore the twelve signs of the zodiac displayed round the circumference, on each of which the Manoiple or Arranger had placed a dish of suitable and appropriate viands: on the Ram ram's-head pease, on the Bull a piece of beef, on the Twins fried testicles and kidneys, on the Crab simply a Crown, on the Lion African figs, on a Virgin a sow's haslet, (on Libra a balance with a tart in one scale and a cheese-cake in the other, on Scorpio a small sea-fish, on Sagittarius an eye-seeker, on Capricornus a lobster, on Aquarius a wild goose, on Pisces two mullets. In the middle was a sod of green turf) cut to shape and supporting a honeycomb. Meanwhile an Egyptian slave was carrying bread round in a miniature oven of silver, crooning to himself in a horrible voice a song in praise of wine and laserpitium.

Seeing us look rather blank at the idea of attacking such common fare, Trimalchio cried, "I pray you gentlemen, begin; the best of your dinner is before you." No sooner had he spoken than four fellows ran prancing in, keeping time to the music, and whipped off the top part of the tray. This done, we beheld underneath, on a second tray in fact, stuffed capons, a sow's paps, and as a centrepiece a hare fitted with wings to represent Pegasus. We noticed besides four figures of

Marsyas, one at each corner of the tray, carrying little wine-skins which spouted out peppered fish-sauce over the fishes swimming in the Channel of the dish.

We all join in the applause started by the domestics and laughingly fall to on the choice viands. Trimalchio, as pleased as anybody with a device of the sort, now called out, "Cut!" Instantly the Carver advanced, and posturing in time to the music, sliced up the joint with such antics you might have thought him a jockey struggling to pull off a chariot-race to the thunder of the organ. Yet all the while Trimalchio kept repeating in a wheedling voice, "Cut! Cut!" For my part, suspecting there was some pretty jest connected with this everlasting reiteration of the word, I made no bones about asking the question of the guest, who sat immediately above me. He had often witnessed similar scenes and told me at once, "You see the man who is carving; well; his name is Cut. The master is calling and commanding him at one and the same time."

Unable to eat any more, I now turned towards my neighbour in order to glean what information I could, and after indulging in a string of general remarks, presently asked him, "Who is that lady bustling up and down the room yonder?" "Trimalchio's lady," he replied; "her name is Fortunata, and she counts her coin by the bushelful! Before? what was she before? Why! my dear Sir! saving your respect, you would have been mighty sorry to take bread from her hand. Now, by hook or by crook, she's got to heaven, and is Trimalchio's factotum. In fact if she told him it was dark night at high noon, he'd believe her. The man's rolling in riches, and really can't tell what he has and what he hasn't got; still his good lady looks keenly after everything, and is on the spot where you least expect to see her. She's temperate, sober and well advised, but she has a sharp tongue of her own and chatters like a magpie between the bed-curtains. When she likes a man, she likes him; and when she doesn't, well! she doesn't.

"As for Trimalchio, his lands reach as far as the kites fly, and his money breeds money. I tell you, he has more coin lying idle in his porter's lodge than would make another man's whole fortune. Slaves! why, heaven and earth! I don't believe one in ten knows his own master by sight. For all that, there's never a one of the fine fellows a word of his wouldn't send scutting into the nearest rat-hole. And don't you imagine he ever buys anything; every mortal thing is home grown,— wool, rosin, pepper; call for hen's milk and he'd supply you! As a matter of fact his wool was not first rate originally; but he purchased rams at Tarentum and so improved the breed. To get home-made Attic honey he had bees imported direct from Athens, hoping at the same time to benefit the native insects a bit by a cross with the Greek fellows. Why! only the other day he wrote to India for mushroom spawn. He has not a single mule but was got by a wild ass. You see all these mattresses; never a one that is not stuffed with the finest wool, purple or scarlet as the case may be. Lucky, lucky dog!

As the dinner party becomes increasingly farcical, Trimalchio requests to see the clothes he will be buried in.

Without a moment's delay, Stichus produced a white shroud and a magistrate's gown into the dining-hall, and asked us to feel if they were made of good wool.

Then his master added with a laugh, "Mind, Stichus, mice and moth don't get at them; else I'll have you burned alive. I wish to be buried in all my bravery, that the whole people may call down blessings on my head." Immediately afterwards he opened a pot of spikenard, and after rubbing us all with the ointment, "I only hope," said he, "it will give me as much pleasure when I'm dead as it does now when I'm alive." Further he ordered the wine vessels to be filled up, telling us to "imagine you are invited guests at my funeral feast."

The thing was getting positively sickening, when Trimalchio, now in a state of disgusting intoxication, commanded a new diversion, a company of horn-blowers, to be introduced; and then stretching himself out along the edge of a couch on a pile of pillows, "Make believe I am dead," he ordered. "Play something fine." Then the horn blowers struck up a loud funeral dirge. In particular one of these undertaker's men, the most conscientious of the lot, blew so tremendous a fanfare he roused the whole neighbourhood. Hereupon the watchmen in charge of the surrounding district, thinking Trimalchio's house was on fire, suddenly burst open the door, and rushing in with water and axes, started the much admired confusion usual under such circumstances. For our part, we seized the excellent opportunity thus offered, snapped our fingers in Agamemnon's face, and away helter-skelter just as if we were escaping from a real conflagration.

THE ERUPTION OF VESUVIUS

Letters, 6.16

Pliny the Younger

Translated by Daisy Dunn, 2018

Most writers in antiquity believed that Mount Vesuvius was a mountain, or at most an extinct volcano. It had been dormant for around 700 years when, in AD 79, it erupted catastrophically. Thousands of people died at Pompeii, Herculaneum, and across the Bay of Naples. This is the account of a senator and lawyer named **Pliny the Younger** (AD *c.* 62–*c.* 113) who witnessed the eruption at the age of seventeen and survived it. Writing almost thirty years after the disaster, he describes in this letter to the historian Tacitus (see Stories 72 and 73) how his uncle, Pliny the Elder, an admiral and natural historian, launched a rescue operation but died at Stabiae, a town close to the volcano. He later wrote a second letter describing his own experience of the disaster.

You ask that I write to you of my uncle's death so that you might pass the truth down to posterity. Thank you. For I can see that, if his death is recorded by you, then immortal glory is assured him. For although he died in an unforgettable disaster which destroyed the most beautiful parts of the earth, as well as cities and their people so, in a sense, he was bound to live on, and although he produced a great number of enduring works of his own, the inextinguishable nature of your writing may still do much to perpetuate his name. Lucky, I think, are those men with a god-given gift for doing what deserves to be written about or writing what deserves to be read – and very lucky are those who can do both. Through his own books and yours, my uncle will be one of these. I'm only too pleased to write this account, for in fact I'm eager for what you enjoin me to do.

My uncle was at Misenum where he was commander of the imperial fleet. On 24 August, at around midday, my mother alerted him to a cloud, both strange and enormous in appearance. He had taken some sun, had a cold bath, lunched while reclining and was then at his studies; he called for his shoes and made his way up to a spot from which he could obtain the best view of the phenomenon. The cloud was too far away from where we were watching for us to be certain of which mountain it was rising from (it was afterwards known to be Vesuvius), but its shape was closest to that of an umbrella pine tree quite specifically. For it was raised high on a kind of very tall trunk and spread out into branches, I suppose because it was freshly pushed out by air and then weakened as the air subsided or, overcome by its own weight, filtered out across the sky, white one moment, dirty and grey-spotted the next through the earth or ash it bore. To a scholarly man like my uncle, it was obvious that, to understand more about it, he needed to get closer.

He gave orders for a galley to be fitted out; he asked if I wanted to come with him. I replied that I would prefer to study, for he himself happened to have given me something to write. He was on the point of leaving the house when he received a written message from Tascius' wife Rectina, who feared imminent danger, for her villa lay beneath Vesuvius and there was no escape, except by boat. She urged him to rescue her from this grave situation. He changed his plan and what he had begun as an intellectual pursuit he completed with all he had. He had the quadriremes drawn up and embarked with the intention of bringing help not only to Rectina, but to many people, for the exquisite coast was highly populated. He pushed forward in the direction from which others were fleeing, and held course, steering straight into the danger zone, so fearless as he went that he described and noted down every movement, every shape of that evil thing, as it appeared before his eyes.

Now ash began to fall on the ships, hotter and thicker the nearer they got; now pumice and even black stones, burned and broken by fire; now, suddenly, in the shallows, the waste the mountain had ejected was blocking the way to the shore. Having hesitated briefly as to whether to turn back, my uncle said to the helmsman who favoured this course: "Fortune favours the brave: make for Pomponianus".

He was cut off at Stabiae by the curve of the bay (for a gently rounded shore surrounds it and is filled by the sea); although the danger was not yet approaching there, it was nonetheless clear that it would get nearer as it intensified in size. Pomponianus had stowed his baggage aboard a ship, set on flight if the opposing wind settled.

My uncle, conveyed by this favourable breeze, embraced his trembling friend, consoled him, jollied him along and, so as to relieve his fear through his own confidence, asked to be taken to the baths. After washing he lay down and dined; either he was content, or he showed a semblance of contentment, which was just as great-hearted. Meanwhile flames shot out all over from Mount Vesuvius and glowed bright and lit up the night sky, their blazing brightness illuminated by the shadows of darkness. To soothe their fears my uncle kept telling them that these were merely the bonfires of peasants, abandoned through terror, and empty houses on fire. Then he went to rest and fell into a deep sleep. For the motion of his breath, which was rather heavy and noisy on account of the portliness of his body, could be heard by those who were keeping watch outside his doorway. And the terrace which led out from his room was now filled with ash mixed with pumice so the ground level was raised; if he had lingered in his bedchamber any longer he would not have been able to escape.

Awakened, he made his way out and reconvened with Pomponianus and the others who had stayed up. They deliberated together over whether to stay inside or venture out into the open. For the buildings were shaking due to frequent and violent earthquakes and seemed almost to be moving from their foundations, shunted this way and then that. On the other hand, there was the fear of the pumice fall, even though it was light and porous; they opted for this as the lesser of the dangers. For my uncle, reason prevailed, but for the others, fear. They put pillows on their heads and tied them in place with pieces of cloth: this was their protection against the falling debris.

Now, elsewhere, it was daylight, but here it was still night but blacker and denser than all the nights there have ever been. But they tried to overcome it with a number of torches and various lamps. My uncle decided to go down to the shore to see close-up whether they might now escape by sea; the swell was still against them. Lying down there on a cloth, he asked again and again for cold water and drank. Then flames and the smell of sulphur that suggested there were more flames to come put the others to flight but roused him. Leaning on two slaves for support he stood up but at once fell, I imagine because his breathing was impeded by the thick smog and his windpipe – which was habitually weak and narrowed and often inflamed – was blocked. When daylight returned (this was on the third day from the last one he'd seen) his body was found – intact and unharmed and clothed as he had been: he looked more asleep than dead.

My mother and I, meanwhile, were at Misenum – but that is of no historical consequence and you didn't want to know about anything other than my uncle's death. And so I end here. I add only that I have included everything that I witnessed for myself and heard straight after the event, when the truth is most remembered. You can excerpt the highlights; for a letter one writes to a friend is one thing, but the history one writes for everyone, quite another. All best.

ON LAMPSTANDS, THE DISCOVERY OF GLASS, ON THE DOLPHIN

Natural History

Pliny the Elder

Translated by Daisy Dunn, 2018

On Lampstands

> **Pliny the Elder** (AD 23/4–79), who died in the eruption of Vesuvius in AD 79, was the author of a remarkable thirty-seven-volume encyclopaedia. The earliest encyclopaedia to survive from the Graeco-Roman world, the *Natural History* contains observations on animals and plants, accounts of art and monuments, and cures and remedies for a huge range of ailments. In this passage, taken from the thirty-fourth book, Pliny the Elder offers a delightfully esoteric tale of the origins of lampstands.

Aegina specialised in finely crafting the tops of candelabra and Tarentum their stems. Recognition for their manufacture is therefore shared between them. People are unashamed of paying a military tribune's salary for these candelabra, even though, as the name suggests, they merely hold lights. At the sale of one such candelabrum Clesippus, a clothes-washer with a hunched back and ugly countenance besides, was added to the lot at the instruction of the public crier Theon. The two were bought by a certain Gegania for 50,000 sesterces. She showed off what she had purchased at a party, with Clesippus displayed nude to make everyone laugh. After taking him into her bed in an outpouring of shameless lust, however, she added him to her will, and in his newfound wealth he took to cultivating the candelabrum as if it were a god. This story became associated with Corinthian lampstands. Morality was only recovered when a proper tomb was erected for Gegania with the result that the memory of her misconduct lived on forever and became only more notorious across the world.

The Discovery of Glass

Pliny the Elder believed that 'no book is so bad that there is nothing to be taken from it'. He drew on a vast range of sources when compiling his encyclopaedia and cited a great many of them. But not everything he recorded was strictly accurate. His *Natural History* is all the more colourful for the errors and eccentricities it contains. This story may not tell of the very earliest creation of glass, but it does capture in some detail a discovery of glass. The fact that it is described as a chance discovery on sand gives the story a ring of truth.

There is a part of Syria which is known as Phoenicia, bordering Judaea, which contains, between the slopes of Mount Carmel, a swamp called Candebia. This is believed to be the source of the River Belus, which covers a distance of five miles before emptying into the sea beside the colony of Ptolemais. This river is slow in it course, unclean to drink, but sacred for religious purposes, muddy, deep, and reveals its sands only when the tide is out, for they glisten once the motion of the waves has removed their dull impurities. It is thought that the sand is cleansed by the bite of the seawater and only then, and not a moment sooner, becomes useful.

The coast isn't more than half a mile in extent but was nonetheless the only place for producing glass for many centuries. The story goes that a ship that traded in soda put in here and its men spread out along the shore and began to prepare a meal. Finding they had no way of propping up their cauldrons for lack of rocks, they placed lumps of soda from their ship under them instead, and when these were kindled and began to merge with the sand of the beach, streams of a novel kind of translucent liquid began to flow, and this was the origin of glass.

Soon, as is usual where creative genius is concerned, man was not satisfied with mixing in soda alone; loadstone started to be added, since it was predicted that it might attract liquid glass in the same way as it does iron. In much the same way, a variety of shiny pebbles began to be used, then shells and sand. Writers say that in India it is made of broken crystal, on account of which nothing compares with Indian glass.

On the Dolphin

In his encyclopaedia, **Pliny the Elder** described the dolphin as 'the very fastest of animals, not only of sea creatures, faster than a bird'. It has a wide short tongue which, he wrote, was 'not unlike a pig's'. Dolphin stories were popular in antiquity. One of the most famous featured a musician named Arion, who was said to have plunged into the sea to escape some evil sailors who were pursuing him, only to be saved by a dolphin. The first story in this passage from the *Natural History* is set in the Bay of Naples, where Pliny the Elder served as admiral of the imperial fleet. The second story also appears in a letter written by his nephew, Pliny the Younger, decades later.

The dolphin is an animal that is well-disposed not only to man but to the art of music as well. He is soothed by harmonious song and especially by the sound of the water-organ. He is not frightened of man as of a stranger, but comes to greet ships, enjoys playfully leaping about them, and indeed races them even when they're in full sail.

In the rule of Divine Emperor Augustus, a dolphin was swept into the Lucrine Lake and developed the most marvellous affection for a poor man's son, who used to travel from Baiae to Puteoli to go to school. The boy would linger there in the middle of the day and call the dolphin by the name of Simo, coaxing him with pieces of bread, which he carried expressly for the purpose. I'd be ashamed to relate this story had it not been entrusted to me in the letters of Maecenas and Fabianus and Flavius Alfius and many others. Whatever the time of day the dolphin was called by the boy, regardless of whether it was hidden far beneath the surface, it would spring from the depths, feed from his hand, and offer its back for him to mount, concealing the sharper bits of his fins in their sheath, so to speak. And having taken him up he would carry him over a vast expanse of sea to the school at Puteoli and carry him back again in the same way over several years, until the boy suddenly died of an illness. And yet the dolphin would return to the usual place, mournful and full of sorrow, until he too died – of heartache – a fact that no one could doubt.

Within the same period another dolphin, this one at Hippo Diarrhytus on the coast of Africa, used in much the same way to be hand-fed and offer himself up to be stroked. It would play among the swimmers and carry them on his back. It was smothered in perfume by Flavianus, the proconsul of Africa, and was lulled to sleep, or so it seemed, by the novelty of the fragrance, after which it floated as if it were dead. For several months the dolphin avoided contact with humans as if it had suffered at their hands. Soon, however, it returned to its old habits to the same wondrous display. Eventually, however, the ill effects that resulted from tourists coming to see this sight drove the people of Hippo to put the dolphin to death.

THE MADNESS OF HERCULES

Hercules Furens

Seneca the Younger

Translated by Jasper Heywood, 1559–1561

We tend to think of Hercules as a hero. In this tragedy by **Seneca the Younger** (4 BC–AD 65) we see him in a very different light, as victim of the vengeance of Juno, queen of the gods, who had always hated him because he was the product of an affair her husband Jupiter had with the mortal Alcmene. First Hercules had to complete twelve fiendishly difficult 'Labours' or challenges (see Story 33). Now, upon his return from the last of his labours, which required him to lead to the upper world Cerberus, the three-headed dog who guarded the entrance to the Underworld, Hercules succumbs to the madness Juno incites in him. As this passage begins, Hercules has just defeated Lycus, king of Thebes. He is reunited with his friend Theseus, his 'father' Amphitryon, his wife Megara, and their children. This passage comes from the lyrical translation of a sixteenth-century Jesuit priest named Jasper Heywood.

> [...] HERCULES. I wyll
>   the prayers make, for mee
> And Jove full meete. yn his due place
>   Lette stande the haughty skye,
> And lande, and ayre, and lette the starres
>   dryue foorthe eternallye
> Their course unstayde: let restfull peace
>   keepe nations quietlye,
> Let labour of the hurtlesse lande
>   all yron nowe occupye,
> And swoordes lye hydde: let tempest none
>   full vyolent and dyre
> Disturbe the sea: let from the skyes
>   no flashe of lyghtnyng fyre
> Fall downe whyle Jove full angry is:
>   nor yet with wynter snowe
> Encreased floode the grownde upturnde

and fieldes quight overthrowe.
Let poysons cease: and from hensfoorth
   let up from grownde aryse
No greevous herbe with hurtfull sappe:
   nor fierce and fell lykewyse
Let tyrantes raygne: but yf to syght
   some other mischiefe bryng
The grownde yet shall, let it make haste:
   and any monstrous thyng
If it prepare, let yt bee myne.
   but what meanes this? myd daye
The darknes have encloasde abowt,
   lo Phoebus gothe his waye
With face obscure withowt a clowde.
   who dryues the daye to flyght,
And turnes to east? from whence doth now
   his dusky hed the nyght
Unknown bryng forth? whēce fyl the poale
   so many rownde about
Of daytyme starres? lo here beholde
   my labour fyrst full stoute
Not in the lowest parte of heaven
   the lyon shyneth bryght,
And fervently dothe rage with yre,
   And byttes prepares to fyght.
Even now loe he some starre wyl take:
   with mouthe full wyde to see
He thretnyng stands, and fyres out blowes
   and mane up rustleth he
Shaking with necke. the harvest sadde
   of shape, what ever thyng,
And what soever wynter collde
   in frosen tyme doothe bryng,
He with one rage wyll overpasse,
   of spryng tyme bull he wyll
Bothe seeke, and breake the neckes at once.
   AMPHITRYON. What is this sodayne yll?
Thy cruell cowntnance whether sonne
   Doste thou caste here and there?
And seeste with troubled daselde syght
   false shape of heaven appere?
HER. The land is taemde, the swellyng seas
   theyr surges dyd asswage,
The kyngdomes lowe of hell lykewyse
   have felte and knowne my rage,
Yet heaven is free, a labour meete
   for Hercules to prove.

To spaces hygh I wyll bee borne
   of hawghtye skyes abdue:
Let th'ayre be skaelde, my father dooth
   me promyse starrs t'obtayne.
What yf he it denyde? all th'earthe
   can Hercles not contayne,
And geeves at length to godds. me calls
   of owne accorde beholde
The whole assembly of the godds,
   and dooth theyr gates unfolde,
Whyle one forbydds. receyuste thou me,
   and openest thou the skye,
Or els the gate of stubborne heaven
   drawe after me doo I?
Do I yet doubte? I even the bondes
   from Saturne wyll undoe,
And even agaynst the kyngdome prowde
   of wycked father loe,
My grandsyre loase. let Titans nowe
   prepare agayne theyr fyght
With me theyr captayne ragyng: stones
   with woodes I wyll downe smyght,
And hye hylles topps with Centaures full
   in ryght hande wyll I take.
With double mountayne nowe I wyll
   a stayre to godds up make.
Let Chiron under Ossa see
   his Pelion mowntayne grette:
Olympus up to heaven above
   in thyrde degree then sette
Shall come it selfe, or ells bee caste.
    AM. Put farre awaye from thee
The thowghts that owght not to be spoake:
   of mynde unsownde to see,
But yet full great, the furyows rage
   asswage and laye awaye.
HER. What meaneth this? the gyantes doe
   pestiferous armes assaye,
And Tityus from the sprights is fledde,
   and bearyng torne to see
And empty bosome, lo howe neere
   to heaven it selfe stoode hee?
Cythaeron falles, the mountayne hye
   Pallene shakes for feare,
And torne are Tempe. he the toppes
   of Pindus cawght hathe here,
And Oethen he, some dredfull thyng

threatnyng doothe rage abowt
Erinnys bryngyng flames: with strypes
   she soundes nowe shaken out,
And burned brandes in funeralls,
   loe yet more neare and neare
Throwes in my face: fearce Tisyphone
   with head and ugly heare
With serpents sette, nowe after dogge
   fet owt with Hercles hande,
That emptye gate she hathe shette up,
   with bolte of fyry brande.
But loe the stocke of enmiows kyng
   doothe hydden yet remayne,
The wycked Lycus seede: but to
   your hatefull father slayne
Even nowe this ryght hande shall you sende
   let nowe his arrowes lyght
My bowe owt shoote: it seemes the shaftes
   to goe with suche a flyght
Of Hercles. Am. Whether doothe the rage
   and fury blynde yet goe?
His myghty bowe he drewe with hornes
   togyther dryven loe,
And quyver loaste: great noyese makes
   with vyolence sente owt
The shafte, and quyght the weapon flewe
   his myddle necke throwghowt,
The wownd yet left. Her. His other broode
   I overthrowe wyll quyght,
And corners all. What stay I yet?
   to me a greater fyght
Remaynes then all Mycenes loe,
   that rockye stones shoulde all
Of Cyclops beeyng ouertnrnde
   with hande of myne, downe fall.
Let shake bothe here: and there the house,
   with all staves overthrowne,
Let breake the poasts: and quight let shrinke
   the shaken pyller downe:
Let all the palayce fall at once.
   I here yet hydden see
The sonne of wycked father. Am. Loe
   his flattryng handes to thee
Applyeng to thy knees doothe crave
   his lyfe with pyteous mone.
O wycked gylte, full sadde, and eke
   abhorde to looke uppone,

His humble ryght hande caught he hath,
    and ragyng rownde abowt
Him rolled twyse, or thryse hath cast,
    his head resoundeth owt,
The sprynkled howses with the brayne
    of hym throwne owt are wet.
But shee poore wretche her lyttle sonne
    in bosome hydyng yet
Loe Megara, lyke one in rage
    doothe from the corners flee.
HER. Thowgh runnagate in bosome of
    the thundrer hydde thou bee,
This ryght hande shall from every where
    Thee seeke, and bryng to syght.
AM. wher goest thow wretch? what lurkyng
    seekste thou to take, or flyght?
No place of savegarde ys yf once
    bee Hercles styrde with yre:
But doo thou rather hym enbrace,
    and with thy meeke desyre
Assaye t' asswage hym. MEG. Husbande spare
    us I beseeche thee nowe,
And knowe thy Megara, this sonne
    thy cowntenaunce doothe showe,
And bodyes pytche: beholdst thow howe
    his hands up lyfteth hee?
HER. I holde my stepdame: followe on
    dewe penawnce paye to mee,
And bownden Jove from fylthy bonde
    delyver free awaye:
But I before the mother wyll
    this lyttell monster slaye.
MEG. Thou mad man whither goest thow?
    wylte thou thyne owne bloode sheade?
AM. Th'infant with fathers fyry face
    astonnyde all for dreade,
Dyed even before the wownde: his feare
    hath tooke away his lyfe.
And nowe lykewyse his heavy clubbe
    is shaken towarde his wyfe:
He broaken hath the bones, her head
    from blocklyke bodye gone
Is quight, nor any where it stayes.
    darste thow this looke uppone
To long lyude age? yf mournyng doo
    thee greue, thou hast then loe
The deathe preparde. Doo thou thy breast

uppon his weapons throe,
Or ells this clubbe with slaughter staynde
   of monsters slayne that bee,
Nowe hyther turne. thy parent false,
   unfytte for name of thee
Ryd hens away, least he shoulde be
   to thy renowne a let.
THE. Which waie ye father toward thy death
   dooste thow thy selfe caste yet?
Or whyther goest thou madde man? flee,
   and lye thow cloasely hyd,
And yet from handes of Hercules
   this onely myschiefe ryd.
HER. Tis well, the howse of shameful kyng
   ys nowe quyght overthrowne.
To thee O spowse of greattest Jove
   I have loe beaten downe
This offred flocke: I gladly have
   fulfyllde my wyshes all
Full meete for thee, and Argos nowe
   geeve other offryngs shall.
AM. Thow hast not sonne yet al performde,
   fyll up the sacrifyse.
Loe th'offryng doothe at th'aultars stande,
   it waytes thy hande lykewyse
With necke full prone: I gyve my selfe,
   I roon, I followe loe.
Mee sacrifyce. what meaneth this?
   his eyes rolle to and froe,
And heavynesse doothe dull his syght.
   see I of Hercules
The tremblyng hands? down falles his lace
   to sleepe and quietnes,
And weery necke with bowed head
   full faste doothe downewarde shrynke,
With bended knee: nowe all at once
   he downe to grownde doothe synke,
As in the woodes wylde asshe cut downe,
   or bulwarke for to make
A haven in seas. Lyuste thow? or els
   to deathe doothe thee betake
The selfe same rage, that hath sent all
   thy famylye to deathe?
It is but sleepe, for to and froe
   doothe goe and come his breathe.
Let tyme bee had of quietnesse,
   that thus by sleepe and reste

Greate force of his disease subdewde,
    may ease his greeved breste.
Remove his weapons servantes, least
    he madde gette them agayne.

CHORUS

Let th'ayre complain, & eke ye parent great
of haughty sky, & fertile land throughout,
And wandryng wave of ever mouing freate.
And thow before them all, which lands about
And train of sea thy beams abroad dost throe
with glyttryng face, & makst ye night to flee,
O fervent Titan: bothe thy settyngs loe
and rysyng, hath Alcides scene with thee:
& known likewise he hath thy howsen twayn.
from so great yls release ye nowe his brest,
O godds release: to better turne agayne
his ryghter mynde. and thow O tamer best
O sleepe of toyles, the quietnesse of mynde,
of all the lyfe of man the better parte,
O of thy mother astrey wynged kynde,
of hard and pinyng death that brother arte,
With truth mingling the false, of after state
The sure, but eke the worste foreteller yet:
O father of all thynges, of lyfe the gate,
Of light the rest, of nyght and felowe fytte,
that comst to kyng, and servant equallye,
And gentlye cherysshest who weerye bee,
All mankynde loe that dredfull is to dye,
thou doost constrain long deth to learn by thee,
keepe him fast bound with heavy slepe opprest,
Let slomber depe his limmes untamed bynde,
Nor sooner leave his unryght ragyng brest,
The former mid his course again may fynd.
Lo layd on ground with lull fierce hart yet styll
His cruell sleepes he turnes: and not yet is
The plague subdewde of so great raging yll:
And on great clubbe the weery head of his
He woont to lay, dothe seeke ye staffe to fynde
With empty hand, his armes owt castig yet
withmoving vayn: nor yet all rage of mynde
he hath laid down: but, as with southwind gret
The wane once vext, yet after kepeth styll
his ragyng long, & though the wind now be

Asswaged, swells. shake of these madde & yll
tossyngs of mynde, returne let pietee,
And vertue to the man, ells let be so
his mynd with moving mad tost every way:
Let errour blynde, where it begoon hath, go.
for nowght els now but only madnes may
Thee gyltlesse make: in next estate it stands
to hurtles hands, thy mischief not to knowe.
Now strooken let with Hercules his hands
thy bosoms sound: thyne armes ẏ world alow
wer wont to bear, let grevous strips now smite
with conquryng hand: & loude complaining cries
Let th'aire now here: let of dark pole & night
the quene them heare, & who ful fiersely lyes
That bears his necks in mighty chains fast
low lurking Cerberus in depest cave. (bound,
Let Chaos all with clamour sad resound,
and of broade sea wide open wafting wave.
And th'ayre that felt thy weapons better yet,
But felt them thowgh.
The brestes with so greate yls as these beset,
with litle stroake they must not beaten be.
Let kyngdoms three sound with one plait & cry,
and thow neckes honowr, & defence to se,
His arrowe strong long hanged up on hye,
& quivers light, ye cruel strypes now smyght
on his firce back, his shoulders strong & stowt
let oken clubbe now stryke, & poaste of might
with knots full harde his brests loade al about,
let even his weapons so greate woes complain.
Not you poore babes mates of your fathers
with cruel woud revenging kings agai: (praise,
not you your lims in argos barriars plaies,
Are taught to turn with wepon strong to smight,
& strong of hand: yet even now daring loe
the weapon of the Scythian quiver light
With steady hand to paise sent out from bowe,
and stags td perse ẏ save them selves by flyght,
and backes not yet full maend of cruel beast.
To Stygian havens goe ye of shade & night,
goe hurtles souls, whom mischief hath opprest
Even in first porche of lyfe but lately hadde,
And fathers furye. goe unhappy kynde
O little chyldren, by the way full sadde
Of journeye knowne.
Goe, see the angrye kyngs.

THE FYFTHE ACTE

HERCULES, AMPHITRYON,
    THESEUS.
What place is this? what region?
    or of the worlde what coaste?
Where am I? under ryse of sonne,
    or bonde els uttermoste
Of th'ycy beare? or els doothe here
    of sea of Hesperye
The fardest grownde appoynte a bonde
    for th'ocean sea to lye?
What ayre drawe we? to weery wyght
    what grownde is undersette?
Of truthe we are returnde from hell.
    whence in my howse downe bette
See I these bloudy bodyes? hath
    not yet my mynde of cast
Thinfernall shapes? but after yet
    returne from hell at last
Yet wander dooth that helly heape
    before myne eyes to see?
I am ashamde to grawnte, I quake,
    I knowe not what to mee,
I can not tell what grevous yll
    my mynde before dooth knowe.
Where is my parent? where is shee
    with goodly chyldrens showe
My noble hartye stomakt spowse?
    why dothe my lefte syde lacke
The lyons spoyle? whiche waye is gone
    the couer of my backe?
And selfe same bed full softe for sleepe
    of Hercules also?
Where are my shaftes? where ys my bow
    Them from me lyuing who
Cowlde plucke awaye? who taken hathe
    the spoyles so greate as thes?
And who was he that fearyd not
    even sleepe of Hercules?
To see my conquerour me lykes,
    yt lykes me hym to knowe:
Ryse victor up. what newe sonne hath
    my father gotten nowe
Heaven beeynge left? at byrthe of whome
    myght ever stayed bee
A longer nyght, then was in myne?

what myschiefe do I see?
My chyldren loe do lye on grownde
   with bloodie slawghter slayne:
My wyfe is kyllde: what Lycus clothe
   the kyngedome yet obtayne?
Who durst so heynous gyltes as these
   At Thebes take in hande
When Hercles is returnde? who so
   Ismenus waters lande,
Who so Acteons fieldes, or who
   with dowble seas beset
The shaken Pelops kyngdomes doste
   of Dardan dwell on yet,
Healpe me: of cruell slawghter showe
   who may the author bee.
Let rage my yre on all: my foe
   he ys, who so to mee
Showes not my foe. doste thou yet hydd
   Alcides victour lye?
Come foorthe, even whether thow revenge
   the cruell chariots hye
Of bloudy Thracian kyng, or yf
   thow Geryons catell quyght,
Or lordes of Libya, no delaye
   there ys with thee to fyght.
Beholde I naked stande, althowgh
   even with wy weapons loe
Thow me unarmed sette uppon.
   wherfore fleeth Theseus soe
And eke my father from my syght?
   theyr faces why hyde they?
Deferre your weepyngs, and who dyd
   my wyfe and chyldren sley
Thus all at ones, me tell. Wherfore
   O father doest thow whushte?
But tell thow Theseu, but Theseu
   with thy accustomde truste.
Eche of them sylent hydes awaye
   their bashefull cowntnawnces,
And pryuelye they shedde their teares.
   In so greate yls as thes,
Of what owghte we ashamde to bee?
   dothe ruler yet of myght
Of Argos towne, or hatefull bande
   Of sowldyars apte to fyght
Of Lycus dyinge, us oppresse
   with such calamytee?

By prayse of all my noble actes
    I do desyre of thee
O father, and of thy great name
    approvde to me alwaye
The prosperous powre, declare to me,
    who dyd my housholde slaye?
Whose praye laye I? A. Let thus thyne yls
    in sylence overpas.
HE. That I shoulde unrevenged bee?
    AM. Revenge ofte hurtfull was.
HE. Dyd ever man so grevows ylles
    without revenge sustayne?
A. Whos'ever greater feard. H. Then these,
    O father yet agayne
May any greater thing, or els
    More grevows feared bee?
AM. How greate a parte is it thow wotst,
    Of thy calamitee?
HER. Take mercy father, lo I lyfte
    to thee my humble handes.
What meaneth this? my hand Heeth backe,
    some privye gylte here standes.
Whēce coms this blood? or what doth mean
    flowyng with deathe of chyllde
The shafte, enbrewde with slawghter once
    of Lerney monster kyllde?
I see my weapons nowe, the hande
    I seeke no more to wyt.
Whose hand could bend this bow but myne?
    or what ryght arme but yt
Coulde stryng the bowe, that unto me
    Even scantely doothe obaye?
To you I tourne: O father deere,
    is thys my gylte I praye?
They healde theyr peace: it is myne owne.
    AM. Thy greevous woe is there,
The cryme thy stepdames: this myschawnce
    no fawte of thyne hath here.

THE SIEGE OF JOTAPATA

Jewish War, Book III

Josephus

Translated by H. St. J. Thackeray, 1926

In AD 66, sixty years after the Romans transformed Judaea into a Roman province, the Jews revolted. The Jewish War with Rome lasted until AD 73/4 and resulted in the destruction of Jerusalem and its Temple. Nero put his general Vespasian at the head of the campaign. The Roman-Jewish historian **Josephus** (AD 37–c. 100) – who had commanded the Jewish forces against the Romans at the Siege of Jotapata (Yodfat) before being captured and enslaved – later told the story of the siege in the third book of his *Jewish War*. His description of how he avoided having to die is justly famous.

But Josephus, when the city was on the point of being taken, aided by some divine providence, had succeeded in stealing away from the midst of the enemy and plunged into a deep pit, giving access on one side to a broad cavern, invisible to those above. There he found forty persons of distinction in hiding, with a supply of provisions sufficient to last for a considerable time. During the day he lay hid, as the enemy were in occupation of every quarter of the town, but at night he would come up and look for some loophole for escape and reconnoitre the sentries; but, finding every spot guarded on his account and no means of eluding detection, he descended again into the cave. So for two days he continued in hiding. On the third, his secret was betrayed by a woman of the party, who was captured; whereupon Vespasian at once eagerly sent two tribunes, Paulinus and Gallicanus, with orders to offer Josephus security and to urge him to come up.

On reaching the spot they pressed him to do so and pledged themselves for his safety, but failed to persuade him. His suspicions were based not on the humane character of the envoys, but on the consciousness of all he had done and the feeling that he must suffer proportionately. The presentiment that he was being summoned to punishment persisted, until Vespasian sent a third messenger, the tribune Nicanor, an old acquaintance and friend of Josephus. He, on his arrival, dwelt on the innate generosity of the Romans to those whom they had once subdued, assuring him that his valour made him an object rather of admiration, than of hatred, to the commanding officers, and that the general was anxious to bring him up from his retreat, not for punishment—that he could inflict though he refused to come forth—but from a desire to save a brave man. He added that Vespasian, had he intended to entrap him, would never have sent him one of his friends, thus using the fairest of virtues, friendship, as a cloak for the foulest of crimes, perfidy; nor would he himself have consented to come in order to deceive a friend.

While Josephus was still hesitating, even after Nicanor's assurances, the soldiers in their rage attempted to set fire to the cave, but were restrained by their commander, who was anxious to take the Jewish general alive. But as Nicanor was urgently pressing his proposals and Josephus overheard the threats of the hostile crowd, suddenly there came back into his mind those nightly dreams, in which God had foretold to him the impending fate of the Jews and the destinies of the Roman sovereigns. He was an interpreter of dreams and skilled in divining the meaning of ambiguous utterances of the Deity; a priest himself and of priestly descent, he was not ignorant of the prophecies in the sacred books. At that hour he was inspired to read their meaning, and, recalling the dreadful images of his recent dreams, he offered up a silent prayer to God. "Since it pleases thee," so it ran, "who didst create the Jewish nation, to break thy work, since fortune has wholly passed to the Romans, and since thou hast made choice of my spirit to announce the things that are to come, I willingly surrender to the Romans and consent to live; but I take thee to witness that I go, not as a traitor, but as thy minister."

With these words he was about to surrender to Nicanor. But when the Jews who shared his retreat understood that Josephus was yielding to entreaty, they came round him in a body, crying out, "Ah! well might the laws of our fathers groan aloud and God Himself hide His face for grief—God who implanted in Jewish breasts souls that scorn death! Is life so dear to you, Josephus, that you can endure to see the light in slavery? How soon have you forgotten yourself! How many have you persuaded to die for liberty! False, then, was that reputation for bravery, false that fame for sagacity, if you can hope for pardon from those whom you have fought so bitterly, or, supposing that they grant it, can deign to accept your life at their hands. Nay, if the fortune of the Romans has cast over you some strange forgetfulness of yourself, the care of our country's honour devolves on *us*. We will lend you a right hand and a sword. If you meet death willingly, you will have died as general of the Jews; if unwillingly, as a traitor." With these words they pointed their swords at him and threatened to kill him if he surrendered to the Romans.

Josephus, fearing an assault, and holding that it would be a betrayal of God's commands, should he die before delivering his message, proceeded, in this emergency, to reason philosophically with them.

"Why, comrades," said he, "this thirst for our own blood? Why set asunder such fond companions as soul and body? One says that I am changed: well, the Romans know the truth about that. Another says, 'It is honourable to die in war': yes, but according to the law of war, that is to say by the hand of the conqueror. Were I now flinching from the sword of the Romans, I should assuredly deserve to perish by my own sword and my own hand; but if they are moved to spare an enemy, how much stronger reason have we to spare ourselves? It would surely be folly to inflict on ourselves treatment which we seek to avoid by our quarrel with them. 'It is honourable to die for liberty,' says another: I concur, but on condition that one dies fighting, by the hands of those who would rob us of it. But now they are neither coming to fight us nor to take our lives. It is equally cowardly not to wish to die when one ought to do so, and to wish to die when one ought not. What is it we fear that prevents us from surrendering to the Romans? Is it not death? And shall we then inflict upon ourselves certain death, to avoid an uncertain death, which we fear, at the hands of our foes? 'No, it is slavery we fear,' I shall be told. Much liberty we enjoy at present! 'It is noble to destroy oneself,' another will say. Not so, I retort, but most ignoble; in my opinion there could be no more arrant coward than the pilot who, for fear of a tempest, deliberately sinks his ship before the storm.

"No; suicide is alike repugnant to that nature which all creatures share, and an act of impiety towards God who created us. Among the animals there is not one that deliberately seeks death or kills itself; so firmly rooted in all is nature's law—the will to live. That is why we account as enemies those who would openly take our lives and punish as assassins those who clandestinely attempt to do so. And God—think you not that He is indignant when man treats His gift with scorn? For it is from Him that we have received our being, and it is to Him that we should leave the decision to take it away. All of us, it is true, have mortal bodies, composed of perishable matter, but the soul lives for ever, immortal: it is a portion of the Deity housed in our bodies. If, then, one who makes away with or misapplies a deposit entrusted to him by a fellow-man is reckoned a perjured villain, how can he who casts out from his own body the deposit which God has placed there, hope to elude Him whom he has thus wronged? It is considered right to punish a fugitive slave, even though the master he leaves be a scoundrel; and shall we fly from the best of masters, from God Himself, and not be deemed impious? Know you not that they who depart this life in accordance with the law of nature and repay the loan which they received from God, when He who lent is pleased to reclaim it, win eternal renown; that their houses and families are secure; that their souls, remaining spotless and obedient, are allotted the most holy place in heaven, whence, in the revolution of the ages, they return to find in chaste bodies a new habitation? But as for those who have laid mad hands upon themselves, the darker regions of the nether world receive their souls, and God, their father, visits upon their posterity the outrageous acts of the parents. That is why this crime, so hateful to God, is punished also by the sagest of legislators. With us it is ordained that the body of a suicide should be exposed unburied until sunset, although it is thought right to bury even our enemies slain in war. In other nations the law requires that a suicide's right hand, with which he made war on himself, should be cut off, holding that, as the body was unnaturally severed from the soul, so the hand should be severed from the body.

"We shall do well then, comrades, to listen to reason and not to add to our human calamities the crime of impiety towards our creator. If our lives are offered us, let us live: there is nothing dishonourable in accepting this offer from those who have had so many proofs of our valour; if they think fit to kill us, death at the hands of our conquerors is honourable. But, for my part, I shall never pass over to the enemy's ranks, to prove a traitor to myself; I should indeed then be far more senseless than deserters who go over to the enemy for safety, whereas

I should be going to destruction—my own destruction. I pray, however, that the Romans may prove faithless; if, after pledging their word, they put me to death, I shall die content, for I shall carry with me the consolation, better than a victory, that their triumph has been sullied by perjury."

By these and many similar arguments Josephus sought to deter his companions from suicide. But desperation stopped their ears, for they had long since devoted themselves to death; they were, therefore, infuriated at him, and ran at him from this side and that, sword in hand, upbraiding him as a coward, each one seeming on the point of striking him. But he, addressing one by name, fixing his general's eye of command upon another, clasping the hand of a third, shaming a fourth by entreaty, and torn by all manner of emotions at this critical moment, succeeded in warding off from his throat the blades of all, turning like a wild beast surrounded by the hunters to face his successive assailants. Even in his extremity, they still held their general in reverence; their hands were powerless, their swords glanced aside, and many, in the act of thrusting at him, spontaneously dropped their weapons.

But, in his straits, his resource did not forsake him. Trusting to God's protection, he put his life to the hazard, and said: "Since we are resolved to die, come, let us leave the lot to decide the order in which we are to kill ourselves; let him who draws the first lot fall by the hand of him who comes next; fortune will thus take her course through the whole number, and we shall be spared from taking our lives with our own hands. For it would be unjust that, when the rest were gone, any should repent and escape." This proposal inspired confidence; his advice was taken, and he drew lots with the rest. Each man thus selected presented his throat to his neighbour, in the assurance that his general was forthwith to share his fate; for sweeter to them than life was the thought of death with Josephus. He, however (should one say by fortune or by the providence of God?), was left alone with one other; and, anxious neither to be condemned by the lot nor, should he be left to the last, to stain his hand with the blood of a fellow-countryman, he persuaded this man also, under a pledge, to remain alive.

Having thus survived both the war with the Romans and that with his own friends, Josephus was brought by Nicanor into Vespasian's presence. The Romans all flocked to see him, and from the multitude crowding around the general arose a hubbub of discordant voices: some exulting at his capture, some threatening, some pushing forward to obtain a nearer view. The more distant spectators clamoured for the punishment of their enemy, but those close beside him recalled his exploits and marvelled at such a reversal of fortune. Of the officers there was not one who, whatever his past resentment, did not then relent at the sight of him. Titus in particular was specially touched by the fortitude of Josephus under misfortunes and by pity for his youth. As he recalled the combatant of yesterday and saw him now a prisoner in his enemy's hands, he was led to reflect on the power of fortune, the quick vicissitudes of war, and the general instability of human affairs. So he brought over many Romans at the time to share his compassion for Josephus, and his pleading with his father was the main influence in saving the prisoner's life. Vespasian, however, ordered him to be guarded with every precaution, intending shortly to send him to Nero.

On hearing this, Josephus expressed a desire for a private interview with him. Vespasian having ordered all to withdraw except his son Titus and two of his friends, the prisoner thus addressed him: "You imagine, Vespasian, that in the person of Josephus you have taken a mere captive; but I come to you as a messenger of greater destinies. Had I not been sent on this errand by God, I knew the law of the Jews and how it becomes a general to die. To Nero do you send me? Why then? Think you that [Nero and] those who before your accession succeed him will continue? You will be Caesar, Vespasian, you will be emperor, you and your son here. Bind me then yet more securely in chains and keep me for yourself; for you, Caesar, are master not of me only, but of land and sea and the whole human race."

As Josephus predicted, Vespasian become emperor, ruling from AD 69 *to* 79, *and was succeeded by his son Titus, who was succeeded in turn by his brother Domitian. Freed by Vespasian, Josephus became a Roman citizen and lived out the rest of his life in Rome, where he wrote* The Jewish War *and other works of Jewish history.*

THE COLOSSAL TURBOT

Satires, IV

Juvenal

Translated by William Gifford, 1817; revised by John Warrington, 1954

Juvenal was one of the great satirists of ancient Rome. He flourished in the troubled times of Emperor Domitian (ruled AD 81–96), the 'last Flavian' and 'bald-pate Nero', who exiled him to the Egyptian desert after he made a particularly mocking reference. The AD 80s and 90s were fraught with anxieties. Political informers flourished until Domitian was assassinated in AD 96. Juvenal jests about Domitian's hair loss in this satire about a very expensive fish. The shady but wealthy Crispinus, a member of Domitian's staff, crops up in several of Juvenal's satires.

When the last Flavian, drunk with fury, tore
The prostrate world, which bled at every pore,
And Rome beheld, in body as in mind,
A bald-pate Nero rise, to curse mankind,
It chanced that where the fane of Venus stands,
Reared on Ancona's coast by Grecian hands,
A turbot in the Adriatic main
Filled the wide bosom of the bursting seine.
Monsters so bulky from its frozen stream
Maeotis renders to the solar beam,
And pours them, fat with a whole winter's ease,
Through the bleak Euxine into warmer seas.
The mighty draught the astonished boatman eyes,
And to the Pontiff's table dooms his prize.
For who would dare to sell it, who to buy,
When the coast swarmed with many a practised spy—
Beachcombers, prompt to swear the fish had fled
From Caesar's ponds wherein it erstwhile fed;
And, thus recaptured, claimed to be restored
To the dominion of its ancient lord?
Nay, if Palfurius may our credit gain,
Whatever rare or precious swims the main
Is forfeit to the Crown. Our boatman chose
To give what, else, he had not failed to lose.

Now were the dog-star's sickly fervours o'er;
Earth, pinched with cold, her frozen livery wore;
The sick of quartan fevers 'gan to speak,
And fiercely blew the blasts of winter bleak,
Keeping the turbot fresh. The boatman flew
As if the sultry South corruption blew;
And now the lake, and now the hill he gains,
Where Alba, though in ruins, still maintains
The Trojan fire which, but for her, were lost,
And worships Vesta, though with less of cost.
The wondering crowd, that gathered to survey
The enormous fish and barred the fisher's way,
Satiate at length retires; the gates unfold;
Murmuring, the excluded senators behold
The envied dainty enter. On the man
To 'great Atrides' pressed, and thus began:
'This, for a private table far too great,
Accept. The day as festive celebrate.
Make haste to load your stomach and devour
A turbot destined for this happy hour.
I sought him not: he marked the toils I set,
And rushed, a willing victim, to my net.'
Was flattery e'er so rank? Yet *He* grows vain,
And his crest rises at the fulsome strain.
When to divine a mortal power we raise,
He credits all hyperboles of praise.
But when was joy unmixed? No dish is found
Capacious of the turbot's ample round!
In this distress he calls the chiefs of state,
At once the objects of his scorn and hate,
In whose pale cheeks distrust and doubt appear,
And all a tyrant's friendship breeds of fear.
Scarce was the loud Ligurian heard to say:
'He sits, 'ere Pegasus was on his way;
Yes, the new bailiff of the affrighted town
(For what are Prefects more?) had snatched his gown
And rushed to council. From the ivory chair
He dealt out justice with no common care,
But yielded oft to those licentious times
And, when he could not punish, winked at crimes.
Then old, facetious Crispus tripped along,
Of gentle manners and persuasive tongue:
None fitter to advise the lord of all,
Had that pernicious pest, whom thus we call,
Allowed a friend to soothe his savage mood,
And give him counsel, wise at once and good.
But who shall dare this liberty to take

When, every word you hazard, life's at stake,
Though but of stormy summers, showery springs?
For tyrants' ears, alas! are ticklish things.
So did the good old man his tongue restrain,
Nor strove to stem the torrent's force in vain.
Not one of those who, by no fears deterred,
Spoke the free soul and truth to life preferred,
He temporized. Thus fourscore summers fled,
Even in that court, securely o'er his head.

    Next him appeared Acilius hurrying on,
Of equal age, and followed by his son
Who fell, unjustly fell, in early years,
A victim to the tyrant's jealous fears.
But long ere this were hoary hairs become
A prodigy among the great at Rome:
Hence I would rather owe my humble birth,
Frail brother of the giant brood, to Earth.
Poor youth! in vain the ancient sleight you try;
In vain, with frantic air and ardent eye,
Fling every robe aside and battle wage
With Numidian bears upon the Alban stage:
All see the trick, and, spite of Brutus' skill,
There are who count him but a trifler still;
For in his day it cost no mighty pains
To gull a prince with much more beard than brains.

    Rubrius, though not, like thee, of noble race,
Followed with equal terror in his face;
And, labouring with a crime too foul to name,
More than the pathic satirist lost to shame.
Montanus' belly next, and next appeared
The legs on which his monstrous pile was reared.
Crispinus followed, daubed with more perfume,
Thus early, than two funerals would consume;
Then bloodier Pompey,* practised to betray,
And quietly whisper noble lives away.
Fuscus,† an arm-chair strategist, is there,
Whose corpse the Dacian vultures wait to tear.
Last, shy Veiento with Catullus‡ came,
Deadly Catullus, who, at beauty's name,
Took fire, although unseen: a wretch whose crimes
Struck with amaze e'en these prodigious times;
A base, blind parasite, a murderous lord,
Raised from the bridge-end to the council-board;
Yet fitter still to dog the travellers' heels

---

* An informer.
† Cornelius Fuscus, Prefect of the Praetorian Guard, killed in Domitian's Dacian Wars, AD 86–8.
‡ Fabricius Veiento and Catullus Messalinus, both informers under Domitian.

And whine for alms to the descending wheels,
To blow soft kisses to the cars until
They reach the foot of steep Aricia's hill.
None dwelt so largely on the turbot's size,
Or raised with such applause his wondering eyes;
But to the *left* (Oh, treacherous want of sight!)
He poured his praise—the fish was on the *right*!
Thus would he in the amphitheatre sit
And shout with rapture at some fancied hit;
And thus applaud the stage machinery; where
The youths are rapt aloft and lost in air.
 Nor fell Veiento short. As if possessed
With all Bellona's rage, his labouring breast
Burst forth in prophecy: 'O Prince, I see
The omens of some glorious victory!
Some monarch taken prisoner of war:
Arviragus hurled from his British car!
The beast's a foreigner: there is no lack
Of prickles bristling all along his back.'
Proceed, Fabricius, and what remains untold
(The turbot's age and birth-place) next unfold.
 The emperor now the important question put:
'How say ye, Fathers? Shall the fish be cut?'
'Oh, far be that disgrace,' Montanus cries;
'No, let a dish be formed of amplest size,
Within whose slender sides the fish, dread sire,
May spread his vast circumference entire.
The matter's urgent; someone is required—
Prometheus—to see the oven's fired.
Bring, bring the tempered clay, and let it feel
The quick gyrations of the plastic wheel.
But, Caesar, thus forewarned, make no campaign
Unless your potters follow in your train.'
Montanus ended; all approved the plan,
And all the speech, so worthy of the man.
Versed in the old court luxury, he knew
The feasts of Nero and his midnight crew,
Where oft, when potent draughts had fired the brain,
The jaded taste was spurred to gorge again.
And in my time none understood so well
The science of good eating: he could tell
At the first relish if his oysters fed
On the Rutupian or the Lucrine bed;
At first sight of a sea-urchin he'd name.
The country, nay the district, whence it came.
 Here closed the solemn farce. The Fathers rise,
And each, submissive, from the presence hies—

Pale, trembling wretches, whom the Prince in sport
Had dragged, astonished, to the Alban court,
As if the stem Sycambri were in arms
Or the fierce Chatti threatened new alarms;
As if ill news by flying posts had come
And gathering nations sought the fall of Rome.
    Oh, that such scenes (disgraceful at the most)
Had all those years of cruelty engrossed,
Through which his rage pursued the great and good
Unchecked, while vengeance slumbered o'er their blood.
And yet he fell; for when he changed his game
And first grew dreadful to the vulgar name,
They seized the murderer, drenched in Lamian gore,
And hurled him headlong to the infernal shore.

CANNIBALS IN EGYPT

Satires, XV

Juvenal

Translated by Niall Rudd, 1991

Juvenal was not wholly complimentary about the customs of Egypt, where he found himself exiled during the reign of Emperor Domitian (see Story 79). In his satirical story of cannibalism, he nods to Odysseus' tales of his travels in Homer's *Odyssey* (see Story 6). While the cannibals of Homer were mythical, the cannibals of Egypt were, for Juvenal, only too real. Perhaps he really did witness an act of cannibalism, but there is little evidence for it in the historical sources. Juvenal addresses the story to a friend from the Roman province of Bithynia, on the north coast of what is now Turkey.

Volusius, my Bithynian friend, everyone knows
what monsters the mad Egyptians worship. Some of them honour
the crocodile, others bow down to the ibis bulging with snakes;
the long-tailed ape is sacred, with its gleaming golden image,
where lyre-strings magically echo from Memnon's mangled statue,
and ancient Thebes, with its hundred gates, is a heap of ruins.
In one place cats, in another fresh-water fish, in another
dogs are worshipped by entire towns; Diana by no one.
It's sin and sacrilege to sink your teeth in a leek or an onion
(a holy country indeed where such divinities grow
in gardens!); wool-bearing quadrupeds are strictly avoided
by guests at table; it's a sin to slit the throat of a kid.
The consumption of human flesh is in order. Ulysses, describing
a crime like that to the astonished Alcinous as they sat over dinner,
elicited anger, or in certain quarters possibly laughter,
as a spinner of lying yarns: 'Will nobody throw the fellow
into the sea? He deserves the horror of a real Charybdis—
he and his preposterous Cyclopes and his Laestrygonians!
I'd sooner believe in his Scylla, or those Cyancan rocks
that clash together, and the mighty winds tied up in a wine-skin,
or how Elpenor was struck with an elegant tap by Circe,
who packed him off to grunt amongst the swinish oarsmen.
Does he take the folk of Phaeacia for such a witless lot?'

That would have been a fair response from a guest, still sober,
who had drunk no more than a sip of wine from a jar of Corcyra;
for the Ithacan told that tale on his own; there was none to confirm it.
I have a story which, strange as it sounds, recently happened
when Iuncus was consul, beyond the town of sweltering Coptus.
Mine's a *collective* story; the stage can boast nothing like it.
You may look through all of tragedy's wardrobe from Pyrrha on,
but you'll find no *people* guilty of outrage. Now hear this example
of appalling barbarity, which has come to light in modern times.

Ombi and Téntyra are neighbours; but an old, long-standing feud
blazes between them still. It's an open wound and a source
of undying hatred. The madness infecting the two communities
comes from the fact that each detests the other's religion,
convinced, as it is, that the only deities worth the name
are those it worships itself. When one of the towns was holding
a sacred feast, the enemy's chiefs and leaders resolved
to a man that the chance should be seized to prevent the folk
      from enjoying
the happy auspicious day; they must not be allowed the pleasure
of a splendid banquet, with tables set at Cross-road and temple,
and couches that knew no sleep by night or day and were sometimes
found in place by the sun on his seventh circuit (yes, Egypt
to be sure is uncouth; but in self-indulgence its barbarous mob
aspires as high, or so I have found, as scandalous Canopus).
Victory, too, would be easy over a wine-sodden enemy,
slurred in his speech and reeling drunkenly . Here there were menfolk
prancing about to a negro piper, complete with perfumes
(such as they were) and flowers and garlands over their eyebrows.
There stood hunger and hate. It began with noisy insults;
but when tempers are boiling, these are the bugle that starts the fray.
Raising a common cry, they charged. In the absence of weapons
bare fists flew; and scarcely a jaw was left unbroken.
From the press of battle few, if any, emerged with a nose
that was not smashed in. Through all the ranks you could see men's faces
mangled, with unrecognizable features; cheek-bones poking
through gaping wounds, knuckles covered with blood from eyes.
And yet the combatants think it is just a game—like children
playing at soldiers—because no bodies are there to stamp on.
What is the point of a host of thousands starting a fight
if no one is killed? And so the attack grows fiercer; they look for
stones on the ground; then, bending their arms, they proceed to hurl
      them—
the type of weapon normally used by rioting crowds,
not great rocks of the size propelled by Turnus and Ajax,
and not so heavy as that with which the son of Tydeus
smashed Aeneas' hip, but such as the hands of today

can manage to throw, hands of a kind so different from theirs.
For the human race was already declining in Homer's time.
Now the earth gives birth to such nasty and puny creatures
that any god who observes them is moved to laughter and loathing.

After that brief digression our story continues. When one side
was joined by reserves, suddenly swords appeared in their hands;
they at once stepped up the attack with showers of deadly arrows.
As Ombi advanced, those who reside in the shady palmgrove
of nearby Téntyra turned their backs and fled in disorder.
One, as he ran in mindless panic, happened to trip,
and was seized. He was promptly chopped into countless bits
        and pieces,
so that a single corpse might furnish numerous helpings.
After that, the victorious mob devoured the lot,
and picked his bones. They didn't boil him in a seething cauldron
or roast him on spits. It seemed too long and too slow a business
to wait for a hearth. They were happy to eat the carcase raw.
One can only be grateful here, that they didn't profane the fire
which you, Prometheus, stole from the highest courts of heaven
and gave to earth. Three cheers for that element! And I imagine
you share my pleasure. But, to the man who chewed the corpse,
that was the most delicious meat he had ever tasted.
Nor, in this horrid act, would I leave you wondering whether
it was only the leader's gullet that experienced pleasure. The man
who had stood on the edge of the scrimmage, when nothing was left of
        the carcase,
scratched the ground with his nails to obtain a lick of the gore.

The Váscones, so the story goes, turned to such victuals
to prolong their lives. But the case was different; for over there
they had to contend with a hostile fortune, the disasters of war,
desperate conditions, the appalling distress of a lengthy siege.
It was when they had eaten every plant and creature and object
to which the pangs of a famished stomach drove them, when even too
their enemies pitied their pallor and their wasted skeletal limbs,
that they tore at another's flesh in their hunger; they were ready
        to swallow
even their own. What man or god could withhold indulgence
from bellies reduced to such frightful, and such outlandish, extremities,
bellies which could be forgiven by the very ghosts of the people
whose bodies they used as food? Now, of course, we know better
thanks to the teachings of Zeno, but who would expect a Spaniard
to be a Stoic, at least in the days of old Metellus?
Today the entire world has its Graeco-Roman culture;
smooth-tongued Gaul has been coaching British barristers; now
there's talk of hiring a rhetoric-teacher in Timbuctoo!

The community mentioned, however, was noble. It was matched by
    Zacynthus in valour and loyalty, and indeed outweighed in the scale
    of disaster.
But what excuse does Egypt have for being more savage
than Crimea's altar? (For the Tauric founder of that ghastly rite,
if one accepts the poets' tradition as worthy of credence,
contents herself with human sacrifice. Therefore the victim
has nothing more hideous to fear beyond the knife.) What affliction
recently goaded them? What ravenous hunger, what army
besieging their city walls impelled them to hazard an outrage
so revolting? What more could they do, if the land of Memphis
were parched with drought, to shame the lazy Nile into rising?
Neither the dreaded Cimbrian hordes, nor the barbarous Britons,
nor the grim Sarmatians, nor yet the wild Agathyrsi raged
with the utter frenzy displayed by that soft and worthless rabble
who are used to setting their tiny sails on earthenware vessels,
and to bending over their miniature oars in painted potsherds.

You will never match such a crime with punishment, or devise
    retribution
to suit communities such as these; for in *their* way of thinking
hunger and anger are one and the same. By giving tears
to the human race Nature revealed she was giving us also
tender hearts; compassion is the finest part of our make-up.
She therefore moves us to pity the accused, as he pleads his case
unkempt in body and dress, or the orphan who brings to court
his swindling guardian, and whose face, streaming with tears, and
    framed
by his girlish hair, invites the question 'Is he a boy?'.
It is Nature who makes us cry when we meet the cortège of a girl
on the eve of marriage, or a little child too small for the pyre
is laid in a grave. For what good man—the sort who deserves
the initiate's torch and lives as the priest of Ceres would have him—
believes that any woes are remote from *him*? It is this
that marks us off from the brutish herd. Moreover, we only
possess an intellect worthy of homage, have god-like powers,
and are able to learn and practise the arts of civilization,
because we received that gift, sent down from the castle in heaven,
which is lacking in four-footed creatures that stare at the ground.
    To them,
when the world began, our common creator granted no more
than the breath of life; to us, a soul as well. He intended
that our fellow-feeling should lead us to ask and offer help;
to gather scattered inhabitants into communities, leaving
the ancient woods, and deserting the groves where our ancestors lived;
to put up houses, placing another man's dwelling beside
our own abode, ensuring that we all slept safe and sound

in the knowledge that each had a friend next door; to shield with our
  weapons
a fallen comrade or one who reeled from a shocking wound;
to sound the call on a common trumpet; to man the turrets
in joint defence, and fasten the gate with a single key.

But nowadays snakes maintain a greater harmony. Spotted
animals spare their spotted kin; when did a stronger
lion tear the life from a weaker? Was there ever a forest
where a boar was killed, gashed by the tusks of a larger boar?
In India, one ferocious tigress lives with another
in constant peace; and savage bears observe an agreement.
To man, however, it is not enough to have forged his deadly
blades on an evil anvil. Early smiths were accustomed
to spend their energies fashioning only hoes and scuffles,
mattocks and ploughshares; they hadn't the skill to produce a sword.
But here is a people whose fury is not appeased by an act
of simple murder, who regard trunks, and arms, and faces
as a kind of food! What, one asks, would Pythagoras say?
Would he not take flight to no matter where, on witnessing these
enormities—that man who refused all meat, as though it were human,
and denied himself even the pleasure of certain vegetable dishes?

ACHILLES BECOMES A GIRL

Achilleid, Book I

Statius

Translated by D. R. Shackleton Bailey, 2003

> The *Achilleid*, an epic poem by **Statius** (*c.* AD 45–*c.* 96), is an unfinished Latin 'biography' of the Greek hero Achilles, tracing his life from his earliest childhood. Achilles' mother, Thetis, is a sea nymph or 'Nereid'. She has divine connections but seems entirely human as she tries desperately to prevent her son from going to fight at Troy, where she knows he is fated to die. A prequel, of sorts, to Homer's *Iliad*, the poem even has Patroclus, Achilles' closest friend in the epic, feature in his early life.

Icy pallor rivets the Nereid. The lad was there, much sweat and dust made him bigger, and yet amid weapons and hurried labours he was still sweet to look upon. A bright glow swims in his snow-white face and his hair shines fairer than tawny gold. Nor yet is his first youth changing with new down, the lights in his eyes are tranquil and much of his mother is in his face: like Apollo the hunter when he returns from Lycia and quits his fierce quiver for the quill. By chance too he comes rejoicing (ah how much does happiness add to beauty!): he had struck with steel a lioness newly whelped under Pholoë's crag and left her in her empty cavern, bringing home the cubs and provoking their claws. But when his mother appears on the trusty threshold, he throws them aside, picks her up and encircles her with greedy elbows, already powerful in his embrace and of height to match her. Patroclus follows, linked even then by a great love. He strains to rival such mighty deeds, equal in youthful zeal and manners but far behind in strength; yet he too was to see Pergamus, alike doomed.

Forthwith in a swift leap he approaches the nearest stream and freshens his steaming cheeks and hair in its water, like Castor entering the shallows of Eurotas with panting steed and furbishing the weary ray of his star. The ancient wonders at him, spruces him up, stroking now his chest, now his strong shoulders. Her joys torture the mother. Then Chiron* begs her to taste victuals and Bacchus' gift, weaving various delights for her amazement. At last he draws out his lyre, moving the care-comforting strings, and after making light trial of them with his

---

* *Chiron is the half-man, half-horse tutor to the young Achilles.*

thumb hands them to the boy. Willingly he sings mighty seeds of glory: how many commands of his proud stepdame Amphitryon's son accomplished, with what a glove Pollux crushed cruel Bebryx, with how strong a grip the son of Aegeus encircled and broke the limbs of Minos' bull, and finally his mother's marriage bed and Pelion weighed down by the High Ones. Here Thetis' anxious countenance yielded in a smile. Night draws to slumber. The huge Centaur collapses on stone and Achilles fondly twines himself about his shoulders, though his faithful mother is there, preferring the familiar bosom.

But Thetis in the night stands beside the sea-sounding rocks. Her mind is split this way and that as she turns over what secret place she should choose for her son, in what lands she should decide to conceal him. Thrace is nearest, but much given to Mavors' pursuits. Nor does the hardy race of Macedonians please, nor yet the children of Cecrops (they would spur him to glory). Sestos and the bay of Abydos are too much in the way of ships. She decides to go through the crowding Cyclades. Here she spurns Myconos and lowly Seriphos and Lemnos, to men unfriendly, and Delos, hospitable to all peoples. A while back she had heard from Lycomedes' unwarlike palace bevies of girls and the sound of their play along the shore, while on a mission to follow Aegaeon as he relaxed his harsh bonds and to number the god's hundred chains. This land pleases, this is safest for the fearful mother. Even so a bird, near to giving birth, already careful, already afraid, wonders on what branch to hang her vacant house; here she foresees winds, here thinks anxiously of serpents, here of men; finally as she doubts, a shady place takes her fancy; scarce has she alighted on the stranger boughs and all at once she loves the tree.

Another care remains for the sad goddess' weary pondering: should she herself take her son through the waters in her embrace or use mighty Triton, call on the swift winds to aid or Thaumas' daughter, wont to feed upon the sea? Then from the deep she summons her team, a pair of dolphins, bridling them with sharp seashells. Great Tethys had reared them for her in the Atlantic ocean, deep in an echoing sea hollow. No denizen of Neptune's watery kingdom has such beauty of grey-blue form, such power of swimming, or more of human mind. She tells them to halt in the full sea verge, so that contact with bare earth do them no hurt. Then she herself carries Achilles, his bosom all relaxed in the sleep of boyhood, down from the crags of the Haemonian cave to the placid waters and the shore commanded to be silent. Cynthia shows the way, shining out with all her orb. Untroubled by the sea, Chiron follows the goddess on her path and begs speedy return, hiding his moist eyes and gazing out from horse erect as they are suddenly carried away and presently hidden from sight, where for a little while foam the white traces of flight and the track dies upon the liquid flood. Him now sad Pholoë, now cloudy Othrys lament, no more to return to Thessalian Tempe, likewise Sperchios in thinner flow and the learned ancient's muted cavern. The Fauns miss his boyish songs and the Nymphs bewail long hoped-for nuptials.

Now day presses down the stars and Titan rolls his dripping steeds from out the low and level waters and the sea raised by his chariot falls from the vast sky. But the mother had already crossed the waves and was safe on Scyros' shore, the weary dolphins had left their mistress' yoke, when the boy's sleep was shaken and his wide eyes felt daylight pouring in. At first sight of sky he was stunned:

what place is this, what waves, where is Pelion? Everything he sees is changed and strange, and he doubts to recognize his mother. She hastens to caress the frightened lad and lovingly addresses him:

'Dear boy, if a kindly lot had brought me the marriage it proffered, I should be holding you in my embrace as a grand star in the celestial regions; of the great heaven should I have borne my child nor feared lowly fates and earthly dooms. As it is, my son, your birth is unequal and death's path blocked only on your mother's side. Ay, and the time of danger approaches, perils moved close to the final turning point. Let us give way. Lower a little your manly spirit and deign to wear my raiment. If the Tirynthian carried Lydian wool in his hard hand and womanish spears, if Bacchus it beseems to sweep his footsteps with a gold-embroidered robe, if Jupiter donned a virgin's limbs, and doubtful sexes did not rob great Caeneus of his manhood, pray allow me this way to escape the threat and the baleful cloud. Soon I shall give you back your fields once more, once more the Centaur's wilds. I beg you by your handsome looks and future joys of youth: if for your sake I made trial of land and a lowly spouse, if I armed you at birth with the stern Stygian river (and would it had been all of you!), for a little while take safe clothing, that will do no harm to your spirit. Why do you withdraw your face, what purpose is in your eyes? Are you ashamed to soften in this dress? I swear to you, dear boy, by my kindred sea, Chiron shall not know of this.'

So she wrought on his rough heart, coaxing in vain. Against her plea stands his father and his huge foster sire and the raw rudiments of a great nature: as though one were to try to subject a horse, haughty with the fire of unbridled youth, to his first harness; long delighting in field and river and proud beauty, he bends not his neck to the yoke nor his fierce mouth to the bit, loudly indignant to pass captive under a master's command, marvelling to learn new courses.

What deity bestowed artful trickery on the baffled mother? What mood diverted stubborn Achilles? It fell out that Scyros was celebrating a day in honour of Pallas of the Beach. The sisterhood, daughters of mild Lycomedes, had left their native walls on the holy morning (a rare licence) to give spring's riches to the goddess and bind her austere tresses with foliage and scatter flowers upon her spear. All possessed surpassing beauty, all were dressed alike; they had reached the term of tender modesty, their maidenhood, their burgeoning years, were ripe for the marriage bed. But as Venus overwhelms the green Sea Nymphs when she joins them, as Diana's shoulders outtop the Naiads, so far does Deidamia, queen of the fair choir, shine out eclipsing her lovely sisters. Purple is fired by her rosy face, her gems have more brilliance, her gold more allure. Her form equals the goddess' own, would she but lay aside her bosom's snakes and pacify her countenance, helmet removed. When the truculent boy, whose heart no stirring had ever assailed, saw her leading her attendant column from far ahead, he stiffened and drank novel flame in all his bones. Nor does his draught of love stay hidden; the brand waving in his inmost parts goes to his face and tinges the brightness of his cheeks, wandering over them with a light sweat as they feel the impulse. As when the Massagetae darken their cups of milk with scarlet blood or when ivory is tainted with purple dye, such is the sudden fire manifest by various signs, paling and blushing. He would go forward and wildly disrupt the rituals of his hosts, careless of the crowd and oblivious of his years, did not modesty and reverence for the mother by his side hold him back. As when the future father and leader of the herd, whose horns have not yet finished their full circle, looks upon the snow-white heifer who shares his pasture, his spirit takes fire and first love foams through his mouth, while the merry cowherds watch and oppose him.

His mother is already aware of his secret; seizing her moment, she makes her move: 'My son, is it so hard to feign to dance among these girls and join hands in play? What is there like this beneath chilly Ossa and the heights of Pelion? Oh if only it were mine to join loving hearts and carry another Achilles in my bosom!' He is softened and blushes for joy, casting sly, wanton glances, and lightens the hand that pushes the garments away. His mother sees his indecision, sees that he would fain be forced, and throws the folds over him. Then she softens the stiff neck, lowers the weighty shoulders, loosens the strong arms; she subdues the unkempt hair, fixing and arranging, and transfers her necklace to the beloved neck. Constraining his steps with an embroidered hem, she teaches him how to walk and move and how to speak with modesty. As wax that an artist's thumb will bring to life receives shape and follows fire and hand, such was the semblance of the goddess as she transformed her son. Nor did she struggle long. Charm is his in plenty and to spare, though manhood demur, and doubtful sex cheats the observer, hiding in narrow divide.

They go forward. Gently Thetis cautions and presses, over and over again: 'So then, my son, will you bear your step, so face and hands, copying your companions in fashions feigned, lest the ruler suspect you nor let you join the soft quarters and the falsehood of our artful enterprise go for nothing.' So she speaks, nor ceases her trimming and touching. So when Hecate returns weary from virginal Therapne to her father and brother, her mother attends her as she walks, herself covering shoulders and bared arms, herself relieving of bow and quiver, drawing down the girt-up gown and proudly ordering the dishevelled locks.

Forthwith she accosts the king and there calling the altars to witness she speaks: 'I give this girl, oh king, the sister of my Achilles (see you not how fierce she looks, how like her brother?) into your keeping. High-mettled, she asked for weapons on her shoulders and a bow, asked to shun wedlock Amazon fashion. But I have enough to worry about on my man-child's account. Let her convey the baskets and the holy things, do you rule and tame the froward wench and keep her in her sex, till it is time for marriage and relaxing of modesty. Don't let her practice wanton wrestlings or wander in woodland wilds. Raise her indoors, shut her among girls like herself. Especially be sure to keep her away from the beach and the harbour. You saw the Phrygian sails the other day. Ships have now learned to cross the sea and violate mutual laws.'

The father assents to her words and accepts Achilles disguised by parental craft—who should resist divine deceits? He even reverences her with suppliant hand and thanks her for choosing him. The flock of duteous Scyrian girls continue to stare relentlessly at the new maiden's face, marvelling how she outtops them by neck and hair, how broad she spreads her chest and shoulders. Then they urge her to share their dances and join their chaste rituals, yielding her place and rejoicing in the contact. As with Idalian birds when they break soft clouds, long congregated in their home and in the sky: if a stranger bird coming from a distant region join her feathers, at first they all wonder and fear, but presently they fly closer and closer and still in the air little by little they make her one of their own, merrily circling her with auspicious flap of wing, leading her to their lofty roost.

The mother lingers long at the threshold as she leaves, repeating her admonitions, planting secret mutterings in his ears and giving last words with muted countenance. Then the waters receive her and she swims away.

Achilles went on to have a son by Deidamia. When the truth of his gender was revealed, he had no choice but to join the fighting at Troy.

THE IMPORTANCE OF BREAST MILK

Attic Nights

Aulus Gellius

Translated by the Rev. W. Beloe, 1795

Aulus Gellius (*c.* AD 125–*c.* 180), who was brought up in Rome but spent several years of his life in Greece, was sufficiently interested in the debate over breast milk to include it in his commonplace book, *Attic Nights*. Named for their compiler's evenings of quiet study in a villa near Athens, the *Attic Nights* are a repository of the work of writers who would otherwise be forgotten, and a rich source of information about life in the second century AD. Women today, if not then, may well object to many of the views set out below.

Word was brought once to Favorinus the philosopher, when I was with him, that the wife of one of his disciples was brought to-bed, and a son added to the family of his pupil. "Let us go," says he, "to see the woman, and congratulate the father." He was a senator, and of a noble family. We, all who were present, followed him to the house, and entered with him. Then, at his first entrance, embracing and congratulating the father, he sat down, and enquired whether the labour had been long and painful. When he was informed that the young woman, overcome with fatigue, was gone to sleep, he began to converse more at large, "I have no doubt," says he, "but she will suckle her son herself." But when the mother of the lady said, that she must spare her daughter, and find nurses for the child that to the pains of child-birth might not be added the toilsome and difficult talk of suckling the child; "I entreat you, madam," said he, "allow her to be the sole and entire mother of her own son. For how unnatural a thing is it, how imperfect and half-sort of motherly office, to bring forth a child, and instantly to send him from her; to nourish in her womb, with her own blood, something which she has never seen, and not with her own milk to support that offspring which she now sees endued with life and human faculties, and imploring the tender care of a mother. And do you suppose," he continued, "that nature has given bosoms to women only to heighten their beauty, and more for the sake of ornament, than to nourish their children. For on this account (which be it far from you) many unnatural women endeavour to dry up and extinguish that sacred fountain of the body, and nourishment of man, with great hazard turning and corrupting the channel of their milk, lest it should render the distinctions of their beauty less attractive. They do this with the same insensibility as those who endeavour by the use of quack medicines to destroy their conceptions, lest they should injure their persons and their shapes. Since the destruction of a human being in its first formation, while he is in the act of receiving animation, and yet under the hands of his artificer, nature, is deserving of public detestation and abhorrence; how much more so must it be to deprive a child of its proper, its accustomed and congenial nutriment, when now perfect and produced to the world. But it is of no consequence, it is said, provided it be nourished and kept alive, by whose milk it is. Why does not he who affirms this, if he be so ignorant of the processes of nature, suppose like wife that it is of no consequence from what body or from what blood an human being is formed and put together? Is not that blood, which is now in the breasts, and has become white by much spirit and warmth, the same as that which was in the womb? But is not the wisdom of nature evident also in this instance, that as soon as the blood, which is the artificer, has formed the human body within its penetralia, it rises into the upper parts, and is ready to cherish the first particles of life and light, supplying known and familiar food to the new-born infants? Wherefore it is not without reason believed, that as the power and quality of the seed avail to form likenesses of the body and mind, in the same degree also the nature and properties of the milk avail toward effecting the same purpose. Nor is this confined to the human race, but is observed also in beasts. For if kids are brought up by the milk of sheep, or lambs with that of goats, it is plain, by experience, that in the former is produced a harsher sort of wool, in the latter a softer species of hair. So in trees, and in corn, their strength and vigour is great in proportion to the quality of the moisture and soil which nourish them, rather than of the feed which is put into the ground. Thus you often see a strong and flourishing tree, when transplanted, die away, from the inferior quality of the soil. What, I would ask, can be the reason then that you should corrupt the dignity of a new-born human being, formed in body and mind from principles of distinguished excellence, by the foreign and degenerate nourishment of another's milk? particularly if she whom you hire for the purpose of supplying the milk be a slave, or of a servile condition, or, as it often happens, of a foreign and barbarous nation, or if she be dishonest, or ugly, or unchaste, or drunken; for often, without hesitation, any one is hired who happens to have milk when wanted. And shall we then suffer this our infant to be polluted with pernicious contagion, and to inhale into its body and mind a spirit drawn from a body and mind of the worst nature? This, no doubt, is the cause of what we so often wonder at, that the children of chaste women turn out neither in body or mind like their parents. Wisely and with skill has our poet Virgil spoken in imitation of these lines in Homer,—

Sure Peleus ne'er begat a son like thee,
Nor Thetis gave thee birth: the azure sea
Produc'd thee, or the flinty rocks alone
Were the fierce parents of so fierce a son.

He charges him not only upon the circumstance of his birth, but his subsequent education, which he has called fierce and savage. Virgil, to the Homeric description, has added these words:

> And fierce Hyrcanian tygers gave thee suck.

Undoubtedly, in forming the manners, the nature of the milk takes, in a great measure, the disposition of the person who supplies it, and then forms from the seed of the father, and the person and spirit of the mother, its infant offspring. And besides all this, who can think it a matter to be treated with negligence and contempt, that while they desert their own offspring, driving it from themselves, and committing it for nourishment to the care of others, they cut off, or at least loosen and relax, that mental obligation, that tie of affection, by which nature binds parents to their children? For when a child is removed from its mother, and given to a stranger, the energy of maternal fondness by little and little is checked, and all the vehemence of impatient solicitude is put to silence. And it becomes much more easy to forget a child which is put out to nurse, than one of which death has deprived us. Moreover, the natural affection of a child, its fondness, its familiarity, is directed to that object only from which it receives its nourishment, and thence (as in infants exposed at their birth) the child has no knowledge of its mother, and no regret for the loss of her. Having thus destroyed the foundations of natural affection, however children thus brought up may seem to love their father or mother, that regard is in a great measure not natural, but the result of civil obligation and opinion." These sentiments, which I heard Favorinus deliver in Greek, I have, as far as I could, related, for the sake of their common utility. But the elegancies, the copiousness, and the flow of his words, scarcely any power of Roman eloquence could arrive at, least of all any which I possess.

DO IT YOURSELF

Attic Nights

Aulus Gellius

Translated by the Rev. W. Beloe, 1795

Aulus Gellius was one of Aesop's greatest admirers. In this snippet from his commonplace book, the *Attic Nights* (see Story 82 above) he retells a fable of Aesop's whose message is that if you want something done, you should do it yourself.

Aesop the fabulist of Phrygia, has justly been reckoned a wise man. He communicated his salutary admonitions, not, as is the custom of philosophers, with a severity of manners and the imperiousness of command; but by his agreeable and facetious apologues; having a wife and and salutary tendency, he impressed the minds and understandings of his hearers, by captivating their attention. His fable, which follows, of the bird's nest, teaches with the most agreeable humour that hope and confidence, with respect to those things which a man can accomplish, should be placed not in another but in himself.

"There is a little bird," says he, "called a lark; it lives and builds its nest amongst the corn, and its young are generally fledged about the time of the approach of harvest. A lark happened to build among some early corn, which therefore was growing ripe when the young ones were yet unable to fly. When the mother went abroad to seek food for her young, she charged them to take notice if any unusual thing should happen or be said, and to inform her when she returned. The master of the corn calls his son, a youth, and says, 'You see that this corn has grown ripe, and requires our labour; tomorrow therefore, as soon as it shall be light, go to our friends, desire them to come and assist us in getting in our harvest.' When he had said this, he departed. When the lark returned, the trembling young ones began to make a noise round their mother, and to entreat her to hasten away, and remove them to some other place; 'for the master,' say they, 'has sent to ask his friends to come to-morrow morning and reap.' The mother desires them to be at ease; 'for if the master,' says she, 'refers the reaping to his friends, it will not take place to-morrow, nor is it necessary for me to remove you to-day.' The next day, the mother flies away for food: the master waits for his friends; the sun rages, and nothing is done; no friends came. Then he says a second time to his son: 'These friends,' says he, 'are very tardy indeed. Let us rather go and invite our relations and neighbours, and desire them to come early to-morrow and reap.' The affrighted young tell this to their mother: she again desires them not to be at all anxious or alarmed. 'There are no relations so obsequious as to comply instantly with such requests, and undertake labour without hesitation. But do you observe if any thing shall be said again.'—The next morning comes, and the bird goes to seek food. The relations and neighbours omit to give the assistance required of them. At length the master says to his son, 'Farewell to our friends and relations; bring two sickles at the dawn of day; I will take one, and you the other, and to-morrow we will reap the corn with our own hands.'—When the mother heard from her young ones, that the master had said this: The time is now come,' says she, 'for us to go away; now what he says will undoubtedly be done; for he rests upon himself, whose business it is, and not on another, who is requested to do it.' The lark then removed her nest; the corn was cut down by the master."— This is the fable of Aesop concerning confidence in friends and relations, generally vain and deceitful. But what else do the more sententious books of philosophers recommend, than that we should make exertions for ourselves, nor consider as ours, nor at all belonging to us, what is external with respect to ourselves and our minds? Ennius has given this apologue of Aesop in his Satires, with great skill and beauty, in tetrameters. The two last, I think, it is well worth while to have impressed on the heart and memory.

"Always have in mind this sentiment, Expect not from your friends what you can do yourself."

ANDROCLES AND THE LION

Attic Nights

Aulus Gellius

Translated by the Rev. W. Beloe, 1795

The 'Appion' described as the earlier teller of this tale was Apion, an Egypt-born Greek writer of the first century AD. The story of Androclus – or 'Androcles' – and the lion is also found in Aesop and has been retold many times. It inspired, among others, George Bernard Shaw's play of 1912, in which Androcles is explicitly characterised as a Christian undergoing punishment for his faith.

Appion, who was called Plistonices, was a man of great and various learning, and had also very extensive knowledge of Greek. His books are said to have had considerable reputation, in which almost every thing is to be found that is most extraordinary in the history of Aegypt. But in those things, which he affirms that he either heard or read himself, from a reprehensible desire of ostentation, he is somewhat too talkative, being indeed, as to the propagation of his own doctrines, a boaster. But what follows, as it is written in his fifth book of Aegyptian Things, he does not affirm that he either heard or read, but saw with his own eyes in the city of Rome.

"In the largest circus,' he relates, "a shew of a very great hunting contest was exhibited to the people. Of this, as I happened to be at Rome, I was a spectator. There were many savage animals, beasts of extraordinary size, and of unusual form and ferocity. But, beyond all the rest," he observes, "the size of the lions was most wonderful, and one in particular was most astonishing. This one lion, by the strength and magnitude of his body, his terrific and sonorous roar, the brandishing of his mane and tail, attracted the attention and the eyes of all present. Among others who were introduced to fight with the beasts, was a Dacian slave, belonging to one of consular rank. His name was Androclus. When the lion observed him at a distance, he suddenly stopped as in surprize, and afterwards gradually and gently approached the man, as if recollecting him. Then he moved his tail with the appearance of being pleased, in the manner of fawning dogs: he next embraced, as it were, the man's body, gently licking with his tongue the arms and the legs of the man, half dead with terror. Androclus, in the midst of these blandishments of the ferocious animal, recovered his lost spirits, and gradually turned his eyes to examine the lion. Immediately, as if from mutual recollection, the man and the lion were to be seen delighted, and congratulating each other. This matter, in the highest degree astonishing, excited," as he relates, "the greatest acclamations from the people. Androclus was sent for by Caesar, who asked him the reason why this lion, fierce above all others, had spared him alone. Then Androclus told what is really a most surprising circumstance:—'When my master,' said he, 'had obtained the province of Africa as his proconsular government, by his unjust and daily severities I was compelled to run away; and, that my place of retreat might be safer from him, the lord of the country, I went to the most unfrequented solitudes and deserts; and if food should fail me, I determined to take some method of destroying myself. When the sun was at midday most violent and scorching, having discovered a remote and secret cave, I entered and concealed myself within it. Not long afterwards this lion came to the same cave with a lame and bloody foot, uttering groans and the most piteous complaints from the pain and torture of his wound.' He proceeded to declare, 'that when he saw the lion first approach, his mind was overcome with terror. But when the lion was entered, and as it appeared into his own particular habitation, he saw me at a distance endeavouring to conceal myself; he then approached me in a mild and quiet manner, and with his foot lifted up appeared to point and reach it out to me, as soliciting my aid. I then,' said he, 'plucked from the bottom of his foot a large thorn, which there stuck; I cleared the corruption from the inner wound, and more carefully, and without any great apprehension, entirely dried and wiped away the blood. He then, being relieved by my care and aid, placing his foot betwixt my hands, laid down and slept. From this day, for the space of three years, the lion and I lived together in the same den, and on the same food. Of the beasts which he hunted, the choicest limbs he brought to me in the den, which I, not having any fire, roasted in the mid-day sun, and ate. But being tired of this savage life, one day, when the lion was gone out to hunt, I left the den, and after a journey of three days was discovered and apprehended by the soldiers, and brought by my master from Africa to Rome. He instantly condemned me to a capital punishment, and to be given to the beasts. I understand,' he continued, 'that this lion also, after my departure, was taken, and now he has shewn his gratitude to me for my kindness and cure.'

Appion relates, that this narrative was told by Androclus, who explained all this to the people, inscribed and handed about on a tablet. Therefore, by the universal request, Androclus was discharged and pardoned, and, by the voice of the people, the lion was given him. "We afterwards," he relates, "saw Androclus, and the lion, confined only by a slight cord, go round the city and to the taverns. Money was given to Androclus, the lion was covered with flowers, and all who met them exclaimed, "This is the lion who was the man's friend! This is the man who was the lion's physician!"

PERSEUS AND MEDUSA

The Library, Book II

Apollodorus

Translated by Sir James George Frazer, 1921

The *Library* is a collection of Greek myths and heroic legends which bears the name of **Apollodorus**, a Greek scholar of the second century BC, but it is much more likely that it dates to the second or early third century AD. Authorship of the *Library* is therefore usually attributed to 'Pseudo-Apollodorus'. This story begins with Acrisius, King of Argos, and his daughter Danaë, and ends with Danaë's son Perseus and his beheading of the monster (Gorgon) known as the Medusa. These myths were famous long before they were boiled down to their bare essentials by Pseudo-Apollodorus.

When Acrisius inquired of the oracle how he should get male children, the god said that his daughter would give birth to a son who would kill him. Fearing that, Acrisius built a brazen chamber under ground and there guarded Danae. However, she was seduced, as some say, by Proetus, whence arose the quarrel between them; but some say that Zeus had intercourse with her in the shape of a stream of gold which poured through the roof into Danae's lap. When Acrisius afterwards learned that she had got a child Perseus, he would not believe that she had been seduced by Zeus, and putting his daughter with the child in a chest, he cast it into the sea. The chest was washed ashore on Seriphus, and Dictys took up the boy and reared him. Polydectes, brother of Dictys, was then king of Seriphus and fell in love with Danae, but could not get access to her, because Perseus was grown to man's estate. So he called together his friends, including Perseus, under the pretext of collecting contributions towards a wedding-gift for Hippodamia, daughter of Oenomaus. Now Perseus having declared that he would not stick even at the Gorgon's head, Polydectes required the others to furnish horses, and not getting horses from Perseus ordered him to bring the Gorgon's head. So under the guidance of Hermes and Athena he made his way to the daughters of Phorcus, to wit, Enyo, Pephredo, and Dino; for Phorcus had them by Ceto, and they were sisters of the Gorgons, and old women from their birth. The three had but one eye and one tooth, and these they passed to each other in turn. Perseus got possession of the eye and the tooth, and when they asked them back, he said he would give them up if they would show him the way to the nymphs. Now these nymphs had winged sandals and the *kibisis*, which they say was a wallet. But Pindar and Hesiod in *The Shield* say of Perseus:—

> "But all his back had on the head of a dread monster, The Gorgon, and round him ran the *kibisis*."

The *kibisis* is so called because dress and food are deposited in it. They had also the cap of Hades. When the Phorcides had shown him the way, he gave them back the tooth and the eye, and coming to the nymphs got what he wanted. So he slung the wallet (*kibisis*) about him, fitted the sandals to his ankles, and put the cap on his head. Wearing it, he saw whom he pleased, but was not seen by others. And having received also from Hermes an adamantine sickle he flew to the ocean and caught the Gorgons asleep. They were Stheno, Euryale, and Medusa. Now Medusa alone was mortal; for that reason Perseus was sent to fetch her head. But the Gorgons had heads twined about with the scales of dragons, and great tusks like swine's, and brazen hands, and golden wings, by which they flew; and they turned to stone such as beheld them. So Perseus stood over them as they slept, and while Athena guided his hand and he looked with averted gaze on a brazen shield, in which he beheld the image of the Gorgon, he beheaded her. When her head was cut off, there sprang from the Gorgon the winged horse Pegasus and Chrysaor, the father of Geryon; these she had by Poseidon. So Perseus put the head of Medusa in the wallet (*kibisis*) and went back again; but the Gorgons started up from their slumber and pursued Perseus: but they could not see him on account of the cap, for he was hidden by it.

Being come to Ethiopia, of which Cepheus was king, he found the king's daughter Andromeda set out to be the prey of a sea monster. For Cassiepea, the wife of Cepheus, vied with the Nereids in beauty and boasted to be better than them all; hence the Nereids were angry, and Poseidon, sharing their wrath, sent a flood and a monster to invade the land. But Ammon having predicted deliverance from the calamity if Cassiepea's daughter Andromeda were exposed as a prey to the monster, Cepheus was compelled by the Ethiopians to do it, and he bound his daughter to a rock. When Perseus beheld her, he loved her and promised Cepheus that he would kill the monster, if he would give him the rescued damsel to wife. These terms having been sworn to, Perseus withstood and slew the monster and released Andromeda. However, Phineus, who was a brother of Cepheus, and to whom Andromeda had been first betrothed, plotted against him; but Perseus discovered the plot, and by showing the Gorgon turned him and his fellow conspirators at once into stone. And having come to Seriphus he found that his mother and Dictys had taken refuge at the altars on account of the violence of Polydectes; so he entered the palace, where Polydectes had gathered his friends, and with averted face he showed the Gorgon's head; and all who beheld it were turned to stone, each in the attitude which he happened to have struck. Having appointed Dictys king of Seriphus, he gave back the sandals and the wallet (*kibisis*) and the cap to Hermes, but the Gorgon's head he gave to Athena. Hermes restored the aforesaid things to the nymphs and Athena inserted the Gorgon's head in the middle of her shield.

WAR ON THE GIANTS

The Library, Book I

Apollodorus

Translated by Sir James George Frazer, 1921

> Often celebrated in art, the war between the gods and giants belongs to early mythological history. **Pseudo-Apollodorus** clearly relished imagining the size of the giants relative to the landmarks on earth. Throughout antiquity, the strange rumblings of the earth and mountains were often explained by the existence of giants.

But Earth, vexed on account of the Titans, brought forth the giants, whom she had by Sky. These were matchless in the bulk of their bodies and invincible in their might; terrible of aspect did they appear, with long locks drooping from their head and chin, and with the scales of dragons for feet. They were born, as some say, in Phlegrae, but according to others in Pallene. And they darted rocks and burning oaks at the sky. Surpassing all the rest were Porphyrion and Alcyoneus, who was even immortal so long as he fought in the land of his birth. He also drove away the cows of the Sun from Erythia. Now the gods had an oracle that none of the giants could perish at the hand of gods, but that with the help of a mortal they would be made an end of. Learning of this, Earth sought for a simple to prevent the giants from being destroyed even by a mortal. But Zeus forbade the Dawn and the Moon and the Sun to shine, and then, before anybody else could get it, he culled the simple himself, and by means of Athena summoned Hercules to his help. Hercules first shot Alcyoneus with an arrow, but when the giant fell on the ground he somewhat revived. However, at Athena's advice Hercules dragged him outside Pallene, and so the giant died. But in the battle Porphyrion attacked Hercules and Hera. Nevertheless Zeus inspired him with lust for Hera, and when he tore her robes and would have forced her, she called for help, and Zeus smote him with a thunderbolt, and Hercules shot him dead with an arrow. As for the other giants, Ephialtes was shot by Apollo with an arrow in his left eye and by Hercules in his right; Eurytus was killed by Dionysus with a thyrsus, and Clytius by Hecate with torches, and Mimas by Hephaestus with missiles of red-hot metal. Enceladus fled, but Athena threw on him in his flight the island of Sicily; and she flayed Pallas and used his skin to shield her own body in the fight. Polybotes was chased through the sea by Poseidon and came to Cos; and Poseidon, breaking off that piece of the island which is called Nisyrum, threw it on him. And Hermes, wearing the helmet of

Hades, slew Hippolytus in the fight, and Artemis slew Gration. And the Fates, fighting with brazen clubs, killed Agrius and Thoas. The other giants Zeus smote and destroyed with thunderbolts and all of them Hercules shot with arrows as they were dying.

When the gods had overcome the giants, Earth, still more enraged, had intercourse with Tartarus and brought forth Typhon in Cilicia, a hybrid between man and beast. In size and strength he surpassed all the offspring of Earth. As far as the thighs he was of human shape and of such prodigious bulk that he out-topped all the mountains, and his head often brushed the stars. One of his hands reached out to the west and the other to the east, and from them projected a hundred dragons' heads. From the thighs downward he had huge coils of vipers, which when drawn out, reached to his very head and emitted a loud hissing. His body was all winged: unkempt hair streamed on the wind from his head and cheeks; and fire flashed from his eyes. Such and so great was Typhon when, hurling kindled rocks, he made for the very heaven with hissings and shouts, spouting a great jet of fire from his mouth. But when the gods saw him rushing at heaven, they made for Egypt in flight, and being pursued they changed their forms into those of animals. However Zeus pelted Typhon at a distance with thunderbolts, and at close quarters struck him down with an adamantine sickle, and as he fled pursued him closely as far as Mount Casius, which overhangs Syria. There, seeing the monster sore wounded, he grappled with him. But Typhon twined about him and gripped him in his coils, and wresting the sickle from him severed the sinews of his hands and feet, and lifting him on his shoulders carried him through the sea to Cilicia and deposited him on arrival in the Corycian cave. Likewise he put away the sinews there also, hidden in a bearskin, and he set to guard them the she-dragon Delphyne, who was a half-bestial maiden. But Hermes and Aegipan stole the sinews and fitted them unobserved to Zeus. And having recovered his strength Zeus suddenly from heaven, riding in a chariot of winged horses, pelted Typhon with thunderbolts and pursued him to the mountain called Nysa, where the Fates beguiled the fugitive; for he tasted of the ephemeral fruits in the persuasion that he would be strengthened thereby. So being again pursued he came to Thrace, and in fighting at Mount Haemus he heaved whole mountains. But when these recoiled on him through the force of the thunderbolt, a stream of blood gushed out on the mountain, and they say that from that circumstance the mountain was called Haemus. And when he started to flee through the Sicilian sea, Zeus cast Mount Etna in Sicily upon him. That is a huge mountain, from which down to this day they say that blasts of fire issue from the thunderbolts that were thrown.

THE METAMORPHOSIS OF CERAMBUS

Metamorphoses

Antoninus Liberalis

Translated by Francis Celoria, 1992

In the second century AD the author **Antoninus Liberalis** assembled an anthology of stories featuring metamorphosis. Myths involving the transformation of mortals into plants, animals or landscape features by angry gods and goddesses were popular throughout antiquity (see also Stories 59 and 64–66). This particular story had originally been published in the now lost Metamorphoses of Nicander, a Greek poet of the second century BC. In this concise retelling, Cerambus, a shepherd, is disturbed from his work on the slopes of Mount Othrys, which lies to the north-east of Lamia in central Greece. Pan, the sylvan god, issues him some advice.

Cerambus, son of Eusirus, who was the son of Poseidon and of Eidothea the nymph of Othreis, lived in the land of the Melians on the spurs of Mount Othrys. He had numerous flocks and herded them himself.

Nymphs would help him since he delighted them as he sang among the mountains. He is said to have been the best singer of those days and was famous for his rural songs. In those hills he devised the shepherd's pipes and was the first of mankind to play the lyre, composing many beautiful songs.

It is said that because of this the nymphs one day became visible to Cerambus as they danced to the strumming of his lyre. Pan, in goodwill, gave him this advice: to leave Othrys and pasture his flocks on the plain, for the coming winter was going to be exceptionally and unbelievably severe.

Cerambus, with the arrogance of youth, decided – as though smitten by some god – not to drive his beasts from Othrys to the plain. He also uttered graceless and mindless things to the nymphs, saying they were not descended from Zeus, but that Deinó had given birth to them, with the River Spercheius as the father. He also said that Poseidon, for lust of one of them, Diopatra, had made her sisters put down roots and turned them into poplars until, satiated with his desires, he had returned them to their original shapes.

Thus did Cerambus taunt the nymphs. After a short while there came a sudden frost and the streams froze. Much snow fell on the flocks of Cerambus and they were lost to sight as well as were the trees and paths. The nymphs, in anger against Cerambus because of his slanders, changed him into a wood-gnawing Cerambyx beetle.

He can be seen on trunks and has hook-teeth, ever moving his jaws together. He is black, long and has hard wings like a great dung beetle. He is called the ox that eats wood and, among the Thessalians, Cerambyx. Boys use him as a toy, cutting off his head, to wear as a pendant. The head looks like the horns of a lyre made from a tortoiseshell.

FIRST LOVE

Daphnis and Chloe

Longus

Translated by George Thornley, 1657

Set on the island of Lesbos, the birthplace of the love poet Sappho, *Daphnis and Chloe* is a Greek novel of the late second or early third century AD. The young protagonists of this pastoral romance must overcome a series of impediments to their happiness. Their story, which is presented in the novel as a description of a scene in a picture, has often been considered too rude to print in full. Nothing is known of the life of its author. This translation captures the atmosphere of the original. The story of Daphnis and Chloe spawned a taste for pastoral writing in sixteenth- and seventeenth-century Europe and was a direct inspiration for Edmund Spenser's *Faerie Queene* (1590) as well as a ballet by Maurice Ravel (1912).

Mitylene is a City in Lesbos, and by ancient Titles of honour, it is the Great, and Fair Mitylene. For it is distinguisht, and divided (the Sea flowing in) by a various Euripus, and is adorn'd with many Bridges built of white and polisht Marble. You would not think you saw a City, but an Iland in an Iland. From this Mitylene some twenty furlongs, there lay a Mannor of a certain rich Lord, the most sweet and pleasant prospect under all the Eyes of Heaven. There were Mountains, stored with wild Beasts for Game; there were Hills, and Banks that were spread with Vines; the Fields abounded with all sorts of Corn; the Valleys with Orchards, and Gardens, and purles from the Hills; The Pastures with Sheep, and Goats, and Kine; the Sea billows dashed to the shore as it lay extended along in an open horizon, with a soft and glittering sand. In this sweet Countrey, the field and farm of Mitylene a Goat-herd dwelling, by name Lamo, found an Infant-boy exposed; by such a chance (it seems) as this. There was a Laun, and in it a place of thick Groves, and many brakes, all lined with wand'ring Ivie, the inner ground furred over with a finer sort of grasse, and on that the Infant lay. A Goat coming often hither, neglecting still her own Kid, to attend the wretched child. Lamo observes her frequent outs and Discursations, and pittying that the Kid should be so forsaken, follows her even at high-noon; and anon he sees the Goat walking carefully about the child, holding up, and setting down her feet softly, lest she should chance to tread upon it, or to hurt it with her hooves; and the Infant drawing milk as from the breast of a kind mother. And wondering at it, (as well he might) he comes nearer, and finds it a manchild, a lusty boy, and beautifull; with pretious accoutrements about him, the monuments and admonitions of a secret noble Stem. His mantle, or little Cloak was purple, fastened with a Golden button; and by his side, a little dagger, the handle polisht Ivory. He thought at first to take away the fine Things, and take no thought about the child. But afterwards conceiving shame within himself if he should not imitate the kindnesse and philanthropy that he had seen in that Goat, waiting till the night came on, he brings all to Myrtale his Wife, the boy, his pretious Trinkets, and the Goats. But Myrtale all amazed at This, What (quoth she) do Goats cast boyes? Then he fell to tell her all; namely, how he had found him Exposed; how suckled, how overcome by meer shame he could not leave the sweet child to dye in that forsaken thicket. And therefore when he discerned Myrtale was of his mind, the things exposed together with him, are laid up carefully and hid; they say the boy's their own child, and put him to the Goat to nurse. And that his name might be indeed a Shepherds name, they agreed to call him Daphnis. And now when two years time was past, a shepherd of the neighbouring fields, had the luck to see such sights and find such rarities as Lamo did. There was a Nymphaeum, a solitary, sacred Cave of the Nymphs, a huge rock, hollow and vaulted within, but round without. The Statues, or Images of the Nymphs were cut out most curiously in stone, bare-footed, and bare-legg'd; their arms naked up to the shoulders; all their hair loose and playing carelessly, their eyes and lips smiting the Moediama, the proper sweetnesse of the Nymphs; their vests, and lawnie-petticoats tied, and tuckt up at the waste. The whole presence made a figure as of a divine ammusing Dance, or Masque. The mouth, and sieling of the Cave reacht the midst of that great rock. And from below out of the Chasme, gusht a strong Chrystal Fountain into a fair current or brook, and made before the holy Cave, a fresh green, and flowery Mead. There were hanged up, and consecrated there, the milking-pailes of fair Maids; Shepherds-pipes, ho-boyes, whistles, and reeds, the Gifts and Anathema's of the ancient Shepherds. To this Cave the often gadding of an Ewe, made the Shepherd often think, that she undoubtedly was lost. Desiring therefore to correct the straggler, and reduce her to her rule; of a green With, he made a snare, and lookt to catch her in the Cave. But when he came there, he saw things he never dreamed of. For he saw her giving suck from her duggs in a very humane manner; and an Infant, without crying, greedily to lay, first to one dugge, then the t'other, a most neat and fair mouth: for when the Child had suckt enough, the careful Nurse lickt it still, and trimmed it up. That Infant was a Girle, and in such manner as before, was trickt and harnessed out with fine and rich advertisements of her origin and Extraction: on her head she wore a Mitre embroider'd with Gold; her shoes were Gilded; her blankets and Mantle cloth of Gold. Wherefore Dryas thinking with himself that this could not come about without the providence of the Gods, and learning mercy from the Sheep, takes her up into his arms, puts her Monuments into his Scrip, and prayes to the Nymphs he may happily preserve, and bring up, their Suppliant, and Votary. Now therefore when it was time to drive home his flocks, he comes to his Cottage, and tells all, that he had seen, to his Wife; shews her what he had found; bids her think she is her daughter; and however, nurse her up, though uncertain, though unknown. Nape, that was her name, began presently to be a Mother, and with a kind of Jealousie would appear to love the Child, lest that Ewe should get more praise; and all in haste gives her the pastoral Name of Chloe, to assure us, it's their own. These Infants, grew up apace, and still their beauty appeared too excellent to suit with rusticks, or derive at all from Clowns. And Daphnis now is fifteen, and Chloe younger two years. Upon a night Lamo and Dryas had their visions in their sleep. They thought they saw those Nymphs, the Goddesses of the Cave, out of which the Fountain gusht out into a stream; and where Dryas found Chloe; That they delivered Daphnis and Chloe to a certain young boy, very disdainfull, very fair; one that had wings at his shoulders, wore a bowe, and little darts; and that this boy did touch them both with the very self-same dart; and commanded it from thenceforth, one should feed his flock of Goats; the other keep her flock of sheep. This dream being dreamed by both, they could not but conceive grief, to think that Daphnis and Chloe should be nothing but Goat-herds like themselves, when they had read them better fortune from their Infant Swaddling cloaths; and for that cause, had both allowed them bolted bread, with a finer sort of meat, and bin at charge to teach them to read a ballad in the Lesbian Tongue; and whatsoever things were passing brave, among the rurall Swains and Girls. Yet neverthelesse it seemed fit, that the Mandats of the Gods concerning them, who by their providence were saved, should be attended, and obeyed. And having told their dreams to one another, and sacrificed in the cave of the Nymphs to that winged boy (for his name they knew not yet:) They set them out Shepherds with their flocks; and to every thing instructed: how to feed before high-noon, and when the scorching Glare declined; when to drive their flocks to water; when to bring them to the folds; what cattell was disciplin'd with the Crook; what commanded by the Voice. And now this pretty pair of young Shepherds, are as jocund in themselves as if they had got some great Empire, while they sit looking over their goodly flocks; and with more than usual kindnesse, treated both the Sheep and Goats. For Chloe thankfully referred her preservation to a Sheep: and Daphnis had not forgot to acknowledge his to a Goat.

It was the beginning of Spring, and all the flowers of the Launs, Meadowes, Valleyes, and Hills, were now blowing; all was fresh, and green, and odorous. The Bee's humming from the flowers, the Bird's warbling from the groves, the Lamb's skipping on the hills, were pleasant to the ear, and eye. And now when such a fragrancy had filled those blest and happy fields, both the old men and the young, would imitate the pleasant things they heard, and saw; and hearing how the birds did chant it, they began to carroll too; and seeing how the Lambs skipt, tript their light and nimble measures; then to emulate the Bees, they fall to cull the fairest flowers. Some of which in toysome sport they cast in one anothers bosoms, and of some plaited Garlands for the Nymphs. And always keeping near together, had, and did all things in common: for Daphnis often gathered in the straggling sheep; and Chloe often drove the bolder ventrous Goats from the crags, and precipices; and sometimes to one of them, the care of both the flocks was left, while the other did intend some pretty knack, or Toysome play. For all their sport, were sports of children, and of Shepherds. Chloe scudding up and down, and here and there picking up the windlestrawes; would make in plats, a Trap to catch a Grasshopper; and be so wholly bent on that, that she was carelesse of her flocks. Daphnis on the other side, having cut the slender reeds, and bored the quils, or intervals between the joynts, and with his soft wax joyned and fitted one to another; took no care but to practise, or devise some tune, even from morning, to the twilight. Their wine, and their milk, and whatever was brought from home to the fields, they had still in common. And a man might sooner see all the Cattel separate from one another, than he should Chloe and Daphnis, asunder. But while they are thus playing away their time, to sweeten pleasure, afterwards Love procures them these Cares: A Wolf that had a kennel of whelps, came often ravenous upon the fields, and bore away many cattel, because she needed much prey, to keep her self and those cubs. The Villagers therefore meet together, and in the night they dig a ditch of a proportinall Length, and Depth, and Breadth; the earth flung up they scatter all abroad at a good distance, by handfulls; and laying over-crosse the Chasm, long, dry, and rotten sticks, they strow them over with that earth which did remain: that if a Hare did but offer to run there, she could not choose but break those rods, that were as brittle as the stubble; and then would easily make it known, that that indeed was not true, but only Counterfeited Soil. Many such Trap-ditches were digg'd in the Mountains, and the fields; yet they could not take this Wolf, (for she could perceive the Sophi-stick, and commentitious ground:) but many of the Sheep and Goats were there destroyed; and there wanted but a little, that Daphnis too was not slain; and it was on this chance: Two he-goats were exasperated to fight, and the shock was furious. One of them, by the violence of the very first Butt, had one of his horns broke; upon the pain and grief of that, all in a fret and mighty chase, he betakes himself to flight: but the victor pursuing him close, would not let him take breath. Daphnis was vext to see the horn broke, and that kind of male-pertnesse of the Goat; up he catches his club and pursues the pursuer. But, as it frequently happens when one hastes away as fast as possibly he can, and the other with ardency pursues; there was no certain prospect of the things before them, but into the Trap-ditch both fall, first the Goat, then Daphnis. And indeed it was only this that served to save poor Daphnis, that he flunder'd down to the bottome of the ditch a cock-horse on the rough Goat. There in a lamentable case he lay, waiting, if perchance it might be some body to draw him out. Chloe seeing the accident, away she flyes to weep over Daphnis his grave, and found he was alive, though buried there, and calls for help to a herdsman of the adjoyning fields. When he was come, he bustled about for a long Cord: but finding none, Chloe in a tearing haste, pulls off her hair-lace and her fillet, gives him them to let down; and standing on the pit brim, both began to draw and hale; and Daphnis holding fast by it, nimbly followed Chloe's line, and so ascended to the Top. They drew up too the wretched Goat which now had both his horns broke (so fiercely did the revenge of the victor pursue him,) and they gave him to the herdsman as a reward of the rescue, and redemption of their lives. And if any body mist him at home, they would say it was the Invasion of the Wolf: and so returned to their Sheep and Goats. And when they had found that all were feeding orderly, according to the precepts of Lamo and Dryas; sitting down upon the Trunk of an Oak, they began curiously to search, whether he had hurt any limb in that terrible fall; but nothing was hurt, nothing bloodied; onely his head, his bosome, and some other parts, were durtied by the soil which covered over, and hid the Trap. And therefore they thought it best before the accident was made known to Lamo and Myrtale, that he should wash himself in the Cave of the Nymphs. And coming there together with Chloe, he gives her his Scrip, his Jacket, and his Shirt to hold while he washt.

Chloe kisses Daphnis, who is then abducted by pirates. Chloe plays a tune which incites some cows to capsize the pirate ship. Daphnis is rescued. At the time of the grape harvest, an old man called Philetas talks to the young couple of love.

And, what is Love (quoth Chloe then)? Is he a boy, or is he a bird? And, what can he do, I pray you, Gaffer?

Therefore again—thus Philetas: Love (sweet Chloe) is a god, a young Youth, and very fair, and wing'd to flye. And therefore he delights in youth, follows beauty, and gives our phantasie her wings. His power's so vaste, that that of Jove is not so great. He governs in the Elements, rules in the Stars, and domineers even o're the gods, that are his Peers. Nor have you only dominion o're your Sheep and Goats, for Love has there his range too. All flowers are the works of Love. Those Plants are his creations, and Poems. By him it is that the rivers flow, and by him the winds blow. I have known a Bull that has been in Love, and run bellowing through the Meadows, as if he had been prickt with a Goad; a he-goat too so in Love with a Virgin-she, that he has followed her up and down, through the woods, through the Launs. And I myself, when I was young, was in love with Amaryllis, and forgot to eat my meat, and drink my drink; and for many tedious nights, never could compose to sleep: my panting heart was very sad and anxious, and my body shook with cold: I cryed out oft, as if I had bin thwackt and basted back and sides: and then again, was still and mute, as if I had layen among the dead: I cast my self into the Rivers, as if I had been all on a fire: I call'd on Pan, that he would help me, as having sometimes bin himself catcht with the Love of peevish Pitys: I praised the Echo, that with kindnesse it restored, and trebbled to me, the dear name of Amaryllis: I broke my Pipes, because they could delight, and lead the sturdy herds which way I would, and could not draw the froward girle. For there is no med'cine for Love, neither meat, nor drink, nor any Charm, but only Kissing, and Embracing, and lying naked together.

The young couple continue kissing. Some young men from a city on Lesbos arrive and beat Daphnis when his goats eat the willows which tether their ship to the shore. Daphnis is separated from Chloe for the winter before being reunited with her.

But Chloe asking him, whether anything remain'd more than kissing, embracing, and lying together upon the ground; or what he could do by lying naked upon a naked Girle?

That (quoth he) which the Rams use to do with the Ewes, and the he-Goats with the She's. Do you not see, how after that work, neither these run away, nor those weary themselves in pursuit of them; but afterwards how enjoying a common pleasure, they feed together quietly. That... as it seems is a sweet practice, and such as can master the bitternesse of Love.

How Daphnis? And dost thou not see the she-Goats and the Ewes, the he-Goats and the Rams, how these do their work standing, and those suffer standing too; these leaping and those admitting them upon their backs? And yet thou askest me to lye down, and that naked. But how much rougher are they than I, although I have all my Clothes on?

Daphnis is persuaded, and laying her down, lay down with her, and lay long; but knowing how to do nothing of that he was mad to do, lifted her up, and endeavour'd to imitate the Goats. But at the first finding a mere frustration there, he sate up, and lamented to himself, that he was more unskilfull than a very Tup in the practice of the mystery and the Art of Love. But there was a certain neighbour of his, a landed man, Chromis his name, and was now by his age somewhat declining. He married out of the City a young, fair, and buxome girle, one that was too fine and delicate for the Country, and a Clown: Her name was Lycaenium; and she observing Daphnis as every day early in the morning he drove out his Goats to the fields, and home again at the first twilight, had a great mind to purchase the youth by gifts to become her sweetheart. And therefore once when she had sculkt for her opportunity, and catcht him alone, she gave him a curious fine pipe, some pretious honey-combs, and a new Scrip of Stag-skin: but durst not break her mind to him, because she could easily conjecture at that dear love he bore to Chloe. For she saw him wholly addicted to the girle: which indeed she might well perceive before, by the winking, nodding, laughing and tittering that was between them: but one morning she made Chromis believe that she was to go to a womans labour, and followed softly behind them two at some distance, and then slipt away into a thicket and hid herself, and so could hear all that they said, and see too all that they did; and the lamenting untaught Daphnis was perfectly within her reach. Wherefore she began to condole the condition of the wretched Lovers, and finding that she had light upon a double opportunity; this, to the preservation of them; that, to satisfie her own wanton desire, she projected to accomplish both by this device. The next day making as if she were to go a Gossipping again, she came up openly to the Oak where Daphnis and Chloe were sitting together; and when she had skilfully counterfeited that she was feared, Help (Daphnis) help me, (quoth she), An Eagle has carried away from me the goodliest Goose of twenty in a flock, which yet, by reason of the great weight, she was not able to carry to the top of that her wonted high crag, but is fallen down with her into yonder Cops. For the Nymph's sake, and this Pan's, do thou Daphnis go in to the Wood, and rescue my Goose. For I dare not go in my self alone. Let me not thus lose the Tale of my Geese. And it may be thou mayest kill the Eagle too, and then she will scarce come hither any more to prey upon the Kids and Lambs. Chloe for so long will look to the flock; the Goats know her as thy perpetuall Companion in the fields. Now Daphnis suspecting nothing of that that was intended, gets up quickly, and taking his staff followed Lycaenium, who lead him a great way off from Chloe. But when they were come to the thickest part of the wood, and she had bid him sit down by a Fountain: Daphnis (quoth she) Thou dost love Chloe, and that I learned last night of the Nymphs. Those tears which yesterday thou didst pour down, were shewn to me in a dream by them, and they commanded me, that I should save thee, and teach thee the secret practices of Love. But those are not Kisses, nor embracing, nor yet such things as thou seest the Rams, and the he-goats do. There are other leaps, there are other friskins than those, and far sweeter than them. For unto these there appertains a much longer duration of pleasure. If then thou wouldst be rid of thy misery, and make an Experiment of that pleasure, and sweetnesse which you have sought, and mist so long, come on, deliver thy self to me a sweet Schollar, and I, to gratifie the Nymphs, will be thy Mistris. At this Daphnis as being a rustick Goat-herd, a Sanguin Youth, and burning in desire, could not contain himself for meer pleasure, and that Lubency that he had to be taught; but throwes himself at the foot of Lycaenium, and begs of her, that she would teach him quickly that Art, by which he should be able, as he would, to do Chloe; and he should not only accept it as a rare and brave thing sent from the gods, but for her kindnesse he would give her too a young Kid, some of the finest new-milk Cheeses; nay, besides, he promised her the dam her self. Wherefor Lycaenium now she had found the Goat-herd so willing and forward beyond her expectations, began to instruct the Lad thus—She bid him sit down as near to her as possibly he could, and that he should kisse her as close and as often as he used to kisse Chloe; and while he kist her to clip her in his arms and hugg her to him, and lye down with her upon the ground. As now he was sitting, and kissing, and lay down with her; She, when she saw him itching to be at her, lifted him up from the reclination on his side, and slipping under, not without art, directed him to her Fancie, the place so long desired and sought. Of that which happened after this, there was nothing done that was strange, nothing that was insolent: the Lady Nature and Lycaenium shewed him how to do the rest. This wanton Information being over, Daphnis, who had still a Childish Pastorall mind, would presently be gone, and run up to Chloe, to have an experiment with her, how much he had profited by that magistery, as if indeed he had bin afraid lest staying but a little longer, he could forget to do his trick. But Lycaenium intercepted him thus: Thou art yet Daphnis, to learn this besides. I who am a woman, have suffered nothing in this close with thee, but what I am well acquainted withall. For heretofore another Youth taught me to play at this sport, and for his pains, he had my maidenhead. But if thou strive with Chloe in this list, she will squeak, and cry out, and bleed as if she were stickt. But be not thou afraid of her bleeding; but when thou hast persuaded her to thy pleasure, bring her hither into this place, that although she should cry and roar, no body can hear; and if she bleed, here's a clear Fountain, she may wash; and do thou, Daphnis, never forget it, that I before Chloe made thee a man. These advertisements given, Lycaenium kist him, and went away through another glade of the Wood, as if still she would look for her Goose. But Daphnis considering with himself what had been said, remitted much of that impetuous heat he had to Chloe. For he durst not venture to presse her beyond his former kissing and embracing; because he could not endure that she should make an outcry, as against an Enemy, or shed tears for any grief or anguish from him, and much lesse that she should bleed, as if she had bin slain by Daphnis. For he himself not long before had had some experience of that when he was beaten by the Methymnaeans; and therefore he abhorred blood, and thought verily that no blood could follow but onely from a wound.

Too disturbed to make love with her, Daphnis decides that Chloe should remain a virgin. His hackles are raised when other suitors try to court her. His desire to marry her is aided by the discovery that he is not a poor man's son at all. He was exposed at birth by an aristocratic father whose family was already large enough. Chloe similarly turns out to be the daughter of a wealthy family. A rich life in the city does not appeal to the young couple, who return to a jolly wedding in the countryside. They are united, at last, by Love. Their future children will be shepherds.

Then when it was night, and Venus rising up the horizon, they all lead the Bride and Bridegroom to their Chamber, some playing upon Whistles and Hoboyes, some upon the oblique Pipes, some holding great Torches.

And when they came near to the door, they chang'd their tone, and gave a grating harsh sound, nothing like the Hymenaeus, but as if the Virgin Earth had bin torn with many Tridents.

But Daphnis and Chloe lying naked together, began to clip, and kisse, and twine, and strive with one another, sleeping no more than birds of the night; and Daphnis now did the Trick that his Mistris Lycaenium had taught him in the thicket. And Chloe then first knew, that those things that were done in the Wood, were only the sweetest Sports of Shepherds.

A SHAM SACRIFICE

Leucippe and Clitophon

Achilles Tatius

Translated by Anthony Hodges, 1638

Achilles Tatius was a Greek novelist of the second century AD from
Alexandria in Egypt. His tale of Leucippe and Clitophon, of unknown
date, shares many similarities with Longus' *Daphnis and Chloe*. The young
lovers have eloped only to run into trouble. When they are shipwrecked
they attempt to make their way to Alexandria. Some Egyptian bandits
– or 'theeves', in Anthony Hodges's dramatic seventeenth-century translation – set upon them and kidnap Leucippe with the intention of offering
her as a human sacrifice. Cue the highly theatrical series of events in this
extract from the novel.

... these theeves had built an altar of clay, and digged a sepulchre, two of them
led a virgin bound toward the altar, whom because they were in armour I knew
not, but the virgin I discerned to bee Leucippe; they poured oyle on her head,
and omitted not any ceremony; while an Aegyptian Priest sung an hymne, for
so I ghest by his making of faces and wry mouthes: immediately a watch-word
was given, and each man stood a pretty distance from the altar, then one of those
which led her made her fast to a stake (like Marsyas whom the potters frame
in clay bound to a tree) who stabbing her in the breast ript her downewards till
hee came to the paunch, so that her entrailes started out, which they snatching
up, speedily threw upon the altar, and when they had boiled them, cut them in
peeces, and eate them up, dividing to each man a share.

When the souldiers and Captaine saw this, they could not chuse but cry out at
the horridnesse of the fact, but I was amazed and astonisht at it, for the unusuall
greatnesse of the wickednesse had quite bereft me of sense, which made me give
more credit to that tale of Niobe, who conceiving some extraordinary griefe for
the death of her children, gave occasion to the fable. After this part of the tragedy
was acted (as it seemed to me to be) having laid her in the sepulchre, and covered
her with earth, they pull'd downe the altar, and departed, never looking backe
againe on the place.

About the evening the trench betwixt them and us was filled up, so our souldiers went over and pight their tents on the other side, this being done we went to
supper. Charmides perceiving mee much grieved in minde, sought by all meanes
possible to comfort mee, but prevailed not, for about the first watch of the night,

finding them all asleep, I tooke my sword and went to the sepulchre, intending to slay my self theron, which when I had drawne out, thus I spake: O wretched Leucippe, and the unhappiest of all women, I grieve not so much that thou diedst so farre from thine owne countrey a violent death, or that those salvage villaines made such a May-game of thy murther; but this it is augments my misery, that thou shouldst bee made an expiation for such polluted slaves that they should rippe thee up alive, that their unhallowed hands should violate thy chaste wombe, that they should erect thee an altar, and digge thee a grave, wherein 'tis true, thy carcasse lyes, but where are thy bowels? had they beene consumed with fire, the calamity had beene the lesse, but when in stead of a sepulchre, they shall lye buried in those paunches of these lewd miscreants, what patience is equall for so great a burthen of sorrow! a strange and unheard of banquet was it, could the gods see it & not blush? But to pacifie thy ghost, O Leucippe, I will offer my self a sacrifice to the infernall gods: Having said thus, I set the sword to my breast, when suddenly I espied two poasting towards mee in all haste, (for the moone shone) wherfore thinking them to bee theeves, and therefore the more willing to bee slaine by them, I held my hand, when they came neare they shouted to me; now who doe you thinke these two men were but Satyrus and Menelaus? whom with all the rest of my friends I had given over for dead, yet though they came so unexpectedly, I was so far from imbracing them, that I tooke no comfort me thought at the sight of them, the bitternesse of my griefe had so dejected me. They went to take my sword out of my hand; but I replyed, by all the gods you shall not envy me not the glory of so rare a death, nor detaine from mee that which is the only medicine of all my sorrowes; though you should compell mee to live, I cannot, Leucippe being dead; what though you take my sword from me by violence, yet there is a sting of griefe within mee which will torment me, would you have me still wounded and never die? If this bee all the cause why you would lay violent hands on your selfe (quoth Menelaus) I sweare by Hercules you may forbeare; for Leucippe is still alive, and shall straightway appeare unto you: at that fixing mine eyes very wishfully upon him, Is it not enough said I that I am in this distresse, but must I also bee derided and mocked? this is against the laws of all Hospitality: Then Menelaus beating on the sepulchre with his foote, bad Leucippe testifie whether shee were alive or not, when hee had smote the urne two or three times, I heard a very still voice, whereat looking steadfastly on Menelaus, I supposed him to bee some Magician, but he uncovered the urne and straightway came Leucippe forth, a most gastly creature, for shee was unbowelled from top to bottome, shee casting her selfe upon mee imbrac't me, and I her also, at which sudden meeting wee both swoun'd.

I was scarce come to my selfe, but straightway I turn'd to Menelaus, and asked him why he would detaine the truth of this matter from me? is not shee which I hold by the hand, and heare speake, mine owne Leucippe? What did I then see yesterday, either this or that was a dreame, and yet me thinkes againe this is a true and lively kisse, such a one as I use to have of my Leucippe: what say you, quoth Menelaus, if I finde her bowels againe, and heale this great wound without leaving any scar behinde? cover your face, for I must invoke the aide of Proserpina to the effecting of it, (whereat beleeving that hee was able to performe what hee promised) I did so, and while he utter'd some strange bombast words, hee tooke away that device which they had put before her breast to delude the theeves, and Leucippe was as whole as ever shee was; then hee bid mee looke backe, which I would scarce doe, fearing that Proserpina was there indeed, at length I turned about and uncovered my face, and saw Leucippe sound: At which wondring more and more, I told Menelaus if hee were some god he should tell us, then Leucippe intreated him that hee should hold mee no longer in suspence, but relate unto mee the whole carriage of the matter; so hee began.

If you be remembred Clitophon at our first acquaintance in the ship, I told you I was an Aegyptian; now the greatest part of my possessions and lands lye neare to this Citie; the chief governours whereof are my friends: What time wee then suffered shipwracke, I was cast on the Aegyptain shore, where Satyrus and I were taken by the Pirats of this Citie, but some of them which knew me, led mee to their governour, by whom I was freed from my bonds, kindely intreated, and desired to bee an assistant to them in such enterprizes as they should undertake; finding so much favour at their hands I begged Satyrus freedome also, but they replyed unto me ere they granted mee that, I was to performe some noble exploite, wherein I might give sufficient testimony of my valour. At that time they had a strict command from the Oracle to offer up a Virgin, as an expiation for the Citie which they inhabited, and that they should eat part of the liver of the sacrifice, then bury the body, afterwards depart; and all this was to keepe the enemie back from assaulting them, what followed I pray will you tell Satyrus. So thus hee continued the story. When first I came to the Campe (Master) understanding what was like to befall Leucippe, I wept, and desired Menelaus to thinke on some meanes to free her; in which businesse I know not what god was propitious to us, for the very day before the sacrifice was to be don, we were both by the sea side, very pensive, thinking upon some way to deliver her: while we were in these dumps, the thieves espying a ship, which not knowing those coasts, had lost its way, set upon it; they who were in it seeing they were assaulted by Pirats, indevour'd to flie, which course failing them, they fought it out: In that ship was one who used to recite Homers Poems in the theatre, attir'd in the same manner as he used to be at recitation; he with the rest of his company gave them a shrewd onset, but the theeves having a fresh supply of gallies, and other long boats, quickly slew all the men, and brake the ship; a piece whereof did swim toward us, and in it a little cabinet, which had escaped the hands of those which ransackt the ship: this Menelaus tooke up, and going aside opened it, wherein I thought there had beene no smal treasure, but in it we found nothing but a short cloake and a knife, the handle whereof was foure handfulls long, but the blade not above three fingers; while Menelaus handled this knife, hee pulled unawares a great part of the blade out of the handle, wherein as in a sheath it was hid, so we straightway supposing that this was the weapon which that juggling fellow made people beleeve he stabd himselfe withall; wherefore turning me to Menelaus, I said, Now beat thy braines a little, and wee doubt not by the gods assistance but wee shall free the virgin, and the theeves never discover our device: wee will sow a very thinne sheepskinne in the forme of a wallet, about the bignesse of a mans belly, and filling it with the bloud and entrailes of some beast, put it before her, so when she hath her long garment on, and is adorned with garlands and flowers, our device cannot bee discovered, in which matter wee are much furthered by the

Oracle, which gave strict charge that she being cloathed in a long robe, should bee led to the altar, there to be cut up; besides, this knife is made so, that the beholders will thinke it runs into her body when it runnes into the handle; so there is but just enough to cut the counterfeit belly, which neverthelesse when it is drawne out, you would thinke had beene sheathed in her body; if we doe this, the theeves can never detect us, for the skin shall be covered, and the entrailes at the first stroke shal start forth, which we presently snatching up wil fling on the altar – nor shall the standers by bee suffered to come neare the body, which we will prevent, by burying it. The meanes how wee shall come to have the chiefe care of the sacrifice is this: The King, if you be remembred, not long since enjoyned you some exploit, ere you could obtaine my enfranchisement, wherefore goe straight to him, and tell him you are ready for this enterprise.

Having thus said, I conjured him by Iuppiter the hospitable, and by our familiarity, and the shipwracke we suffered together.

THE DREAM OF LUCIAN

Lucian: His Life or His Dream

Lucian

Translated by Francis Hickes, 1634

'There's nothing more boring than other people's dreams', so the saying goes. This story is certainly an exception. **Lucian** of Samosata (Samsat, Turkey), a Greek satirist of the second century AD, describes his boyhood dream with immense charm. The ancients tended to believe in the significance of dreams. Lucian's apparently led him to change his career path from artist's apprentice to rhetorician and writer. His seventeenth-century translator, the Oxford-educated Francis Hickes, renders his story compellingly.

After I had given over going to schoole, and was grown to be a stripling of some good stature, my father advised with his friends, what it were best for him to breed mee to: and the opinion of most was, that to make mee a scholler, the labour would be long, the charge great, and would require a plentifull purse: whereas our meanes were poore, and would soone stand in need of speedy supply: but if he would set mee to learn some manuall art or other, I should quickly get by my trade enough to serve my owne turne, and never be troublesome for any diet at home, if I were placed abroad, neither would it be long before I should make my father a glad man, to see mee daily bring home with mee what I had got by my labours.

This being concluded upon we begunne to consult againe what trade was best, soonest learned, and most fitting a freeman, that would be set up with an easie charge, and bring in a profitable returne. With that, some began to commend one trade, some another, as every mans fancie or experience led him, but my father casting his eyes upon mine uncle (for my uncle by the mothers side was there present, an excellent workman in stone, and held to be one of the best statuaries in all the country by no meanes, (said he) can I endure that any other art should take place, as long as you are in presence: take him therefore to you (shewing him mee) and teach him to be a skilfull workman in stone, how to joynt them together neatly, and to fashion his statues cunningly: he is able enough for it, and his nature inclinable enough to it; this he conjectured, because he had seene some toies of mine made out of waxe; for I could no sooner come home from schole, but I should be tempering waxe together, and out of it counterfeit the shapes both of oxen, horses, and men, and (as my father thought) hansomely enough, which my masters were wont to whip me for, though now it turned to my commenda-tion: but those kinde of figments put mee in good hopes that I should learne my trade the sooner; and that very day was thought luckie for mee to be initiated into the art, whereupon I was committed to my uncle, and to confesse the truth, not much against my will: for I thought it would prove but a kinde of sport, and that I should be thought a brave fellow among my companions, if I could carve out gods, and pretty puppets, both for my selfe, and those lads I best liked of. But it fell out with mee, as with other yong beginners: for my uncle putting a carving toole into my hand, bad mee therewith to strike a table that lay before mee, softly and gently, adding withall this old proverbe What's well begunne is halfe done: but my ignorance was such, that I smote too hard, and the table burst in peeces: which put him so farre out of patience, that he gave mee hansell in a harsh measure, as I thought, and exceeding the bounds of due correction, insomuch that teares were the proeme of my occupation, and I ranne away as fast as I could, crying out with full eyes, telling how I had been lasht, and shewing the prints which the stroakes had made upon me, exclaiming upon such crueltie, and adding this of mine owne, that it was onely for envie, lest in the end I should prove a better workman then himselfe: this greeved my mothers heart, and shee railed bitterly against her brother for using me with such extremitie: but when night came I went to bed, though swolne with teares, and all the night long it would not out of my minde: what I have hitherto delivered, is meerely ridiculous and childish: but now, Gentlemen, you shall heare matter not to be discommended, but what deserves attentive auscultation: for to say with Homer, A heavenly dreame seised upon mee, as I slept in the dead time of the night, so directly, that it failed nothing of truth it selfe; for even to this day, after so long a distance, the figures of the apparition sticke still in mine eyes, and the voice of that I heard soundeth in mine eares, every thing was delivered so plainly and apparently.

Mee thought two women laid fast hold on my hands, and either of them drew mee to her selfe with all the strength shee had, and contended so earnestly for mee, that I was almost torne in pieces betweene them: sometimes the one would have the better hand, and get me almost wholly into her clutches: within a while after the other would seise upon me as surely, still scolding and brawling one against another, the one saying I was hers, and she would keep possession of mee, the other answering, it was a follie for her to lay claime to that she had nothing to do withall. Now indeed, the one of them was a homely sturdie dame, with her haire ill-favourdly drest up, and her hands overgrowne with a hard skinne, her garment was tuckt up about her, all full of lime and morter, for all the world such another as mine uncle when he was about his worke: the other was a well faced wench of comely proportion and handsomely attired: in the end they referred the matter to mee, which of them I would betake my selfe unto: and first that sturdy manly drudge begunne with mee in this manner. I, sweete boy, am that art of carving, to which you professed your selfe an apprentise yesterday, a trade familiar to you, and tyed to your house by succession: for your grandfather (delivering the name of my mothers father) was a carver and so were both your uncles, and by that meanes came to be men of note and reputation: if thou wilt therefore renounce the fopperies and idle vanities that this female would lead thee into (pointing to the other) and follow mee as one of my family, first thou shalt be maintained in a plentifull fashion, thou shalt continue good strength of body, keep thy self evermore free from envie, & never be forced to forsake thy friends and country, & betake thy self to a forrain soile, nor be commended by all men for words onely: disdaine not then the meannesse of my person, nor the basenesse of my apparell, for such beginnings had Phidias, that carved Jupiter, and Polycletus who made the Image of Juno, and the renowned Myron, and the admired Praxitiles, who now are honoured as if they were gods: and if it be thy fortune to become such another, thou must needs be famous among men of all degrees, thy father shall be held for a happy man, and thou shalt adde a great deale of glory to thy country.

This and much more was babled and blundred out by that art, and hudled one in the necke of another (because she would faine have wrought upon me,) which I cannot now call to minde, for the most is quite out of my remembrance. But as soone as shee had given over, the other begunne in this sort:

And I, sweete child, am Learning, which thou hast long beene acquainted withall, and well knowne unto thee, though thou never cam'st to attain the full end and perfection of mee: what thou shalt get by the art of carving, shee hath told thee alreadie her selfe: but take this from mee, thou shalt never be any better then a peasant, and a bodily labourer, and therein must thou repose the whol hope of thy life, which can be but obscure, thy gettings small and simple, thy mind dejected, thy commings in poore, and thou neither able to patronage a friend, nor crie quittance with a foe, nor worthy to be emulated by other citizens, only a meer drudge, one of the common rascalitie, ready to give way to thy better, and waite upon him that can speake in thy behalfe, living the life of a hare: and great luck if ever thou light upon a better: for, say thou come to be as cunning as Phidias, or Polycletus, and worke many wonderous pieces, thy Art will certainly bee commended by all men, but not one that lookes on them, if hee love himselfe, will wish to be such an other as thou: for bee what thou canst be, thou shalt be but a mechanicall fellow, one of a manuall Trade, that hath no meanes to live, but by his handy-labour. But if thou wilt be ruled by me, I will acquaint thee with all the famous Acts, and memorable exploits of men of former time: I will make thee know all that hath beene spoken or delivered by them, so that thou shalt have a perfect insight into all things: thy minde, which is the lordly part within thee, I will beautifie and garnish with many excellent ornaments, as temperance, justice, pietie, clemencie, wisdome, patience, the love of good things, and desire to attaine to matters of worth: for these indeede are the ornature of the minde that shall never decay: nothing whatsoever it be ancient or moderne shall escape thy knowledge: and by my assistance, thou shalt also foresee what is yet to come: and to conclude, I will in a short space make thee learned in all things divine and humane: so thou that art now so poore and simple, the son of a meane person, that lately was like to bee put to a base and ignoble Art, within a while shalt bee emulated and envied by all men, reverenced, commended and celebrated for thy good parts, and respected by those that are of an high ranked both for nobilitie and riches: then shalt thou be clad in such a garment as this is (shewing mee the mantle shee wore her selfe, which was very gorgeous to the eye) and thought worthy of all honour and preheminence: if it shall be thy fortune to travell into any forraine place, thou shalt never arrive there as a person unknowne and obscure, for I will set such markes and tokens upon thee, that every one that seeth thee shall jogge the next stander by on the elbow, and point out his finger toward thee saying, This is the man: If any occasion of urgencie betide thy friends, or the whole Citie, they all shall cast their eyes upon thee: when thou art to make a speech in any place, the whole multitude shall stand gaping to heare thee, admiring and wondring at thee, blessing the powerfulnesse of thy deliverance, and thy fathers happinesse to beget such a sonne: And as it is said of some men, that they shall continue immortall, the same will I effect in thee: for when thou shalt depart this life, thou shalt perpetually converse with learned men, and keepe company with the best: hast thou not heard of Demosthenes, what a poore mans sonne he was, and what a fellow I brought him to be? remembrest thou not Aeschines, the sonne of a Taberer? yet how did King Philip observe him for my sake? yes Socrates himselfe, though he were bred up in this art of carving, yet as soone as he made a better choice, and gave that trade the bagge, to be intertain'd as a fugitive by me, you know how much he was magnified by all men: and wilt thou forsake men of such excellent worth, such glorious exploits, such powerfull speeches, such decent attire, honour, glory, praise, precedencie, power, authority, commendation for good words, admiration for wisedome, and in leiw of all this, cover thy skinne with a base garment, cast a thread-bare cloak upon thy backe, have thy hands full of carving tooles, fit for thy trade, thy face ever more bent downewards towards thy worke, so continuing a sordide, slavish, and abject life, never able to lift up thy head, or to entertaine any manly or free thoughts, but all thy care must bee to have thy worke handsome and proportionable, respecting not a rush thine owne good, but making thy selfe of lesse value then a stone?

Whilest she was yet speaking, I could hold no longer for my life, but rising up, declared my selfe for her, and abandoning that ugly drudge, betooke me to learning with a glad heart, especially when I bethought my selfe of the lash, and the many stripes I received for my welcome the day before: she that was forsaken, tooke it haynously, clapt her hands at me, gnasht her teeth together against mee, and in the end, like a second Niobe, was wholly congealed and turned into a stone: you may thinke it strange, but distrust not the truth; for dreames can produce as unlikely matters as this. But the other, casting her eye upon me, What recompence shall I make thee (saith shee) for passing thy censure with such discretion? come hither and mount this chariot, (shewing me a chariot drawne with certaine horses, winged and shaped like Pegasus) that thou mayst see how many rare wonders thou shouldst have beene ignorant of, if thou hadst not followed me: When I was got up, she drave away, and supplyed the place of a Coachman, and being raised to a full height, I looked every way round about me, beginning at the East, and so to the West, beholding Cities, and Nations, and people: and like Triptolemus, sowed somewhat down upon the earth; yet can I not remember my selfe what seede it should be: only this, that men from below looked up towards me, applauded me, and with acclamations brought me onward to those whom I was to visite in my flight: and when shee had shewed these things to me, and me to them that praysed and commended me, she brought me backe againe, not clad in the same garment I wore in my voyage, yet I thought my selfe apparrelled handsomely enough: and at my comming home, I found my father standing and attending for me, to whom I shewed my apparrell and my selfe, and what a brave fellow I was returned, giving him a little item withall, how he had been like to have bestowed me the day before.

This I remember I saw, when I was little bigger then a boy, and, as I thinke, terrified in my sleepe with the blowes I had before received. But whilest I am telling this unto you, good god, (may some man say) this was a long dreame indeed, and stuffed with judicious matter. Some winters dreame I warrant you (sayes another) when the nights are at the longest: or it may be the length of three nights, the time of Hercules begetting: what comes in his head to trouble us with these fooleries, & tell us his ancient apish dreames, that are now growne old with age? this dull narration is stale and out of date: doth hee take us for some kinde of dreame readers? Nothing so good sir: for Xenophon, when hee reported a dreame that appeared unto him, as hee thought, in his fathers house, and other visions else, you know, the apparition was held for no fiction, nor hee condemned for a trifler in repeating it, though it were in the time of warre, when his case was desperate, and hee round beset with enemies: but the relating of it wanted not his fruit. So I, for my part, have repeated this dreame unto you, because I would have yong men take the better way, and sticke to learning, especially hee, whom povertie enforceth to a wilfull neglect of himselfe, and to incline to worse courses, so depraving the good condition of his nature: for I know the hearing of this tale will encourage him much, and that hee will propose mee, as a sufficient patterne for him to imitate, when hee shall consider how poore a snake I was, and yet affected the highest fortunes, and fixed my desire upon learning, and would not be discouraged with the povertie I was then opprest withall. And in what condition I am now returned amongst you, though it be not all of the best yet I hope I am no worse a man then a Carver.

PRAXITELES AND THE GODDESS

Erotes

Pseudo-Lucian

Translated by M. D. MacLeod, 1967

Praxiteles was one of the most talented artists of ancient Greece. In the fourth century BC he made two sculptures of Aphrodite. In one the goddess was modestly veiled. The other showed her nude and coquettishly semi-covering her crotch. The people of Kos bought the former and the people of Knidos the latter. This story, which was formerly attributed to Lucian but is now considered to be of uncertain authorship, describes the extremes of passion the nude inspired after it was placed in a temple to the goddess. The tale reveals the power of art and skill of Praxiteles, whose Knidian Aphrodite is known today from Roman copies. Ancient writers alleged that Praxiteles modelled her on his lover, Phryne, a prostitute who was said to have shown her naked breasts before a jury after she was accused of revelling inappropriately and inventing a new god. She clearly had something of Aphrodite's divine beauty, for she was acquitted.

I had in mind going to Italy and a swift ship had been made ready for me. It was one of the double-banked vessels which seem particularly to be used by the Liburnians, a race who live along the Ionian Gulf. After paying such respects as I could to the local gods and invoking Zeus, God of Strangers, to assist propitiously in my expedition to foreign parts, I left the town and drove down to the sea with a pair of mules. Then I bade farewell to those who were escorting me, for I was followed by a throng of determined scholars who kept talking to me and parted with me reluctantly. Well, I climbed on to the poop and took my seat near the helmsman. We were soon carried away from land by the surge of our oars and, since we had very favourable breezes astern, we raised the mast from the hold and ran the yard up to the masthead. Then we let all our canvas down over the sheets and, as our sail gently filled, we went whistling along just as loud, I fancy, as an arrow does, and flew through the waves which roared around our prow as it cut through them.

But it isn't the time to describe at any length the events serious or light of the intervening coastal voyage. But, when we had passed the Cilician seaboard and were in the gulf of Pamphylia, after passing with some difficulty the Swallow-Islands, those fortune-favoured limits of ancient Greece, we visited each of the Lycian cities, where we found our chief pleasure in the tales told, for no vestige of prosperity is visible in them to the eye. Eventually we made Rhodes, the island of the Sun-God, and decided to take a short rest from our uninterrupted voyaging.

Accordingly our oarsmen hauled the ship ashore and pitched their tents near by. I had been provided with accommodation opposite the temple of Dionysus, and, as I strolled along unhurriedly, I was filled with an extraordinary pleasure. For it really is the city of Helius with a beauty in keeping with that god. As I walked round the porticos in the temple of Dionysus, I examined each painting, not only delighting my eyes but also renewing my acquaintance with the tales of the heroes. For immediately two or three fellows rushed up to me, offering for a small fee to explain every story for me, though most of what they said I had already guessed for myself.

When I had now had my fill of sightseeing and was minded to go to my lodgings, I met with the most delightful of all blessings in a strange land, old acquaintances of long standing, whom I think you also know yourself, for you've often seen them visiting us here, Charicles a young man from Corinth who is not only handsome but shows some evidence of skilful use of cosmetics, because, I imagine, he wishes to attract the women, and with him Callicratidas, the Athenian, a man of straightforward ways. For he was pre-eminent among the leading figures in public speaking and in this forensic oratory of ours. He was also a devotee of physical training, though in my opinion he was only fond of the wrestling-schools because of his love for boys. For he was enthusiastic only for that, while his hatred for women made him often curse Prometheus. Well, they both saw me from a distance and hurried up to me overjoyed and delighted. Then, as so often happens, each of them clasped me by the hand and begged me to visit his house. I, seeing that they were carrying their rivalry too far, said, "Today, Callicratidas and Charicles, it is the proper thing for both of you to be my guests so that you may not fan your rivalry into greater flame. But on the days to follow—for I've decided to remain here for three or four days—you will return my hospitality by entertaining me each in turn, drawing lots to decide which of you will start."

This was agreed, and for that day I presided as host, while on the next day Callicratidas did so, and after him Charicles. Now, even when they were entertaining me, I could see concrete evidence of the inclinations of each. For my Athenian friend was well provided with handsome slave-boys and all of his servants were pretty well beardless. They remained with him till the down first appeared on their faces, but, once any growth cast a shadow on their cheeks, they would be sent away to be stewards and overseers of his properties at Athens. Charicles, however, had in attendance a large band of dancing girls and singing girls and all his house was as full of women as if it were the Thesmophoria, with not the slightest trace of male presence except that here and there could be seen an infant boy or a superannuated old cook whose age could give even the jealous no cause for suspicion. Well, these things were themselves, as I said, sufficient indications of the dispositions of both of them. Often, however, short skirmishes broke out between them without the point at issue being settled. But, when it was time for me to put to sea, at their wish I took them with me to share my voyage, for they like me were minded to set out for Italy.

Now, as we had decided to anchor at Cnidus to see the temple of Aphrodite, which is famed as possessing the most truly lovely example of Praxiteles' skill, we gently approached the land with the goddess herself, I believe, escorting our ship with smooth calm waters. The others occupied themselves with the usual preparations, but I took the two authorities on love, one on either side of me, and went round Cnidus, finding no little amusement in the wanton products of the potters, for I remembered I was in Aphrodite's city. First we went round the porticos of Sostratus and everywhere else that could give us pleasure and then we walked to the temple of Aphrodite. Charicles and I did so very eagerly, but Callicratidas was reluctant because he was going to see something female, and would have preferred, I imagine, to have had Eros of Thespiae instead of Aphrodite of Cnidus.

And immediately, it seemed, there breathed upon us from the sacred precinct itself breezes fraught with love. For the uncovered court was not for the most part paved with smooth slabs of stone to form an unproductive area but, as was to be expected in Aphrodite's temple, was all of it prolific with garden fruits. These trees, luxuriant far and wide with fresh green leaves, roofed in the air around them. But more than all others flourished the berry-laden myrtle growing luxuriantly beside its mistress and all the other trees that are endowed with beauty. Though they were old in years they were not withered or faded but, still in their youthful prime, swelled with fresh sprays. Intermingled with these were trees that were unproductive except for having beauty for their fruit—cypresses and planes that towered to the heavens and with them Daphne, who deserted from Aphrodite and fled from that goddess long ago. But around every tree crept and twined the ivy, devotee of love. Rich vines were hung with their thick clusters of grapes. For Aphrodite is more delightful when accompanied by Dionysus and the gifts of each are sweeter if blended together, but, should they be parted from each other, they afford less pleasure. Under the particularly shady trees were joyous couches for those who wished to feast themselves there. These were occasionally visited by a few folk of breeding, but all the city rabble flocked there on holidays and paid true homage to Aphrodite.

When the plants had given us pleasure enough, we entered the temple. In the midst thereof sits the goddess—she's a most beautiful statue of Parian marble—arrogantly smiling a little as a grin parts her lips. Draped by no garment, all her beauty is uncovered and revealed, except in so far as she unobtrusively uses one hand to hide her private parts. So great was the power of the craftsman's art that the hard unyielding marble did justice to every limb. Charicles at any rate raised a mad distracted cry and exclaimed, "Happiest indeed of the gods was Ares who suffered chains because of her!" And, as he spoke, he ran up and, stretching out his neck as far as he could, started to kiss the goddess with importunate lips. Callicratidas stood by in silence with amazement in his heart.

The temple had a door on both sides for the benefit of those also who wish to have a good view of the goddess from behind, so that no part of her be left unadmired. It's easy therefore for people to enter by the other door and survey the beauty of her back.

And so we decided to see all of the goddess and went round to the back of the precinct. Then, when the door had been opened by the woman responsible for keeping the keys, we were filled with an immediate wonder for the beauty we beheld. The Athenian who had been so impassive an observer a minute before, upon inspecting those parts of the goddess which recommend a boy, suddenly raised a shout far more frenzied than that of Charicles. "Heracles!" he exclaimed, "what a well-proportioned back! What generous flanks she has! How satisfying an armful to embrace! How delicately moulded the flesh on the buttocks, neither too thin and close to the bone, nor yet revealing too great an expanse of fat! And as for those precious parts sealed in on either side by the hips, how inexpressibly sweetly they smile! How perfect the proportions of the thighs and the shins as they stretch down in a straight line to the feet! So that's what Ganymede looks like as he pours out the nectar in heaven for Zeus and makes it taste sweeter. For I'd never have taken the cup from Hebe if she served me." While Callicratidas was shouting this under the spell of the goddess, Charicles in the excess of his admiration stood almost petrified, though his emotions showed in the melting tears trickling from his eyes.

When we could admire no more, we noticed a mark on one thigh like a stain on a dress; the unsightliness of this was shown up by the brightness of the marble everywhere else. I therefore, hazarding a plausible guess about the truth of the matter, supposed that what we saw was a natural defect in the marble. For even such things as these are subject to accident and many potential masterpieces of beauty are thwarted by bad luck. And so, thinking the black mark to be a natural blemish, I found in this too cause to admire Praxiteles for having hidden what was unsightly in the marble in the parts less able to be examined closely. But the attendant woman who was standing near us told us a strange, incredible story. For she said that a young man of a not undistinguished family—though his deed has caused him to be left nameless—who often visited the precinct, was so ill-starred as to fall in love with the goddess. He would spend all day in the temple and at first gave the impression of pious awe. For in the morning he would leave his bed long before dawn to go to the temple and only return home reluctantly after sunset. All day long would he sit facing the goddess with his eyes fixed uninterruptedly upon her, whispering indistinctly and carrying on a lover's complaints in secret conversation.

But when he wished to give himself some little comfort from his suffering, after first addressing the goddess, he would count out on the table four knuckle-bones of a Libyan gazelle and take a gamble on his expectations. If he made a successful throw and particularly if ever he was blessed with the throw named after the goddess herself, and no dice showed the same face, he would prostrate himself before the goddess, thinking he would gain his desire. But, if as usually happens he made an indifferent throw on to his table, and the dice revealed an unpropitious result, he would curse all Cnidus and show utter dejection as if at an irremediable disaster; but a minute later he would snatch up the dice and try to cure by another throw his earlier lack of success. But presently, as his passion grew more inflamed, every wall came to be inscribed with his messages and the bark of every tender tree told of fair Aphrodite. Praxiteles was honoured by him as much as Zeus and every beautiful treasure that his home guarded was offered to the goddess. In the end the violent tension of his desires turned to desperation and he found in audacity a procurer for his lusts. For, when the sun was now sinking to its setting, quietly and unnoticed by those present, he slipped in behind the door and, standing invisible in the inmost part of the chamber, he kept still, hardly even breathing. When the attendants closed the door from the outside in the normal way, this new Anchises was locked in. But why do I chatter on and tell you in every detail the reckless deed of that unmentionable night? These marks of his amorous embraces were seen after day came and the goddess had that blemish to prove what she'd suffered. The youth concerned is said, according to the popular story told, to have hurled himself over a cliff or down into the waves of the sea and to have vanished utterly.

CUPID AND PSYCHE

The Golden Ass

Apuleius

Translated by Walter Pater, 1885

Psyche is the youngest and most gorgeous of a king's three daughters. As news spreads of her beauty, people begin to worship her and neglect Venus, the beautiful goddess of love. Psyche's father obtains an oracle that advises him to set her on a rock, for she is to wed a winged serpent. Psyche is brought to the rock but then events take a very different turn. The story of Cupid and Psyche, extracted here, is told within the *Golden Ass*, a Latin novel by **Apuleius** (*c.* AD 124–*c.* 170). Walter Pater's translation from the late nineteenth century is rendered in exquisitely stylish prose, well befitting a founding father of the Aesthetic movement.

The wretched parents, in their close-shut house, yielded themselves to perpetual night; while to Psyche, fearful and trembling and weeping sore upon the mountain-top, comes the gentle Zephyrus. He lifts her mildly, and, with vesture afloat on either side, bears her by his own soft breathing over the windings of the hills, and sets her lightly among the flowers in the bosom of a valley below.

Psyche, in those delicate grassy places, lying sweetly on her dewy bed, rested from the agitation of her soul and arose in peace. And lo! a grove of mighty trees, with a fount of water, clear as glass, in the midst; and hard by the water, a dwelling-place, built not by human hands but by some divine cunning. One recognised, even at the entering, the delightful hostelry of a god. Golden pillars sustained the roof, arched most curiously in cedar-wood and ivory. The walls were hidden under wrought silver:—all tame and woodland creatures leaping forward to the visitor's gaze. Wonderful indeed was the craftsman, divine or half-divine, who by the subtlety of his art had breathed so wild a soul into the silver! The very pavement was distinct with pictures in goodly stones. In the glow of its precious metal the house is its own daylight, having no need of the sun. Well might it seem a place fashioned for the conversation of gods with men!

Psyche, drawn forward by the delight of it, came near, and, her courage growing, stood within the doorway. One by one, she admired the beautiful things she saw; and, most wonderful of all! no lock, no chain, nor living guardian protected that great treasure house. But as she gazed there came a voice—a voice, as it were unclothed of bodily vesture—"Mistress!" it said, "all these things are thine. Lie down, and relieve thy weariness, and rise again for the bath when thou wilt. We thy servants, whose voice thou hearest, will be beforehand with our service, and a royal feast shall be ready."

And Psyche understood that some divine care was providing, and, refreshed with sleep and the bath, sat down to the feast. Still she saw no one: only she heard words falling here and there, and had voices alone to serve her. And the feast being ended, one entered the chamber and sang to her unseen, while another struck the chords of a harp, invisible with him who played on it. Afterwards the sound of a company singing together came to her, but still so that none were present to sight; yet it appeared that a great multitude of singers was there.

And the hour of evening inviting her, she climbed into the bed; and as the night was far advanced, behold a sound of a certain clemency approaches her. Then, fearing for her maidenhood, in so great solitude, she trembled, and more than any evil she knew dreaded that she knew not. And now the husband, that unknown husband, drew near, and ascended the couch, and made her his wife; and lo! before the rise of dawn he had departed hastily. And the attendant voices ministered to the needs of the newly married. And so it happened with her for a long season. And as nature has willed, this new thing, by continual use, became a delight to her: the sound of the voice grew to be her solace in that condition of loneliness and uncertainty.

One night the bridegroom spoke thus to his beloved, "O Psyche, most pleasant bride! Fortune is grown stern with us, and threatens thee with mortal peril. Thy sisters, troubled at the report of thy death and seeking some trace of thee, will come to the mountain's top. But if by chance their cries reach thee, answer not, neither look forth at all, lest thou bring sorrow upon me and destruction upon thyself." Then Psyche promised that she would do according to his will. But the bridegroom was fled away again with the night. And all that day she spent in tears, repeating that she was now dead indeed, shut up in that golden prison, powerless to console her sisters sorrowing after her, or to see their faces; and so went to rest weeping.

And after a while came the bridegroom again, and lay down beside her, and embracing her as she wept, complained, "Was this thy promise, my Psyche? What have I to hope from thee? Even in the arms of thy husband thou ceasest not from pain. Do now as thou wilt. Indulge thine own desire, though it seeks what will ruin thee. Yet wilt thou remember my warning, repentant too late." Then, protesting that she is like to die, she obtains from him that he suffer her to see her sisters, and present to them moreover what gifts she would of golden ornaments; but therewith he ofttimes advised her never at any time, yielding to pernicious counsel, to enquire concerning his bodily form, lest she fall, through unholy curiosity, from so great a height of fortune, nor feel ever his embrace again. "I would die a hundred times," she said, cheerful at last, "rather than be deprived of thy most sweet usage. I love thee as my own soul, beyond comparison even with Love himself. Only bid thy servant Zephyrus bring hither my sisters, as he brought me. My honeycomb! My husband! Thy Psyche's breath of life!" So he promised; and after the embraces of the night, ere the light appeared, vanished from the hands of his bride.

And the sisters, coming to the place where Psyche was abandoned, wept loudly among the rocks, and called upon her by name, so that the sound came down to her, and running out of the palace distraught, she cried, "Wherefore afflict your souls with lamentation? I whom you mourn am here." Then, summoning Zephyrus, she reminded him of her husband's bidding; and he bare them down with a gentle blast. "Enter now," she said, "into my house, and relieve your sorrow in the company of Psyche your sister."

And Psyche displayed to them all the treasures of the golden house, and its great family of ministering voices, nursing in them the malice which was already at their hearts. And at last one of them asks curiously who the lord of that celestial array may be, and what manner of man her husband? And Psyche answered dissemblingly, "A young man, handsome and mannerly, with a goodly beard. For the most part he hunts upon the mountains." And lest the secret should slip from her in the way of further speech, loading her sisters with gold and gems, she commanded Zephyrus to bear them away.

And they returned home, on fire with envy. "See now the injustice of fortune!" cried one. "We, the elder children, are given like servants to be the wives of strangers, while the youngest is possessed of so great riches, who scarcely knows how to use them. You saw, sister! what a hoard of wealth lies in the house; what glittering gowns; what splendour of precious gems, besides all that gold trodden under foot. If she indeed hath, as she said, a bridegroom so goodly, then no one in all the world is happier. And it may be that this husband, being of divine nature, will make her too a goddess. Nay! so in truth it is. It was even thus she bore herself. Already she looks aloft and breathes divinity, who, though but a woman, has voices for her handmaidens, and can command the winds." "Think," answered the other, "how arrogantly she dealt with us, grudging us these trifling gifts out of all that store, and when our company became a burden, causing us to be hissed and driven away from her through the air! But I am no woman if she keep her hold on this great fortune; and if the insult done us has touched thee too, take we counsel together. Meanwhile let us hold our peace, and know naught of her, alive or dead. For they are not truly happy of whose happiness other folk are unaware."

Psyche's husband, whom she has never seen face to face, warns her against her scheming sisters and informs her that she is carrying his child. Psyche's sisters come to visit her and treacherously deceive her into thinking that her husband is the vile serpent of which the oracle had spoken. They advise her to chop off his head while he is sleeping. Psyche approaches him but is struck, upon seeing him for the first time, by his dazzling beauty.

At sight of him the very flame of the lamp kindled more gladly! But Psyche was afraid at the vision, and, faint of soul, trembled back upon her knees, and would have hidden away the steel in her own bosom. But the knife slipped from her hand; and now, undone, yet ofttimes looking upon the beauty of that divine countenance, she lives again. She sees the locks of that golden head, pleasant with the unction of the gods, shed down in graceful entanglement behind and before, about the ruddy cheeks and white throat. The pinions of the winged god, yet fresh with the dew, are spotless upon his shoulders; the delicate plumage wavering over them as they lie at rest. Smooth he was, and, touched with light, worthy of Venus his mother. At the foot of the couch lay his bow and arrows, the instruments of his power, propitious to men.

And Psyche, gazing hungrily thereon, draws an arrow from the quiver, and trying the point upon her thumb, tremulous still, drave in the barb, so that a drop of blood came forth. Thus fell she, by her own act, and unaware, into the love of Love. Falling upon the bridegroom, with indrawn breath, in a hurry of kisses from her eager and open lips, she shuddered as she thought how brief that sleep might be. And it chanced that a drop of burning oil fell from the lamp upon the god's shoulder. Ah! maladroit minister of love, thus to wound him from whom all fire comes; though 'twas a lover, I trow, first devised thee, to have the fruit of his desire even in the darkness! At the touch of the fire the god started up, and beholding the óverthrow of her faith, quietly took flight from her embraces.

And Psyche, as he rose upon the wing, laid hold on him with her two hands, hanging upon him in his passage through the air, till she sinks to the earth through weariness. And as she lay there, the divine lover, tarrying still, lighted upon a cypress tree which grew near, and, from the top of it, spake thus to her, in great emotion. "Foolish one! unmindful of the command of Venus, my mother, who had devoted thee to one of base degree, I fled to thee in his stead. Now know I that this was vainly done. Into mine own flesh pierced mine arrow, and I made thee my wife, only that I might seem a monster beside thee—that thou shouldst seek to wound the head wherein lay the eyes so full of love to thee! Again and again, I thought to put thee on thy guard concerning these things, and warned thee in loving-kindness. Now I would but punish thee by my flight hence." And therewith he winged his way into the deep sky.

Psyche, prostrate upon the earth, and following far as sight might reach the flight of the bridegroom, wept and lamented; and when the breadth of space had parted him wholly from her, cast herself down from the bank of a river which was near. But the stream, turning gentle in honour of the god, put her forth again unhurt upon its margin. And as it happened, Pan, the rustic god, was sitting just then by the waterside, embracing, in the body of a reed, the goddess Canna; teaching her to respond to him in all varieties of slender sound. Hard by, his flock of goats browsed at will. And the shaggy god called her, wounded and outworn, kindly to him and said, "I am but a rustic herdsman, pretty maiden, yet wise, by favour of my great age and long experience; and if I guess truly by those faltering steps, by thy sorrowful eyes and continual sighing, thou labourest with excess of love. Listen then to me, and seek not death again, in the stream or otherwise. Put aside thy woe, and turn thy prayers to Cupid. He is in truth a delicate youth: win him by the delicacy of thy service."

So the shepherd-god spoke, and Psyche, answering nothing, but with a reverence to his serviceable deity, went on her way. And while she, in her search after Cupid, wandered through many lands, he was lying in the chamber of his mother, heart-sick. And the white bird which floats over the waves plunged in haste into the sea, and approaching Venus, as she bathed, made known to her that her son lies afflicted with some grievous hurt, doubtful of life. And Venus cried, angrily, "My son, then, has a mistress! And it is Psyche, who witched away my beauty and was the rival of my godhead, whom he loves!"

Therewith she issued from the sea, and returning to her golden chamber, found there the lad, sick, as she had heard, and cried from the doorway, "Well done, truly! to trample thy mother's precepts under foot, to spare my enemy that cross of an unworthy love; nay, unite her to thyself, child as thou art, that I might have a daughter-in-law who hates me! I will make thee repent of thy sport, and the savour of thy marriage bitter. There is one who shall chasten this body of thine, put out thy torch and unstring thy bow. Not till she has plucked forth that hair, into which so oft these hands have smoothed the golden light, and sheared away thy wings, shall I feel the injury done me avenged." And with that she hastened in anger from the doors.

And Ceres and Juno met her, and sought to know the meaning of her troubled countenance. "Ye come in season," she cried; "I pray you, find for me Psyche. It must needs be that ye have heard the disgrace of my house." And they, ignorant of what was done, would have soothed her anger, saying, "What fault, Mistress, hath thy son committed, that thou wouldst destroy the girl he loves? Knowest thou not that he is now of age? Because he wears his years so lightly must he seem to thee ever but a child? Wilt thou for ever thus pry into the pastimes of thy son, always accusing his wantonness, and blaming in him those delicate wiles which are all thine own?" Thus, in secret fear of the boy's bow, did they seek to please him with their gracious patronage. But Venus, angry at their light taking of her wrongs, turned her back upon them, and with hasty steps made her way once more to the sea.

A distraught Psyche is terrified that Venus is in pursuit of her. She calls upon the goddesses Ceres and Juno to take pity, but they refuse out of loyalty to Venus. Psyche is eventually found and brought before Venus, who attacks her and sets her a series of challenges. Cupid is locked in a chamber. Psyche retrieves a box from the Underworld.

And Cupid being healed of his wound, because he would endure no longer the absence of her he loved, gliding through the narrow window of the chamber wherein he was holden, his pinions being now repaired by a little rest, fled forth swiftly upon them; and coming to the place where Psyche was, shook that sleep away from her, and set him in his prison again, awaking her with the innocent point of his arrow. "Lo! thine old error again," he said, "which had like once more to have destroyed thee! But do thou now what is lacking of the command of my mother: the rest shall be my care." With these words, the lover rose upon the air; and being consumed inwardly with the greatness of his love, penetrated with vehement wing into the highest place of heaven, to lay his cause before the father of the gods. And the father of gods took his hand in his, and kissed his face and said to him, "At no time, my son, hast thou regarded me with due honour. Often hast thou vexed my bosom, wherein lies the disposition of the stars, with those busy darts of thine. Nevertheless, because thou hast grown up between these mine hands, I will accomplish thy desire." And straightway he bade Mercury call the gods together; and, the council-chamber being filled, sitting upon a high throne, "Ye gods," he said, "all ye whose names are in the white book of the Muses, ye know yonder lad. It seems good to me that his youthful heats should by some means be restrained. And that all occasion may be taken from him, I would even confine him in the bonds of marriage. He has chosen and embraced a mortal maiden. Let him have fruit of his love, and possess her for ever."

Thereupon he bade Mercury produce Psyche in heaven; and holding out to her his ambrosial cup, "Take it," he said, "and live for ever; nor shall Cupid ever depart from thee." And the gods sat down together to the marriage-feast. On the first couch lay the bridegroom, and Psyche in his bosom. His rustic serving-boy bare the wine to Jupiter; and Bacchus to the rest. The Seasons crimsoned all things with their roses. Apollo sang to the lyre, while a little Pan prattled on his reeds, and Venus danced very sweetly to the soft music. Thus, with due rites, did Psyche pass into the power of Cupid; and from them was born the daughter whom men call Voluptas.

A PICTURE OF PHAËTHON

Imagines

Philostratus the Elder

Translated by Daisy Dunn, 2018

The *Imagines* of the third-century AD Greek sophist **Philostratus the Elder** and his grandson Philostratus the Younger purport to be a series of descriptions of paintings hanging in an art gallery in Naples. The pictures, whether real or imaginary, are windows onto stories drawn from myth. The subject of this painting-story is Phaëthon, who drove the chariot of his father, the Sun god Helios, to his own destruction. The story had been told by Ovid a few centuries earlier and was picked up in the sixteenth century by the artist Michelangelo, who drew Phaëthon's fall and the metamorphoses of his mourning sisters for a young nobleman named Tommaso de' Cavalieri.

Golden are the tears of the Heliades, daughters of the Sun god Helios. The story goes that they flow for Phaëthon. For in his eagerness to drive, this son of Helios decided to entrust his life to his father's chariot, but failed to keep hold of the reins and stumbled and fell into the River Eridanus. Wise men take this story as a sign that there is too much fire in the atmosphere. Poets and painters, for their part, visualise the horses and chariot – and the skies confounded.

For look! Night is driving Day from the meridian, and the round sun drags along the stars as it dips towards the earth. The Horae leave the gates behind as they flee towards the darkness approaching them, and the horses throw off their yokes and tear along, all wild. But the Earth sinks away and raises her hands as the furious flames draw near her. And the young chap falls and is borne down, down, for his hair is ablaze and his chest burning – he will fall into the River Eridanus and lend his legend to the water.

For indeed swans will exhale, now here, now there, sweet songs about the young man, and a wedge of swans will soar to sing this tale to the Cayster River and the Danube. No place will fail to hear this wondrous tale. The swans will be accompanied in their song by Zephyrus, the light-footed wayside wind god. For he is said to have come to an agreement with the swans to join with them in singing funeral songs. Such is Zephyrus' harmony with the birds that you can see him playing them now as he would a musical instrument.

And they say that the women on the banks of the Eridanus, the daughters of Helios, not yet metamorphosed into trees, did, on account of their brother, change into trees, and wept.

This painting shows an understanding of the tale, for there are roots at their extremities, and some are trees up to the navel, and others have branches instead of hands. Alas! Their hair is wholly black poplar! Pity! Their tears are golden. The teary flood shines in the brightness of their eyes and sort of attracts rays of light and gleams as it reaches the cheeks and the blush that fills them, but the tears which drip down their chests are already gold.

Even the river grieves as it rises from the whirlpool and holds out its lap to Phaëthon – for it is in the shape of one who receives – and at once cultivates the daughters of Helios. For with the breezes and chills it releases it will turn to stone the pieces which fall from the poplars and carry them through its radiant waters to the barbarians in Oceanus.

THE WEDDING FEAST

Deipnosophistae

Athenaeus

Translated by C. D. Yonge, 1854

> Written in the third century AD by **Athenaeus**, an Egyptian who lived in
> Rome, the *Deipnosophistae* or 'Dining Sophists' is a peculiar collection
> of descriptions of food, symposia and banquets. Here a narrator from
> Macedonia describes a particularly extravagant wedding feast hosted by
> a fellow Macedonian named Caranus in the fourth century BC.

In Macedonia, then, as I have said, Caranus made a marriage feast; and the
guests invited were twenty in number. And as soon as they had sat down, a
silver bowl was given to each of them as a present. And Caranus had previously crowned every one of them, before they entered the dining-room, with
a golden chaplet, and each chaplet was valued at five pieces of gold. And when
they had emptied the bowls, then there was given to each of the guests a loaf
in a brazen platter of Corinthian workmanship, of the same size; and poultry,
and ducks, and besides that, pigeons, and a goose, and quantities more of the
same kind of food heaped up abundantly. And each of the guests taking what
was set before him, with the brazen platter itself also, gave it to the slaves who
waited behind him. Many other dishes of various sorts were also served up to
eat. And after them, a second platter was placed before each guest, made of silver, on which again there was placed a second large loaf, and on that geese, and
hares, and kids, and other rolls curiously made, and doves, and turtledoves, and
partridges, and every other kind of bird imaginable, in the greatest abundance.
Those also, says Hippolochus, we gave to the slaves; and when we had eaten to
satiety, we washed our hands, and chaplets were brought in in great numbers,
made of all sorts of flowers from all countries, and on each chaplet a circlet of
gold, of about the same weight as the first chaplet. And Hippolochus having
stated after this that Proteas, the descendant of that celebrated Proteas the son of
Lanice, who had been the nurse of Alexander the king, was a most extraordinary
drinker, as also his grandfather Proteas, who was the friend of Alexander, had
been; and that he pledged every one present, proceeds to write as follows:—

"And while we were now all amusing ourselves with agreeable trifling, some
flute-playing women and musicians, and some Rhodian players on the sambuca
come in, naked as I fancied, but some said that they had tunics on. And they
having played a prelude, departed; and others came in in succession, each of them

bearing two bottles of perfume, bound with a golden thong, and one of the cruets was silver and the other gold, each holding a cotyla,[1] and they presented them to each of the guests. And then, instead of supper, there was brought in a great treasure, a silver platter with a golden edge of no inconsiderable depth, of such a size as to receive the entire bulk of a roast boar of huge size, which lay in it on his back, showing his belly uppermost, stuffed with many good things. For in the belly there were roasted thrushes, and paunches, and a most countless number of fig peckers, and the yolks of eggs spread on the top, and oysters, and periwinkles. And to every one of the guests was presented a boar stuffed in this way, nice and hot, together with the dish on which he was served up. And after this we drank wine, and each of us received a hot kid, on another platter like that on which the boar had been served up, with some golden spoons. Then Caranus seeing that we were cramped for the want of room, ordered canisters and bread-baskets to be given to each of us, made of strips of ivory curiously plaited together; and we were very much delighted at all this, and applauded the bridegroom, by whose means we were thus enabled to preserve what had been given to us. Then chaplets were again brought to us, and another pair of cruets of perfume, one silver and one gold, of the same weight as the former pair. And when quiet was restored, there entered some men, who even in the Potfeast[2] at Athens had borne a part in the solemnities, and with them there came in some ithyphallic dancers, and some jugglers, and some conjuring women also, tumbling and standing on their heads on swords, and vomiting fire out of their mouths, and they, too, were naked.

And when we were relieved from their exhibition, then we had a fresh drink offered to us, hot and strong, and Thasian, and Mendaean, and Lesbian wines were placed upon the board, very large golden goblets being brought to every one of us. And after we had drunk, a glass goblet of two cubits in diameter, placed on a silver stand, was served up, full of roast fishes of every imaginable sort that could be collected. And there was also given to every one a silver breadbasket full of Cappadocian loaves; some of which we ate and some we delivered to the slaves behind us. And when we had washed our hands, we put on chaplets; and then again we received golden circlets twice as large as the former ones, and another pair of cruets of perfume. And when quiet was restored, Proteas leaping up from his couch, asked for a cup to hold a gallon; and having filled it with Thasian wine, and having mingled a little water with it, he drank it off, saying—

He who drinks most will be the happiest.

And Caranus said—"Since you have been the first to drink, do you be the first also to accept the cup as a gift; and this also shall be the present for all the rest who drink too." And when this had been said, at once nine of the guests rose up snatching at the cups, and each one trying to forestall the other. But one of those who were of the party, like an unlucky man as he was, as he was unable to drink, sat down and cried because he had no goblet; and so Caranus presented him with an empty goblet. After this, a dancing party of a hundred men came in,

1   A cotyla held about half a pint.
2   Held on the thirteenth day of the month Anthesterion; being the first day of the great festival Anthesteria.

singing an epithalamium in beautiful tune. And after them there came in dancing girls, some arranged so as to represent the Nereids, and others in the guise of the nymphs.

And as the drinking went on, and the shadows were beginning to fall, they opened the chamber where everything was encircled all round with white cloths. And when these curtains were drawn, the torches appeared, the partitions having been secretly removed by mechanism. And there were seen Cupids, and Dianas, and Pans, and Mercuries, and numbers of statues of that kind, holding torches in silver candlesticks. And while we were admiring the ingenuity of the contrivance, some real Erymanthean boars were brought round to each of the guests on square platters with golden edges, pierced through and through with silver darts. And what was the strangest thing of all was, that those of us who were almost helpless and stupefied with wine, the moment that we saw any of these things which were brought in, became all in a moment sober, standing upright, as it is said. And so the slaves crammed them into the baskets of good omen, until the usual signal of the termination of the feast sounded. For you know that that is the Macedonian custom at large parties.

And Caranus, who had begun drinking in small goblets, ordered the slaves to bring round the wine rapidly. And so we drank pleasantly, taking our present liquor as a sort of antidote to our previous hard drinking. And while we were thus engaged, Mandrogenes the buffoon came in, the descendant, as is reported, of that celebrated Strato the Athenian, and he caused us much laughter. And after this he danced with his wife, a woman who was already more than eighty years of age. And at last the tables, to wind up the whole entertainment, were brought in. And sweetmeats in plaited baskets made of ivory were distributed to every one. And cheesecakes of every kind known, Cretan cheesecakes, and your Samian ones, my friend Lynceus, and Attic ones, with the proper boxes, or dishes, suitable to each kind of confection. And after this we all rose up and departed, quite sobered, by Jove, by the thoughts of, and our anxiety about, the treasures which we had received.

But you who never go out of Athens think yourself happy when you hear the precepts of Theophrastus, and when you eat thyme, and salads, and nice twisted loaves, solemnizing the Lenaean festival, and the Potfeast at the Anthesteria. But at the banquet of Caranus, instead of our portions of meat, we carried off actual riches, and are now looking, some for houses, and some for lands, and some of us are seeking to buy slaves."

CUPID CRUCIFIED

Cupid Crucified

Ausonius

Translated by Deborah Warren, 2017

Ausonius (*c.* AD 310–*c.* 395) was a Latin poet and teacher from Bordeaux, known in Gallo-Roman times as Burdigala. He was also a Christian, which may come as a surprise, for his poetry often feels thoroughly pagan. Among his many careers, Ausonius served as tutor to the future emperor Gratian (ruled 367–383 AD). Like the Greek novelists before him, Ausonius took a picture as the inspiration for this intriguing tale of the distress that Cupid – love – has caused women in literature. Here, love finally gets his comeuppance.

Preface

From Ausonius to my dear "son":

Have you ever seen a picture painted on a wall? You've certainly seen one and remember it. Naturally this painted picture in Zoilus's dining room in Treves: lovesick women fix Cupid to a cross—not women of our time, who sin of their own free will, but those heroines who excuse themselves and blame God—some of whom our Virgil lists in the Fields of Mourning. I admired this painting for its beauty and subject. Afterwards I translated my dazzled admiration into the ineptitude of my poetry: except for the title, nothing pleases me; still, I send you my meanderings. We love our own warts and scars and, not content to fail alone in our defects, we seek that they be loved by others. But why do I defend this little poem so zealously? I'm sure you'll like whatever you know is mine: this I hope more than that you praise it. Farewell, and remember your "father" affectionately.

Cupid Crucified

In heaven's fields, which Virgil's muse describes,
where a myrtle grove conceals distracted lovers,
heroines held their rituals—and each one
bore her mark of her long ago death—
wandering through vast woods in grudging light,

through reedy goat's-beard, heavy flowering poppy,
and silent, still lakes and unmurmuring streams
whose flowers sigh through banks in misty light,
mourning the names of youths and kings of old:
gazing Narcissus; Oebalus' Hyacinth;
gold-haired Crocus; Adonis, purple-dyed;
Ajax of Salamis, limned with tragic pain.
All the griefs that spur sad memories
after death, with tears, sorrowing loves
call heroines back again to their lost lives:
pregnant Semele, deceived, moans in birth and destroys
a burning cradle, and brandishes the fire
of a thunderbolt. Mourning her worthless gift,
Caenis grieves—changed back to her former shape,
having been pleased with her gender as a man.
Procris, stabbed, is tending to her wounds
and even now loves Caephalus's deadly hand.
The girl at Sestus goes headlong from the tower
bearing her smoking clay lamp; and mannish Sappho,
who'd die from the barbs of love for a man of Lesbos,
threatens to leap to death from cloud-wrapped Leucas.
Sad Eriphyle shuns Harmonia's necklace,
doomed by her son, unlucky in her marriage;
the whole tale also of Minos's lofty Crete
flickers, a faint image of a depicted scene:
Pasiphae follows the tracks of the snow-white bull;
deserted Ariadne holds the ball of threads,
in her hand; regretful Phaedra recalls her tablet
left behind. One bears a noose, one the sham
of a vain crown; it shames the third to enter
and hide in Daedalus's heifer. Laodamia
laments two stolen nights of doomed delights
with dead and living lovers; in another place
others, fierce with drawn swords, Thisbe, Canace
and Tyrian Dido loom: one bears her husband's sword,
the second her father's, the third her guest's.
And horned Luna, with torch and starry crown,
strays as once over Latmos' rocks,
having pursued the sleeping Endymion.
A hundred others dwelling on love's old wounds
re-live the torments with sweet and gloomy plaints.
Between them reckless Cupid on rattling wings
has scattered the shadows of black fog. All of them
knew the boy and, memory returning,
saw their common offender, though the damp clouds
obscured his belt gleaming with golden studs
and his quiver and the flame of his bright red torch.

They recognize him, though, and try to vent
their vain force on their one foe—met in a place
not his own where he'd wield wings ineffective
in thick gloom—and they press him as a swarm:
they pull him trembling and vainly seeking refuge
into their mass, mid-throng.
                              A myrtle is chosen,
familiar in that sad grove, loathed as the gods' revenge—
with this, once, spurned Proserpine tortured Adonis
who thought of Venus. Hanged on its high branch,
chained, hands behind his back, feet bound,
they grant the weeping Cupid no lesser sentence.
Love, accused, is condemned with no trial or judge.
Each, eager to absolve herself of blame,
shifts her own guilt into another's crime.
All, blaming him, argue the indications
for his justifiable killing. They consider
their attack a sweet vengeance that seeks to redress their grief
each in the way she was ruined. One holds a noose;
one shows the false spectre of a sword; another
a rough cliff, ghost-river, threat of the ocean, a sea
though calm in its depths, raging: some brandish flames
and wield torches hissing flameless. Myrrha opens
her full womb—hurls at the trembling boy her tears
shining as amber drops of a weeping tree. A few intend
mere mockeries but in the guise of pardons,
so a sharp shaft under his pierced skin can draw out
tender blood from which the anemone springs
or their lamps move wanton lights toward the boy.
Even Venus herself, his mother, guilty
of similar sin, enters this fray unafraid.
Not rushing to plead for her surrounded son,
she redoubles his terror and kindles their wavering rage
with bitter goads, and blames her own disgrace
on her son's crimes, since she suffered the hidden chains—
caught with Mars; since for her shame at her child,
the stigma of Priapus from the Hellespont
was mocked; and Eryx, cruel, and Hermaphroditus
only half-man. Words weren't enough:
with her red wreath Venus beat the boy, suffering
and fearing worse; she pressed red dew from his body struck
with repeated blows, roses fastened together,
already red, drew blood more fiery red.
The fierce threats died away, the punishment having seemed
now greater than his own offenses, and Venus
about to become the offender. The heroines
themselves intervene and each prefers to blame

her own death on cruel Fate. Then the fond mother
gives thanks at their having withdrawn their grievances
and forgiven her boy and pardoned his crimes.
And then such visions in nocturnal shapes
upset his sleep, disturbed by empty terror,
which Cupid, having suffered most of the night—
the fog of sleep at last dispelled—flees, leaves
the ivory gate and flies up to the gods.

A CLASSICS STUDENT

Confessions, Book I

Saint Augustine

Translated by Peter Constantine, 2018

Augustine (354–430 AD) wrote his *Confessions* after he became a bishop in Hippo, a Roman city in what is now Algeria, in North Africa. He used the work to reflect on his life experience, especially the misdemeanours of his youth, prior to his discovery of God. His mother was a Christian but his father was not. In many respects Augustine represents the union of classicism and Christianity. In this extract he recounts his struggles to learn – and more importantly enjoy – classical literature. He can quote from Virgil's *Aeneid*, particularly the episodes surrounding Dido's suicide (see Story 49), but Homer, he recalls, was a struggle. Like many pupils, his feelings towards the subject he was studying were influenced by his feelings towards its teachers; his Greek tutors, he writes, 'goaded me with fierce threats and punishments'. He nevertheless recognised 'the sweetness of the Greek heroic tales'. Saint Augustine evidently enjoyed a good story.

I have still not managed to fathom the reasons why I hated Greek, which I studied as a boy. Yet Latin I truly loved; not what my first masters taught me, but what I later learned from the men we call grammarians. For I considered my first lessons of reading, writing, and arithmetic as great a burden and punishment as any Greek lesson. And yet, as I was flesh, a passing breath that does not return, did this not come from the sin and vanity of life? The first lessons were in fact better than the later ones, because they were more sound. Through them I acquired, and still retain, the ability to read whatever I find written and to write whatever I want; whereas in my later lessons I was forced to retain the strayings of an Aeneas I did not know, forgetting my own, and to weep over a dead Dido who killed herself for love; while I, without a tear, was prepared to pitiably die away from You through such works, my God, my life.

What is more pitiable than a pitiful being who does not pity himself but weeps at the death of Dido for love of Aeneas; a pitiful being who does not weep over the death he is suffering because he does not love You, O God, light of my heart, bread of the mouth deep within my soul, vigor that impregnates my mind and the vessel of my thoughts. I did not love You, and fornicated against You, and as I did so I heard from all around cries of "Well done! Well done!" for the friendship of this world is fornication against You; and "Well done! Well done!" is what they shout in order to shame a man who is not like them. For all this I did not weep, but wept for Dido, "who with a dagger did the lowest ends pursue," just as I, having forsaken You, pursued the lowest of Your creations, dust turning to dust. Had I been forbidden to read these works, I would have suffered at not being able to read what made me suffer. And such foolishness is considered a higher and better education than that by which I learned to read and write.

But now may my God call out in my soul, Your Truth proclaiming to me, "This is wrong, this is wrong! Your first lessons were better by far!" For I would readily forget the strayings of Aeneas rather than forget how to read and write. The doors of the grammarians' schools are indeed hung with precious curtains, but this is not so much a sign of high distinction as a cloak for their errors. Let not those whom I no longer fear cry out against me while I confess to You what my soul seeks, finding peace in condemning my evil ways and loving Your good ways. Let not the sellers and buyers of high learning cry out against me. If I ask them whether it is true that Aeneas once came to Carthage, as the poet says, the less learned will reply that they do not know, while the more learned will say that he never did. But if I ask with what letters the name "Aeneas" is written, everyone who has learned this will answer me correctly, according to the agreement and decision that men have reached concerning these signs. Likewise, if I should ask which was the greater inconvenience, forgetting how to read and write or forgetting those poetic fictions, who would not know what answer someone in possession of his senses would give. Thus as a boy I sinned, preferring empty learning to learning that was more useful, going so far as to love the former and hate the latter. "One plus one is two, two plus two is four" was a hateful incantation, while the sweetest dream of my vanity was the wooden horse filled with armed men, the burning of Troy, and even the ghost of Creusa.

So why did I hate Greek literature, which also sings of such feats? Homer too is skilled at weaving such tales, delusive in the sweetest way, and yet when I was a boy he was bitter to my taste, as I suppose Virgil might be to Greek boys forced to study him as I was forced to study Homer. Clearly it was the difficulty of learning a foreign tongue that sprinkled as if with gall the sweetness of the Greek heroic tales, I did not know a word of Greek, and to make me learn, my tutors goaded me with fierce threats and punishments. As an infant I had not known a word of Latin either, but I learned it from cooing nurses and their jesting and laughing and happy games; I learned it by paying attention, without torment or dread. I learned Latin without the threat of punishment, for my heart goaded me to bring its concepts to life, something I could not have done had I not already learned a few words—not from tutors, but from those who talked to me, and in whose ears I also strove to bring forth what I thought and felt. This clearly proves that free curiosity has a greater power to make one learn than severe enforcement. And yet enforcement curbs the unbridled wandering of that curiosity by way of Your laws, O God, Your laws from the tutor's cane to the martyr's trial, Your laws that mix for us a wholesome but bitter potion, calling us back to You from the pestilent delight that has drawn us away from You.

Lord, hear my prayer: that my soul not falter under Your discipline, nor that I falter in avowing before You the mercies through which You have rescued me from my most evil ways; I pray that You become sweet to me beyond all the seductions I pursued, that I may love You most fervently and clasp Your hand with all my heart, and that You will rescue me from all temptation, even to the end. O Lord, my King and God, may whatever I learned that was useful in my childhood serve You: my speaking, writing, reading, and counting. For when I was learning all that was worthless You gave me Your discipline and forgave my sin of delighting in those vain things. These things did give me many useful words, though they can also be learned in things that are not worthless, the safe path along which children should walk.

But woe to you, torrent of human custom! Who can resist you? When will you run dry? How long will you drag the sons of Eve down to that vast and dreadful sea which even those who cling to wood can barely cross? Did I not read in you of Jupiter the thunderer and adulterer—he surely could not have been both, but was presented as such so that a fictitious thunder might mimic and pander to real adultery. For who among our robed orators will lend a sober ear to a colleague from his own forum crying out: "These are Homer's inventions, transferring human qualities to the gods; how much better if Homer had transferred divine qualities to us!" It would have been truer to say that these are indeed Homer's inventions, but that he is attributing a divine nature to dissolute men so that their shameful acts will no longer be shameful, and that those who commit them are seen to be imitating not fallen men but celestial gods.

And yet, O infernal torrent, it is into you that the sons of men are cast along with the fees for their studies, in order for them to learn all that is worthless; and it is given great importance when publicly, in the forum, within sight of the inscriptions of the laws decreeing the tutors' salaries from public funds, the pupils' extra fees to their tutors are decreed. Infernal torrent, you lash at your rocks and roar: "This is why words are learned, this is why eloquence is acquired, the eloquence so vital to inducing others to do one's will and implement one's purpose." It is as if we would not have known expressions such as "shower of gold," "lap," "deceiving," "temples of heaven," had not Terence in his play brought a lewd young man onto the stage who takes Jupiter as his model for debauchery as he gazes at a mural "that shows the god sending forth, as in the legend, a shower of gold into Danae's lap," and so deceiving the woman? And look how the young man is incited to wanton lust through celestial guidance: "Such a great god!" he says. "He rocks the temples of heaven with his thunder! And I, little man that I am, should not do as he did? I did so, and with pleasure." Words are certainly not learned more easily with the help of such vileness, but through such words vileness is committed with greater confidence. I do not reproach the words, for they are precious and exquisite chalices, but I reproach the wine of error that was offered us in these chalices by drunken tutors; and if we did not drink this wine of error we were beaten, and had no sober judge to whom we could appeal. And yet, my God, before Whom I now recall this without fear, I learned all this readily, and, wretch that I was, delighted in what I was learning, and was called a boy of great promise.

Permit me, my God, also to say something about my innate talent, Your gift, and the foolishness on which I squandered it. I was set a task that greatly worried me because of the prospect of praise or shame, and the dread of being beaten:

the task was to speak the words of Juno as she raged and grieved, unable as she was to "keep the Prince of Troy from seeking the shores of Italy," even though I knew she had never spoken such words. But we were forced to go astray in the footsteps of those poetic creations, and to say in plain speech what Virgil had said in verse. The declaimer who was most praised was the one who best brought forth, shrouded in the most fitting words, the grandeur of the feigned characters in their passion of rage and grief. What is it to me, my God and true life, that my declamation was applauded over that of so many of the pupils of my age and in my class? Is all this not smoke and wind? Was there nothing else on which to exercise my talent and my tongue? Your praises, Lord, Your praises through Your Scriptures, would have trellised the young vines of my heart, and foolish nonsense would not have snatched at it, vile prey for winged scavengers. There is more than one way for man to pay homage to fallen angels.

THE PHOENIX

'Idyll 1'

Claudian

Translated by A. Hawkins, 1817

Claudian (*c.* AD 370–*c.* 404) was probably born in Alexandria in Egypt, but travelled to Italy, where he became court poet to the emperor Honorius, who ruled from 393 to 423 and whose reign witnessed the sack of Rome by the Visigoths. Claudian also wrote in praise of Honorius' regent, a Roman general named Stilicho. This story takes Claudian back to his Egyptian roots.

In Orient realms, beyond where Indus flows,
A wood, with Ocean round, in verdure grows,
The panting coursers of the god of day
First touch the foliage in their rapid way,
When humid gates with dewy chariot quake,—
The whistling whips, the lofty branches, shake,—
The rising ray discloses glances red,—
The glitt'ring wheels, resplendent brightness, spread,—
And NIGHT, far off, turns pale, constrained by light,
Her sable robe draws in, and takes to flight.
   THE solar bird, within this happy clime,
Resides, protected by the FLAME SUBLIME,
Possesses tracts, frail animals ne'er trace,
And feels no suff'rings of the human race;
Immortal as the pow'rs, that dwell on high:
Eternal like the stars of azure sky;
The constant waste, which rolling ages view,
Replenished is with limbs that rise anew.
To satiate hunger or his thirst assuage,
No food nor liquids e'er, his sight, engage;
Him nourishment, the SUN's pure heat procures:
From vapours Tethys, fluids thin, assures.
His eyes are ever darting secret rays:
Encircling beams of flame, his beak displays.
A tuft arises o'er his lofty crown:
Thence lustre shines, that rivals SOL's renown,

And pierces darkness with impressive force;—
His legs in purple, decked from Tyrian source;—
Wings, swifter than the winds, blue tints, unfold;—
And, o'er his back, the plumes adorned with gold.
To no conception he existence owes,
The father and the son at once he shows,
Alternately resuming youthful breath,
As oft as passing through the scene of death.
For when a thousand years has Summer run,—
As often Winter equal course begun,—
And Spring, the husbandman, brought shady store,
Which Autumn from the spreading branches tore,—
The Phenix then, oppressed by weight of years,
To sink at length beneath the load, appears.

   So, overpow'red by storms, the lofty pine
Inclines his top on Caucasus' high chine;
A part, to winds' incessant shock, gives way:
The rest to beating rains and time's decay.

   DIMINISHED now is seen this lustre bright;—
Old age's languid chill pervades his sight.
Thus Cynthia, when the clouds obscure her face,
No longer shows, of dubious horns, the trace.
His wings, accustomed, ether, to explore,
Above the humid ground can scarcely soar.
Then, conscious that his age is near the end,
He preparation makes new life to lend,
Selects the dryest plants from temp'rate hills,
With fragrant leaves the pile Sabaean, fills,
A tomb composes for himself on earth,
Where, breath resigned, he takes his future birth.
Here sits the bird and, now more feeble grown,
Salutes the beaming Sun in flatt'ring tone,
Prayer mixes with the plaintive song he sings,
Desiring flame, that back, fresh vigour, brings.
When Phoebus sees him, as his chariot rolls,
He stops, and thus, the fav'rite bird, consoles:

   "O PHENIX! ready on the pile of death,
"At once to render up thy aged breath,
"And, thus prepared at length to meet thy doom,
"Gain natal changes from fallacious tomb,
"Who, from destruction, art produced again,
"And, through departed life, dost bloom obtain;—
"Resume beginning:—worn out frame, forsake;—
"And, by mutation, form more active, take."

   THIS said, with moving head gold beams he darts,
And, vital splendour to the bird, imparts.
The Phenix willingly receives the fire:

Joy feels to die, and then anew respire;
The heap of perfumes burns with solar rays,
And ancient features perish 'mid the blaze.
Th' astonished MOON restrains her bullocks' course;
The HEAV'NS, dull wheels, no longer forward force;
All NATURE in solicitude appears;—
Lest lost th' eternal bird, disclosing fears;—
Fans faithful flames that freely they may burn;—
Th' immortal glory of the world, return.

AT length the scattered frame new vigour shows;
Through ev'ry vein, the blood repassing flows;
The ashes of themselves begin to move;
And, full of plumes, the shapeless embers prove.
Just what the father was, forth comes the son,
And now, of life, a fresh career's begun.
Fire interposed, with momentary space,
Divides the line where doubly life we trace.

AN anxious wish at once his breast pervades,
To consecrate, on Nile, paternal shades,
And bear to regions of Egyptian earth,
The heap of ashes whence derived new birth;
To foreign clime he flies on rapid wing,
Intent, remains in grassy tomb, to bring.
Innumerable birds, his flight, attend:
Battalions thick, through air, their pinions bend,
The feathered cohorts, closed on ev'ry side,
His varying course along the welkin hide.
Nor one among the multitude around,
To cross the path audaciously is found;
But, to the fragrant monarch, all give way,
And highest adoration freely pay.
The hawk and THUND'RER's bird, fierce war, neglect;—
Pacifick compact, springing from respect.

THE Parthian king thus leads BARBARIAN ranks,
From undulating Tigris' yellow banks;
Proud of rich dress and gems around him spread,
He, royal garlands, places on his head;—
Reins formed of gold, his noble courser, guide:—
Robe, from Assyrian needle, purple dyed;
'Mid troops that servilely, commands, obey,
Himself he shows elated with his sway.

IN Egypt's clime a famous city* lies,
Which, sacrifices, for the SUN, supplies;
The Phenix thither, to the temple goes:
The dome, a hundred Theban columns, shows;

---

* Heliopolis.

There he deposits relicks of his sire;—
Adores the god;—his burden, gives the fire;
And, of himself, the germ and last remains,
He consecrates where holy fervour reigns.
From myrrh, through all the limits, lustre flies.
And fumes divine upon the altars rise;
The Indian odours reach Pelusium's* fen,
The nostrils, titillate:—yield health to men;
And vapours, by the richest perfumes, fed,
O'er Nile I sev'n mouths, more sweet than Nectar, spread.
   O HAPPY bird! that from thyself canst spring;
Death's blows, to all besides, destruction bring;
And while to others lengthened life's denied,
With strength and vigour new art thou supplied.
On thee through ashes is fresh birth conferred:
Age dies,—but thou immortal art averred.
Whatever *was* has passed before thy sight:
The witness of revolving periods' flight;—
O'er lofty rocks the swelling waters hurled;—
The year that Phaeton inflamed the world.
No slaughters ever thee deprive of breath;—
Escaped:—EARTH vanquished vainly asks thy death;
Thy thread of life the Parcae ne'er divide:
No pow'rs of hurting thee, with them reside.

---

*   At the farthest part of the Nile.

THE TWICE-BORN GOD

Dionysiaca, Book VII

Nonnos

Translated by W. H. D. Rouse, 1940

Zeus or 'Cronion' ('Son of Cronos') once abducted Europa by disguising himself as a bull (see Story 38). In this story, Eros (Cupid) fills him with passion for Semele, daughter of Cadmus, the founder-king of Thebes. The episode comes from the longest surviving poem in Greek. Little is known of its author, **Nonnos**, other than that he came from Panopolis in Egypt and worked in the fifth century AD. This story was as such a late response to an early myth. Dionysus, the god of wine and revelry, was embraced as a life force. Semele's dream presaged what was to come. The myth of Semele had also appeared in Ovid's *Metamorphoses*, some four centuries before.

While Eros was fluttering along to the house of Zeus, Semele also was out with the rosy morning, shaking the cracks of her silver whip while she drove her mules through the city; and the light straight track of her cartwheels only scratched the very top of the dust. She had brushed away from her eyes the oblivious wing of sleep, and sent her mind wandering after the image of a dream with riddling oracles. She thought she saw in a garden a tree with fair green leaves, laden with newgrown clusters of swelling fruit yet unripe, and drenched in the fostering dews of Zeus. Suddenly a flame fell through the air from heaven, and laid the whole tree flat, but did not touch its fruit; then a bird flying with outspread wings caught up the fruit half-grown, and carried it yet lacking full maturity to Cronion. The Father received it in his kindly bosom, and sewed it up in his thigh; then instead of the fruit, a bull-shaped horned figure of a man came forth complete over his loins. Semele was the tree!

The girl leapt from her couch trembling, and told her father the terrifying tale of leafy dreams and fiery blast. King Cadmos was shaken when he heard of Semele's fireburnt tree, and that same morning he summoned the divine seer Teiresias son of Chariclo, and told him his daughter's fiery dreams. As soon as he heard the seer's inspired interpretation, the father sent his daughter to their familiar temple of Athena, and bade her sacrifice to thunderhurling Zeus a bull, the image of likehorned Lyaios, and a boar, vine-ravaging enemy of the vintage to come.

Now the maiden went forth from the city to kindle the altar of Zeus Lord of Lightning. She stood by the victims and sprinkled her bosom with the blood; her body was drenched with blood, plentiful streams of blood soaked her hair, her clothes were crimsoned with drops from the bull. Then with robes discoloured she made her way along the meadow deep in rushes, beside Asopos the river of her birthplace, and plunged in his waters to wash clean the garments which had been drenched and marked by the showers of blood.

Erinys the Avenger flying by in the air saw Semele bathing in the waters of Asopos, and laughed as she thought how Zeus was to strike both with his fiery thunderbolt in one common fate.

There the maiden cleansed her body, and naked with her attendants moved through the water with paddling hands; she kept her head stretched well above the stream unwetted, by the art she knew so well, under water to the hair and no farther, breasting the current and treading the water back with alternate feet.

There she received a new dress, and mounting upon the neighbouring river-bank, by the eastern strand which belonged to Dionysos the Guardian Spirit, she shook off into the winds and waters all the terror of her dreams. Not without God she plunged into the water, but she was led to that river's flow by the prophetic Seasons.

Nor did the allseeing eye of Zeus fail to see her: from the heights he turned the infinite circle of his vision upon the girl. At this moment Eros stood before the father, who watched her, and the inexorable archer drew in the air that bow which fosters life. The bowstring sparkled over the flower-decked shaft, and as the bow was drawn stretched back the poet-missile sounded the Bacchic strain. Zeus was the butt—for all his greatness he bowed his neck to Eros the nobody! And like a shooting star the shaft of love flew spinning into the heart of Zeus, with a bridal whistle, but swerving with a calculated twist it had just scratched his rounded thigh with its grooves—a foretaste of the birth to come. Then Cronion quickly turned the eye which was the channel of desire, and the love-charm flogged him into passion for the girl. At the sight of Semele, he leapt up, in wonder if it were Europa whom he saw on that bank a second time, his heart was troubled as if he felt again his Phoinician passion; for she had the same radiant shape, and on her face gleamed as born in her the brightness of her father's sister.

Father Zeus now deceitfully changed his form, and in his love, before the due season, he flew above River Asopos, the father of a daughter, as an eagle with eye sharp-shining like the bird, as he were now presaging the winged bridal of Aigina. He left the sky, and approaching the bank of the near-flowing river he scanned the naked body of the girl with her lovely hair. For he was not content to see from afar; he wished to come near and examine all the pure white body of the maiden, though he could send that eye so great—such an eye! ranging to infinity all round about, surveying all the universe, yet he thought it not enough to look at one unwedded girl.

Her rosy limbs made the dark water glow red; the stream became a lovely meadow gleaming with such graces. An unveiled naiad espying the nymph in wonder, cried out these words:

"Can it be that Cronos, after the first Cypris, again cut his father's loins with unmanning sickle, until the foam got a mind and made the water shape itself into a selfperfected birth, delivered of a younger Aphrodite from the sea?

Can it be that the river has rivalled the deep with a childbirth, and rolled a torrent of self-pregnant waves to bring forth another Cypris, not to be outdone by the sea? Can it be that one of the Muses has dived from neighbouring Helicon into my native water, and left another to take the honeydripping water of Pegasos the horse, or the stream of Olmeios! I spy a silverfooted maiden stretched under the streams of my river! I believe Selene bathes in the Aonian waves on her way to Endymion's bed on Latmos, the bed of a sleepless shepherd; but if she has prinked herself out for her sweet shepherd, what's the use of Asopos after the Ocean stream? And if she has a body white as the snows of heaven, what mark of the Moon has she? A team of mules unbridled and a mule-cart with silver wheels are there on the beach, but Selene knows not how to put mules to her yokestrap—she drives a team of bulls! Or if it is a goddess come down from heaven—I see a maiden's bright eyes sparkling under the quiet eyelids, and it must be Athena Brighteyes bathing, when she threw the skin back at him after the old victory over Teiresias. This girl looks like a divine being with her rosy arms; but if she was the glorious burden of a mortal womb, she is worthy of the heavenly bed of Cronion."

So spoke the voice from under the swirling waters. But Zeus shaken by the firebarbed sting of desire watched the rosy fingers of the swimming girl. Unrestingly he moved his wandering glance, now gazing at the sparkling rosy face, now bright eyes as full as a cow's under the eyelids, now the hair floating on the breeze, and as the hair blew away he scanned the free neck of the unclad maid; but the bosom most of all and the naked breasts seemed to be armed against Cronides, volleying shafts of love. All her flesh he surveyed, only passed by the secrets of her lap unseen by his modest eyes. The mind of Zeus left the skies and crept down to swim beside swimming Semele. Enchanted he received the sweet maddening spark in a heart which knew it well. Allfather was worsted by a child: little Eros with his feeble shot set afire this Archer of Thunderbolts. Not the deluge of the flood, not the fiery lightning could help its possessor: that huge heavenly flame itself was vanquished by the small fire of unwarlike Paphia; little Eros faced the shaggy skin, his magical girdle faced the aegis; the heavy-booming din of the thunderclap was the slave of his lovebreeding quiver. The god was shaken by the heartbewitching sting of desire for Semele, in amazement: for love is near neighbour to admiration.

Zeus could hardly get back to his imperial heaven, thinking over his plans, having now resumed his divine shape once more. He resolved to mount Semele's nightly couch, and turned his eye to the west, to see when sweet Hesperos would come. He blamed Phaethon that he should make the afternoon season so long, and uttered an impatient appeal with passionate lips:

"Tell me, laggard Night, when is envious Eos to set? It is time now for you to lift your torch and lead Zeus to his love—come now, foreshow the illumination of night-ranging Lyaios! Phaëthon is jealous, he constrains me! Is he in love with Semele himself and grudges my desire? Helios, you plague me, though you know the madness of love. Why do you spare the whip when you touch up your slow team? I know another nightfall that came very quickly!

If I like, I will hide you and the daughter of the mists together in my clouds, and when you are covered Night will appear in the daytime, to speed the marriage of Zeus in haste; the stars will shine at midday, and I will make rising Hesperos, instead of setting Hesperos, the regular usher of the loves. Come now, draw your own forerunner Phosphoros to his setting, and do grace to your desire and mine; enjoy your Clymene all night long, and let me go quick to Semele. Yoke your own car, I pray, bright Moon, send forth your rays which make the trees and plants to grow, because this marriage foretells the birth of plant-cherishing Dionysos; rise over the lovely roof of Semele, give light to my desire with the star of the Cyprian, make long the sweet darkness for the wooing of Zeus!"

Such was the speech of Zeus, even such commands as desire knows. But when in answer to his eagerness, a huge cone of darkness sprang up from the earth and ran stretching into the heights, bringing a shadow of darkness opposite to setting Eos, Zeus passed along the starry dome of the sky to Semele's bridal. Without leaving a trace of his footsteps, he traversed at his first bound the whole path of the air. With a second, like a wing or a thought, he reached Thebes; the bars of the palace door opened of themselves to let him through, and Semele was held fast in the loving bond of his arms.

Now he leaned over the bed, with a horned head on human limbs, lowing with the voice of a bull, the very likeness of bullhorned Dionysos. Again, he put on a shaggy lion's form; or he was a panther, as one who begets a bold son, driver of panthers and charioteer of lions. Again, as a young bridegroom he bound his hair with coiling snakes and vine-leaves intertwined, and twisted purple ivy about his locks, the plaited ornament of Bacchos. A writhing serpent crawled over the trembling bride and licked her rosy neck with gentle lips, then slipping into her bosom girdled the circuit of her firm breasts, hissing a wedding tune, and sprinkled her with sweet honey of the swarming bees instead of the viper's deadly poison. Zeus made long wooing, and shouted "Euoi!" as if the winepress were near, as he begat his son who would love the cry. He pressed love-mad mouth to mouth, and beaded up delicious nectar, an intoxicating bedfellow for Semele, that she might bring forth a son to hold the sceptre of nectareal vintage. As a presage of things to come, he lifted the careforgetting grapes resting his laden arm on the firebringing fennel; or again, he lifted a thyrsus twined about with purple ivy, wearing a deerskin on his back—the lovesick wearer shook the dappled fawnskin with his left arm.

All the earth laughed: a viny growth with self-sprouting leaves ran round Semele's bed; the walls budded with flowers like a dewy meadow, at the begetting of Bromios; Zeus lurking inside rattled his thunderclaps over the unclouded bed, foretelling the drums of Dionysos in the night. And after the bed, he saluted Semele with loving words, consoling his bride with hopes of things to come:

"My wife, I your bridegroom am Cronides. Lift up your neck in pride at this union with a heavenly bedfellow; and look not among mankind for any child higher than yours. Danaë's wedding does not rival you. You have thrown into the shade even the union of your father's sister with her Bull; for Europa glorified by Zeus's bed went to Crete, Semele goes to Olympos. What more do you want after heaven and the starry sky? People will say in the future, Zeus gave honour to Minos in the underworld, and to Dionysos in the heavens! Then after Autonoë's mortal son and Ino's child—one downed by his dogs, one to be killed by a sonslaying father's winged arrow—after the shortlived son of mad Agaüe, you bring forth a son who shall not die, and you I will call immortal. Happy woman! you have conceived a son who will make mortals forget their troubles, you shall bring forth joy for gods and men."

Envy struck Zeus' wife Hera, who proceeded to strike pregnant Semele with a thunderbolt. The messenger god Hermes rescued the baby from his mother's womb and gave him to Zeus to incubate in his thigh until he reached full term. Dionysus was therefore known as 'Twice Born'.

INTRIGUES AT THE PALACE

Secret History

Procopius

Translated by Richard Atwater, 1961

The *Secret History* is one of the most salacious books from antiquity. Written by a prominent Christian historian, **Procopius** of Caesarea (*c.* AD 500–*c.* 554), in the mid-sixth century AD, it describes life in the Late Eastern Roman Empire under Emperor Justinian and his wife Theodora. While Procopius elsewhere documented Justinian's wars and building projects without malice, in this book he let loose. Justinian is a cruel villain; Theodora a harlot. The author is no kinder in his characterisation of the wife of his patron Belisarius. Antonina, the daughter of a charioteer and theatre actress, is described as having used magic to charm Belisarius into marrying her, only to prove shamefully unfaithful to him. Procopius had served under Belisarius in Justinian's war on the Vandals in North Africa, and his loyalty to his former commander is patent. The Constantine referred to in this story is an officer of Belisarius, and Photius is Antonina's son by a previous relationship.

There was a youth from Thrace in the house of Belisarius: Theodosius by name, and of the Eunomian heresy by descent. On the eve of his expedition to Libya, Belisarius baptized this boy in holy water and received him in his arms as a member henceforth of the family, welcoming him with his wife as their son, according to the Christian rite of adoption. And Antonina not only embraced Theodosius with reasonable fondness as her son by holy word, and thus cared for him, but soon, while her husband was away on his campaign, became wildly in love with him; and, out of her senses with this malady, shook off all fear and shame of God and man. She began by enjoying him surreptitiously, and ended by dallying with him in the presence of the men servants and waiting maids. For she was now possessed by passion and, openly overwhelmed with love, could see no hindrance to its consummation.

Once, in Carthage, Belisarius caught her in the very act, but allowed himself to be deceived by his wife. Finding the two in an underground room, he was very angry; but she said, showing no fear or attempt to keep anything hidden, "I came here with the boy to bury the most precious part of our plunder, where the Emperor will not discover it." So she said by way of excuse, and he dismissed the matter as if he believed her, even as he saw Theodosius's trousers belt somewhat unmodestly unfastened. For so bound by love for the woman was he, that he preferred to distrust the evidence of his own eyes.

As her folly progressed to an indescribable extent, those who saw what was going on kept silent, except one slave, Macedonia by name. When Belisarius was in Syracuse as the conqueror of Sicily, she made her master swear solemnly never to betray her to her mistress, and then told him the whole story, presenting as witnesses two slave boys attending the bed-chamber.

When he heard this, Belisarius ordered one of his guards to put Theodosius away; but the latter learned of this in time to flee to Ephesus. For most of the servants, inspired by the weakness of the husband's character, were more anxious to please his wife than to show loyalty to him, and so betrayed the order he had given. But Constantine, when he saw Belisarius's grief at what had befallen him, sympathized entirely except to comment, "I would have tried to kill the woman rather than the young man." Antonina heard of this, and hated him in secret. How malicious was her spite against him shall be shown; for she was a scorpion who could hide her sting.

But not long after this, by the enchantment either of philtres or of her caresses, she persuaded her husband that the charges against her were untrue. Without more ado he sent word to Theodosius to return, and promised to turn Macedonia and the two slave boys over to his wife. She first cruelly cut out their tongues, it is said, and then cut their bodies into little bits which were put into sacks and thrown into the sea. One of her slaves, Eugenius, who had already wrought the outrage on Silverius, helped her in this crime.

And it was not long after this that Belisarius was persuaded by his wife to kill Constantine. What happened at that time concerning Presidius and the daggers I have narrated in my previous books. For while Belisarius would have preferred to let Constantine alone, Antonina gave him no peace until his remark, which I have just repeated, was avenged. And as a result of this murder, much enmity was aroused against Belisarius in the hearts of the Emperor and all the most important of the Romans.

So matters progressed. But Theodosius said he was unable to return to Italy, where Belisarius and Antonina were now staying, unless Photius were put out of the way. For this Photius was the sort who would bite if anyone got the better of him in anything, and he had reason to be choked with indignation at Theodosius. Though he was the rightful son, he was utterly disregarded while the other grew in power and riches, they say that from the two palaces at Carthage and Ravenna Theodosius had taken plunder amounting to a hundred centenaries, as he alone had been given the management of these conquered properties.

But Antonina, when she learned of Theodosius's fear, never ceased laying snares for her son and planning deadly plots against his welfare, until he saw he would have to escape to Constantinople if he wished to live. Then Theodosius came to Italy and her. There they stayed in the satisfaction of their love, unhindered by the complaisant husband; and later she took them both to Constantinople. There Theodosius became so worried lest the affair became generally known, that he was at his wit's end. He saw it would be impossible to fool everybody, as the woman was no longer able to conceal her passion and indulge it secretly, but thought nothing of being in fact and in reputation an avowed adulteress.

Therefore he went back to Ephesus, and having his head shaved after the religious custom, became a monk. Whereupon Antonina, insane over her loss, exhibited her grief by donning mourning; and went around the house shrieking and wailing, lamenting even in the presence of her husband what a good friend she had lost, how faithful, how tender, how loving, how energetic! In the end, even her spouse was won over to join in her sorrow. And so the poor wretch wept too, calling for his beloved Theodosius. Later he even went to the Emperor and implored both him and the Empress, till they consented to summon Theodosius to return, as one who was and would always be a necessity in the house of Belisarius.

But Theodosius refused to leave his monastery, saying he was completely resolved to give himself forever to the cloistered life. This noble pronouncement, however, was not entirely sincere, for he was aware that as soon as Belisarius left Constantinople, it would be possible for him to come secretly to Antonina. Which, indeed, he did.

Antonina continues her affair with the young man, aided by the Empress Theodora, who conceals him in the palace for her until his premature death from dysentery.

A MEETING WITH LADY PHILOSOPHY

The Consolation of Philosophy

Boethius

Translated by Queen Elizabeth I, 1593

Boethius was born in Rome in the late fifth century AD at around the time
the last Western emperor was deposed. A Christian, he also had a keen
scholarly interest in paganism, particularly ancient Greek philosophy,
which he cultivated in his work. Boethius saw Italy come under the sway
of an Ostrogothic king named Theodoric, under whom he served as
magister officiorum (Master of Offices) until he was arrested on suspicion
of being implicated in treasonous acts. It was while he was in his cell
that Boethius wrote his *Consolation of Philosophy*. The dialogue, in
which Boethius converses with a personification of Philosophy, was
especially popular in the Middle Ages and Renaissance. Queen Elizabeth
I produced the translation from which this extract comes in 1593 when
she was sixty years old. Her decision to translate the text (provided here
in a modern-spelling version) has sometimes been seen as a reflection of
her anxieties and frustrations upon hearing that year of the conversion
of King Henri IV of France to Catholicism. Boethius was ultimately
tortured and executed.

Meter 1

[...]
The glory once of happy, greeny youth,
    Now Fates of grunting age, my comfort all.
Unlooked-for Age, hied by mishaps, is come,
    And Sorrow bids his time to add withal;
Unseasoned, hoary hairs upon my head are poured,
    And loosèd skin in feeble body shakes.
Blessèd Death, that in sweetest years refrains,
    But, oft called, comes to the woeful wights;
O with how deaf ear she from wretched, wries,
    And wailing eyes, cruel, to shut denies.

While guileful Fortune with vading goods did cheer,
    My life well nigh the doleful hour bereaved;
When her false look a cloud hath changed,
    My wretched life, thankless abode protracts.
Why me so oft, my friends, have you happy called?
    Who falleth down, in steady step yet never stood.

Prose 1

While of all this, alone in silence I bethought me, and tears-full complaint in style's office meant, over my head to stand a woman did appear. Of stately face, with flaming eyes of insight above the common worth of men; of fresh color and unwon strength, though yet so old she were that of our age she seemed not be one. Her stature such as scarce could be discerned, for somewhile she scanted her to the common stature of men, straight she seemed with crown of head the heavens to strike; and lifting up the same higher, the heavens themselves she entered, beguiling the sight of lookers-on.

Her weeds they were of smallest threads, perfect for fine workmanship and lasting substance as, after by herself I knew, was by her hands all wrought. Whose form, as to smoky images is wont, a certain dimness of despised antiquity overwhelmed. Of these weeds, in the lowest skirts π, in the upper side a θ, was read, all woven. And between both letters, ladder-wise, certain steps were marked, by which, from lowest to highest element, ascent there was. Yet that self garment the hands of violent men had torn and pieces such as get they could, away they stole. Her right hand held a book, the left a scepter.

Who, when she spied poets' Muses standing by my bed, and to my tears inditing words, somewhat moved, inflamed with gloating eyes: "Who suffered," quoth she, "these stage's harlots approach this sick man, which not only would not ease his sorrow with no remedies, but with sweet venom nourish them? These they be, that with barren affections' thorns destroys the full ears of reason's fruit, and men's minds with disease inures, not frees. But if of vain man, as vulgar wonts, your allurements had deprived me, with less grief had I borne it. For by such, our work had got no harm. But this man have you touched, whom Stoic and Academic study brought out. Get you away, Sirens, sweet till end be seen. To my Muses leave him for cure and health."

To this, the checked rabble, with look downcast with woe, with blush confessing shame, doleful out of doors they went. But I, whose sight, drowned in tears, was dimmed, could not know what she was, of so imperious rule; and settling my eyes on ground, what she would more do, in silence I attended. Then she, drawing near, on my bed's feet sat down. And viewing my look of heavy woe and with my dole to the earth thrown down, in verses these, of my mind's pain, complaineth thus:

Meter 2

Oh, in how headlong depth the drowned mind is dimmed;
    And, losing light, her own, to others' darkness turns,
As oft as, driv'n with earthly flaws, the harmful care upward grows.
    Once this man, free in open field, used the skies to view:
Of ros[y] sun the light beheld,
    Of frosty moon the planets saw;
And what star else runs her wonted course,
    Bending by many circles, this man had won
    By number to know them all,
Yea, causes each: whence roaring winds the seas perturbs;
    Acquainted with the spirit that rolls the steady world;
And why the star that falls to the Hesperia's waters
    From his reddy root doth raise herself;
Who that gives the spring's mild hours their temper,
    That with rosy flowers the earth be decked;
Who made the fertile autumn, at fullness of the year,
    Abound with grape, all swoll'n with ripest fruits.
He, wonted to search and find sundry causes of hidden Nature,
    Down lies, of mind's light bereaved,
With bruisèd neck, by overheavy chains,
    A-bowèd-low look, by weight-bearing
Driven, alas, the seely earth behold.

Prose 2

"But fitter time," quoth she, "for medicine than complaint." Then, fixing on me her steady eyes: "Art thou the same," quoth she, "who once nourished with my milk, fed with our food, art grown to strength of manly mind? On whom we bestowed such weapons as, if thou hadst not cast away, had saved thee with invincible strength? Dost thou me know? Why art thou dumb? Is it shame or wonder makes thee silent?" But when she spied me not only still but wordless and dumb, on my breast gently laid her hand. Said: "There is no danger; he is entered in a lethargy, a common disease of mind distract. He hath a little forgotten himself. Easily his memory will return when first he hath remembered me. And, that he may, a little let us wipe his eyes overdimmed with cloud of earthly things." Thus speaking, my eyes flowing with tears, folding her garment, she dried.

Meter 3

Then night o'erblown, the darkness left me,
    And former strength unto my eyes returned.
As when the heav'ns astound with headlong wind,
    And pole amidst the cloudy mists,
The sun is hid, and in the heav'ns appears no stars:
    From high, the night on earth is spread.
The same if Boreas, sent from his Thracian den,
    Doth strike and opens the hidden day.
Shines out, and with his sudden light, Phoebus, shaken,
    With his beams strikes all lookers-on.

Prose 3

No otherwise, mists of my woe dissolved, to heaven I reached, and raised my mind to know my curer's face. Then, when on her I rolled my eyes, and look I fixed, my nurse I saw, in whose retired rooms in my youth I dwelt. "And how," quoth I, "art thou come to the solitariness of our exile, O pedagogue of all virtues? Fallen from the highest step, shalt thou with me be tormented too with false crimes?"

"Shall I," quoth she, "O scholar mine, thee leave? And not to ease thy burden, which, for my sake thou bearest, in easing thy labor with fellowing of thy pain? It ill becomes Philosophy to leave alone an innocent's way. Shall I dread mine own blame, and, as if any novelty had happed, shall I fear? Are you now to know how, among wicked folks, Wisdom is assailed with many dangers? Have we not wrestled with Folly's rashness among the elder sort afore our Plato's age, and made therewith great battle? Yea, he alive, his master Socrates unjustly claimed the victory of death when I was by. Whose inheritance, when after the vulgar Epicurean and Stoic and all the rest, each man for his part meant to bereave me, sundered (as, in part of their prey) my garment, though I resisted and exclaimed: for, being the workmanship of mine own hand, they, plucking some rags from it (supposing they had all), departed from me. Among which, for that some prints of my garment appeared, folly, supposing they were my familiars, abused some of them with error of the vain multitude.

"Though thou hast not known Anaxagoras's flight, nor Socrates' venom, nor Zeno's torment, because they are strange, yet Caniuses, Senecas, Soranuses thou mayst know, for they are not cowards nor of unhonored memory. Whom nothing else to their bane brought, but that, instructed with our conditions, they seemed unlike the wicked's endeavors. Thou oughtest not, therefore, to wonder, if in the sea of life we be tossed with many a tempest rising, whose purpose is this, chiefest, to dislike the wickedest. Whose army, though it be great, ought to be despised, as whom no guide rules, but hurled rashly with a dim error. Which, if once setting battle against us, should fortune to prevail, our guide will draw our troops to castle while they be busy to raven unprofitable baggage. And we from high shall scorn them while they spoil that is vile, sure from the furious tumult and safe in such a trench whither these foolish raveners may never attain."

ACKNOWLEDGEMENTS

I am extremely grateful to Richard Milbank, Florence Hare, Clémence Jacquinet, Jessie Price, Leah Jespersen, Anthony Cheetham, Georgina Capel, Rachel Conway, Irene Baldoni, Michael Bond, Dan Jones, Amanda Short, Jeremy Danziger, Alice Dunn and all the talented translators who have kept these stories alive.

EXTENDED COPYRIGHT